What People Are Saying about *Torchbearers*...

Torchbearers is inspirational and informational! The lineup is like heaven's hall of fame. The contents stirred my soul!

—*Dr. Cecil Todd*
Founder/President, Revival Fires Ministries

These ordinary people with an extraordinary God will stretch your faith and allow you to be the champion God intended you to be.

—*Sid Roth*
President, Messianic Vision

Torchbearers brings the heroes of the faith to life. How crucial it is in our fast-paced, indulgent society to be reminded of those who have sacrificed all for the cause of Christ. This book will surely inspire future generations to share the living message of Jesus with the world.

—*Ron and Shelley Blackwood*
Blackwood Brothers Quartet

As you read this book, you will feel the fire lifting from the pages into your heart. It is my prayer that God will use this fire to light a torch of revival across the world.

—*Sonny Holland*
Sonny Holland Evangelism Outreach Ministries

I highly recommend *Torchbearers* to challenge readers interested in changing their world through rugged spiritual character.

—*Ralph Sutera*
Cofounder, Sutera Twins Ministry

Torchbearers is a truly fascinating book with a dynamic message of faith and courage. I believe the book will be a tremendous blessing to Christians throughout the world.

—*Dwight Kinman*
Author, The World's Last Dictator

Several of our customers have told us that *Torchbearers* is the best book they have ever read.

—*Thomas LeBlanc*
President, Solid Rock Books, Inc.

Torchbearers is TERRIFIC! What a unique style—highly interesting and informative.

—*David Mayo*
Manager, WHBR TV, Pensacola, FL

I have shared many passages from *Torchbearers* with my friends and family...The story is so interesting, I could not put it down. I recommend this book to any person carrying the torch for Jesus who has ever felt alone, rejected, or just in need of a little encouragement.

—*Rosey Bryan*
Wife of Andy Bryan, Andy Bryan Ministries

I was totally awestricken by *Torchbearers*. The encouragement one can receive from reading this book is much needed.

—*Quinton Mills*
Evangelist, Songwriter

Torchbearers is the most relevant book I have seen for the twenty-first-century church. In a religious world that is marked by disappointment, discouragement, and defection, modern believers have found little lasting encouragement. This is the book we have been waiting for!

—*Paul Vick*
Pastor, Harvest Christian Fellowship
Paul Vick Ministries

Wow! What a journey! I felt like I was running right along with John the Baptist, Peter, Paul, Augustine, John Wyclif, John Wesley, Martin Luther...

—*Brother Bob Harrington*
Chaplain of Bourbon Street

BASED ON THE LIVES OF
HEROES OF THE FAITH

TORCHBEARERS

A Historical Novel by
CAROLYN WILDE

In some cases, the dates given for historical figures are approximate.

Dave, his relatives, his friends, and his acquaintances are fictional. However, the historical characters are part of our rich Christian heritage. The accounts are based on each character's teachings and recorded history, though aspects have been fictionalized for the sake of brevity and narrative style.

Scripture quotations are taken from the King James Version of the Holy Bible. However, when Bible verses are included in dialogue, the language has been updated from words such as *thee* and *thou* to *you* and *your*.

TORCHBEARERS

ISBN-13: 978-0-88368-793-2
ISBN-10: 0-88368-793-3
Printed in the United States of America
© 1994, 2005 by Carolyn Wilde

1030 Hunt Valley Circle
New Kensington, PA 15068
www.whitakerhouse.com

Library of Congress Cataloging-in-Publication Data
Wilde, Carolyn.
Torchbearers / by Carolyn Wilde.
p. cm.
ISBN-13: 978-0-88368-793-2 (trade pbk. : alk. paper)
ISBN-10: 0-88368-793-3 (trade pbk. : alk. paper)
1. Olympic games—Fiction. I. Title.
PS3623.I535T67 2005
813'.6—dc22   2005014721

1 2 3 4 5 6 7 8 9 10 11 ⨇ 12 11 10 09 08 07 06 05

HISTORY'S TORCHBEARERS...

Chapter One

DAVE

~Present Day~

Know ye not that they which run in a race run all, but one receiveth the prize? So run, that ye may obtain.

—1 Corinthians 9:24

The sudden silence of the crowd seemed even louder than the previous dull roar. Every eye was riveted on the taut bodies of the runners. The hush would last only until the blast of the gun shattered it.

The shot rang out, and the race began.

Dave fought to shut out the noise and keep his mind wholly centered on the race, but it was impossible. His brain was cluttered with unbidden thoughts.

He had lived for this moment for the past four years. The fact that the race would be over in just a few minutes terrified him, especially since its outcome would judge those four pressure-packed years either a total waste or his most profitable.

He watched his teammate run, agony contorting his face, his mouth open wide in a desperate gasp for air. Dave's eyes dropped to the hand that gripped the baton...the baton that would soon be passed to him. But even as he watched, his mind remained a jumble of conflicting thoughts.

He had been too excited to get a good night's sleep.

Could he win?

He had to win!

This was his last chance! He couldn't let his coach down.

He'd show the hateful press with their unrelenting insults and naysaying that he could win.

Dave tried desperately to stop his thoughts. This was no time to dwell on the insults of the media!

One teammate was just about to pass the baton to another. He saw both their bodies stretched to their limit as the exchange was made. His eyes moved to the runners encircling the track. It would be his turn soon.

The runners were closer now. Dave could hear their jagged breaths and panting groans. The news media was right. The team they had predicted would win was out in front.

We aren't too far behind, Dave thought. But he didn't enter this race to be behind. Maybe others were satisfied with just the thrill of being in this race, but the thrill wasn't enough to satisfy him. Neither were the silver or the bronze. He was here for the gold.

His physical condition would never be better. If he didn't win today, he never would. He was all too aware of his weak areas, but the body is a complex structure. There would always be at least one muscle or tendon that was sore or in the process of recovering from being pushed or stretched to its limit.

He struggled to quit thinking and to focus on the race. He had expected his teammates to do better. Perhaps they too had trouble with the high of this race. None of his training had prepared him for this. *His training...*

He had kept running with his swollen foot bulging out of his shoe. He had kept running when he was sure that his throbbing side would rupture.

He had kept going when his lungs ached for more oxygen and his parched mouth hung open in a soundless scream for water. He had kept running when his whole body begged to collapse, and his mind shrieked for him to give up.

He had slowed to a crawl through a bog, but he had not stopped. He had kept running through ankle-deep mud, while lightning zigzagged through the blackened sky and rain smarted his face and stung his eyes.

He had kept running when every joint and muscle was in agony.

He had run while sick, with sweat streaming from his pores even as his body shook with chills.

He had kept running when the cheers of the crowd changed to jeers as he fell behind.

He was out running while other runners were sleeping and still others playing.

He had continued to run when everyone but his coach had told him there was no way this race was worth the sacrifice.

He had kept running to prepare for this one moment in time. How, then, could he now feel so totally inadequate and unprepared?

He had laughed off the ridicule of the press. Why now, of all times, did he suddenly believe they were right? Who was he to be among the world's best athletes? What had given him the idea that he was good enough to win?

He felt the icy claws of fear grip his heart.

He stood riveted, staring, unseeing, wanting to run—not in the race, but far away from the arena and the defeat of his dream.

It was nearly his turn now.

It was not until just seconds before reaching out to grasp the baton that Dave's years of training rose up within him to meet the challenge.

A barrier settled around his mind, blocking out all thoughts of panic.

Dave could no longer hear the dull roar of the crowd. He didn't hear the voices of those around him.

He was totally unaware of his stance or the tension building in his body.

He saw nothing. Nothing but the baton in the hand of his teammate—the baton that was his to take to the finish line.

It no longer mattered who was ahead of him. He would simply pass them, for Dave had come to win.

Just before turning off his light, Dave looked up at the gold medal encased in glass on the shelf. He lay back in bed, grinning foolishly.

Would the thrill of snapping that ribbon against his chest ever wear off? Nearly seven months had passed since the race, but since then every day had ended the same way. He could not sleep without first savoring his win. Night after night, he felt all over again the triumph of victory.

His next memory was of the pain of his lungs screaming for air and hearing nothing but the sound of his own heaving gasps for breath and the booming thud of his heart.

He remembered becoming aware of people helping him in his struggle to sit up so he could breathe.

He recalled sensing that the crowd had risen to its feet, though he did not break focus to look toward the stands. He remembered hearing the crowd suddenly burst again into a thundering roar that reverberated through his entire body.

He remembered how his eyes had slowly focused on his coach kneeling beside him, roughly sponging his face. A huge grin split his coach's face.

He kept repeating the same words, and finally the sense of them came with their sound.

"We did it, Dave. We did it!"

He could still taste the thrill of victory coursing through his body, instantly expelling all weakness and pain.

Dave was no longer an Olympic runner. He was now an Olympic champion.

Dave could still feel himself being lifted to his feet by his teammates. He saw pictures later of their hands clasped and raised as victors. They were smiling through their tears.

He couldn't remember their walk to the victors' platform. But he would never forget the feeling he had while standing there, surrounded by multiplied thousands of cheering people. Nothing in his life had even come close to the indescribable feelings of pride, awe, and thanksgiving, all mixed together, that he experienced at that moment. He had tried to sing his national anthem, but instead found himself alternately weeping and grinning.

And that was the moment when every pain-filled day and torture-wracked night, four years of sacrifice and deprivation, had paid off.

For he had won.

Dave fell asleep, still smiling.

He did not yet realize that this was the night he would be called into yet more training...

by the unsurpassed Coach of all time

to the race of all races

for the greatest prize of all.

Chapter Two

DAVE

~Present Day~

---

*Ye did run well; who did hinder you that
ye should not obey the truth?*

—Galatians 5:7

*Now they do it to obtain a corruptible crown;
but we an incorruptible.*

—1 Corinthians 9:25

Dave fumbled for the lamp switch and looked at his watch lying on the bed stand. Two a.m. Why was he so wide awake? And why this sudden urge to read the Bible?

He turned the light off and tried to get back to sleep. After tossing restlessly for a few minutes, he got up to search for his Bible. He finally found it on the bottom shelf of a bookcase. He sat holding it for a few minutes without opening it. He didn't have to open its worn cover to remember the inscription written inside.

To Dave, on the day of your new birth. May this book be a lamp unto your feet and a light unto your path as you begin your new life with Christ.

With my heartfelt love and fervent prayers, Pastor Whyte

Dave realized he was gripping the book so hard his knuckles had turned white. How long had it been since he had devoured its truths? How many years had it been since he had knelt and talked to his God?

He recalled the nights he had prayed for the strength and power to be an effective witness to his family and friends. Pleasing Jesus had been all that mattered to him.

He hadn't consciously left Christ behind when he began training for the Olympics. But, somehow, the race had become his all-encompassing goal and running had replaced Christ as his first love. God, like the Bible, had been hidden away on the bottom shelf of his life. He opened the book and absentmindedly read the first verse he came to.

Wherefore seeing we also are compassed about with so great a cloud of witnesses, let us lay aside every weight, and the sin which doth so easily beset us, and let us run with patience the race that is set before us. (Hebrews 12:1)

The race...
Let us run the race...
Dave was instantly alert, his mind fully on the words he had just read. His eyes scanned them again and again.

Dawn was just breaking in the eastern sky when Dave finally rose from his knees. Consenting to enter this spiritual race had not been easy for him. He hadn't wanted to make the lifetime commitment that it demanded of its runners.

He was tired of Olympic training and having someone else make his rules and plan his days.

For the past four years he had faithfully followed orders, sometimes willingly and sometimes rebelliously. It was finally over, and he was looking forward to living his life as he chose. He hadn't been sure what to do with his life, but he had made one firm decision. He would answer to no one. The last thing he wanted was the constant discipline and unquestioning obedience a coach demanded.

Then Jesus had come, demanding not only his next four years, but the rest of his life.

Dave had fought bitterly.

"My whole life! It's too much for You to ask!"

He that findeth his life shall lose it: and he that loseth his life for my sake shall find it. (Matthew 10:39)

"But why me? I am not qualified! You need someone smarter, full of wisdom, someone who is a great orator! Surely You don't need me!"

God hath chosen the foolish things of the world to confound the wise...that no flesh should glory in his presence.
(1 Corinthians 1:27, 29)

Dave grinned. "When You put it that way, I guess I do qualify after all."

Then he sobered.

"What will my family think? I've all but ignored them for the past four years, and I am just now getting close to them again!"

He that loveth his father or mother more than me is not worthy of me. (Matthew 10:37)

"Lord! Lord! This is not what I planned to do with my life."

Why call ye me, Lord, Lord, and do not the things which I say? (Luke 6:46)

Dave had been careful not to address Jesus as Lord again.

"But my friends...what will they think when they see me running with Your torch? This race is not a popular one right now."

Whosoever therefore shall be ashamed of me and of my words in this adulterous and sinful generation; of him also shall the Son of man be ashamed, when he cometh in the glory of his Father with the holy angels. (Mark 8:38)

Dave had literally groaned aloud. "It's going to be so hard."

Whosoever will come after me, let him deny himself, and take up his cross, and follow me. (Mark 8:34)

"I am weak in areas. You must know I am not good at public speaking. I would never want You to ask me to do that!"

My strength is made perfect in weakness. (2 Corinthians 12:9)

"Could I just try it for awhile, and if it doesn't work, I'll just go back to my plans?"

No man, having put his hand to the plough, and looking back, is fit for the kingdom of God. (Luke 9:62)

Remember Lot's wife. (Luke 17:32)

Dave felt almost crushed with the weight of the decision. He said, half to himself, "It would be easier if I didn't know what You're asking of me. But I do know what this means. It means giving up everything and everyone that means anything to me."
He hadn't expected an answer, but received a quick reply.

Whosoever he be of you that forsakes not all that he hath, he cannot be my disciple. (Luke 14:33)

Dave thought of the friendships he had renewed in the past few months. He enjoyed having a good time, free at last from the responsibilities of training and running. He swallowed bitterly. "My friends will no longer want to be around me. I'll be all alone."

I am with you alway, even unto the end of the world.
(Matthew 28:20)

Dave was still for a few minutes, and then the full impact of the call made him speak once more.
"But I will never have all the things that I hoped to have!"

For what shall it profit a man, if he shall gain the whole world, and lose his own soul? (Mark 8:36)

A question became his answer, and with it, Dave ran out of arguments.

Dave was silent for a long while.

Then he asked hesitantly, "Where do You want me to go?"

"Follow Me."

So the Lord would chart the course. Who knew where it would lead? He thought of the path others had run, and he shuddered. "This race can be dangerous. Several have died running for You."

Be thou faithful unto death, and I will give thee a crown of life. (Revelation 2:10)

"What exactly is it that You want me to do?"

Let your light so shine before men, that they may see your good works, and glorify your Father which is in heaven.
(Matthew 5:16)

Dave pictured himself holding high his flaming torch as he ran through a sin-blackened world. A small flicker of excitement stirred within him as he realized how desperately the world needed light. "And I will represent You?"

"You will be My ambassador."

Dave's voice was almost a whisper, but he had to ask one more question that was troubling him.

"What about my support? I have to eat...I have some bills..."

The words of the Lord interrupted him.

Take no thought for your life, what ye shall eat, or what ye shall drink; nor yet for your body, what ye shall put on...But seek ye first the kingdom of God, and his righteousness; and all these things shall be added unto you. (Matthew 6:25, 33)

There were no more excuses. There was nothing else to say. The Word of God offered man no alternative to total surrender.

The chair where Dave knelt became an altar. Dave offered himself as the sacrifice. His words at the end were simple. "Here I am, my Lord. Send me."

He was totally unprepared for what happened next. Electrifying joy filled him to overflowing. He had expected a misery to settle within him that would only be liberated by death itself. Instead, he was weeping and laughing both at the same time, thanking God for choosing him to run with the torch.

The thrill of winning the Olympics was nothing compared to this! It reminded him of the words King David had penned thousands of years before:

In thy presence is fulness of joy; at thy right hand there are pleasures for evermore. (Psalm 16:11)

This then was the blessing that came from surrendering to Jesus! He could feel His presence, almost see His outstretched hands and hear His cheerful words, "Dave! Enter into the joy of the Lord!"

Looking up, tears shining on his radiant face, he whispered reverently, "How I love You, my Lord. Forgive me for straying from You. Please help me to never again make anyone or anything my first love. I thought a commitment to You would bring pain. But I have never been as happy as I am right now."

If ye know these things, happy are ye if ye do them. (John 13:17)

Dave was silent, basking in the presence of his Lord.

Finally he spoke. "Lord, I hardly dare believe that I have made You happy by agreeing to run for You. But I know I have. Is it Your pleasure that has made me so happy? Lord, I never knew a happiness like this even existed.

"I love You. I give You my life, my strength. I give You my mind, my soul, my heart. I present my body to You, a living sacrifice. I forsake this world, Lord, to choose You.

"Please make me a good runner. I ask for nothing but Your continued pleasure. My Lord, I will run for You, and You alone."

The altar. The sacrifice. The fire.

The three always go together.

Dave's torch was set aflame by the touch of God.

Chapter Three

DAVE

~Present Day~

And the light shineth in darkness; and the darkness comprehended it not.

—John 1:5

I t was often a lonely run. Perhaps Dave remembered too well the thrill of the Olympics, with its massive arena, thousands of fans, deafening cheers, news reporters competing with one another for an interview...

Dave hadn't realized how different this race would be. There were no reporters, no cheering fans. Not even the members of his own family showed interest in this race.

When Dave had mentioned his new race to some of his family and friends, they had laughed and scoffed. Only one great-uncle had clasped Dave's hand with approval. "Dave, you will find your new life to be one of total commitment. You will also find this an unpopular race. But there is nothing you can do with your life that will be more profitable to you in the long run. Nothing."

He was silent then, and Dave began to speak. His uncle interrupted in a low voice that broke with emotion. Dave leaned forward, straining to hear his words.

"Dave, the Lord called me to this race when I was about your age. I was afraid to say no. So instead I just ignored Him.

"The years of my life have passed so quickly. All the time, in the back of my mind, I thought maybe someday I would answer

19

the call of God. But I never did. I just drifted, busy with the day-to-day affairs of living.

"Now my life is nearly over. I should be looking forward to meeting Christ. Instead, I wonder what I am going to say to Him. What concerns me more is wondering what He will say to me. I would love to hear, 'Well done, good and faithful servant.' But I will never hear those words."

He looked up, tears filling his eyes.

"Don't concern yourself with your family's opinions. You have made the decision I should have made, but didn't. I wasted my life."

Dave was relieved when Uncle Joe walked away, for he hadn't known what to say. What words could ease the pain of an unanswered call, a squandered life?

Uncle Joe was the only relative who had spoken favorably of Dave's race. Dave hadn't expected his family to be excited about his decision, but neither had he expected their bitter reaction. Some had responded with a curse, some with disgust, some with a lecture, and some with total disinterest. They now avoided him when possible.

He would have to run alone, misunderstood and criticized by both friends and family. This run was proving to be far different from the one that began in Olympia of ancient Greece.

He remembered beginning his training for that race. He could still hear his coach's lecture. "Dave, you must be single-minded! You have to have one goal, and only one. All these other concerns and ambitions of yours have got to go."

So, one by one, they went. His family had grown used to Dave's absence at events and gatherings they considered important. His girlfriend had dropped him in disgust after just a few weeks of training. While his friends were out enjoying life—getting good jobs, pretty girls, fast cars, and having fun—Dave was training. He had tried to slip off now and then to look up his old friends, but his coach had reminded him in no uncertain terms of his priority. His family and friends had scoffed at his rigid lifestyle, but he knew secretly they were all pulling for him. They wanted him to make the Olympic team, and when he had, they talked of nothing else. No one could have asked for more enthusiastic supporters.

This time it was different. Again they were scoffing at his rigid lifestyle. But they weren't pulling for him now. They were embarrassed when their acquaintances learned he had entered the race. He remembered his brother's sneer.

"You don't look like a runner for God."

Dave had answered with a question.

"What are God's runners supposed to look like, bro?"

His brother hadn't bothered to answer.

Dave had been so proud when they had all gathered around enthusiastically to see his Olympic medal. They had passed it around almost reverently, awed by its six grams of gold. It seemed strange to Dave that they were not in the least bit interested in a place where gold was so abundant that it was used to pave the streets.

The Lord had forewarned His runners of the difficulties of this race. He had clearly informed them in advance that there would be conflict with their families.

What could be clearer than, *"A man's foes shall be they of his own household"* (Matthew 10:36)?

And yet it was painful. However, no amount of pain inflicted by the world could ever overshadow the joy of pleasing Jesus.

Joy in the presence of Christ had caused John the Baptist to leap while still in the womb!

John. What a runner!

Dave grinned. *My brother has some preconceived idea about what runners should look like,* he thought. *He would have been shocked if he could have seen John!*

Then he sobered. John's race had not ended in a blaze of glory. What hurts had he experienced? Had loneliness plagued him? Was he misunderstood—forsaken by those he loved?

I think I will take a look at the great runners of the past, he thought. *It might be interesting.*

He decided to begin that evening, not realizing that his search through the centuries would introduce him to mass murderers, desolate slaves, prosperous merchants, destitute failures, aged men, fearless professors, courageous women, helpless invalids, elderly women, sharp lawyers, drunken teenagers, hardworking housewives, dying men, respectable counts, sneering agnostics, vile blasphemers, and despised priests. And these were just a few of God's torchbearers!

He would meet runners of distant lands, of other times, discovering them in slave ships, hog pens, battlefields, prisons, teepees, mansions, orphanages, forests, and dungeons.

His search began that evening with the simple words,

There was a man sent from God, whose name was John.

(John 1:6)

Chapter Four

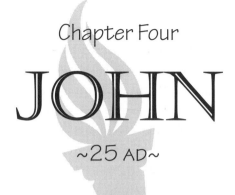

JOHN

~25 AD~

Behold, I will send my messenger, and he shall
prepare the way before me.

—Malachi 3:1

T he Jordan River. Could there be a stranger place to run the race? It was the lowest river in the world, and probably the ugliest. Its swirling waters and threatening currents made its crossing a challenge.

No wonder Naaman had cringed at the thought of his dip in the Jordan River. The trek to it was anything but pleasant. He had to fight his way through the dense, half-tropical jungle inhabited by wild boars. Nearer the clay banks, poisonous reptiles and tormenting insects hid among wild grasses and reeds.

By the time a person reached the dirty, yellow waters, he was bitten, scratched, and filthy.

The river bed did not invite waders. Mud seeped around the ankles, making each step a chore.

A strange river...

A stranger runner...

His beard was full and untrimmed. His eyes were fierce and fixed straight ahead. Not only was he covered in his own hair, but he was also clad in camel-hair garments, making him look even more wild.

There were a few people nearby the day he made his first appearance. They stared as the man emerged from the wilderness

Torchbearers

and half walked, half slid down the river bank. John waded into the river without hesitation, then suddenly turned and stared straight at them. Their conversation ceased abruptly.

His eyes blazed. They jumped when they heard his piercing words, "Repent! Repent! Repent, you sinners! The kingdom of heaven is coming! The Lord is coming! Get rid of your sins and get ready for Him!"

Little children ran to hide behind their mothers, and the teenagers just sort of eased themselves backward to stand with their families.

The wild man continued to rant about their sins, and the people fled the area. In a short time, the news had spread.

Speculation ran wild.

"Who is he?"

"Where did he come from?"

"Could he be a prophet?"

"Do you think he is still there?"

Some men of the area got together and went to see.

He was there. He was still standing in the river, yelling at one lone fisherman to repent.

They all listened to him intently, transfixed by his eyes. Then they began to listen to his words. The longer they listened, the more sense he made.

"Come. Get baptized, and confess your sins," he shouted.

After listening for about an hour, one young man broke away from the group. He ran down the embankment and waded out to John.

John watched as he came, his eyes never leaving the man's face. When the man had almost reached him, John stopped him with the command, "Confess your sins, man. When you've confessed them all, I will baptize you."

The young man began to confess his sins to God, one by one. Midway through his confession, tears were streaming down his face. His heart was heavy with shame. He felt naked before a holy God.

24

He finally lifted his head and looked again into the savage man's blazing eyes.

And he stared. The eyes that had looked so harsh just minutes before had softened and were radiating love. John reached out to him. His fear was gone as he was almost compelled to John's side. John dipped him into the river and lifted him up.

Waves of relief swelled through him. "My God!" he prayed. "I feel clean for the first time in my life!"

He turned and made his way back to the river bank, up through the tangled brush, to his friends.

They stood staring at him. "You look different," one of his friends finally said.

"I feel great...different...and clean!"

He wanted to run, shout, dance, and leap for joy. He was free! Free from a load that had been piling up and weighing him down since birth!

He didn't understand what had happened to him. He only knew that the guilt was no longer there. God had done a work.

It was the unconcealed joy on his face that caused two of his friends to warily approach John for the same experience.

When they later made their way back home, their wives and children tried to sort out their words.

So John was a messenger from God. Prophets were nothing new to Jews who knew their history. Yet it was so much easier to believe in the prophets of old than to be confronted with a live one!

The following day, the men took their families, neighbors, and friends to the river bank, hoping and praying that John would be there.

He was sitting on the bank of clay eating locusts when they arrived. When he saw them coming, he dipped his finger into a comb of honey and then sucked it. Then he waded into the river and again began shouting.

It was about an hour before the men convinced their families to get into the river and approach him. But his message, coupled with their transformed husbands and fathers, finally motivated them to be baptized. When they waded from the river, their faces radiant with joy, other families made the trek to John.

The word spread. More people arrived daily, seeking God's messenger.

The Jordan, for centuries the violent boundary that divided the holy from the unholy, now became the divider between the old ways and the new. Men joined John in the task of baptizing the crowds.

The crowds...

They flocked to John and away from the priests, who were quickly losing control.

The priests were incensed. How dare this man claim to be a messenger from God? Jehovah already had His priests to speak for Him.

"Stay away from the river! Stay away from the man! Ignore his message," they warned. But the people were replacing death with life, and they took no heed of the priests' bitter counsel.

The day was hot, heavy with humidity. Mobs thronged the area. Suddenly, there was a stir. Fingers pointed and voices whispered. The priests had arrived, their robes snagged, the hems soiled.

The people's eyes shifted from the priests to John. There would surely be a confrontation now.

John didn't even seem to notice them. Instead he continued to baptize.

Then, with a swift movement, he faced the priests. The crowd gasped. The eyes that they had seen filled with love just seconds before were now blazing with fire. He stared into the eyes of each of their leaders. One stared back defiantly, but the others lowered their heads or turned away. He waited silently until every eye was back on him. A hush came over the crowd. Even the children stared at this John they had almost learned not to fear.

Everyone jumped as his shout penetrated the silence. "You snakes! You vipers! You serpents! What are you doing here? If you do not bring forth good fruit, you will be cut down by the ax of God and cast into the fire!"

The men stared at him. Who did this man think he was? How dare he speak to them like this, especially in front of their people? And he wouldn't quit! His voice continued to rave. They turned and nearly ran from him.

John turned to the crowd as they were leaving. "There is someone coming who will lead you," he said gently. "I'm not even good enough to untie His shoes. I can only baptize you with water. He will baptize you with the Holy Spirit and with fire."

Then his voice stopped abruptly. His eyes left the crowd, and he stood staring at a man who came walking toward him.

The face that had so recently changed from anger to compassion was now filled with awe. He seemed to shrink before the One who was now making His way closer.

He turned to the spectators. "Look," he said, pointing at the man approaching him. "This is the Lamb of God, who will take away the sin of the world. This is the One I've been telling you would come."

The crowd glanced at the One coming, but then turned back to stare at John. Where was the John they knew—the one who fearlessly exposed sin and condemned sinners? John had been intimidated by no man. He had rebuked the king, challenged the soldiers, and denounced the priests. But now...now he stood trembling before the man who had reached his side.

They peered closely at the stranger. They could see nothing in Him that would inspire such deference in John.

"Baptize Me, John."

John's head dropped.

"I can't," he answered. "I'm not worthy to baptize You."

The crowd was shocked at his answer.

"Now," the man answered.

John hesitated, then reached out to baptize Him. He didn't even ask Him to first confess His sins, as he had demanded of everyone else. He simply baptized Him.

The crowd got up to their feet as this stranger rose from the water. He literally radiated light!

Suddenly a dove swooped from the clouds, flew directly toward them, and then settled upon the stranger's shoulder.

A voice thundered from the heavens, "This is My beloved Son, in whom I am well pleased."

It was a day earth would not forget.

Things changed for John after that day. He had begun his race with vigor and uncompromising boldness. He ran hard, and the crowd was amazed at his stamina. But after that day, he simply slowed his pace. What had been the greatest day of his life also seemed to be the beginning of a decline. Some of his best helpers left him that day. They just turned and followed the man who had been declared by a voice in the heavens to be the Son of God.

Most of the people left too.

Some stayed.

"Why is everyone leaving the river, John?" some asked him.

"I told you I was not the one to follow. I was just the one sent here to announce His coming."

John watched as more of the crowd left.

John wasn't sad that they were leaving him. He knew that he had come to prepare people for the coming of God's Son, and he felt good about having done that. He felt something like the best man in the wedding. It was great to be a part of the wedding, but it wasn't his big day. The groom was the one with the bride!

He looked at the stragglers still on the bank and smiled one of his rare smiles that lit up his face. "He must increase; I must decrease," he told them. "I am a man from this earth. He is a man who has come from heaven. God has sent Him to you and filled Him with His Spirit. God is His Father, and He loves His Son, and has given Him all power and all authority. If you will believe and trust Him, you will have everlasting life. If you reject Him, God's wrath will be toward you."

He turned and made his way out of the river, up the bank, and into the woods. He was still smiling.

John entered a dark area in his race then, so tangled and thick that no sunlight could penetrate. It began with his arrest. He was accused of speaking against the king. He had only spoken the truth; even as guards shackled and dragged him to prison, he denounced the sins of the king. "King Herod has broken the law of God! He too needs to confess his sins! He is living with his sister-in-law! She is married to his brother, Philip, and he has no right to take her!"

Herod and his wife were infuriated when they were told of John's denunciation! The king confessed to no one!

"Kill him!" Herod ordered.

"We will have an uprising if we kill him, Your Majesty," one of his subjects advised. "The people believe he is a messenger from their God. They refer to him as a prophet."

"Then lock the man up!"

This part of John's race was the toughest yet. It was too dark in the musty cell to see the rats, but he both heard and felt them. His wrists, waist, and ankles were shackled with chains that were embedded in the stone wall. They prevented him from stretching out or sitting, except in a crouched position.

His former helpers came when they could, making their way down the musty corridors. He identified them by their voices at the small, square opening to his cell. They prayed with him and kept him informed of the news.

As time dragged on, John became bitterly discouraged. He had trained for this race as far back as he could remember. From his earliest childhood, he had known this race was his destiny and had hardly been able to wait for it to begin.

But it had come to this. He was told about Jesus and the crowds that were beginning to follow Him. The news was good. So why was he abandoned and forgotten?

Was his race over? The weeks dragged on. Insects filled John's matted beard. Rat bites covered his weakened body.

One morning—or was it evening?—he heard a voice telling him more about Jesus. He listened eagerly.

Jesus. Just the mention of His name brought hope and a surge of strength. Another voice interrupted. There were two men at the door, both excitedly describing the crowds, the miracles, the Master.

John's ravaged body ached with pain. He spoke with an effort. "Ask Him...ask Him..."

He paused. Dare he ask the question that plagued him in the black, lonely hours? Yes. For he had to know the answer. It seemed so long since that day when the heavens opened and the sign of the dove was given. "Ask Him...tell Him I have to know for sure that He is the One. Or is there another we should look for?"

He heard the messenger gasp. "John! You know He's the One! You yourself told us He was the one! You saw the dove light on Him! You heard God's voice speak from heaven!"

John sighed heavily. "Please ask Him for me...and hurry back to give me His answer."

Exhausted with the effort of speech, he closed his eyes.

How many hours, days, or weeks passed before the answer finally came? He didn't know. In this place of blackness, days and nights all blended together.

"John! John! We told Jesus what you said! Do you want to hear His answer?"

"Yes! Oh, yes. Tell me—quickly!"

"John! Jesus told us to come and tell you what we are hearing and seeing. Blind people are seeing for the first time in their lives! People who have never walked are walking and jumping and running! He has healed lepers with just His touch! Deaf people are hearing! John, even dead people are coming back to life! Jesus is preaching the gospel to the poor!

"And, John..."

"Yes?"

"Jesus said everyone would be blessed who is not offended because of Him."

They waited for his answer.

"My Lord," he prayed silently. "Don't let me be offended by this prison cell."

"Did He say anything else?" he asked when he was able.

"He began telling the crowd what a great man you are. We didn't stay to listen to all that He was saying about you. We did hear Him say you were a messenger sent from God. Then we left and came running to you with His answer."

"Thank you. Thank you," John whispered.

Hours after they left, he still lay thinking about their message. If this Jesus was raising the dead and healing lepers, He could surely release him from prison. He undoubtedly would be out of this wretched place soon. He slept peacefully for the first time in weeks.

Things continued as they were, but John was no longer troubled. It helped so much just knowing that Jesus remembered him. Jesus had praised him to the people as a great runner. It was enough. If God should choose that he never preach again, if he should finish his race in the stench of this hole, then he would die at peace. For he had done his work faithfully, announcing the Christ to all who awaited His coming.

A few evenings later, he heard the feet of soldiers outside his cell. The door burst open, and John looked up expectantly. Three soldiers stood over him, one with his sword drawn. Another soldier placed his shoe on John's head, crushing the side of his face into the floor. His hoarse scream, the final reaction of his tortured body, ended abruptly as his head was severed.

The Herods of this world esteem neither the race nor its runners. This race is only in, not of, this world.

And while earth derides, heaven applauds.

An angel had announced the birth of John with the message, *"He shall be great in the sight of the Lord"* (Luke 1:15).

And he was. The Lord Himself had paid him His highest compliment:

> *Among them that are born of women there hath not risen a greater than John the Baptist.* (Matthew 11:11)

Chapter Five

DAVE

~Present day~

Thine ears shall hear a word behind thee, saying, This is the way,
walk ye in it, when ye turn to the right hand, and
when ye turn to the left.

—Isaiah 30:21

D ave's heart was pounding as his thoughts returned to the present...his time, his call, his race. "Oh, God," he breathed. "I don't know if I can survive this race! What if the course You set for me takes me where You took John? I don't think I can go through what John did! And God, if John was so great, why did You let his race end in such a violent death?"

The words of Jesus reverberated through Dave's mind, answering his question in the way He often did: with a question of His own. "Dave, do you seek the glory of men—or do you seek to fulfill My will for your life?"

Dave didn't answer until he had searched his heart.

Then his quiet answer came. "I seek only Your will, my Lord."

Wasn't that what John had sought? He did not seek approval from man!

Hadn't his race ended in a blaze of glory? For what greater glory could a man have than the stamp of approval given him by the Master he had lived to please?

Dave recalled the way the Lord had described John to the people.

What went ye out into the wilderness to see? A reed shaken with the wind? But what went ye out for to see? A man clothed in soft raiment? behold, they that wear soft clothing are in kings' houses. But what went ye out for to see? A prophet? yea, I say unto you, and more than a prophet. For this is he, of whom it is written, Behold, I send my messenger before thy face, which shall prepare thy way before thee. Verily I say unto you, Among them that are born of women there hath not risen a greater than John the Baptist.   (Matthew 11:7–11)

"Oh, Lord," Dave sighed. "Let me live my life as John did." A Bible verse he had memorized as a teen suddenly came back to him.

Thy word is a lamp unto my feet, and a light unto my path.
    (Psalm 119:105)

The words had never meant much to Dave. But now their message filled him with joy and relief. The Bible would light his way, beaming its rays upon the course he should run! He didn't have to worry about this race. He would just simply follow the light, as other runners had before him. If a prison cell or a sword was in his future, then so be it. He, like John before him, would be concerned only with pleasing the Lord.

He picked up the Bible from the table beside him. Opening it randomly, he read,

Looking unto Jesus the author and finisher of our faith; who for the joy that was set before him endured the cross, despising the shame, and is set down at the right hand of the throne of God.   (Hebrews 12:2)

Look to Jesus, the Author...
There was no doubt about Jesus being the Author of his race. He surely would never have chosen it on his own!
And Jesus, the Finisher?

The Lord obviously wouldn't start something He didn't intend to finish. Dave would trust His leadership one day at a time, one step at a time, until he crossed his finish line.

Look to Jesus, Dave. Look to Jesus...

Chapter Six

JESUS

~From Eternity to Eternity~

His lightnings enlightened the world: the earth saw, and trembled.

—Psalm 97:4

E arth had never seen a runner like Jesus. He did not just carry a torch. He *was* the Torch.

His race began with an explosion of light. Angels left the heavens to announce His birth to shepherds. The night air lit up with their awesome presence, and the shepherds followed their directions to the stable to welcome God's Lamb.

Wise men from the East followed the same path, lit for them by a star, and worshiped at His crib.

His mother knew He was destined to run the race, and she spent many of His childhood hours watching Him, contemplating His future in the privacy of her heart.

At twelve years of age, He was already in training, announcing to whomever cared to listen, "I must be about My Father's business."

He was thirty when God Himself announced Him to this earth as His chosen runner. Those at His baptism trembled at the introduction. "This is My beloved Son, in whom I am well pleased," God's voice reverberated from the heavens. And His race began.

He ran until He was exhausted, but He did not once falter. Crowds gathered and stared at this runner, transfixed. The dead came off their funeral biers and out of their graves when He spoke their names. Lepers crept from their caves and, at His touch, were no longer lepers. The brilliance of His presence penetrated blinded eyes, and the first sight they gazed upon was His face. The stooped and bent straightened to attention when they heard His name. The crippled ran, danced, and leaped. Demons screamed through their human cages, but were silenced by His rebuke.

He ran past a cemetery, freeing a tormented lunatic from over four thousand demons. Demons, terrified at being evicted from their home, clawed their way into a herd of two thousand swine. Jesus, in return for His act of compassion, was begged by those whose only concern was with the loss of their hogs to continue His race elsewhere. He ran from their coasts, leaving behind Him a new runner who held his torch high, lighting all around him.

He preached fearlessly as He ran; the deaf listened raptly while those who could hear stopped their ears.

As He ran through the multitudes, sinners discovered their Savior and the righteous discovered their sin.

Everyone and everything touched by this Torch was forever altered. Those who ran to Him were themselves transformed from darkness to light. Those who fled His presence found themselves groping in unimaginable, horrible blackness. Water became wine when lit by this Torch. A lad's small lunch became food for five thousand hungry men.

Howling winds grew silent at His command for peace. The sea lost its power to pull man to its depths as He ran nonchalantly across its surface.

The religious leaders came to question, sneer, and scoff, but they ended up fleeing from Him, trembling with rage and fear. His friends tried to stop His race, calling Him mad. Scribes, priests, and Pharisees, fueled with envy, incited the mobs to push Him from cliff edges as He ran. He escaped their fury and kept running.

"Vipers! Serpents!" He shouted vehemently to the jealous leaders.

Then His focus would invariably leave them. Turning tenderly to the sick, lame, possessed, hungry, thirsty, and needy, He gently called them His lambs and His little children.

He ran into Jerusalem's temple, shocking those in attendance as He drove out both the money changers and their customers with a whip, dumped their money on the floor, tipped over their tables, upended their cages of doves, and threw out their sheep and oxen. By ridding the temple of its profiteers, He further incurred the rage of His enemies.

Earth was not prepared for a runner such as this. His light was blinding, exposing man's weaknesses, frailty, faults, and sins. The world had never liked this race or its runners, but men particularly despised this One. He entered and ran through the world as someone more than human, and men realized they would either have to bow to Him or kill Him. They chose death, not realizing it was the path He Himself chose.

Earth's cry gained volume in one mighty crescendo: "Stop this runner!"

Jesus was praying one evening in the solitude of a hillside olive garden. The peace was suddenly shattered by the noise of a multitude. They advanced with torches and lanterns, but what were lanterns compared to the presence of Light?

Men approached their Creator armed with swords, but as Jesus walked toward them, simply declaring, "I am He," they fell backward, their bodies and their useless weapons littering the ground.

His trial was a mockery. Running in this race was not unlawful, and everyone involved knew it. He submitted meekly to His creation, stretching His body out on a tree He had made. He winced as hands He had formed wielded the hammer, driving nails through His hands and feet. His cross was set on a hill He had shaped.

He looked upon His hovering army of angelic warriors awaiting His nod to advance and destroy. Then He stopped His troops with a shake of His head and hung in agony as blood streamed from His wounds.

God turned His face, and the earth turned black, heaving and trembling.

The crucifixion of Christ was man's worst hour...and God's best. Only matchless mercy stayed the avenging hand of a loving God.

"It is finished," Jesus cried in His agony, and the veil in the temple separating unholy man from holy God ripped in half, from top to bottom.

A terrified soldier and his men could only say, "Truly this was the Son of God."

The runner of all runners was down. The race was over. The runners who had been in training to carry the torch wept in defeat. Satan and man had together succeeded in extinguishing the Light that had lit a sin-blackened world. Satan and his demons howled in glee. They had won.

But Christ lay in a borrowed tomb. He had no plans to remain there. Because how can Life be killed? And how can Light be darkened? And how can Resurrection be buried?

Satan, his devils, and his human agents would soon learn that they had attempted the impossible and failed. They had claimed their victory prematurely.

For Jesus' race was not over.

He was on a journey, and His first stop was hades. He arrived, an unexpected and uninvited guest. Light blazed into hell that day, shattering darkness. Demons shrieked as Jesus advanced triumphantly through the earth's bowels. Satan cringed with terrible comprehension.

Life had blazed a path through Death.

All that remained of the war then were the final skirmishes. Satan had lost.

A vicious hatred boiled up within him. Satan may have received the death blow, but he would fight to the end. He would use every cunning wile, every deceitful lie, and every evil torture he could devise to drag one man, woman, or child to hell with him. His scream of rage became a battle cry that echoed throughout the universe. No follower of Jesus Christ would get to heaven without a vicious warfare!

Jesus ignored both him and his cowering demons. Traveling through the corridors of darkness, Light ran. His brilliance lit up paradise. Prisoners of war, held in the black bowels of death, squinted and shielded their eyes as Light marched toward them.

"O Lord! My Strength! My Redeemer!" the psalmist cried.

"He has come to get us at last," John gasped.

A mighty crescendo of shouts merged with theirs. Their hopes had not been in vain! He had come to liberate them!

Satan shuddered as the saints' shouts of joy and the praise from Jesus' followers met somewhere between heaven and earth.

Fire leaped from the serpent's eyes as his avowed enemy led the redeemed to their new home in the heavens. He could imagine their homecoming. He had been evicted. Now mere humans were being ushered in with a celestial welcome.

There was nothing he could do about them. They were home safe. But he vowed he would do everything in his power to prevent any more people from getting there. He glared at the screeching demons surrounding him. They were beginning to comprehend the awful purpose of Christ's death and their impending doom. A snarl twisted his features. He would use his legions to fill the earth with sin and misery until the end. He would have to hurry. He didn't have long.

Jesus was not threatened by Satan's empty threats and hopeless schemes. He was even then alone with His Father in the most holy place. No human being had ever dared to approach the throne of God. Jesus, the Son of Man and the Son of God, now knelt before His Father, presenting to Him His own blood as the ransom for the souls of fallen man. His offering was received. Man's debt was paid in full.

How I despised the shame of the cross, He thought. *But, oh, the joy, the joy that I have now!*

He looked at Noah, Abraham, and Moses savoring heaven's beauty. He smiled upon David as he sat caressing his tiny son, stolen from him by sin and death. And John. He was freed from man's prison at last. Jesus didn't want to leave them even for a second. But He still had work to do on earth. He must meet with His torchbearers.

God dispatched an angel from heaven, and he arrived as a streak of lightning at the grave site. With a touch of his finger, he removed the stone, not so Jesus could get out, but so man could get in. For we all needed to know that His tomb was empty.

Arriving back on earth, the Lord ran to the seashore to find His men out fishing in the sea.

"Children," He called, "have you any meat?"

"No!" came the weary reply from the ship. They had fished the whole night, but they had caught nothing.

The Creator of the sea, the fish, and the men shouted back, "Cast the net on the right side of the ship, and you shall find!"

The words sounded familiar. But more concerned with the business of catching fish than remembering the words of their former Master, the disciples cast their net. Bringing it up again, they struggled with its weight. John stared at the swarming net, then at Peter.

"Peter! It's the Lord!"

Peter's eyes grew wide in wonder. Then, grabbing a coat, he dove overboard and began to swim ashore.

Jesus had a fire going before the ship landed. "Bring the fish!" Jesus called. It took all of them to drag in their catch.

Jesus set out the bread and grilled the fish. When the meal was ready, He invited, "Come and dine!"

They were still stunned. Even Peter was tongue-tied. No one dared to approach either Christ or the food. Jesus looked upon these rugged men. He knew they were fearful and embarrassed. Had they not hidden from the murderous mob and left Him to face His torturers alone?

He divided the bread and the fish and served them. They could feel His love as they ate together.

"Peter," He said after they finished eating.

Here it was then. The reproof. The shame.

"Feed my sheep, Peter. Feed my lambs."

Peter immediately lost all desire to do anything else.

The disciples leaned forward, listening intently to His final instructions.

"Don't leave Jerusalem until I baptize you with the Holy Spirit and with fire."

Then He just stood there, gazing with a tender love upon His people.

And as they gazed back, they realized their eyes were slowly lifting to the heavens. They stared in awe as their Champion Runner rose in the air. A cloud enfolded Him. He was no longer visible.

And still they stood, staring into the heavens, stretching for just one more glimpse of Him. It took a voice to call them back to earth. Two men, clothed in snow-white garments, asked them, "Why do you stand here gazing up into heaven?"

Why? Why!

Jesus had come!

They had watched Him die!

He had been resurrected!

And now He was gone again!

They all turned and stared at the two angels. One question was written on all their faces.

Will He come back?

The angels answered their unspoken question.

This same Jesus, which is taken up from you into heaven, shall so come in like manner as ye have seen him go into heaven.
                                                    (Acts 1:11)

They sighed in pleasure. He would come back. That promise would keep them going to their finish line.

Peter was already running in place, anxiously waiting for his baptism of fire.

Chapter Seven

DAVE

~Present Day~

Let us run with patience the race that is set before us, looking unto Jesus the author and finisher of our faith.

—Hebrews 12:1–2

Dave knelt before Jesus. "Lord," he prayed softly, "don't ever let me lose sight of You. You are the Author of this race. And You alone are the Finisher of it. If I ever get proud of my accomplishments, Lord, please remind me that all is darkness without You, for You are the Light. And remind me that all is death without You, for You alone are Life."

Dave paused, thinking about the runners through the centuries who had run with the torch. There were so many...and they were so different. The Lord never seemed to choose the ones Dave would expect Him to pick. There were the old ones and the young, the weak ones and the strong, the poor ones and the rich, the educated and the uneducated, some wicked and vile, and others pompous and arrogant.

"Lord," he said aloud, "You gave strength to the weak and weakness to the strong. You made the poor rich and the rich poor. You renewed the old and matured the young, gave knowledge to the uneducated and a child's faith to the educated. You made the wicked righteous and the arrogant humble.

"You have always had runners carrying the torch, through every generation, in every century. During the blackest hours, You had Your light on earth. Though all the forces of evil gathered together to stop the race, You have always kept someone running with the blazing torch. And when his race was over, You had another ready to take his place.

"What an awesome race! It never quits, and it never will, until Your shout of triumph echoes throughout the universe. When You fill all of heaven and earth with light, the need for a mere torch will be eliminated."

Dave felt small and unworthy as he thought about the runners who had preceded him. Who was he in such a company? But then again, who were any of them without Christ?

What could the great prayer warriors have accomplished without God to pray to? And what would the renowned preachers have preached, if God had not given the message? Could the famed revivalists have convicted a sinner or created a new heart?

"All of us are but men," Dave said softly, "from the greatest to the least. Only Christ can hold our universe together, send the sun across the sky, prevent the oceans from overflowing, grow a harvest from a seed—and anoint a runner with His awesome Spirit."

Dave wondered where his race would lead him. He knew it wouldn't be easy. He had been studying the lives of the past runners, and not one had had an easy race. All the forces of hell were determined to stop the smallest flicker of light from breaking the darkness that enveloped the earth.

But the enemy wasn't what really bothered Dave. His main concern was himself. He was all too aware of his weaknesses. Would it be his explosive temper that would defeat him? How many times had it gotten him into trouble?

"Lord," he prayed sincerely, "are You sure You want me in this race? If You are going to make a runner out of me, You have lots of work to do."

Dave sighed and picked up his Bible. He read,

The spirit indeed is willing, but the flesh is weak.

(Matthew 26:41)

And then he began to read about the runner called Peter.

Chapter Eight

PETER

~30 AD~

And the Lord said, Simon, Simon, behold, Satan hath desired to have you, that he may sift you as wheat: but I have prayed for thee, that thy faith fail not: and when thou art converted, strengthen thy brethren.

—Luke 22:31–32

P eter could not believe he was sitting in this room waiting for the fire of God to light his torch so he could begin his race. He thought he had forfeited his right to run. He had left the training field, cursing Jesus to anyone who cared to listen to his ranting. He had even claimed that he never knew Him to a woman who questioned his friendship with Jesus. Jesus had warned him it would happen.

"Peter, this night, before the cock crows, you will deny Me three times."

Peter knew Jesus had missed it this time. There was no way he would ever deny his Master. Ever. And then, with soldiers pressing thorns into Jesus' head, sneering at Him and brandishing their swords, he had. He had denied Him, not once, but three times. The rooster had crowed, even as he had cursed.

Even now, the sound of a rooster crowing sent shudders of shame reverberating through his body. In fact, the crow of a rooster not only reminded him of his failure to stand for Jesus, but also reminded him of himself, strutting around in his pride, believing he could get through anything, with or without God's help.

It had been a heady experience being with Jesus. From the time Jesus had called him from working on his dad's boat, his ego had steadily inflated. No other apostle had walked on water. Sure, he had begun to sink, but he had done it, while the others stood gaping from the ship.

He recalled the time he had fished the whole night and had caught nothing. Then Jesus had told him to go back out in the lake and let down his nets. Peter had boldly argued with Him. Jesus was no fisherman. He was a carpenter! Who was He to tell Peter, one of the best fishermen in his time, how to fish?

He had argued, but then had decided to pacify Jesus. "I'll let down the net," he sighed. "One net," he muttered as he headed back out to sea.

If he had let down both nets that day, as Jesus had instructed, he would not have broken the first one with the heavy weight of swarming fish they pulled from the sea.

He could only fall at the feet of Jesus when he finally reached the shore, saying, "I am a sinful man, Lord."

He should have realized that Jesus knew all about fish. How else could He have earlier sent Peter to the sea with a pole and hook and with a promise that the first fish he caught would have money in its mouth?

Jesus had certainly proved to him in no uncertain terms that He knew more about the sea and its fish than mere men ever knew. If Peter wanted to be a successful fisher of men, he would have to go to his Creator for help!

He had been the one with the revelation of who Christ really was, and Jesus had commended him for it. His pride had been deflated a few minutes later, though, when he began to lecture Jesus about His prophecy of His untimely death. Jesus had turned to him with eyes of fire, commanding sternly, "Get behind me, Satan! You are an offense to me!"

Peter had stayed in the background for a few days, but then Jesus had asked him and James and John to climb a mountain with Him. He hadn't asked the others to go along, so Peter knew he was still in the Lord's favor.

He would never forget that mountain scene. Jesus had told them before that He was the Light of the world, but that day Peter saw Jesus literally transformed into light itself. He knew for certain then that Jesus was no mere man.

He was brighter than the sun, and His clothing was almost blinding in its brilliance. As he stood there radiant, Moses and Elijah appeared, and the three of them talked together. Peter remembered with embarrassment how he had blurted out the suggestion that three tabernacles be built right there on the mountaintop: one for Moses, one for Elijah, and one for Jesus.

While he was still babbling, without the benefit of much thought, the voice of God Himself had interrupted him with the announcement, "This is My beloved Son, in whom I am well pleased; hear Him!"

Peter recalled falling on his face, trembling with fear. He stayed on his face until Jesus touched him, saying gently, "Get up; don't be afraid."

He and the two brothers, James and John, had gotten unsteadily to their feet, not knowing what they would see. When they looked around, only Jesus stood with them. Moses and Elijah were nowhere to be seen. Peter now realized that he had been out of order in suggesting three temples be built. The law, represented by Moses, and the prophets, represented by Elijah, had both been fulfilled in the person of Jesus Christ. God Himself had thundered from the heavens to point this out to him.

Thinking back, he wondered how Jesus had put up with his brashness.

Jesus had been so patient. Peter had reminded Jesus that he and the other apostles had forsaken everything to follow Him. Then he had come right out and asked Him what they were going to get out of their sacrifice. Jesus had calmly reassured him that they were not following Him in vain.

He thought back to the time he had vehemently stated, "Though I should die with You, yet will I not deny You."

He had been so arrogant while he trained for his race. "I'd die with You before I would deny You!" he had insisted to Jesus. Jesus had warned him to pray for strength, as he was too weak to face the battle to come. But he had been so sure of his spiritual strength that he had slept the evening away. He had slept when, just a few feet away from him, Jesus was agonizing in prayer.

When Judas had come leading the soldiers to arrest Jesus, he had jumped to his feet, whipped out his sword, and cut off Malchus' ear. Jesus hadn't even glanced his way as He stooped, picked up the ear, and gently placed it back on Malchus' head.

His arrogance was inconceivable to him now. He had been so sure of himself, only to discover he couldn't even stand strong against a servant girl.

"I recognize you!" she said loudly. "You were with Jesus!"

He was immediately the center of attention in the courtyard full of people.

"I don't know what you are talking about," he yelled.

She had no sooner left, when another servant girl spotted him.

After staring for a moment, she turned to the crowd and announced shrilly, "This fellow was also with Jesus of Nazareth!"

"I don't know the man!" Peter cried.

Peter noticed a group of men staring at him after being pointed out the second time. Finally they came over to him.

"You are one of them! We can tell by your speech!"

Peter had begun cursing and shouted, "I don't know the man!"

It was then that the rooster had crowed.

Then he remembered Jesus' words, and he felt them pierce the very depths of his soul. Never had he felt such shame. He ran from the courtyard, sobbing bitterly.

He never wanted to face Jesus again. Never! But just a few days later, Mary Magdalene had run to him and the rest of the apostles with the two words that forever changed his mind and his life. Mary was so electrified from her experience at the sepulchre that she could hardly relate the angel's message for them.

Finally she had calmed down enough to tell them what the angel had said.

"Go on your way. Tell Jesus' disciples and Peter..."

And Peter.

And Peter!

Those two words would thrill him to his dying day.

The angel had singled him out. There was hope that he was still eligible to run the race!

When he went to eat with Jesus on the seashore later, Jesus drew him aside and asked, "Do you love Me?"

Peter assured Jesus of his love.

Jesus simply answered, "Feed My lambs."

Jesus then asked, "Peter! Do you love Me?"

Peter replied, "Yes, Lord! I love You!"

"Feed My sheep."

The third time Jesus's words pierced his very soul. "Do you love Me, Peter?"

"You know I love You," Peter had said with hurt in his voice.

He pondered that conversation for days. Had Jesus questioned his love one time for each time he had denied knowing Him? He determined in his heart to run his race well. He would spend the remaining days of his life feeding the lambs and sheep of the Lord's pasture.

He waited now in this upper room. He didn't know what was supposed to happen. So far, nothing had, and he was getting restless.

Suddenly the room grew still with an unearthly hush. Something supernatural was about to happen, and Peter could feel it.

A strange noise filled the heavens, and a mighty wind surged through the room. Tongues of fire appeared as if from nowhere and settled on each one present. Peter was aware of an awe-inspiring Presence in the room, and for once in his life, though his mouth opened in amazement, he had nothing to say. Then he realized he was speaking—but in words he did not even recognize.

Peter's torch had been set aflame by God Himself.

And he began to run.

He ran down the steps and out the door. He preached with power and authority. People's hearts were filled with guilt, and they cried out, "What will we do?"

The beginning of Peter's race was explosive. Three thousand people repented of their sins and were baptized the first day.

Peter ran to the temple to pray and found a man over forty years old who had never walked. Peter lifted him to his feet, boldly demanding, "In the name of Jesus Christ of Nazareth, get up and walk!"

He didn't just walk! He leaped, jumped, and bounded into the temple, praising God!

Religious leaders, believing they had stopped the race at last, raged in fury at another miracle, another runner. They fumed as they saw Peter's torch held high and made their devious plans to kill this ignorant man. They arrested him, but Peter ran to his cell with joy. He was celebrating! Five thousand more people had now turned to Jesus.

Those who conspired to stop the race threatened Peter, but they dared not stop him by force yet. He was surrounded by too many cheering spectators. They could only release him, knowing he would just run harder and faster.

Peter ran in the newly formed church, rebuking Ananias and Sapphira fearlessly for their shameless lies, watching them fall dead at his feet.

He ran through the streets, and crowds thronged him, carrying their sick friends and relatives on stretchers to lay them in his shadow. All were instantly healed.

He ran through Joppa, pausing long enough to listen to the mournful wails around the cold and lifeless body of Tabitha. He knelt to pray and then summoned her back to life with two words, "Tabitha, arise." He ran from the room, where ashes had become beauty, mourning had become joy, and the spirit of heaviness had been clothed with the garment of praise. He ran, laughing with delight.

Then he changed his course.

"No runner has ever run there," spectators called.

But Peter had received a vision from God and began to run among the Gentiles. God alone charted his course.

He paused in his race only momentarily when a bystander called out some shocking news. "Herod has killed James! He is determined to stop this race! He is searching for you!"

Peter's pace slowed, but only for a moment, before committing his life to the race anew. He had backed down in the face of death previously. With God's help, he would never back down in fear again. He realized he would one day be stopped. But until that day, he would run with all the strength God gave him.

He thought it was all over the day he was arrested by sixteen of Herod's soldiers.

That dark night, he lay sleeping. Yes, he was chained to two cruel soldiers. Yes, guards stood alert at the prison doors to prevent his escape. Yet his sleep was sweet because his race, its course, and its length were all in the hands of his Master.

He awoke with a jerk as he felt a smack on his side. He looked up to see the prison lit up like the day. A stranger was reaching down to lift him to his feet, urging, "Get up quickly!"

Simultaneously the chains locking him to the soldiers fell from his hands.

"Get dressed, Peter! Put on your shoes! Follow me!"

Peter got dressed in a daze, convinced he was dreaming.

They hurried from the prison. The locked iron gate swung open of its own accord before they even reached it. Peter thought of Isaiah's words:

I will go before thee....: I will break in pieces the gates of brass, and cut in sunder the bars of iron. (Isaiah 45:2)

He looked up to grin at the stranger, but he wasn't there. Peter stood alone in the middle of the dark city.

Peter trembled as he realized an angel of the Lord had been dispatched from heaven to deliver him from his prison cell and certain execution.

He was even more fearless after that day.

He ran through Asia, holding his torch high. He ran valiantly, crying, "Christ left us an example! Follow His steps!"

He ran until his enemies, intent on stopping his race, came upon him violently.

Even as they sought to forever extinguish his light, he cried to those watching his race, "If you suffer for righteousness' sake, you will be happy! Do not be afraid of their terror, and do not be troubled! If any man suffers as a Christian, do not let him be ashamed; but let him glorify God because of it! So then, let those who suffer according to the will of God commit the keeping of their souls to Him in well doing, for He is a faithful Creator!"

Then one day he penned these words:

Shortly I must put off this my tabernacle, even as our Lord Jesus Christ hath showed me. (2 Peter 1:14)

He realized he was about to cross the finish line. He was tired. He had run hard and well. He remembered Jesus had warned him that in his old age he would be carried to a place he would not go of his own accord. He had often wondered about that. Perhaps he would be crucified, suffering the death his Lord had suffered. Even as he quaked at the possibility, he determined in his heart that if he was to be crucified, he would request to be hung upside down. He was unworthy to even die the same death as his precious Lord.

One thought gave him peace of mind: Jesus had assured him that he would glorify God in his death. Jesus had then gently repeated the same two words that He had spoken to call him into this race: "Follow Me."

He had been faithful.

When the time came for Peter to cross his finish line, he was untroubled. All he could think about was the excitement of being with Jesus again. As life ebbed from his body, and the torch fell from his limp hand, Peter was still smiling.

Chapter Nine

DAVE

~Present Day~

Except the LORD build the house, they labour in vain that build it:
except the LORD keep the city, the watchman waketh but in vain.
It is vain for you to rise up early, to sit up late, to eat the bread of
sorrows: for so he giveth his beloved sleep.

—Psalm 127:1–2

Dave leaned back in his chair, grinning. "Wow! Lord, You really changed Peter, didn't You? Somehow You made a mighty runner out of him! He went from chopping off a man's ear to being led meekly to his execution! He went from cursing You to singing praises to You! He didn't even have enough faith to let down his nets—but You gave him enough faith to lift up that crippled man!

"You took a coward who had denied You before a servant girl and made him into a fearless runner who lit up the darkness wherever he ran! Do it for me, too, Lord! Make a faithful runner out of me. Turn my temper into gentleness. Turn my weakness into strength! Help me to be faithful to the end, even if it means my death!

"...and Lord...I just now remembered who You said You are. You said You are the Beginning—and the End! So, I think I'll just call it a night and leave the end of my race in Your hands! Goodnight, Lord."

Dave dreamed he was back in high school. He hadn't studied the night before and the teacher had just asked him for a synopsis of the chapter he should have read. Then the bell rang. It kept ringing...and ringing...and ringing. Dave finally woke up enough to realize it was the telephone. He reached for it and muttered a halfhearted hello.

"Dave, this is Rev. Norton. We've never met, but I would like to change that. Could you come to my church office today at 4:30?"

Dave assured Rev. Norton he would be there and spent the rest of the day wondering why Rev. Norton would want to talk to him. His church was huge. Dave had attended his cousin's wedding there.

Someone must have told the pastor that Dave had entered the race. Perhaps he had a place in his church for Dave to serve. This day could be the beginning of a great ministry!

Dave wondered how Rev. Norton had gotten his name—who had told him that he had dedicated his life to the race? No one Dave knew seemed even remotely interested except Uncle Joe. He surely wouldn't have discussed Dave's race with Rev. Norton.

Shortly after four, Dave arrived at the church. He looked up at the huge pillars that seemed to dwarf the men entering through the doors below. He was shown into an office area by a polite secretary, who instructed him to wait. Exactly at 4:30, she came back to lead him to Rev. Norton's office.

Dave felt awkward in the presence of this distinguished man, but the noted preacher greeted him with a smile.

"Dave," said Rev. Norton, "please be seated. Someone close to you is very concerned about your welfare and asked me to talk with you."

"Concerned?" Dave asked. "May I ask who requested that you talk to me, sir?"

"That is confidential information, Dave. I will tell you that their concern is that you may be heading in a wrong direction.

Could you tell me your thoughts about the Bible and how it relates to your life?"

Dave's eyes lit eagerly. Here was a subject he was glad to talk about! "Rev. Norton, I was not raised in a Christian home. My family never went to church. We had a family Bible in our library, but none of us ever read it. Then I met Jesus Christ, and..."

"Dave, please forgive me for interrupting you, but I feel I must. How is it that you met Jesus Christ?"

"Sir," Dave answered, smiling, "I learned that Jesus had shed His blood on the cross of Calvary for me and that He wanted to be my Savior. I knelt before Him..."

"Did you see Him, Dave?"

"No, sir, not in the same way I see you. However, I did see Him, and I asked Him to be my Savior and to come into my heart..."

"Dave!" Rev. Norton said firmly. "I must again interrupt your tirade and inform you that you have been misled and deluded by the uneducated and ignorant. It is little wonder that those close to you are concerned about your mental welfare. I have only listened to you a few minutes, and I can already see that you are not rational in your thinking."

"Sir, don't you believe the words that Jesus Christ Himself spoke in John 1:12?"

Rev. Norton momentarily lost his poise. His face reddened, and he slammed his hand on his desk. He struggled to regain control of his expression. Then he smiled, but his eyes remained cold.

"I will ask you to refrain from quoting Bible verses to me, young man!" he said in a stiffly controlled voice.

"Sir, you opened this conversation by asking me to tell you my thoughts about the Bible!"

"Yes, David, I did," Rev. Norton answered coldly. "I was referring to your thoughts about the book itself, not to your uneducated interpretation of specific verses. You see, Dave, the Bible is a valuable book for its history and many of its beautiful passages of poetry. It is hardly a book relevant for today or for your life. Many people make a grave mistake by assuming the Bible is a book they can base their lives upon. These are people who border on the edge of fanaticism. Now the advice I have for you is..."

Dave stood to his feet, his eyes flashing. "I am sorry to interrupt you, but I will not listen to you or your lies another minute. You can tell those who are so concerned about me to consider instead their own eternal destiny and their own relationship with God."

Dave hurried from the stifling office, sweeping past the startled secretary and out of the church. He tried to slam the door, but it eased shut behind him.

He walked for a couple of miles at a brisk pace until he finally began to cool off. How could a man like that stand behind a pulpit Sunday after Sunday? He could think of no reason why anyone would attend such a church.

"I'm certainly glad I'm not like that man," he muttered.

Then he frowned as a verse from Scripture filled his mind:

The Pharisee stood and prayed thus with himself, God, I thank thee, that I am not as other men are. (Luke 18:11)

"That verse surely doesn't pertain to me," Dave mumbled.

All the high hopes and peace of the day were gone. Finally, he turned toward home. He avoided the Bible. He was afraid that if he tried to read it, it would open right to the verses dealing with anger and wrath—or even self-righteousness.

Self-righteousness? Could that describe him? Well, he just didn't want to think about it right now. He would get his mind on other things. But nothing he did stilled his troubled thoughts.

Finally he picked up his Bible and opened it to the passage that kept churning in his mind. He remembered reading just yesterday about the Pharisee and the sinner who had gone to the temple to pray. He dreaded reading it, but knew he would have no peace until he did.

*And he spake this parable unto certain which trusted in them-
selves that they were righteous, and despised others.* (Luke 18:9)

"All right, Lord. I admit it. I don't like that man. I also don't
appreciate my family insinuating that I am mentally unstable."

He set his Bible down and looked around the room for a
job that would keep him too busy to think. How could today be
so miserable when he had gone to sleep so peacefully the night
before? He had felt so close to the Lord just last night!

He slammed around the house, completing various chores
he had put off for months, but his accomplishments brought him
no joy.

He stood looking out the window for some time, thinking.
Which one of his family members or his former friends had
called Rev. Norton? Could it have been his own parents? There
was no doubt that they were upset over the direction his life had
taken, but it hurt him more than he cared to admit that they
would consider him mentally unbalanced.

Finally he turned and went into his room. Kneeling by his
bed, he opened his Bible again. His eyes grew wide as he read
and reread the words before him.

*And when his friends heard of it, they went out to lay hold on
him: for they said, He is beside himself.* (Mark 3:21)

For neither did his brethren believe in him. (John 7:5)

"Jesus! Your family didn't believe in You? Your friends
thought that You were beside Yourself? I didn't realize that You
went through these same things!

"Lord, I am so sorry. Just yesterday I told You I would go
with You to death. Today I am slamming around and all upset
because someone close to me cannot understand the race and my
call to it. Please forgive me for my unwillingness to suffer persecution for You. I need Your help if I am going to run this race
right. Please change me, Lord!"

He felt a little better, but still something was standing between him and the Lord. "What is it, Lord?" he whispered.

Then he knew.

"Lord, I can't love that man! I know Your Word tells me to love my enemies and pray for those who despitefully use me. How do I pray for him? What can I say? Rev. Norton is too proud to turn to You for salvation! How could that man ever be part of Your race? He is so sure of himself, even while he is leading people away from salvation! He belittles Your runners and doesn't even believe in You or Your Word! He wraps himself up in religion and calls himself a spiritual leader!"

Dave knew his praying wasn't getting him anywhere, so he turned off his light and went to bed. He tossed restlessly, and finally he turned his light back on and, picking up his Bible, began to read words that Paul had penned centuries ago.

> *After the most straitest sect of our religion I lived a Pharisee...I verily thought with myself, that I ought to do many things contrary to the name of Jesus of Nazareth. Which thing I also did in Jerusalem: and many of the saints did I shut up in prison, having received authority from the chief priests; and when they were put to death, I gave my voice against them. And I punished them oft in every synagogue, and compelled them to blaspheme.* (Acts 26:5, 9–11)

Dave closed his Bible with a groan. So Paul, a religious man, took pleasure in getting Christians to blaspheme their Lord.

And did anyone ever run a better—or more exciting—race than Paul ran?

Dave wondered what it must have been like to be smuggled out of a city in a basket.

Paul—what a runner!

Chapter Ten

PAUL

~39 AD~

*He is a chosen vessel unto me, to bear my name before the Gentiles,
and kings, and the children of Israel: for I will show him
how great things he must suffer for my name's sake.*

—Acts 9:15–16

The evening calm was shattered as a messenger burst through the door into the room where Paul sat visiting with disciples of Christ.

"They're waiting to capture Paul when he leaves Damascus!" the messenger cried. "They've posted guards around the clock at every gate of the city!"

Everyone talked at once, grasping at wild ideas for Paul's escape. Paul's thoughts were racing, too, but every suggestion that was presented would only result in his capture and execution.

"Oh, God," he half prayed and half sighed, "is my race to end so soon?"

Out of the tumult, he heard from the corner, "Yes, that just may work."

He pulled his chair nearer to the two men. As they discussed the pros and cons of the plan, Paul interrupted them. "What might work?"

"Paul! It's risky, but we may be able to lower you outside the city wall in a basket tied to a rope, escaping the guards at the city gates."

A few hours later, under the cloak of night, Paul climbed gingerly into the basket. He looked anxiously at the rope, hoping and praying that it would hold his weight—and that the men would hold the rope!

And to think he had once thought this race would be dull! He often relived the experience he had had while travelling the road into this city three years ago. His encounter with Jesus Christ would be forever etched in his mind. He had started his trip to Damascus with great expectation. He had despised followers of Jesus. Someone had to stop their lies, and if no one else would do it, he would. His whole life was fueled by his hatred. His very breath exhaled threats. Christians were a plague in the streets and in the synagogues, and he would not rest in peace until they were all exterminated from the earth.

His craze had compelled him to appear before the high priest, begging for authority to arrest believers in Christ. He then would bring them to Jerusalem to be tried for their blasphemous heresy. He planned to capture them, dead or alive, child or adult, man or woman, infirm or healthy, old or young. The thrill of the hunt ahead of him had made his journey seem longer than usual.

Then it had happened. One second everything was normal. The next, a blinding light enveloped him and he literally crashed to the earth with a thud.

Out of the light, a voice spoke, ringing with power and authority.

"Saul, Saul, why are you persecuting Me?"

Paul remembered trembling in fear as he asked, "Who are You, Lord?"

The next words sent terror through him. "I am Jesus, whom you persecute."

Jesus. Jesus, whom he hated. Jesus, whose followers he wanted to massacre. Jesus, whose church he was determined to destroy.

Jesus, who had lit up the whole area, knocked him to the earth with an unseen hand, and was now demanding to know why Paul was persecuting Him.

"Rise! Stand on your feet!" Paul leaped to his feet. He still saw nothing but blinding light, far brighter than the sun itself. He squeezed his eyes shut, but still the light penetrated his body and soul.

Jesus continued speaking. "I have appeared unto you for this purpose: to make you a minister and a witness. I send you to the Gentiles; to open their eyes and to turn them from darkness to light, and from the power of Satan unto God, that they may receive forgiveness of sins and inheritance among them who are sanctified by faith that is in Me."

The light left as abruptly as it had arrived. Paul remembered opening his eyes, and then shutting and opening them again and again, but still he saw nothing. He reached out, groping, until he felt the arm of one of his fellow travelers.

"Did you see the light? Did you hear the voice?" Paul asked in a voice still shaking with terror.

It was several seconds before the voice of the man whose arm Paul gripped answered weakly. "I heard a voice. But I didn't see anything."

Paul remembered how the men had gathered around him. They took his hand gently and led him like a child to Damascus.

Paul had remained in a room in the house of a man named Judas for three days. He refused to eat or drink anything served to him. He recalled pondering all that had happened to him. Jesus, famous for making blind eyes see, had appeared to him, making his seeing eyes blind. Why? Over and over again he recalled the message that Jesus had given him.

"I will make you a minister. I will make you a witness. I will send you to the Gentiles to open their eyes, to turn them from darkness to light, and to turn them from Satan to God."

There was no way to misunderstand that message. He himself would be a runner in the despised race. He had no choice. He would carry the torch.

Three days later, Paul heard his door open and someone walking toward him. Then he felt a hand on his head and the stranger spoke in a strong, clear voice. "Brother Saul, the Lord, even Jesus, who appeared to you in the way as you came, has sent me, that you might receive your sight and be filled with the Holy Ghost."

Paul could almost feel that strange sensation all over again—the scales cracking and peeling from his eyes. As they fell away, his sight was completely restored.

Then God lit his torch, and Paul began to run.

He ran first to the synagogue of Damascus, not to arrest disciples of Jesus as he had planned, but to announce himself as a runner.

He ran throughout the city, confounding Jews everywhere, proving that Jesus is the Christ.

And now he was climbing into a basket to escape certain death.

"God be with you, Paul," someone spoke, as the basket was lifted carefully over the wall to begin its descent. The basket swung against the wall several times on the way, jarring Paul, but it finally hit the ground with a thud. Paul was out and running almost immediately.

He ran to Jerusalem, then on to Caesarea, and then to Tarsus.

He ran tirelessly, holding his torch high. He ran along the seashores, in cities, in streets, in houses, in synagogues, in churches. He was chased from cities but, shaking the dust from his feet, ran on to others.

He ran out of Iconium and into Lystra to escape being stoned. He ran past a cripple, and as he passed by, shouted, "Stand upright on your feet!" He scarcely paused to watch as the man leaped up and ran behind him.

A crowd, witnessing the wonder, chased him, desiring to worship him. He turned and ran among them, his cry ringing, "Worship God!"

They turned on him, hurling stones as he ran. His pace slowed and then stopped as he crumpled to the ground. They dragged his limp body outside their city and left it there to rot.

Other runners of the race stopped their dash long enough to gather around him. Their torches cast light upon his bruised and bleeding body. Paul stirred and, rising to his feet, began to run again. He ran through the city, leaving a trail of his flabbergasted would-be murderers behind him.

He ran toward Bithynia, but God redirected his course to Troas. There Paul saw in a night vision a Macedonian, pleading, "Come to Macedonia, and help us!"

Paul ran to Macedonia, down by a riverside, then on through the city. He was followed by a girl, out of whom he cast an evil spirit. A multitude chased him. Magistrates caught him, beat him brutally, and cast him into an inner prison. Enemies of the race thrust his feet in stocks, cruelly bringing his race to a standstill.

Paul's back was bruised and bleeding. The dirt hole stank with dung, and rats moved in the darkness. Paul reflected on his experience. He was not bitter. He gloried in his adversities. But no matter how many afflictions he suffered, they would never wipe out the scene that came back to him in the night hours.

"Oh, Stephen. Stephen. God, I'm so sorry about what I did to Stephen."

Would he ever quit seeing that young man, radiating with life and power, cut off just as his race began? Paul squeezed his eyes shut, but he could still see him. He had been so serene and calm during the mockery of his trial, even while being accused of blasphemy. His face itself had become the torch, lighting the entire room with unnatural radiance.

The men, crazed with their lust to murder, took their coats off and laid them at Paul's feet. Paul not only consented to the death of this valiant runner, but exulted in it. Would the next scene never be erased from his mind? Paul tried to will the memory away, but he looked yet again at the blood pouring from Stephen's eyes, his nose, his ears, until his wrenching body had finally stilled, his race finished.

If only he could forever wipe away his triumphant smile of pride. If only he could forget his arrogant determination to incite a mob to stone every runner and extinguish every torch.

Paul shook his head, and his thoughts returned to the present.

"I will glory in my infirmities," he resolved in his heart. "I am glad I was beaten! I will take pleasure in this prison!"

It was pitch-black. Paul saw nothing. But he heard Silas, his fellow runner, softly moaning.

"Silas," Paul whispered, "are you okay?"

"I'm sore all over, Paul. And you?"

"Yes. But Silas—we're alive! We're alive! Yes, we suffered for Jesus! But He suffered for us! Yes, we've been persecuted! But Silas, we're not forsaken! Can this persecution separate us from the love of Christ? No! We are more than conquerors through Him!"

"You're right, Paul. Surely we will be killed in the morning."

"To be absent from the body is to be present with the Lord, Silas. And if we suffer, we shall also reign with Him."

"Yes," Silas breathed.

Paul was quiet for a few minutes, then he spoke again.

"Silas, let's pray."

Before Silas could respond, Paul began praying softly, his love for God pouring from his heart.

His prayer soon turned into a sweet song of praise. Silas joined him after a few words, and the two sang weakly at first; then their voices gained both strength and volume. They sang their worship, unaware that the other prisoners were listening intently.

Never had singing been heard in this prison. Prisoners crept nearer the sound at the midnight hour, listening, wondering.

Suddenly the song was interrupted by the screams and curses of the inmates as the building began to quake and the floor to heave. The doors of every cell swung open with a crash, and the chains shackling the prisoners snapped.

The inmates, released from their bonds, were held captive by fear.

Leaping to his feet, Paul ran to the doorway and saw the keeper of the prison staring wild-eyed at the scene. The man slowly drew out his sword to kill himself.

"Do yourself no harm! We're all here!" Paul prevented his suicide with a shout.

Paul prepared to run again, pausing long enough to explain his race and his torch to the jail keeper and his family. The keeper, notorious for his cruelty, knelt to wash the caked blood from Paul's back. Then, kneeling before Jesus, he asked Him to wash away his sins.

After baptizing the family and being released by the city's magistrates, Paul lifted high his torch and ran.

He ran to Thessalonica, to Berea, and then on to Athens. He ran past their idols, into their synagogues, through their marketplaces. He ran on to Corinth, where Jesus encouraged him during the night hours, "Be not afraid, but speak, and hold not your peace. For I am with you, and no man shall set on you to hurt you; for I have many people in this city."

He ran past the sick, leaving them well, past those chained to darkness, now lit by the light of his torch.

A spectator called out as he ran, "Paul, did you hear about the fire? Jews and Greeks of Ephesus turned to Jesus and have burned satanic books and symbols worth fifty thousand pieces of silver!"

Paul laughed as he ran on. Yes, this race was a difficult one, but the world was not as black now. More and more runners were joining the race, their torches penetrating its darkness. As for

Paul, his life was complete, his spirit at peace. He found this race exhilarating!

He ran into Ephesus, through a crowd of people who worshiped the goddess Diana. Demetrius had presented the image he created to the ignorant, claiming the idol had fallen to earth from the planet Jupiter.

As Paul ran, scattering the crowd, a riot erupted. The Ephesians despised Paul and his torch. His light exposed them, leaving them naked without their cloak of darkness.

Crowds thronged the sidewalks, screaming, "Great is Diana of the Ephesians!"

"There are no gods made with hands," Paul yelled above the din. It took the town clerk to restore peace to the city.

Paul then turned toward Jerusalem.

"Paul!" he was warned repeatedly. "Don't run in that direction! Your life is in danger!"

"None of these things move me. I do not consider my life precious to myself." He dismissed their warnings with a shrug. "I'll finish my course with joy!"

Who were men to set his course? His route was determined by God Himself!

He ran to Jerusalem, was stopped by an angry mob, and was beaten unmercifully. A chief captain strode into the tumult, bound him with chains, and carried him away. But the howling mob followed, chanting, "Away with him! Away with him!"

Paul quieted the multitude with a sweep of his hand, telling them why he was now running this race. He preached fervently and fearlessly, and when he finished, they cried as one enraged voice, "Away with such a man from the earth! It is not fit for him to live!"

The captain, fearing Paul would literally be pulled to pieces by the mob, carried him to a castle for refuge.

Jesus was already there. He came to Paul's room that night. "Be of good cheer, Paul! You have testified of Me in Jerusalem; so must you bear witness also at Rome!"

Paul slept peacefully, his lips forming a smile.

Over forty Jews vowed they would neither eat nor drink until they had killed this runner. They either broke their vow or died of starvation. That night the captain smuggled Paul to Caesarea. He was accompanied by two hundred soldiers, seventy horsemen, and two hundred spearmen.

Paul ran past governors. He carried his torch before kings and queens!

He was thrown on a ship full of convicts. An angel of God was aboard, waiting for the runner. Paul gripped his torch as a hurricane roared, tossing the ship like a match and breaking it in half. Paul swam to an island, his torch still held high, its fire still burning.

Paul ran on the island. He shook off the deadly snake that attached itself to his hand, intent on breaking his hold on the torch. Flinging the viper into the fire, Paul continued to run, passing those who lay dying and diseased, his life-giving torch restoring them to health.

He ran into Rome, still clutching his torch, shouting in triumph, "If God is for us, who can be against us?"

Paul ran to the point of exhaustion. Lying on the ground, he panted, "Christ will be magnified in my body, whether it be by life or by death. For me, to live is Christ, and to die is gain."

He lay still a moment, then whispered his wish. "I desire to depart and be with Christ."

He lay limply, listening, looking up at the heavens. The sky was full of beautiful, snow-white clouds, drifting, drifting...

The clouds slowly transformed into the faces of previous runners who had finished their course and were now watching him, all their expectations fixed on him.

There was Abel. Abel, who, prompted by his thankful heart, had offered God the best of his flock. Abel, who had enjoyed the pleasure of God, but had incurred the wrath of his brother and become the first victim of murder.

"Lord," Paul whispered. "I understand how it was with Abel now. I have been placed in peril by my own countrymen, my own people. I have been threatened by false brethren. And their hatred hurts. I am tired."

He recognized another face, the face of Enoch. Enoch, who had simply been translated to heaven without taking the death route that other men traveled. Enoch had pleased God. "I want to please you, too, my Lord," Paul breathed, as the face faded from view.

Was that Abraham? Yes! Abraham was there, watching him intently. Abraham, who had run his race without wavering, his eyes fixed on the finish line and beyond the finish line, looked steadily toward the city whose Builder and Maker is God.

Abraham reached it—and I can too, Paul thought.

He searched the other faces.

"Moses, is that you?" Paul asked, as he recognized Moses in the stands, viewing Paul's race with rapt attention. Paul felt tears filling his eyes as he sensed Moses' love and concern for him.

Who was he to be cheered on by Moses? Moses had walked away from all of Egypt's treasures to endure suffering and hardship as he ran the race for Christ!

The faces of the crowd of spectators were too many for Paul to contemplate individually. He had so often felt alone, not realizing that while the race was being run on earth, the heavens were filled with a multitude of spectators, watching, cheering, sometimes weeping, often breaking into a thunderous applause.

Paul felt new vigor and a faint stirring to get up and continue in spite of his weariness. For wasn't he being watched and applauded and urged on by a vast company of those heroes who had finished before him? They had not quit! Dare he?

They were drifting from his view now. He strained to identify others. Gideon, Samson, David, and Samuel were all there. Daniel was in the stands, a champion who had faced lions and had been lifted from their den, praising the Lord for victory over every foe, be it man or beast!

There were spectators he didn't know, but he heard their shouts of victory.

A woman he could not identify spoke to those near her in a triumphant voice. "If only the runners will keep their faith! I saw the dead raised during my race!"

Others came into focus and one by one stated the trials they had endured.

"We were tortured!"

"I was stoned!"

"We were killed with the sword!"

A man called out in a voice ringing with victory, "I was sawed apart!"

After a sudden hush, a father said almost gently, "I and my family were cast out of our home. We wandered in mountains. We lived in dens and caves. We wore skins of sheep and goats. But, by faith, we kept running."

Their voices then seemed to blend into one mighty crescendo as they worshiped their Savior and King.

Paul knelt below, weeping. "My Christ, the sufferings that I have endured are not worthy to be compared to the glory that will be revealed in me when I finish my course! This light affliction, which is but for a moment, will win me a reward of eternal glory!

"My God," he continued, tears streaming down his face, "I didn't realize I was surrounded by this huge cloud of witnesses! I didn't know so many spectators were watching this race! Lord, help me to run even better! Help me to rid myself of all weights that slow me down! Free me of every sin! Give me patience to run this race well!"

A peace settled over Paul as he thought about all the trials that champion runners before him had endured. His race, like theirs, had not been an easy one. He had endured one trial after another. His body was scarred by the one hundred and ninety-five vicious lashes of the brutal scourge. He had been beaten sadistically with rods, not once, but three times. Angry mobs had hurled stones, bruising his pain-wracked body, their wrath unspent until he lay at their feet as dead. He had survived three shipwrecks and had spent a night and a day in the open sea. He had run on dusty, hot roads, his parched mouth craving water. Thieves had robbed him of all but his faith. He was hunted as a common criminal by his own people. He had run until his body was worn out, and he often had wondered how he could keep going. He recalled days of gnawing hunger, cold nights when he lay shivering without shelter, the shameful time when he had been stripped even of his clothing.

But he had kept running.

For, through it all, Jesus was there. Jesus had told him right at the beginning that He would never forsake him. And He hadn't.

"Jesus," Paul whispered, "tribulation, distress, persecution, famine, nakedness, peril, the sword—none of these things have ever been able to keep me from running for You. I have felt Your love through them all!

"I am now persuaded that nothing—not death, life, angels, principalities, powers, things present, things to come, height, depth, nor any creature will ever be able to separate us!

"Yes, I've been troubled on every side—but I'm not in distress. I have been perplexed—but You have kept me from despair! I have been persecuted—but You have never forsaken me! Men have cast me down, but You have kept them from destroying me! In all of these things, because of You, Jesus, I have been more than a conqueror!"

Paul remembered the sneers and ridicule of his friends as he had walked away from the world and its riches to run this race for Christ, and he laughed aloud. "All this world has to offer is dung!" he proclaimed to anyone who cared to listen. Few did.

Paul felt strength displace his weakness.

He looked up to the heavens and spoke, even though the spectators were no longer visible.

"They finished. And I will too. I will run until my Lord says my course is finished. Until that final day, I will press on toward the goal for the prize of the high calling of God in Christ Jesus!"

Paul rose to his feet, renewed vigor surging through his body. He knew the time of his departure was at hand. He also now knew that he would continue to run, teaching the next runners all he had learned about this race, preparing them to carry the torch.

He ran, even while imprisoned, writing, always writing, the fire in his torch transformed to words that would burn their way into the hearts of his readers down through the centuries.

Paul's body weakened steadily, but his spirit thrived with power. As he fell across the finish line, he expended every ounce of energy left in his spent body to shout, so all in the stands could hear:

"I have fought a good fight!

"I have finished my course!

"I have kept the faith!

"Lord, I am coming for my crown!"

Paul laughed as he faced his executioner. He had just one more thing to say before he crossed his finish line. The sword was stayed as Paul's cry pierced the silence with words that would echo down through the ages to future runners. "Death, where is your sting? Grave, where is your victory? The sting of death is sin; and the strength of sin is the law! Thanks be to God, who gives us the victory through our Lord Jesus Christ!

"Therefore, my beloved brothers, be steadfast, unmovable, always abounding in the work of the Lord! Your labor is not for nothing in the Lord! I have not run in vain!"

His shout of triumph was severed with the sword. Paul's words would themselves fan the flames in the torches carried by future runners.

Runners like Dave...

Chapter Eleven

DAVE

~Present Day~

Whosoever shall smite thee on thy right cheek,
turn to him the other also.

—Matthew 5:39

Recompense to no man evil for evil.

—Romans 12:17

I want to be able to make the same claim that Paul did when my race is over, Lord," Dave prayed. "I too want to fight a good fight. And I want to finish the course You have set for me."

Dave dreaded tomorrow, for he knew what he had to do. He was not going to let anyone—not even Rev. Norton—point to his temper in order to discredit the message of the gospel.

The next morning, Dave prayed that God would give him wisdom both to speak and to keep silent. "Lord, You know how that man aggravates me. Please help me to see him with Your eyes of mercy and Your heart of love."

The pillars seemed even bigger than before as Dave walked into the church.

The secretary's eyes seemed to narrow as she watched him enter the office. "Yes?" she asked.

Dave smiled, but her expression remained cold.

"I am here to see Rev. Norton. I need only a couple of minutes with him."

"Do you have an appointment?"

"No, ma'am. But I will wait."

"Yes, you will," she answered, turning back to her work.

Dave was finally summoned after nearly an hour and a half had passed.

"Lord, give me courage," he prayed silently as he made his way to the office.

Rev. Norton was barely civil as he greeted Dave.

"Rev. Norton," Dave said, "I have come to apologize for the anger I displayed yesterday. I was rude and..."

"David," Rev. Norton interrupted coldly, "are you trying to say that you have considered what I said and have come to your senses?"

Dave smiled. "No, sir. Jesus Christ gave His life for me, and I could do no less than give my life back to Him. I will base my life and stake my eternity on His holy Word..."

"Then why are you here? We have nothing to discuss. You are wasting both my time and yours."

"As I said, Rev. Norton, I have come to apologize..."

"You are repeating yourself, David. If that is all you have come for, you may leave."

Rev. Norton pressed a button to summon his secretary. The door opened so swiftly that Dave decided she must have been listening at the door.

"Send in my next parishioner, Doris."

Dave extended his hand, but Rev. Norton ignored it and began rearranging papers on his desk.

"Thank you, Rev. Norton. God bless you," Dave said as he turned and left the office.

He caught himself whistling even before he reached the massive doors of the church. He looked up at the pillars as he went down the steps. They didn't look so big after all! Above them floated beautiful, fluffy, snow-white clouds. Above them was the endless blue sky. And above the sky the sun shone, sending its blazing light and warmth to the earth. But what was the sun compared to the Son, who sent His brilliant light and warmth into the hearts of men? For far above the universe was the heaven of heavens, where the Creator of it all reigned over His vast creation. It was to Him that Dave spoke, and by faith he could see the tender love in the eyes that gazed straight into his heart.

"I feel so good, Lord! I never would have dreamed that apologizing to someone could make me feel like this. Guilt is a heavy load to carry. Why do I let it weigh me down, when with just a few simple words, I can be free of it? Rev. Norton didn't accept my apology, but what does that matter? For You did, Lord. You did. And You know, that's beginning to be all that really matters!"

Chapter Twelve

DAVE

~Present Day~

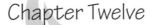

---

*Withhold not good from them to whom it is due, when
it is in the power of thine hand to do it.*

—Proverbs 3:27

D ave could hardly wait to begin the day. He didn't often
sing aloud as he ran. He had tried it a few times. Those
who had the misfortune of hearing him said he sang off
key more often than on. But today was made for singing! Hadn't
God made the crows to caw as well as the nightingales to sing?
He figured God must just make one big symphony out of it and
somehow enjoy the sounds of His creation.

"Please guide my steps today, Lord," Dave prayed. "Lead me
to people I can serve."

Dave felt like shouting praises as he began his morning jog
around the neighborhood. He just knew that the Lord had tremendous victories in store for him.

He had run only a block when he stopped abruptly and slowly
retraced his steps. He stood looking at the dark house before
him and sighed deeply.

"All right, Lord. I'm here because You told me to come back. I
don't know exactly what You want me to do, so please direct me."

Dave looked at the neglected lawn as the doorbell echoed in
the house. Finally the door opened just a crack, and two fearful
eyes peered out.

"Mrs. Arnold, I am your neighbor from across the street. My name is Dave. I've heard your husband is very ill. Could I just come in and visit him for a moment?"

She opened the door just wide enough for him to squeeze into the dark foyer. He looked into the living room beyond and saw the wasted body of an old man lying on a bed.

Dave walked over and picked up a gnarled hand.

"Mr. Arnold, I am your neighbor, Dave. I have come to visit with you and your wife and to see if there is anything you need."

He thought he saw a flicker in the man's eyes, but he wasn't sure. Had he even heard?

"Mrs. Arnold, may I pray for your husband?"

He hoped the barely imperceptible movement of her head meant yes, and began praying.

"Lord, You are needed here. Please come and strengthen and encourage Mr. and Mrs. Arnold. Bless this home, in Jesus' name, Amen."

Dave laid the limp hand back on the sheet and turned to Mrs. Arnold.

"Mrs. Arnold, is there anything I can do for you?"

Her sagging chin lifted and the eyes in her wrinkled face flashed.

"There is nothing we need, young man. We are getting along fine," she said, walking to the door and opening it wide, making sure Dave would have no trouble leaving.

As Dave left, he said, "God bless you, Mrs. Arnold. Please feel free to call me if you need anything."

As he resumed his jog, he prayed silently.

"Lord, I don't think I accomplished much there. At least I did what You told me to do."

Then the Lord's voice penetrated Dave's heart.

"It is you who are needed in that home. It is through you that I choose to bless the Arnolds."

Dave couldn't believe what he was hearing.

"Lord, I told them if they needed anything to call me!"

"Did you see any needs?"

Dave recalled the broken porch step and the overgrown lawn.

"Yes."

He knew the conversation was finished. Again he turned around, and this time he went back home. Minutes later he came out of his driveway dressed in old work clothes and carrying a rake.

He chuckled. "This is hardly the high hope I had for today, Lord."

Hours later, Dave wiped the sweat from his eyes. He hadn't realized how bad this yard was. He wondered how many years the leaves, branches, and debris had been accumulating. He hadn't seen Mrs. Arnold, and he was sure she hadn't seen him either. Her drapes remained tightly closed.

He would have to make arrangements to haul the piles of trash away. He surely wouldn't get this job done all at once, but if he kept at it a little bit each day, he would eventually see some progress.

Dave looked across the street as a car pulled up to his apartment. It was his aunt. Why would she visit him? She never had.

He called out to her as she got out of the car.

"Aunt Marie? I'm over here. I'm coming!"

She looked at him critically as he approached.

"David," she stated firmly, then continued stiffly, "I wasn't aware that you had been reduced to yard work."

Dave laughed.

"Come on in while I wash up."

He didn't have long to wonder why she had come. As usual, she got right to the point.

"David, your family is very upset with the direction your life is taking. You are bright, and we all have had high hopes for you. Now look at you. We were told you had entered some new kind of race, but raking lawns hardly seems like a respectable profession to me. What kind of nonsensical race is this?"

Dave breathed a silent prayer before he answered.

"Aunt Marie, I cannot expect you to understand the change in my life. No one can, unless they are acquainted with my Lord. I have given my life to Jesus Christ. He tells me how to live, and if He directs me to rake elderly neighbors' lawns, then that is all part of my new life."

"What is all this about a race?"

"Aunt Marie, you watched my relay race on television. You saw the runners carrying the torch through the host nation before the Olympics began.

"The race I am now running is a spiritual race. Down through the ages, in every century, there have been men, women, and even children who have carried the torch for Christ in their generation. I have been called to carry it in mine."

Dave could see his aunt was unimpressed, and her next words verified his conclusion.

"It all sounds very noble, David, but the fact of the matter is that you are standing in front of me in old work clothes, covered with dirt from a neighbor's yard. I hardly think you are making much of an impact on your generation.

"If you refuse to think about yourself, then consider your parents, David. They have made many sacrifices so you could obtain a good education and have a financially stable life. It is time you repaid them with some common sense."

She was gone before Dave even realized she was leaving. He stood by the window for a moment, contemplating her mission. Then he prayed quietly.

"Lord, thank You for my family. My parents have made many sacrifices for me, and I thank You for Dad and Mom and the home they provided. But You alone are the One who made the ultimate sacrifice on the cross. You bought me with the price of Your own precious blood. My life does not belong to my family, or even to myself. I belong to You, now and forever."

Dave lifted his head and grinned.

"Even if I have to spend my days raking yards!"

Dave cleaned up and ran toward the park. Maybe there would be some boys there playing basketball. He'd seen them before, but he had never stopped to talk to them.

There were six boys there, about fourteen or fifteen years old. Dave stood and watched them for a few minutes, and then he grew restless. He never had been good at watching others play. He wanted to get out there and play himself.

"Do you mind if I join you?"

They stopped and stared, but one finally shrugged.

After several minutes, he finally got the ball and sent it through the net. They made sure he didn't get the ball again.

The game ended, and Dave sat down on a picnic table near the boys. Two girls walked by, and before they were even beyond hearing distance, obscene filth poured from the boys' mouths. They laughed and joked and then looked at Dave. Their grins changed to scowls as they noticed he wasn't laughing.

"Hey, what kind of guy are you anyway?" one asked.

Dave looked at each boy steadily before answering, and then he spoke directly to Tom, the boy who seemed to be the leader of the others.

"I am glad you asked me that question because I *am* different. You see, I am a follower of Jesus Christ. You must know who He is; you have referred to Him consistently in your conversation. Do you realize that He is God? I have heard you ask God to damn one another, but Jesus didn't come to earth to damn anyone. He came instead to save you from your sins and to give you eternal life."

Tom underwent a transformation right before Dave's eyes. His eyes narrowed to slits and filled with a hatred and rage that Dave had seldom seen even in an older person. Vile blasphemy, curses, and threats poured from his mouth.

Dave knew he was no longer listening to the words of a fourteen-year-old boy, but to a deranged demon, whose hate-filled eyes looked out from a child who desperately needed deliverance.

Dave looked fearlessly past the venomous devil and into the heart of the captive boy.

"Jesus loves you, Tom. And I love you too. Jesus Christ alone can deliver you from the bondage of Satan and save you from your sins and eternal death. The devil is a loser. The precious blood given on the cross of Calvary by Jesus Christ caused the devil's defeat.

"Tom, I want you to know that I will be praying for you— every single day."

Dave left the deceptively peaceful park and the screams of profanity that filled the air. He was heartsick.

"My Lord," he cried. "What has happened to our children? What has Satan done to this generation?"

He was still heavyhearted when he entered the door of the church. He was a little late, and when he slipped into a pew, people were already singing.

It took a few minutes for the music to penetrate his soul. He looked around at the people as they worshiped the Lord in singing. And then his eyes settled on a young boy, about the age of the boys he had just left. Dave noticed tears glistening on his face as he lifted his voice in song,

> *Let the temple be filled with His glory.*
> *Let the courts be filled with His praise.*
> *Let the people sing praises in the holy of holies,*
> *Zion rejoices again!*

"My sweet Lord," Dave prayed. "I know there is hope for this generation—but only in You. Please help me to somehow reach Tom with the life-changing message of the gospel. And Jesus...I want to tell You how much I appreciate this beautiful church and these beautiful people. Thank You for my pastor who encourages

Your runners and so faithfully teaches us Your Word. Thank You for my brothers and sisters in Christ.

"This race is not easy. In fact, it seems to get harder each day. You knew how desperately we would all need to meet together in Your name and encourage and strengthen one another. It is so refreshing to come out of the world of darkness, hatred, and profanity, and enter into this place of light, love, and worship."

When the service was over, Dave told his pastor how much the church meant to him.

"Dave," the pastor said, "thank you for appreciating your church family and our ministry to the believers. You said that it is harder today to run this race than at any other time. This race, Dave, has never been easy for God's true people. The apostles faced constant persecution. God's prophets were killed. The blood of Christian martyrs has been spilled throughout the world in every generation.

"I often think of one of the most beloved pastors who ever lived. He did not waver in the heat of the battle. He left his congregation not only an example of righteous living, but also an example of facing death with dignity and courage. Let me tell you about a pastor who has been an inspiration to me."

Chapter Thirteen

POLYCARP

~70 AD–156 AD~

I will give you pastors according to mine heart, which shall feed you with knowledge and understanding.

—Jeremiah 3:15

The world succeeded in purging itself of the twelve apostles and Paul, hoping to forever end the despised race. But for every drop of blood planted by faithful martyrs, a crop of new runners grew. Their courage and joy, even when facing torture and death, caused many to pick up the torch. Ignited by the fire from God's censer, runners carried light throughout the earth.

Polycarp, born about 70 AD, was one of many who ran gallantly, casting light in dark places.

Polycarp had spent hours, days, even weeks, with the apostle John, drinking in his every word as he talked about Jesus. Others sat with them, but Polycarp was the last to leave, never tiring of hearing about his Master. When John's voice would grow hoarse and his body tired, Polycarp would urge him to tell him more.

John smiled tenderly at the eager face before him and said, "Polycarp, Jesus did so many things! If they were all written, I suppose that even the world itself could not contain all the books."

Polycarp thirsted to know more and more of Jesus. He had fallen in love with Him when he was only nine years old.

The dark day came when John was gone, captured by the enemies of the race and banished to Patmos, the island of convicts.

It was then that Polycarp realized it would never be enough to just hear about Jesus from another. So he himself reached up to the hand of the Lord, and with great trembling and much humility, took the torch that Christ held out to him.

The fire of God coursed through his body, burning, filling him with light. He had not known a touch from the Master would be like this! All that John had told him could not compare to this one touch! He was totally and unexpectedly consumed with a love he had never known. He loved everyone. He was thrilled to be part of the race and wanted to share with the world the news that Jesus lives and Jesus saves!

He ran to Smyrna, gathering together slaves and aristocrats alike, loving them all fervently, helping them to love one another.

He pastored this flock, leading his people gently, pointing them always to his Savior.

His congregation grew until all Asia Minor watched in horror as the fire spread. The dreaded light radiated throughout the entire area. It seemed that no family was exempt from its influence. Hatred began to ferment in the hearts of men.

"This man refuses to give the Roman gods the honor due them," they ranted. "Don't listen to him!" The mob responded with a cry of fury.

"Polycarp, the destroyer of our gods, must himself be destroyed!"

He paid no attention to the wrath of his enemies. And that enraged them all the more.

"There is only one way to stop this race! Polycarp cannot be allowed to run! His preaching must be silenced! His writings must be banned! We cannot allow him to produce more torchbearers! Even members of our governor's staff have joined his church!"

The voice grew louder as Polycarp continued to run. When he was eighty-six years of age, and still running strong, the voices became deafening.

It was then that his adversaries decided he would no longer be allowed to run. The Roman governor sent guards to seize him, but they searched for him in vain. Polycarp lay in the upper room of a cottage, nourished by his concerned congregation.

"We need you. Please hide for our sake," they had pleaded. Out of his love for them, he had conceded.

When his friends warned him that mounted police were on their way to search the cottage, he refused to be moved to another farm.

"The will of God be done," Polycarp said.

The police found him there and gathered around their prey. Polycarp rose to his feet, speaking calmly to his captors.

"Would you be my guests at dinner?"

The Roman guards joined their prisoner for a feast. As they ate, they looked questioningly at their host. He gazed back at them, love in his eyes. Never had they been this close to one carrying the torch. They felt naked in its light.

When they finished eating, Polycarp rose to his feet. "Please give me one hour to talk to my Lord."

They looked at one another, shrugging, then nodded.

While they sat watching him intently, Polycarp looked upon the face of his beloved Friend and Savior, totally absorbed in his conversation with Him. For one hour, he prayed passionately.

As the guards sat in the glow of his torch, listening to the prayer of this condemned, aged man, they cursed themselves for having captured this brave and loving runner. They now had no choice but to carry him to the governor. They found themselves dreading his fate.

The governor was thrilled, and yet troubled, when Polycarp was brought to him. What should he do with such a renowned prisoner? Would his execution stop other runners? Or would they just lift their torches higher, as in the past, and run with renewed vigor?

He realized that victory would be his only when Polycarp himself chose to extinguish his torch. He must persuade him to reject Jesus and embrace Caesar.

He faced Polycarp.

"Save yourself!" he demanded. "Admit that Caesar is Lord!"

"Jesus is my Lord," Polycarp answered.

"Offer incense to Caesar! Carry your torch for him!"

Polycarp calmly shook his head.

"Have respect for your age," the governor pleaded. "Swear by the divinity of Caesar! Repent!"

All his begging availed nothing.

Polycarp's reply remained unmovable. "Jesus is, and forever will be, my Lord!"

It would take more than begging to break this runner.

The governor called soldiers to drag Polycarp into the stadium. A bloodthirsty crowd sat waiting impatiently to be entertained by the sport of murder.

The governor noticed Polycarp looking at the crowd.

"Take the oath of Caesar!" he implored. "I will still let you go!"

Polycarp turned toward him, his face set, his heart fixed. His torch still lit the darkness around him, exposing all those in its path.

The governor grew impatient. He hated standing in this cursed light. And he despised anyone who dared to carry it. He determined to extinguish it by any means. How much better it would be if Polycarp would lay down his torch! He would try just once more.

"Polycarp, curse your Christ. I have the authority to set you free!"

Polycarp looked upon him with pity, and then his eyes rested on the restless crowd. Men, women, children—all eyes were upon him, eagerly awaiting his execution.

He shook his head wearily. His race was nearly at an end, and he would finish on the run, his torch held high.

He turned again toward the anxious governor.

"For eighty-six years," he said in a strong, firm voice, "I have been His servant. Christ has never done me wrong. How can I blaspheme my King who saved me?"

The governor stared at him. Polycarp's eyes bored right back into his, unwavering. The governor stood trembling, but Polycarp calmly awaited his sentence, no fear in his eyes. It made the governor boil with anger.

If Polycarp would run to the end, then let the end come.

"I have wild beasts!" he yelled viciously.

Polycarp stood unmoved.

"If you make light of them, I will have you destroyed by fire!"

A hush had settled over the crowd. Even the children were still as Polycarp answered. His gentle eyes seemed as fire. He shouted in a voice that echoed throughout the stadium. "The fire you threaten burns for a time and is soon extinguished. There is a fire you know nothing about—the fire of the judgment to come and of eternal punishment, the fire reserved for the ungodly!"

He continued to look at the crowd, who sat unconcerned and unmoving. Then he turned toward the governor.

"Why do you hesitate? Do what you want to me."

The governor stared at this valiant runner.

He could not gaze long into his eyes. Turning abruptly, he shouted, "Crier! Go to the center of the arena and announce three times: 'Polycarp has confessed that he is a Christian!'"

The crier ran with his message.

> *Polycarp has confessed that he is a Christian!*
> *Polycarp has confessed that he is a Christian!*
> *Polycarp has confessed that he is a Christian!*

The crowd seemed to writhe with anticipation as adults and children alike thundered in one mighty voice, "Burn Polycarp alive!"

Soldiers tied him to the stake, piling wood around his feet.

He stood unresisting, praying to the Christ he knew would soon enfold him in a welcoming embrace.

His prayer was heard by all in the arenas of both earth and heaven.

"O Lord God Almighty, the Father of Your beloved and blessed Son Jesus Christ, by whom we have the knowledge of You, the God of angels and powers, and of every creature, and of the whole race of the righteous who live before You: I give You thanks that You have counted me worthy of this day and this hour, that I should have a part in the number of Your martyrs, in the cup of your Christ, unto the resurrection of eternal life."

He smiled as he spoke his last "Amen." The crowd stared in horror as flames encircled his body like an arch. He stood untouched, unburned, in their midst.

"Pierce him with a sword!"

The executioner obeyed the order but leaped back quickly to avoid the flow of blood that came from Polycarp's body. The blood gushed in a supernatural torrent, and the fire was instantly extinguished.

His remains were burned, but the mob was in turmoil. Many realized that they had not only witnessed, but had also participated in, the grisly murder of one of the world's most gallant runners. Unanswered questions began to echo in men's minds.

What race was this, that its runners would embrace death with gladness rather than throw down their torches?

What caused these runners to be unmovable and fearless before the powerful rulers of the world?

How could this race ever be stopped with such runners sprinting throughout the entire earth, leaving more runners, more torches burning in their wake?

There had been no joy in the execution of Polycarp. His death had brought no victory for Rome.

Many people, inspired by this faithful runner, held their torches aloft to be lit by heaven's fire.

Polycarp, now one of heaven's witnesses to earth's race, remembered the words spoken to him by his beloved friend, John. The words were both a prayer for those still carrying the torch and a victory cry of his own.

Whatsoever is born of God overcometh the world: and this is the victory that overcometh the world, even our faith. Who is he that overcometh the world, but he that believeth that Jesus is the Son of God? (1 John 5:4–5)

The world passeth away, and the lust thereof: but he that doeth the will of God abideth for ever. (1 John 2:17)

Chapter Fourteen

DAVE

~Present Day~

Now ye are the body of Christ, and members in particular.
—1 Corinthians 12:27

There was silence as Dave stood quietly thinking about Polycarp's life and death. Then the pastor spoke.

"Dave, I like to look back at the lives of previous runners. Many of their lives have challenged me to soar to new heights. What a blessing it is to learn that God has never failed one of His own! I can count on every one of His promises. I have never had to face torture, but I know God gives courage and grace to face even death as a martyr. I have read that Stephen smiled while being stoned. Many runners down through the centuries have faced both life and death victoriously. Their triumphant entry into the courts of heaven overshadowed their painful exit from this sin-sick world.

"Polycarp is an inspiration to me as a pastor because he was a single-minded shepherd over his flock. He chose to love his people. His people, in turn, chose to love him. As he faced arrest, he chose to love his enemies. Even as he was given the choice of saving his life by denying his Savior, he chose to serve his beloved Lord unto death.

"Dave, you will face many challenges during the course of your run. Only one Runner has ever run the perfect course and left us the perfect example. That is Jesus Himself. But the runners who have carried the torch before us can be a great inspiration for those of us who carry it today. Many ran a triumphant race, their sole purpose to please their Lord."

He sighed and shook his head. "We do not have enough runners today whose lives challenge us to new heights in Christ."

He smiled gently at Dave, then said earnestly, "I pray, Dave, that you will become one.

"Let me leave you with one thought before you go home this evening. I may not get another chance to share with you a lesson I have learned during my race."

"I would love to hear it! I appreciate the time you are giving me," Dave answered. "And I value your counsel."

The pastor smiled and continued.

"Dave, our Lord treats us all as individuals. He will make a unique runner out of each one of us. We only need a glance at His creation to see that truth. God has filled this earth with millions of species of fish, birds, animals, plants, flowers, and even insects.

"Billions of snowflakes fall to this earth, remain for a short time, and then melt. Each is a marvel of God's handiwork. Wilson Bentley dedicated forty-six years of his life to photograph snowflakes. He lived alone in a shack battling the fierce Vermont winters, but he never tired of his work. Each snowflake was a fresh and beautiful new design.

"Billions of people inhabit this earth, but each one is unique. Every individual can be identified by just his fingerprints. You too are unique, Dave. There is only one you. Don't pattern your life or your race after another's. Simply let our Master Designer make you into His own special design for His service.

"As you run, you will meet other runners, each one unique in our Master's plan. Just like the snowflake, each one, though different, is beautifully designed by the Master Creator. God values each one and speaks of His people as His precious jewels. The church will renew its first love when we value and love one another as our Lord loves us.

"Let me tell you about a runner whose name was Lawrence. He was a runner with a message for the people of his day—and ours."

Chapter Fifteen

LAWRENCE

~258 AD~

A book of remembrance was written before him for them that feared the LORD, and that thought upon his name. And they shall be mine, saith the LORD of hosts, in that day when I make up my jewels.

—Malachi 3:16–17

Lawrence enjoyed his race. He ministered to God's flock faithfully, caring for both their physical and spiritual needs. He knew his race would be short, for he ran when running was forbidden.

Valerian, the emperor of Rome, had ordered in the year 258 that all bishops, priests, and deacons be executed, and that the laity and civil servants lose their privileges and be reduced to slavery.

Then he added the order that excited Marcianus, who managed the Roman government for Valerian: All church property was to be confiscated!

Marcianus was a ruthless and cruel man who enjoyed killing the runners he despised. But he searched in vain to locate the treasures of the despised sect.

He knew there had to be a treasury. How else could the Christians continue to eat and stay clothed? The government had made every effort to crush them, but still their needs were supplied. Someone, someplace had to have a vast storehouse to continuously supply the Christians with provisions.

He asked questions, sometimes discreetly, often using torture. The answer was always the same: Lawrence. For Lawrence, men claimed, was the runner in charge of distributing goods to the poor. He could lead him to the church's treasure. Marcianus longed to capture Lawrence, not only to rid the earth of one of its faithful runners, but also to take for himself the wealth of the Christians.

Lawrence was running, his torch held high, when he was approached and halted by Marcianus. Lawrence looked with pity upon the cruel countenance of the one standing before him, seeing in him both hatred and raw greed.

"Lead me to your treasures," Marcianus demanded coldly.

"Marcianus," Lawrence answered calmly, "it will take me three days to gather the treasures of the church in one place. I will meet you then and show you our treasures."

"Three days then," Marcianus answered curtly.

Lawrence didn't even waste a moment to watch Marcianus and his attendants leave.

He knew he had only three days left to run.

He ran throughout the city, the hillsides, the marketplace.

Then his three days were spent. He went to meet the ruthless persecutor and thief.

Marcianus marched to the appointed place surrounded by his guards.

He found not one runner, not one torch, but many runners and many torches. He cringed in the light.

"What is this?" he demanded of Lawrence.

Lawrence smiled, then turned to those he had gathered together. He looked gently upon the poor of the earth, the despised, the persecuted, those tossed away by the world as its refuse. He walked over and joined them, stretching out his arms, and turned back to Marcianus. "These, Marcianus, are the precious treasures of the church.

"These are the treasures indeed, in whom Jesus Christ has His mansion place. What more precious jewels can Christ have than those in whom He has promised to dwell? What greater riches can Christ our Master possess than the poor people in whom He loves to be seen?

"These are truly the precious treasures, in whom the faith of Christ reigns!"

Marcianus was mad with fury! He stomped; he glared; he literally foamed at the mouth!

Lawrence looked upon him with pity.

This mere servant of an earthly emperor saw only rabble standing before him. And at the same time, the King of Kings and Lord of Lords looked down from His throne of gold and, with love in His eyes, saw priceless jewels.

Lawrence would love and serve King Jesus unto death.

Marcianus turned his bulging eyes back to Lawrence. Then he turned toward his guards.

"Kindle the fire!" he cried. "Has this villain deluded the emperor? Away with him, away with him! Whip him with scourges, beat him with rods, buffet him with fists, brain him with clubs, ye tormentors!"

Lawrence looked upon this maniac and prayed, "God, help him."

He thanked God that he was the persecuted, not the persecutor. He thanked God that he was the one hated rather than the one full of hatred. He thanked God that he would be the martyr rather than the murderer. He would soon be ushered before the King of Kings and Lord of Lords, who looked upon His followers not as just part of a worthless mob, but as the priceless treasures of His kingdom.

Those who watched his hand finally grow limp, and his torch fall to be picked up by another, said later that Lawrence did not seem consumed by pain, but merely at rest in the everlasting arms of the King, for whom he had joyfully run.

Chapter Sixteen

DAVE

~Present Day~

See that ye love one another with a pure heart fervently.

—1 Peter 1:22

*If any man defile the temple of God, him shall God destroy;
for the temple of God is holy, which temple ye are.*

—1 Corinthians 3:17

T he pastor paused, then said, "Dave, there aren't many Christians like Lawrence who see God's people as God sees them. If God's people are His precious jewels, as indeed they are, then don't ever handle His priceless treasures without the utmost care. As you see your sisters and brothers in Christ as God sees them, they will become precious to you also."

He sighed. "Dave, if the church today could just learn what Lawrence knew back in the year 258..."

Tears filled Dave's eyes as the pastor gripped his hand and prayed that God would bless his race.

As Dave left the church, he prayed, "Lord, if the church today had more men like Polycarp, like Lawrence, and like my pastor— men who really love Your people—what a church it would be!"

He stopped and lifted his hands and face to the heavens. "My Lord," he breathed, "please give me love for each one of Your precious jewels! May I never treat one carelessly. Help me to realize that Your people are Your temple. Help me to value each one as You do."

Chapter Seventeen

DAVE

~Present Day~

*For every one that doeth evil hateth the light, neither cometh
to the light, lest his deeds should be reproved.*

—John 3:20

D ave was running down a side street when his face broke
into a huge grin. Two of his old friends from school were
approaching him, laughing and talking together. Their
laughter faded abruptly when they saw him. One stared at Dave's
torch, then cursed. They ignored his warm greeting and passed
by without a word.

It hurt.

What a contrast that encounter was to meeting a fellow
runner! The fire leaping from two torches mingled and created
a warmth—even among strangers.

Dave smiled, thinking about the boy he often met on another
street. He felt close to him, even though all he knew about him
was that his name was Jack. He guessed he was about seventeen
years old.

Dave stopped suddenly. He hadn't seen Jack the last four
or five times he had run through the area. He turned around
and slowly retraced his steps. He walked down the street he
had just left, gazing at the houses. He remembered seeing Jack
come out of one of them a couple of times. They all looked
alike to him.

"Lord, if You want me to find Jack, please lead me to the right house," he prayed.

A door opened at the house just in front of him, then quickly closed. A figure had started out, seen Dave, and then ducked back in.

"Thank You, Lord!"

Dave knocked a long time before Jack came to the door.

He looked different. The friendly grin was gone. His eyes were dull, his shoulders slumped. His hand held his barely flickering torch loosely. It looked ready to drop.

He grudgingly motioned Dave to follow him inside.

The conversation was strained. Actually there was no conversation. Dave just kept talking and Jack answered with a barely perceptible nod now and then.

Finally Dave bluntly asked, "Jack, I see your torch is about to drop. Why?"

For the first time, Jack looked into Dave's eyes.

Then a torrent of pent-up frustration poured from him.

"Do you know what it is like to have your whole family turn against you? Do you know what it is like to have your parents wish you would get out of their lives? Do you know how hard it is to stay close to Christ in a house filled with cursing, filth, blasphemy, drunkenness, drugs, and constant screaming and fighting? Do you know how hard it is to keep smiling when everyone shuns you and ridicules you?

"Do you know what it's like today to carry the torch in school? The school I attend denies God, ridicules His Word, and forbids our prayers. Oh, the name of Jesus Christ is spoken of often—constantly, in fact. But the only ones who can freely speak of Him without censure are those who curse His name.

"Can you even imagine, Dave, how they despise my torch? Even the teachers and coaches who were my friends don't want to have anything to do with me. The custodian won't even speak to me!

"My cousin stayed around me for awhile. He sneers with the rest now. Dave, I just don't think I've got what it takes to finish this race! I hate being hated!"

Silence filled the room.

Finally Dave said, "Jack, I know only a little bit of what you are going through. I've been shunned and ridiculed by my family and cursed at by my friends. But my answer to your questions is no. I haven't been through all the things you face in your home and school. I can tell you about one who has.

"His name was Martin. He's gone down in history as Martin of Tours..."

Chapter Eighteen

MARTIN OF TOURS

~316 AD–397 AD~

My son, if sinners entice thee, consent thou not.

—Proverbs 1:10

Martin tried to keep from overhearing his parents' conversation. His dad, as usual, was shouting. His mother's voice was raised in anger too. The fury of both was directed at Martin.

"...ever since he joined these Christians, he has changed! He refuses to sacrifice to our gods or join our festivities. He's always wanted to be a soldier like me—but not now! Oh, no! The Roman soldiers are too brutal for him! I can feel his disapproval when I curse in my own home! The boy is only ten years old, and I have lost control of him! We have to keep him away from Christians! Without their influence, he'll get back to normal."

Martin sighed. He would never be able to please both Christ and his family. He hated causing his parents pain. And they had been furious when he denounced their pagan gods and received both salvation and his torch from Christ. He was forbidden to mention His name at home. But everyone else was free to curse Him.

The years passed slowly. As Martin grew in the Lord, the tension grew in his home.

He was only in his mid-teens when his dad forced him to join the Roman army.

"My Lord," Martin prayed the night before he had to leave. "Deliver me! I cannot become a Roman soldier! You have called me to give people life, not death!"

His prayer, as usual, ended in desperation. "Christ, what am I to do?"

He hoped for deliverance, but the answer he received was, "I am with you always. I will never leave you. I will never forsake you."

It was enough.

Martin was dressed in the uniform of Rome. A sword was thrust into his reluctant hand. He hoped and prayed he wouldn't be forced to use it.

His dad was relieved. He was an officer in the army, and he knew it wouldn't take long for his son to forsake Christ in the company of the blaspheming soldiers.

He smiled. "And he is finally away from those horrible Christians," he muttered. It wouldn't be long before he had his son back.

Martin was miserable. Fellow soldiers despised both Martin and his torch. Curses and obscenity colored the very atmosphere. Christ and His followers were mocked. Martin was ridiculed for refusing to treat people with cruelty.

The years dragged by. Martin's parents had little hope for their son now. The dreaded torch was still in his hand.

Martin petitioned the Roman emperor to release him.

"I am Christ's soldier," he said simply. "I am not allowed to fight."

The news of his request spread among the soldiers.

"Coward," they yelled fiercely, knowing there was nothing cowardly about him. For years he had stood alone, one Christian in their midst. They had never heard him curse, but they had heard him pray. They had never seen him treat anyone cruelly, but they had watched him share his food, his clothing, and his money with the needy. While they roughly shoved children out of their way, they could see him stooping down before them, smiling kindly, speaking gently. They had tried everything in their power to reduce him to their level. But still he continued to serve the Christ they hated.

Their failure to corrupt him filled them with rage.

Their voices swelled into one mighty shout.

"Coward! Coward! Coward!"

Martin faced them all head-on. There was a sudden hush as he spoke in a firm voice.

"I will be glad to stand in front of the battle line with all of Rome's soldiers lined up against me. My only weapon will be the cross."

They turned away in defeat. As far as they were concerned, he and his cross could both leave the army. Rome had no use for a soldier who refused to fight.

He was thrown into prison. Even there, his light exposed darkness. They discharged him in disgust.

His family turned away from their disgraceful son. They too had lost the battle.

Martin was finally free to do what he was called to do. He ran to the Balkan Peninsula to evangelize there.

"You came to preach Christ? We already follow Christ!" he was told. But no one held a torch. "We believe Christ is one of the prophets," they explained.

"Jesus Christ is not merely one of the prophets," Martin replied. "Jesus Christ is God!"

But the doctrine of Arianism had preceded him here. He was expelled from the country.

Undaunted, Martin ran to Italy, and then on to Gaul.

There he founded a monastery. He had faced loneliness all his life. He knew how desperately torchbearers needed fellowship, strength, encouragement, and a place to study the Scriptures together. Many weary and footsore runners stopped by for rest and renewal.

Martin was used to being alone in a crowd. So he ran to places where people had never heard of Christ. He demolished pagan shrines and idols with an ax.

Then a smile lit his face as he preached about the Love of his life and His great salvation. He ran throughout the French countryside, spreading the gospel wherever he went.

And he left behind an example of courage for the one with the torch who stands alone—in the home, in the classroom, at work, among family, among classmates, or among soldiers.

Chapter Nineteen

DAVE

~Present Day~

I have somewhat against thee, because thou hast left thy first love.
Remember therefore from whence thou art fallen, and repent.

—Revelation 2:4–5

Jack sat with his head bowed. The room was quiet.

Dave finally spoke softly. "Jack?"

Jack ignored him and began talking softly to God. "Jesus," he began. "I am so sorry for the way I've been acting. It's been so long since I've even talked to You. I was feeling so sorry for myself. I forgot...I forgot how it used to be before I knew You. I was always lonely then. I had friends—but I was so empty inside.

"Lord, I told Dave that I hate being hated. I want You to know that I love being loved by You more than I hate being hated by people. No one ever cared for me like You have."

His voice broke, and there was a long pause. Finally he continued his prayer. "I love You, my Christ. Please help me to be brave like Martin. Keep me company during the lonely times.

"And Jesus...thanks so much for sending Dave to get me back on track."

He looked up. His brilliant smile was back, shining through his tears, lighting his face. Flames leaped from his torch.

"You know, Dave, I didn't get lonely when I stayed close to Christ. I talked to Him constantly. He spoke to me as I read the Bible. We ran together.

"Then, somehow, I just quit talking to Him and spending time with Him. That's when I got lonely. I realized when I was praying...I wasn't really lonely for my friends or my family. I was lonely for my Jesus."

Dave clasped his shoulder.

"Jack," he said quietly, "I suppose most runners have gotten their eyes on their troubles and on people, instead of keeping them on the Lord. Peter sure did when he ran across the water!"

Jack nodded soberly. "Yes. And Peter started to sink too."

Dave nodded. "You're right, Jack, he did start to sink—but only low enough to jolt him into looking up!"

He chuckled.

"Peter was the only one who started to sink because he was the only one brave enough to get out of the boat."

Dave was already running down the street when Jack called out, "Hey, Dave! I'm going to look up that Martin when I finish my race!"

Dave turned around with a grin and a wave.

"Jack," he called back, "I think you and Martin are going to spend your eternity surrounded by friends!"

Chapter Twenty

DAVE

~Present Day~

*Keep that which is committed to thy trust, avoiding profane and
vain babblings, and oppositions of science falsely so called:
which some professing have erred concerning the faith.*

—1 Timothy 6:20–21

D ave gripped his torch more tightly as he ran on to the
university campus. The darkness was oppressive. Light
from his torch was able to penetrate only a small area of
the thick blackness. He ignored the many jeers as he made his
way to the dormitory to visit Phil.

"Phil!" Dave cried, glad to see his childhood friend again.

Phil glanced at his roommates, embarrassed to have a torchbearer coming to visit him. Sure, he and Dave had gone to church
together as kids, but he had left his childish friends and beliefs
behind years ago. He glanced warily at the torch Dave carried. It
made him uneasy. His friends laughed scornfully as Phil introduced Dave.

"This is great, Dave! We've heard about this race but have
never met a runner our own age!"

They looked him over, amused looks on their faces. They
seemed especially interested in his torch.

"Tell us, Dave, how can you be so naive? Do you seriously
believe that Bible you carry is the Word of God? Don't you realize
it's full of outdated principles? This is a new day! The so-called

Word of God you live by is nothing but antiquated mythology and fables! Modern knowledge has taken us far beyond its teachings."

Dave smiled at them, then looked at Phil. Phil looked quickly away, and Dave knew his old friend no longer believed in Christ. He turned back to Phil's friends.

"Do you really believe this is a new day?"

Without invitation, he sat on the nearest bed. His eyes seemed to look into the past.

"Let me take you back to another time...another place..."

Chapter Twenty-One

AUGUSTINE

~354 AD–430 AD~

Wherewithal shall a young man cleanse his way?
by taking heed thereto according to thy word.

—Psalm 119:9

It was a day made for the young and their pleasure. The rigid restrictions that had bound their parents and grandparents were no longer binding this generation, and the young people enjoyed the freedom to live their lives as they pleased. Fornication and adultery were included in most everyone's lifestyle, and few labeled them sin. Teenagers reveled in lust and bragged openly of their conquests. Young men and women simply lived together, delaying marriage to pursue their careers. Unplanned pregnancies and unwanted babies were terminated by means of abortion. The divorce rate was skyrocketing.

Teens and adults alike lived for pleasure. Sports were the craze. To maintain their popularity they had to become ever more brutal.

Complaints were heard continually about the excessive spending of the extravagant government. No one was willing, however, to make the necessary sacrifices to curtail increasing taxes.

Resentment was brewing throughout the world against Rome and its powerful, long-reaching tentacles. Vast amounts of money had to be spent to build gigantic armaments for protection.

The people chose the guidance of astrologers rather than God, for astrologers did not demand a holy life of their followers.

There were the few voices warning that the enemy that would finally destroy the powerful nation lay within rather than without. Modern men had decided that both God and His laws were obsolete. Anyone who cared to look could see that, with the removal of God from their nation, a deep moral decay had set in. Rome was in the process of rotting.

Restless vandals, dissatisfied with their station in life, set fire to cities, laughing as men's houses and livelihoods turned to ashes.

Christianity, the religion many claimed but few lived, was attacked both physically and intellectually.

Into this world, in the year 370, marched a brilliant sixteen-year-old youth. All his teachers were impressed with his superior intelligence. But if a subject did not come easily to Augustine, he dismissed it as unworthy of his attention. There was no way he was going to waste his teen years studying. For he, like his peers, was caught up in the pursuit of pleasure. Unbridled lust gripped him. Since he had no wish to be loosed, he surrendered himself completely to its control. His father was amused. His mother, a Christian who clung stubbornly to the old-fashioned values of the Bible, was troubled.

Augustine cared nothing about her disapproval of his life-style. If she chose to live by the laws of God, let her.

"It's a new day, Mom," he laughed, as she tried to reason with him. "This is The New Morality!"

His mother wept, praying that her son would one day see that this so-called new morality was nothing more than the old immorality.

Augustine mocked her Christ and the Bible she faithfully followed, with its warnings of sin and judgment. He found a perverse pleasure in doing whatever was forbidden in the Scriptures.

"The Bible is merely a book of fables," he jeered.

A wealthy pagan watched this brilliant young man closely, listening to his bold defiance of God.

"I wish Augustine to be my protégé," he remarked to his friends. "This young man, with the right training, could very well become the philosopher Rome needs to turn its Christians back to paganism!"

Augustine's parents were not wealthy, but no financial sacrifice was too great to send their son to the best of universities.

So, Augustine left home, without a backward glance, to attend college at Carthage. When he was seventeen years old, he looked forward to college life with great anticipation. What young man wouldn't be excited? Carthage was the most sophisticated and worldly city in North Africa!

He has been on campus only a short time when he met a beautiful woman and fell hopelessly in love.

"I mean to have her!" he declared to his friends.

They laughed at him. "Augustine! She is not a suitable wife! You know she is beneath your social standing! She would do nothing to further your career!"

"Oh, I don't plan to marry her," he laughed. "I realize she would hurt my career! But I do plan to take her as my mistress!"

And he did. He lived with her for the next thirteen years. She bore him a handsome son.

He had no shame about his relationship with her. Most of his friends had mistresses. After all, it was a new day.

His career flourished, and Augustine became a popular college professor. The brightest of his students became his faithful followers. He consulted astrologers to guide his every decision.

He lived life to the fullest. He loved his mistress and their son. Even though he was now a success and had reached many of his career goals, however, he realized she would still be a detriment to him socially if he were to marry her. He vowed to do nothing that would damage his career.

He lived in Rome, esteemed by the elite of the city as a great man of influence. He had carefully formed friendships with senators and others who had political status in Rome. He envied their position and became obsessed with the desire for their power. He was even willing to claim their pagan gods as his own.

Rome considered itself a Christian nation, but an altar to the Goddess of Victory still stood in the Senate chamber. Romans were willing to include Christ in their worship, but they had no wish to exclude their gods. Many of Augustine's senator friends worshiped Jupiter and Juno. Most of them didn't take their worship too seriously but didn't want to take a chance on offending any god.

Augustine willingly worshiped whatever god was popular with the crowd he longed to impress.

Steadily he climbed the ladder of success. He was in constant contact with Valentinian II, the young emperor of Rome. He finally managed to win his favor. Valentinian was impressed with the brilliant young professor and asked him to become his speech writer. Augustine was thrilled! To write speeches for the emperor was beyond his wildest dreams!

Dave paused. The silence in the room made the students uncomfortable.

Finally one said, "Life was really like that back in the fourth century?"

Dave smiled. "Did you really believe that this generation had invented a new style of living? Have you not read the words penned by King Solomon, the world's wisest sage? He wrote:

The thing that hath been, it is that which shall be; and that which is done is that which shall be done: and there is no new thing under the sun. Is there any thing whereof it may be said, See, this is new? it hath been already of old time, which was before us. (Ecclesiastes 1:9–10)

111

Phil looked down. One of his friends said, "Well, Dave, you've got us sort of interested in this Augustine. You may as well tell us the rest of the story. I'm sure it doesn't end there, right?"

"No, his story doesn't end there. If it had, we would know nothing of him today. He would be just another one of the men in his generation who lived and died and was buried under mountains of rubble, forgotten through the centuries of time.

"But something happened to Augustine that changed his life..."

Augustine finally felt secure enough in his career to marry. His mother arranged a marriage with an heiress. He watched as his mistress was forced to leave her lover of over thirteen years. He listened to her sobs as she hugged her beloved son good-bye. It had been a simple legal maneuver for Augustine to get custody of him. He would miss her, and he knew she would desperately miss her son, but life must go on.

Life go on? Augustine panicked at the thought of living alone until he was married. Then he grinned. He knew exactly what he would do! He would find himself another mistress and ask her to move in until his wedding day! And he did.

He tried to get excited about his fiancée and wedding, but he was depressed.

His career was flourishing, but his personal life was in shambles. He was restless, engaged to marry a woman he did not love, and deeply troubled. He could no longer sleep at night. The success he craved had brought him neither peace nor joy. His gods had not calmed his endless mental torment. Astrology had not brought him the assurance that his decisions were the right ones.

He had to get out of his house. Just before leaving, his eyes fell upon a Bible. He picked it up, almost without thinking, and left for a walk.

He wandered aimlessly, finally stopping in a garden. There he faced the fact that he was one of the most miserable men who had ever lived. Why was he so unhappy? Would nothing bring him contentment? Was he to spend his entire life dissatisfied and with this emptiness within him? Was anything or anyone worth living for? Was there to be no peace of mind for him?

Peace of mind... He doubted there even was such a thing, but then he remembered his best friend.

Again the scene he had tried to forget replayed itself in his mind. Could he never erase the memory?

Their friendship began when they were both children. They had grown up together, and as they neared manhood, they found a perverse pleasure in ridiculing Christ. They had fun thinking up new ways to mock Christianity, with its denunciation of so-called sin.

Then the dark day had come when his friend was struck with a sudden sickness and fell into a coma. Augustine was devastated.

He remembered rushing to his friend's room, and then stopping short as he viewed the scene before him. His friend lay perfectly still, his eyes wide and unseeing. A priest was leaning over him—baptizing him!

Augustine stared and then rushed up to the bedside.

"How dare you baptize him?" he raged, shaking with anger. "He wants nothing to do with your Christ! Now that he lies in a coma, unable to stop your foolishness, you dare to baptize him!"

Augustine turned and hurried from the room.

The following day, he was called to his friend's room. He dreaded seeing his friend in his comatose state.

He entered the room slowly, and then a huge smile lit his face. His friend greeted him with a grin. He had miraculously recovered! Augustine rushed to his bed, laughing.

When he had greeted him, he joked, "Can you believe a priest baptized you while you were in your coma?"

The smile on his friend's face immediately vanished. "I received Christ and His atonement for my sins, Augustine," he answered, a new sincerity ringing in his voice.

Just two weeks later, Augustine stood weeping as his friend again began his journey through death's unknown valley. Augustine was in turmoil, but his friend faced death without fear. He seemed to be filled with a strange and beautiful peace. He drew his last breath and passed beyond Augustine's reach.

The vivid memory still haunted Augustine. He and his friend had mocked and blasphemed Christ and His offer of salvation so many times. Christ had come with His offer of peace when he needed it most. What did Augustine have to offer his friend as he lay on his deathbed, facing eternity?

Augustine forced himself to answer the question he had avoided all these years, for he knew he had nothing to offer anyone, himself included, in the face of death.

He was unable to calm the inner storm of unrest that raged within him and could no longer ignore it. He threw himself prostrate under a fig tree, his body wrenching violently and uncontrollably with sobs.

Augustine found himself crying out to God, "End my uncleanness, O Lord! End my uncleanness!"

Between his praying and weeping, he heard the voice of a child in a nearby house begin to chant, "Take up and read! Take up and read!"

Augustine remembered the Bible he had brought with him. With shaking hands, he opened it in obedience to the voice of the unseen child. He read:

> *Not in rioting and drunkenness, not in chambering and wantonness, not in strife and envying: but put ye on the Lord Jesus Christ, and make not provision for the flesh, to fulfil the lusts thereof.* (Romans 13:13–14)

Not in rioting and drunkenness... He had partied since the days of his youth.

Not in chambering... He had lived a life of fornication and fathered a son outside of marriage.

Not in wantonness... His mind was a filthy pit of unclean thoughts.

Not in strife and envying... He had spent his whole life striving for power and status. He envied everyone in a higher position than he held.

Put ye on the Lord Jesus Christ... He had done nothing but mock and jeer the only One who loved him enough to die for him.

Make not provision for the flesh... He had cared for nothing and no one, concerned only with his own fleshly and self-centered desires.

To fulfil the lusts thereof... His whole being was saturated with lust.

His inner core of rottenness was exposed by the light of God's Word. He had never seen himself as he really was. He cringed at the stench of vile filth within him. For the first time in his life, he stood alone, naked in spirit, before the piercing gaze of a holy God.

"Oh, my God! End my uncleanness! End my uncleanness, O Lord!"

And God opened a fountain for cleansing sin and uncleanness, the precious blood of His only begotten Son. Augustine became a new creation in Christ.

Light literally blazed into his heart, driving out darkness and all other gods with its presence.

"Oh, my Christ," Augustine prayed in wonder and awe. "Let me live the rest of my life only to please You."

Men stared as Augustine ran from the garden, his face lit from within, his torch held confidently.

"I have no need to ever consult another astrologer," he cried. "Yes, I consulted these impostors, but Christ is and forevermore will be my Guide!"

All his craving for worldly success was gone. The esteem of men meant nothing to him. Why should he marry an heiress he did not love? He broke his engagement. He resigned his position as professor and retreated to a country villa to write.

Shortly after beginning his new life, his restlessness returned. He turned to the Scriptures for help, and daily grounded himself in the Word of God. The restlessness was again replaced with a beautiful peace.

Within a few months, his mother, his son, and one of his best friends died. But death no longer held him in its grip of fear and bondage. He had met the One who holds the keys of death and found Him faithful even in life's most trying hour.

Men had accepted the pleasure-mad, lustful, ambitious Augustine. He was one of their own. But men recoiled from this new Augustine. They plotted to murder him.

A group of people was gathered around Augustine one day when one of the group called out, "Augustine! Did you know that men who used to be your friends are planning to kill you?"

Augustine was unconcerned about their plans. He was ready and willing to both live and die for Christ.

"But why, Augustine?" he was asked. "Why must a Christian endure these persecutions? Why are Christians so hated? Why does God allow so many to be killed?"

"Many Christians were slaughtered and put to death in a hideous variety of cruel ways," he answered. "Well, if this is hard to bear, it is assuredly the common lot of all who are born into this life! Of this at least I am certain: No one has ever died who was not destined to die sometime. They who are destined to die need not inquire about what death they are to die, but into what place death will usher them!"

"So many Christians have lost all their possessions," another voice stated. "Why would a loving God allow His people to lose everything?"

Augustine answered without hesitation. "Our Lord's injunction is the following:

Lay not up for yourselves treasures upon earth, where moth and rust corrupt, and where thieves break through and steal.
(Matthew 6:19)

"Oh, the joy of those who, by the counsel of their God, have fled with their treasure to a fort that no enemy can possibly reach...

"The tragedy is not the loss of one's possessions, but the love one had for the possessions in the first place. If in losing them one no longer loves them, he has received a significant gain!

"You say that they lost all they had? Did they then lose their faith? Their godliness? The possession of the hidden man of the heart, which in the sight of God is of great price? Did they lose these? For these are the wealth of the Christian!

"The Scriptures contain no promise to Christians of all-comfortable lives or freedom from suffering. And who is so absurd and blinded as to be audacious enough to affirm that in the midst of the calamities of this mortal state, God's people, or even one single saint, does live, or has ever lived, or shall ever live, without tears or pain?"

A cultured voice filled his pause.

"Do you then have an aversion to wealth?"

The crowd turned to stare. The man and his servants stood a little apart from the rest. Everyone knew they required space. His servants were clad better than they. He was dressed in a tunic of fine silk, embroidered with a border of spun gold. His girdle was inlaid with gems. Matching bracelets encircled his arms and ankles.

No one was surprised at his question.

Augustine looked upon the poor among the crowd, then turned back to him with his answer.

"That bread which you keep, my friend, belongs to the hungry. That coat that you preserve in your wardrobe, belongs to the naked. Those shoes that are rotting in your possession—give them to the shoeless. The gold that you have hidden in the ground, distribute to the needy."

"Augustine!" a listener challenged. "How is it that you, a mocker of Christ, now claim to understand scriptural truth?"

Augustine smiled.

"To understand scriptural truth, my friend," he answered, "you must have faith. You are not required to understand in order to believe, but to believe in order to understand! And I now believe in Christ and the Scriptures."

"Our priest," a woman stated in her cultured voice, "tells us that we will enjoy only peace and prosperity if we have faith. We will not have problems and setbacks!"

Augustine's face clouded with sternness.

"May the Lord deliver His church from the eloquence that prophesies falsehood, yet inspires the priests to clap their hands and the people to love their words. May this madness never happen to us!"

"What about abortion, Augustine?" a young woman asked. "Is a baby a human being at the time of its conception?"

Augustine slowly shook his head. "I can't assuredly say at exactly what point human life begins."

A pained expression then crossed his face.

"But anyone who looks upon the cut-up remains of an aborted baby, as I have, has to recognize that this has been a human life."

A doctrinal dispute arose in the group. Voices increased in volume as each claimed to belong to the only group that was right.

Suddenly they were aware of a silence and, looking at Augustine, saw his eyes, black with anger, boring into theirs.

"The essence of the church is in the union of the whole church with Christ, not in the personal character of certain select Christians. The house of the Lord shall be built throughout the earth; and these frogs sit in their marsh and croak, 'We are the only Christians'!

"I bring against you the charge of schism, for you do not communicate with all the nations of the earth, nor with those churches that were founded by the labor of the apostles."

"But Augustine, did not Christ call Peter the rock?" a youth inquired.

"Christ did not name Peter the rock upon which He would build His church," Augustine answered. "Our Lord said, 'On this rock I will build my church,' because Peter had said, 'You are the Christ, the Son of the living God.' On this rock, therefore, He said, which you have confessed, I will build my church! The Rock is Christ!"

"You apparently forget that Peter alone was given the promise of the keys!" a church leader argued.

"Peter represented the universal church. Tell me, sir," Augustine said, "did Peter receive those keys and Paul not receive them? Did Peter receive them, and John and James and the rest of the apostles not receive them? Peter was symbolically representing the church, and what was given to him singly was given to the entire church!"

"Augustine," a woman questioned. "Why didn't you marry your mistress?"

Augustine looked down for a moment, then lifting his head, answered truthfully, "I was not so much a lover of marriage as a slave to lust."

He paused, thinking quietly about his promiscuous lifestyle as a young teenager, his mistress of thirteen years, his engagement to an heiress for the sake of convenience, and the mistress he took while waiting for his wedding day.

"From a perverted act of my will," he confessed, "desire grew, and when desire was given satisfaction, habit was forged; and when habit passed unresisted, a compulsive urge set in.

"The arrogance of pride, the pleasure of lust, and the poison of curiosity are movements of a soul that is dead—not dead in the sense that it is motionless, but dead because it has forsaken the Fountain of Life and is engrossed in this world and conformed to it.

"My heart was always restless, until it found its rest in Jesus Christ.

"You see, God's being is in Himself; man's being is in God. Foolishly, man tries to be like God and find rest in himself. He cannot."

"Do you believe we are saved by our works?" a quiet voice spoke from the crowd.

"God surely does not save us by good works," Augustine responded. "But remember this. Good works are always present in those who believe!"

"Augustine," an authoritative voice questioned, "is it not true that Rome is falling because so many Romans have offended the pagan gods by turning to this Christ?"

The speaker looked at the group of people, an arrogant smile on his face.

Augustine waited until the speaker looked back at him, then answered sharply.

"Rome's vulnerability has come from internal decay and moral decadence, not some pagan god's rebuke for not being worshiped. No nation can stand. No nation will ever stand! Only the City of God will stand forever!"

"Augustine," a young man inquired. "If God is a God of love, as you teach, why is there so much evil in this world?"

"Young man, sin is the corruption of God's very handiwork," Augustine explained. "You see, evil is a hopeless parasite. It does not exist in its own right, but only as a corruption of something good.

"You ask me about the love of God. Even the life and vital power of wicked angels and wicked people depend on the continuing gifts of God.

"There are two cities, made by two loves. The earthly city is built by the love of self unto the contempt of God. And the heavenly city is made by the love of God unto the contempt of self.

"The city of God is inhabited by God's people, whose citizenship is determined by a personal relationship to God, through Jesus Christ.

"The earthly city is inhabited by sinners who reject God.

"They are combatants in the age-old struggle between righteousness and wickedness.

"The founder of the earthly city was Cain. Overcome with envy, he slew his own brother, who was a citizen of the eternal city and a sojourner on earth. As were the relations in the beginning, so will they be even unto the end. The church will continue to go forward, amid the persecutions of the world. God knows who are citizens of the one city, and who are citizens of the other. An unmistakable and eternal barrier shall be set up between them at the day of judgment."

A moment's silence, as the crowd pondered his words, was broken by a shrill voice.

"Is it right to worship deceased persons whom we consider saints?"

"Let me assure you," Augustine answered quickly, "that by the Christian Catholics, no deceased person is worshiped!"

"Augustine, you are always telling us to give," an elderly woman said. "What should we give?"

The crowd turned to stare at her. Her appearance made it obvious that she had little to give. They turned back to Augustine as he began to speak.

"Give alms to the poor. Give forgiveness freely to all who wrong you. And," Augustine said, a smile warming his face, "give to your own self what you need most—Christ."

Augustine turned to walk back home.

A young man caught up to him and walked beside him.

"Augustine, please answer just one more question that is bothering me! What should I do about the sins I have in my life?"

"Confess your sins before God, young man! Never let sin become comfortable in your life. Struggle with it!

"Seek God, and God alone! Be not conformed to this world. Restrain yourself from it. The soul's life is in avoiding those things that are death to seek!"

Augustine turned into his villa and resumed his writings. He wrote for a short while, and then he paused for a moment, remembering how proud he had been as he wrote speeches for the emperor of Rome. He had been the envy of every writer.

But when he had met Christ, he turned from the emperor and fame without a backward glance.

Men mocked his decision, but Augustine rejoiced at his promotion. For he now wrote for the King of Kings and Lord of Lords!

Augustine died at the age of 76, leaving for us 758 songs and poems and 242 books that would bless multitudes down through the ages. People have studied Augustine's teachings for over 1,600 years. But does anyone remember even one word spoken by Emperor Valentinian II?

Dave looked at each one in the silent room.

Then he said softly, "You give your lives for the pursuit of earthly success, wealth, position, pleasures. But worldly pleasures cease the instant you draw your last breath. Every possession you have accumulated will be owned by another. The position you have strived for will be filled by another. Are these things really worth giving your life for?

"The Bible you ridicule says it best:

For what is your life? It is even a vapour, that appeareth for a little time, and then vanisheth away. (James 4:14)

For all that is in the world, the lust of the flesh, and the lust of the eyes, and the pride of life, is not of the Father, but is of the

world. And the world passeth away, and the lust thereof.
(1 John 2:16–17)

Dave paused, and then continued quietly, "You mock the race and its runners who carry the torch. Do you believe that Augustine wasted his life? Do you consider me a fool?

"Anyone with any foresight at all knows that this world passes away from the grasp of everyone who lives and dies. But friends, God's Word says that he who does the will of God abides forever."

Dave stood to his feet. "Good-bye, Phil," he said quietly. Nodding at the others, he left the room. He was already outside when he heard Phil call out to him.

"Dave! Dave!"

He turned.

"I just wanted to say good-bye. I don't understand this race you're in. And I'll admit your torch puts me on edge. But don't quit running, Dave. And who knows? Maybe someday I'll join you!"

Someday, Dave thought, as he left the dark campus.

How many people, both young and old, had he met who gambled their eternal destiny on the uncertainty of a tomorrow?

A beautiful peace seemed to descend and literally fill him with its presence.

"My Lord," he breathed. "Sometimes this race gets lonely. There are times I feel so far away from You. And I confess I get tired of the trials along the way. But seeing Phil and his friends tonight, Lord, made me realize that without You, the life of man is meaningless.

"I just want You to know, Lord, that there is nothing I'd rather do than carry Your torch!"

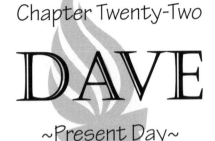

Chapter Twenty-Two

DAVE

~Present Day~

Bless them that curse you...For if ye love them which love you, what reward have ye?

—Matthew 5:44, 46

Therefore if thine enemy hunger, feed him; if he thirst, give him drink.

—Romans 12:20

The sun had not yet risen, but Dave, unable to sleep, knelt by his bed, his Bible open before him. He had read the same words over and over:

Love your enemies.

Bless them that curse you.

Do good to them that hate you.

Pray for them which despitefully use you, and persecute you.

(Matthew 5:44)

"Who is it, Lord?" Dave asked simply.

He knew immediately. Sometime today he would check the park and see if Tom was there.

"Now."

"But, Lord, surely Tom will be in bed! Everyone probably is but me!"

Dave got back in bed, but sleep was out of the question. Throwing back the covers, he got back up. The sun was just rising when he began his walk to the park.

The birds were welcoming the new day, the only sound in the otherwise silent park. There was no noise of a basketball bouncing, no curses, no shouts. The park was empty.

Dave turned and started back home, feeling foolish. Then he stopped and walked slowly back into the park. He would find a bench and begin his day here in prayer.

Suddenly he stopped and stared. A boy was curled up on the bench in front of him. His head rested on a wadded up sweatshirt, and his thin arms were wrapped around his chest as he tried to keep warm.

It was Tom. Dave stood looking down at him. There were no obscene sneers now—just a pitiful, skinny child, alone and cold in the park. Why wasn't he home in bed?

Dave left quietly. A few minutes later, he sat down at a table near the bench where Tom still lay. Noisily, he opened a sack. Out of the corner of his eye, he saw Tom spring to his feet. Dave turned toward him just in time to see insolence settle over his face.

"Oh, hello," Dave said, as he laid the contents of his sack on the table. "I came to meet someone here, but he didn't show. Do you want to help me eat all of this food?"

Tom neither spoke nor moved. Dave placed half of the food on the other side of the table. Then, ignoring Tom, he began eating. He was nearly done when Tom picked up the food and sauntered over to a tree and leaned against it, eating.

By the time Dave finished his last few bites, Tom had finished his meal and was walking away.

"Tom!" Dave called, following him.

The boy turned, his eyes cold with a challenge that Dave could plainly read: "Don't you dare ask me if I live in this park. Don't you dare."

Dave smiled and said softly, "I just wanted to say God bless you. I want you to know that I am still praying for you. If I can ever do—"

His words were cut short by a vicious curse, and Tom was gone.

Dave slowly made his way home, thinking about another time...another torchbearer. One whose race took him straight into the land of his enemies...

Chapter Twenty-Three

PATRICK

~389 AD–461 AD~

For by thee I have run through a troop; and by my God have I leaped over a wall.

—Psalm 18:29

Patrick was not quite sixteen years old when the wild raiders from Ireland invaded his town. They shackled him and dragged him from his home near the west coast of Britain to Ireland.

Patrick looked at the other young boys who had been captured along with him. He saw raw fright in their eyes and wondered if his eyes looked the same. He realized they must, for he was nearly wild with fear. Where was he being taken? And what would happen to him when he reached his destination?

He was prodded rudely by one of the raiders as he stumbled along with the rest.

They finally reached Ireland, where brutal men herded the boys to the town's center. Men gathered around them. One grabbed him roughly, and Patrick realized with horror that he had been purchased by him. Patrick was now a slave, no longer free to live the life he would choose, but owned by another.

When they reached his master's farm, he was taken to the pigpen. As he realized that his new job was herding and feeding swine, all his hopes and ambitions for his future were lost in hopeless despair.

Patrick made his home with pigs for the next six years. He often thought back to his Christian home and his godly parents. Time after time, they had told him about their Savior, but Patrick had no faith in God and no desire to make the acquaintance of His Son. And now, like the Prodigal Son Jesus had referred to, he was reduced to feeding hogs in a far country.

Finally, with all hope gone, Patrick came to himself in the pigpen like the wayward son of old. And it was there that he found the Lord.

Years later, he would write of his experience: "The Lord opened the understanding of my unbelief so I would remember my faults and turn to the Lord, my God, with all of my heart."

Though he was still a slave of man, he was now gloriously set free from sin. Patrick's days were now joyful ones, spent in intense and persistent prayer. He was no longer alone. "God strengthened and comforted me there as a father does his son," he recalled later.

When Patrick was twenty-two years old, God helped him escape. It was night, and Patrick lay sleeping on the hard ground. He awoke suddenly, hearing the Lord's voice.

"I will help you escape from here. You are to leave and run to the sea. I will have a ship waiting to take you home when you arrive at the port."

Patrick jumped up and, in the cloak of night, began to run. When he reached the port, he found a ship prepared to sail to France. Its cargo was filled with hounds. Patrick was welcomed aboard. Someone was needed to care for the dogs!

He returned to Britain, praising God for His deliverance.

"My Lord set me free!" he testified to all who would listen. "He told me exactly how and when to escape!"

Friends and strangers alike looked at him skeptically when he claimed he heard the voice of God. Patrick was amazed that they doubted his testimony.

"Have you never read the words of Jesus?" he cried. "For He said, 'My sheep know My voice'!"

Patrick knew the voice of his Shepherd. He had heard His voice often while serving pigs!

"Jesus," he whispered, surrounded by his cynical friends, "I am so glad I know Your voice! Thank You for setting me free!"

He shrugged off the opinions of men and continued to find comfort in the Lord.

Then God spoke to him once again, this time in a dream. He saw a man coming toward him out of Ireland, a bundle of letters in his hands. He handed one to Patrick, and as he opened it to read, he suddenly heard the voices of many people near the western sea, calling out, "Please, holy boy, come and walk among us again!"

Their cry pierced his heart, and he woke from his sleep, trembling.

"My Lord, what does this mean?" he prayed. "Am I to go back to the land of my captivity and preach Your gospel?"

As he lay pondering the message of his dream, he remembered a similar vision given to the apostle Paul. Patrick found the account in the book of Acts and read,

A vision appeared to Paul in the night; there stood a man of Macedonia, and prayed him, saying, Come over into Macedonia, and help us! (Acts 16:9)

Patrick's heart began to pound. He read on:

After he had seen the vision, immediately we endeavoured to go into Macedonia, assuredly gathering that the Lord had called us for to preach the gospel unto them. (verse 10)

Rising from his bed, Patrick knelt before the Lord he loved.

"My God," he prayed. "Could You be calling me? I am not well educated! I am not fit for such a task!"

Finally he prayed, "I will go."

God reached down into that humble home that night and lit the torch of the young man who had come to know Him in a pigpen.

Patrick ran to Ireland. There he found a people bound in paganism. They were worshiping the sun, moon, wind, water, fire, and rocks. Their faith was in the good and evil spirits that they believed lived in the trees and the hills. They were obsessed with magic. They not only sacrificed animals to pacify evil spirits, but also regularly sacrificed humans.

Patrick looked upon the druids and the priests and the demonic rituals these blind leaders were performing to deceive their blind followers.

They looked back at this one who had dared to run into their territory, and they hated him, his message, and his torch. Frantically casting their evil spells and enchantments against him, they tried to force him to leave Ireland.

Patrick faced the druids fearlessly, and it was they who began to tremble as he cried, "Jesus said, 'All power is given to Me in heaven and in earth!'

"My Lord said to His followers, 'I give to you power to tread on serpents and scorpions, and over all the power of the enemy; and nothing shall by any means hurt you.'"

The druid chiefs, like the Egyptian magicians who used their magic in their struggle with Moses, found they were up against a greater power than they possessed.

Many Irishmen, watching this power struggle, were amazed that the powerful druid chiefs could not stop one runner armed only with a torch. Many turned away from the druids and their dark religion and were born again through the blood of Jesus Christ into the kingdom of light. Eventually, even some of the druid chiefs made their way to the cross and knelt there.

"God," they cried, "we come to You in the name of Your only begotten Son, Jesus the Christ! Set us free from sin and from

Satan's dark kingdom! We receive Jesus as our Savior and our Lord!"

Patrick established a church for the new Christians, and then he moved to new areas that had never heard the gospel. "I have not come to turn you to an organization!" he proclaimed. "God has sent me here to make you disciples of Jesus Christ!"

By 447 AD, after fifteen years of preaching, much of Ireland was evangelized by Patrick and the converts who had found Christ through his ministry.

Enemies of the gospel despised him and determined to kill him. He was kidnapped and held for two weeks before escaping his captors and certain death. Twelve times God miraculously spared him from being murdered.

He boldly kept running. He established two hundred churches and baptized one hundred thousand converts. Then, working diligently with these new Christians, he grounded them in the Scriptures with intensive training.

"You must grow in Christ!" he counseled them. "And you must become involved in the ministry. God is calling you to bring light to this dark world!"

He lived a simple life, totally unselfish in his devotion to the race. He was amazed that God had called him. So many others, with their education and learning, were better suited for the job.

Just before he crossed his finish line, he wrote,

I pray those who believe and fear God, whosoever has deigned to scan or accepts this document, composed in Ireland by Patrick the sinner, an unlearned man to be sure, that none should ever say that it was my ignorance that accomplished any small thing...but let it be most truly believed, that it was the gift of God. And this is my confession before I die.

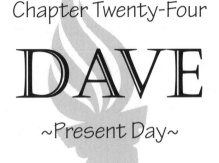

Chapter Twenty-Four

DAVE

~Present Day~

Beloved, let us love one another: for love is of God; and every one that loveth is born of God, and knoweth God.

—1 John 4:7

If Patrick could serve the people who left him in a pigpen for six years, I guess I can feed people who curse at me, Dave thought.

Before his study, he had known only thing about Patrick—that he was Irish. He smiled to himself. *Since my study of him,* he thought, *I've learned a lot more. He wasn't even a native Irishman! But he was a fantastic runner who lived out the Lord's words,*

> *Do good to them who hate you, and pray for them which despitefully use you, and persecute you.*   (Matthew 5:44)

Dave's Ireland would be the park.

Dave was absentmindedly running along the outskirts of the city when the words of Jesus began to trouble his mind.

> *I was...in prison, and ye visited me not.*   (Matthew 25:43)

Dave did not even have to ask the Lord what He meant. He just turned around and began running back toward the prison he had passed about thirty minutes earlier.

"Is there anyone here who might like a visit?" Dave asked the guard. The guard looked closely at Dave, at the torch, then at Dave again. "I'll bring Sam," he said. "He hasn't had a visitor in twenty-three years."

He motioned Dave to follow and led him to a small room, the steel doors clanging shut behind him. Dave breathed a prayer for wisdom, wondering what this Sam would be like.

The door opened and a huge, burly man shuffled in. Dave put out his hand, but the man ignored it.

"Sam, I'm Dave," Dave began. "I have come to bring you good news. You can be set free!"

Sam looked at him, but quickly lowered his head, not willing to look a torchbearer in the eye.

Dave began telling Sam that God loved him so much that He had sent Jesus to set him free. Sam began to shake his head vigorously.

"No," was the first word he spoke to Dave. "Heaven is not for me. If there is a hell, that's where I'm headed. This jail has been my home for over twenty-three years, and it will be my home until I die. I'm in for murder."

"Sam," Dave said, "just let me tell you about three of the greatest men in the Bible who are now in heaven! There was Moses, who killed an Egyptian and had to flee for his life to the desert. Then there was King David, a man who plotted the death of a beautiful woman's husband so he could marry her. And finally there was Paul. Before Paul met Jesus, he was full of hate. He encouraged the stoning and slaughter of many Christians. But God forgave and received every one of them, and even used them in the ministry!

"And Sam, let me tell you about a man named Columba."

Chapter Twenty-Five

COLUMBA

~521 AD–597 AD~

The way of the wicked is as darkness: they know not at what they stumble.

—Proverbs 4:19

Let us cleanse ourselves from all filthiness of the flesh and spirit.

—2 Corinthians 7:1

K ing Brude did not want to look out the window as he walked past, but his eyes just seemed to turn that way. And there he was. Did the man never sleep?

Ever since he had forbidden Columba to enter his city, the persistent man had come every single day to the city gate. He spent his days on his knees, obviously praying for the king to change his mind. King Brude was finding it more and more difficult as the days passed by to put the kneeling figure from his thoughts.

Columba claimed to have some message to give to his people about someone called Jesus. The people surely wouldn't be affected by whatever Columba had to say. What harm could he do anyway?

King Brude motioned to his servant. "Tell Columba I have decided that he may come into my city and preach whatever message it is that he has come to preach."

The news was carried to Columba, and he leaped to his feet, a smile lighting his face. Lifting his hands to heaven, he praised God.

King Brude shook his head as he watched from the window. "Strange fellow," he murmured as he walked away. "I wonder who this Jesus is anyway."

Reports of converts to Jesus spread throughout his kingdom from that hour. King Brude's disgruntled servants were smiling now. People he had known all his life were somehow transformed. They were literally radiating joy, love, and peace.

And then the day came that Columba requested an audience with King Brude. The king consented to see him the following day. He was anxious to hear what Columba had to say, but it was always good not to appear too anxious. When Columba was brought before him, the king assumed an uninterested expression.

Columba opened the Scriptures and began to preach the gospel of Jesus Christ to the king. "He is the only begotten Son of the living God!" Columba declared. "He is Life! Only through receiving His blood as atonement for your sins will you be justified before God!"

The gospel message penetrated the heart of the king, and he turned to Jesus Christ for cleansing from his sin and salvation for his soul.

Columba was thrilled as he left the presence of the King. But as always, his joy was shadowed by his memory of another king, and he remembered the home he had been forced to flee.

Columba was born in Ireland in 521 in the midst of revival fires that had been burning ever since the days that Patrick had run through the land with the torch. He was raised among Christians whose entire lives were spent in serving their beloved Savior. They had been gloriously liberated from the dark practices of the druids and were now dedicated to telling everyone about Christ and His salvation. They feared no danger and believed that no hardship was too much to suffer for the Lord they loved. They willingly followed Him whenever and wherever He led them. Columba had heard about those who had left

Ireland and were running with their torches throughout Europe and as far north as Iceland.

Columba decided that he too would run in this thrilling race. He began to preach from the Scriptures. The Word did its work, and many who heard his message turned to Christ.

But there was a part of Columba that he was unable to control and unwilling to yield to God. For, lurking like a coiled serpent, in the deep recesses of his heart, lay a dark and vicious temper. He tried to subdue it, but it seemed to always get the best of him. It had gotten him into one fight after another, and his testimony was ruined time and again by his outbursts of wrath.

"He is both a saint and a fighter," some said of him. All who knew him were very careful not to offend this huge and powerful man. Even strangers kept their distance when they heard his mighty voice. When and where would this man erupt next? Everyone was surprised when his temper lashed out to strike a king.

Columba had never had any respect for King Diarmuid or his decisions, but slowly a hatred began to grow within him. It first simmered, then began to boil, and finally exploded in Columba's determination to kill him.

He fueled hatred in others against the king, and the day came that Columba, leading a gang of seething men, marched to confront him. A vicious and bloody battle was fought. When it was all over, Columba had won, but five thousand men lay dead. Columba, his anger spent, stared in horror at the corpses littering the battlefield.

Leaving the devastation, he found a place to be alone with God. "My God!" he cried. "What have I done?"

He was victorious in battle with the king, but would there never be victory over his violent temper?

He finally realized that this battle could never be won in his own strength and, crying out for mercy, gave his temper to God to conquer. At last he arose, cleansed and set free in Christ, a torch now in his hand.

He realized he would never again be respected in Ireland. He left his home country in 563, weighed down with the burden that his uncontrollable temper had caused the death of five thousand men. Yes, his gracious God had forgiven him for his terrible sin, but he had a determination burning in his heart. He knew that he would never rest again until he had won five thousand souls to Jesus Christ.

He ran to Scotland, where the powerful druids fought him fiercely. He faced them fearlessly, challenging them openly with the power of God. They backed away as they saw the miracles that accompanied his ministry, and many of their followers found their way to the old rugged cross.

He made his home in Iona, a barren island just off the coast of Scotland. Most days his home was enveloped in fog, and throughout the year the small island was battered by the pounding waves of the sea.

Columba and his twelve followers dedicated their lives to fasting and prayer and study of the Scriptures. He trained evangelists and sent them out to preach the everlasting gospel of Jesus Christ. He and his followers diligently translated and copied portions of Scriptures and hymns and distributed them among the people.

Columba kept careful count of those who turned to Christ.

He left his island home often to run throughout the land. Then one day, he ran into the Scottish highlands to bring the gospel to their inhabitants, the Picts.

It was there that he had been stopped by King Brude.

And now...now King Brude himself had turned to Christ for salvation! Columba knew he could never atone for his past. Only the blood of Jesus could blot out that dark stain. He praised the Lord as he left the palace, which now glowed with the Light of the world.

"Thank You, my Lord. Thank You for bringing King Brude into Your heavenly kingdom through my ministry. My temper caused a king to be alienated from You, but now another king has come to You. My temper caused the death of five thousand men, but, Lord, I will come before Your throne bringing at least five thousand precious souls with me."

Columba spent his life living Psalm 126:6:

He that goeth forth and weepeth, bearing precious seed, shall doubtless come again with rejoicing, bringing his sheaves with him.

He had left his homeland weeping, and had faithfully scattered the precious seed of the Word of God. As Columba crossed his finish line, he was rejoicing, bringing an abundant harvest of many more than five thousand souls to his merciful Master.

Chapter Twenty-Six

DAVE

~Present Day~

The darkness is past, and the true light now shineth.

—1 John 2:8

The shouts and curses echoing throughout the prison could be clearly heard, but there was an unearthly stillness in the room with Dave and Sam.

Sam sat with his head bowed, while Dave silently prayed. Then Sam looked up, and the light of Dave's torch fell upon his face.

"There is hope for me. I can be set free from my sins and my guilt. I too want this Jesus."

Together Dave and Sam knelt on the cement floor. Sam poured out his heart before God, tears streaming down his face, often stopping in his prayer because he was too choked up to continue. When they rose to their feet, Dave was amazed at Sam's transformation. Sam was glowing from within, and a brilliant smile lit his face.

Dave reached out to shake his hand, but Sam gripped him in a powerful bear hug, thanking him for coming to visit him.

Dave had been tired when he first turned back toward the prison. But now he felt renewed vigor surging through him, as he ran again down the highway, singing praises to God, thanking Him for once again reaching down to set a lonely captive free.

Chapter Twenty-Seven

DAVE

~Present Day~

Let this mind be in you, which was also in Christ Jesus: who, being in the form of God...took upon him the form of a servant.

—Philippians 2:5–7

Dave was just about to cross the street to work on the Arnolds' lawn when he noticed a blue Ford coming toward him. He waved and grinned, and the car slowed.

Uncle Joe rolled down the window and shook Dave's hand vigorously. Dave's family seldom came to see him, so Dave wondered if Uncle Joe was just driving through the neighborhood or actually stopping for a visit.

"I came to see how you're doing!" Uncle Joe explained. His eyes went to Dave's torch, and he smiled. "I see you're still running the race!"

"Come on in, Uncle Joe! I'll tell you about my race," Dave invited.

His uncle shook his head.

"I don't want to keep you from doing something important. Where were you headed when I arrived?" he asked.

Dave pointed to the Arnolds' house. "I was just going over to work in their yard."

"Did they hire you for the job?"

Dave grinned. "No...but God did."

"Well, go ahead. We'll talk while we work."

Uncle Joe made the time go by quickly. Dave rarely spent time alone with him. The family was always around when they were together.

"You've tackled quite a job here, Dave," he commented.

"You're right about that!"

They worked on in silence.

Finally Joe stood erect, wiping his brow with his sleeve. "Dave."

Dave looked up.

"What exactly did you mean when you said God hired you to clean up this yard? Does He ask His runners to do jobs like this?"

Dave leaned on his rake. "You know, Uncle Joe," he answered, "I didn't think He would when I first started running. I thought I'd be doing bigger, more important work. But when the Lord started asking me to do things like this, I looked in the Bible for some answers."

Joe looked at the piles of leaves, Dave's rake, and then at Dave.

"Son," he said, "I don't remember reading anything in the Bible about runners doing yard work."

"Well, Uncle Joe, I don't either," Dave answered. "But the runners did do a lot of things we wouldn't consider to be too important. The disciples served dinner to the multitudes. Stephen helped take care of needy widows. Paul gathered up sticks to throw on a fire to keep shipwrecked prisoners warm. And Jesus..."

Dave's voice softened, and Joe noticed he spoke with love in his voice and a light in his eyes.

"...Jesus sat on the edge of a well and talked to a Samaritan woman. He made wine for a wedding reception. He took time to pick up babies and small children and bless them. He went to lunch with Zacchaeus. He knelt and washed His disciples' feet. He grilled a fish dinner and then served it to His disciples."

Joe thought Dave had finished talking. He was about to resume raking when Dave continued. "Uncle Joe, do you know what amazes me most about Jesus? When Jesus comes back to earth, He will have all those who watched for Him sit down to eat. Luke 12:37 tells us that Jesus will gird Himself and serve His people!

"When I think about the King of Kings serving food to sinners He died for, how can I expect to be anything but a servant to people? Serving is what running this race is all about!"

Not answering, Uncle Joe walked away and attacked another area of the yard.

A short time later, he went over to Dave and patted him on the shoulder. "I'm proud of you, son," he said softly. Then he was gone.

Dave went home tired, but happy. Uncle Joe would probably never know how much his visit and his kind words meant to him.

"Thank you, my God," he prayed softly. "Bless Uncle Joe. He thinks his life is nearly over. Show him it's not too late to commit what time he has left to serve You! And Lord, You told us we'd be happy when we serve You by serving people. I just want to tell You that I never knew anyone could be as happy as You have made me!"

Dave glanced down at his open Bible.

He that is greatest among you shall be your servant.

(Matthew 23:11)

The greatest among you...

Dave thought about Gregory, a pope who went down in history as Gregory the Great.

Chapter Twenty-Eight

GREGORY THE GREAT

~540 AD–604 AD~

And call no man your father upon the earth: for one is your Father,
which is in heaven. Neither be ye called masters:
for one is your Master, even Christ.

—Matthew 23:9–10

Rome was ravaged by both floods and war. The floods had claimed their share of victims, homes, and possessions. The war had taken its toll on husbands, sons, and fathers.

Then the plague struck the reeling city.

The sickness began innocently enough, with just a slight sore throat. When the blackness erupted, the end followed swiftly. Its victims left this world screaming in agony. Insanity claimed many who escaped the plague but were unable to cope with the deaths of loved ones.

The people of the weary city tried in vain to close their ears to the continual screams of suffering and wails of mourning. They turned their heads away from the steady stream of carts making their way through the streets to pick up and dump their cargos of corpses.

The pope was one of the plague's victims. His office was left vacant for six months. Church leaders searched frantically for even one who carried a torch. Their eyes at last settled on a frail, balding man of fifty, by the name of Gregory.

Gregory had just finished preaching from Ezekiel when he learned of his election as pope. He listened in horror to the messenger.

He could think of only one thing to do. So, without hesitation, attempting to conceal his face with his cloak, he fled through the city to the forest. Finding the densest spot available, he cowered, hiding among the trees and brush.

Meanwhile, the church leaders made their way to the monastery with their pronouncement. Not finding Gregory there, they frantically formed a search party.

Gregory heard them coming, and his heart sank. "My God," he prayed frantically, "don't punish me by making me pope!"

He was discovered, and was dragged back to Rome, protesting all the way.

It had come to this. He would be forced into the papal position. How he dreaded it! He looked at the depressed city as he was propelled through its streets by his captors.

He sighed deeply. His future was too much to think about. His mind drifted to his past.

His family had governed in the senate for longer than he could remember. Some may have envied the wealth he had inherited by birth, but it meant little to him.

He was only thirty-three years old when he became the mayor of Rome. His responsibilities included overseeing the entire economy of the thriving city. He directed its grain supplies, ran its welfare programs, supervised its new constructions, and kept the baths and sewers functioning and the riverbanks beautiful.

Then his father died, leaving his vast wealth to him.

He was rich—but only long enough to give his entire inheritance away. He founded seven monasteries for the education of the clergy. He gave everything else to the poor. He moved into a monastery and cheerfully dined on raw fruits and vegetables.

While others slept their nights away, he chose to spend his praying. He spent his days cheerfully doing jobs that others shunned.

But now...now he was the pope.

Sighing, he contemplated his awesome task. He knew of only one way to begin. For there was no way to accomplish anything without God's helping hand.

He walked through the streets ceaselessly for three days, praying and singing hymns.

Gregory looked around with despair.

"Surely the end of the world is at hand," he groaned.

"Everywhere," he later wrote, "we see tribulation, everywhere we hear lamentation. The cities are destroyed, the castles torn down, the fields laid waste, the land made desolate. Villages are empty, few inhabitants remain in the cities, and even these poor remnants of humanity are daily cut down. The scourge of celestial justice does not cease, because no repentance takes place under the scourge. We see how some are carried into captivity, others mutilated, others slain. If we love such a world, we love not our joys, but our wounds."

No repentance takes place under the scourge...

Finally the plague subsided.

Gregory didn't have much energy. His health was poor, and many days he was unable to rise from his bed.

One of those days, he wrote weakly to a friend, "I have been unable to rise from my bed. I am tormented by the pains of gout. A kind of fire seems to pervade my whole body. To live is pain, and I look forward to death as the only remedy. I am daily dying, but never die!"

He expended what energy he had to labor among a broken people. He had no desire to be great in the world. He desired only to serve God.

He was enraged at the titles men heaped upon him as the pope.

"Universal pope!" he fumed. "What an assumption. I want this title revoked. It is a foolish, proud, profane, wicked, pestiferous, blasphemous, and diabolical usurpation! Anyone who uses it can be compared only with Lucifer! I nor any one else ought to be called anything of the kind. Away with words which inflate pride and wound charity!

"Do you want to call me by a title? I will give you my title. Call me the servant of the servants of God."

He both despised and fought against pride.

"Pride," he wrote in his commentary on the book of Job, "which we have called the root of vices, far from being satisfied with the extinction of one's virtue, raises itself up against all the members of the soul, and as a universal and deadly disease corrupts the whole body."

His thoughts turned to the pompous bishops and clergy who craved the praise of man.

He shuddered and decided to write a book on what a real pastor should be like.

Dipping his quill, he penned the title: *Pastoral Care.*

Part of his counsel would extend through the centuries as wise advice to future shepherds of flocks.

"A spiritual leader should never be so absorbed in external cares as to forget the inner life of the soul, nor neglect external things in the care of his inner life. Our Lord continued in prayer on the mountain, but wrought miracles in the cities."

Dave spoke softly, "Lord, I pray for all Your runners. Help us to be filled with Your love and power during our times in the mountains alone with You. Only then will we be able to return to the people and give them Your love."

His thoughts drifted back to Gregory.

How Gregory would have disdained the pompous claims of succeeding popes, fifteen of whom would not only take his name, but also arrogantly embrace the titles he had spurned.

Centuries later, Pope Innocent III made a claim that Gregory would have dismissed as conceited arrogance: "I, as pope, am the judge of the world," he declared, "set in the midst of God and man, below God, above man. I am the supreme authority, not only of earth, but over all the souls of men departed to eternity."

Gregory VII echoed these words, then added his own haughty announcement. "I am the mediator between God and man. As such," he proclaimed, "I will judge all and be judged by no one." He then threatened his critics with excommunication.

The people responded with questions. Could a man deprive their souls of the grace essential for their salvation? Was it possible for a mere man, whatever his position, to prevent them from being washed in the blood of the Lamb?

"Yes," the decree from Rome echoed throughout the land. "Not only can we excommunicate you from the church and thus from heaven, but we can also excommunicate angels if we so desire!"

Many began to examine the Scriptures closely. A faint voice began to swell against such unscriptural claims.

Popes looked down with contempt upon those who dared to challenge their supremacy.

"Scriptural claims?" they sneered. "Do you not realize that we have the authority to change and modify the laws of God Himself?"

The earth darkened as greedy men, garbed in the cloaks of Christianity, appointed themselves as runners. They held no torch. They brought no light.

Intent on stopping runners who did both, they joined forces and announced new rules for the race and its runners! They, not God, would appoint and approve future runners. They, not God, would map future courses.

Yes, God's forgiveness and Christ's salvation would still be distributed to the masses—but now with a price attached. What God offered freely, man dared to merchandise. They ran, but for an earthly kingdom, not a heavenly one. They ran for the gold.

In the thirteenth century, Thomas Aquinas approached Pope Innocent II while he was absorbed in counting a huge sum of money.

Smiling at the treasure heaped before him, the pope said, "See, Thomas, the church can no longer say like Peter, 'Silver and gold have I none.'"

Thomas stared at the mass of wealth, then sadly shook his head.

"True," he replied. "But neither can she now say, 'Arise, and walk.'"

Over the centuries, two or three men jostled for the powerful position of pope at a time, each claiming to succeed Saint Peter. Rivals were often murdered.

Popes proudly wore the title of Chief King of Kings. How different from the title Gregory had insisted upon being called— simply God's servant of servants.

Chapter Twenty-Nine

DAVE

~Present Day~

Be thou faithful unto death, and I will give thee a crown of life.

—Revelation 2:10

Dave was running in an area that seemed blacker than usual. It was so dark that his torch penetrated only a small area.

He felt like shouting, "Will somebody here please turn on the lights?"

It had never been this dark in the past. What had changed? Then he remembered. One store had been lit up by the twin torches carried by a beautiful young couple. Perhaps they'd sold the store and moved. It was a rough area.

He groped his way to the store.

They were both inside. Neither carried a torch. They greeted him coldly, shielding their eyes from his light.

"What happened?" he asked simply.

They looked embarrassed. Tension filled the awkward silence. Dave calmly waited for one of them to answer.

Finally the husband spoke.

"It got pretty tough carrying a torch here. Business dropped..."

He glanced at his wife for help with his explanation, but she remained silent.

He looked back at Dave, then almost shouted, "Look, man, we don't owe you an explanation. It just got too hard, that's all.

Runners have a lot of enemies they don't ask for. We don't expect you to understand, but if we had kept holding the torch here, it could have cost us not only our business, but also our lives!"

Dave answered softly. "Do you two have time to talk for a few minutes?"

The wife laughed harshly. "Time? We have time, all right. We lost nearly all the customers we had. We're trying to recover, but business is still slow."

Dave prayed for wisdom as he leaned on the counter and began talking.

"The purpose of a torchbearer is to shine the light of Christ in this black world. If it wasn't a black world, there would be no need for God to turn on some lights.

"Some areas are blacker than others. Down through history, there were some really black times.

"Can you imagine how it must have been for a runner going into a country or city that didn't have even a flicker of light? Only the bravest ran, and many of them were savagely murdered by those who preferred darkness.

"Let me tell you about just a few of the thousands of courageous runners who faced darkness, demons, and death.

"One of the boldest was Boniface..."

Chapter Thirty

BONIFACE

~675 AD-754 AD~

---

*A man was famous according as he had lifted
up axes upon the thick trees.*

—Psalm 74:5

B oniface stood beneath the enormous oak tree looking up at its branches, which were bigger than most tree trunks. It was a splendid creation of God. Under different circumstances, he would admire its beauty.

He sighed and glanced at the silent crowd surrounding him. Someone had convinced them that this tree was sacred to Thor, their so-called thunder god, so now they bowed before it, prayed to it, sacrificed to it, and worshiped it. He would never understand why men worshiped the creation rather than the Creator.

Well, he had better get on with his job, for certainly he wasn't going to convert this crowd of pagans to Christianity as long as they idolized a tree.

He could feel the awe and fear of the heathen crowd as he picked up his ax. He knew they expected Thor to thunder with vengeance from the heavens and strike him dead before his ax could smite their sacred tree.

Boniface had no fear of their nonexistent god. He lifted his ax and sent it crashing against the oak. His mission gave him strength as he continued to chop. Wood flew as he cut deeply into the monstrous trunk. After hours of labor, the final blow was at last struck, and the tree crashed to the ground. The Hessians stood transfixed, awestruck by this bold Englishman who had come to Germany and destroyed their idol. But what bothered them most was that Boniface was still very much alive. Where was Thor? Was he not their mighty god of war who defended all their other gods with his enchanted hammer? How could he stand by and do nothing against this mere man who had defied his deity?

Boniface had come to Germany for just one purpose: to introduce men and women to the living God and to persuade them to worship Him as their Savior. If he had to chop down a tree to accomplish his goal, then so be it. He would do anything he possibly could to reach men for Christ.

Hadn't God told His prophet Jeremiah to "root out, pull down, destroy, throw down, build, and plant"? Sometimes things like this old oak tree had to be destroyed, and only then could the building and the planting begin.

Now that the destroying was done, he would build a church on this very site, and he would use this very oak to begin construction.

The Hessians left the scene, grumbling with disappointment in their impotent god. By the time Boniface left to seek out more of the lost in another part of Germany, thousands were worshiping the living God in their new church.

For thirty-nine years, this fearless missionary ran through Germany demolishing pagan temples, preaching Christ, building churches on the ruins of idolatrous structures, and baptizing over one hundred thousand converts.

At the age of seventy-five, he was still running. With his age came physical infirmities. He had tried to slow his pace, but as long as there were Germans worshiping idols rather than Christ, Boniface could not rest.

He ran to the Netherlands, considered by many to be the most dangerous mission field on earth. There he won thousands of

Frisians to Christ. Wherever he went, pagan leaders were incensed. And this fact led to his death.

Boniface and fifty-two companions were on their way to confirm a group of Frisians. As he approached his designated meeting place, he looked up to see not his new Christian brothers and sisters, but a raging crowd of savages advancing menacingly toward him.

My race is finished, he thought, as he waited calmly for his death. He looked with love upon the fifty-two companions who accompanied him.

Boniface had courageously withstood every enemy who opposed the Lord, and now he would boldly confront death, the last enemy to be destroyed.

As the howling mob came nearer, he turned calmly toward his friends.

"They are coming to bring us our crown of life! Let us wait for them here."

Chapter Thirty-One

DAVE

~Present Day~

They that sow in tears shall reap in joy. He that goeth forth and weepeth, bearing precious seed, shall doubtless come again with rejoicing, bringing his sheaves with him.

—Psalm 126:5–6

Dave paused. Then Ron spoke. "He was brave, all right. But Dave, I think I could keep going if I saw results like he did. You said he won over one hundred thousand people to the Lord!"

He paused and glanced at his wife. She was looking down.

"Ann and I haven't seen one person turn to Christ—oh, unless we count a couple of children and one old homeless lady who repented a few weeks before she died. We ran faithfully for seven months! It gets discouraging!"

Dave smiled.

"I'm sure Jesus will count the children and lady. He is no respecter of persons; He loves them all the same. I think I'll tell you about a runner named Anskar. He's known as the Apostle of the North. With that title, we would assume he had tremendous results like Boniface. But that assumption would be wrong. He actually experienced some of the same discouragements you face. There was one major difference. Anskar held on to his torch."

Chapter Thirty-Two

ANSKAR

~801 AD–865 AD~

---

*Let us not be weary in well doing: for in due season
we shall reap, if we faint not.*

—Galatians 6:9

The Apostle of the North. Anskar sighed deeply. He was now sixty-five, tired, and, yes...deeply disappointed. He knew his run was nearly done.

God had given him a huge task. All the heathen of northern Europe were his mission field.

He had begun his race with such high hopes. Born in France, he began his education at five years of age in a monastery founded centuries before by Columba.

His life had been one of constant troubles and trials.

He was twenty-six years old when he carried the torch into Denmark. Three years of exhausting efforts had followed. He still felt the heartache and pain as he and his message were both expelled from the country. Denmark was content with its darkness.

He had turned toward Sweden then.

Sweden.

What a challenge! The gospel had never been preached there. The country was black with idolatry and paganism. Satanic practices filled the land. Some Swedes worshiped a dead king. Others worshiped tribal gods, and still others, the sun and the moon. Charms were carried as protection from sickness and misfortune. Both animals and humans were sacrificed to Odin, their demonic god.

Before he even arrived in this unwelcoming country, pirates attacked his ship and sailed away with all his possessions. He held nothing but his torch when he landed on Sweden's shores.

King Bjorn and his people had never seen a torchbearer, for none had ever run in Sweden. Anskar was the first.

Oh, the king had been cordial. The people had listened to his message. Many responded eagerly and converted to Christianity with joy.

I was so thrilled with their response, Anskar thought.

It hadn't taken long to realize they were just temporary converts, as were described by Jesus in Mark 4:16.

And these are they...which are sown on stony ground; who, when they have heard the word, immediately receive it with gladness.

Soon they had come to the same end as the seed on the stony ground. Jesus had predicted the outcome of both.

They...have no root in themselves, and so endure but for a time: afterward, when affliction or persecution ariseth for the word's sake, immediately they are offended. (verses 16–17)

They'd been offended all right. They had apparently only received Christ so He would help them win their many wars.

As long as they won their battles, they were faithful Christians. When they were defeated, they rebelled against Christ and returned to their pagan gods.

Their fickleness led Anskar to spend long days and nights praying and fasting.

He spent his days preaching the Word.

Prayer and fasting are vital to the ministry, he thought, *but never at the expense of useful activity.* He had faithfully done both.

He had left Sweden then. He'd become an archbishop when he was thirty-three. The new city of Hamburg, Germany, became his base.

Just about the time the work he had begun in Denmark was revived, the Vikings stormed into Hamburg and set the entire city on fire. His headquarters were reduced to ashes in the inferno.

So, he became the bishop of Bremen.

He returned to Sweden in 853 and 854, and he rejoiced as the king turned to the Lord. Perhaps this time...

He and other missionaries preached with power and liberty. Powerful pagan priests were angered by the presence of Christ. They plotted a rebellion that would overthrow the kingdom so they could expel Anskar and the gospel from their land.

After thwarting their evil plot, Anskar returned to Bremen.

Rumors about the Apostle of the North had spread quickly. He scoffed when they credited him with great miracles.

"The greatest miracle in my life," he responded, "would be if God ever made a thoroughly pious man out of me!"

I spent my life trying to win Sweden and Denmark to Christ, he thought. He was so disappointed. *Now both have returned to their pagan practices.*

Anskar crossed his finish line, never having seen the fruit of his labors. He did not know that the light he had taken to the black lands yet burned...

Chapter Thirty-Three

DAVE

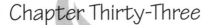

~Present Day~

He which converteth the sinner from the error of his way shall save a soul from death, and shall hide a multitude of sins.

—James 5:20

Ann spoke for the first time since Dave had entered their store. "He accomplished something then?"

Dave's eyes met hers squarely.

"There has never been a runner who did not accomplish something. And Anskar was no exception. Even though he died without seeing a harvest, he left behind a flicker here, an ember there. And fire will do one of two things. It will either go out or spread."

Ron and Ann both glanced guiltily at their empty hands.

"Before I leave, I want to tell you about another runner who was almost too discouraged to go on. Have either of you heard of Mr. Kimball?"

Ron and Ann both shook their heads.

"Well, I would tell you all about him, but I don't know much. I don't know where he was born or where he died. I don't know what he did for a living. All I know is that he was a very discouraged Sunday school teacher in Boston. He saw no results. He could have easily laid down his torch and simply given up. And that's what he nearly did. But if he had, the entire world would have been much blacker today."

"The world? What did this Mr. Kimball do?"

"He told an eighteen-year-old shoe clerk named Dwight about Jesus. Then they prayed together, and the clerk received Jesus into his heart. Mr. Kimball was no doubt happy that the clerk had turned to Christ for salvation. But the young man didn't hold much promise. He had been only four years old when his father died, leaving his mother with nine children to raise, all under the age of thirteen. His entire schooling was about the equivalent of a fifth-grade education today. Mr. Kimball probably felt about the same way you do. He saw no results—just one young shoe clerk.

"He didn't know that Dwight L. Moody would look up at his Savior, then at his pain-filled world, and cry, 'The world has yet to see what God can do with a man fully consecrated to Him. By God's help, I am to be that man.'"

Dave smiled. "Mr. Kimball's insignificant shoe clerk ran more than one million miles and preached about Jesus Christ to more than one hundred million people.

"Moody's course took him to England in 1879, where Frederick B. Meyer, a pastor of a small church, was set ablaze.

"F. B. Meyer carried the torch to an American college campus, where a student by the name of J. Wilbur Chapman was born again. Chapman later hired a young man by the name of Billy to do evangelistic work as an extension of the YMCA.

"Billy Sunday was an orphan who worked as an undertaker's assistant before he entered professional baseball. He gave up running the bases to run the race...and a million people found Christ as their Savior.

"He was running through Charlotte, North Carolina, when a group of men was set aflame. They invited a runner named Mordecai Hamm to Charlotte to preach in their city after Billy left.

"During Hamm's meeting, a young man joined the race. His name is Billy Graham."

He smiled. "I think you've both heard of him."

"And it all started with one discouraged runner who was about to lay down his torch," Ann said thoughtfully.

"Think about it, Ron and Ann," Dave continued. "God sent fire from heaven to light the torches of the one hundred and twenty praying disciples gathered in an upper room—and thus started His church. The reformation of the church began as Martin Luther taught a few students at Wittenberg. John Wesley found Christ at a back alley prayer meeting at Aldersgate. Charles H. Spurgeon joined the race in a tiny chapel.

"I think that settles the question of giving up in despair when you don't see results. Now let's talk about running through dangerous areas."

Ron glanced at the door. "I don't see any customers breaking down the door in their rush to get in," he laughed. "You might as well keep talking."

"Then let's start with Adalbert."

Chapter Thirty-Four

ADALBERT

~997 AD~

Be thou faithful unto death, and I will give thee a crown of life.

—Revelation 2:10

I s there no end to my troubles?" cried Adalbert. He sighed bitterly, glancing at his still flickering torch. He had done everything he could think of to bring his people to holiness. But still they stubbornly refused to conform to God's holy Word.

There was tension in the country and tension in the church. Was there anyone who did not hold a bitter grudge of hatred? He could not stand to work among such people! His own torch had died down to embers.

He was wasting his time and energy. "I will resign my position as bishop of Prague," he decided. "My work from now on will be to convert the infidels."

He turned to the heathen Prussians on the shores of the Baltic. They listened to the message of the gospel with joy. Many turned to Christ with their hearts...and their lives!

Pagan priests eyed Adalbert with murder in their hearts. As more and more people turned to Christ, they turned away from their old beliefs and religious leaders. The priests could no longer control the people with their dark superstitions. He would have to be stopped...and quickly. They joined to plot his murder.

With a cry of rage, they fell upon him. Moments later, Adalbert crossed his finish line. The devil had used his ministers to pierce Adalbert's body with darts.

Their fury spent, the pagan priests looked up.

And their faces darkened.

Adalbert had left runners behind, faithfully carrying their torches throughout the land. Would the earth never be rid of them?

Chapter Thirty-Five

DAVE

~Present Day~

*Fear not them which kill the body, but are not able to kill the soul:
but rather fear him which is able to destroy
both soul and body in hell.*

—Matthew 10:28

D ave paused and looked at the two faces staring at him in horror.

They both started to talk at once, but Dave silenced them by lifting his hand.

"Please wait before you say anything. This has never been an easy race. Jesus warned us of its dangers. He said in Matthew 11:12 that the kingdom of heaven suffers violence, and the violent take it by force.

"Paul told us to endure hardness, as a good soldier of Jesus Christ. We are in a war between Christ and Satan, good and evil, light and darkness. The battle is fierce. And yes, many runners have died on the battlefield.

"Even as we talk, runners are suffering in prisons. Some are being tortured. Others are being murdered. Over ten thousand Christians have been killed every year since 1950, due to clashes with anti-Christian mobs, infuriated relatives, state-organized death squads, and so on. Dave Barrett of the World Evangelization Research Center tells us that martyrdoms are increasing. In 1900, an estimated 35,000 laid down their lives for the Lord, and in 1990 there were 260,000! Barrett goes on to say, 'All the long-term underlying factors that produce martyrdoms seem to be gradually increasing in our day.'

"Yes, Adalbert died a horrible death. Has there ever been a war without casualties?

"He left us an example not only in living, but also in dying for Christ. So many left us an example in courage.

"Runners like Alphage, Gerard, and Stanislaus."

Chapter Thirty-Six

ALPHAGE

~1012 AD~

The good shepherd giveth his life for the sheep. But he that is an hireling, and not the shepherd, whose own the sheep are not, seeth the wolf coming, and leaveth the sheep, and fleeth.

—John 10:11–12

A lphage. His name brought a gentle smile to the faces of young and old alike. They loved him simply because he loved them.

There weren't many men like Alphage.

He could have chosen them as his servants. He was born into a wealthy family and was far better educated than most. He chose instead to serve them as their beloved pastor.

He was archbishop of Canterbury when the Danes invaded England. News of the attack reached the city. Cities and villages were ravaged, their inhabitants slaughtered.

The messenger had reached Canterbury just ahead of the invaders. The city's leaders would have just enough time to escape with their lives.

Snatching their prized possessions, they began to flee the city.

"Hurry!" they called to Alphage.

"I am not leaving. My people need whatever help and encouragement I can give them."

The fleeing men were horrified.

"Don't be a fool, Alphage! You will be killed!"

But his eyes were already fixed on the people he loved.

The city's leaders had barely escaped when the Danes poured into the city, killing and plundering.

Alphage hurried from his home. Everywhere there were victims, some already dead, others writhing in pain. Men, women, children, the aged, babies—the Danes had mercy on none.

The city was thick with smoke. Flames leaped to the skies and piercing screams added to the chaos. Alphage gazed at the carnage. Then he turned toward the savage soldiers. Their curses and shouts filled the air. They were laughing as they killed— clearly enjoying the slaughter.

He walked steadily toward them.

They paused to stare. Who was this who dared to approach them? Did he have no fear?

"Save the people!" he pleaded. "Do what you will with me, but save the people! Please. Spend your rage on me."

They laughed sadistically as they seized him.

They tied his hands together and marched him to his church.

"Watch," they mocked, as they set it afire.

The flames spread quickly. Monks ran from the building to escape the inferno. Alphage cringed as they were cruelly massacred.

"Save the people?" the soldiers sneered. "We will save your precious people. One out of ten!" Then, brutally and systematically, they killed nine of every ten.

By day's end, 7,236 people lay dead.

All that remained were four monks, eight hundred laymen... and Alphage.

He lay bound in a dungeon. The Danes found pleasure in tormenting him for several months.

"Give us money," they demanded. He had no money to give. He had long ago distributed it to the people he loved.

Finally they dragged what was left of him to Greenwich for a mock trial.

"Oh, my friends," he implored. "Forsake your idolatry! Embrace Christ! Let Him cleanse you from your sins!"

One soldier did.

The Danes were incensed. Would they never silence this voice? Would nothing they did extinguish his dreaded light?

They dragged him outside the city and beat his tortured body unmercifully.

Then they beheaded him.

Alphage had given himself first to Christ, then to Christ's people.

How Satan despised such a runner!

How he hated every runner!

The race had lasted ten centuries so far. Still Satan had devised no torture, no mockery, no method to stop it. He had used ridicule, making the runners a laughingstock before the people. He had used pain, torturing their riddled bodies. He had isolated them in dungeons. He had finally killed them in frustration, only to have them forever out of his reach.

And still, valiant runners carried the torch.

Darkness raged, but was no match for their light.

Light was always the victor, even in death.

Chapter Thirty-Seven

GERARD

~1045 AD~

So also is the resurrection of the dead...It is sown in dishonour; it is raised in glory: it is sown in weakness; it is raised in power.

—1 Corinthians 15:42–43

Gerard knew the dangers of the race. He had loved Christ as a small child. He loved Him still. Nothing the world had to offer attracted him. He was destined to run.

He read of the Lord's race with a longing in his heart. He wanted to travel from Veneci to the Holy Land and trace his beloved Master's footsteps.

Finally he left Italy to fulfill his dream. Detouring into Hungary, he met Stephen, the king. A friendship formed between the two men.

"Stay," Stephen pleaded.

Gerard did, and he became the bishop of Chonad.

Stephen's kingdom was overthrown. Violent rivals fought for the throne. Kings came and went. Finally, Andrew was offered the crown, but with one condition.

Andrew was eager to meet the condition, whatever it was. It turned out to be an easy one. He simply had to abolish Christianity from Hungary.

"Done," agreed Andrew.

When Gerard heard the news, he quickly called four bishops. "We will go and try to talk to him," he said.

"My God," he prayed as he made his way to the king. "Use me to persuade King Andrew to stop this violence against Your people!"

He was about to cross the Danube River when he was halted by a party of soldiers.

Sneering, they hurled stones at him.

They lifted his bleeding body and beat him unmercifully.

Finally, they speared him with their lances.

The soldiers grinned, gazing with pleasure at their grisly accomplishment.

"We have finally rid the world of these hateful runners," they bragged.

But the torch would be picked up and carried by other courageous runners, undaunted by persecution, unmoved by the persecutors.

Chapter Thirty-Eight

STANISLAUS

~1030 AD–1079 AD~

Arise, shine; for thy light is come, and the glory of the LORD *is risen upon thee. For, behold, the darkness shall cover the earth, and gross darkness the people; but the* LORD *shall arise upon thee, and his glory shall be seen upon thee.*

—Isaiah 60:1–2

King Bolislaus shouted furiously at his soldiers, "Kill Stanislaus! I want him dead!" A malevolent smile curled his lips. How dare Stanislaus warn him that God would judge his crimes if he didn't repent? Was he not the king of Poland? He confessed his sins to no one.

How he hated these insolent torchbearers. He waited impatiently for the news of Stanislaus' death.

The soldiers looked forward to their bloody task. They found the bishop just out of town, all alone in St. Michael's chapel.

He greeted them warmly. They in turn stared at their prey.

Their prey...

Gentle, loving Stanislaus.

He had helped so many of them. He had gently taught their children, given liberally to the poor, helped the elderly, nursed the sick, strengthened the weak. He spent his life helping and giving.

The soldiers glanced at his torch, then back at him. They turned as a group and marched back to their king.

He was anxiously waiting to hear the gruesome details of their mission.

He listened in shock as they announced, "We refuse to kill such a man."

He turned purple with rage and stormed violently at them, cursing. Snatching a dagger from the nearest soldier, he ran furiously to the chapel.

Stanislaus was at the altar, kneeling before his King.

Hatred boiled within the king. If no one else would stop this runner, he would! Running to the altar, he plunged the dagger viciously into Stanislaus' heart.

The psalmist's decree rang out against this pitiful king, even as Stanislaus was crowned with victory in the heavens.

The kings of the earth set themselves, and the rulers take counsel together, against the LORD, and against his anointed, saying, Let us break their bands asunder, and cast away their cords from us. He that sitteth in the heavens shall laugh: the Lord shall have them in derision. (Psalm 2:2–3)

Stanislaus was home safe. His fallen torch would be picked up. All hell had been loosed against Christ and His runners, but all of the forces of earth and hell combined were unable to crush the race.

Yes, some were hurled violently across their finish line, but they were not left there.

Angels gathered them gently in their arms and carried them into the courts of heaven, where a cheering crowd and a loving King welcomed them.

Heaven...there they were forever out of reach of depraved men and vile demons.

Satan's vicious hatred accomplished nothing.

For always—without fail—there were more runners who would pick up the fallen torch and begin to run with the despised light.

Satan was finding it impossible to stop this race, for it was directed by God Himself.

How he hated the words spoken to him and his diabolical warriors by Tertullian:

> The oftener we are mown down by you, the more in number we grow. The blood of Christians is seed.

Seed.

There was always another crop of Christians springing up from the blood-soaked ground.

The darkness grew black as midnight as the devil dressed his ministers in the robes of Christianity itself.

But still the dreaded light continued to conquer.

In the eleventh century, the torch was carried by Berengarius. He and his followers, the Berengarians, refused to pollute or dilute the message of the gospel. They ignored the counterfeit runners with their empty torches. They just continued to run, fervently, fearlessly, faithfully.

These believers were followed by Henry of Toulouse and his disciples. Discarding the bondage of man-made traditions, they held aloft the Scriptures.

"This is the Word given by God," they proclaimed. "Jesus Christ, and Jesus alone, is the Way, the Life, the Truth."

Light banished darkness wherever a runner was found. It was the twelfth century now, and still the race continued.

Ah, yes, the light sometimes grew dim. But the fire never went out. For God was in the heavens, conducting His race.

Chapter Thirty-Nine

DAVE

~Present Day~

Ye shall be hated of all men for my name's sake: but he that endureth to the end shall be saved.

—Matthew 10:22

Ron reached out and took Ann's hand. "Dave," Ron began. "Ann and I have some praying and confessing to do. The Lord put us in this race, and we can't just walk away from it when it gets tough. Many of the runners you told us about didn't even have a partner."

He smiled at Ann and squeezed her hand gently.

"At least we have one another, babe."

She nodded as Ron added, "I think I speak for both of us. We're in this race, for better or worse, for richer or poorer—right now it seems we're experiencing the poorer part—and we're going to keep running, no matter what."

He looked at Ann. "Even if it means the death of one or both of us. I don't mean to be dramatic, but in this neighborhood, you never know."

Ann nodded again. "I feel the same way."

"Dave," Ron asked, "are you in a hurry to get someplace, or do you want to go in the back room and pray with us?"

About an hour later, Dave left their store.

Ron and Ann stood at the door, their arms around each other, smiles lighting their faces.

Their torches cast a warm glow over their neighborhood.

Dave was on his way home. He was running past the park when he noticed Tom with his gang of boys. As soon as they saw him, they once again began their tirade of obscene filth and cursing.

Tom turned toward the other boys and stopped them savagely with a curse. There was sudden quiet.

Dave simply ignored them. He wasn't gaining much headway with Tom. However, it was encouraging that Tom had gone from initiating the harassment to putting a stop to it.

He had again shared his food with Tom earlier that morning. That was all he shared. As usual, Tom had eaten the food in sullen silence. Dave spent the time reading his New Testament. He had looked up once and caught Tom staring at him, but Tom had only scowled and looked quickly away.

He was still thinking about Tom when he turned onto his street. He noticed Uncle Joe's car parked in his driveway, and he ran to invite him into his house. The car was empty. Uncle Joe couldn't be in the house. The door was locked.

He glanced over at the Arnolds' yard. His uncle wasn't anywhere in sight. He looked both ways on the street. Then he saw him standing in the window of the Arnolds' house, motioning to him.

Uncle Joe opened the door before Dave could knock, his finger to his lips.

"I'll be over soon, Dave, if you're going to be home," he whispered.

"Uncle Joe," Dave whispered back. "What are you doing here?"

"I came over to sit with Ed. He's in a lot of pain, and his wife needed some sleep. Go on now. I'll be over shortly."

"Wait!"

But Uncle Joe closed the door.

By the time Uncle Joe knocked at Dave's door, Dave had the coffee perking.

Dave asked several questions at once.

"How did you know Mr. Arnold was in pain and his wife was exhausted? Were you there to work on their yard? How did you even get in their house?"

Uncle Joe took his time drinking his coffee before answering.

"I just knocked on the door to tell Mrs. Arnold that I was there to work on her yard for my nephew."

"Uncle Joe! She doesn't even know that I work on her yard!"

Uncle Joe smiled.

"That's what you think. She told me how many hours you've spent there, how hard you work, how much trash you've hauled away. I think she may have even calculated the number of leaves you have raked up. She also told me about the prayer you prayed for her husband.

"That's when I said I wasn't much good at praying but I would pray for him too if she liked. She invited me in. He was moaning and restless, but when I finished praying, he was quiet. When I opened my eyes, he was looking straight at me.

"She said, real quiet like, 'I can't believe it.' I looked at her. She looked all done in. So I told her to go and get some rest and I'd sit with him. She wasn't going to accept it, but then I told her I was too old for all this yard work you had me doing. I told her that it would be a whole lot easier for me to sit with her husband and leave the heavy work to you. So, she went and took a nap while I sat with Ed."

"How do you know his name is Ed?"

Uncle Joe looked at him strangely. "What do you mean, how do I know? I asked him his name, and he told me!"

"You mean he talks?"

"Well, of course he talks! Do you think people lose their voice when they get old?"

"No...I mean...well...he didn't tell me his name."

"I'm sure he didn't. And I'm just as sure you never asked him."

Dave changed the subject. "How long were you there, Uncle Joe?"

Joe looked at his watch, then quickly stood up. "Much too long. Most of the day, in fact! I've got to get home!"

"Wait! Just one more thing. Did he stay calm after you prayed?"

Joe was already out the door but turned to answer. "No. He got restless several times."

His uncle had the car running and was ready to leave when Dave asked the next question. "Did you pray again when he got restless?"

"You ask too many questions, son. But if you must know, I read him this." He patted the New Testament in his shirt pocket.

Dave saw his uncle's car in the Arnolds' driveway often after that day.

He saw other things too...

Their drapes were open much of the time now. More than once, Mrs. Arnold was on the porch rocking in her chair while Uncle Joe sat inside with her husband.

Then there was the beautiful day that Dave ran home early to do some work on their yard. He stopped and stared. Two rockers were going. Between them was a roll-away cot. A shriveled figure lay on it. Dave walked slowly toward the porch, almost hating to interrupt the trio.

His uncle grinned at him. Mrs. Arnold nodded. And Mr. Arnold...he didn't even look like the same man. Oh, his body was still shriveled, but a radiant smile lit his face and Jesus looked out from his eyes.

Dave looked from him to Uncle Joe.

Joe was caught off guard and hoped he had turned his head before Dave saw the tears trickling down his face.

He brushed them roughly away with his sleeve and looked back at Dave. But Dave wasn't looking at his face at all—he was staring at his hand.

For Uncle Joe was finally carrying his torch.

Chapter Forty

DAVE

~Present Day~

*Labour not for the meat which perisheth, but for that
meat which endureth unto everlasting life.*

—John 6:27

"
Dave! Dave! Please wait for me!"

Dave stopped running and turned around. A young
man came running toward him. As he came closer, Dave
noticed his expensive jogging suit and tennis shoes. His dark,
wavy hair was styled perfectly. He wiped the sweat from his fore-
head with a monogrammed handkerchief as he reached out to
shake Dave's hand. A friendly grin warmed his handsome face.

"Dave, my name is Jim. I was hoping I could run with you.
I was listening as you spoke to the young people at the park the
other night. What you said about life and its purpose made a lot
of sense to me. I decided I too would follow this Jesus. Please let
me run with you!"

Dave liked this young man. He saw in his eyes a sincere
desire to follow Christ.

"I would love to have you run with me, Jim!" he answered
warmly.

They ran well together, both in their physical run and in their
spiritual one. Jim shared his vibrant testimony with those they witnessed to. He was as thrilled as Dave was when people responded

to the age-old gospel message. But at about six that evening, Jim said, "Dave, I've got to leave you. I have an appointment at seven that I can't miss. I'll meet you in the morning at ten."

Dave hid his surprise and agreed to meet Jim the following morning.

He was standing at the designated place a little before ten the next morning when a young woman approached him.

"Are you Dave?" she asked.

"Yes."

"I'm Jim's secretary. He sent me to tell you that he won't be able to run today. A business meeting was called that he can't miss. He asked that you be here this evening at seven."

Dave agreed, without hesitation. He knew Jim had great potential as a runner, and he was willing to adapt his schedule to meet him.

Jim was there early. He met Dave eagerly, anxious to run again.

"Where are we going, Dave? I'm ready to talk about my Lord to anyone who will listen!"

Dave began telling him his plans for the evening when Jim interrupted.

"Wait, Dave! I can only run for an hour! I have an appointment with a client at 8:30! I've been trying to get a meeting with him for several months. His business will be a big break for me! It will mean long nights at the office, but it will really pay off."

Dave looked into Jim's friendly eyes, and then seemed to look straight into his heart, seeing what was at its center.

"Dave!" Jim cried. "I have to be there!"

"Jim, I want to meet you tomorrow morning at the coffee shop at eight. Please...I want you there. You go on to your appointment now. Don't come with me tonight; we will just get started, and then you will have to excuse yourself to leave. I'll see you tomorrow."

Dave stood watching as Jim walked away.

The next morning, Jim was already at a table when Dave entered the coffee shop. He jumped up eagerly when he saw Dave and pumped his hand.

"Dave!" he said, excitement in his voice. "Last night was a turning point in my business! And I was able to witness too! After the man agreed to transfer his business to my firm, I shook his hand and said, 'God bless you, sir!'"

Dave sat down, and replied, "Sit back down, Jim. I want to tell you about two young men who remind me of you. They wanted to run for Christ too. The first one lived while Jesus was walking the earth. Let me tell you what happened on the day he had a face-to-face encounter with Jesus Christ..."

Shouts of "Jesus is here!" reverberated throughout the city.

A woman rushed out of her house and approached a teenage boy.

"Jesus? Jesus who heals lepers and raises the dead?"

"Yes! Look! He has His twelve with Him. The people push and shove just to get close! I heard a mother running home to get her baby say that He was blessing children!"

"Jesus!" a young man breathed.

Without a word to his friends, he began to run down the road. As he got closer, his pace slowed, for many people were coming from all directions. He made his way through the crowd persistently. He had heard so much about Him. He had to talk to Him! Finally he made it through the crowd to Jesus. As he stood staring at Him, Jesus suddenly turned and looked fully into his face, His eyes seeming to pierce into his very soul. He radiated light!

The young man hadn't planned to bow before Him, but somehow he found himself on his knees. He was in awe and barely able to ask the question that had always kept him from having peace of mind and enjoying life to its fullest.

"Good Master," he said, "what good thing can I do in order to have eternal life?"

Jesus talked to him for a few minutes. Then He spoke the words that would rob him of his peace of mind until his dying day. "If you will be perfect, go and sell what you have, and give to the poor, and you will have treasure in heaven and come and follow Me!"

The young man could not meet the penetrating eyes of Jesus, for they seemed to light the one dark area of his heart and expose it before everyone. He would give anything to follow this Jesus. Anything...but his wealth. It was his security! He had worked so long and so hard for it! Why, of all things, had Jesus demanded this of him? He slowly stood to his feet, turned around, and walked away, his heart nearly overwhelmed with grief.

He turned once to look back and saw Jesus still looking at him, an expression of tender love on His face. He didn't look back again.

Jim looked down. His brow was furrowed, his expression troubled. Dave continued.

"Jim, let me tell you now about Waldo..."

Chapter Forty-One

WALDO

~1157 AD–1217 AD~

The law of thy mouth is better unto me than
thousands of gold and silver.

—Psalm 119:72

It started out just like any other day in 1174. Waldo had kept appointments with both wholesalers and retailers. It was business as usual.

He loved his active life here in Lyons, France. It was a thriving community, and he had a good working relationship with nearly every store and business in town. Lately, he had been received by the leaders of the city. He hadn't planned to become part of the inner political circle here, but he welcomed the new respect he was given and the influence he was beginning to have among the people.

But everything changed that evening when Jesus came. He spoke quietly to Waldo.

"One thing you are missing. Go your way! Sell your belongings, and give to the poor. Then you will have treasure in heaven! Then come, take up the cross, and follow Me!"

Waldo's heart leaped. Jesus was asking him to give up his earthly wealth and influence to walk with Him? There was not even a question or a moment's hesitation in his mind. His possessions would never mean anything to him again! He had come face-to-face with the priceless Pearl! When Waldo looked into His face, he knew beyond all doubt that he had found the treasure he had been searching for. What did business and politics and money mean, compared to Jesus? Waldo knew in his heart that all the earth had to offer would never satisfy him. If he turned and walked away from Jesus, his life would never have meaning again.

Then he saw the torch Jesus held. Waldo had learned in business that when opportunity came, it was not wise to hesitate. Life would not be worth living without Jesus. He reached out for the torch. The expression on Jesus' face brought tears to his eyes. He thought it had been alight before! Now His brilliant smile literally filled the entire room with joy!

Waldo smiled back and looked at the torch that he now held in his hand. When he looked back to Jesus, he could no longer see Him. But He was here. He was here! Never again would Waldo be alone! What a small price to pay! His worldly goods were nothing compared to the awesome presence of Christ!

The flaming torch was still in his hand. He couldn't wait until people got up to begin their day. He decided to go wake up the town. He had a lot of work to do! He ran throughout the city, giving away everything he owned. He marveled at how the poor rejoiced as he gave them his possessions. Didn't they know that these material things would never bring the peace and joy they sought? He longed for this day to be over, so he could offer everyone the real treasure.

He ran into his business and greeted his faithful employees.

"Draw up deeds," he shouted happily. "I'm giving you my business! I have met Jesus!"

When the day was over, Waldo had nothing. His Master would now have to provide for him. He was happier than he had ever been in his entire life. In fact, he couldn't quit smiling. What an uproar he had caused in Lyons! He knew that his relatives and friends were convinced he was crazy, even though they had been careful not to express their opinions to him. They didn't want him to change his mind about giving away his wealth until they owned a piece of it!

He had given some of his money to a printing company, commissioning it to translate several books of the Bible from Latin to French. He wanted plenty of Bibles on hand to give away!

He opened his Bible now to his favorite passage. He had read these words of Jesus many times before, but tonight he could almost see Jesus sitting on the mountain, enjoying the view, and then turning to smile at His disciples and teach them His ways.

> *Blessed are the poor in spirit.* (Matthew 5:3)

Waldo was richly blessed!

> *Let your light so shine before men.* (verse 16)

He glanced at his torch.

> *Give to him that asketh thee, and from him that would borrow of thee turn not thou away.* (verse 42)

Waldo smiled. He planned to spend the rest of his life giving to those in need.

> *Where your treasure is, there will your heart be also.*
> (Matthew 6:21)

His treasure was Jesus now. He would seek nothing and no one else.

> *Take no thought for your life, what ye shall eat, or what you shall drink; nor yet for your body, what ye shall put on.*
> (verse 25)

Waldo knew that everyone who had joined this race had been provided for. Why should he worry? His Lord would take care of him! He was a runner now!

The following day, Waldo ran through Lyons. One friend approached him warily.

"Waldo! What has happened to you? The things I heard... they're not true, are they?"

Waldo's face lit with a smile.

"I have decided to live by the words of the gospel. I am going to live the Sermon on the Mount and the commandments of Jesus Christ! I will live for my Lord in poverty. For the first time in my life, I will have absolutely no concern for tomorrow!"

A crowd gathered around them, and Waldo told them of his encounter with Christ, mixing with his testimony the Scriptures that meant so much to him.

When he saw the hunger in their eyes, he said, "Won't you repent of your sins, turn to Jesus Christ, and be saved?"

While some bowed in prayer, repenting of their sins and receiving Jesus as their Lord and Savior, one man broke away from the group and rushed to report Waldo to the archbishop.

"Waldo is in the streets, preaching the gospel in public!"

"He'll get over this," the archbishop replied. "I've heard that he has been carried away by his excitement."

But Waldo continued to walk the streets, talking, sharing, preaching.

"This has to be stopped," the archbishop finally decided. He sent for Waldo.

"I am warning you to stop your preaching! You have no right to speak of Jesus to the people. You are not ordained by the church to speak the Word!"

But even as he was speaking, Waldo was looking not upon him, but upon the face of the Lord. He smiled and then lowered his eyes to face his accuser.

"It is better to obey God than man," he answered simply. Then he returned to the streets to proclaim the gospel to men, women, and children.

Waldo did not intend to oppose the church. He did not plan to found another sect. Nor did he wish to build himself a name or gain a following. He had no new revelations to share. He merely wanted to live as Jesus told His followers to live. He continued to run.

Again he was called before the archbishop.

"Do you still not understand that only the clergy has the right to preach? I have told you that the church alone can give a man authority to preach, and you have been given no such power!"

Waldo met his eyes steadily. His voice was polite but firm as he replied, "I preach the gospel, not because the church has commissioned me, but because Christ has commissioned me."

The archbishop seemed to undergo a transformation right before Waldo's eyes. Rage and raw hatred contorted his features. He spoke in a low voice, through clenched teeth.

"Then get out of my city! And don't ever enter Lyons again! You are excommunicated from the church! You and your followers are nothing but heretics!"

Years later, a police report was found among the church documents in Carcassonne, France. Perhaps the voice of one of Waldo's enemies will most clearly portray his life.

Waldo was a rich man but, abandoning all his wealth, he determined to observe a life of poverty and evangelical perfection, as the apostles. He arranged for the Gospels and some other books of the Bible to be translated in common speech. Infatuated with himself, he presumes to preach the gospel in the streets, where he made many disciples, and involving them, both men and women, has sent them out, in turn, to preach.

These people, ignorant and illiterate, went about through the towns, entering houses and even churches, spreading many errors round about. The archbishop of

Lyons had forbidden such presumption, but they by no means wished to obey him, cloaking their madness by saying that they must obey God rather than men, since God had commanded the apostles to preach the gospel to every creature.

Because of this disobedience and their undertaking a task which did not pertain to them, they were excommunicated and expelled from their country.

So light spread throughout the land. Many runners, banished from France, settled in the Alps of Italy. They chose to live their lives in the same way the one who led them to Christ did, simply living Christ's sermon given to His disciples on the mountain.

As the world hated Jesus and His disciples, it will hate anyone who follows their example. Many "Waldensians," as Waldo's followers were called, were cruelly massacred. But in spite of massive extermination campaigns to rid the earth of those who followed Waldo's example of following Christ, the chain of souls born into the kingdom of God through his ministry has survived for over eight hundred years.

Chapter Forty-Two

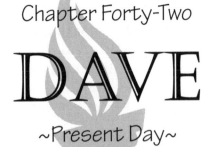

DAVE

~Present Day~

How long halt ye between two opinions? if the
LORD be God, follow him.

—1 Kings 18:21

Jim was silent for several moments after Dave finished. He still looked down, not wanting to meet Dave's eyes.

"Jim," Dave said softly, "you need to make a decision. Our Lord told us clearly that we would not be able to serve God and mammon. Mammon is the wealth of this world. But mammon is even more than that, Jim. It's the personification of money. It's a god of this world, with seducing and enticing power, compelling people to give their entire lives to it, rather than to Christ.

"The first young man chose to serve mammon. He made the wrong choice, Jim. All the lands and riches that he accumulated in his lifetime are now either buried under mountains of rubble or owned by someone else.

"Waldo forsook mammon, took the torch, and ran for Christ. His treasures are still accumulating today. He is rich for eternity.

"Jim, you alone can decide whom you will follow. Christ demands one thing of His torchbearers. He requires each one of them to love and follow Him, with all their heart, with all their soul, with all their mind, and with all their strength."

Dave stood up and laid his hand on Jim's shoulder. "I'll pray for you, Jim. You would make a great runner."

"Thanks, Dave," Jim mumbled. He remained sitting with his head bowed as Dave left to resume his run.

"Oh, God," Dave breathed, "may Jim see through the deceptive outer splendor of mammon to its inner rottenness. May he one day say, like Paul, 'I have suffered the loss of all things, and I count them but dung, that I may win Christ!'"

The campus lay in darkness. Dave noticed only one glow of light to the right. He had hoped to bring Jim along. But, as usual, he was alone.

He knocked on the dorm door, wondering which one of Phil's friends would answer. He was shocked to see that it was Ray, the one who had scoffed more than the others the night he had visited Phil. It didn't seem like today's reception was going to be any warmer.

Dave extended his hand and said, "Phil called and said you wanted me to come talk with you."

Ray ignored his hand and shrugged. "I wouldn't put it exactly like that. I made a few comments after you left. Phil told me to shut up about you and your torch. This morning I said something that set him off. He stormed out the door and told me you would be here to talk to me tonight. I was going to leave but couldn't think of anyplace to go that interested me."

Dave sighed. He didn't know whether to stay or leave.

"What kind of comments were you making?"

"Oh, nothing to get all riled up about. All I said this morning is that at least you have something to live for."

He shrugged and made a half-hearted attempt to smile. Dave thought he looked better with his perpetual frown.

Dave decided to stay.

"Do you want me to talk, Ray? Or do you want to question me?"

"Neither, really. But since you're here, I do have one question. It's bad enough for an Olympic champion who has everything going for him to run around waving a torch. But that old book you're carrying—that's too much."

Dave looked at his Bible, then at Ray. "What is your honest opinion about this old book?"

"I told you before. It's an antique. It's irrelevant to life. It's meaningless to me. What's your opinion of it?"

"It's the Word of God."

"Oh, come on, Dave! Do you believe God sent the book from heaven on the wings of an angel?"

"I realize my belief that God anointed men to write a message to His creation brands me as a fool in your mind. But I also realize I wouldn't be sitting here with you if you had all the answers to life. You're still searching for truth. And you're right about one thing. I have found life worth living. And I found the answers in the pages of this book."

Ray laughed. "You're a fool."

Dave smiled. "Yes...one of many. If you don't mind, I'll name a few."

"Go ahead. Rattle off your list of old ladies, prissy girls, and feeble-minded men."

Dave ignored his comment as he removed a paper from the back of his Bible. "I'll read these quotes so they will be accurate.

"George Washington said,

It is impossible to rightly govern the world without God and the Bible.

"John Quincy Adams agreed with him. He said,

So great is my veneration of the Bible, that the earlier my children begin to read it the more confident will be my hope that they will prove useful citizens of their country and respectable members of society.

"A friend of Andrew Jackson asked for his opinion of the Bible. He answered,

That book, sir, is the rock on which our republic rests.

"Was Abraham Lincoln a fool? Hear his words.

I believe the Bible is the best gift God has ever given to man. All the good from the Savior of the world is communicated to us through this book.

"Horace Greeley recommended the Bible, saying,

It is impossible to mentally or socially enslave a Bible-reading people. The principles of the Bible are the groundwork of human freedom.

"Woodrow Wilson asked the audience he was addressing to make a commitment to read the Bible every day.

I ask every man and woman in this audience that from this day on they will realize that part of the destiny of America lies in their daily perusal of this great book.

"Douglas MacArthur ended every day by reading the Bible. Listen to his words.

Believe me, sir, never a night goes by, be I ever so tired, but I read the Word of God before I go to bed.

"Herbert Hoover joins the others in his praise of the book:

The whole of the inspiration of our civilization springs from the teachings of Christ and the lessons of the prophets. To read the Bible for these fundamentals is a necessity of American life.

"Benjamin Franklin added his counsel.

Young man, my advice to you is that you cultivate an acquaintance with, and a firm belief in, the Holy Scriptures.

"Next in the lineup of old women, prissy girls, and feeble-minded men are the founders of Yale, Princeton, and Harvard. Yale College was granted a new charter in 1745. There was nothing peculiar about reading the Bible then. Included in its regulations were these words:

> If any scholar shall deny the Holy Scriptures or any part of them to be the Word of God, or be guilty of heresy or any error directly tending to subvert the fundamentals of Christianity, and continuing obstinate therein after the first and second admonition, he shall be expelled.

> All scholars shall live religious, godly, and blameless lives according to the rules of God's Word, diligently reading the Holy Scriptures, the fountain of light and truth...

> That the president, or in his absence one of the tutors, shall constantly pray in the college hall every morning and evening, and shall read a chapter or suitable portion of the Holy Scriptures.

"Princeton's first president, John Witherspoon, said,

> Cursed be all learning that is contrary to the cross of Christ. Cursed be all learning that is not coincident with the cross of Christ. Cursed be all learning that is not subservient to the cross of Christ.

"Harvard University clarified its main educational priority in its Rules and Precepts, adopted in 1646:

> (1) Every one shall consider the main end of his life and studies to know God and Jesus Christ, which is eternal life.

> (2) Seeing the Lord giveth wisdom, every one shall seriously by prayer in secret seek wisdom of Him.

(3) Every one shall so exercise himself in reading the Scriptures twice a day that they be ready to give an account of their proficiency therein, both in theoretical observations of languages and logic, and in practical and spiritual truths."

Dave replaced the paper and looked straight at Ray.

"Isn't it amazing, in the light of that lineup, that America has forbidden the Bible to be read in its schools?"

He paused reflectively.

"Ray, only governments that wish to take their people's freedom despise this book. Confiscation of the Bible was one of the first things on the Communist agenda to enslave a people. It's rather frightening to me that America's Supreme Court has declared it illegal for a teacher to even place one on his desk!"

Dave tapped his Bible with his forefinger.

"It may surprise you to know that in past centuries men and women alike were not only excommunicated, but also strangled, imprisoned, and burned at the stake—not by the government, but by the church—simply for translating and distributing the Bible! Tell me...why this hatred and fear for what you refer to as just 'another old book'?

"Let me introduce you to a brilliant scholar who held a doctorate from Oxford University. He was hated so intensely by his enemies that they referred to him as the child of the devil..."

Chapter Forty-Three

JOHN WYCLIF

~1334 AD–1384 AD~

And the LORD answered me, and said, Write the vision, and make it plain upon tables, that he may run that readeth it.

—Habakkuk 2:2

T he light of the Word of God did not shine on the masses of England in that day. The only word they could know was that chosen by their priests to give to them.

Out of this gripping darkness stepped a tall, thin scholar, clothed in a long black gown. He had a full, flowing beard, and his eyes were clear and penetrating. His appearance was one of lofty earnestness, dignity, and character. And John Wyclif carried a torch.

People gasped as he emerged from the shadows. Oxford University was Europe's most outstanding university in the fourteenth century, and John Wyclif, having studied for sixteen years to obtain his doctorate of divinity, was its leading theologian and philosopher.

This priest had one consuming goal. He loved his Christ, and he had become acquainted with Him through the Scriptures. He wanted everyone to be able to feast on the Word of God!

He wrote, "The Bible is necessary for all men, not for priests alone. It alone is the supreme law that is to rule church, state, and Christian life, without human traditions and statutes.

His purpose was met with the fury of the church! "Heresy!" was the outcry.

John ignored the threats and sat down at his desk. He opened his Latin Bible, a handwritten copy of a thousand-year-old translation. He faced his awesome task with anticipation. Dipping his pen into ink, he began to translate the first Bible in the English language.

Waiting outside were men, their own torches burning, ready to take the Word of God throughout the countryside. They were committed to their task, preparing to spend their lives living and dressing simply, preaching wherever there was even one person to hear them. John kept at his work diligently, pausing only long enough to distribute to these itinerant preachers portions of the Word.

The leaders of the church were stunned.

A Catholic chronicler, Henry Knighton, began to fight John viciously with his pen and ink.

> Christ gave His gospel to the clergy and the learned doctors of the church so that they might give it to the laity and to weaker persons, according to the message of the season and personal need. But this Master John Wyclif translated the gospel from Latin into the English, making it the property of the masses and common to all and more open to the laity, and even to women who were able to read! The pearl of the gospel is thrown before swine and trodden underfoot...What used to be the highest gift of the clergy and the learned members of the church has become common to the laity!

The light of God's Word had begun to spread, and no man and no church could quench the fire.

People received the Bible hungrily, devouring the Word of God. John Wyclif was summoned to London to answer the charges of heresy. Pope Gregory XI denounced him.

He was expelled from his teaching position at Oxford University. But he kept writing.

Along with his translation of the Bible, John wrote other materials, stressing that the head of the church was Christ, not man. He also stressed the need for renewed spiritual life through the teachings of Christ. He preached that each individual needed a direct relationship with God through Jesus Christ.

He clashed with the church, declaring that every Christian had the right to know the Bible. He longed for the day that every Christian would understand that Christ alone is the way of salvation.

Pope Gregory XI described him as a deadly pest "who must be plucked up by the roots, who hath gone to such a pitch of detestable folly, that he feareth not to teach, and publicly preach, or rather to vomit out of the filthy dungeon of his breast false conclusions!"

John, ignoring the avalanche of accusations raging against him, wrote a tract in English for his followers to distribute.

A Short Rule of Life

First, when you are fully awake, think upon the goodness of your God...

Second, think on the great sufferings and willing death that Christ suffered for mankind.

Third, think how God has saved you from death and other mischief. And for this goodness and mercy, thank God with all your heart. Pray Him to give you grace to spend in that day, and evermore, all the powers of your soul (as mind, understanding, reason, and will) and all the powers of your body (as strength, beauty, and your five senses) in His service and worship, and in nothing against His commandments, but in ready performance of His works of mercy, and to give good example of holy life, both in word and deed, to all men about you.

Be well occupied, and no idle time, for the danger of temptation.

Besides this, do right and equity to all men, your superiors, equals, and subjects, or servants; and stir all to love truth, mercy, true peace, and charity; and help all people to be in harmony with one another.

Most of all, fear God and His wrath; love God and His law, and His worship: and ask not principally for worldly reward, but maintain a virtuous life.

At the end of the day, think about how you have offended God, and amend it while you may. And think how graciously God has saved you; not for your desert, but for His own mercy and goodness. And pray for grace that you may dwell and end in His true and holy service, and real love, and according to your skill, to teach others to do the same.

"Preaching," John explained to his followers, "is to spread God's Scriptures!"

When people of John's parish came to him, he counseled, "It is not confession to man but to God, who is the true Priest of souls, that is the great need of sinful man. Private confession and the whole system of medieval confession was not ordered by Christ and was not used by the apostles, for of the three thousand who were turned to Christ's law on the day of Pentecost, not one of them was confessed to a priest! It is God who is the forgiver!"

People gathered from all walks of life to receive the Word from this torchbearer. "What of our faith?" cried out one of the crowd gathered to hear him preach.

John turned to him. "Trust wholly in Christ; rely altogether on His sufferings; beware of seeking to be justified in any other way than by His righteousness. Faith in our Lord Jesus Christ is sufficient for salvation."

John crossed his finish line at home in bed on New Year's Eve. He had completed his task. He laid his torch down joyfully, knowing that its light was spreading throughout his country, lighting both huts and mansions.

While John Wyclif rested from his labors with the Lord he loved and served, his enemies had no rest. The archbishop of Canterbury fumed, "That pestilent and most wretched John Wyclif, of damnable memory, a child of the old devil, and himself a child or pupil of Antichrist, who, while he lived, walking in the vanity of his mind...crowned his wickedness by translating the Scriptures into the mother tongue!"

His hatred for John Wyclif consumed him. The Word of God was being read and preached everywhere! Doctrines taught by the church but not found in the Scriptures were no longer passively accepted.

He summoned a council meeting of clergymen, and in 1408 this decree was published:

> We decree and ordain that no one shall in future translate on his authority any text of Scripture into the English tongue or into any other tongue, by way of book, booklet, or treatise. Nor shall any man read, in public or in private, this kind of book, booklet, or treatise, now recently composed in the time of the said John Wyclif under penalty of the greater excommunication.

Hatred against his memory intensified as men, both rich and poor, discovered in the Bible that they too could be runners who carried the torch for Christ! Light was being turned on everywhere, exposing the corrupt leaders' greed and lust for power.

"John Wyclif must be condemned as a heretic!" demanded those who vainly attempted to put out the embers from his torch.

Thirty-one years after John Wyclif died, he was condemned as a heretic at the Council of Constance on 260 different counts.

"Burn his writings!" came the order. "Exhume his bones! Cast them out of consecrated ground!"

His body was dug up and banished to ground unsanctified by the church. But still his enemies were not satisfied.

Thirteen years later, nearly half a century after John Wyclif's death, the pope gave the command to dig up his remains a second time, burn them, and scatter the ashes into the river Swift.

Men rushed to carry out the pope's order. But the burning of Wyclif's body did nothing to extinguish the light his torch had brought to the world.

Fuller, a historian, contemplated John Wyclif's life and death, thinking about the waters carrying Wyclif's ashes throughout the world. Then he thought about the Word of God now bringing light throughout a dark world. Another one of heaven's great runners had finished a great race. Fuller wrote,

> They burnt his bones to ashes and cast them into the Swift, a neighboring brook running hard by. Thus the brook hath conveyed his ashes into Avon; Avon into Severn; Severn into the narrow seas; and they into the main ocean. And thus the ashes of Wyclif are the emblem of his doctrine, which now is dispersed the world over.

The fires that destroyed John Wyclif's body were unable to destroy his writings. For those who hungered to hear God's Word were running with them, dispersing them throughout the land. Some would find their way into Prague, Czechoslovakia, where they would burn their way into the heart of another John, a priest who would become a heroic runner in this unceasing race.

Chapter Forty-Four

DAVE

~Present Day~

Many pastors have destroyed my vineyard, they have trodden my portion under foot, they have made my pleasant portion a desolate wilderness...For the pastors are become brutish, and have not sought the LORD.

—Jeremiah 12:10; 10:21

R ay shrugged. "I don't understand. I thought it was the church that pushed the Bible on the rest of the world. Now you're telling me that the church outlawed it."

Dave prayed silently for wisdom to explain.

"Ray, there is the church...and then there is the true church. Wyclif was part of the true church, founded by Christ Himself. He loved and taught the Scriptures—and he carried a torch.

"A government can exist to serve its people or to enslave its people. A church can also either serve or enslave its people. Do you remember Horace Greeley's words? He said, 'It is impossible to mentally or socially enslave a Bible-reading people. The principles of the Bible are the groundwork of human freedom.'"

Dave opened his Bible. "Jesus said,

If ye continue in my word, then ye are my disciples indeed; and ye shall know the truth, and the truth shall make you free.

(John 8:31–32)

He looked at Ray.

"Now do you see, Ray, why the government or the church that desires to enslave its people despises the Bible?

"When a government or church begins to attack the Bible and writes laws against it, it has marked itself as an institution whose ultimate desire is to totally dominate its people. Any man who dares to go among the people of that church or nation with the Bible will be marked for destruction.

"Thank God for brave men who were willing to incur the wrath of tyrannical leaders. They blazed a path of freedom for future runners.

"John Hus was one who gave the ultimate sacrifice at the hands of cruel and sadistic men..."

Chapter Forty-Five

JOHN HUS

~1372 AD–1415 AD~

*Princes have persecuted me without a cause: but my
heart standeth in awe of thy word.*

—Psalm 119:161

John Hus looked across the multitude and felt pity for them.
They wouldn't have much longer to wait before seeing his
body consumed by fire. Even now wood and straw were
being piled around his feet and legs.

Today was his forty-third birthday. Events of his life flashed
before him.

He was born in 1372 in a village in Bohemia, a region in
what is now the Czech Republic. His parents were not wealthy,
but they were determined he would be well educated. Teachers
and professors in both the private school he attended and the
University of Prague were impressed by their brilliant young
scholar. He received his bachelor of divinity degree and became
the pastor of Bethlehem Chapel and the dean and rector of the
prestigious University of Prague. It was then that his life began
to change—for it was then that he began reading Scriptures and
messages distributed by Wyclif. And they began to burn their way
into his soul.

He saw sin as God saw it, in all its raw ugliness. He looked
within his heart and recoiled in horror, for it fit Jeremiah's description:

The heart is deceitful above all things, and desperately wicked. (Jeremiah 17:9)

"God," he cried. "I am a sinner in need of a Savior!" And God lifted his sins from him and clothed him in the righteousness of His only begotten Son.

His congregation, faculty, and students gasped as they saw their pastor and dean running toward them, lighting both the church and the campus with his presence. He preached with authority, his message now the life-changing, sin-cleansing gospel of Jesus Christ.

The truth of Psalm 119:9 had become reality in the life of John Hus.

Wherewithal shall a young man cleanse his way? by taking heed thereto according to thy word.

The archbishop of Prague stared at this new runner. "How dare Hus bring the Scriptures and Wyclif's heresy into my jurisdiction?" he raged. "He must be silenced! Send out a decree! Suppress by any means possible the further spreading of Wyclif's writings!"

Students and faculty alike reacted to the decree in outrage. They called a meeting to decide what to do.

"We will not give up the Scriptures," they decided. "We will instead increase our efforts to circulate them! For who is the one," they reasoned, "who would dare confiscate the letters written by a king to his queen? The Bible is a letter written by the Lord God, the King of Kings, to His bride! How dare man confiscate God's letter to His beloved?"

John joined their cry, informing the archbishop, "You are putting unlawful bonds upon the Word of God!"

The archbishop responded in fury.

"Wyclif's writings and Scripture translations are condemned," he declared. "I want all his writings delivered to me.

Anyone who refuses to deliver the copies in their possession will henceforth be forbidden to preach in any church!"

John refused to give up his Scriptures and Wyclif's messages.

"Why do you insist on reading the writings of Wyclif, the heretic?" the infuriated archbishop asked him.

John Hus answered calmly, "I am attracted by his writings, in which he expends every effort to conduct all men back to the law of Christ, and especially the clergy, inviting them to let go pomp and dominion of the world, and to live, like the apostles, according to the law of Christ. I am attracted by the love he has for the law of Christ, maintaining its truth and holding that in no point can it prove to be false."

"Then you will no longer preach at Bethlehem Chapel—or anywhere," came the reply.

John thought about the apostles facing authorities of their day, fourteen hundred years earlier. They too had been commanded to quit preaching the gospel of Jesus Christ. Their stand gave John courage, for they had answered their accusers boldly.

> *Whether it be right in the sight of God to hearken unto you more than unto God, judge ye. For we cannot but speak the things which we have seen and heard.* (Acts 4:19–20)

John Hus would follow their example.

After he was excommunicated from the church, he moved to the village of his birth, where he continued to run—preaching, writing, and distributing the gospel message. For what man can stop the race God Himself has established? And what runner, commissioned by God, dare take orders from mere men?

He was watched constantly by his enemies. They called a meeting of the General Council in 1414 and summoned John to Constance, Germany.

His friends, concerned for his safety and fearing that authorities might stop him from leaving Constance, pleaded with the emperor on his behalf, "John Hus needs a letter from you, assuring him of his safety. He will not be allowed to return home without it."

The emperor called for his scribe and dictated,

Receive the honorable man, Master John Hus, whom we have taken under our protection and safeguard, and under that of the Empire. When he arrives among you, receive him kindly and treat him favorably. Let him freely and securely pass, sojourn, stop, and return.

John's friends were elated and ran to give him the emperor's letter. John read it, then looked at the friends surrounding him. He appreciated their efforts, but the letter he held in his heart was the only one that truly assured his safety. For it was written by the King of Kings and Lord of Lords, and read,

I will never leave thee nor forsake thee...Lo, I am with you always, even unto the end of the world.
(Hebrews 13:5; Matthew 28:20)

John knew in his heart he would not return from Germany, but would instead die there for the Lord. No earthly emperor could see him safely through the portals of death, but Jesus would. He alone gave John comfort.

As he made his way to Germany, John was amazed to see the streets and roads lined with people, honoring him, praying for him.

"I thought I had been an outcast," he told his fellow travelers. "But I now see my worst friends are in Bohemia."

His adversaries had reached Constance before him and were already at work, poisoning the minds of those who would judge him.

Guards were stationed to await his arrival. As they watched the road, they saw in the distance a runner approaching, his torch shining brightly. They arrested him as soon as he reached them. He offered no resistance, but his companions cried, "Look at this letter from the emperor! This man is not to be arrested!"

The guards looked at one another, confused by two conflicting orders.

"We will lock him in a palace chamber," they decided. "Then we will show this letter to the proper authorities."

They took it to the pope. He scarcely glanced at it before dismissing it with a wave of his hand. "I am not bound to the pledge of the emperor," he scoffed.

John was taken before the Council, where he spoke fearlessly. The members of the Council jeered loudly, drowning out the message they hated. John ignored their derision and calmly continued proclaiming the Word of God, not regarding the fact that it was branding him a heretic in their eyes.

"Union with Jesus Christ is the essential condition of membership in His church," he proclaimed. "For Christ alone is the Head of the church."

"Heresy," the mockers screamed.

"The Scriptures are our only source of truth," he replied with composure.

"Oh!" answered one Council member. "So you will obey the apostolic commands?"

"I surely will," John agreed.

Then he looked his accusers in the eye unflinchingly and added, "Understand me, gentlemen! I term the doctrine of Christ's apostles the only true apostolic commands! So far as the commands of the pope of Rome agree with that doctrine and those commands, I am willing to obey them gladly; but when I see the contrary, I shall not obey, even if you place before me fire to consume my body."

"Take him to the dungeon," the men yelled.

He was grabbed and dragged to a foul dungeon. The guards opened the door and threw him in, closing it quickly to escape the awful stench. They left John there for days. John was only forty-two years of age, but no man could retain his health in such rancid living conditions.

His body deteriorated rapidly. It wasn't long before his imminent death was reported by the guards to their superiors.

"Move him to a better cell," they ordered. "He needs to be kept alive for his execution."

Shortly afterward, his trial began. The council had met earlier to plot their strategy.

"We must prevent Hus from speaking, for he will continue to quote Scripture," they declared.

This was to be John's trial, not their own, yet God's Word condemned them, rather than him. They had to reach a verdict swiftly and condemn John to death. They must force him to be silent.

They dressed John in priestly garments, and a chalice was given to him to hold. He was brought into the room and seated before the Council.

A bishop thrust documents into his hands.

"These are your teachings," he was told. "We will read them aloud. Then you will be given the opportunity to retract them or approve them."

John listened in shock as the Articles were read. Heresy had been filtered in with the scriptural teachings. He was given no opportunity to differentiate between the false and the true.

He tried to interject a few sentences at intervals during the reading but was sharply reproved.

When the reading was completed, his judges looked upon him sternly. "Retract or acknowledge these Articles!" he was commanded.

John did not dare to denounce the Articles, as some were the truths of the Scriptures. Neither did he dare agree with them, as many of the Articles were outright lies.

He lifted his head to face his accusers.

"I refuse to denounce the Articles," he stated.

"Then you are condemned to die," came the verdict.

John fell to his knees when he heard his sentence and prayed, "Lord Jesus Christ! Pardon all my enemies, I pray, for the sake of Your great mercy. You know that they have falsely accused me, brought forward false witnesses, and concocted false articles against me. Pardon them for the sake of Your infinite mercy."

The Council grew even angrier as John prayed. They looked on this man they were unable to dominate and his torch they were unable to extinguish.

"Strip him of his priestly garments!" they screamed. "Remove the chalice from his cursed hand!"

As a bishop grabbed the chalice from his hand, he spoke to John furiously, "We take from thee, accursed Judas, the cup of salvation."

John replied fervently, "I trust in God, my almighty Father. He will not take from me the cup of His salvation, and I have a steadfast hope that I will today drink it in His kingdom."

The council was enraged. How could they humiliate this man?

They called for paper, painted devils on it, fashioned it into a miter, and then inscribed on it, "A Ringleader of Heretics."

John smiled as they placed it upon his head. He turned toward the laughing Council, but their mirth died abruptly as he said, "My Lord Jesus Christ, for my sake, did wear a crown of thorns; why should not I then, for His sake, again wear this light crown, be it ever so ignominious? Truly I will do it, and willingly."

The bishop was infuriated. The time he had longed for was at hand. He snarled, "Now we commit thy soul unto the devil."

"But I," John answered, his eyes lifted toward heaven, "do commend into Thy hands, O Lord Jesus Christ, my spirit which Thou hast redeemed."

He had been dragged mercilessly to the stake and secured to it with a rusty chain. Even then he had smiled. "My Lord Jesus Christ was bound with a harder chain than this for my sake," he said, "and why then should I be ashamed of this rusty one?"

The time had come for John Hus to cross his finish line. His race was nearly completed. He had blazed a trail for others to follow in life. He must now blaze a trail that future runners could follow in death.

His thoughts returned to the present. The wood and straw were piled up to his neck now.

If he had known his life would end like this, would he have changed the way he had lived, altered the message he had preached? No, he would have lived as he had lived, preached as he had preached, run as he had run, carrying the torch regardless of whom it offended.

He turned his attention to the man standing before him.

"Abjure!" the man was demanding of him. "Abandon your beliefs!"

"No," John answered, without hesitation. "What I taught with my lips, I now seal with my blood."

The wood and straw were set aflame, and a hush settled over the crowd. They listened intently to the crackling of the fire. What was this they heard? Their minds could scarcely comprehend what their ears were hearing. For John Hus was loudly and cheerfully singing a hymn.

Would this heretic never be silenced?

Finally the singing stopped as the fire of his torch mingled with the flames that consumed his body.

His enemies looked upon the pile of ashes, and they couldn't stand the sight of anything that remained of this runner.

"Gather his ashes together!" they commanded. "Cast them into the Rhine!"

They left then, but somehow they did not feel the victory they had anticipated. Yes, the earth was rid of one more torchbearer. But would the joyful hymn he had sung as fire consumed his body ever quit echoing in their minds?

Chapter Forty-Six

DAVE

~Present Day~

I send unto you prophets, and wise men, and scribes: and some of them ye shall kill and crucify; and some of them shall ye scourge in your synagogues, and persecute them from city to city.

—Matthew 23:34

D ave glanced at Ray—and looked again. Dave had previously thought Ray's scowl was permanent, but now it was replaced with unadulterated anger.

Ray spoke with a barely controlled voice seething with fury.

"How dare the church treat its own runner that way?"

"I told you, Ray. There are some churches whose only desire is to enslave their people. God's true people are here only to serve."

Dave paused, then said, "Perhaps you will understand better if I tell you about a mighty preacher by the name of Girolamo Savonarola. The church leaders could think of only one way to stop his scathing sermons. And stop him they must, for his finger pointed straight at their corruption."

Chapter Forty-Seven

GIROLAMO SAVONAROLA

~1452 AD–1498 AD~

And when they had left their gods there, David gave a commandment, and they were burned with fire.

—1 Chronicles 14:12

A visitor to Florence walked toward the sound of singing. He didn't know what was going on, but he aimed to find out. Ever since his arrival, people had been rushing about. Many carried clothing and furniture. Was the whole city moving?

He found the mob at the main square, placing their things at the foot of a giant wooden pyramid. It was a happy crowd, alternately talking and singing.

He pushed through them for a closer look at the piles heaped around the pyramid. There were cards, carved gaming tables, a few books, dresses, wigs, paintings, jewelry, and many pornographic pictures.

He stepped back just as a song ended.

Young men torched the straw surrounding the pyramid—and it exploded. He discovered later it was laced with gunpowder. The mob cheered as the structure and their possessions burned.

"What is going on here?" he asked the man standing next to him.

"We are burning our vanities," he replied, looking at him closely. "You must not be from here. We have done this often since Savonarola became the prior of St. Mark's."

The stranger smiled.

So this was the work of Girolamo Savonarola.

The friars had never heard such a scorching sermon.

"Repent! If Italy does not repent, terrible catastrophes will befall us! God will pour out His wrath upon this sinful and wicked country!

"We are governed by tyrants who heap abuse on the poor.

"People have replaced the worship of God with humanistic paganism! It has corrupted our manners, our art, our poetry... and yes, even our religion!

"The Roman court is vile! Its only concern is its power and wealth. The gold and silver hoarded by the church should be sold to feed the poor!

"And the pope! His private life is scandalous!"

A shock rippled through the congregation of friars. It was common knowledge that Pope Alexander VI was corrupt. It was obvious to everyone that he cared nothing about spiritual matters. He sought only the world, with its pleasures and fortunes. Pope Alexander didn't even attempt to hide his enormous wealth or all the children he had fathered.

One scandal would scarcely be over before another one would begin. News of his depravity had rocked the church at first. Now the people scarcely noticed.

Yet...how dare Girolamo denounce the pope?

Had he gone too far this time? His words would surely reach Rome. The pope would be enraged. Had Girolamo forgotten the Unam Sanctum of 1302 that said every human being is subject to the pontiff of Rome? Did Girolamo not know the meaning of the three-tiered crown—the lower tier signifying his rule over departed souls in hell, the middle tier signifying his rule over all souls on earth, and the top tier showing he also ruled over all the souls in heaven?

Girolamo was unimpressed.

"The church desperately needs reforming," he continued to preach fearlessly.

He paused in his sermon to talk to God.

"My Lord," he cried. "As a child I have not been able to suffer the blind wickedness of the peoples of Italy! Our only hope is for You to intervene. Chastise us with Your scourge!"

He remained silent a moment, then looked at the friars and prophesied, "The church will be scourged. Following its scourging, the church will be renewed."

The pope issued Girolamo an official letter, forbidding him to preach. Ignoring it, he taught the books of Ruth, Micah, and Ezekiel.

He further incurred the wrath of the church by selling much of its property. He sent friars out to distribute the proceeds to the poor.

"The friars under Girolamo are so different than they used to be," the people remarked. "They are living like holy men. They are truly servants of God!"

Government officials discussed ways to stop Girolamo's preaching. They gathered the rabble and incited riots against him. Absorbed in his Bible study and prayer, he paid no attention to them.

He began a series of sermons from Exodus, preparing his congregation for his own exit from the world.

His departure came swiftly. He was seized like a common criminal. A commission of his worst enemies was appointed to examine him by savage torture. As blood poured from his wounds, he remembered the offer he had spurned: The church had decided to stop his rebukes by promoting him to a cardinal.

"We will give you the red hat," they bribed.

"A red hat?" he had scoffed. "I want a hat of blood."

He had one now. He would not exchange it for all that the world or a corrupt church had to offer.

Unable to find sufficient evidence to brand him a heretic, they falsified records to charge him with crimes.

They hanged his broken and bruised body, then burned his remains. Dumping his ashes in the river, they heaved a sigh of relief.

Girolamo's detestable sermons would be heard no more.

But future generations would have reason to remember his prophecy.

The church will be scourged.

Following its scourging, the church will be renewed.

Chapter Forty-Eight

DAVE

~Present Day~

They kept not the covenant of God, and refused to walk in his law.

—Psalm 78:10

The nation and kingdom that will not serve thee shall perish; yea, those nations shall be utterly wasted.

—Isaiah 60:12

A nother Bible thumper put to death," Ray said.

Dave was angry at Ray's flippant comment, but he remained silent.

Ray glanced at the Bible Dave held. "It must be a pretty powerful book," he observed.

"This is the only book in America that has been declared illegal in schools by the federal government. A teacher breaks the law by reading it to students or even referring to its wisdom. It has been removed from many school libraries. Portions of it have been torn from our school walls. Doesn't that tell you something?"

Ray nodded grimly, then answered. "Two things, as a matter of fact. One, as I said, it must be a pretty powerful book. Two, the United States government is in the beginning stages of enslaving its people."

Dave nodded, for the first time thinking maybe he was getting somewhere with Ray. "This country didn't start out this way. The Confederation of the United Colonies of New England met in Boston in 1643 to adopt a resolution. It stated, in part:

Whereas we all came into these parts of America with one and the same end and aim, namely, to advance the kingdom of our Lord Jesus Christ and to enjoy the liberties of the gospel in purity with peace.

"William Penn, the overseer of the founding of Pennsylvania, said,

If we will not be governed by God, we must be governed by tyrants.

Dave leaned forward. "Ray, have you been to a middle school or high school recently?"

"No."

"I have. An armed security guard walked the grounds. Another one stood by the main entrance. A police car patrolled the parking lots. Their presence indicated violence brewing inside. Students armed with weapons are common today, and teachers and students alike fear assaults, rapes, thefts, and murder.

"Martin Luther made a statement about universities that applies to our present grade schools. He said,

I am much afraid that schools will prove to be the great gates of hell unless they diligently labor to explain the Holy Scriptures, engraving them in the hearts of youth. I advise no one to place his child where the Scriptures do not reign paramount. Every institution in which men are not increasingly occupied with the Word of God must become corrupt!"

Ray leaned forward. "I've never paid any attention to all this Bible banning. Where did it all begin?"

"It began with the Board of Education of Union Free School District Number 9 of Hyde Park, New York."

"What did they do?"

"They asked that the schools in their district begin their day by having the students repeat a prayer every morning. Someone complained, and the courts declared the prayer illegal."

"It must have been a very biased prayer!"

Dave smiled. "Biased? This was the prayer. You judge."

Almighty God, we acknowledge our dependence upon Thee, and we beg Thy blessings upon us, our parents, our teachers, and our country.

"That's it?"

"That's it."

"Seems general enough to me," Ray mused.

"The United States Supreme Court upheld the decision in 1962 with a vote of six to one. That decision became the precedent that banned both prayer and Bible reading from America's schools.

"Let me ask you a question, Ray. How far do you think America will go in banning this book? How far will it go to prevent not only schools, but also parents, from teaching its truths to their children? Will parents be imprisoned...tortured...even killed?"

"That's absurd!"

"Is it, Ray?

"Let's take a look at another time, another nation, a pushing crowd, and a horrible scene..."

Chapter Forty-Nine

WILLIAM TYNDALE

~1494 AD–1536 AD~

They are of those that rebel against the light; they know not the ways thereof, nor abide in the paths thereof.

—Job 24:13

The crowd shifted, shoving one another in their eagerness to watch a woman and six men set aflame.

"What is their crime?" a stranger asked the man standing beside him.

He turned and stared. "Don't you know? They have taught their children the Lord's Prayer, the Ten Commandments, and the Apostles' Creed—in the English language!"

"That is a crime that deserves death?" the stranger asked.

"It surely is a crime to translate the Bible into the English language—and well it should be!" the man answered firmly, turning back to view the twisting, blistering bodies.

It was just seven years later, in 1526, that William Tyndale stood in a small room, fascinated by the marvelous invention of Johannes Gutenberg. It was a tremendous printing machine, accomplishing in moments what took scribes years to do! Ever since William had first seen one, he had devoted his life to the dream that today had finally become a reality.

He thought about his past few years as he stood watching the first printed English New Testaments roll through the press. He remembered vividly his frustration at Oxford and Cambridge Universities.

It had all begun the day he had listened in horror to a clergyman. He could scarcely believe the statements he was making. They were in direct opposition to the Scriptures! And finally, he could stand listening to his lies no longer.

"Why do you teach these things?" William asked. "Do you not realize that what you are saying is in direct opposition to the Bible?"

The clergyman had looked at him with a look of utter bewilderment. "What do you mean?" he asked.

As William showed him passages of God's Word, he realized from the confusion on the man's face that he was totally ignorant himself of scriptural truths.

Other renowned clergymen joined their conversation.

"What do these things matter?" one asked William.

"What do they matter?" William declared vehemently. "Our authority for our faith is based solely upon the Word of God!"

"Our authority comes solely from the church!" the clergymen replied. They walked away from him, shaking their heads.

William knew the world would remain in darkness without the light of the Scriptures to guide man's path. The clergymen who were sent out from the universities to teach men the ways of God were themselves ignorant of God's truths. What hope was there for the common people? They had no Bibles and never would have them! They could never know the truths of the blessed Scriptures! There were scattered portions of Scripture that John Wyclif had translated and had men faithfully smuggle to the people. But William dreamed of the day when the English Bible would be available to every man.

God had commended the Jews of Berea because they searched the Scriptures daily to see if Paul preached the truth! Congregations did not have that privilege today—for the church had declared it illegal to translate the Bible into English! All people had to rely upon were the sermons of men who neither knew nor respected the Bible themselves!

"The universities have ordained that no man shall look on the Scripture until he is steeped in heathen learning for eight or nine years, and armed with so many false principles that he is completely shut out of the understanding of the Scripture," William declared to his fellow clergymen. They remained unconcerned and could see no reason for his distress.

William's heart was deeply troubled.

"My God!" he cried. "People need to be able to read Your Word!"

In response, God came to him, and William knew immediately why He had come. A torch was in His outstretched hand. William also realized that if he took the extended torch, he was signing the warrant for his own death.

He did not hesitate, nor did his hand waver as it closed around the torch. His world needed a runner, and he was honored to be called to the race!

The very next day, he boldly declared his intention to the clergyman he had argued with.

"If God spares my life, before many years pass, I will cause a boy who drives the plow to know more of the Scripture than you do!"

"The fellow is demented," the man muttered, as he hurried away from the light cast from William's torch.

William Tyndale did not waste time worrying about the opinions of men. He spent his time faithfully laboring over the one task God had appointed to him. Verse by verse, he translated the Scriptures into the English language.

He was mocked.

"Who are you to translate the Scriptures? Will they be the words of William when you finish with them?"

"I call God to record against the day we shall appear before our Lord Jesus, that I never altered one syllable of God's Word against my conscience, nor would to this day, if all that is in earth, whether it be honor, pleasure, or riches, might be given me," William Tyndale replied.

And he toiled on.

And now...now the first copies of the New Testament were rolling from the press. The common man would at last be able to have a Bible to read. Those seeking God and longing to know His ways would no longer be dependent upon blind leaders to guide them to truth.

Bishops raged as their congregations began reading the Scriptures. Doctrines that were contrary to the Bible were now being rejected by the common people! The authority of the church was being undermined by the Word itself!

"Stop Tyndale!" William Warham, the archbishop of Canterbury, roared.

Men plotted to destroy the press.

A young boy overheard their plans and ran to William, who even then labored over the printer. "Mr. Tyndale! They're coming to destroy your printer and your New Testaments!"

William hastily grabbed the unfinished copies that had just been printed and fled, escaping just in time.

The archbishop was infuriated.

"Buy every single New Testament you can find and bring them all to me!" he yelled, while dumping money into the hands of his men.

They dashed away to search for New Testaments to buy. People, including William himself, offered them their copies at vastly inflated prices. While the men rushed back to Warham to burn them, William lifted his hands in praise to God.

"God! I have prayed for money to finance a better and bigger second edition! But who would have dreamed that You would cause the archbishop himself to pay for it!"

Catholic priests preached furiously against William's illegal English Bible. Copies that could be found were confiscated and ceremoniously burned at St. Paul's Cathedral.

There was only one way to stop the work. William himself must be caught. But where was he? Several English agents were sent throughout Europe to search for him. William Tyndale knew he was a hunted man, and he barely escaped capture time and again, slipping in and out of their hands.

Henry Phillips arrived in Antwerp. He worked his way into the hearts and lives of many of William's friends. They didn't realize that his sole mission was to deliver William to the authorities. He desperately needed the money William's arrest would bring him, and he didn't care how long it took to fulfill his ambition.

Henry was dining at the home of a friend one evening when William Tyndale was announced. Henry tried to subdue his excitement. At last he was about to meet his prey face-to-face. During the dinner, Henry turned all of his charm upon William. Before long, William, who was kind to everyone, became Henry's close friend.

As they were going to lunch one day, William and Henry walked together down a narrow, twisting alley, darkened by overhanging buildings on each side. Henry suddenly shoved William roughly ahead of him. William, startled by the action of his friend, looked back at him just in time to see his finger pointing him out to two men who were waiting in the shadows. Almost before he realized what was taking place, William was grabbed and quickly bound with ropes.

He had always known it would come to this. This was part of running the race. But the shock of being betrayed by his friend was almost too much for him to bear.

He was carried to a state prison six miles north of Brussels. William looked at the castle looming ahead of him, with its moat, seven towers, three drawbridges, and massive walls. He knew he would never escape this place.

"My God," he breathed, "I will continue to serve You...even here!"

He was thrown into a foul-smelling, damp dungeon. William stared at the dripping walls and the rats that would be his cell mates for the next two years.

The cell was both wet and cold. William shivered through the days and long nights. It didn't take long for his health to fail, but he spent every bit of the strength he had in work for the Lord.

Dim light penetrated the gloomy prison only a few hours a day. During the time he was able to see, William continued writing and translating the blessed Scriptures. He would gladly rot in a cell and give his life to proclaim the Word of God!

The day came that he was dragged to trial. He listened as the charges against him were read.

"First, you have maintained that faith alone justifies! Second, you have maintained that to believe in the forgiveness of sins and to embrace the mercy offered in the gospel are enough for man's salvation."

And the list went on and on...

The Bible, for which he was being condemned, came to comfort him now.

If ye suffer for righteousness' sake, happy are ye: and be not afraid of their terror, neither be troubled. (1 Peter 3:14)

If ye be reproached for the name of Christ, happy are ye; for the spirit of glory and of God resteth upon you: on their part he is evil spoken of, but on your part he is glorified! (1 Peter 4:14)

If any man suffer as a Christian, let him not be ashamed; but let him glorify God on this behalf. (1 Peter 4:16)

He looked squarely at his accusers, even as he lifted his torch higher. His body was weak, ravaged by sickness, clothed in foul rags, the stench of the prison clinging to him. He was a man condemned by men, an object of ridicule. But he had no shame, and he would leave this wretched world glorifying the Lord.

He was branded a heretic. That accusation by the Catholic church sealed his sentence.

He submitted quietly as he was taken away and dressed in priestly robes. He was then taken to the town square. He glanced at the high platform where a great assembly of prominent doctors and dignitaries proudly sat in all their pomp and splendor.

A huge crowd had gathered to watch the degrading ceremony. His thoughts drifted to the words penned by Paul, who had so bravely run in his day:

We are made a spectacle unto the world...We are made as the filth of the world, and are the offscouring of all things.
(1 Corinthians 4:9, 13)

Paul was in heaven now, and it was up to William to be the spectacle today. Branded a heretic, he would now go through the formalities of being cast from the church.

His thoughts were interrupted by an arrogant voice.

"Kneel!" he was commanded.

He was struck to his knees, and the ritual of scraping his hands with a knife began.

"You have now lost the benefits of the anointing oil with which you were consecrated to the priesthood," a man's voice intoned.

William glanced at his torch, still shining brightly in the darkness. He knew his anointing had not been given to him by man and could never be taken away from him by man.

He was jerked to his feet and was ceremoniously stripped of his priest's robes.

He submitted calmly, for he knew man could never strip him of the fine, clean, white linen that Christ had clothed him with.

What did earthly robes matter, compared to the blessed robes of righteousness?

Man's ritual was finally over, and man no longer considered William Tyndale a priest.

But what a comfort to know that Jesus, by His own blood, had made him not only a priest, but also a king unto God! Was man so foolish that he thought any threat could persuade him to forsake that holy office?

William was handed over to the authorities for punishment. They sent him back to his cold dungeon for two more months.

One early morning in October 1536 William was again led from the prison to the town square.

So this was the day he would cross his finish line! He was ready!

A vast crowd of onlookers was already gathered around a circle of stakes to celebrate his final disgrace. Men, women, and children, some with a devilish glee in their eyes, parted as he was led through the circle to the large pillar of wood in the form of a cross.

He glanced at the chain hanging from the top and noticed the noose threaded through a hole.

The attorney walked over to him.

"You are to be given one final chance to recant."

William looked at him steadily, then lifted his head toward the God he loved and served, and prayed one last prayer.

"Lord," he cried, "open the king of England's eyes."

Two soldiers bound his feet cruelly to the stake. Another fastened the iron chain around his neck and placed the noose at his throat. Piles of wood were heaped around him.

They stepped back, and the executioner came forward. He yanked the noose down, and within seconds, William was strangled. The torch fell from his hand even as the attorney set the wood aflame. The spectators watched as the fire raged. Even as

the body of William Tyndale burned, the spirit of the victorious runner was being ushered into the courts of heaven, where angels were assembled to cheer his triumphant entrance into the celestial arena.

Chapter Fifty

DAVE

~Present Day~

*So shall my word be that goeth forth out of my mouth: it shall not
return unto me void, but it shall accomplish that which I please,
and it shall prosper in the thing whereto I sent it.*

—Isaiah 55:11

So, was his prayer answered?" Ray asked, a cynical expression on his face.

"What prayer are you referring to, Ray?"

"Tyndale's! His last prayer. He asked God to open the king of England's eyes."

"Yes, as a matter of fact it was. Less than one year later, King Henry gave his official approval for the distribution of an English Bible. He didn't realize nearly 70 percent of it was William Tyndale's translation! King Henry proclaimed, 'If there be no heresies in it, let it be spread abroad among all the people!'"

Ray's cynical expression faded.

Dave looked at him.

No scowl. No anger.

Ray was even beginning to look interested in the conversation.

"So Wyclif, Hus, Tyndale...they all accomplished what they set out to do."

Ray seemed to be thinking, so Dave kept quiet. Finally Ray broke the silence with a question.

"What do you think will happen in the United States, Dave?"

"What do *you* think will happen here, Ray?"

He shrugged. "I'm not sure. Churches that are more concerned about their power over people than...than..."

"God," Dave inserted.

"...Okay, we'll call him God. As I was saying, power-hungry churches will probably just sort of put the Bible on a back shelf. Possibly the courts will ban the Bible in more places—the workplace, perhaps. Maybe the public library. Who knows how far they'll take this thing. Before it's finished, the Bible and prayer and God Himself may be banned from America!"

"They could try, Ray, but it will never work."

"Why? It worked in the schools."

"No, Ray, it didn't. The courts might as well enact a law against oxygen or declare it illegal for the sun to shine. No court can keep a teacher or a student from praying. I've prayed to God several times since I've been here with you. Nothing you could have done or said would have been able to stop me. As long as I live, I can pray. Laws can forbid prayer and ban the Bible, but God's people will still pray.

"As far as banning the Bible, it is hidden safely in the hearts of God's people. No search party can find it, and no nation can destroy it. All they can do is kill God's people."

Ray interrupted with a snort. "I'd say that's enough!"

"Not really. Christians don't shun death. When their race is done, the hard part is over, and they are finally with God—not to mention being out of Satan's reach. But let's not get on the subject of Satan right now. Let me illustrate the statement I made about the Bible being hidden in the hearts of God's people with a true story.

"In the 1930s, a humble villager in eastern Poland was given a Bible by Michael Billester, a peddler of religious books. The villager read it and was converted to Christ. He passed the book on to others. Two hundred more became believers.

"When the peddler returned to the town in the summer of 1940, the group gathered to worship and listen to him preach.

"Billester said, 'Instead of giving the usual testimonies, I wonder if each of you could recite a verse of Scripture.'

"A man stood and asked, 'Perhaps we have misunderstood. Did you want us to recite just a verse—or a chapter?'

"Billester replied, 'Do you mean to say there are people here who can recite entire chapters of the Bible?'

"The man asked, 'Do you mean entire chapters—or books?'

"Billester soon learned that the villagers had memorized whole books of the Bible. Thirteen of them knew Matthew and Luke and half of Genesis. One could quote the entire book of Psalms. Together the two hundred Christians could quote the complete Bible. The worn-out book had been passed from family to family and carried to their Sunday gatherings. Its words were barely legible."

Ray picked up the Bible and flipped through its pages reflectively. Giving it back to Dave, he commented, "That's a lot to memorize."

"Ray, Christians throughout the whole world have portions of this book memorized. There was one monk who could quote nearly all of the New Testament and much of the Old. He caused a reformation that literally shook the foundations of the church. Believe me, the church desperately needed shaking! Girolamo's prophecy was about to come true..."

Chapter Fifty-One

MARTIN LUTHER

~1483–1546~

---

*See, I have this day set thee over the nations and over the
kingdoms, to root out, and to pull down, and to destroy,
and to throw down, to build, and to plant.*

—Jeremiah 1:10

The people gaped at the dark figure emerging from the
shadows. He was clothed in the garb of a monk. His deep-
set eyes and brows were dark black.

His eyes...

One who tried to look into them remarked, "They sparkle
and burn like stars so that I can hardly bear looking at them."

Anger radiated from him. Even the flames in his torch
seemed to rage and leap in anger. "Yes, I am angry!" he cried.
"I was born to war with fanatics and devils! I must root out the
stumps and trunks, hew away the thorns and briar, fill in the
puddles! I am the rough woodsman, who must pioneer and hew
a path!

"I was born to war with fanatics and devils," he repeated.
And his finger pointed straight at Tetzel.

"How dare this fraud travel around selling sin?" he raged.

Martin's parishioners had joined the mad rush to follow Tetzel when he had arrived in Wittenberg, Germany, where Martin's parish was. They had returned excitedly, waving their documents. They could now indulge in sin and God wouldn't punish them. Did they not have a written guarantee, backed by the pope himself? The rich among them purchased not only indulgences for themselves, but also releases from purgatory for their deceased loved ones.

The carnival-like procession had begun with a parade. Bells pealed and banners flew. With the papal decree displayed on a pillow of gold and scarlet and the stacks of printed letters of indulgence nearby, Tetzel began his disgusting performance. He painted a vivid picture of deceased parents whose wails of pain could be stilled only when their children gave liberal offerings.

A huge sign was propped in front of Tetzel's money box.

As soon as the coin in the coffer rings,
The troubled soul from purgatory springs.

"Just deposit your twenty silver coins here," his assistants called to the swarming crowds. They were kept busy hauling money.

Half of the money was rushed to Rome to finish building St. Peter's Basilica. The other half went toward paying an enormous debt at Fugger's banking house, for Albert of Mainz had borrowed heavily to buy his office of archbishop from the pope.

If Martin hadn't discovered a Bible in the library years earlier, he would have blended into the blackness along with the rest. Before he began to study the Scriptures, he, like Tetzel, was a monk without a torch.

Martin had settled into the life of a monk easily enough, wearing the robes and beret of a doctor of theology. But as far as his relationship with God went, he simply had none.

He had done everything possible to become righteous. He remained celibate. He renounced his family and his possessions. He trudged eight hundred miles to say masses at Rome. He fasted. He confessed every sin he could imagine. He abased himself, he lay prostrate before the altar, he did penance, he studied, he sang, he labored, he faithfully taught theology to his students at the university in Wittenberg...and he prayed.

It was when he tried to pray that he came face-to-face with the bitter truth. No matter what he did or how he lived, Martin knew—and Martin knew that God knew—that he was a vile sinner.

He dreaded prayer. Who was he to approach a holy God? Guilt hounded his every waking moment and prevented his sleeping ones. Others might be able to fool themselves, but he couldn't. Hopelessness nearly overwhelmed him. He was miserable.

Then he had discovered the Bible.

Day after day, month after month, for ten years, Martin devoured its pages. When he lay on his cot at night, he still pondered the words.

For therein is the righteousness of God revealed...The just shall live by faith.   (Romans 1:17)

Live by faith? Faith in what? Faith in whom?

He read about others who strived for righteousness but remained in the depths of sin.

For they being ignorant of God's righteousness, and going about to establish their own righteousness... (Romans 10:3)

"I try so hard to be righteous," he groaned. Sighing bitterly, he read on.

...have not submitted themselves unto the righteousness of God. For Christ is the end of the law for righteousness to every one that believeth.   (verses 3–4)

For therein is the righteousness of God revealed...The just shall live by faith...

That's all then? he thought. *Is salvation simply...faith in the finished work of Jesus Christ for my soul?*

"Yes," the Scripture declared.

"Yes," his heart responded.

"Yes!" he finally shouted.

"At this," he later recorded, "I felt myself to have been born again, and to have entered through open gates into paradise itself!"

He penned his personal testimony in a victorious second verse to "A Mighty Fortress Is Our God."

> *Did we in our own strength confide,*
> *Our striving would be losing,*
> *Were not the right Man on our side,*
> *The Man of God's own choosing.*
> *Dost ask who that may be?*
> *Christ Jesus! It is He!*

His joy and relief had to overflow. He wanted the world to know—especially the poor—that the wondrous gift of salvation was free! For the poor could not afford the perverted gospel offered by the church.

The church...

How it had corrupted the simple truth of the Scriptures. Trusting people filled the coffers of a church growing rich by peddling redemption.

Martin snorted. How could a church claiming Peter as its head promote such blasphemy? Did they never read Peter's words?

> *Ye know that ye were not redeemed with corruptible things, as silver and gold...but with the precious blood of Christ.*
> (1 Peter 1:18–19)

Martin's rage kept him from sleep. How could the church stoop to such a spurious fund-raising scheme? The more Martin thought about it, the angrier he became.

Peter's prophecy had surely come true in his generation:

Through covetousness shall they with feigned words make merchandise of you. (2 Peter 2:3)

His fury could not be silenced. He had to speak.

Dipping his pen, he began to write. He would fight with his pen and post his beliefs on the door of Castle Church. When people gathered there to read the daily news and announcements, they could read his views along with it. Perhaps no one would notice, but he would feel better. Number 1...

When our Lord and Master Jesus Christ said, "Repent," He willed the entire life of believers to be one of repentance.

He attacked the church viciously for its sale of indulgences. If the pope knew the sharp practices of the indulgence purveyors, he would prefer to have St. Peter's collapse in ruins rather than build it with the skin and flesh and bones of his sheep.

He sighed. Obviously the pope was fully aware of the scheme. He had authorized the indulgences.

If, for the sake of money, the pope can free suffering souls from purgatory, why not for the sake of love empty out purgatory altogether?

The list grew. And still he wrote. Number sixty-two...

The true treasure of the church is the most holy gospel of the glory and the grace of God.

He was nearing the end now.

Being a Christian involves embracing the cross and entering heaven through tribulation.

He would surely have his share of tribulation if anyone read this edict! Finally he dropped his pen and leaned back in his chair. It was finished. It had taken ninety-five theses to bare his soul.

He glanced at the calendar. October 31, 1517—as good a day as any to begin his war against heresy.

A few passersby glanced his way as he nailed his theses to the university chapel door.

It took just four weeks for all hell to break loose. Someone translated his theses into German and rushed it to John Gruenenberg, the printer. Copies were distributed among the people. Groups of the illiterate crowded around as those who were more educated stood on the streets reading the theses aloud.

The sound of the hammer pounding Martin's theses to the church door echoed throughout Europe!

The archbishop of Mainz forwarded the documents to Rome with his urgent request: "This man must be stopped!"

"Impeach Luther!" screamed the Dominicans.

Slowly but surely the dreaded word *heretic* was attached to his name.

"Drag him to Rome in chains!" some advised.

Martin's days and weeks became a hectic flurry of meetings, interrogations, and trials. He was denounced by one crowd and hailed as a hero by another.

"Burn Luther's books!" was the decree. His writings and his effigy lit up Rome in a mighty bonfire.

"Recant!" Rome commanded.

"Reform!" he thundered back.

A jagged streak of lightening had scared him into the ministry, causing him to promise to be a monk if St. Anne would save him from the storm. Now he himself became a lightning bolt, part of the mighty storm that shook the church.

Man insisted Martin denounce his beliefs, but he was bound by the Word of God to cling to them. Other leaders and laymen joined him in his protest against unscriptural practices. A new word began to be heard in the land to describe them—Protestants.

He had to be stopped. The pope issued a decree, giving him sixty days to recant or be excommunicated. On the sixty-first day, Martin tossed the decree into the fire.

He was forced into hiding, a hunted outlaw. Wanted posters were scattered throughout the land. Would his life end at just thirty-three years of age?

Well-meaning friends faked a kidnapping and smuggled him to a remote castle. He shed his monk's garb and let his hair and beard grow long to conceal his face.

He spent his days working at a furious pace. He wrote fourteen works and translated the entire New Testament from Greek to German in just eleven weeks. How he loved the Scriptures! He could quote most of the New Testament and large sections of the Old by memory. But he was so restless. He dubbed the isolated castle "Land of the Birds," for they were his only companions. He endured the loneliness and frustration for nearly a year, when he could stand no more. Had he been called to run with the torch or cower in a castle?

He ran back to his church. If Rome wanted him, let them come to Wittenberg, where he was under state protection, and get him. Until then, he planned to preach. He announced his typical weekly teaching schedule to his congregation.

Sunday at 5 a.m.:	Pauline Epistles
Sunday at 9 a.m.:	The Gospels
Sunday Afternoon:	The Catechism
Monday:	The Catechism
Tuesday:	The Catechism
Wednesday:	The Gospel of Matthew
Thursday:	The Epistles
Friday:	The Epistles
Saturday:	The Gospel of John

He taught, preached, sang, strummed his lute, and played his flute. He turned his entire congregation into his choir, further enraging his enemies. Did he not know that only the clergy were allowed to sing?

He shed his monk's garb with finality.

His rebellion against the church was complete when he married Katherina, a feisty, redheaded, twenty-six-year-old ex-nun. He was forty-two.

His marriage shocked even himself. "There's a lot to get used to in the first year of marriage," he wrote. "One wakes up in the morning and finds a pair of pigtails on the pillow that were not there before."

Katie took some getting used to. "If I should ever marry again," he told a friend, "I would hew myself an obedient wife out of stone."

Six noisy children soon filled his house. He and Katie adopted four more.

There were times he longed for silence. He once locked himself in his study for three days, but Katie simply took the door off its hinges.

He invited needy students to move in with them, along with the homeless, the sick, and the dying. His home was open to scholars, exiled clerics, and visiting dignitaries. He refused to concern himself with the problem of financing the growing household. He simply left it all to God and Katie.

So Katie cared for the orchard, the fish pond, and the barnyard. She harvested the fruit and caught the fish and slaughtered the pigs. There were usually about twenty-five or thirty people gathered around her table to eat.

Martin gave away what money he had. "God divided the hand into fingers so that money would slip through," he explained.

"Do you love her, Martin?" he was asked by his friends.

"Of course! A Christian is supposed to love his neighbor, and since his wife is his nearest neighbor, she should be his deepest love."

Then he laughed. "In domestic affairs, I defer to Katie. Otherwise, I am led by the Holy Ghost."

Katie paused in her work long enough to notice her husband was unsuccessfully battling a deep discouragement. He was constantly bombarded with betrayals, friends' misunderstandings, vicious rumors, hatred from enemies, endless debates, threats of excommunication by the church, and threats of death. Besides enduring poor health, he was branded a heathen, a wild boar, and the devil incarnate. The load slowed his run to a crawl. Katie looked at him closely. His eyes had lost their glow. His torch hung at his side.

He finally became too depressed to walk, much less run. His concerned friends gathered around to encourage him, but all left in defeat.

So Katie took matters into her own hands.

He heard her wails the moment he entered the house. He followed the noise and found her dressed in mourning clothes. She was too lost in grief to even notice him. "Who died, Katie?" he cried. "Who died?"

She finally quieted enough to answer him between her wrenching sobs. "Oh, Martin! God is dead! I can't bear it, for all His work is overthrown."

His face flushed in anger. "That is utter blasphemy, Katherina!" he raged.

Her sobs ceased abruptly. "Well, Martin," she said sternly, "you have been going around acting as if God is dead, as if God is no longer here to keep us. So I thought I ought to put on mourning to keep you company in your great bereavement."

Her words, as usual, hit their mark. He straightened his shoulders and picked up his torch.

He was unmoved by the threats of a representative from the pope.

"Do you not understand how much power the pope has?" he warned menacingly. "Don't you realize that the day will come when your supporters will all desert you? Tell me, Martin, where will you be then?"

Martin grinned.

"Then, as now, in the hands of Almighty God," he replied.

Enemies surrounded him. Their opposition to his message only stirred him to run faster.

"God has used my enemies to compel me to raise my voice even more insistently," he claimed. "I must speak, shout, shriek, and write till they have had enough!"

"What is Martin Luther really like?" someone asked one of Martin's close friends.

"Go see for yourself," came the quick reply. "Martin Luther hides nothing from anyone. His life is an open book, and he speaks freely to everyone about himself."

The friend laughed and added, "And if you want to know what he thinks of somebody else, ask him that as well. He will give you his honest opinion and hold back nothing!"

Martin was at work in his study when one of his students burst in with good news.

"Your followers are calling themselves Lutherans!"

Martin's black eyes bored into the messenger. "Lutherans?" he thundered. "What is Luther? The teaching is not mine. Nor was I crucified for anyone. How did I, poor stinking bag of maggots that I am, come to the point where people call the children of Christ by my evil name?"

Martin ran at a furious pace. He preached four thousand sermons and penned over sixty thousand pages. Both his preaching and his writing kept his enemies stirred up.

"Couldn't you try to keep from offending people?" his friends asked.

"What good does the edge of the sword do if it does not cut?" he scoffed.

He was forty-seven when he went on strike against his own congregation. "I refuse to preach to you!" he announced. "You remain godless. It annoys me to keep preaching to you!"

When the shocked congregation mended their ways, he returned to his pulpit.

His barber and lifelong friend, Peter, asked him simply, "How should I pray, Martin?"

Martin Luther responded with a pamphlet.

A Simple Way to Pray

It is a good thing to let prayer be the first business of the morning and the last at night. Guard yourself carefully against those false, deluding ideas which tell you, "Wait a little while. I will pray in an hour; first I must attend to this or that." Such thoughts get you away from prayer into other affairs which so hold your attention and involve you that nothing comes of prayer for that day.

Do not leave your prayer without having said or thought, "Very well, God has heard my prayer; this I know as a certainty and a truth." That is what Amen means!

It is of great importance that the heart be made ready and eager for prayer. What else is it but tempting God when your mouth babbles and the mind wanders to other thoughts?

A good and attentive barber keeps his thoughts, attention, and eyes on the razor and hair and does not forget how far he has gotten with his shaving or cutting. If he wants to engage in too much conversation or let his mind wander or look somewhere else, he is likely to cut his customer's mouth, nose, or even his throat. How much more does prayer call for concentration and singleness of heart!

Hopefully his barber took his advice.

Once someone innocently referred to his doctrine in his presence—and faced his wrath head-on.

"It is not my doctrine," he cried, his voice rising and his eyes snapping. "Dear Lord God, it was not spun out of my head, nor grown in my garden. Nor did it flow out of my spring, nor was it born of me. It is God's gift, not a human discovery!"

He summed up his race in the third verse of his most famous hymn, "A Mighty Fortress Is Our God."

> *And though this world with devils filled*
> *Should threaten to undo us,*
> *We will not fear, for God has willed*
> *His truth to triumph through us!*

He had just turned sixty-two when he left Wittenberg for Mansfeld. Suffering in the winter's cold, he was violently ill by the time he reached Eisleben. He knew his race was nearly finished. He spent his remaining few days settling a dispute, preaching four sermons, ordaining two pastors, founding a school, writing letters to his beloved and worried Katie, and jotting down notes for another treatise.

Even as his voice faded in death, he crossed his finish line quoting John 3:16:

> **For God so loved the world,** *that he gave his only begotten Son, that whosoever believeth in him should not perish, but have everlasting life.*

Chapter Fifty-Two

DAVE

~Present Day~

I will run the way of thy commandments,
when thou shalt enlarge my heart.

—Psalm 119:32

Ray leaned back in his chair smiling. "No wonder churches and governments don't particularly like the Bible. When they're corrupt, that old book causes them quite a few problems."

"It causes a corrupt person quite a few problems too," Dave answered.

Ray quit smiling abruptly. "What exactly do you mean?"

Dave stood to his feet and was prepared to leave. At the door, he turned and handed Ray his Bible. "Take it."

Ray stepped back. "I'm not taking your Bible!"

"I want you to have it. I have another one at home. Please."

Reluctantly Ray took the Bible and turned around to toss it nonchalantly on his bed. When he turned back, Dave was gone.

He was left alone...with God and whatever message He had for him in His awesome book.

People of nearly every description crowded the sidewalk near the bus stop. A woman dressed in a suit sat on a bench near a stooped and tattered woman who looked as though she carried all her worldly possessions in her bag. A young man with a shaved head bulldozed through a group of college students. A few women looked as though they were returning from a shopping trip. Briefcases carried by impeccably groomed young men and women bumped against legs clad with torn jeans. A child held on to his mother's jacket, tugging on and playing with the zipper.

This mixture of humanity waited for a bus at the corner. Standing near them was a young man with a clipboard and a pen, taking a survey. Most swept on past, ignoring him. Some who had nothing better to do while waiting for their bus answered his questions.

Dave had no plans to stop—but then he caught the last words of the question.

"...heaven when you die?"

Dave edged closer to hear. The young man was talking now to a woman whose attire advertised her trade. Layers of makeup failed to conceal her years of sin, but she answered haughtily.

"Of course I am going to heaven! I was saved as a child!" With a look of disgust, she turned her back on him.

He spoke to a young man with rippling muscles and a shaved head. Dave had to admire the man's nerve. Who could tell how this one would respond?

"Do you believe you will go to heaven when you die?"

He let out a foul curse, followed by, "If anybody goes, I will. I'm as good a Christian as anybody who goes to church!"

Dave shuddered as he listened to the same answer, over and over again. They were all planning to be welcomed into heaven... drunks, students, prostitutes, housewives, drug addicts, blasphemers, and businesspeople alike.

Dave waited until the bus came and the young man took a break. When he got closer to speak to him, he noticed he was no more than eighteen or nineteen years old.

"It's your turn now," Dave said. "I have a question for you."

"Go ahead," the boy answered, grinning.

"Why are you taking this survey?"

The young man looked into Dave's eyes, and he recognized a fellow runner. "Let's have a cup of coffee together, and I'll tell you about it," he answered, pointing to a nearby restaurant.

When they were seated, he said, "My name is Dan. I've been out here for over two hours today. The answer is always the same. Everyone plans on making heaven their home. I guess they think living in 'Christian America' gives them a ticket.

"I felt the same way they did. Then I met Jesus Christ and invited Him into my heart and life. He not only saved me from my sins, He also delivered me. I am no longer in the drug scene. Christ turned my life from darkness to light, from sin to righteousness, from death to life.

"I wanted to tell everyone about Jesus. I started with my family and friends."

He shook his head slowly. "I discovered pretty quickly that they couldn't understand what the big deal was. According to them, they had been Christians all their lives. Of course, Jesus was never mentioned in our home except when His name was used to curse someone. I never saw anyone talk to Him in prayer. No one read His book or lived by His commandments. If any of them had met Him, Jesus obviously hadn't made a big enough impact on them to change their way of living one bit. It was the same thing with my friends.

"So I got curious. Was it just my family and my crowd that professed Christianity while ignoring Christ?

"I decided to find out. What better place could there be than here in this city? I can meet all kinds right here! This is my third day here, and the answer is always the same. A lot of people don't bother to answer me, but the ones who do assure me in no uncertain terms that they are on their way to heaven. I've even asked, 'Are you born again?' They all assure me they are.

"It's pretty discouraging to realize that all these people have no fear of judgment and no desire for cleansing from their sins. Some are really insulted when I ask them if they know Jesus

Christ, the Son of God. Sure they know Him! They celebrate Christmas, don't they?

"I know you are a runner, Dave. So can you tell me something? What have these people heard in church? How can they think they are Christians without Christ?"

Dave thought a minute before answering slowly.

"Many you have questioned have probably never attended church. I'm sure that some were raised in church from childhood, and possibly some still attend regularly.

"This isn't a problem unique in our society. Christianity has always had its share of both professors and possessors. Dan, have you ever heard about a young man by the name of Auguste Francke?"

"I haven't heard of hardly anyone yet. I just met Jesus three weeks ago!"

"Then let me tell you about him. He was raised in church. In fact, his life revolved around church services. If you had interviewed him today, he would have assured you that he was on his way to heaven.

"Then came the day that the very foundations of his faith were shaken. It was not until Auguste realized he was an atheist that he came face-to-face with Jesus Christ, the God he had professed but had never met."

Chapter Fifty-Three

AUGUSTE HERMANN FRANCKE

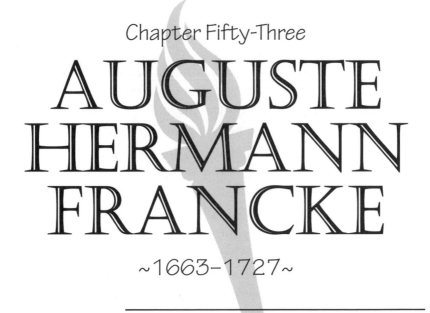

~1663–1727~

Ye cannot be partakers of the Lord's table, and of the table of devils.

—1 Corinthians 10:21

These are written that ye might believe that Jesus is the Christ, the Son of God; and that believing ye might have life through his name. (John 20:31)

Written that ye may believe...

Auguste Francke tried to shut the verse from his mind. Why, with all the verses in the Bible, did it have to be this verse that kept crowding its way again and again into his head, interrupting his thoughts and even keeping him from sleep?

Auguste quit his restless pacing and sat down, his head in his hands.

That ye might believe that Jesus is the Christ, the Son of God.

"Well, I don't believe Jesus is the Son of God. I don't believe there even is a God. So how can I believe in a Son who supposedly saves souls? In fact, I don't believe I even have a soul to be saved!"

There. He had admitted it.

"I guess this makes me an atheist," he mumbled. What would his church friends think if they knew that he was an atheist? Everyone in the Church of St. John thought he was a believer. In fact, he had thought so himself until he was asked to preach a sermon on Sunday.

He groaned as he remembered his response. He was just twenty-four years old. He knew he could not only preach a suitable sermon, but could also undoubtedly preach a much better sermon than most preachers he had heard. *I surely will look better than most of them,* he had thought with a smile, trying to decide which of his elegant suits to wear.

He decided to favor the congregation with an eloquent speech that would keep them praising him for weeks.

And I will also attempt to build up the listeners with my sermon, he decided as an afterthought.

That was when the verse had taken over his waking thoughts. The more he had pondered the text, the more troubled he had become.

Now it had all come to this. All the doubts he had pushed aside for years suddenly demanded his attention.

Thinking of himself as an atheist seemed strange. His family and most of his friends attended church, so he had made church a big part of his life too. Being a member of the church had never truly affected his life, though, except for maybe giving him a better image. He remembered praying now and then that God would improve him so he would be respected by everyone who had the opportunity to meet him. It hadn't taken much to act religious while he was with the church crowd. And when his other friends were around, he joined in their sin with reckless enthusiasm.

Now that he thought about it, he realized he had tried to grasp heaven with one hand and earth with the other.

Well, if he was going to give up one, he supposed it must be heaven since he realized now it didn't exist. He certainly would never give up the world. He loved the world and its pleasures, and the world in turn loved him.

But what should he do about this wretched sermon? The Sunday he was to preach would be here all too soon. Should he back out of his commitment? What would people think? What explanation could he give? He certainly could not tell his church friends that he didn't believe there was a God!

What should he do?

Almost without thinking, Auguste got on his knees. Looking up to the heavens and seeing no one, Auguste said, "God, if indeed You are a true God, save me from this miserable state of unbelief!"

The God he had denied both heard and instantly answered his simple prayer. God literally filled the heart and life of Auguste with a glory he would never be able to describe. Joy and peace and an unshakable assurance that vanished all his doubts nearly overwhelmed him!

"My God!" he cried. "You are real! You are full of mercy and grace and love! You have given Jesus, Your only begotten Son to save my soul! I love You! I will serve You all the days of my life! You are not only my God, You are also my beloved Father!"

Auguste laughed and cried. He felt as if a stream of unspeakable, glorious joy was running through his entire being. How could he even describe the peace that flooded his soul?

"Never again will I distrust You, my Father," he prayed, "for I have met You personally. I would give up my blood without fear for such a God as You!"

Finally, rising from his knees, he went to bed and tried to sleep. But how could anyone this happy sleep?

"My God," he breathed. "You are the living God! You are my new Father, through Your Son, Christ Jesus! I honor You! I adore You! Thank You for revealing Yourself to me! I love You so much!"

Auguste closed his eyes for a few moments, trying to sleep, but then began praising God again.

"My Father," he whispered. "I can't sleep! I feel as if I have spent my entire life in a deep sleep! Everything I have experienced up to now has been only a dream! I have just now been awakened! I feel as if I have been dead and am just now alive!"

Auguste leaped out of bed and again began praising God.

"You angels in heaven," he shouted, "praise the name of the Lord with me! Praise the Lord who has shown me such mercy!"

After a wonderful time of praise and worship to his new-found God, Auguste again went to bed and tried to sleep. He remembered the words penned by Martin Luther—words that for the first time in his life made sense to him.

> Faith is a living, moving trust in God's grace, so certain that one would die for it a thousand times. And such trust and knowledge in divine grace makes one joyous, bold, and delighting in God and all creatures; this the Lord God does in faith!

> Faith is a divine word in us that changes us and gives us new birth from God and makes us completely other men in our hearts, minds, thoughts, and all our powers and brings the Holy Spirit with it.

I understand now what Luther was saying, Auguste thought, *for I have experienced this wondrous faith for myself.*

Sleep never did come. Auguste spent the entire night worshiping Christ.

The next morning, Auguste, with tears of joy streaming down his face, told his friends that he had met God. Some laughed and cried with him. Others just stared, wondering, nervously backing away from the brilliant light of his testimony that exposed their own unbelief.

The world stared at Auguste even as Auguste stared back at the alien world he had been so comfortable in just yesterday.

"I am a new person in Christ," Auguste realized. "I care nothing for promotion, honor, or visibility in this world. I no longer desire riches and worldly pomp. And where is my idol of education? Why, faith the size of a mustard seed counts for more than a hundred sacks full of learning! All the knowledge learned from the wisest of men is as dirt beside the superabundant knowledge of Jesus Christ, my Lord!"

He had a sermon to preach now! His life would be meaningless if he did not dedicate all his strength and days to telling everyone he met about God and His beloved Son.

Why wasn't I told by the teachers and pastors of my church that I must be born again? he wondered. *Could it be that some of them are as I was? How many have no faith, no new birth, no Savior? How many of them have no joy, no peace, no life, no message?*

His experience with Christ drove him to his knees, led him to the pulpit, and moved him to found an educational community to train pastors and teachers for the ministry.

"You spiritual leaders must go into your communities with a burning message born of your own experience," he counseled them.

"For only when we preach this marvelous new birth," he continued, "will we see a life changed, a church revived, a nation reformed, and a world evangelized."

Chapter Fifty-Four

DAVE

~Present Day~

Ye that love the LORD, hate evil...Light is sown for the righteous.
—Psalm 97:10–11

A church revived. A nation reformed. A world evangelized. And it all begins with a life changed," Dave said.

Dave and Dan sat thinking for a moment, then Dave spoke again. "Dan, people who meet Jesus Christ and receive Him as their Lord change. Jesus and John were both still in the womb when their mothers met. John leaped even then, just because he was in the presence of Christ!

"Wise men knelt at His crib, fishers of fish became fishers of men, lepers were cleansed, and Mary Magdalene was delivered of seven devils. Lazarus came out from his tomb, Zacchaeus gave away half his riches, and Paul became a leader of the church he had despised.

"The two on the road to Emmaus looked at one another and said, 'Didn't our hearts burn within us while He talked with us?'"

Dave shook his head. "Dan, when Auguste met Christ personally, he became a new man. But the people you questioned today claim to know Him, and yet their lives have not been affected in the least."

Dan shrugged. "That is exactly what bothers me. So how do you suggest we introduce people to someone they already claim to know?"

Dave looked around at the people in the restaurant. He heard a man at the counter make a suggestive remark to a waitress. She responded with a laugh and a lewd remark of her own. He heard the Lord's name mentioned by a businessman at the table next to his, but he realized it was spoken as a curse.

He thought of Christ's words to John in Revelation 3:17 about a group he would one day spit from his mouth.

Thou sayest, I am rich, and increased with goods, and have need of nothing; and knowest not that thou art wretched, and miserable, and poor, and blind, and naked.

He turned to Dan.

"Dan, some of these people may realize they don't have Jesus in their lives when they face a crisis they can't handle and desperately need His help. Others may have a friend or relative who will meet Jesus and be transformed. The change in that one's life may cause them to question their own salvation.

"But I'm afraid most people won't realize they are lost until they stand before Him in judgment. It will be too late for them then. He said many would travel the broad road to destruction."

Dave stood and extended his hand to Dan. "Dan, you've made me realize more than ever that we torchbearers have a big job to do. I am going to take Jesus to as many as I can, while I can."

He smiled. "Don't be discouraged, friend. There are still men, women, and children today who have met Jesus and whose lives will never be the same. I am one of them."

Chapter Fifty-Five

DAVE

~Present Day~

My heart panteth, my strength faileth me: as for the light of mine eyes, it also is gone from me.

—Psalm 38:10

D ave ran wearily, neither knowing nor caring which direction he took. He no longer derived joy from the race. The excitement was gone. Days lengthened into weeks, and he ran on mechanically.

How long have I been running like this? he wondered to himself.

It didn't really matter. He ran simply because he had answered the call of God and was committed to the race. He would continue to run until he died.

But the thrill of running was gone.

He looked ahead, knowing that the scorn of the unbelievers would never end, and wondered how he could keep going.

He thought he saw a gleam of light in the distance. But then it vanished. He was approaching another hill, and his pace slowed.

He finally reached the top and paused to rest. He was tired so much of the time lately. He looked ahead. Yes, there was a light. Another torchbearer was running toward him. But Dave experienced no leap of joy at the thought of the meeting. He remembered the days when he would have run forward in

anticipation, thrilled with the thought of sweet fellowship with another runner.

Today his pace slowed to a walk.

"Dave! Dave!"

The shout grew louder as the runner grew closer. Dave didn't recognize him, but apparently they had met somewhere in the past.

Finally their paths crossed at the bottom of the hill. The runner pumped Dave's hand enthusiastically. Dave worked at being polite.

After awkward attempts at conversation, the runner grew silent, looking past Dave's eyes and into his very soul. Then he looked at Dave's torch and back again. Dave looked away.

"Dave."

Dave's eyes met the runner's. He saw love and compassion. And there was something else. Was it concern?

"Dave, how long have you been running like this? The light you carried was brilliant, and you were an inspiration to all of us. But look at your torch now, Dave. There are just a few sparks left, and they are about to go out. What has happened to you?"

Dave couldn't answer. He lowered his torch and stared at it. The runner was right. Only a few embers remained. How long had he been carrying it this way?

The runner led Dave to the side of the road.

"Dave, sit here with me for awhile. You have encouraged so many of us by your stories of valiant runners who ran before us. Let me remind you of the way Count Zinzendorf found renewed power and vigor during his race when he grew weary."

Dave simply nodded, and the runner began his story.

Chapter Fifty-Six

COUNT ZINZENDORF

~1700–1760~

Is not this the fast that I have chosen?...Is it not to deal thy bread to the hungry, and that thou bring the poor that are cast out to thy house?...Then shall thy light break forth as the morning.

—Isaiah 58:6–8

Count Zinzendorf is the beast of the book of Revelation!
Count Zinzendorf is the beast of the book of Revelation!
Count Zinzendorf is the beast of the book of Revelation!

The angry cry shattered the peace as it echoed throughout the lush estate at Berthelsdorf. When the dreadful words were carried to Count Zinzendorf, he silently bowed his head, walked to his study, and shut the door. He sat quietly for the next few hours, reflecting on his life.

He recalled the life-changing commitment he had made when he was just twenty years old, while on a tour of France. He would never forget standing in the art museum at Dusseldorf, gazing at the painting by Domenico Fetis entitled *Ecce Homo (Behold, the Man)*. He could not take his eyes away from the portrait of Jesus. He stared at the wounds caused by the thorns that crowned the head of the King of Kings. His eyes drifted to the inscription.

I have done this for you; what have you done for Me?

He stared until the question was no longer simply engraved below the painting but reverberated throughout his entire being, piercing his heart. He realized his Savior was using this painting to personally ask him the question: "I have done this for you; what have you done for Me?"

He knew the living Christ required his answer.

He trembled as he gazed at the picture. He still remembered the prayer he had prayed when only four years old.

Dear Savior, do Thou be mine and I will be Thine!

Finally he answered the Lord. "I have loved You for a long time. But I have never actually done a single thing for You. From now on, I will do whatever You lead me to do."

And Christ placed a torch in Count Zinzendorf's hand.

Just a few months later, he purchased his grandmother's huge estate at Berthelsdorf in southeastern Saxony.

It was there that his work began.

He smiled as he remembered the day he had greeted the stranger at the door of his manor. His eyes had been immediately drawn to his burning torch.

"I am Christian David," the runner announced himself.

Christian wasted no time but boldly stated his mission. "I have come to ask for your help. Christians are being severely oppressed and persecuted. They are fleeing for their lives from Bohemia, Moravia, Germany, and beyond! Many are in desperate need of a place such as this for a refuge!"

Count Zinzendorf smiled. "My Lord has my life," he told Christian David, "and along with my life, all my possessions."

Ten Moravians came with Christian David just a few days later. When they first arrived, they scarcely looked at their new home, for their thoughts were filled with their escape and those they had left behind. But the next day, they gazed at their new home in wonder.

There were evergreen woods on two sides of the rising ground. On the other sides were beautiful, well-tended gardens. Just a short distance away, lofty hills dominated the spectacular view.

Someone softly broke the silence.

"Let us call this beautiful refuge Herrnhut."

Herrnhut. The word could be translated two ways: "Under the Lord's watch" or "On the watch for the Lord."

Yes, this land would be called Herrnhut.

Christian David returned again and again, leading Christians who had left all their possessions behind them, stealing them across borders by night, placing them safely in Herrnhut.

And Christian did his work well. By 1726, there was a community of three hundred people living in two hundred houses on the Count's estate. Count Zinzendorf, along with twelve elected elders, served as the town council. There was the home for single brethren and another for single sisters. A boarding house for orphaned children had been built, and there was now an academy, a print shop, and an apothecary. The Christians had been industrious, anxious to work. There were woolen mills. Linen was woven and sold. Potters toiled, along with the carpenters, farmers, bakers, and cooks.

Count Zinzendorf sighed. He had not once regretted his decision to turn his estate into a haven for Christians. He had committed his life and his wealth to serving Christ by serving His oppressed people.

But along with the beautiful people of God had come the wolves, always seeking the tender lamb, the weakened sheep.

Even now a wolf was stalking the community, howling that Count Zinzendorf was the beast referred to in the book of Revelation!

"My Lord," Count Zinzendorf groaned aloud, "show me what to do!"

And instantly he knew. "We must move out of our new manor," he told his wife and children. "We will make our home in the orphanage."

They lived in the midst of the community, and the count spent hours each day going from house to house, reading the Scriptures and counseling the believers in the ways of the Lord.

Still the peace that Count Zinzendorf longed for was shattered by constant division, bitter grudges, accusations, and strife. He grew so weary of it.

Again he knelt before the Lord. "Lord, I long to see this place a haven of rest and peace and love! My Lord, where is Your power among this people? My heart yearns for You to move among us!"

Again the answer came from the Lord.

Count Zinzendorf was just twenty-seven years of age when he called twenty-four couples together.

"We must pray," he told them. "And we must pray without ceasing."

It was on August 27, 1727, that twenty-four men and twenty-four women began praying one hour each day.

Day after day, night after night, they prayed. Herrnhut literally became God's house of prayer.

There was not a moment that prayer was not ascending from that community of believers to the throne room of God.

God in turn descended upon Herrnhut.

The Count's vision of peace and power at last became a reality. His fatigue was replaced with renewed vigor. Love and sweet fellowship replaced bickering and dissension.

Power swept through the community of believers and began to spread across its boundaries.

The prayers continued. Unending. Unceasing.

Others joined in the prayer watch.

At Herrnhut and abroad, on land and at sea, history's longest prayer meeting continued. And revival began in the hearts of the prayer warriors themselves.

After just six months of this hourly intercession, Count Zinzendorf challenged the Christians to march across Greenland,

Hours later, Dave looked up. The runner was gone.

Dave looked at his torch. Fire blazed from it, casting a glow over the entire area.

"My God," he breathed, his face glowing in the light of his torch. "Lead me daily in the direction You want me to go. And help me never again—ever—to run a single day without first coming to You for power, to have my torch refilled with the fire of the Holy Spirit!"

Strength coursed through his being, filling him with anticipation for what lay ahead. Eagerly he began to run, his voice shouting and singing praises to the Master, whom he loved with his entire being.

His torch cast a glow over a vast area. He looked ahead with pleasure, his spirit soaring with new vitality.

"Lord Jesus," he breathed. "I love You! I want You to know that there is nothing I would rather be doing than running for You! And Lord...there is no one I would rather run with than You.

"Thank You. Thank You for refilling me with Your love, Your power, and Your awesome presence."

Chapter Fifty-Eight

DAVE

~Present Day~

He that taketh not his cross, and followeth after me, is not worthy of me.

—Matthew 10:38

The old man's pace had slowed. Pain filled his eyes as he limped along. His hair was snow white, and deep furrows lined his face. But still he ran.

Dave greeted him warmly, but he made no response. Dave was running on by when something about the man made him pause.

"Sir, could we talk for a few moments?" Dave asked.

The man looked at the young runner sharply, then gave him a curt nod. Slowly, they made their way together to a nearby bench.

The gentleman sighed deeply as he sat down. He bent and removed his shoes from his swollen and gnarled feet.

"How beautiful are the feet of them that preach the gospel of peace, and bring glad tidings of good things," Dave quoted softly from Romans 10:15.

The man gave no indication that he had heard. Leaning back against the bench, he closed his eyes.

Dave sat quietly. A deep voice suddenly penetrated the silence. "They are not the same today."

Dave waited for him to continue, but when there were no further comments, he asked, "Who, sir?"

"The young ones. The new ones. They come to the mission field expecting, always expecting."

Dave finally spoke into the lengthening pause.

"Expecting what, sir?"

The man's eyes snapped open and seemed to stare right into Dave's soul.

Dave saw something more in those eyes now. He had noticed the pain, the weariness, earlier. But now shining through them was a clear and discerning mind. The man sat erect then and spoke sharply.

"Young man, don't be one of them. Don't run this race for what you can get out of it. Run expecting only to give all that you have to give, even if it means your life.

"The young runners expect too much today. They want riches, fame, the applause of men, comfort, ease. They expect a harvest even before they have tilled the land and sown the seed! They are going overseas in the name of Christ for an adventure, a thrill!

"When will they quit saying, 'What can I get,' and say instead, 'Ah, my Lord! What can I give?'"

The man leaned back again. Dave's heart ached for this weary man whose flame still soared from his torch, but whose arm was nearly too exhausted to lift it.

A few minutes passed.

Dave thought the man was sleeping, so he just sat quietly, breathing a prayer for him.

Again the man broke the silence. "I wish every young runner could have been at the ordination service of my friend. It was there that I entered the race. It was back in 1920. Dr. John Lake was the speaker. Young man, as long as I live, I will never forget his challenge to us that night. How I wish every beginning runner could hear it!"

His eyes pierced into Dave's. "Young man, you are one who will."

The Message Given by Dr. John G. Lake

(1920)

The thirteenth chapter of Acts tells us the story of the ordination and sending forth of the apostle Paul, his ordination to the apostleship. Paul never writes of himself as an apostle until the thirteenth chapter of Acts. He had been an evangelist and teacher for thirteen years when the thirteenth chapter of Acts was written, and the ordination took place that is recorded there. Men who have a real call are not afraid of apprenticeships.

There is a growing up in experience in the ministry. When Paul started out in the ministry, he was definitely called of God and was assured of God through Ananias that it would not be an easy service, but a terrific one, for God said to Ananias,

Arise, and go into the street which is called Straight, and inquire in the house of Judas for one called Saul, of Tarsus: for, behold, he prayeth...He is a chosen vessel unto me, to bear my name before the Gentiles, and kings, and the children of Israel: for I will show him how great things he must suffer for my name's sake. (Acts 9:11, 15–16)

That is what Jesus Christ, the crucified and glorified Son of God, told Ananias to say to the apostle Paul. He was not going to live in a holy ecstasy and wear a beautiful halo and have a heavenly time and ride in a limousine. He was going to have a drastic time, a desperate struggle, a terrific experience. And no man in biblical history ever had more dreadful things to endure than the apostle Paul. He gives a list in his letter to the Corinthians of the things that he had endured.

Of the Jews five times received I forty stripes save one. Thrice was I beaten with rods, once was I stoned, thrice I suffered

*shipwreck, a night and a day I have been in the deep; in jour-
neyings often, in perils of waters, in perils of robbers, in perils
by mine own countrymen, in perils by the heathen, in perils
in the city, in perils in the wilderness, in perils in the sea, in
perils among false brethren; in weariness and painfulness, in
watchings often, in hunger and thirst, in fastings often, in
cold and nakedness.* (2 Corinthians 11:24–27)

They stripped him of his clothing, and the executioner lashed him with an awful scourge, until bleeding
and lacerated and broken, he fell helpless and uncon-
scious and insensible. They doused him with a bucket
of salt water to keep the maggots off and threw him in
a cell to recover. That was the price of apostleship. That
was the price of the call of God and His service. But God
said he shall "bear my name before the Gentiles, and
kings, and the children of Israel." He qualified as God's
messenger.

Beloved, we have lost that character of consecration here manifested. God is trying to restore it in
our day. He has not been able to make much progress
with the average preacher on that line. "Mrs. So-and-
so said so-and-so, and I am just not going to take it."
That is the kind of preacher, with another kind of call,
not the heaven call, not the God call, not the death
call if necessary. That is not the kind the apostle Paul
had.

Do you want to know why God poured out His
Spirit in South Africa like He did nowhere else in the
world? There was a reason. This example will illustrate. We had one hundred and twenty-five men out on
the field at one time. We were a very young institution;
we were not known in the world. South Africa is seven
thousand miles away from any European country. It is

ten thousand miles by way of England to the United States. Our finances got so low under the awful assault we were compelled to endure, that there came a time I could not even mail to these workers at the end of the month a ten-dollar bill. It got so I could not send them two dollars! The situation was desperate. What was I to do? Under these circumstances I did not want to take the responsibility of leaving men and their families on the frontier without real knowledge of what the conditions were.

Some of us at headquarters sold our clothes, sold certain pieces of furniture out of the house, sold anything we could sell, to bring these one hundred and twenty-five workers off the field for a conference.

One night in the progress of the conference, I was invited by a committee to leave the room for a minute or two. The conference wanted to have a word by themselves. So I stepped out to a restaurant for a cup of coffee and came back. When I came in, I found they had rearranged the chairs in an oval with a little table at one end, and on the table was the bread and wine. Old Father Van der Wall, speaking for the company, said, "Brother Lake, during your absence, we have come to a conclusion. We want you to serve the Lord's Supper. We are going back to the fields if we have to walk back. We are going back if we starve. We are going back if our wives die. We are going back if our children die. We are going back if we die ourselves. We have but one request. If we die, we want you to come and bury us."

The next year, I buried twelve men and sixteen wives and children. In my judgment not one of the twelve, if they had had a few things a...man needs to eat, but what might have lived. Friends, when you want to find out why the power of God came down from heaven in South Africa like it never came down before since the days of the apostles, there is your answer.

Jesus Christ put the spirit of martyrdom in the ministry. Jesus Christ Himself instituted His ministry with a pledge unto death. When He was with the disciples on the last night, He took the cup, "when He drank, saying." Beloved, the *saying* was the significant thing. It was Jesus Christ's pledge to the twelve who stood with him, "This cup is the New Testament in My blood." Then He said, "Drink ye all of it."

Friends, those who were there and drank to that pledge of Jesus Christ entered into the same covenant and purpose that He did. That is what all pledges mean. Men have pledged themselves in the wine cup from time immemorial. Generals have pledged their armies unto death. It has been a custom in the race. Jesus Christ sanctified it to the church forever, bless God.

"My blood is the New Testament. Drink *ye all* of it!" Let us become one in our purpose to die for the world. Your blood and mine together. "My blood in the New Testament. It is My demand from you. It is your high privilege."

Dear friends, there is not an authentic history that can tell us whether any one of them died a natural death. We know that at least nine of them were martyrs, possibly all. Peter died on a cross, James was beheaded, for Thomas they did not even wait to make a cross— they nailed him to an olive tree. John was sentenced to be executed at Ephesus by putting him in a caldron of boiling oil. God delivered him and his executioners refused to repeat the operation and he was banished to the Isle of Patmos. John thought so little about it that he never even tells of the incident. He says, "I was in the Isle called Patmos, for the Word of God, and for the testimony of Jesus Christ." That was explanation enough. He had committed himself to Jesus Christ for life or death.

Friends, the group of missionaries that followed me went without food and went without clothes, and once when one of my preachers was sunstruck and had wandered away, I tracked him by the blood marks of his feet. Another time I was hunting for one of my missionaries, a young Englishman, twenty-two years of age. He had come from a line of Church of England preachers for five hundred years. When I arrived at the native village, the old native chief said, "He is not here. He went over the mountains, and you know mister, he is a white man and he has not learned to walk barefooted."

That is the kind of consecration that established Pentecost in South Africa. That is the reason we have a hundred thousand native Christians in South Africa. That is the reason we have 1,250 native preachers. That is the reason we have three hundred and fifty churches in South Africa. That is the reason that today we are the most rapid growing church in South Africa.

I am not persuading you, dear friends, by holding out a hope that the way is going to be easy. I am calling on you in the name of Jesus Christ, you dear ones who expect to be ordained to the gospel of Jesus Christ tonight, take the route that Jesus took, the route that the apostles took, the route that the early church took, the victory route, whether by life or by death. Historians declare, "The blood of the martyrs was the seed of the church." Beloved, that is what the difficulty is in our day—we have so little seed. The church needs more martyr blood.

If I were pledging men and women to the gospel of the Son of God, as I am endeavoring to do tonight, it would not be to have a nice church and harmonious surroundings and a sweet do-nothing time. I would invite them to be ready to die. That was the spirit of early Methodism. John Wesley established a heroic call. He demanded every preacher to be "ready to pray, ready to preach, ready to die." That is always the spirit of Christianity. When any other spirit comes into the church, it is not the spirit of Christianity. It is a foreign spirit. It is a sissified substitute.

I lived on corn meal mush many a period with my family and we did not growl...When my missionaries were on the field existing on corn meal mush, I could not eat pie. My heart was joined to them. That is the reason we never had splits in our work in South Africa. One country where Pentecost never split. The split business began to develop years afterward, when pumpkin-pie-eating missionaries began infesting the country. Men who are ready to die for the Son of God do not split. They do not holler the first time they get a stomachache.

Bud Robinson tells a story of himself. He had went preach in the southern mountains. It was the first time in his life that no one invited him to go home and eat with them. So he slept on the floor and the next night and the next night. After five days and five nights had passed and his stomach began to growl for food terribly, every once in awhile, he would stop and say, "Lay down, you brute!" and he went on with his sermon. That is what won. That is what will win every time. That is what we need today. We need men who are willing to get off the highway. When I started to preach the gospel, I walked twenty miles in the night when I got through. I did it for years for Jesus and souls.

In early Methodism an old local preacher would start Saturday and walk all night and then walk all night Sunday night to get back to his work. It was the common custom. Peter Cartwright preached for sixty dollars per year and baptized ten thousand converts.

Friends, we talk about consecration and we preach about consecration, but that is the kind of consecration that my heart is asking for tonight. This is the kind of consecration that will get answers from heaven. That is the kind that God will honor. That is the consecration to which I would pledge Pentecost. I would strip Pentecost of its frills and fall de ralls. Jesus Christ, through the Holy Ghost, calls us tonight not to any earthly mansion and a ten thousand dollar motor car, but to put our lives—body and soul and spirit—on the altar of service. All hail! Ye who are ready to die for Christ and this glorious Pentecostal gospel. We salute you. You are brothers with us and with your Lord.

The stirring voice ceased. Dave looked at his companion, amazed. He did not even seem like the same man! His eyes were ablaze, and rather than being spent by delivering the message, he was full of vitality and vigor.

"Young man, what is your name?"

"David."

"Ah. David." Pointing a bony finger straight under Dave's nose, he said, "Are you acquainted with David Brainerd, the young man who labored in your country and literally laid down his life, crawling at times to reach one more soul for Christ?"

Dave shook his head. "I don't know about David, sir."

"Then listen. And don't forget him. We need Davids today who will run this race to give of themselves, not to get for themselves."

He looked at Dave critically. Then he shook his head slightly.

"I don't know. You may share the same name, but perhaps you won't even want to be like David when you hear his story."

Chapter Fifty-Nine

DAVID BRAINERD

~1718–1747~

We ought to lay down our lives for the brethren.
—1 John 3:16

My God," whispered the dying old man, "there is a dark cloud upon the work of the gospel!" He lay silent for a few moments, and then he sighed his last prayer.

"Lord, revive and prosper the work and grant that it may live when I am dead."

"Revive the work, Lord," was the cry of John Eliot's heart.

Known as the Apostle to the Indians, John's work was in eastern America. He had left his job as a schoolmaster in England to take Jesus to the Indians who lived in the vicinity of Massachusetts Bay. He had trudged along countless trails, through dense forests, and across rushing rivers to find their villages. He had struggled with learning their languages. He had faithfully preached to them about Jesus Christ. He had even purchased land and built entire towns for them. With great expectations he had named one town Noonatomen, the Indian word for "Rejoicing."

There had been little cause for rejoicing.

Though his labors had been rewarded with many Indians receiving Christ—and he rejoiced to see their transformed lives—still the widespread move of God for which John Eliot had dedicated his entire life had never come.

The torch lay where he dropped it, even as his final prayer ascended to the heavens and made its way to the throne of God.

Nearly twenty years later, a boy was born in Connecticut who would be the answer to John's prayer. His father died when he was eight. Six years later, his mother died.

In 1743, David Brainerd picked up John Eliot's torch and held it aloft to be lit by the Christ who baptizes with fire. Then David began running as John had before him, through the states of New Jersey, New York, and Pennsylvania, thrilled to be bringing the gospel to the Seneca and Delaware Indians.

It did not take long for David Brainerd to become as discouraged as his predecessor. He had not even been running a year, and he was weary and depressed. David wondered if he would ever have cause to rejoice. He sat dejectedly on a log, his diary in one hand, his other pressing against his throbbing head.

How could he continue to take money from the Scottish Missionary Society who supported his work?

For he was a dismal failure.

He had come with noble hopes and dreams—at first. He had doggedly fought his way through swamps, forests, streams, and storms. He had forded the Hudson River, plodded on through drenching rains, and walked his nearly dead horse through unfamiliar swampland in the blackness of night. More than once he had wrung out his clothes, put them back on his shivering body, and struggled forward.

It all had taken a toll on his body. He had always been weak and sickly, but now his head ached constantly. He had a persistent fever, and his strength was drained by a wracking cough.

How many nights had he tried to sleep on a bundle of straw or a few branches in the dense woods during the cold winter?

But the physical difficulties were not what sunk his spirit into depression. He had expected them when he volunteered for his work. The one thing he could no longer tolerate was his spiritual failure.

Where were the longed-for results? Where were the answers to his hours, days, and long nights of prayer?

He loved the Indians, but how desperately they needed the salvation Jesus offered! Could he ever forget the scenes he saw the night he lay hidden on a hilltop? The Indians had carefully arranged their offering of ten deer on the altar of fire. He watched in fascinated horror as they writhed and leaped their frenzied, sacred dance, their demonic screams piercing the air. Finally, the satanic ritual completed, they had eaten the flesh of their sacrifice before falling into an exhausted stupor.

How would he ever persuade them to turn to Christ for salvation? For he knew they had no desire to give up their idolatrous practices to worship the white man's God.

Could he blame them?

They had seen firsthand the treachery of the white men, and they believed every white man was a Christian. They had been raided by white thieves, slaughtered by white murderers, given "firewater" by white men who coveted their land. The white man's firewater had made them lash out cruelly at one another, quarreling and killing, the peace in their families and tribes shattered by drunkenness. But even while hating the devastation that came with this drink, they were giving up all they owned to get more of the white man's venom.

Alcohol held them in the white man's power. Alcohol was steadily stripping them, leaving them with no hope, no possessions. They would awake from their drunken stupors and discover that they were deeply in debt to the white traders who supplied the drink. They would then be arrested for their debt, and thrown into prison, where they were offered freedom only by signing over all their possessions to the white men. Worst of all was the never-ending ridicule as these evil men called Christians stole their goods, their lands, and their very way of life.

Was it any wonder that David had been unable to persuade even one Indian to listen to Christ's offer of salvation?

How would his feeble efforts ever bear fruit? Of all the despised "palefaces" he had ever met, he was the palest of them all!

Yes, the Indians had allowed him to build his strange little log and turf huts in their villages. Still he knew they watched him warily, believing that soon they would learn what evil motive lay behind his kindness.

In a few villages, he had been invited into their wigwams, but the thick smoke had sent him running back out, coughing fitfully. He sighed. Why couldn't he have been strong and healthy? He was pitifully weak and sickly. Often he was so exhausted by the time he dismounted in their villages that he could not even stand.

Full of disappointment, he wrote his decision in his diary.

"If at the end of this year there are still no results, I will resign my mission."

Lying back down on the ground, he slept. With the brightness of the morning came a stirring of renewed hope. Prostrate before the Lord, David once again poured out his desires to God in prayer, promising Him he would patiently, and even cheerfully, suffer all things if only God would bless his labors with converts to Christianity.

When David finished praying, he slowly got to his feet. He was still in his twenties, but his body was so weak that it was a great effort to mount his horse.

"One more thing, Lord," he prayed as he made his way to the closest village. "How am I ever going to learn their languages?"

It had taken thirty-six letters just to write down one tribe's word for *question*. It seemed to him that they could have thought of a simpler word than *kremmogkodonaltootiteavreganumeouash*!

His *kremmogkodonaltootiteavreganumeouash* was how he would ever pronounce, let alone memorize, such words! And for every Indian village, there was another dialect to learn!

At the end of the year, David began receiving invitations from several churches.

"David, come be our pastor! You will have a home and will no longer have to work among unreachable people in such deplorable conditions."

David struggled with his decision. What did he have to show for his efforts? All his accomplishments could be counted in a few scattered Indians, mostly women and children, who had received Christ. His health had deteriorated so rapidly that he often thought it would be a great relief just to die. His constant coughing kept him awake night after night. But burning inside his heart was the dream that if he continued his labors, God would do a mighty work among the Indians.

"My Lord," he prayed. "I am not yet ready to abandon this work. But how desperately I need Your help!"

Prayer had become as natural to David as breathing. He often awoke realizing that, even as he had slept, he had dreamed he was praying!

His most urgent prayer had been that God would send him an interpreter who would travel with him, for he realized that he was incapable of learning the language. He had often used a fifty-year-old Indian who knew English and most of the Indian dialects, but Tinda was drunk more often than he was sober. And how could David know what he was even saying to the people?

Then came the morning Tinda came to David, greatly distressed.

"I dreamed," he said, "that to be saved I had to climb a huge mountain. I tried over and over and over to reach the top. Finally

I gave up, knowing it was impossible to climb. I was lost with no hope to be saved. Then I heard a voice calling to me and saying, 'There is hope! There is hope!' And I knew that you are the one to show me the way to be saved."

Tears ran down David's face as he knelt with Tinda, his new brother in Christ! Tinda added Moses to his name on the day of his baptism. And Moses Tinda Tautamy became a faithful interpreter, touched by the anointing of God.

No longer did David have to worry about Tinda being drunk. Now he was as excited about preaching as David was, and he interpreted David's messages with power and zeal.

David never knew exactly when it all happened. But suddenly, wherever he went, Indians crowded around him, asking him to show them how to be saved.

Before he could even dismount from his horse in the villages, they would come running from every direction, crowding around his horse, all talking at once. Tinda's face would light up, and he would say, "David! They all want you to tell them about Jesus!"

The magicians, called powwows, were enraged. More than once they dressed in their skins, put their knives in their belts, and, brandishing their spears, danced before David and his converts in a frenzied fury, shaking their rattles and trying to scare them into renouncing Christ.

Something was wrong. David and the Christians were not dying from the poison of their spells. These followers of Jesus were immune to their curses. The powwows shook their rattles harder, cut themselves deeper, and screamed louder to the devils they served.

But their spells were ineffective. Many of them came humbly before David, offering to him their worthless rattles and charms.

David gave them to his Indian brothers in Christ, who burned them while the medicine men knelt and invited Jesus to become their personal Savior and Lord.

One beautiful June Sunday afternoon, David and Tinda began to preach about the agonizing death Jesus had endured because He loved the Indians so much. Sitting in front of them, eagerly listening to their every word, were three to four thousand Indians, tears streaming down the faces of even the most hardened warriors. When David asked how many wanted to receive Jesus into their hearts, hundreds immediately responded!

From that day on, David got no rest. When he came out of his hut in the mornings, Indians were waiting outside, eager to learn more about Jesus.

One morning he saw a group of Indians, all sobbing bitterly. "What do you want Jesus to do for you?" he asked them quietly.

They answered simply, "We want Him to wipe our hearts clean!"

David himself could scarcely believe the scene before him. Tribes came from far and wide—children, men, and women. As David preached, nearly all who listened wept over the state of their souls. One young Indian woman lay prostrate before God for hours, praying over and over, "Guttummaukalummeh wechaumeh kmeleh Nolah!" David was told that she was crying out to Christ, "Have mercy on me, and help me to give You my heart!"

White men came to see "this babbler" who was ruining their liquor business among the Indians. When they heard his preaching, they openly laughed at the idea of redskins becoming Christians. Some disturbed the meeting, but other scoffers found themselves on their knees being saved!

Families and entire villages were transformed! Where there had been fighting and drunkenness and idolatry, there was now love and peace.

One day a young man ran to David.

"David," he said excitedly. "There is a tribe that has settled not too far from here! They have never heard about Jesus!"

"Call the Christians together," David instructed.

When they stood before him, he said, "I need to go to them. I ask that you pray with me that this tribe will listen to the gospel and receive Christ."

David had a victorious meeting, and when he returned to the village, he learned that everyone in the village had spent the entire night in prayer!

Prayer became a way of life for whole villages. One woman told David the day she was water baptized, "I am so thankful for the kind Christians in Scotland who sent you to us! My heart loves these good people so much," she said, "that I can scarcely help praying for them all night."

"Never," David wrote later, "have I seen such a display of Christian love among any people."

Sometimes David would go to sleep while listening to the Indians singing hymns. They often sang until after midnight.

David's health was giving out completely. He had worked among the Indians for just less than three years and had traveled by foot or on horseback over three thousand miles during that time. His body was ravaged by tuberculosis. He knew he did not have long to live and welcomed his impending death, even though he was not yet thirty years of age. Only one question plagued him. Who would continue his work among his beloved Indians?

Then John, David's brother, came to visit him. His heart was broken when he saw the state of David's health.

"David," John promised. "You may die in peace. I will carry on your work among the Indians."

David gazed at his beloved brother. Seeing the torch in his hand, he knew God had answered yet another prayer.

David spent his last days in the home of Jonathan Edwards, the preacher who brought thousands to their knees with his acclaimed sermon, "Sinners in the Hands of an Angry God."

"David," Jonathan said one day, "thank you for letting me read your diary. It needs to be read by all men. It has been a great encouragement to me and will be to others. Please allow me to publish it."

David was horrified at the thought of people reading his diary. He had recorded his innermost prayers, his private confessions, his daily struggles. The pages he wrote were for God's eyes alone. He wanted no glory, no praise, no honor for his name.

But he reluctantly consented with the prayer that someone, somewhere, would be encouraged by his life.

Jonathan Edwards counted it a great privilege to have David in his home for his nineteen final weeks. He wrote,

> I and my family were richly blessed by David's dying behavior, hearing his dying speeches, receiving his dying counsels, and benefitting by his dying prayers.

David Brainerd died as he lived, breathing a prayer with his last breath on October 9, 1747.

Chapter Sixty

DAVE

~Present Day~

Take, my brethren, the prophets, who have spoken in the name of the Lord, for an example of suffering affliction, and of patience.

—James 5:10

W ell?" Dave was brought abruptly back to the present and the old man sitting next to him.

"Sir?"

"Well, are you willing to go through the same kinds of things David Brainerd went through?"

"Yes, sir."

The old man was still unsure. "Jonathan Edwards published David's diary," he went on. "There was a young man in England who literally poured over that diary, receiving strength from its pages. After reading it, he advised every minister he met, 'Let every preacher of the gospel read carefully the life of David Brainerd!'

"Do you know who that young man was?" the old man asked, his black eyes boring into Dave's.

Dave reluctantly admitted he didn't.

The old man shook his head disgustedly. "That young man was John Wesley, a runner who changed his world as he ran with his torch. Men and devils alike joined forces to stop him, but he just kept running."

He snorted. "I would tell you about his life, but young people today need to study for themselves."

He grew silent as he stared into Dave's eyes.

Dave knew the conversation was ended.

As far as the old man was concerned, it was time for Dave to get up and get running.

Chapter Sixty-One

DAVE

~Present Day~

It is not the will of your Father which is in heaven,
that one of these little ones should perish.

—Matthew 18:14

D ave was deep in thought as he ran toward his house and nearly ran into Uncle Joe's car parked in his driveway. Uncle Joe was just crossing the street, heading for the Arnolds' house.

"Uncle Joe! What are you doing out so early?"

"Ed had a bad night. I just stopped by to pray with him. What are you doing out so early?"

"I go to the park every morning to eat my breakfast."

"Well, I'll stop by in a bit, and we'll talk if you're still home when I finish here."

Dave answered with a quick nod and returned to his uneasy thoughts. *Where was Tom?*

This was the first day he hadn't come to eat since Dave had started buying food for him. Dave knew it was probably foolish to worry, but he couldn't shake the idea that something was wrong.

He was just leaving his house to return to the park when Uncle Joe walked up the driveway.

"Ed's sleeping now," Uncle Joe called to Dave.

"That's great, Uncle Joe," Dave replied absently, his mind on Tom.

"Uncle Joe, why don't you come along with me to the park? We'll talk on the way."

Joe nodded, and Dave started out the drive.

"Wait!" he called. "You mean...walk?"

"Yes, walk!"

"Get in," Joe commanded, motioning to his car. "I never walk when I can ride."

There were several police cars and an ambulance in the roped off park. Dave jumped out of the car and hurried through the bystanders.

"What happened?" he asked a bystander who looked as if he'd been there for a while.

"Someone said a boy was stabbed. I don't know if he's dead or not."

There were two boys with the policemen. One saw Dave and walked over to him. Dave recognized him as one of Tom's gang. He didn't look so tough today. He looked like a badly frightened small boy. "It's Tom," he said. "We found him lying on a bench bleeding when we got here this morning."

Dave's stomach lurched.

Tom had been just a few steps from him, possibly dying. And Dave hadn't even known he was there.

The ambulance sped away.

"Follow it, Uncle Joe," Dave said, jumping back in the car.

"Is he someone you know?" Joe asked, as he tried to keep the ambulance in sight.

"We eat together every morning in the park," Dave answered simply.

Joe parked at the hospital, and they hurried into the emergency entrance.

A policeman overheard Dave telling the receptionist that he was there for the stab victim.

"Are you a relative?" he asked.

"No, a friend. How is he?"

"He's still alive. We're trying to identify him. All we've got so far is Tom. What's his last name?"

"I don't know. All I know him by is Tom."

"Well, you're the only one who has shown up. We need to find out who he is and where he lives so we can notify his family."

"I can tell you where he lives, sir," Dave offered. "His home is the park. He sleeps on one of the benches."

The burly man sighed heavily. "Great. Another one. Is he a runaway? Or doesn't he have parents?"

"I don't know. But I'm going to wait here. If he's able to see someone, I'm available."

The policeman glanced at Dave, then at his torch, then back again. He nodded.

Dave and Joe settled in a waiting room. Dave wondered about Tom.

If he was a runaway, what had caused a thirteen- or fourteen-year-old boy to run away from home? A house filled with violence and abuse? A mother with an endless procession of live-in boyfriends? A home whose only relief came when the dad passed out in a drunken stupor? A kitchen with empty cupboards and refrigerator because all the grocery money went to buy crack or cocaine?

Was Tom just one of an endless procession of children whose gnawing physical hunger equaled their craving for love?

Dave's burden for Tom became a heart-wrenching prayer for all such children.

"Dear Lord, give us godly mothers. Give us mothers who will face the hardships of life and yet keep their hands firmly in Yours. Give us mothers who will fill their homes with love for their children and their children with love for You."

He remembered reading about a mother in Russia who raised her children during the reign of Communism. Her children were

forced to attend the state schools, where atheism was daily drilled into their minds. But she was determined that Satan would not rob her precious children of their faith in God. She faithfully spent six hours, every single evening, teaching her children the Word and the ways of God.

"Give us more mothers like that dedicated Russian mother, and more women like Susanna..."

Chapter Sixty-Two

SUSANNA AND JOHN WESLEY

~1669–1742 and 1703–1791~

*These words, which I command thee this day, shall be in thine heart:
and thou shalt teach them diligently unto thy children, and shalt talk
of them when thou sittest in thine house, and when thou walkest by
the way, and when thou liest down, and when thou risest up.*

—Deuteronomy 6:6–7

Susanna Wesley stood transfixed, staring in horror as her house burned to the ground. She looked, yet did not really see, as roaring flames devoured all her earthly possessions. Her mind's eye saw only John, her beloved six-year-old son. He was alone inside the fiery grave.

Her husband, Samuel, had tried again and again to reach him but was driven back by the blaze. Finally, in exhausted defeat, he knelt on the ground and committed John's soul to the Lord.

Susanna still stood frozen in shock, a silent scream repeating her son's name over and over in her mind. She stared at the flames, stupefied, and then her eyes focused on a window.

Could it be John, or was her mind cruelly deceiving her? No! It was John! She watched a neighbor run through the scorching heat and pull him from the house just seconds before the burning roof collapsed.

Susanna and Samuel knelt with their eight children and their neighbors, thanking God for sparing the family.

What did it matter that their three-story, seven-room house was reduced to ashes? Their clothes and furniture could be replaced! Their library, purchased over the years at a great sacrifice, would never be restored—but what were books, compared to people?

Susanna stole a look at her son while kneeling on the ground with her husband. His escape was truly a miracle. Silently, she made a promise to God concerning John.

"My Father," she prayed, "I will be more careful of this child's soul, which You have so mercifully provided for! I will endeavor more than ever to instill into his mind the principles of Your true religion and virtue! You surely have some great purpose for him!"

When the flames settled to ashes, the family sifted through the remains. All that they found were two bits of charred paper from their library. One was the song, penned by Samuel, "Behold, the Saviour of Mankind."

The other was just a fragment of their beloved Bible with only this sentence still legible:

Sell whatsoever thou hast:...take up the cross, and follow me.
(Mark 10:21)

Samuel, later writing to a friend about the fire, added, "All this, thank God, does not sink my wife's spirits."

Susanna was no stranger to hardship. The youngest in a family of twenty-five children, she herself bore nineteen children. Only nine lived to adulthood. One child died in his sleep. Susanna, her first daughter, died. Then death claimed her precious twins. In the four years from 1697 to 1701, five more of her babies died. The carelessness of a maid caused another daughter to be deformed for life. She nursed several of her children through smallpox. Her firstborn son did not speak until he was nearly six years of age. She battled disease, and this was not the first fire that had claimed her earthly possessions.

Days were a constant struggle to provide for her family. There was the time when the full responsibility of her family fell upon her, for her husband was imprisoned because of accumulated debts. Samuel was a minister, but an impractical man, unconcerned about the management of his financial affairs.

She was thankful for her dairy herd during this devastating period of her life, for the cows were her main means of support. Then came the dark morning that she viewed their corpses littering the field. One of Samuel's enemies had slaughtered them all during the night.

Tragedy caused Susanna, a physically frail woman, to cling more tightly to her Savior's hand, to immerse herself more fully in His Word, and to spend more hours on her knees in prayer.

Her one purpose was to raise her children in such a way that their souls would be saved from the eternal fires to come. And she was now determined to spend extra hours training her fifteenth child, John, for she knew in her heart that God had destined him for a special work.

Her days were full.

On Sunday evenings during her husband's many prolonged absences, Susanna led a special service in her home. It had begun as a simple service for her children, but then her friends and neighbors had asked if they could join her family. Susanna read a sermon, prayed, and talked of Jesus, her Lord and her Friend. At first only a few people gathered in her kitchen, but soon over two hundred people filled her house and overflowed into the barn!

After the birth of her ninth child, Susanna set aside two hours each day for private time with the Lord.

She spent six hours of every day for twenty years teaching her children. She began guiding them when they were still infants, teaching each one obedience to his parents. She taught them to cry softly and to eat and drink whatever was given to them. She did not allow drinking or eating between meals, unless they were ill. The family ate promptly at six each evening, following family prayers. The children were sent to bed at eight and were instructed to go to sleep. All who visited Susanna's home were amazed at the large family of happy and playful yet quiet children.

Then there was the spiritual training. She wrote three religious textbooks for their studies.

Having invested so much time and energy in her children, Susanna's heart ached when several of her daughters, eager to leave their lives of poverty behind them, chose unworthy, but wealthy, husbands.

Her faith did not waver when Mary, her crippled daughter, died in childbirth a year after her marriage, or when her daughter Kezia died at the age of thirty-two.

She lived to see the fulfillment of God's promise:

Let us not be weary in well doing: for in due season we shall reap, if we faint not.   (Galatians 6:9)

Susanna reaped a bountiful harvest for her labors. John, in whom Susanna had invested so much of her time, lived a life of strict discipline all through his childhood and young years.

Then came the day at age thirty-five when he met Christ. With his new birth, his life was transformed.

The year Samuel died, John and his younger brother, Charles, prepared to leave as missionaries to Georgia to preach to the Indians and the settlers of the New World. John was concerned about leaving his newly widowed mother, but she assured him he was making the right choice.

"Had I twenty sons," she said cheerfully, "I would rejoice if they were all employed so, though I might never see them again!"

John returned to England heartsick, feeling that his efforts to evangelize had miserably failed. Not one Indian had received Christ through his ministry.

And then John experienced the mighty touch of God that revolutionized his ministry. He recorded the event in his journal:

Monday, January 1, 1739, [I] and my brother Charles were present at our love feast in Fetterlane, with about sixty of our brethren. About three in the morning, as we were continuing instant in prayer, the power of God came mightily upon us, insomuch that many cried out for exceeding joy, and many fell to the ground. As soon as we recovered a little from that awe and amazement at the presence of His majesty, we broke out with one voice, "We praise Thee, O God, we acknowledge Thee to be the Lord!"

After that day, there was a powerful anointing upon John, and wherever he preached, huge crowds gathered to hear him. A mighty conviction of sin smote the hearts of the multitudes.

During the last half of the eighteenth century, he preached and taught every day, making an annual circuit from London to Bristol to Newcastle and back to London, with many side trips along the way.

He and Charles introduced hymn singing in public worship.

Charles wrote over 6,500 hymns and has been referred to as "the greatest hymn writer of all ages." He penned "Jesus, Lover of My Soul," "O for a Thousand Tongues to Sing," "Hark! the Herald Angels Sing," and "Love Divine, All Loves Excelling."

Crowds of over twenty thousand people lined the hillsides to hear John proclaim the gospel. Countless lives, families, and villages were transformed as people turned to Jesus Christ for salvation.

He ordained men to go into the world and preach. They were called "Methodists."

"Give me a hundred men," John cried, "who fear nothing but sin and desire nothing but God, and I will shake the world! I care not a straw whether they are clergymen or laymen. Those one hundred men alone will overthrow the kingdom of Satan and build up the kingdom of God on earth!"

Theologians around the world were amazed by this 5-foot, 3-inch, 128-pound man who drew the huge crowds. Finally one dared to ask him, "Wesley! How do you attract these crowds?"

John's answer was quick and sure. "I simply set myself on fire, and the people come to see me burn."

Could any godly mother fail to be pleased with such a son? He described himself as "a man of one Book"—the Bible. Yet he wrote over two hundred books, edited a magazine, compiled dictionaries in four languages, and composed a home medical handbook—all in his own handwriting!

He traveled over two hundred and fifty thousand miles on horseback—the equivalent of riding ten times around the world along its equator! He preached more than forty thousand powerful sermons!

John, like his mother, was no stranger to adversity. He married a widow at the age of forty-eight, but her greatest pleasure was to torment and annoy her faithful husband. Finally, unable to break him, she deserted him, taking with her some of his prized journals and papers.

John was constantly heckled and jeered. He was riding along a road one day when it occurred to him that three whole days had passed in which he had suffered no persecution! No bricks had been thrown—he had not even been bombarded with an egg!

He immediately stopped his horse with a shout and fell to his knees.

"My Lord," he cried. "Show me my fault! Am I backslidden? Have I sinned?"

A man on the other side of the hedge heard his prayer and recognized him. "I'll fix that Methodist preacher," he said, picking up a brick and throwing it at him.

The brick fell short of its mark, but John leaped to his feet and joyfully shouted, "Thank God! It's all right! I still have His presence!"

John's ministry transformed not only men's hearts, but also the country itself.

One day, as he rode his horse through the countryside, he noticed the drabness of the land and the ugliness of the villages.

I will bring beauty to England, he thought to himself. From then on, John carried flower seeds with him. Distributing them to housewives, he offered them prizes for the most beautiful gardens. Today the English countryside is one of the most colorful places in the world!

There were other lasting changes.

A British nobleman, passing through a village in Cornwall, England, searched in vain for a drink. In desperation, he finally stopped a villager. "How is it that I cannot get a glass of liquor in this wretched village of yours?" he asked.

The old man, recognizing the rank of the stranger, respectfully removed his cap, bowed, and then replied, "My lord, over a hundred years ago a man named John Wesley came to these parts."

In her seventies now, Susanna stood beside her son as he preached to the crowd filling the hillside. Her mind traveled back to the six-year-old child who had appeared at the window of the house when it was engulfed in flames, and the promise she had made to plant the Word of God firmly in his heart.

Could she have spent her life in any more profitable way than this? Yes, trials and hardships had been ever present. But God had sustained her through them all.

"My God," she sighed, "we are of yesterday and know nothing. But Your boundless mind comprehends, at one view, all things past, present, and future. As You see all things, You understand what is good and proper for each individual—and for me—in relation to both worlds."

Her last words to her loved ones were, "Children, when I am gone, sing a song of praise to God."

And John had faithfully followed in her footsteps. At eighty-three years of age, he complained that he could no longer read or write more than fifteen hours a day without his eyes hurting. He regretted that he had to limit himself to two sermons a day. He was ashamed to confess that he had an increasing tendency to lie in bed until 5:30 a.m.!

His blueprint for living was:

> Do All the Good You Can,
> By All the Means You Can,
> In All the Ways You Can,
> In All the Places You Can,
> At All the Times You Can,
> To All the People You Can,
> As Long as Ever You Can!

A lady once asked him how he would spend his time if he knew he would die at midnight the following day.

He seemed bewildered at her question, then answered, "Why, madam, just as I intend to spend it now. I would preach this evening at Gloucester, and again at five tomorrow morning; after that I would ride to Tewkesbury, preach in the afternoon, and meet the societies in the evening. I would then go to Martin's house...talk and pray with the family as usual, retire to my room at ten o'clock, commend myself to my heavenly Father, lie down to rest, and wake up in glory."

What a legacy Susanna and John Wesley have left not only to the Methodists, but to every mother, to every son, and to every child of the living God!

Preach the Word
by John Wesley

Shall I, for fear of mortal man,
The Spirit's course in me restrain?
Or, undismayed, in deed and word
Be a true witness to my Lord.

Awed by a mortal's frown, shall I
Conceal the Word of God most high?
How then before Thee shall I dare
To stand, or how Thine anger bear.

Shall I, to soothe the unholy throng
Soften Thy truths, and smooth my tongue?
To gain earth's guilded toys, or flee
The cross, endured my Lord by Thee.

What then is he whose scorn I dread,
Whose wrath or hate makes me afraid?
A man! an heir of death, a slave
To sin! a bubble on the wave!

Yea! let men rage, since Thou wilt spread
Thy shadowing wings about my head;
Since in all pain Thy tender love
Will still my sure refreshment prove.

Give me Thy strength, O God of power;
Then let winds blow or tempests roar;
Thy faithful witness will I be;
'Tis fixed; I can do all through Thee.

Chapter Sixty-Three

DAVE

~Present Day~

When he saw him, he had compassion on him, and went to him, and bound up his wounds, pouring in oil and wine.

—Luke 10:33–34

Dave's thoughts were interrupted by a tap on his shoulder. He looked up to see a nurse. "Tom is very restless and frightened. We have him stabilized and are preparing him for surgery. Since you're the only one here who knows him, we were hoping you would to talk to him before we take him in."

Dave followed her to the bed behind the curtain, wondering what Tom's reaction would be when he saw him.

Tom hadn't noticed him, so Dave just stood looking at him for a moment. He looked so vulnerable. Tears were sliding down his colorless face. An IV dripped its fluid steadily into his vein. Tom turned and saw Dave and grabbed his arm.

Dave suddenly knew Tom was going to be all right. He was not only going to live, but he would also one day live for the Lord. Dave couldn't say how he knew. He just knew.

"Tom," he said. "I'm here to pray for you. I love you. Jesus loves you too. I will stay right here and be in your room when you wake up."

Tom grew still as Dave prayed for him. Dave had to gently remove Tom's hand from his arm when an orderly came to take him to surgery. He kept his panic-filled eyes on Dave until the elevator door closed behind him.

Uncle Joe went home, and Dave settled down for a long stay in the surgery waiting room.

About an hour later, a policeman came into the waiting room.

"They said you were still here," he greeted Dave. "We still don't have any idea who this boy belongs to." He shrugged and added, "If he doesn't tell us himself, we may never know."

He left and Dave was again alone with his thoughts. A short time later, Joe came back.

"How's the boy, son?" he asked.

Dave smiled. "He'll be okay, Uncle Joe. What brings you back?"

"I got to wondering about you and the lad. Here, I brought you a sandwich." He handed Dave a bag.

It was late afternoon when a doctor came into the waiting room looking for Dave.

"Are you here for Tom?" he asked Dave.

Dave stood. "Yes. How is he?"

"He'll make it. The knife missed his heart by less than an inch. He's going to be in the hospital for a good while though. He's in recovery now. You can see him in about an hour or so."

Dave was given his room number nearly three hours later. Tom was sleeping and looked even whiter than before. Dave napped but woke up suddenly when Tom grabbed his arm. His grip was weaker this time.

Tom drifted back to sleep, and Dave slipped out quietly to tell his uncle he planned to spend the night.

Tom and Dave were both asleep when a nurse came in with the policeman the next morning.

"Tom!" the nurse said, shaking him gently. "Tom, there is someone here to ask you a few questions."

Tom's eyes filled with fear when he saw the policeman. He closed his eyes and kept them and his mouth firmly shut.

"Just tell me where to find one of your parents, Tom."

"Did you see who assaulted you?"

"What is your last name?"

Tom remained silent. Finally they left the room and Tom instantly opened his eyes.

"Tom," Dave began, "someone needs to notify your family."

Tom's eyes narrowed.

"Why?" he asked softly. "You're the only one who cares."

Tom was sleeping when Dave left word at the nurses' station to tell Tom he would return later that afternoon.

Dave was about to enter Tom's room when he heard voices through the half-opened door. Looking in, he saw Uncle Joe. He was holding Tom's hand. Dave listened in shock to the sentences he kept repeating. "It'll be okay, son. Dave will take care of you."

Dave quickly backed out.

I guess I will at that, he thought. *Tom might just as well eat at my table as the park table.*

All kinds of objections flooded his mind. He brushed them aside and was smiling when he entered the room. Tom grinned back through the maze of needles and tubes.

They all talked for awhile before a nurse came in. Joe and Dave moved to the hall and Joe said, "It's about like you figured, son. Tom and I have had a long talk. His mother is spaced out on drugs. Her house is a gathering place for addicts."

He shook his head.

"Believe me, it's no place for kids. Tom left almost six months ago."

"Has Tom been living in the park for half a year?" Dave asked.

"No, he moved and slept wherever he found a place to bed down. He decided to stay at the park when he discovered a hot breakfast was served there every morning."

Dave ignored the remark.

"Who attacked him?"

"A couple of older teens looking for kicks."

"Uncle Joe, Tom has been a wild kid. He doesn't have much going for him. I'm not sure why, but I know he will be in the race someday."

Joe nodded. "I wouldn't be surprised. He's already praying."

"Praying!"

"Sure. He and I had a prayer meeting this afternoon while you were gone."

"Tom prayed?"

"It sounded like a prayer to me. Oh, it wasn't anything with fancy words, but he was sincere. He confessed a lot of sins. But he only broke down and wept when he told the Lord he was sorry for cussing at you. Then he asked the Lord if He would come into his heart and make a new person out of him. He told the Lord he wanted to be just like you. So, when he finished praying, I told him you would take care of him."

Tom continued to improve under Joe's watchful eye. The afternoon came that Dave made his daily run to the hospital room and found it empty. Fighting panic, he went to the nearest nurse.

"Where did they take Tom?"

"He was released."

"Where did he go? He has no home!"

She looked puzzled.

"Why, he went with his uncle, of course. We all referred to the gentleman as Uncle Joe."

Dave dialed Joe's number.

"Where is Tom?" was his greeting.

"Settle down, Davey. He's here with me, of course. I've fixed the spare bedroom for him. As soon as he's feeling better, we're going shopping for some things he needs, and we want you to go with us. We'll let you know when we're going."

"Uncle Joe, I thought you wanted me to..."

"Tom and I talked. We agreed you had work to do. As for me, I don't have anything but lots of time on my hands. Believe me, we'll be calling on you often enough."

"Uncle Joe, Tom isn't an innocent..."

"Well, of course he isn't! Neither am I! Quit worrying like an old woman, will you? We're getting along fine. He's in there now teasing his new dog."

"Dog! You hate dogs!"

There was a silence.

Joe finally broke it with a low, "I never cared much for boys either, Dave. But Jesus and Tom have changed all that. We'll be okay. Now go run someplace."

A click and the dial tone followed his words. Dave was left staring at the telephone.

There was no doubt about it. His uncle was surely carrying a torch.

Chapter Sixty-Four

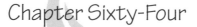

DAVE

~Present Day~

Discretion shall preserve thee, understanding shall keep thee:...to deliver thee from the strange woman, even from the stranger which flattereth with her words; which forsaketh the guide of her youth, and forgetteth the covenant of her God.

—Proverbs 2:11, 16–17

D ave picked up his journal. He hadn't made an entry in over three months. He skipped all the blank pages and found the current date. He picked up his pen and prepared to write down the events of this day.

But instead of writing, he again leafed through the blank pages. Lost days. Lost weeks. Lost months. What people and events could have filled the pages if he hadn't run in the wrong direction?

He thought about the time he had lost. The moments and hours and weeks all seemed to blur together. He wished he could erase them or just keep them blank like these pages in his journal. But they were part of his life. Turning back to the first blank page, he began to write.

> I was tired. I had been tired before, but it was different this time. My fatigue was coupled with a gnawing loneliness. Almost daily, I passed husband and wife teams running together, their hands clasped. Each time I glanced their way, I was conscious of my solitary run.

301

Finally I was consumed by an intense hunger that would only be satisfied by finding a mate to run with me.

I had run only a few steps after making my decision to find a wife, when I heard someone running behind me. I turned and stared at the beautiful woman approaching me. She was vibrant, literally pulsing with life, and laughing as she tried to catch up with me. I slowed my pace and finally stopped. That was my first mistake. Then I made my second.

I ran toward her. Her hair was windblown, and she laughed with joy as she tilted her face toward me. All the restlessness of the last few weeks vanished as I took her hands in mine.

How many weeks passed? I don't know. I only know my heart pounded with fear of her answer the night I asked, "Will you run with me?"

"I have come to run with you," she replied, her expression one of love.

My joy was complete. I was captivated by my beloved. I took time to thank the Lord for sending her to me. I realized that He had sensed my need and had sent me the desire of my heart. "Thank You, Lord, thank You," I whispered, as I walked hand in hand with the one who would soon be my running mate. "But I will need to quit running, just temporarily, in order to wed my lovely one."

My family and friends were ecstatic when they met her and learned of our decision. They could fellowship with me while my torch was lowered, its rays no longer blinding them. They helped me prepare for the wedding.

I had not known life could be so exhilarating. I delighted in the presence of my beloved, even as I became

302

familiar with her personality and diverse moods. I discovered she could carry sorrow. At those times, I gently wiped away her tears. But nearly always, I found her radiating joy and delight.

One evening, while she was preparing for the wedding day with friends, I was alone. Alone?

I asked my Lord where He had gone. I kept calling for Him, but I received no reply. I cried loud and long, but my pleading availed nothing. I finally fell into bed, exhausted with my search, and slept. It was that night that my Lord came and gave me His Word.

Be ye not unequally yoked together with unbelievers.

(2 Corinthians 6:14)

I pondered his message. "Lord! Are you talking about my fiancée? She is not an unbeliever! She talks about You! She approves of my race! She has promised to carry the torch with me!"

But the heavens were silent, and my Lord was gone again. I tossed and turned all night but could not find rest for my soul. It was dawn before I finally slept. When I awoke, words of Scripture filled my mind.

Now concerning spiritual gifts, brethren, I would not have you ignorant. (1 Corinthians 12:1)

What were these words to me? I tried to ignore them, but the words refused to leave. Over and over again they echoed. Finally I reached for my Bible and searched for the list of spiritual gifts. I read them from the twelfth chapter of 1 Corinthians, not knowing what it was that I was searching for.

Three words leaped from the page, became flames, and burned their way into my heart. They were included in the list of spiritual gifts.

Discerning of spirits. I knew this was the gift God meant for me to have. I prayed, "God, I need this gift! I need to be able to distinguish between right and wrong and good and evil. I need to perceive the spirit of man."

Then I knew. I fought the prayer I knew I must pray. I battled long and hard.

Finally I lay prostrate on my face before God and wept and prayed the hardest prayer I have ever prayed: "Please, Lord, help me to discern the spirit of my beloved."

I was supposed to pick her up for lunch that same day. The hours dragged until the time came for me to leave. I was frantic.

I rang her doorbell, and she came to the door. I looked at her with despair.

Was this my beloved, who had enchanted me with her beauty? She was dressed in filthy, tattered garments. I lifted my eyes from her despicable clothing and stared into the eyes that had so often melted their way into my heart. They were unseeing. There was no light in them. Darkness emanated from this wretched and miserable creature. I looked at the hands that I had held so tenderly. They hung at her side. She carried no torch.

Had she changed so much? No. My Lord had given my blinded eyes sight. For the first time I was looking not at her flesh, but at her spirit.

I turned to flee. As I stumbled away from her, she called out, "But Dave! I believe! I will run with you! I believe in your Lord too!"

I turned to face her one last time and quoted James 2:19–20.

You believe that there is one God; you do well: the devils also believe, and tremble. But will you know...that faith without works is dead?

I ran from her, and as I ran, her curses followed me.

"God," I whispered, "I thought You had sent me this one. Now I know she was sent by our enemy, and I was deceived by her beauty. Lord, if You want me to run with a mate, please send one to me. But until then, I will be content with You. I thought I was lonely before, but I have never known the meaning of loneliness until I called for You and discovered You had left me."

My Lord answered immediately.

Lo, I am with you alway, even unto the end of the world.

(Matthew 28:20)

"But Lord, You didn't come when I called!"

Lo, I am with you alway.

He had not left me. I was the one who had turned around and walked away from my Lord in order to follow my fiancée. Without a backward glance, I had continued to wander farther and farther away from my Lord.

And even there, and even then, my precious Savior had come to me in the evening hours, drawing me back. How I love Him!

Dave laid his leather journal and pen on the desk. Falling to his knees, he cried, "Lord, can You forgive me for leaving You? Please help me never to leave You again. And Lord? Thank You! Thank You for giving me discernment and understanding. Thank You for putting me back in the race!"

The love of God gently enclosed him until he felt nearly overwhelmed by the Lord's embrace. Never had he felt love like this.

No earthly love could compare. Dave laughed aloud as renewed vigor surged through him.

He would begin his run again. He would once more raise his torch to the heavens. His sweet Savior would forevermore be his First Love.

Dave lay on his bed later that night, alternately thinking and praying. He wondered if he would marry someday. He thought about runners whose lives were enriched by a faithful running partner. He remembered the fiery founder of the mighty Salvation Army, William Booth. William's motto was "Go for souls, and go for the worst!"

Catherine, his partner, was a dedicated torchbearer who helped him fulfill that mission. Catherine vowed, "While women weep, as they do now, I'll fight; while little children go hungry, I'll fight; while men go to prison, in and out, in and out, as they do now, I'll fight; while there is a drunkard left, while there is a poor lost girl upon the streets, while there remains one dark soul without the light of God—I'll fight! I'll fight to the very end!"

And war she did—hand in hand with her beloved William. They formed an army to wage war against the hosts of hell. Their troops suffered casualties of vicious and brutal murders, beatings, and stonings. They marched through the streets singing, playing music, and preaching. Together they met the needs of a decaying humanity, crushed by sin. Their brass instruments were often battered beyond repair by those who tried in vain to stop their music, but they sang their way home, dripping with a combination of blood, mud, and egg yolks.

They kept singing while storming into territory long held by demon forces. They marched through barrooms, prisons, and dark alleys. They stormed their way into danger-filled ghettos and homes filled with violence.

William traveled over five million miles to preach sixty-thousand sermons. Catherine ran with him, preaching, writing, warring, studying, organizing, and training a workforce of women to bring relief to hurting people.

In the couple's spare time, they reared their eight children and adopted a ninth. Seven of them became well-known preachers, leaders, and songwriters.

They ran, hand in hand, for thirty-five years—a team, one in purpose, each enriched by the other.

Dave recalled the wise counsel of Martin Luther:

> Whoever intends to enter married life should do so in faith and in God's name. I should pray God that it may prosper according to His will and that marriage may not be treated as a matter of fun and folly. It is a hazardous matter and as serious as anything on earth can be. Therefore we should not rush into it as the world does, in keeping with its frivolousness and wantonness and in pursuit of its pleasure. Before taking this step, we should consult God, so that we may lead our married life to His glory.

"Thank You again, my Lord, for sparing me a life of heartache," Dave prayed.

He thought about John Wesley, a champion runner whose marriage was a miserable failure. His wife was not a blessing, but a hindrance. She didn't run with him but chose instead to war against him.

"In spite of her rage, Lord, he just kept running for You."

Dave thought of Max, a faithful runner he knew who smiled through his tears, daily bearing the load of a divided marriage. His wife had grown bitter with hatred against the race. Now she hated him.

Dave decided to remind Max of John Wesley the next time he saw him.

Just before drifting off to sleep, Dave murmured, half to himself and half to the Lord, "I'm so glad I didn't marry her."

Chapter Sixty-Five

DAVE

~Present Day~

The drunkard and the glutton shall come to poverty:
and drowsiness shall clothe a man with rags.

—Proverbs 23:21

The sounds and sights of the night filled the city. A siren wailed, then began to fade from view and hearing. As the sound grew fainter, Dave heard the soft strains of a song.

Amazing grace, how sweet the sound!

Dave turned toward the music, foreign in this city of profanity, screams, revelry, and weeping. He followed it to a small mission sandwiched between the barred windows of a pawn shop and a theater.

Dave slipped in and sat in the back. The hollow sound of an old upright piano accompanied an elderly man's quavering words:

We've no less days to sing God's praise
Than when we first begun.

Dave looked at the men scattered in the room. The dismal, unadvertised side effects of drugs and liquor sat in these seats. They had no interest in the music or the message. They were here simply to secure their free meal and cot for the night. Dave was surprised that so many young were among the old.

The speaker's words caught his attention.

"Will you do it, sir?"

The man was looking straight at him.

Dave hadn't been listening. Was the man speaking to him?

Dave looked questioningly at the speaker, and he kindly repeated his question. "I am glad you have joined us. Do you have a message for these men?"

Dave was about to shake his head when he realized that he did have something to say.

He walked slowly to the front of the cheerless room and faced the hopeless faces before him.

Sighing his prayer, he said simply, "I was drawn into this building by the song that has been sung throughout the world in many languages...'Amazing Grace.'"

His eyes rested on each man before continuing.

"I looked for hope in your eyes, but it's no longer there. Somewhere along the road of life, you have lost it. I don't know what disappointments, troubles, and heartaches have brought you here. But I do know that there is not one man in this place who was more miserable or more destitute than a man named John."

Chapter Sixty-Six

JOHN NEWTON

~1725–1807~

He brought me up also out of an horrible pit, out of the miry clay,
and set my feet upon a rock, and established my goings.
And he hath put a new song in my mouth.

—Psalm 40:2–3

A man named John Newton made his way early one morning to his favorite spot on the hillside. He sat down on a log and began to talk to God. He looked at the sea in the distance and remembered—oh, God, it was so painful to remember—his days at sea...

His life at sea had begun at just eleven years of age. What a wicked sailor he had been! His godly mother had faithfully taught him the Scriptures, but just before his seventh birthday, she had died. And John, no longer under her influence, had rejected God, religion, and the Bible.

He had not been content with merely ignoring God, but had delighted in mocking Him. Blasphemy and profanity literally poured from his mouth, ridiculing all that even hinted of religion. It wasn't long before his heart seemed as stone. He became cruel. Murderous thoughts filled his mind. He had no fear of God, no regard for man, no conscience. He lived a totally depraved and abandoned life. And he lived it to the fullest. He was never satisfied with just being vile himself. Instead, his greatest pleasure in life was seducing others away from God and into sin.

He sailed to Africa to purchase slaves. He enjoyed shackling them with chains, bolting them together, dragging them onto the ship, throwing them into the hold, and then selling those who survived for a big profit.

He had begun to be infatuated with the occult practices of Africa. He turned to charms, black magic, sorcery, and divination.

In all his travels with ungodly sailors, he had never met a more daring blasphemer than himself. He daily invented new oaths to mock God. Even the sailors shunned and despised his company.

"God," he cried from the hillside. "I was like one infected with a pestilence, spreading the disease of sin wherever I went!"

John thanked God for bringing him out of such depths of sin. His heart overflowed with love, and tears streamed down his face as he remembered how blind he had been to the love and mercy of God!

"God," he prayed. "Thank You for Your grace—Your amazing grace."

Opening his diary, he began to write,

Amazing grace! (how sweet the sound!)
That saved a wretch like me;
I once was lost, but now am found;
Was blind, but now I see.

He stopped for a moment then, remembering the night his heart had first begun to turn toward God for mercy.

It was during a voyage he would never forget, back in 1748. He was twenty-three then. The ship he was on was unfit for sailing in stormy weather. He was sleeping when the force of a violent wave broke upon the ship. He awoke with a start as his cabin began to fill with water.

He heard a frantic shout from the deck, "The ship is going down!" He ran to the ladder, where he met his captain.

"Go back to your cabin and get your knife," the captain yelled. A sailor took John's place on the ladder as he returned to his cabin. When John came back with the knife, he found that the sailor who had taken his place had been instantly washed overboard.

John joined the sailors who were plugging their clothes and bedding into the leaks, nailing pieces of boards over the holes, and frantically manning the pumps.

John laughed as he pumped, remarking, "In a few days, we will be drinking and laughing about this!" A sailor looked at him, his eyes wide with fear, tears streaming down his face.

"No, it is too late now," he replied in a trembling voice.

Fear struck his heart as he realized that he was on a sinking ship. He ran to speak with the captain and then returned frantically to the pumps. Without thinking he screamed, "If this does not work, the Lord have mercy on us!"

As he continued to pump, almost every passing wave broke over his head. He was roped to the deck to keep from washing away. Every time the ship descended into the sea, he expected it to rise no more.

The words he had just uttered, "The Lord have mercy on us!" echoed unceasingly in his troubled mind.

"'The Lord have mercy on us!' Why did I say that? For what mercy can there be for me?" he asked himself.

Even the mercy of God would not be enough for him, for he was the greatest and most wretched of all sinners. The God he had so proudly blasphemed could never forgive him. He had made the life, and even the death, of Jesus Christ the subject of profane ridicule.

Now he knew God had just one message for him. It came from the dark recesses of his mind and repeated itself over and over as he pumped water from the doomed ship.

> *Because I have called, and ye refused; I have stretched out my hand, and no man regarded; but ye have set at nought all my counsel, and would none of my reproof: I also will laugh at your calamity; I will mock when your fear cometh; when your fear cometh as desolation, and your destruction cometh as a whirlwind; when distress and anguish cometh upon you. Then shall they call upon me, but I will not answer; they shall seek me early, but they shall not find me: for that they hated knowledge, and did not choose the fear of the LORD: they would none of my counsel: they despised all my reproof. Therefore shall they eat of the fruit of their own way, and be filled with their own devices.* (Proverbs 1:24–31)

He was surrounded with black, unfathomable despair.

The ship was finally emptied of water. The wind died. Would the damaged ship be able to reach port? The sails were reduced to a few tattered rags. And what would the sailors eat? All the livestock had been washed overboard. All that remained were a few fish and some food that had been set aside for the hogs.

At his first break from the pumps, John picked up the Bible he had scorned and read from Luke 11:13:

> *If ye then, being evil, know how to give good gifts unto your children: how much more shall your heavenly Father give the Holy Spirit to them that ask him?*

He read the verse over and over. "If this book I am trying to read was written by this Holy Spirit, then I need to ask for the Spirit to help me to understand it. And if this book is true, then this verse is true. So I will ask and see what happens."

He expected to die at any moment. The crew was dressed inadequately for the frigid cold, and there was only half of a salted cod each day for twelve sailors. Pumping continued endlessly, and between incessant labor and little food, the sailors were wasting away. One died.

Fear was John's constant companion. He knew he would either starve to death or resort to cannibalism.

The captain continuously eyed John. John knew why. The captain had often remarked that he looked upon John as a modern-day Jonah. "A curse is present on every ship you board," he had once told him. John began to fear that the captain, in desperation, would throw him overboard in order to save the ship.

Finally, after four weeks of keeping the damaged ship afloat, they sailed into port, the last of their food boiling in the pot. All who looked upon the battered ship knew it would not have lasted even one more night at sea.

The rest of the sailors forgot God and their prayers when the danger was past—but John didn't. He continued to read the Bible. He read 1 Timothy 1:12–13 over and over again, a little ray of hope growing each time he read it. It was the testimony of Paul, the apostle who had himself suffered shipwreck.

And I thank Christ Jesus our Lord, who hath enabled me, for that he counted me faithful, putting me into the ministry; who was before a blasphemer, and a persecutor, and injurious: but I obtained mercy, because I did it ignorantly in unbelief.

So Paul had been a blasphemer. He had persecuted Christians and had hurt the gospel of Jesus Christ. But he had obtained mercy. Perhaps there was hope for John too.

That tiny ray of hope had grown into a prayer, and the prayer into a cry for forgiveness; and slowly, slowly, his heart of stone began to melt, and the light of Christ began to penetrate his dark soul.

John marveled at the grace of God as he again bent to write in his diary.

'Twas grace that taught my heart to fear,
And grace my fears relieved;
How precious did that grace appear
The hour I first believed!

He could have so easily died before finding Christ. There were so many times that God had miraculously spared him from death.

He was thrown from a horse at twelve years of age, landing just a few inches from a wood pile.

There was the Sunday he planned to go sailing with his friend. He had arrived just a few minutes too late for the venture, but just on time in God's providence. The boat was overturned, and his friend and several others drowned.

He had been deathly sick and unable to sail on one voyage. His captain had left him on a small, sandy island plantation in the care of a black woman, the captain's mistress. She had despised him and fed him only the leftovers from her plate. He remembered crawling through the plantation during the night hours, pulling up roots and eating them raw to keep from starving to death. When he was too sick to crawl, he was kept alive by slaves who shared their own small amount of food with him.

After many weeks of delirious fever, he recovered enough to attempt walking. The woman called her slaves to look at him as he staggered and fell, and urged them to mimic his clumsy movements. They tottered along with him, clapping their hands, sneering, and throwing limes and stones at him.

When he was finally well enough to sail away, he was falsely accused by another trader of stealing from his captain.

The captain was furious. "Lock John in chains on deck every time I leave the ship!" he ordered.

John was given a pint of rice and left in the cold and rain until the captain returned from his trips to shore. He lost his fierceness during those times. He became depressed, but still his cold heart seethed with hatred against God.

There was the time he had gone shooting with friends. He had climbed a steep bank, pulling his shotgun after him. It went off so near his face that it burned away the corner of his hat.

He remembered his many treks through the jungles. Many of his companions had been poisoned by the natives. He had miraculously escaped.

There were the countless times he had been dragged to land half dead after being pitched overboard.

He remembered the night he was about to embark in a small boat to go to shore to perform his duties there. He was ready to let go of the ropes when he heard his captain shout, "John! Get back in the ship."

Another sailor was sent in his place. The boat had sunk, and the man who had replaced him had drowned. The captain, when later questioned, had no explanation for his change of plans.

He remembered the night onboard that he had instigated a drinking contest. He drank until his brain was on fire. He danced about the deck like a madman, and his hat fell overboard. He threw himself over the rail, his only thought to recover his hat. A sailor caught hold of his clothes just in time. He was barely able to pull him back inside the ship. In his drunken state, John had forgotten he couldn't swim.

"God," he cried now, "how close I came that night to perishing in that dreadful condition and sinking into eternity under the weight of my own curse."

With a heart full of love and gratitude, he wrote,

Through many dangers, toils, and snares,
I have already come;

'Tis grace has brought me safe thus far,
And grace will lead me home.

He had scorned God, mocked Him, blasphemed Him, ridiculed Him, turned others against Him. And God returned all his evil with good.

"Thank You, Lord, thank You," John whispered as he continued to write.

The Lord has promised good to me,
His Word my hope secures;
He will my Shield and Portion be,
As long as life endures.

Yes, when this flesh and heart shall fail,
And mortal life shall cease,
I shall possess, within the vail,
A life of joy and peace.

John, who had been shunned by the most vile members of humanity, was now walking with God, who promised never to leave nor forsake him.

The earth shall soon dissolve like snow;
The sun forbear to shine;
But God, who call'd me here below,
Will be forever mine.

These past years he had preached the gospel that he had tried to destroy. He had proclaimed the love of God that he had shunned. He had invited all to partake of the mercy he had mocked. He had crusaded against the cruelties of slavery that he had profited from. And now, his life nearly over, he looked up to the sky above him.

"I'll be coming home soon, my Father," he breathed.

Who would have believed that the amazing grace of God would reach down into a ship and place a torch in the hand of the vilest of all sailors? But was there anyone who needed light more desperately? Had a blacker one than he ever lived?

What a God! What amazing grace! John would spend an eternity praising Him, but it would never be enough.

He leaned back against a tree, thinking about the glories of heaven that would soon be his, and he bent once again to write.

When we've been there ten thousand years,
Bright shining as the sun,
We've no less days to sing God's praise
Than when we first begun.

John crossed his finish line at the age of eighty-two. As he preached one of his final messages, just before his death, he declared, "My memory is nearly gone, but I remember two things."

His congregation looked at him expectantly, and his eyes filled with tears.

"They are," he stated, "that I am a great sinner, and that Christ is a great Savior."

Chapter Sixty-Seven

DAVE

~Present Day~

---

*But after that the kindness and love of God our
Saviour toward man appeared.*

—Titus 3:4

Dave returned to his seat at the back of the mission. The director nodded at the pianist and stepped to the front of the room.

He didn't even bother to brush away his tears as he stood with his eyes closed, his hands upraised, and began again to sing.

Amazing grace, how sweet the sound...

An old man joined him this time. Dave turned to see the man but was disappointed to see that his eyes were leering. He heard the drunken slur of his words now.

I once was lost, but now am found...

And now a young man began to sing along softly.

Was blind, but now I see.

Dave wept when he singled out this man. For tears streamed down his face, and Dave knew that he was seeing the Savior who had stepped into the life of John Newton and could step into his as well.

The song ended, and the men shuffled toward the dining room—all but one.

Dave went and sat by the man whose head was buried in his hands, and whose body heaved with sobs.

"My God," he heard him pray, "can You save me?"

The room had emptied. The man lifted his head and saw Dave seated beside him.

"Are you sure He'll have me?" he asked.

Dave nodded.

"He came for You, my friend. Did you know that He said, 'All who come to me, I will never cast out?'"

"Then I will come to Him."

I'll come.

Such simple words.

But how low must man descend before he finally speaks them?

The man knelt by his chair. Dave noticed his sin-ravaged body and his frayed, filthy clothing, thinking, *He is so young, and already nearly destroyed by sin.* He could almost hear the heart cry of God for His tormented creation.

O that there were such an heart in them, that they would fear me, and keep all my commandments always, that it might be well with them, and with their children for ever!

(Deuteronomy 5:29)

The mission director came in. He knelt and put his arm around the man's shoulders.

Dave slipped out of the building. The city seemed even blacker in contrast to the dim light of the mission. The garish neon lights inviting fallen humanity to partake of sin and death did nothing to dispel the city's darkness.

Dave had a new bounce to his steps as he ran along the street.

"Thank You, my Christ," he whispered. "Thank You for Your grace that never fails to be amazing."

Chapter Sixty-Eight

DAVE

~Present Day~

And he said, Who art thou? And she answered,
I am Ruth thine handmaid.

—Ruth 3:9

He had seen her so many times...in so many places. The first time he was coming out of the prison while she was going in, her Bible in one hand, her torch in the other.

He had noticed her next coming from a Sunday school class into the sanctuary. A group of eleven- and twelve-year-old girls were gathered around her, jostling for her attention.

He had seen her on a cold day sitting on a bench visiting with a destitute, shivering woman while gently tucking a blanket around her.

Once he had spotted her in the mission serving soup, her hair damp with sweat from the sweltering kitchen.

He had spotted her in a convalescent home reading the Bible to three or four women in the dining room.

Her torch surrounded her with a soft glow wherever she was, separating her from others who lived and walked in darkness.

He had never been in the children's home, but today he noticed the sign as he ran past. Slowly he stopped, turned around, and went in. Perhaps there was a troubled teen he could help.

She was there. A smile lit her face, attracting a group of love-starved children, who swarmed around her.

Her relief was apparent when Dave walked in the room. She handed him a sticky baby and picked up a toddler who clamored for her attention. Dave wasn't sure what to do with the child. The little guy wasn't thrilled with the situation either. He let out a piercing wail.

Dave wondered how so much noise could come from such a small person. He didn't know whether to tighten his grip or just let go. He looked at the girl helplessly. She laughed and seemed to take her time coming to his rescue.

"Here," she said, exchanging the baby for the toddler she was holding. "Maybe this one will like you." He was even stickier.

Dave would never have set foot in this home if he'd known just babies and toddlers were here. Small children baffled him. He wasn't sure how to hold them, didn't know what to do when they wanted his attention, and certainly had no idea how to handle one who cried.

He struggled to hold on to the squirming child without hurting him. He looked at the woman. How did she manage five or six babies and toddlers all at once and keep smiling—and stay beautiful?

Dave looked again.

She was beautiful. Light surrounded her. A radiance shone from her eyes. Her hands were gentle and loving, patting one child while wiping tears from the eyes of another.

She seemed totally unaware that the baby was tugging her golden hair out of place.

Dave remembered all the times and places he had seen her. She was never without her torch.

He sat down on a low stool near the group. He planned to stay until she left. He had to get acquainted with her. Obviously he would have to somehow figure out how to help her with these kids. He was still trying to think of a way when a couple of two- or three-year-old boys dove at him, nearly knocking him backward. Gingerly, he placed one on each knee. *Now what?* He took off his watch, thinking maybe they would take turns listening to it tick. One grabbed it and started eating it. Dave finally wrested it away from him and stood up. This simply wasn't going to work.

He was starting to leave when a tired-looking woman entered the room and gathered the children together. She placed one in a swing, another in a high chair, had one propped on each hip, and the others surrounding her. Dave watched her with respect. There must be a trick to handling children. If there was, no one had ever taught it to him.

"Thank you so much, Ruth," the woman said. "The time you spend here is such a help."

She hugged her and added, "I sometimes don't know how we'd make it without you."

So her name was Ruth. Dave waited for her to pick up her sweater and purse and then held the door open for her.

She laughed. "Thanks so much for your invaluable help with the babies," she said.

"I think it's probably my first and last time," Dave answered with a grin. "I doubt that you noticed, but I'm really not too comfortable with babies or little kids."

"I noticed," she answered, shaking her head.

They walked down the street talking.

They were still talking over coffee in a restaurant two or three hours later. Dave found it easy to talk to her. They shared their experiences, their frustrations, their hurts, their good times, their call to the race, their love for the Lord.

"I have seen you many times in many places," Dave said.

"Can we ever do enough for Jesus?" she answered softly. "When I tire, I think of a torchbearer named Elizabeth, and I keep going. Dave, there are so many needs, so many hurting people, so many sick people, so many neglected children and unwanted elderly, so many lonely people, so many, many people without Christ. And there are so few runners in this race. We desperately need more women like the one who has given me inspiration."

She paused and asked, "Are there torchbearers in the past who have given you inspiration, Dave?"

He smiled. They had so many things in common.

"Tell me about this runner who has inspired you," he answered.

She seemed to forget he was even there as she replied reflectively, "Her name was Elizabeth..."

Chapter Sixty-Nine

ELIZABETH FRY

~1780–1845~

*They are all of them snared in holes, and they
are hid in prison houses.*

—Isaiah 42:22

The obscenities, curses, and shouts were deafening. Three hundred nearly naked women and nearly as many fighting and screaming children pushed and shoved, cooked and ate, lived and slept in four tiny rooms in the infamous Newgate Prison of London. There were no beds, no sheets, no blankets. A few filthy rags served as clothing, and mere scraps of food were the meals. One male attendant and his young son tried, but miserably failed, to keep any kind of order.

Women pushed and shoved viciously for a place at the window gratings, where they begged those who hurried to pass them for shillings to buy liquor. Liquor was their only hope for a few hours of drunken relief.

Into this pot of boiling, foul humanity walked a tall, dignified Quaker. Elizabeth Fry hid her shocked horror as she looked calmly at the women and children. She felt as if she had been thrown into a den of wild beasts.

A few stared back at her, sneering at her plain brown dress with its full skirt, tight waist, and sparkling white cape.

Well, she had asked for this. She had read the words of Jesus, "I was in prison, and you did not visit Me," and they had pierced her soul and stayed there, giving her no peace until she finally appeared before the governor of the prison.

"Sir," she had said quietly, "if you kindly allow me to pray with the women, I will go inside."

The governor smirked as he pictured this stately woman among his clawing, screaming prisoners! Laughing, he granted her permission.

And now here she was. The Lord couldn't tell her on judgment day that she hadn't at least come. The first thing she must do here was to look upon this appalling scene with eyes of mercy, not judgment. She reminded herself she had not come to condemn, but to comfort and relieve.

She removed her bonnet, wiped off a low ledge, sat down, and opened her Bible.

As she began to read, the women started to grow quiet. Even the children were silent, listening to a sound they had never heard in this vile place—a sweet voice reading the words of the living God.

All we like sheep have gone astray; we have turned every one to his own way; and the LORD hath laid on him the iniquity of us all. He was oppressed, and he was afflicted, yet he opened not his mouth. (Isaiah 53:6–7)

Who shall ascend into the hill of the LORD? or who shall stand in his holy place? He that hath clean hands, and a pure heart; who hath not lifted up his soul unto vanity, nor sworn deceitfully. (Psalm 24:3–4)

Hear, O LORD, when I cry with my voice: have mercy also upon me, and answer me. When thou saidst, Seek ye my face; my heart said unto thee, Thy face, LORD, will I seek...When my father and my mother forsake me, then the LORD will take me up. (Psalm 27:7–8, 10)

Wide eyes in filthy faces stared as Elizabeth turned quietly to Psalm 69 and continued reading words never before spoken in this room.

Deliver me out of the mire, and let me not sink...Hear me, O LORD; for thy lovingkindness is good: turn unto me according to the multitude of thy tender mercies...I am poor and sorrowful: let thy salvation, O God, set me up on high...For the LORD heareth the poor, and despiseth not his prisoners. (Psalm 69:14, 16, 29, 33)

Opening to the New Testament, Elizabeth read the words of Jesus.

Blessed are they that mourn: for they shall be comforted. (Matthew 5:4)

Love your enemies, bless them that curse you, do good to them that hate you, and pray for them which despitefully use you, and persecute you; that ye may be the children of your Father which is in heaven. (verse 44)

Elizabeth closed her Bible and looked up. The fierce snarling and blasphemy again filled the room. Had she accomplished nothing?

She slowly made her way home to fix dinner for her husband and eight children. Surely God would call someone else to minister in the prison—someone who did not have a large family to care for.

But she was drawn back again and again. She took clothes with her. Brutal fighting broke out, for there were never enough garments for everyone.

Back at home, looking at her own children, she could not help but see the wild eyes of the children being raised in the prison.

"All right, Lord," she said. "I will teach them."

Gathering together materials, she made her way back to the prison.

"I will teach your children to read," she told the young mothers.

What a nightmare her first class had been! The mothers begged to be taught too. Describing the scene later, Elizabeth wrote, "The railing was crowded with half-naked women struggling together for front places with violence and begging in loud voices for money."

But Elizabeth did not quit. Along with teaching, she brought the women cloth, needles, and thread. She patiently taught them to sew.

And always she read the words of God from her Bible.

At home, Elizabeth knelt and prayed. "O Lord, show me what to do and what to leave undone; then I can humbly trust that a blessing will be with me in my various engagements. Enable me, O Lord, to feel tenderly and charitably toward all my beloved fellow mortals. Help me to have no soreness nor improper feelings toward any. Let me think no evil, bear all things, hope all things, and endure all things. Let me walk in all humility and godly fear before all men, and in Your sight. Amen."

One thing that would have to be left undone was her constant entertaining. She often fed from thirty to sixty at mealtime, as Quakers gathered in her home. She must give that up if she was to continue her work in the prison.

But how could she quit visiting the poor around her? Was not that another of the Lord's commands? And she simply must take time to keep the shelves in her home stocked with an abundant supply of garments and medicines for the sick. Elizabeth sighed as she gathered together an armful of supplies. She walked through alleys and up broken staircases, making her way through children, pigs, and chickens, searching out the sick, the poor, and the lonely who needed her help.

The prison governor did not laugh long at this amazing woman. When Elizabeth invited him to her home to persuade him to hire a matron to supervise the women prisoners, he readily consented.

Day after day, week after week, month after month, year after year, Elizabeth continued her work. Her family grew to eleven children, but the transformation in the prison cells kept her going back and forth between the prison and her house. A drunken, scantily clad, cursing woman was a rare sight now. The women's prison had slowly but steadily been transformed into a place that functioned like a well-regulated family.

Elizabeth had been at her work in the prison for six years when John Randolph, the renowned Virginian congressman, visited London. He wrote to his friend about his visit:

> I saw the greatest curiosity in London! I have seen Elizabeth Fry in Newgate, and I have witnessed there miraculous effects of true Christianity upon the most depraved of human beings—bad women, sir, who are worse, if possible, than the Devil himself. And yet the wretched outcasts have been tamed and subdued by the Christian eloquence of Mrs. Fry. Nothing but religion can effect this miracle!

Elizabeth, having faithfully brought Christ to lost souls, could still not rest from her constant and often exhausting labors. For as long as there was a need, Elizabeth had to do everything in her power to fill it. She learned that many women were loaded onto convict ships and sent to the penal settlement in Australia. She determined that not one ship would leave the Thames River without her praying with the women first. She took materials to them so they could work during their long voyage and would have something to sell when they landed.

She formed a prison committee and appointed one of its members to visit Australia and investigate the conditions the prisoners found upon their arrival there.

"There is no provision for the women!" she was told. "There is neither food nor lodging! In order to survive, the women must turn to crime or prostitution!"

Elizabeth hurried to the English authorities. "You must build barracks for the women! Delay is unacceptable!"

The officials stared at this woman who refused to take no for an answer. She insisted that they build homes immediately—so they did!

Elizabeth's enemies were vocal and powerful. There were many who opposed her work and felt that the prisoners deserved their deplorable living conditions.

Elizabeth turned to the Lord for strength. "I feel the Rock always underneath me," she often told her friends.

She personally investigated prisons in the British Isles and in Scotland. She was informed of vile conditions in other countries, and she corresponded with people in Italy, Denmark, and Russia who wanted to improve prisons in their countries.

She traveled to mental institutions and hospitals in Ireland and obtained an official permit to visit any prison at any time in France. Her Lord's command to visit the prisoners took Elizabeth to Belgium, Holland, Prussia, Switzerland, and Germany. Joseph, her husband, who loved his wife and shared her concern for the needy, often accompanied her.

In the midst of her work among prisoners, she heard that a man had frozen to death in the streets of London.

"O Lord," she cried, "how can I rest happily in my warm home knowing that there are people shivering with cold in the streets?"

She and her committee prepared shelters and stocked them with warm bedding, soup, and bread. They hunted for jobs for the unemployed and organized classes to teach destitute children. She even set up libraries for coastguardsmen in more than five hundred stations around Britain.

She looked around her. There were so many needs and so few laborers—so she opened an institution to train nurses.

The overwhelming needs of people kept her daily in her quiet place of prayer, finding refuge and strength in the Lord. "My Lord, be pleased to help and strengthen me in all this. In all my perplexities, make a way where I see no way," she prayed.

Kings and princes asked Elizabeth for recommendations for prison reform.

She advised the king of France, "When you build a prison, you had better build with the thought ever in your mind that you and your children may occupy the cells."

King Frederick William IV of Prussia asked to visit Newgate Prison with Elizabeth Fry while he was a guest in England.

Elizabeth calmly sat on her ledge and opened her worn Bible to the twelfth chapter of Romans.

The women laid their work aside as she read.

So we, being many, are one body in Christ, and every one members one of another. (Romans 12:5)

Abhor that which is evil; cleave to that which is good. Be kindly affectioned one to another with brotherly love; in honour preferring one another...Bless them which persecute you: bless, and curse not. Rejoice with them that do rejoice, and weep with them that weep. Be of the same mind one toward another. Mind not high things, but condescend to men of low estate. Be not wise in your own conceits. Recompense to no man evil for evil. Provide things honest, in the sight of all men...Be not overcome of evil, but overcome evil with good. (Romans 12:9–10, 14–17, 21)

Closing her Bible, Elizabeth knelt to pray. King Frederick watched as the prisoners got on their knees, and then he too knelt.

"We, being many, are one body in Christ."

331

The Quaker woman, the king of Prussia, and the common prisoners all knelt together before their one Creator, as Elizabeth lifted her voice to God in prayer.

She served her Lord faithfully and kept working until just a few months before her death at age sixty-five. Her last words before saying good-bye to her family were, "I can say one thing. Since my heart was touched at seventeen years old, I believe I never have awakened from sleep, in sickness or in health, by day or by night, without my first waking thought being how best I might serve my Lord."

Chapter Seventy

DAVE

~Present Day~

Who can find a virtuous woman? for her price is far above rubies.

—Proverbs 31:10

I have tried to follow Elizabeth's example," Ruth said softly. "I begin every day asking God to use me to help at least one person."

She smiled. "Elizabeth was a beautiful person."

"You are the most beautiful person I have met," Dave said without thinking. "You not only have outward beauty, you have inner beauty."

Ruth blushed. "We've just met, Dave."

"I feel like I have known you for years, Ruth. You're so easy to talk to. I can't believe how much we have in common."

It was late when Dave got home. "Lord?" he prayed. "She's the one, isn't she?"

A deep peace filled him.

"I was ready to run alone," he added, then smiled. "You have sent me one beautiful running partner!"

He sobered immediately. She may not want to run with him. She seemed to enjoy his company, but she appeared to enjoy everyone's company. She'd been nice to the most miserable of people. He certainly couldn't have made much of an impression with his incompetence in the children's home.

"I think I need Your help, Lord," he said. "Please tell her I'm not so bad, and please, please talk her into running with me!"

Ruth was kneeling at her bed.

"Lord, could you be sending me a running partner? I have seen Dave in different places, always at work for You and always so nice to everyone. He even tried to be sweet to those babies tonight, but he didn't quite know how. I never thought...oh, Lord, if You want me to keep running alone, I will. But I want You to know it was so nice being with him this evening. If it is in Your perfect will, please put us together—soon!"

Chapter Seventy-One

DAVE

~Present Day~

Wherefore is light given to him that is in misery, and
life unto the bitter in soul.

—Job 3:20

Dave ran through the dark subdivision and found the small, white house. He had received an urgent message from a concerned mother. She wanted a torchbearer to talk to her daughter.

A tired-looking woman answered his knock. He noticed the wisps of grey hair, the exhausted sag of her shoulders, her agitated expression.

"Thank you for coming," she said. "My daughter was in an accident. We just brought her home from the hospital three weeks ago. She is confined to a wheelchair and has no desire to live. As far as she is concerned, her life is over at just seventeen. Can you help her?"

Dave breathed a prayer as he followed her to the family room. The girl in the wheelchair glanced at him. Dismissing him as unworthy of her attention, she stared back at the game show on television. Such listless eyes on one so young dismayed Dave. He pulled a chair up to hers.

"I'm Dave," he began, and could tell immediately that neither his name nor his presence made any difference to her.

"What is your name?" he asked softly.

Rather than answering, she tilted her head toward her mother.

"Her name is Charlotte," her mother answered tiredly.

Charlotte!

Dave knew now what he would tell her.

He smiled. "Charlotte, let me tell you about another Charlotte."

As Dave began to talk, the mother slipped over to the TV and turned it off. Charlotte didn't even seem to notice.

Chapter Seventy-Two

CHARLOTTE ELLIOTT

~1789–1871~

And the Spirit and the bride say, Come. And let him that heareth say, Come. And let him that is athirst come. And whosoever will, let him take the water of life freely.

—Revelation 22:17

She had spent the last three years in her bed. The days all seemed to run together, as loneliness and depression nearly overwhelmed her.

She recalled her carefree and joyful life before her health had failed. How she had enjoyed her many friends! Her mother had often said, "Charlotte! Will you never settle down and marry and have children?"

Charlotte had just laughed away her concern. She was having too much fun to settle into the drudgery of caring for a home and family. She was the life of the party, writing humorous poetry to hear her friends laugh. They often gathered around her as she drew or painted their portraits, surrounded by happy friends.

But now...now she could no longer lift her arm to paint pictures of her friends. Now she no longer saw anything humorous in life to write about. For, at just thirty years of age, she had been confined to her bed, a helpless invalid, bitter, and seldom

visited by her friends, who now found her company depressing.

Hours now seemed as days, days as years, and her life
stretched hopelessly before her. She knew her parents were concerned about her mental state, but she had fallen into black
despair, and she saw no way to lift herself out. There was nothing
left to live for.

Charlotte heard her mother come into her room. "Charlotte,"
she said softly, "you have company."

She turned over and faced the wall. "No, Mother! No!
Please—I do not wish to see anyone!"

"Charlotte, Dr. Caesar Malan is here in your room to visit
you."

Charlotte nearly groaned out loud but somehow stifled it. She
had heard of Dr. Malan, the famous evangelist from Switzerland.
Someone had probably sent him to her to see if he could lift her
spirits. She had no desire to hear what he had to say, but she
might as well get this visit over with.

Turning over painfully, she gazed at him. And she was surprised. There was a glow in his eyes that seemed to envelop her
with love and surround her with light.

He began talking to her compassionately about his Best
Friend, Jesus Christ. He spoke of the joy that could be hers—joy
she had never known when she was well.

She longed for his message to be true, but how could it be
for her? No one knew the blackness of her heart and thoughts,
the rebellion and even hatred she held in her heart. And there
was nothing she could do to change herself. She had tried for the
sake of her exhausted parents. But she was too sunk in despair to
make herself worthy to approach God.

Then Dr. Malan spoke the words that would change her life.
"Charlotte, you must come as a sinner to the Lamb of God who
takes away the sin of the world...just as you are."

Come just as you are...

"Will Christ receive me?" Charlotte questioned, her eyes wide. "Just as I am?"

"Jesus shed His blood so He could receive you, Charlotte," Dr. Malan assured her.

Charlotte, her eyes brimming with tears, looked up to Jesus. She saw a blinding Light, His hand outstretched, His eyes literally radiating love and compassion.

"Oh, Jesus!" she cried. "Please be my Savior, my Lord. Don't ever leave my side! Bring light to my dark heart!"

She felt her heart of stone melt when He filled her being.

And her days—oh, how her days had changed from that wondrous moment!

Yes, there had been suffering as before—pain, overpowering weakness, exhaustion—but since that day, Charlotte had never again sunk into depression. Joy such as she had never known filled her to overflowing.

"His grace surrounds me," she declared to all who visited her, "and His voice continually bids me to be happy and holy in His service—just where I am."

Dave prayed silently, "God, use Charlotte's life to reach this Charlotte who needs You so desperately today."

He sat quietly looking at her, and finally, slowly, she lifted her head and looked at him. Tears were rolling down her face.

"I want Jesus too," she said simply.

Dave and Charlotte's mother knelt beside the wheelchair as Charlotte prayed quietly, "God, You know that I am another Charlotte who needs You to change me. Only You and I know how much I need You to forgive me of my sins and come into my heart and make me a new person."

Her mother was too overcome to pray aloud, so Dave prayed for Charlotte. When he again sat in a chair by her side, she said to him, "Jesus did what I asked Him to do. I feel so much lighter. I feel as if a dark presence has left me, and I'm free. But...I didn't understand something you said when you prayed for me. You asked God to use me and make me a runner for Him. How can I run? I can't even walk!"

Dave smiled. "My story about the other Charlotte is not finished. Let me tell you about the rest of her life."

Charlotte woke in the night, her eyes wide, staring.

"My Lord," she breathed.

She heard His tender, yet commanding, voice in her heart. "Charlotte, follow Me."

"Lord, I cannot follow You," she answered. "Do You not see me? Do You want an invalid in Your race? I cannot run—or even walk! I have been confined to this bed for seventeen years! Find a whole person to carry Your torch. I am worthless to You...and to everybody."

Charlotte looked upon her Savior's face. He remained at her bedside, His eyes looking deeply into her soul. Finally she lifted her trembling hand as far as her strength would allow. He gently placed the torch in her hand, and her fingers closed around it.

She no longer saw Him, but she felt His presence still with her. The soft glow of the torch now lit her room.

How can I be expected to run? she wondered. She did not even have enough strength to lift the torch. But she would hold it faithfully in this room, in this bed.

She knew there would be no sleep for her tonight. Excitement surged through her. Who would have thought the Lord would call her to the race? Would He now lift her from her bed as He had with so many in the days He walked the earth with His disciples? For how else could she run?

She looked at her hand clutching the torch. She would learn later that its glow fell on all who entered her room.

Now she could only wonder, *How could an invalid run for the Lord?*

And then it had happened. In the early morning hours, Charlotte reached for her paper and pen. Perhaps if she wrote of her salvation, her words would reach out and help someone. She began to write...

Just as I am, without one plea
But that Thy blood was shed for me,
And that Thou bidd'st me come to Thee,
O Lamb of God, I come! I come!

She thought about her pride, her bitterness, and her rebellion. She remembered how she had cried out to God for cleansing.

Just as I am, and waiting not
To rid my soul of one dark blot,
To Thee whose blood can cleanse each spot,
O Lamb of God, I come! I come!

She recalled the restlessness of her heart, the fears, the rebellion. And she remembered coming to Christ—just as she was.

Just as I am, tho tossed about
With many a conflict, many a doubt,
Fightings and fears within, without,
O Lamb of God, I come! I come!

Charlotte thought of the joy that had replaced her depression, the peace that had replaced her restlessness, the faith that had replaced her fear, and the contentment that had replaced her bitterness. Christ had received her—just as she was!

Just as I am, Thou wilt receive,
Wilt welcome, pardon, cleanse, relieve;
Because Thy promise I believe,
O Lamb of God, I come! I come!

Her hand was weak from writing, but her heart rejoiced.

"Lord," she breathed, "use me, just as I am, to bring light to this dark world."

Singers began to sing the prayer penned by Charlotte.

"Just As I Am" echoed throughout the world, calling the weary, the oppressed, the brokenhearted to Christ.

Thousands of letters from many nations poured into the home where Charlotte lay. They were written by people who had come to Christ through her invitation.

And although Charlotte lived fifty-two years of her life in her bed, embers from her torch have continued to call the heavy laden from all over the world to the Savior for over one hundred and fifty years.

Chapter Seventy-Three

DAVE

~Present Day~

The darkness is past, and the true light now shineth.

—1 John 2:8

A s Dave left Charlotte's home, he ran with a smile lighting his face. Just before he turned the corner, he stopped and looked back at the house. He knew it would never again be the same, for Jesus was now inside, lighting it with His glorious presence.

I will bring Ruth to meet Charlotte, he thought.

Thoughts of Ruth were never far from his mind—her gentle ways, her kind words, the love that shone through her soft, brown eyes.

He picked up the telephone and called to tell her all about Charlotte.

They talked for over an hour before he remembered why he had called.

Chapter Seventy-Four

DAVE

~Present Day~

O God, thou art my God; early will I seek thee: my soul thirsteth for thee, my flesh longeth for thee in a dry and thirsty land, where no water is; to see thy power and thy glory, so as I have seen thee in the sanctuary.

—Psalm 63:1–2

D ave ran into a nearly empty church on a Sunday evening. It was almost as dark inside as it was outside. The singing was spiritless. The pastor asked for testimonies. Two or three people related experiences that had happened several years earlier. By the looks of the rolled eyes and bored expressions, Dave guessed the listeners had heard the same words time and time again. Teens snickered during the service and passed notes. Dave tried to glean something from the sermon but found it difficult. The pastor seemed as bored with his subject as his listeners.

Dave's thoughts wandered, but then he picked up a couple of words.

"...and we're still waiting."

Dave had missed the first part of the sentence. This church was waiting for something, but he wasn't sure what.

He listened closely for a few minutes and realized the church was waiting for a revival. They had been waiting for several years. Dave guessed that, unless their attitudes changed, they would be waiting for several more.

Revival was surely desperately needed.

Dave had a feeling that if Charles Finney were here speaking, he might just tell these people about the starving farmer who watched the seasons come and go from the rocking chair on his porch while wondering why there was no crop to harvest.

His thoughts drifted to the impassioned runner, set aflame by God. What Christian didn't long for a revival such as the one that followed wherever Charles Finney went? Oh, he had his share of critics. Some still accuse him of merely stirring up emotional fervor wherever he went.

"His results were not lasting," they object piously.

Dave smiled and thought, *Tell that to the people in Rochester, New York.*

Dave had just read, in two separate studies, one in 1940 and one finished in 1992, that Rochester was designated the kindest city in America. The citizens had a simple explanation. In 1830, a striking torchbearer had run into their city. He preached daily for six months to Rochester's doctors, lawyers, businessmen, judges, bankers, and workers. Then he sent them running with their torches to the destitute, the sick, the hungry, the captive. The entire city blazed with light. And over one hundred and seventy years later, Rochester is still considered the kindest city in America.

He wondered how this church would react if Charles were to run into this service. Dave could almost see his glowing eyes boring into hardened hearts and his long finger pointing straight at his horrified listeners...

Chapter Seventy-Five

CHARLES FINNEY

~1792–1875~

Who maketh his angels spirits, and his ministers a flame of fire.

—Hebrews 1:7

And, behold, a certain lawyer stood up, and tempted [Jesus], saying, Master, what shall I do to inherit eternal life?

—Luke 10:25

It was another time—the early 1800s—and another place—Adams, New York. And this time, the "certain" lawyer was young Charles Finney. But the age-old tormenting question was the same.

"Master," he cried, "what shall I do to inherit eternal life?"

The question drove him into the woods near his home, and as he made his way into the forest, he vowed, "I will give my heart to God, or I never will come out of here." Charles fell to his knees. Making a log his altar, he prayed fervently, wrestling with God. The minutes stretched into hours. But this young lawyer, who made his profession with convincing words, could not reach the throne of heaven. He was distracted by the sounds of the forest. Each time he heard a rustle of leaves, he jumped up guiltily, fearing that someone walking near him would see him on his knees praying.

He grew increasingly frustrated with himself and this whole business of praying—and with God! He was making an attempt to pray—why did God seem so far away?

He heard another fluttering of leaves, and he quickly looked toward the sound. He finally realized his problem was pride. Why, he was so proud, he was afraid that someone would catch him on his knees—before the Creator of the universe! Why shouldn't he, a mere man, be kneeling before his God?

He began to weep and confessed his pride. Hours later, he left the woods. For the first time in his life, he had peace of mind and heart.

He was alone in his office later that same day when he felt the presence of Jesus Christ enter the room. The room seemed somehow more defined as Christ stood before him. Charles Finney was immediately reduced from a brilliant young lawyer to a sinner in need of a Savior, a child in need of a Father. He fell on his face before his Lord, bathing Christ's feet with his tears.

"Waves of liquid love flowed through my body," he later wrote of his awe-inspiring experience, "cleansing me, baptizing me, filling me!"

Charles ran from his office, gripping the torch that would light his world. The world stared at this new runner. His brows were shaggy, his nose beak-like, his mouth expressive—but it was his eyes that kept men from dropping their gaze. They seemed to literally glow and penetrate hearts with their radiant light.

The next morning began as other mornings. Charles was at work in the law office when a client came in to inquire about his case.

Charles looked at the man and saw not a client who would bring him gain, but a soul who needed a Savior. He realized he would never again be content practicing law.

"Go to another lawyer," was the strange advice this lawyer had for his client. "I will no longer be pursuing a career in law. I am going to become a preacher of the gospel." Closing his books, Charles Finney walked out of his former life.

He knew what his decision would cost. He was leaving behind his pursuit of all the world had to offer him. He fully understood that by running with Christ, he would acquire his enemies. Yet he knew the message that was already burning in him would never be quenched in a law office.

Preparation for running this race differed from preparing for a career in law. His life's work would now be to present the case for Jesus Christ. His congregation would be the jury, and he would bring them to the point of decision. He prepared for the work by fasting and praying, seeking strength from God. Then he began to run.

He ran into churches and into meeting halls. His message was strange, offensive, and unpopular—especially among preachers. They watched in mounting horror as their congregations, along with the unchurched masses, thronged to hear what he had to say. Their voices of opposition grew louder as his crowds grew larger. "There is too much human emotion in your meetings," they accused.

Charles shook his head in amazement at the popular belief that no one should be emotional concerning the state of his soul.

Charles was resting in his home one evening, the open fire warming his tired body. A visitor knocked at his door, and Charles wearily let him in.

"How can you say I can repent and turn to God?" the man asked. "I have no feeling or emotion whatsoever regarding the condition of my soul."

Charles walked over to the fire and picked up a red-hot poker. Turning toward his visitor, he threatened to strike him with it.

His visitor recoiled in terror.

Charles returned the poker to the fire and turned toward his cowering visitor, his eyes penetrating to the man's very heart.

"Sir, you are demonstrating feeling and emotion when you are threatened with a mere poker from my fire. You should demonstrate some feeling about the salvation of your eternal soul that is destined for the raging fires of hell."

His accusers raved on. "He permits women to pray in mixed public meetings!"

Charles continued to allow women to join his prayer meetings and mingle their voices with the men's in prayer. He welcomed the prayers of women and encouraged them to obtain a good education so they could teach their children.

Then Charles incurred further wrath from his enemies by moving a bench to the front of the churches and halls where he preached. "These are our anxious benches," he explained. "I will call those who want to seek salvation through Christ forward to these benches."

"Anxious benches! What will Finney think of next?" the preachers grumbled.

Charles ignored their complaints. And night after night, the benches were filled with people repenting of their sins and receiving Jesus Christ as their Savior.

Church meetings were never held on any days but Sundays... that is, until Charles Finney came to town.

"We will hold services Monday, Tuesday, Wednesday, Thursday, Friday, Saturday—and Sunday," he announced.

The religious leaders who objected to change met together to complain about this strange runner.

"He is holding meetings every day of the week! We all know that church services should be held only on Sundays!"

When these same leaders heard him address God in prayer, they were amazed.

"Have you heard Finney pray? He talks to God in everyday language! He isn't showing reverence by talking to God in such a manner!"

There were always a few in every church who were horrified when some of the city's poor and lowly people came and heard Charles preach that the invitation to receive Christ included them. They were even more dismayed when he insisted they be allowed not only to enter the church, but also to get saved, join the church, and then sit wherever they chose to sit!

"What about our pew rent? He thunders against our churches for charging rent to sit in the pews! He is against our charging high rates to sit in the best pews! Why, we could have the poor sitting in the front of our churches! And without our income from pew rent, how will our church expenses be met? He insists on free seating for anyone who wants to enter the church!"

Charles rebuked them for their conceit and ran on, preaching the message of the gospel to all who would listen.

Men came to his meetings, vowing to kill him. For light from his torch was beginning to shine into homes and into churches where men preferred darkness.

Skeptics went to his meetings to denounce him. Many of them were converted. Others left in disgust, desperate to stop him but not knowing quite how.

Charles ran through villages, towns, and cities. Stores closed so people from all walks of life could attend the controversial meetings.

Professors in the theological seminary in Auburn, New York, wrote to ministers in areas where Charles was scheduled to arrive, warning them to oppose his wretched ministry.

Spies were sent out to find something in his life that could be reported to damage his influence among the people. Charles knew why they had come, but his weapon against them was unwavering love. They cowered as the light from his torch exposed their motives. Many found themselves eagerly sitting on the anxious benches that they had criticized. They returned to those who had sent them with a glowing report of their salvation.

The lawyer who had been training Charles before he entered the race scoffed at both the race and the runner. It was incomprehensible to him that this brilliant young man had abandoned a law career to enter this despicable race. He continuously met friends and acquaintances who had heard Charles preach and were now witnessing to him of their conversion. The prominent lawyer finally decided to make peace with God himself.

"But I will not find God in the woods where Finney found Him!" he declared vehemently. "I will get my torch lit properly, in a church or in my own parlor!"

God would teach him that He did not light men's torches on men's terms. It was not until he walked to those same woods that he was gloriously saved.

Charles announced prayer meetings beginning at daybreak. When attendance at these prayer meetings began to dwindle, he ran to the houses of Christians.

"Wake up! Wake up! Don't you know it's time to pray?" he called loudly, beating on their doors and windows. People jumped guiltily from their beds to make their way sleepily to church to join Finney in prayer.

He ran to a cotton factory at New York Mills. When he got within eight or ten feet of a young woman trying to mend a broken thread, she sank to the floor, bursting into tears. Work stopped in the room as other workers stared at her. Then they too began to weep, until nearly all in the large room were in tears, confessing their sins before God. Conviction of sin spread throughout the mill. The factory owner called his superintendent over to him.

"Stop the mill," he instructed. "Let the people attend to religion; for it is more important that our souls should be saved than that this factory run!"

The workers were called to the mule room, where Charles spoke to them. When he left the cotton mill, the entire factory was ablaze with light.

Charles ran into Rome, New York, and preached on Sunday in a church there. Many people gathered on Monday in a home to listen to him again. Charles began to speak, but there was so much conviction of sins that he simply prayed quietly to his heavenly Father. As he conversed with God, people felt the presence of God fill the room. They began to sob and to sigh. Charles dismissed the service, and they left, weeping, to return to their homes.

Early Tuesday morning, he was called to visit homes all over Rome. The pastor joined him as he went from home to home, leaving them ablaze for God. In the afternoon, families came from every direction of town to gather in a large room. The meeting lasted until night as people crowded in to hear the gospel.

A prayer meeting was held each morning. In the afternoon, he met with people who wanted to be saved. Every evening he preached. And after just twenty days, more than five hundred people had found Christ.

Charles ran to Philadelphia, preaching to the lumbermen who had brought their logs down the Delaware River to sell. Many were converted. As they passed by the shanties of other lumbermen on their way back home, they stopped to tell them of their salvation. Soon over five thousand people in an eighty-mile radius, who had attended no church or revival meeting, and who had heard no preacher, found Christ after simply hearing the joyful witness of these faithful lumbermen.

Charles ran on to Reading, Pennsylvania, passing a merchant whose main business was making whiskey. He had just built a large distillery with all the latest improvements, and it was one of the most modern distilleries of the day. Then he met Jesus Christ, and when Charles left Reading, the merchant was tearing down his distillery, explaining to all who passed, "I will neither work it, nor sell it to be worked!"

Every morning, Charles was up long before daylight, praying. He fasted frequently. He warred against the powers of darkness in prayer. And he saw over one hundred thousand sinners converted in 1830 alone.

He ran into sin-blackened cities, and when he left, each city was blazing with light, its ballrooms and theaters and bars turned into revival centers. The area where Charles ran became known for years afterward as the "Burned-over District."

He ran to London in 1849, where between fifteen hundred and two thousand men, women, and children were saved each evening he was there.

Now there were torches lit all over America and England. The runners, like Charles, were praying and fasting. Between 1858 and 1859, over one million Americans were saved as a direct result of these united prayers.

Only once did Charles' hand falter during his race. Lydia, who had prayed for his conversion, who had become his companion and running partner for twenty-three years, the mother of his three daughters and two sons, his beloved, crossed her finish line triumphantly. Sorrow nearly overwhelmed Charles, leaving him powerless to run, his mind reeling with his loss. He fell on his face before God, and God gently touched His fallen runner. He filled him with love and comfort and renewed him with strength and vigor. Lifting him to his feet, God placed the torch back in his hand.

Charles ran his race well, leaving a glow of light in his wake. At eighty-three years of age, he still stood as erect as a young man, his mind alert, his torch held high and steady.

Two weeks before completing his eighty-third year, he crossed his finish line victoriously.

Charles left behind him not only millions of converts, but also principles that future runners who desire revival in their ministries can follow.

Some of those looking at his life believed that the revivals that accompanied his meetings were miracles sent from God. But

Charles emphatically stated, "A revival is not a miracle! A miracle is an event that does not happen through the established order of the natural world. A miracle is a divine intervention of nature by God.

"When a farmer sows his seed and a crop springs up, we do not consider this a divine miracle," Charles went on. "The growth of the crop is in the natural order of the world that God created.

"A farmer must labor in order to reap a harvest! It is up to him to plow the field, plant the seed, and even bring in the harvest! God will not do the work the farmer must do! A crop cannot be produced without the blessing of God upon it. But God has not chosen to produce a crop in an empty field while the farmer sits idly on his porch!

"Can you imagine the farmers in our land being told that God will give them a crop only when it pleases Him, and that for them to plow and plant and labor as if they expected to raise a crop is very wrong?

"The world is our field. Our seed is the Word of God. Preaching is the sowing of the seed. The results are the springing up and growth of the crop.

"Yes, we need God's blessing, just as the farmer needs plenty of sunshine and rain! That is God's part! But no farmer will reap a harvest without laboring!"

Charles' eyes bored into the hearts of his accusers, exposing their jealousy of the harvests he was reaping.

"You tell me that I am taking the work of revival out of the hands of God and that I am interfering with His sovereignty and going on in my own strength to produce a revival! And now, suppose the farmers would believe such a doctrine. Why, they would starve this world to death!

"The same lack of results will follow from the church's being persuaded that promoting revival and presenting the gospel to the lost is not the responsibility of Christians.

"Because of these teachings, generation after generation of souls have gone down to hell, while the church has been dreaming, waiting for God to save sinners without us doing our part of plowing and planting and reaping!

"This lie has been the devil's most successful means of destroying souls."

His accusers turned away, unable to ensnare or to stop this runner with their arguments against his work.

Charles turned to those who were willing to learn from him and pass the torch to future generations.

"There are principles you must follow to promote a revival," he instructed them.

(It would do us well to listen in.)

1. You must preach messages against sin! It is sin that must be confessed and forsaken!

2. You must teach Christians to obey God! Just as in the case of a converted sinner, the first step for the backslidden Christian is a deep repentance, a breaking down of the heart, a getting down into the dust before God, with deep humility. After one truly repents, his life will be one of daily obedience to God.

3. The church must see the lost state of sinners and their eternal fate. The hearts of many Christians are as hard as marble. The love of God must soften their hearts, so they will begin to labor zealously to bring others to Him. They must be grieved that others do not love God, and they must want everyone to love Him as they do. And they must determine to witness to their neighbors, friends, and families. They must be filled with a tender and burning love for lost souls. They must have a longing desire for the salvation of the whole world. They must be in agony for individuals whom they want to see saved—their friends, relations, enemies. They must not only urge them to give their hearts to God, but they must also intercede for their salvation in prayer.

4. The power and lust of the world must be broken in the lives of the Christians. You must teach them to set their affection on heaven, and not on the charm of this world.

5. When Christians get themselves right with God, sinners will be saved. Harlots, drunkards, infidels, and all sorts of abandoned characters will be converted. The church must welcome them and love them.

Charles paused and looked around at his listeners, shaking his head. "It is no good to preach to people whose hearts are hard and waste and in a fallow state. The farmer might just as well sow his grain on the rock! Seed sowed on rocks will bring forth no fruit!

"You, as well as your listeners, must begin a self-examination of your heart, your life, your actions, your true character. Write down your sins. They were committed one by one—repent of them one by one! Go over them as carefully as a merchant goes over his books. Do not be in a hurry!"

He then gave them a list of headings to write their sins under.

Ingratitude
How often have you received blessings from God and never thanked Him for them?

Lack of Love toward God
God is a jealous God! He wants your unwavering affection and love! How often have you offended Him?

Unbelief
How many times have you charged God with lying by your unbelief of His express promises?

Neglect of the Bible
Neglect of Prayer
Lack of Love for the Souls of Men
Do you have compassion? Do you care that their souls are destined for hell? Are you praying for their salvation?

Neglect of Family Duties

How have you lived before your family? Do they see you praying fervently? Are you a spiritual example for them?

Neglect of Watchfulness over Your Own Life

Have you neglected to watch your conduct and have you sinned before the world, the church, and God?

Neglect to Watch over Your Brethren

Do you bear their burdens? Are you even acquainted with them? Are you meeting their physical and spiritual needs, or just pretending to love them?

Neglect of Self-Denial

Are you willing to deny yourself of comfort and convenience for the Lord? Do you willingly suffer reproach for Christ? Do you deny yourself luxuries to save a world from hell? Do you give out of your abundance—or do you deny yourself and sacrifice willingly for Christ?

Worldly-Mindedness

Do you look at all your possessions as God's—not yours? Do you seek wealth out of lust or ambition?

Pride

Are you more concerned with decorating yourself for church than with preparing your mind for worshiping God? Are you more concerned with how you appear outwardly before men than how your soul appears in the sight of God? Do you seek to divide the worship of the church—to draw attention to yourself and your appearance, rather than to God?

Envy

Are you pained to hear some people praised? Is it more agreeable to you to dwell upon their faults than upon their virtues; upon their failures rather than their successes?

Censoriousness
Do you have a bitter spirit, speaking of Christians without love?

Slander
Do you speak behind people's backs of their faults? Slander can be telling lies or the truth with the design to injure another.

Levity
Have you been reverent in the presence of God?

Lying
Lying is designed deception—making an impression contrary to the truth by your words, looks, or actions.

Cheating
Have you dealt with others in the same way you would have them deal with you?

Hypocrisy
Have you confessed sins you had no intention of forsaking?

Robbing God
Have you misspent your time, squandering the hours God gave you to serve Him? Have you squandered money on your lusts?

Bad Temper
Hindering Others from Being Useful
Have you weakened the influence of others by insinuations against them? Do you hinder the labor of others by destroying people's confidence in them?

"Write down each heading, listing your sins beneath each one. Go over this list four times! Drive the plow through! God does not break up the fallow ground! He told us to!

"Make restitution to those you have wronged! Then, and only then, the soil will bear fruit a hundredfold!"

And so Charles finished his race, leaving behind him not only people, homes, churches, and even taverns and ballrooms ablaze with light, but also a path for other runners to follow that would bring the light of revival to a complacent people, a back-slidden church, a proud society, a sin-laden nation, and a world staggering in darkness.

Chapter Seventy-Six

DAVE

~Present Day~

We are orphans and fatherless.

—Lamentations 5:3

D ave knelt before the wide-eyed girl. "What is your name?" he asked gently.

The small girl shrank back from him, her terror-filled eyes darting quickly to those of the older girl by her side.

"Her name is Jenny."

Dave looked up at the speaker. It was hard to tell how old she was, but he guessed she was no more than ten. Her eyes were already weary of life, and there was a hopelessness about her that wrenched Dave's heart.

He had glanced their way when he passed by them. They were sitting on the city bench looking lost and abandoned. And then, the words spoken by his Master nearly two-thousand years earlier were repeated in his heart.

I was an hungered, and ye gave me no meat: I was thirsty, and ye gave me no drink: I was a stranger, and ye took me not in: naked, and ye clothed me not. (Matthew 25:42–43)

He had retraced his steps and now stood looking at the older of the two children.

"And your name?" he asked softly.

She looked away, as if ashamed to identify herself.

Dave barely heard her mumble, "Beth."

"Well, Beth and little Jenny, will you two wait right here for a few minutes? I don't like to eat alone! I'll just run back to the store down the street and get some food, and we'll have a picnic together."

Jenny's face lit with eager anticipation, but Beth just shrugged.

"I'll be right back," Dave said, as he turned toward the store.

"My Lord," he prayed, brushing the tears from his face. "These children are hungry and dirty and have lost all hope. Where are Your people?"

He stopped, staring at the huge church he was passing. He looked up at the cross atop its spire, its brilliant stained-glass windows, its massive structure.

Then he turned and looked again at the two children sitting alone on the bench. They were less than a block from this church that claimed Jesus as its Lord. Seeing Jenny watching him eagerly, he continued toward the store.

He shopped more carefully than usual, choosing foods that would provide nutrition for several days. Then he hurried back to the girls.

Opening the plastic tablecloth he had bought, he spread it on the ground beside the bench. Jenny jumped down to help him, her eyes on the sacks anchoring it to the ground. He noticed out of the corner of his eye that Beth was watching him, but when he smiled at her, her eyes darted quickly away.

He opened three bottles of fruit juice, peeled back the flaps on the small milk cartons, and polished the apples with a napkin before setting one at each place setting.

He removed the wrapping from the paper plates with jolly clown faces staring up at him. "Happy Birthday" was written across the top. He doubted if either of the girls had a birthday today, but the plates were on sale, and he knew Jenny at least would like them.

Jenny, however, didn't give them more than a quick glance. Her eyes stayed on the bag of food.

Dave felt tears filling his eyes. Why would a child care about a clown when her stomach churned painfully for food?

Quickly he removed bread, cheese, and meat.

"Jenny. Beth. Before we eat, I am going to thank my Father for you and for this food. Sometimes when I talk to Him, I close my eyes. You may join me if you would like to."

Four eyes stared at him intently as he shut his.

"Father," Dave prayed simply. "Thanks so much for my two new friends. I didn't want to eat all alone today. And we all thank You for this food we're going to eat together. Most of all, we thank You for Jesus, your wonderful Son. Amen."

The girls were already eating when he opened his eyes. He nibbled on his apple, studying them openly for the first time. Their attention was solely on their meal, and he knew that both had forgotten he was there. They didn't even notice that he ate only part of an apple. He had just eaten his dinner moments before finding them.

It was hard to keep his eyes off little Jenny. What would this child look like if she was fed and bathed and dressed properly? Her eyes looked hollow in her thin face. Ill-fitting, dirty clothes hung on her body. He wondered how the ugly bruises on her arms had come to be there. Her hair was dull, lifeless, dirty, and uncombed.

He waited until their frantic eating slowed. Then he said quietly to Beth, "Beth, where is your home?"

For the first time her frightened eyes looked straight into his. Then she answered so quietly that he strained to hear her mumbled words.

"We don't have a home now."

"And where is your mother?"

362

She looked down then, and he leaned forward to hear her answer.

"She's looking for work."

Dave hesitated and decided against asking about a Dad. "Where are you staying at night?"

Fear covered the child's face. Jenny filled the silence. "Wherever we can, mister. Last night our mother didn't come for us, so we slept right there," she said, pointing to the ground under a tree.

"Do you stay here until your mother comes?" Dave asked Beth.

Again it was Jenny who answered.

"If people don't tell us we have to leave, we stay where we are. But if they make us leave, we come right back when they go away, so our mother will know where to find us."

He started putting away the leftover food and tried to act casual as he asked, "How long have you been waiting for your mom?"

Jenny looked up at Beth, who mumbled, "Three days."

Dave wrapped the food that remained on his plate in napkins and placed it in a sack. Then he stood up. He could feel the eyes of both girls watching him.

"I have to go now, Beth and Jenny. You have made my dinner a happy one. Now I want you to take these sacks of food. I am a runner and can't be carrying bags of groceries with me."

As he spoke, he set the sack of leftovers and the sack he hadn't opened on the bench. As he turned to leave, he looked into Jenny's eyes and then Beth's.

"Jenny and Beth, I just want to tell you one thing before I leave. There is someone who loves you both very, very much. His name is Jesus. He is the one who told me that it would be good to stop and have dinner with you. I'm so glad He did, because this is one of the most enjoyable dinners I have had in a long time."

Dave ran out of words. How could these two sisters, huddled on a bench, sleeping alone on the ground, their thin bodies craving food, their eyes straining for the sight of their mother, comprehend the love of Jesus?

"My Lord," Dave cried silently as he turned away, "where are Your people who will show these children Your love?"

His steps did not pause as he turned to walk up the granite steps of the church. He did not hesitate as he walked into the ornate, silent cathedral and followed the signs to the office.

A young man greeted him.

"Please, sir," Dave said. "I must see the pastor of this church."

"What is this concerning?" the young man asked.

Dave's eyes softened.

"Two beautiful children who live near this church. Their names are Beth and Jenny."

"Wait here," the man answered and then disappeared.

Dave stood waiting, wondering what kind of man he would be meeting. Just seconds later, he grinned. Standing before him was a large, middle-aged man with warm eyes and a ready smile. Dave knew instantly that this was a man he could open his heart to.

Dave was still grinning when he emerged from a side door, the big man next to him. Together they walked down the block toward the bench. But Dave's grin faded quickly when he saw the bench was empty. He hurried toward the spot. Then he motioned to the man to follow him. The plastic tablecloth was spread under the tree as a bed for the two children, who lay asleep, their arms entwined around the sacks that were placed between them.

The big man stood silently, tears flowing unheeded down his cheeks.

He motioned Dave to the bench, and they sat quietly for a few moments.

Then the man broke the silence.

"I will send someone to get them tonight."

Dave shook his head.

"I doubt that either of them will leave willingly. They're waiting for their mother."

"Then I will send someone to stay with them."

364

The man sighed heavily.

"Dave, what can we do? I want to be like the Samaritan whom Jesus commended, but there are so many needs in this city. Where do we start?"

Dave smiled.

"Sir, you could start with Jenny and Beth."

Both men turned toward the two children.

"How long will you be here, Dave?"

"I was leaving when I saw the children."

"Will you stay and speak to as many board members as I can gather together this evening?"

"I will."

Dave looked at the men gathered before him. He didn't want to prejudge, but they certainly did not look like men who would concern themselves with the plight of two ragged children.

With a prayer for wisdom, he told them about Jenny and Beth.

During a slight pause, one man spoke.

"I believe you plan to ask us to involve ourselves with these two children and probably other children in similar circumstances as well. Don't you realize there are multitudes of these homeless people? Aren't there shelters for them? Do you know anything about their mother? Statistics say she is undoubtedly a drug addict, or a drunkard, and probably selling her body to support her habit. I believe you should know, before you continue, that my personal opinion is that these children should be referred to the appropriate government agencies..."

"Marvin," the booming voice of the pastor interrupted. "Please allow Dave to finish. Then we will discuss our views in this matter."

Dave noticed the flush that heated Marvin's face. He recovered his poise quickly, but not before Dave saw the look of hostility in Marvin's glance toward the pastor. Dave knew then that Marvin would be against whatever the pastor wanted to do.

"Sirs," he said, looking directly at Marvin. "We are all aware that homeless people may be found on many of our nation's streets. If the government agencies were successful at caring for them, I would not have brought this matter to your attention. And Jenny and Beth would not be sleeping less than a block from this church on a plastic tablecloth."

Then he addressed Marvin.

"You, sir, asked what we could do. We could be obedient to our Lord's command to simply feed the hungry, give shelter to the stranger, and clothe the naked."

"It all sounds great," Marvin replied, barely controlling the anger in his voice, "but regardless of appearances, we are not a wealthy church!"

A smile lit Dave's face as he looked at the men seated before him.

"My friends, God does not need a wealthy church to meet the needs of the poor. For you see, he is a wealthy God!

"Please give me just a few minutes of your time. I want to tell you about one man who, by faith, tapped into our God's vast storehouse of endless supplies."

Chapter Seventy-Seven

GEORGE MUELLER

~1805–1898~

And the stranger, and the fatherless, and the widow, which are within thy gates, shall come, and shall eat and be satisfied; that the LORD thy God may bless thee in all the work of thine hand which thou doest.

—Deuteronomy 14:29

The girl was small for her age. Her ragged dress hung loosely on her emaciated little body. It had been days since she had eaten more than a few scraps of food at a time. And she had often fought off dogs and other children to get those! She couldn't remember what it felt like to be without gnawing hunger pains.

Food had often been scarce even when her mother was alive. But there had always been something to partially fill her. Since her mother's death, there had been nothing except what she found thrown away by others. How long had she made her home wherever she happened to wander? Sometimes she had slept under a bench, once or twice in an abandoned building.

She clutched a crumpled paper in her hand as she walked down an unfamiliar street, staring at the numbers on the houses.

Smoothing the paper, she stared again at the words. The message was strange—and probably too good to be true.

It offered a home to girls between the ages of seven and twelve. It said there would be no charge. And it said only orphans would be welcome.

She wasn't sure of her age. Was it eight—or had she turned nine? Her mother would have remembered.

Brushing the tears quickly from her eyes, she knew she was certain about one fact. She was an orphan! There was no one in the world who cared whether she lived or died.

She stared at the house she had nearly passed. The numbers matched. But it was huge! She looked up...one, two, three stories high! *And* the house was beautiful! Dare she knock? What would she find inside—kindness or terror?

She went slowly to its massive door and, standing on her tiptoes, pulled back the knocker. She gripped it tightly for a moment, and then fearfully let it fall.

George jumped to his feet. Someone was knocking! Could it be his first orphan? He had just asked God last evening to send him some orphans!

He chuckled as he nearly ran to the door.

Wasn't that just like God?

Six thousand orphans were living in degradation, vice, and poverty in Bristol's prisons and streets. Somehow their needs had become his. Their hunger had prevented him from enjoying a good meal. Knowing they had no bed hindered him from getting a good night's sleep. Finally, in desperation, he had prayed for a house for thirty children. He had decided to bring in girls between the ages of seven and twelve.

The place had been ready for its orphans for a few days now. He had given out fliers advertising his home all over Bristol—but where were the orphans?

Then he had heard the voice of God speak to his heart. "George, you forgot to pray for the orphans!"

He laughed. He had prayed in the funds to rent this house for a year. He had prayed in good Christian helpers. He had prayed in food. He had prayed in clothing for the girls! Now God expected him to pray in the orphans!

So...last night he had prayed that God would send him the orphans!

He opened the door and looked down at the little ragged girl standing before him, naked fear in her eyes.

A brilliant smile lit his face.

He was so glad she was in rags! She would love the beautiful clothes he had waiting for her upstairs!

And how she needed to eat! Wait until she saw the feast he had prepared for his first guest!

She hesitantly and fearfully handed the smiling man the paper. Could it really mean what it said? Would this beautiful house become her home? Would this kind looking gentleman become her father?

George stepped back, motioning her to enter with a wide sweep of his hand. At the same time he called out behind him, "Come quickly, everyone! Our first little girl is here!"

The girl gazed wide-eyed as the foyer filled with smiling people. They looked at her with love shining through their eyes. They all seemed to be talking at once. She simply stared.

She was the first. The home was soon filled to capacity with thirty chattering, happy girls. George, thirty years old, happily married, and the father of one daughter, was now the busy dad to thirty more girls!

He rose early each morning to pray for their daily needs.

He prayed for spoons, plates, cups, dresses, shoes, bonnets, petticoats, wool, calico, pillowcases, blankets, coal, rent money, apples, bacon, sugar, milk, combs, helpers—and whatever else was needed at the moment. Always the answers came.

There was the gift of money from one poor woman. George knew she herself was nearly destitute. So, taking her gift in his hand, he went to her home to return it.

"I know you yourself have needs and debts," he began.

"But I received a small inheritance from my father!" she interrupted. "And it was enough to pay all my debts and give some to my mother. The rest I gave to you for your orphans!"

"What will you live on?" George asked.

"My heavenly Father will care for me," was her firm answer. "The Lord Jesus has given His last drop of blood for me, and should I not give all the money I have?"

Many days George found money outside his door, placed anonymously in a pan or in a sack.

But his joy in seeing the answers to his daily prayers was clouded by a burden.

For the word about the home had spread. Almost daily now, orphans of every description found their way to his home—little boys, little girls, some bringing with them their tiny little brothers and sisters. George had to turn them away, for his home was filled to capacity.

He went again to his knees. "Father, I need another home for more children," he prayed simply.

In less than a year, thirty-one-year-old George Mueller became the father to sixty orphans.

Still the orphans arrived. And what should he do with the children who had no place to go when they turned thirteen?

Another home was purchased. This one would house forty boys, aged seven and older.

George was thirty-two now. He spent much time on his knees, praying in food, clothing, and shelter for eighty-one children and nine full-time staff members.

In his spare time, he taught three hundred fifty children in day school, three hundred twenty children in Sunday school, and pastored a church!

Some days the responsibility of it all nearly overwhelmed him. These children were looking to him for all their needs! He had no money! Would God continue to provide?

Then one day he read Psalm 68:5 and found the promise that planted unshakable faith in his heart.

A father of the fatherless...is God in his holy habitation.

God—the Father of the fatherless!

If God described Himself as a Father of the fatherless, why, George would never have to worry or be concerned about his orphans again!

For these were not his orphans! They were God's!

And he was not their father! God was!

And fathers, George realized, a smile lighting his face, were obligated to care for their children!

Grabbing a pen and paper, George wrote,

This shall be my argument before Him in the orphans' hour of need. He is their Father, and therefore has pledged Himself to provide for them and to care for them. I have only to remind Him of the need of these poor children in order to have it supplied. This word, "a Father of the fatherless" contains enough encouragement to cast thousands of orphans, with all their needs, upon the loving heart of God!

He continued in prayer for the daily needs of his children, but he never again worried that God would not bring the needed supplies.

A friend once asked him, "George, what would you do if there was no food for the children at mealtime?"

George didn't even hesitate. He had learned the answer to that question long ago!

He replied confidently, "Such a thing is impossible, as long as the Lord gives us grace to trust in Him, for whoever believes in God will not be ashamed! But if we ever forsake the Lord and trust in an arm of flesh or regard iniquity in our hearts—then we may pray and utter many words before Him, but He will not hear us!"

When small items were brought in, George took time to thank his heavenly Father for sending them. He thanked God for every gift, whatever its size or value.

During one six-month period, money and supplies arrived with only minutes to spare before the children sat down to eat.

The cook shook her head wearily, but George, perfectly calm, remarked, "It is worth being poor and greatly tried in faith. For we have every day precious proofs of the loving interest that our kind Father takes in everything that concerns us!"

He now was feeding over one hundred children a day, support-ing two Sunday schools, and giving away Bibles, tracts, and books.

And he couldn't neglect the adults! They had needs too! Four evenings a week, he taught three hundred fifty illiterate adults how to read and write. He prayed in the money for their books and writing materials, so all could freely attend his two adult schools at no charge. At the end of each class, George read the Bible to his students.

George also supported six day schools.

And could he forget the missionaries who had forsaken their countries and homes for Christ? He supported missionaries in Jamaica, Australia, Canada, the East Indies, and China!

And still the orphans came.

At age forty-one, George purchased seven acres and built a home for three hundred children and thirty staff and teach-ers.

At age fifty, George built another house for four hundred girls. When he was fifty-four, he purchased eleven and a half acres and built yet another home to house four hundred fifty more children!

God, truly the Father to the fatherless, sent in daily supplies for 1,150 orphans and their huge staff.

George Mueller, realizing he had tapped into the treasure-house of heaven itself, could not stop praying and providing as long as there was one child in Bristol, England, who had no parents, no home, no food, no bed.

He built two more large homes for eight hundred fifty more children and prayed in the money to purchase eighteen more acres.

He now was responsible for the daily needs of two thousand children and two hundred staff members.

He would never forget the morning they all gathered for breakfast—at an empty table. There was no food in the homes. There was no money to purchase food. George had vowed never to ask man for help. His needs would be made known to God and God alone.

As over two thousand people sat down to eat, George was not prostrate in his prayer closet, weeping before God for food.

Instead, he stood confidently to give thanks to his faithful Father for His daily provision.

"Dear Father," he prayed simply, "we thank You for what You are going to give us to eat."

A knock was heard. The village baker, lying awake with thoughts of George's orphans, had finally dressed and hurried to his bakery at 2:00 a.m., and was now delivering fresh bread for the breakfast of over two thousand people.

And another knock! This time the milkman stood at the door, explaining that his cart had broken down right outside the orphanage. Could he be allowed to empty his cart of milk inside so that he could repair his wagon?

At ninety-one years of age, George Mueller said to a visiting pastor, Charles R. Parsons, "For nearly seventy years, every need in connection with this work has been supplied. The orphans from the first until now have numbered 9,500, but they have never wanted a meal. Hundreds of times we have begun the day without a penny, but our heavenly Father has sent supplies the moment they were actually required. There never was a time when we had no wholesome meal.

"During all these years, I have trusted in the living God alone.

"In answer to prayer, $7,500,000 have been sent to me. We have needed as much as $200,000 in one year, and it has all come when needed. No man can ever say I asked him for a penny.

"We have no committees, no collectors, no endowment. All has come in answer to believing prayer.

"God has many ways of moving the hearts of men all over the world to help us.

"There is no limit to what God is able to do! Praise Him for everything! I have praised Him many times when He has sent me ten cents, and I have praised Him when He has sent me sixty thousand dollars!"

Pastor Parsons asked him, "Did you ever have a reserve fund?"

George looked at his visitor with amazement.

"To do so would be an act of the greatest folly!" he replied emphatically. "How could I pray if I had reserves? God would say, 'Bring out those reserves, George!'

"Oh no, I never thought of such a thing! Our reserve fund is in heaven! I have trusted God for small amounts, and I have trusted him for thousands. I never trusted in vain. Psalm 34:8 says, 'Blessed is the man who trusts in Him.'"

Pastor Parsons hardly dared to ask him the next question. But he had only one hour with this man, and he just had to know his answer.

"You have never thought of saving for yourself?"

George Mueller had been sitting calmly, leaning slightly forward.

But now he jerked erect, and, for what seemed like several moments, searched his interviewer's face, his eyes penetrating to his very soul. He was clearly roused! His eyes flashed fire!

374

Finally he drew from his pocket an old-fashioned purse with rings in the middle separating the coins.

He laid it in the hands of Pastor Parsons and answered quietly, but firmly, "All I am possessed of is in this purse—every penny! Save for myself? Never! When money is sent to me for my own use, I pass it on to God! I do not regard such gifts as belonging to me! They belong to Him, whose I am and whom I serve.

"Save for myself?

"I dare not save! It would dishonor my loving, gracious, all-bountiful Father!"

Pastor Parsons looked at this runner and thought about the works that resulted simply from faith in God's promises.

His faith provided a home for over nine thousand children, supported nearly two hundred missionaries, educated nine thousand scholars in one hundred schools, and prayed in and gave out four million tracts and tens of thousands of Bibles!

Between the ages of seventy and eighty-seven, this man, still pulsing with vigor and energy, had traveled over two hundred thousand miles to forty-two countries, preaching the gospel to over three million people!

Pastor Parsons had yet one more question.

"Do you spend much time on your knees, praying?"

George's face seemed lit from within as he answered, "Hours every day. But I live in the spirit of prayer. I pray as I walk, when I lie down, and when I rise. And the answers are always coming. Tens of thousands of times my prayers have been answered. When once I am persuaded a thing is right, I go on praying for it until the end comes. I never give up!

"In answer to my prayers, thousands of souls have been saved! I shall meet tens of thousands of them in heaven!"

He paused, and when Pastor Parsons was silent, George went on, almost to himself.

"The great point is to never give up until the answer comes. I have been praying every day for fifty-two years for two men, sons of a friend from my youth. They are not converted yet, but they will be! How can it be otherwise? There is the unchanging promise of Jehovah, and on that I rest. The great fault of the children of God is that they do not continue in prayer. They do not go on praying! They do not persevere! If they desire anything for God's glory, they should pray until they get it!

"Oh, how good, kind, gracious, and condescending is the One with whom we have to do! He has given me, unworthy as I am, immeasurably above all I have asked or thought! I am only a poor, frail, sinful man, but He has heard my prayers tens of thousands of times and used me as the means of bringing tens of thousands of souls into the way of truth in this and other lands.

"These unworthy lips have proclaimed salvation to great multitudes, and very many people have believed unto eternal life."

Pastor Parsons again hesitated, and then said softly, "I cannot help noticing the way you speak of yourself."

George Mueller answered instantly.

"There is only one thing I deserve and that is hell! I tell you, my brother, that is the only thing I deserve. By nature I am a lost man, but I am a sinner saved by the grace of God. Though by nature a sinner, I do not live in sin. I hate sin! I hate it more and more, and love holiness more and more!"

As Pastor Parsons left George Mueller, he recalled the story told of George by Charles Inglis, a well-known evangelist:

When I first came to America thirty-one years ago, I crossed the Atlantic with the captain of a steamer who was one of the most devoted men I ever knew. When we were off the banks of Newfoundland, he said to me: "Mr. Inglis, the last time I crossed here, five weeks ago, one of the most extraordinary things happened that has completely revolutionized the whole of my Christian life. Up to that time, I was one of your ordinary Christians. We had a man of God on board, George Mueller, of

Bristol. I had been on that bridge for twenty-two hours and never left it. I was startled by someone tapping me on the shoulder. It was George Mueller.

"Captain," said he, "I have come to tell you that I must be in Quebec on Saturday afternoon." This was Wednesday.

"It is impossible," I replied.

"Very well, if your ship can't take me, God will find some other means of locomotion to take me. I have never broken an engagement in fifty-seven years."

"I would willingly help you, but how can I? I am helpless," I answered.

"Let us go down to the chart room and pray," he said.

I looked at this man and I thought to myself, *What lunatic asylum could the man have come from? I never heard of such a thing.*

"Mr. Mueller," I said, "do you know how dense this fog is?"

"No," he replied, "my eye is not on the density of the fog, but on the living God, who controls every circumstance of my life."

He went down on his knees, and he prayed one of the most simple prayers. I thought to myself, *That would suit a children's class, where the children were not more than eight or nine years of age.*

The burden of his prayer was something like this: "O Lord, if it is consistent with Your will, please remove this fog in five minutes. You know the engagement You made for me in Quebec for Saturday. I believe it is Your will."

When he had finished, I was going to pray, but he put his hand on my shoulder and told me not to pray.

"First," he said, "you do not believe God will do it, and, second, I believe He already has done it. And there is no need whatever for you to pray about it."

I looked at him, and George Mueller said, "Captain, I have known my Lord for fifty-seven years, and there has never been a single day that I have failed to gain an audience with the King. Get up, Captain, and open the door, and you will find the fog is gone."

I got up, and the fog was gone. On Saturday afternoon, George Mueller was in Quebec.

Dave paused, quietly looking at each man gathered before him. Then he went on.

"George Mueller left us not only an example of living by faith, but also its definition.

"When he was asked what faith was, he answered, 'Faith is the assurance that the thing that God has said in His Word is true, and that God will act according to what He has said in His Word. This assurance, this reliance on God's Word, this confidence is faith.

"'Probabilities are not to be taken into account. Many people are willing to believe regarding those things that seem probable to them. Faith has nothing to do with probabilities. The province of faith begins where probabilities cease, and sight and sense fail.

"'Appearances are not to be taken into account. The question is whether God has spoken it in His Word.

"'Trials, obstacles, difficulties, and sometimes defeats, are the very food of faith.

"'There will always be difficulties, always trials. But God has sustained me under them and delivered me out of them, and the work has gone on.'"

Chapter Seventy-Eight

DAVE

~Present Day~

---

*But whoso hath this world's good, and seeth his brother have need,
and shutteth up his bowels of compassion from him, how
dwelleth the love of God in him?*

—1 John 3:17

D ave looked at the members of the church board. None of them returned his gaze. Two got up to refill their coffee cups. The others simply looked down.

A board member named John felt Dave's eyes upon him. Finally he looked up.

"Look, Dave. Your story is great. I'm sure it worked for George. But we're not men of great faith, as he was. We're not..."

"Wait a minute," Dave interrupted. "You don't understand! George Mueller didn't start out any different than any of you! In fact, probably none of you spent your youth as he did! He was a thief, a liar, and a drunkard!

"He wasted his time reading useless novels. He was always in debt. He was even imprisoned as a teenager for running up debts that he had no intention of paying!

"While in college, he faked a robbery by smashing his trunk and guitar case, and then claiming his room had been broken into, just to get money from sympathetic friends and professors!

"His free time was spent in taverns, where he drank ten pints of beer in one afternoon!"

All eyes were back on Dave now.

One man showed interest for the first time. "This same Mueller you were telling us about was a drunk?" he asked.

"This same George Mueller. But when he was twenty years old, he attended a home Bible study with a friend, where he received Christ as his personal Savior and Lord.

"George was a new man! He never again drank in a tavern. His lying ceased! He became a soulwinner on campus, giving gospel tracts to all he met. He visited the sick and prayed with them, held meetings in his dorm, preached in villages and towns surrounding the university, and walked fifteen miles to hear one good sermon. George met Jesus Christ, and he was a new man!

"And this Jesus, gentlemen, whom George met, is the same Jesus you profess to serve!"

Dave looked straight at John, who seemed to be the spokesman for the rest.

"You see, sir, it's not a wealthy church we need here. It's simply a man or a group of men who realize we serve a God of great provision! It's not a man with a huge bank account. It's simply a man who realizes there is an unlimited account in the treasure-house of heaven!

"George Mueller did not begin his work by caring for nine-thousand orphans. He began with one—and his faith grew as the Lord provided for her. You see, friends, a mustard seed of faith grows with the need.

"Couldn't you, as a church, begin a walk of faith by caring for just two small girls who desperately need your love? Couldn't you show them the meaning of the cross that they can see from their bench..."

"Excuse me," the pastor said, his voice, as usual, in full volume. All eyes were upon him as he left the room.

Dave had obviously failed to move these men to action. The pastor, whom he had considered his one ally, was gone. The men simply ignored him and conversed with one another. There was no use in continuing his plea.

The pastor returned after a few minutes, and John moved to adjourn the meeting until the problem of the two children could be looked into further. The motion was immediately seconded by Marvin, and the meeting was brought to an abrupt end.

The men left quickly, leaving only the pastor and Dave.

For the first time since Dave had met the pastor, there was an awkward silence between them.

Finally the man spoke. "Dave, you said what you came to say. I don't know if your story reached the hearts of these men or not. I'm sorry to say that I doubt that it did. I do know that I personally have made a decision today. I will care for Jenny and Beth and any other needy children who wander into my neighborhood—with or without the approval of my church, and with or without my position as pastor of this church."

A big hand reached out to clasp Dave's.

"I will no longer sit in the bleachers and view God's runners! I am going to join old George and run this race myself. Up until now, neither I nor the members of this church have involved ourselves enough to get our hands dirty. It's time we take a look at the real world around our fine sanctuary! Now, let's go see how those two little girls are doing."

He started out the door, but Dave stood still, his heart nearly bursting with joy.

"Well, come on, Dave," the mighty voice filled the room. "What are you waiting for?"

"Can we pray before we go?"

Kneeling in the room, Dave asked God to give the new runner love and courage and a torch that would light up his neighborhood.

The man prayed in the same way that he spoke, his voice thundering out his petitions to God.

Then they ran to the bench together.

Just before reaching the girls, Dave stopped short. A tiny, well-dressed, perfectly groomed woman sat between the two girls, an arm pulling each one close to her immaculate clothing.

A blanket covered their legs against the chill of the evening. She was quietly talking, and both girls were listening with wide eyes. Jenny gripped a cookie.

The new runner looked at Dave and laughed loudly.

"No, that's not their mother. That is my beautiful wife, Doris. I excused myself during the meeting to call her and tell her about these kids. You can continue your run now. There's no need to worry about the kids in our neighborhood. Doris would have been at this business long ago if I hadn't kept her busy with things that really don't matter much. You go on now. We'll take it from here."

The girls didn't even glance Dave's way as he left them.

But he knew there was one who did.

Looking up, he spoke to Him.

"Jesus, it's okay here. You have found a beautiful couple to work through. Jenny and Beth will understand how much You love them now."

He realized he was talking much louder than usual and chuckled as he lowered his voice to its normal volume.

His smile faded as he looked to the towns and cities beyond. "Oh, God, please touch the hearts of Your people. There will always be some who cross the street to avoid those who are hurting. But give us some more Good Samaritans like this beautiful couple I have just met!

"Lord, I guess what I am really asking is that you raise up a George Mueller in every neighborhood! How desperately our children need them!"

Chapter Seventy-Nine

DAVE

~Present Day~

For all the city of my people doth know that thou
art a virtuous woman.

—Ruth 3:11

They were back in the restaurant where they had first gotten acquainted. Ruth had been helping in the children's home again, and Dave had been speaking to a group of young people.

"I met Charlotte," she was saying. "Dave, that girl is an inspiration to me! She has such a beautiful outlook on life. I have never seen a mother and daughter have such a great relationship with one another. They begin each day with prayer and singing...have you ever heard them sing, Dave? Their voices blend perfectly." She sighed. "What I wouldn't give for a voice like Charlotte's!"

Dave flipped open his address book and pointed an address out to her.

"Ruth, are you sure you went to the right house?"

Ruth didn't bother to look at the address.

"Yes, I went to the right house! How many Charlottes in wheelchairs are there whom you won to the Lord?"

Dave closed the book and put it in his shirt pocket. "I was teasing. But the two people you just described don't sound anything like the two people I met."

He smiled. "Of course, I met them BC."

She smiled back. "Before Christ," she said softly. "What were they like then, Dave?"

He shook his head. "Let's just say that you wouldn't have left their house encouraged or inspired by the music they were making together. Did you say you'd gone to see Tom too?"

She nodded. "We went to the park where he used to live. He showed me the bench that was his bed and the table where he met you each morning. He wanted to find some boys he knew, and your Uncle Joe didn't want him to go alone."

"Oh, no! I was hoping Tom wouldn't go back to his old friends!"

"He went back, all right. We found two of them. You should have seen their faces when they saw Tom with a Bible in one hand and a torch in the other!"

"Tom?" Dave asked, pretending to be surprised. Then he grinned. "I know. I know...that was BC. How's Uncle Joe?"

Ruth shook her head. "I love your uncle, Dave. You would never know by being around them that they weren't really related. Uncle Joe was pacing the floor when we got back, but he tried to act as if he wasn't worried a bit. Tom was just as anxious to get home. I think he was afraid Uncle Joe would change his mind about letting him stay there. He told me today that he has never before had a room with a clean bed and three meals a day."

"It's seeing Christ transform people like Charlotte, Uncle Joe, and Tom that makes this run so exciting," Dave remarked. "I realize we need to run and speak the Word even in the places we see no results. But I'm glad God didn't tell me what He told Jeremiah when He called him to run. No wonder they call him the weeping prophet. What a discouraging job he had. Can you imagine responding to a call like his?"

Therefore thou shalt speak all these words unto them; but they will not hearken to thee: thou shalt also call unto them; but they will not answer thee. (Jeremiah 7:27)

"I thank God every day for the Charlottes, Joes, and Toms!"

"I do too," Ruth said thoughtfully. "I feel like Jeremiah on some days and in some places. Then I remember that we run the course God sets for us. Perhaps years down the road someone may remember our witness and turn to Christ. Others may not remember our words until the judgment day, when it's too late. I try to remember at the end of a discouraging day that I have done what God asked me to do, and I need to leave the results to Him."

She paused and then added, "I see very few results at the mission."

She noticed Dave's anxious expression and squeezed his hand, which was holding hers.

"I know you worry about me going to the mission, Dave, but I trust in the Lord's promises just like you do. You're the one who told me to memorize Psalm 91," she reminded him. "He is my refuge and fortress as well as yours!"

Dave frowned. "I guess it's easier for me to trust God to protect me than it is to trust Him to protect you. You're a brave girl."

Ruth shook her head. "I don't feel brave at all. I read about people who are brave and they put me to shame. Think of Corrie ten Boom who hid Jews during Hitler's reign and was imprisoned in Ravensbruck. She ran fearlessly even in a terror-filled German concentration camp. She ran throughout the world when she was sixty and seventy years old. Dave, Corrie landed in foreign airports, not knowing the language or any of the people. God always took care of her!"

"I still say you're a brave girl."

"Brave," she scoffed. "I don't know the first thing about being brave. Let me tell you about a woman who was, though. Her run took her straight up to the coldest, highest mountain range in the entire world. Did you know that, since 1950, people who enter Tibet have to first have their hearts and lungs tested in Beijing? The Lord sent Annie there with a weak heart! Oh, and did I mention that her guide was a murderer? Here's a girl who was truly brave..."

Chapter Eighty

ANNIE TAYLOR

~1855–Unknown Year~

He giveth power to the faint; and to them that have no might he increaseth strength.

—Isaiah 40:29

The doctor stood looking sympathetically at the frail child. "Don't bother educating her," he advised her parents. "Your daughter has valvular heart disease and will die as a child."

But the doctor could not know that God would once again choose the weak of this world to confound those who are mighty. He didn't see ahead to a thirteen-year-old girl. Annie, still frail, knelt in a small church to receive Jesus as her Savior. She chose Him that day for her dearest Friend.

He had no vision of the day that Annie, at age sixteen, would sit listening to a missionary, absorbed as he presented the urgent need for runners in distant and strange lands.

"We need men," he stated. "And they must be strong men, willing to hazard their lives for the Lord!"

Annie leaned back in her seat, sighing with disappointment, knowing she would never qualify for this great race.

She buried her heartfelt desire and chose instead to be educated in the fields of art and medicine. She completed twelve years of intensive training in Italy, Germany, and the London Hospital. But through the years, she was unable to still the voice of the Lord. Finally she knelt at His feet, her weak heart racing wildly, and accepted the torch from His hand.

It was settled. Her load was lifted. She made plans to go to Tibet.

Her announcement was met with shock and dismay. "Annie! Do you realize where you are going?"

"I do," she nodded, smiling. "I am going where God has instructed me to go."

"But Annie! Surely God wouldn't send you to Tibet! Don't you know it is the highest place in the world? Your weak heart will never stand the high altitude of Tibet!"

"I have placed the Great Physician in charge of my heart," Annie replied calmly.

The word spread and more people came with their dire predictions. "Annie, the country of Tibet has the most rugged and difficult terrain in the entire world. The only ones who dare go there are hearty mountain climbers who go to climb Mount Everest."

"And me. I too will go to Tibet." Then she laughed. "There is no need for worry. I have no intention of climbing a 29,000-foot mountain!"

Her eyes took on a faraway look. "Please don't worry. My life is in my Master's hands. Remember, we have received no orders from the Lord that are impossible to carry out, and He has told us to go into all the world!"

On September 2, 1892, Annie's long journey began.

She found a guide, and they joined a caravan of Mongols.

She wore heavy sheepskin, the wool turned toward her body to keep out the frigid winds and bitter gales that raged in the cold mountains throughout the year. Her meals often consisted of raw goat and sheep.

Annie slept wherever shelter could be found—in a cave or tent, often in a snowdrift. She cooked her meat when she was able in her only utensil, a tin basin. More than once, Annie's hand was frozen to the basin's side.

During the trip, she learned that her guide was a murderer. She caught him eyeing her constantly and realized he had marked her as his next victim.

But the God who had summoned her was running with her. She trusted Him to be her shield, buckler, and ever faithful companion.

She awoke some nights gasping for breath, her heart racing. She begged God to stop the palpitation of her weakened heart, so she could continue her course.

Annie ran a route that would make the most valiant and healthy runner tremble. She knew she was not strong, so she held on tightly to the One who was.

Most evenings, she extracted her small diary and pencil from her bundle to write her thoughts, her hand stiff from the bitter cold. One starry evening, Annie paused before writing. Her thoughts returned to her home in England, her fine clothing, her warm house, her delicious meals, her soft bed. Then Annie looked around at her frozen white world, walls of rock jutting above and beyond her.

She smiled as she wrote, "The ground is my bed, the stars my curtain, and the wind pretty bad about my head."

She glanced over at the sleeping form of her ruthless guide, then added, "It is quite safe here with Jesus!"

Annie could hardly contain her excitement as she reached her destination.

Her first stop was a Tibetan monastery. Her smile faded. Formidable statues towered above her, their jewels gleaming. Scores of worshipers lay prostrate before them. Some stood chanting before a repulsive idol, inserting pins into its robes to increase their mental powers.

The floor, ceiling, and walls were covered with paintings and hangings of mythical Buddhist figures. An eerie glow flickered, cast by thousands of butter candles. Pagodas and thrones awaited the demonic rituals of the powerful lamas. Aged women spun their prayer wheels endlessly, tonelessly chanting, chanting, awaiting an answer that would never come from gods who did not exist.

Annie shuddered as the power of evil flowed toward her, threatening to suffocate her in its grip. This was a blackness such as she had never known. The midnight hour of the caves where she had slept did not compare to the spiritual darkness of this night. She reached out frantically for the Lord, then felt His strength and power flow through her.

And Annie lifted her torch.

"Jesus has power over evil spirits!" she cried. "Jesus can set you free!"

The nuns paid her no heed. As she left, she heard their futile chant, knowing it had been prayed for over twelve hundred years. It had never availed anything, and it wouldn't ever avail anything.

O, the jewel in the lotus.

O, the jewel in the lotus.

Annie backed out of the monastery, demons keeping their distance from the light she had dared to bring into their abode.

She ran throughout the forgotten land of Tibet. She met no other runners, for there were none in that strange and dark land.

But the people...how she loved the people. Christ had died for them, and she now lived for them! They were so friendly! They wanted to know all about her. She had never met such curious people! Wherever she walked, children fought for the privilege of holding her hands.

One quarter of all the men and boys were Buddhist monks, trusting in the ceaseless journey of reincarnations to eventually bring them purity.

She told them of Jesus and His amazing love, offering them His free salvation.

Crowds thronged her as she painted the gospel message on story cards. She passed them out to three thousand people.

She gave out a thousand Tibetan and Chinese Bibles. Some copies made their way to the lamas.

Annie recorded joyfully in her diary, "I hear the lamas in all the monasteries are now reading the gospel!"

She introduced many to Jesus. One by one, they began to approach Him, their hands outstretched to receive their own torches. Pockets of light were now scattered throughout the country.

Annie ran valiantly, this girl who was pronounced ineligible for the race by all but the Lord. She ran fearlessly, carrying God's promise in her diseased heart, "Be of good courage, and I shall strengthen your heart!"

Those back home who listened with dread for news from her or about her were sent only reports of victory. They at last realized that a torch shines brightest in the blackest part of the earth, and that Christ's strength is seen most clearly in the weakest of His vessels.

Annie, rejected by the world as unfit for use, ran a path that took her uphill to a forbidding land and a forsaken people. She held gospel meetings, read the Bible, and invited people to prayer meetings. She played a tiny organ, singing the gospel message in her high and cheerful voice. She used her medical training to care for the injured and the sick, many times exhausting herself.

One of her favorite Bible verses was Psalm 2:8:

Ask of me, and I shall give thee the heathen for thine inheritance, and the uttermost parts of the earth for thy possession.

When Annie crossed her finish line, falling into the arms of her beloved Friend, she must have heard His delighted words as He welcomed her home:

"Well done, good and faithful servant. Well done, Annie!"

Chapter Eighty-One

DAVE

~Present Day~

A virtuous woman is a crown to her husband.

—Proverbs 12:4

Wasn't Annie something, Dave?"

Dave nodded. "She was one courageous lady who knew God and trusted Him for protection. You've made your point, Ruth. God takes good care of His people. I'll try not to worry about you."

He laughed. "Just as long as you don't head for Tibet!"

She didn't laugh with him. "I don't know where God will lead me, Dave. I am willing to go wherever He leads. I don't just go where I feel like going and expect Him to follow me. My heart's desire is to follow Him."

Dave nodded. "It's okay if he leads you to Tibet, Ruth. I just hope that wherever He leads us, He will lead us there together."

He leaned forward, taking both her hands in his.

"Ruth, I've fallen in love with you. I thought I was in love with someone once. But I didn't even know what love was until I met you. I can't believe there's a girl like you left in this corrupt world. I never dreamed I would meet someone like you!"

Pleasure colored Ruth's face.

"I love you too, Dave. I loved you the first time I saw you."

"The first time! You couldn't have! I was at my very worst among all those babies!"

She smiled. "It's true. I went right home that night and asked God if it would be possible for us to run together."

"I did the same thing—the first night!"

A waitress walked by to lock the door and officially close the restaurant. One glance at the lovebirds in the corner made her decide to clean the other section first. She noticed they hadn't touched their food.

"Will you be my wife, Ruth?"

She answered softly, quoting the beautiful vow of a Ruth before her:

Whither thou goest, I will go; and where thou lodgest, I will lodge: thy people shall be my people, and thy God my God: where thou diest, will I die, and there will I be buried: the LORD *do so to me, and more also, if aught but death part thee and me.* (Ruth 1:16–17)

The vows in their future wedding would never mean as much to Dave as Ruth's beautiful acceptance of his proposal.

The waitress was vacuuming the floor when Dave and Ruth finally became aware of their surroundings and hurriedly left.

Dave took her in his arms at her apartment door and kissed her. He pulled back quickly. "Ruth! Why the tears?"

She pulled him back to her. "I'm just happy, Dave. Women cry when they're happy."

"I guess I have a few things to learn," he murmured against her hair.

He was halfway home when he started running faster. He had forgotten to tell Ruth about a couple of things that had happened today. He decided to call her the minute he got home.

She laughed when she heard his voice. "I was just wishing you would call, Dave! I thought of something I hadn't told you."

"That's why *I* called! I thought of things I forgot to tell you!"

"You first."

"Uh...let's see. Can you believe it? I can't remember! It seemed important while I was running home. I feel pretty silly. You tell me what you wanted to say."

Silence.

"Ruth?"

"You're not the only one who feels silly. I forgot what was so important too. I think I just wanted to hear your voice."

She laughed. "After all, it's been twenty minutes!"

They talked for another hour or so, and Dave agreed to meet her the next evening, a quiet ending to their busy days. Dave was scheduled to speak at a church and Ruth was conducting a Bible study with a group of women in the inner city.

Ruth looked at the women sitting in front of her. Their clothes were faded and worn, but their faces were glowing with joy. Most of them were still young, but lines were already furrowing their faces. Ruth knew that, in spite of working long and hard hours, they just barely survived financially. How she loved each one of them. Studying with them was one of the high points of her week. They had asked her to be their teacher, but she always left enriched with their wisdom. They mined spiritual gems in God's Word that countless others walked right over.

Following their spirited study, discussion, testimonies, and prayer, they dismissed to chat. Ruth was preparing to leave when Betsy approached her.

"Ruth," she began in her lively voice, "God wants me to run with the torch."

Ruth glanced at the flaming torch Betsy was holding.

"Whatever are you talking about, Betsy? You've been running with the torch ever since you asked Jesus to save you!"

"I know. I guess what I meant to say is that I feel God has called me to be a missionary."

"A missionary! Are you sure?"

"Yes, I'm sure. But I have some big problems to overcome. I never was very smart in school. I had to quit and go to work when I was in tenth grade. Even if I hadn't been forced to quit, I probably would have anyway. I never really read a book until I met Jesus. Now I read the Bible all the time. That's the only book I've ever read cover to cover. As I said, I'm not too smart."

Ruth looked at the tall, strong girl before her. She was the no-nonsense type. She always came straight to the point in her conversation. Her witness was the same. Since she had met Jesus, she simply introduced everyone she met to her beloved Savior and Friend. Ruth could picture her being a very effective missionary. She had already made her own neighborhood her mission field, and several of the women in the Bible study group were brought to Christ by her.

Ruth would never forget the first time she had heard Betsy pray with a friend of hers.

"Jesus, this is Mandy. She wants to meet You like I did, and she needs You to save her like You saved me. I've told her all about You, but I would appreciate it if You would come and meet her for Yourself."

Ruth had smiled the first time she heard the prayer, but she had heard it often since.

"Jesus, this is Lynn...Jane...Belinda...Cindy...Nancy...Sandra...Shelly..."

The list of names went on and on.

Now Ruth often caught herself praying the same way.

"Come sit at the table with me, Betsy. I want to tell you about a parlor maid named Gladys. She wasn't very smart when it came to books either. But wait till you hear what God did with her."

Chapter Eighty-Two

GLADYS AYLWARD

~1902–1970~

Consider what I say; and the Lord give thee understanding in all things.
—2 Timothy 2:7

H er face paled. "But I must go to China! God has told me to go!"

The spokesman for the committee was quickly losing patience.

"Gladys," he said with finality. "You have been studying with this missionary society college for three months. More study will accomplish nothing. You simply will never be able to learn the Chinese language. Never."

He looked at the thirty-year-old woman standing before him. Whatever made her think God would want her in China? She was poor and practically illiterate. She needed to face reality and get back to her job as a parlor maid.

He saw the tears streaking down her face, but remained stern. Sending Gladys to China was out of the question.

Making her way home, Gladys vowed, "Then I will seek support elsewhere."

But the answer was always the same, spoken sometimes rudely, sometimes gently.

All who knew her breathed a sigh of relief when she found employment as a housemaid. She kept to herself, but no one complained, for she was a faithful and hard worker.

The weeks and months passed by. Each payday, Gladys counted and recounted her savings. When she at last had enough, she purchased a one-way ticket to Tientsin, China. She left Liverpool, England, on October 15, 1932, carrying a battered suitcase, filled with food and clothing. She was left almost penniless.

She was forced from the train before it reached China. Gladys gazed at her strange surroundings and listened to conversations she could not understand. Then she straightened her shoulders. God was expecting her in China. She trudged through blizzards, the bitter wind whipping through her thin coat. All around her, soldiers fought the Russo-Chinese War. She miraculously escaped their flying bullets.

The populace of Yancheng, China, gazed in wonder at this bedraggled, smiling figure entering their city.

Love shone from her eyes. She became one with them, rapidly learning to speak, read, and write Chinese fluently. They learned to love her before falling in love with her God.

She was there when the Japanese invaded China. Gathering one hundred children around her, she led them through the mountains to safety.

All around her was the tragic by-product of war: orphans...so many orphans. Her heart went out to them.

Gladys was sixty-eight when she finished her race. She left behind many converts in Yancheng, an orphanage, *and*...the bewildered missionary committee.

Chapter Eighty-Three

DAVE

~Present Day~

Thou therefore endure hardness, as a good soldier of Jesus Christ.

—2 Timothy 2:3

Betsy is so excited, Dave," Ruth told him later that evening. "She thought God only called intellectuals to the race. She didn't know what to do when God called her."

"What did she think of Gladys?"

"She decided that if God could use Gladys, He could use her."

"Did you know I almost didn't run because I felt so inadequate?" Dave said.

"You? What made you feel inferior?"

"I was afraid God would make me speak in front of people. The very thought terrifies me."

"You spoke tonight!"

Dave looked at her blankly.

"Tonight, Dave. You said you were going to speak at a church tonight."

Dave waved his hand. "Oh, that. I wasn't preaching or anything."

"What were you doing then?"

Dave thought a minute.

"Now that I think about it, I guess you could say I was preaching. I've never thought of myself as a preacher and probably never will. If the Lord had asked me to speak when I first started running, I would have run in the opposite direction. But now telling people about Jesus has become my life. I guess it doesn't make much difference whether I'm telling one, ten, or fifty. I can't think of anything I'd rather do.

"You know, Ruth, when we start this race, we have no idea what God will have us do. I don't think Bruchko ever planned to eat live grubs!"

Ruth nearly choked on her sandwich.

"Live grubs!"

"Live grubs. Haven't you heard of Bruce Olson, nicknamed Bruchko by the Motilone Indians?"

"He really ate live grubs, Dave?" Ruth asked in a low voice.

"Sure. He was served a plate full of squirming grubs."

Ruth was quiet, so Dave went on telling her about Bruce.

"God called Bruce at the young age of nineteen out of Minnesota and placed him in the Andes Mountains among the Motilone Indians. No one had ever seen a Motilone Indian before. They were known only by the trail of riddled bodies they left behind when anyone approached their village. They lived in a wild jungle area on the border between Venezuela and Columbia.

"Bruce couldn't get accepted by a mission board either. He was young, broke, and unhealthy; as a child, he couldn't even tolerate the rigors of his Boy Scout activities. He would sneak off whenever possible and read a good book. The mission board was convinced he was best suited to sit in a warm house in a civilized country.

"Instead, God sent him to crawl through a dense jungle in South America. His body was pierced by thorns and covered with red welts from the bites of strange bugs.

"One day, he woke up to the sight of naked men surrounding him. He was pierced with arrows, whipped, and shot in the thigh. He tried to stay friendly while most of his blond hair was pulled out and he was bruised, battered, and tortured.

"Incidentally, Ruth, Bruce didn't like the grubs any better than you would. He tried to eat them to prevent starvation, but the squirming worms didn't stay down."

Dave smiled at her. "Did I mention, Ruth, that each grub was about the size and shape of a hot dog?"

Ruth turned even whiter than she had previously and shuddered as she pushed her plate away.

"I hope the Lord doesn't send Betsy to the Motilones," she said weakly.

"Oh, he won't," Dave answered cheerfully. "He might send some of the Motilones here as missionaries though. The entire village of Motilones are now running with the torch throughout South America. Bruce is still there with them."

"I think Betsy could do it. But I sincerely hope the Lord never puts me to the test."

"To do what?"

"Eat grubs, Dave. The thought of it turns my stomach."

Dave sighed. He had just told her about a great torchbearer, his victorious race, and an entire village lit up as a result. And Ruth was still thinking about grubs. Women were definitely different creatures.

He had to admit, though, she wasn't the only one who hoped never to be served grubs on a platter.

Chapter Eighty-Four

DAVE

~Present Day~

Without shedding of blood is no remission.

—Hebrews 9:22

Dave found himself running through an unfamiliar town one Sunday morning. He joined a group entering a church. He craved fellowship with fellow runners, but he searched the church in vain for just one person carrying a torch.

The congregation was listless, the singing joyless, the prayers poetic words with no expectation of an answer from the throne room of God.

The Scriptures were read, but were themselves dead without the touch of the life-giving Spirit upon them. The church was without Christ, the sermon without power, the service without purpose, the congregation without light.

Dave's mind drifted to an earlier time, another service, another sermon...

Jesus reached out to light her torch.

"No, Lord! Who am I to enter your race? I am old, well beyond the age to run! I am shy—why, everyone knows how timid I am! Please, Lord, find someone else to run for You!"

The Lord gave her no answer. His hand, holding the fire meant for her torch, remained outstretched. She turned away from Him to go about her daily chores. But often, throughout the day, she stopped what she was doing to plead with Him to leave. She reminded Him of others far more capable than she to run in His race. Still He stayed, His eyes seeming to bore into her very soul. She tried in vain to ignore Him.

The hours passed slowly. He remained in her home, patiently waiting for her to come to Him.

Finally she turned and, weeping, crept to Him, kneeling at His feet.

That was the day He lit her torch.

She didn't feel very different, even though her obedience had brought her a great relief. And she still didn't know what He wanted her to do, where He wanted her to run.

So she continued to do just what she had always done, going where she had always gone. Nothing extraordinary happened.

Until that one special day.

Her church was joining others at a large religious service being held at the Golden Gate Exposition in San Francisco. With others in the city, she had anxiously waited to hear the famed speaker who had been invited to preach. But now she listened to the man with mounting horror. He chose his words craftily, eloquently attempting to destroy all faith in the cleansing power of the blood of Jesus Christ!

She looked at the faces around her. Only a few looked disturbed! Many were listening to his words raptly, smiling and nodding as he spoke! The master of deception, Satan himself, was using this man to woo God's people away from the cross!

Her heart pounded and her hands gripped her Bible as she listened.

Then she rose to her feet, unaware of the curious glances and stares of those around her. For her eyes were fixed on a blood-stained cross and a man nailed to its beams, struggling in agony just to draw His next breath. His face was bruised and swollen. Blood poured from His wounds.

She gazed upon the mockers at His feet, ridiculing, taunting, shaking their fists at God's sacrificial Lamb. Slowly those mockers merged into the one today who stood before this vast crowd of people, mocking the Lord Jesus Christ's redeeming blood.

Tears streamed down her upturned face as she lifted high her torch. Without thought or plan, she began to sing softly,

There is a fountain filled with blood
Drawn from Immanuel's veins.
And sinners plunged beneath that flood
Lose all their guilty stains.

As she began the second verse, a hundred people stood to their feet, a hundred voices blended with hers:

The dying thief rejoiced to see
That fountain in his day.
And there may I, though vile as he,
Wash all my sins away.

By the time the second stanza had been sung, a thousand faces had turned from the mocker who stood before them, his voice silenced by one aged woman carrying the torch. A thousand people, their eyes now upon the cross on Calvary's hill, lifted their voices, singing the third stanza triumphantly:

Thou dying Lamb, Thy precious blood,
Shall never lose its pow'r.
Till all the ransomed church of God
Are saved, to sin no more!

Dave didn't know the woman's name. The story had been passed down by those who had attended the exposition, and her name had been lost in its telling. He grinned as he thought how surprised she must have been when she realized that her torch had lit that entire arena with the fire of God.

He returned to the present, where the service was drawing to a close, and the people around him were restlessly preparing to leave.

"Oh, God," he breathed. "Where was Your torchbearer when this church was drawn away from Your cross? Where were Your prayer warriors? Where were Your soldiers, ready to contend for the faith? Did someone here fail to respond when You chose him or her to enter Your race?"

All that remained now was a ritual of death.

Dave slipped quietly out the door.

But even as he grieved for those who dutifully attended a darkened morgue week after week, his heart was joyously singing,

There is a fountain filled with blood...

Chapter Eighty-Five

DAVE

~Present Day~

The people that walked in darkness have seen a great light:
they that dwell in the land of the shadow of death, upon
them hath the light shined.

—Isaiah 9:2

The day didn't seem properly finished without a telephone call to Ruth. They were both enthusiastically sharing their day's events when Ruth said, "Dave! I was visiting my cousin on campus when I noticed a brilliant light. I asked who was carrying the torch, and she laughed and said, 'Oh, that's Ray. Ever since some guy named Dave visited him, all he talks about is Jesus and the Bible.'

"I went over to listen to what he was saying and, Dave, he was preaching—right outdoors! A group was gathered around listening to him. A few of them were asking their ridiculous questions and making their derogatory comments. Ray wasn't phased by anything they said. He had a quick answer for every question. He told them that before he was born again he had made the same foolish remarks. He invited anyone to talk to him anytime, day or night, about his Savior and announced a meeting he is going to hold this weekend to discuss the Bible.

"He held up his Bible and said that people had been tortured and killed to make sure we had copies to read, and we had better start reading it. Most of the crowd drifted away, but two stayed to talk to him. I overheard him tell them that he hadn't had anything to live for until he met Jesus.

"Do you know him? You aren't the Dave he was referring to... are you?"

Dave couldn't believe the news. Could it be Ray—preaching? He couldn't imagine it.

"Ruth, does this Ray have curly black hair and blue eyes, and is he about six feet tall? Does he have sort of a scowl on his face?"

She hesitated before answering. "That may be him. He has curly black hair and I think he has blue eyes. He's probably about six feet. But there definitely wasn't a scowl on his face. This guy was lit up, Dave. He was excited and happy and in love with Jesus. He said he is going to spend the rest of his life telling people about his Savior!"

Dave couldn't visualize Ray without his cynical expression. *Ray...preaching?*

That night, Dave could hardly sleep for excitement. He wondered how Phil had reacted to Ray's salvation.

Who knows what God will do with Ray? Dave thought. *Perhaps he will be another James Stewart.*

It was impossible to think about James without smiling. His race had begun on a soccer field before thousands of fans, and he had blazed a trail of light wherever he ran. He was used to being challenged by scoffing hecklers. In fact, there were times he joined the crowd and became a heckler himself...

Chapter Eighty-Six

JAMES STEWART

~1910–1975~

Go ye therefore into the highways, and as many as
ye shall find, bid to the marriage.

—Matthew 22:9

J ames awoke with a start. He hadn't heard anything, but he could feel the presence of someone in his room. Then he heard a sob.

With disgust twisting his features, he clutched his soccer ball to his chest and turned away from his mother. But even with his eyes closed and his back to her, he could not shut out the picture of her kneeling by his bed, praying silently for his soul.

Why couldn't she just leave him alone and accept him the way he was? Most mothers would be proud that their son was on his way to becoming one of Scotland's greatest soccer players!

While the country had already begun cheering, she sobbed and looked pitiful. He had always loved his mother, but a deep bitterness was swiftly replacing his love.

He patted his soccer ball tenderly. If he couldn't have both soccer and his family, he would choose soccer. He had long since decided he would live for no one and nothing else.

He had been only thirteen when he was chosen to be on Scotland's international team. Coaches and fans alike encouraged his dream of becoming the greatest center forward Europe had ever known.

Soccer...Scotland's national passion.

Hundreds of thousands stood freezing in the bitter cold all night long just to secure tickets to the big games. He would give those loyal fans something to see! His name would one day be praised, not only in Scotland, but also throughout the world.

If his mother wanted to weep about it, then let her weep.

Yes, he was obsessed with the game. How else would he get to the top? He practiced before others woke up in the morning and was still practicing long after they lay asleep. Soccer magazines littered his room. He listened to every word spoken by professionals just to glean one more tip. Then he practiced hours on end to perfect it.

He was fourteen now. Already every senior soccer club had their eyes on him. A tremendous career lay before him and everyone knew it.

"Everyone but Mother," he mumbled bitterly.

Her sobs were getting louder.

"Jim! Jim!"

He faked sleep, but she said her piece anyway.

"Jim, I offered you to God for His service before you were born!"

He snorted. Who was she to offer his life to God? He would live his life as he chose. And he chose soccer, thank you.

"Jim," she continued, as though he had spoken his scorn aloud. "It was not for soccer that God gave you to me. There is only one thing that matters. That is being 100 percent for Jesus Christ."

"That might matter to you," he wanted to shout. Instead he said to himself, "But it matters not one bit to me."

Finally she left the room.

The next night it was more of the same. Would she never leave him alone?

He got used to her presence and was able to sleep right through it until one night. The new urgency in her voice woke him up.

"It's now or never, Jim," she said firmly. "You must surrender all to the claims of Jesus Christ. Now."

Jesus Christ.

There were soccer fanatics. Jesus apparently had His share of fanatics too. Why did his own mother have to be one of them?

As if one wasn't enough in his family, his brother had joined the radicals. David, known as a walking sports encyclopedia, had always amused his friends by spouting out scores and statistics like a ticker tape. Who would ever think he would end up spouting Bible verses instead?

And his father. He sat in his chair every evening, without fail, between nine and ten o'clock, singing hymns out of Sankey's hymn book.

His family wasn't alone. Church services just weren't the same anymore. Staid sermons had become impassioned pleas. Preachers often broke down, weeping for souls. Sinners trembled with conviction, and usually there were between fifty and eighty of them receiving Christ as their Savior...and Lord.

It was the "and Lord" that bothered him.

The preachers never offered salvation to a willful rebel. They gave him just two options: all...or nothing. James realized that the all included his soccer career.

James may not have been a star on the home scene, but he was big in the soccer crowd. Every boy envied him when the director of the leading soccer club gave him a season ticket to the director's box. Sitting in that box in a stadium that accommodated over one hundred thousand people was a heady experience for a fourteen-year-old!

Back in church, James continued to resist the call of God. His awesome Presence permeated every service. Vibrant testimonies by sinners who had surrendered to Christ were followed by joyful songs of praise. James gripped his seat and refused to be budged.

And then...

He expected God to be in church, so it was a real shock to meet Him while playing a championship soccer game. Thousands of people were there. And it was on the soccer field, right in the middle of the game, that God came to James. He didn't ask for his life this time. He demanded it.

It was a bitterly cold night. Yet, while his teammates shivered, sweat poured from his face.

"Oh, Lord," James moaned. "Why here?"

His thoughts raced. *Should I walk off the field? Should I kneel and pray here?*

"God," he prayed silently. "If You will just let me finish this game, I will surrender to You the moment the referee blows his whistle."

James played the rest of the game. The second the final whistle blew, he looked up to heaven and cried, "O God, save me now for Christ's sake. O Lord Jesus, I thank You for shedding Your blood for me that I might be saved. O blessed Holy Spirit, forgive me for all the times I have stifled Your convictions!"

He ran from the stadium, through the shoving crowds, and straight to his mother. Flinging open the door, he cried, "Mother! I'm saved! I'm saved!" And James burst into tears.

His mother merely glanced his way. Quietly she said, "Yes, James, I know. God told me that you would be saved this week. I have arranged for you to give your testimony at an open-air meeting in the center of the city with other Christian young people."

James' love for soccer was replaced with a burning love for souls. He went to work delivering groceries—a position known as a "message boy" in Scotland.

He carried groceries to people's homes and knocked on their doors. Then he stammered, "Friend, I am a message boy, and you know my job is to come and bring provisions to your home.

But I am also a message boy for God, and I have come to ask you to make provision for eternity. Prepare to meet your God!"

He ran to Sunday schools to speak to children who had watched him play soccer. He went door-to-door in his neighborhood, giving out tracts. In those first few weeks, more than a thousand families invited him in to hear his testimony. He preached in the open air wherever he could find an audience. He walked the streets wearing sandwich boards over his shoulders with Scripture texts written on the front and back placards. At other times he carried a leather pouch hung on a strap and tied around his shoulder. He balanced a big heavy pole in the pouch on the upper end of which were his talk texts. They worked like window blinds. As he preached, he pulled them up or down to illustrate his sermons.

It was at his first open-air meeting that a seventeen-year-old youth strode to the front of the crowd of several hundred people. Standing before the men, he shouted, "If God could save James Stewart, he could save the devil!"

The men grinned, waiting for the preacher boy's reaction and hoping for a fight.

"He is right," James said simply. "A mighty miracle has taken place in my life, similar to the miracle John Newton experienced. Let me quote you two verses of the beautiful testimony John put to music. You know the song. It's 'Amazing Grace.'"

In evil long I took delight,
Unaw'd by shame or fear,
Till a new object struck my sight
And stopped my wild career.

I saw one hanging on a tree
In agony and blood,
Who fix'd his languid eyes on me
As near his cross I stood.

James rejoiced as God touched and saved drunkards, men without hope, young people, adults, and children.

He teamed up with Sergeant Wheeler, a famous detective who became a powerful open-air evangelist. Wheeler regarded the teeming masses of all Britain as his congregation. He was a strong man with a booming voice. He was insulted when invited to preach indoors.

"Preaching indoors is child's play, James," he would thunder. "We'll leave that for the softies!"

One of their favorite places to preach was the racetrack. During the twenty-minute interval while bets were being placed for the next race, James and Sergeant Wheeler simply set up church before stands holding ten to twenty thousand people.

One would open the service by shouting, "Well, friends, we are glad you have come! We are sorry to be late, but we will start our service now. We will begin our service this afternoon by singing 'What a Friend We Have in Jesus.'

"What, you haven't got your hymnbooks with you? That is a pity. We will excuse you this time, but don't forget to bring hymnbooks with you tomorrow. Today, we will sing a hymn everyone knows. We will begin with 'Jesus, Lover of My Soul.'

"What? Nobody singing? What's the matter with you all? Are you a bunch of backsliders? Well, we will have to sing a duet for you." And they did.

The racing fraternity regarded them as one of their own. No matter what city the race was being held in, James and the Sergeant would be there first, waiting for the crowds to come hear them preach. They knew of no better way to preach to so many thousands of people without spending money to rent halls and advertise.

James picked up the racing lingo and adapted it to his use. A tipster would move through the crowds shouting, "A dead cert! A dead cert!" Then he would sell bets for the horse certain to win.

James would go walking right behind him shouting, "A living reality! A living reality! It's a dead cert and a living reality that you are going to die! You had better get right with God here!"

Another time he followed a tipster whose cry was, "Two to one, bar one; two to one, bar one; two to one, bar one." James came right behind him yelling, "Bar none! Bar none! Whosoever will may come! If you are barred out of heaven, you bar yourself!"

When the race began with the roar, "They're off," James and the sergeant hurriedly pulled down the gospel banners and knelt and prayed quietly until the race was finished.

They endured punches in the stomach, being knocked to the ground, mocking sneers, and being pelted with overripe tomatoes, the juice oozing down and staining their faces and clothes. None of the ridicule phased either of them.

One bookmaker screamed at the sight of them, "Are you here again? Get out of my sight! The very sight of you makes me sick! Why don't you stay where you belong?"

James replied firmly, "You are going by your racing book, and we are going by our book. We have our marching orders. Our Lord Jesus said to go to all the world and preach the gospel. Isn't this part of the world? Now you just keep quiet while we preach!"

When the races were over, their gospel wagon could be found lumbering to a market square in the heart of whatever city the races were held in. They parked it carefully in their reserved spot. Then they opened up the side of their wagon and preached to one or two thousand shoppers. They did this every evening.

One evening news reached them that the bookmaker who had pleaded with them to leave the racetrack had been gloriously saved and was now a Methodist preacher in northern England!

Many Sunday evenings three to four thousand people gathered in the public park to listen to Sergeant Wheeler and James. The most renowned evangelists of the British Empire counted it a great privilege to stand on the wagon platform with the sergeant.

Crowds of hardened men brushed tears from their eyes as he spoke. At the close of each service, hundreds would kneel on the ground and receive Christ as their Savior.

James ran to Hyde Park of London, where forty or more people often stood on soapboxes, each speaking on different themes. Hecklers were always part of the crowd.

"Scottie, do you believe that the whale swallowed Jonah?"

"Sure I do!"

The heckler would turn triumphantly toward the crowd. "Ha! Did you hear him? He believes the whale swallowed Jonah." Turning back to James he laughed, "We sure don't believe it!"

James was never without a quick answer. "If you don't believe it, that's not my fault. But I'll tell you what I will do. When I get to heaven, I'll ask Jonah!"

"Ha! Suppose he's not there, Scottie boy?"

"Then you can ask him!"

The heckler would be stopped only for a moment.

"Only the fool says in his heart, 'There is no God!'" James would shout. "Do any of you who don't believe in God have more questions? Now not everyone at once! Just one fool at a time. One fool at a time, please."

Finally one would shout from the crowd.

"Where did Cain get his wife?"

"Ah! Now I know what's wrong with you. You are interested in somebody else's wife! If you are not careful, you will get into trouble! Is Cain's wife really your trouble?"

"Yes."

"She is the reason you can't come to Christ?"

"Yes."

"If I tell you who Cain's wife was, will you get converted? Will you accept Christ as your Savior? Will you step out from this crowd and ask God to save your soul?"

"Yes."

"Well then, I will tell you who Cain's wife was. She was Mrs. Cain, of course!"

The crowd kept coming, the hecklers kept heckling, and souls continued getting saved. James was sometimes still there after midnight, persuading lonely people to cast their cares and sins upon a loving Savior.

The leader of an atheistic society in London would stand on the stone wall at Tower Hill quoting famous atheists and mocking the Bible.

If the atheist reached Tower Hill before James, he would set up in James' usual place. The policeman who controlled the mobs would not let James set up. On those days, James simply switched from preaching to heckling.

"How do you know there is no God?" he would call out to the atheist. "How do you know the Bible is not true? Prove to us that death ends it all!"

One such day James turned to the crowd and shouted, "Do you see that man there?" He pointed at the atheist. "One day by the power of God, he is going to stand in that very same place preaching the gospel of the Lord Jesus Christ!"

Only a short while later, the atheist lay dying. He was terrified. Finally he begged God for mercy, and God healed both his soul and body. He returned to his spot and climbed up on his soapbox.

"Jesus saves!" he cried. The crowd stared in shock. Wasn't this new preacher the former atheist? What was he doing carrying a torch? Many turned to Christ.

When most people were home sleeping, James was carrying food and doughnuts to the derelicts who slept on the Thames Embankment or the homeless who sought shelter for the night under the railway arches. He visited one after another, offering doughnuts, friendship, and the love of his Savior.

James turned then to Eastern Europe.

The first signs of war rumbled throughout the nations. While people were fleeing their countries, James Stewart ran cheerfully from one to another. He paid no attention to uniforms or borders. He ignored laws that prohibited the preaching of the gospel.

Then, the first stages of war began to be fought. Undaunted, James ran into Prague and rented the largest music hall in the city. People filled the auditorium, and about four hundred received Christ every evening.

He ran on to Budapest.

Families were homeless and daily battling hunger. People lined the roads, searching through the littered bodies for their lost loved ones.

It was dangerous to leave one's home. Many were murdered for the clothes on their backs.

In the midst of this devastation, James ran into a church to preach. It had been partially demolished. Over two thousand Christians were gathered inside. Thousands more stood outside in the sub-zero temperatures.

Snow fell on the shivering congregation. Yet they stayed, pouring their hearts out to the Lord.

Often James preached to groups of twenty thousand at a time.

James learned the meaning of fervent prayers while with those people. He felt as if he was in the midst of a mighty sob, ascending to the heart of God. The people would pray for two or three hours. They began in unison to praise God for His goodness and glory.

"Don't ask the people to sing, James," he was advised by one preacher. "Our people are too weak from hunger. The exertion of singing will be too much. Many are in the beginning stages of starvation. It takes all their strength just to sit."

James ached with compassion as he looked over the congregation. There was no heat in the building. Actually, the building itself was a mass of solid ice. People were covered with blankets and bundled in coats and hats. The organ was frozen. The organist's hands were so stiff with cold that she could no longer play.

Ushers brought James hot bricks to stand on so he could continue to preach without his feet freezing.

But, oh, what joy! Such hunger for the Word of God!

Crowds followed him home after every service. They stood in the freezing cold at one o'clock in the morning, begging to hear more preaching.

James' interpreter talked to them until daybreak.

The following morning, the building would fill with men for their special service.

James had only one worry.

"Oh, God!" he cried, "am I doing something wrong? Why are things going so well? I am not being attacked by Satan!"

The attack came. He was arrested and accused of being a spy. The Soviets were undecided whether he was a British or Nazi spy. They knew he was one or the other. Why else would he be the most traveled foreigner in Europe?

James cheerfully turned their attempts at interrogation into gospel meetings.

Moscow was unsure what to do with him. America and Britain demanded his release.

"Do not leave! Above all, do not preach!" Soviet officials sternly commanded him.

Finally he was released. He hated to leave, but he knew he was leaving behind him a trail of torchbearers. Even in the midst of Europe's terrible tragedy, the light would not go out.

His race, begun on a soccer field, never slowed.

To his dying day, James faithfully lived his heartfelt prayer:

Let me burn out for Thee, dear Lord,
Burn and wear out for Thee;
Don't let me rust, or my life be
A failure, my God, to Thee.

Use me and all I have, dear Lord,
And get me so close to Thee
That I feel the throb
Of the great heart of God;
Until I burn out for Thee.

Chapter Eighty-Seven

DAVE AND RUTH

~Present Day~

The night is far spent, the day is at hand: let us therefore cast off the works of darkness, and let us put on the armour of light.

—Romans 13:12

The path of the just is as the shining light, that shineth more and more unto the perfect day.

—Proverbs 4:18

The sun shall be no more thy light by day; neither for brightness shall the moon give light unto thee: but the LORD shall be unto thee an everlasting light.

—Isaiah 60:19

It's getting darker, Dave."

Dave squeezed her hand. "I know, love."

"Some runners have quit the race."

"Yes. Paul told us Demas quit too. He loved the present world more than our Lord."

"How could anyone forsake the living Lord for a dying world? Dave, God has been so good to us."

"We serve a faithful and loving God, Ruth. He's been with us every step of the way."

The warmth of his smile lightened her step. "And he has given me a faithful and loving wife. How long have we been running together now?"

"Four years."

"Four years of shared memories."

"Dave, what do you think our future holds?"

"We can't be sure what the next hour holds, hon. But I do know there seems to be growing antagonism against the race. The world is growing blacker and desperately needs more light."

He looked around him as he spoke. "There are so many dark places—neighborhoods, factories, homes, schools, stores, even some churches."

He slipped his arm around her. "Ruth, we know there is only one hope for the world's future. Light will return and darkness will flee His glorious presence. Our Champion Runner has promised to come back again!"

"Oh, Dave, how I long for His coming. We run here and there, trying desperately to bring light. But there is too much darkness and too few lights. Sometimes our task seems overwhelming."

Dave pulled her closer. "Don't ever get discouraged, Ruth. Our race will soon be finished. Jesus will come back in all His splendor and beauty. Ah, what a day! The sun will have no need to shine in the presence of His brilliance."

He looked up to the heavens. "Oh, Lord! I can't wait," he cried. "Come quickly, Lord Jesus!"

Renewed vigor surged through them as they ran in silence, contemplating the triumphant celebration of victory to come. Their Lord would return! The race would be forever won!

Dave spoke quietly in the stillness of the moment. "Until that glorious day, Ruth, I have one more hope for our future."

"What is it, Dave?"

"I pray daily for more torchbearers."

THE CALL OF THE LORD

The harvest truly is plenteous, but the labourers are few; pray ye therefore the Lord of the harvest, that he will send forth labourers into his harvest.

Behold, I say unto you, Lift up your eyes, and look on the fields; for they are white already to harvest.

I must work the works of him that sent me, while it is day: the night cometh, when no man can work.

Watchman, what of the night?
Watchman, what of the night?

A TORCHBEARER'S ANSWER

Then said I, Here am I; send me.

Matthew 9:37–38
John 4:35
John 9:4
Isaiah 21:11
Isaiah 6:8

NOTES

*Exact quotations used in the text are cited first, followed by sources used for general information.

CHAPTER 13

"O Lord God Almighty": Henry C. Sheldon, *History of the Christian Church*, vol. 1, *The Early Church* (Peabody, Mass.: Hendrickson Publishers, 1988), 147.

John Fox, *Fox's Book of Martyrs* (Philadelphia, Pa.: Universal Book and Bible House, 1926), 9.

"Perpetua and Polycarp: Two Heroic Martyrs," *Christian History* 9, no. 27 (1990): 14–15.

Bruce L. Shelley, *Church History in Plain Language* (Dallas, Tex.: Word, Inc., 1982), 52.

Ruth A. Tucker, *From Jerusalem to Irian Jaya* (Grand Rapids, Mich.: Zondervan, 1983), 31–33.

CHAPTER 14

Kenneth Libbrecht, *The Snowflake Winter's Secret Beauty* (Stillwater, Minn.: Voyageur Press, 2003), 30.

CHAPTER 15

"These are the treasures": John Fox, *Fox's Book of Martyrs* (Philadelphia, Pa.: Universal Book and Bible House, 1926), 19.

"Kindle the fire!": Ibid., 20.

CHAPTER 18

The New Encyclopaedia Britannica, 15th ed., s. v. "Saint Martin of Tours."

Justo L. Gonzalez, *The Story of Christianity* (New York, N.Y.: HarperCollins Publishers), 147, 149–50.

Ruth A. Tucker, *From Jerusalem to Irian Jaya* (Grand Rapids, Mich.: Zondervan, 1983), 28.

CHAPTER 21

"Many Christians were slaughtered": Keith Yandell, "The City of God: Augustine's Timeless Classic about the Timeless City," *Christian History* 6, no. 15 (1987): 23.

"Oh, the joy of those": Ibid., 23–24.

"That bread which you keep": "Gallery of Church Fathers and Their Thoughts on Wealth," *Christian History* 6, no. 2 (1987): 35.

"To understand scriptural": Robert P. Sandin, "One of the Best Teachers of the Church: Augustine on Teachers and Teaching," *Christian History* 6, no. 15 (1987): 27.

"The essence of the church": "Fighting Isms and Schisms," *Christian History* 6, no. 15 (1987): 29.

"I bring against you": Henry C. Sheldon, *History of the Christian Church*, vol. 1, *The Early Church* (Peabody, Mass.: Hendrickson Publishers, 1988), 460–461.

"From a perverted act": Herbert Jacobsen, "True Life Confessions: The Precedent-Setting Revelation of Augustine's Restless Heart," *Christian History* 6, no. 15 (1987): 18–19.

The New Encyclopaedia Britannica, 15th ed., s. v. "Saint Augustine of Canterbury."

Randy Petersen, "Augustine's Life and Times," *Christian History* 6, no. 15 (1987): 2–36.

Henry C. Sheldon, *History of the Christian Church*, vol. 1, *The Early Church* (Peabody, Mass.: Hendrickson Publishers, 1988), 548–550.

Augustine, *The Confessions of Saint Augustine* (Westwood, N. J.: The Christian Library, 1984), 22–25.

CHAPTER 23

"I pray those who believe": William J. Federer, *America's God and Country Encyclopedia of Quotations* <http://www.worldnetdaily.com/news/printer-friendly.asp?ARTICLE_ID=26862> (18 May 2005)

The New Encyclopaedia Britannica, 15th ed., s. v. "Saint Patrick."

Henry C. Sheldon, *History of the Christian Church*, vol. 1, *The Early Church* (Peabody, Mass.: Hendrickson Publishers, 1988), 407–410.

Ruth A. Tucker, *From Jerusalem to Irian Jaya* (Grand Rapids, Mich.: Zondervan, 1983), 38–40.

CHAPTER 25

The New Encyclopaedia Britannica, 15th ed., s. v. "Iona."

Ruth A. Tucker, *From Jerusalem to Irian Jaya* (Grand Rapids, Mich.: Zondervan, 1983), 40–42.

AN INTRODUCTION TO
MENTAL
RETARDATION

AN INTRODUCTION TO MENTAL RETARDATION

ROBERT M. SMITH

The Pennsylvania State University

McGraw-Hill Book Company   *New York St. Louis
San Francisco Düsseldorf Johannesburg Kuala Lumpur
London Mexico Montreal New Dehli Panama Rio de Janeiro
Singapore Sydney Toronto*

AN INTRODUCTION TO
MENTAL
RETARDATION

Library of Congress Catalog Card Number 79-137131
07-058903-8

1 2 3 4 5 6 7 8 9 0   MAMM   7 9 8 7 6 5 4 3 2 1

This book was set in Garamond by Monotype Composition Company, Inc., and printed on permanent paper and bound by The Maple Press Company. The designer was Paula Tuerk; the drawings were done by John Cordes, J. & R. Technical Services, Inc. The editors were Nat LaMar and David Dunham. Annette Wentz supervised production.

THIS BOOK

is dedicated to:
Mr. and Mrs. Richard Harbour
of Berkshire, England
and
Dr. William R. Carriker
of Charlottesville, Virginia

CONTENTS

PREFACE

An Introduction to Mental Retardation was written for a number of people who may be interested in the mentally retarded for various reasons. It is directed to those beginning students who are interested in focusing on the mentally retarded in some form of professional endeavor, e.g., as a teacher, speech correctionist, aide, nurse, psychologist, workshop director, or therapist. This book also has pertinence to those persons who have devoted years to managing the retarded but who have not been able to keep up with the current trends, issues, and developments. For this group, it is hoped that the book will serve to stimulate further study and exploration of the professional literature. A large number of the sections have intentionally been planned and written with the parents of retarded children in mind. Every attempt has been made to keep the content nontechnical so that those parents and nonprofessionals with an interest in mental retardation can become familiar with the status of emerging concepts in this field.

An Introduction to Mental Retardation is organized into three sections. Chapter 1 serves as an overview section in which some of the broad topics concerning mental retardation are discussed, general management techniques considered, and some basic questions dealt with. The second section contains five chapters, each of which focuses on a particular developmental period in the life of a retardate. The principal characteristics of a retarded individual during each time period, the diagnoses and management techniques which the literature suggests as being of potential promise at each level, and other relevant issues are focused upon in this section. In the appendixes, several topics are discussed, and a summary statement is presented which offers a challenge to all who are concerned with the mentally retarded.

A further word is in order concerning the format and content of this book. With the exception of the appendixes, *An Introduction to Mental Retardation* was written in a question-and-answer style. Following each answer, a listing of recommended readings is presented so that the serious student will be able to

trace through the literature on each subject in greater depth. Prior to deciding on the content of each question to be considered here, a rather extensive survey was conducted to determine the kinds of questions various persons had about mental retardation. By using personal interviews, telephone surveys, and a brief questionnaire, an extensive list of questions was obtained from parents of the retarded, a randomly drawn sample of people from rural and urban communities, and from teachers of the retarded in institutions and public schools. These data were tabulated and classified, and on this basis the questions which appear in this book were chosen.

Every introductory text excludes some material and lacks the depth desired by academicians. This book is not an exception; certainly the medical and psychological dimensions of mental retardation are covered in only a cursory way, and very little is said about such topics as recreation, camping, administration of programs, professional training, and religious education. These topics were excluded because of the infrequency with which they appeared in the survey and because of a need for brevity.

A number of my colleagues were helpful in various stages of the preparation of this document. Mr. Michael Ross, Professor Gerald Robine, and Dr. Thomas Stich offered advice on a number of topics. The editors of the *American Journal of Mental Deficiency, Mental Retardation,* and *Teaching Exceptional Children* graciously consented to have certain materials reprinted from articles which appeared in the journals. The specific citation for each appears on the appropriate page of this book. Dr. Evelyn Gendel and the National Association for Retarded Children gave permission to reproduce a portion of an excellent article about sex education for retarded adolescents. Mrs. Donna Cone and Miss Karen Lewis were expeditious and thorough in processing the manuscript.

Lastly, my wife, Bette, and sons, David and Andrew, were extremely patient during the period of writing. I appreciate this attitude on their part, and I am especially delighted that they have concern for the many parents, teachers, and others who have not had the professional literature, contemporary ideas, and pertinent theories translated in a fashion which allows them to more effectively and efficiently understand and manage the mentally retarded. I hope that this has been accomplished to some extent here.

Robert M. Smith

AN INTRODUCTION TO
MENTAL
RETARDATION

1
Facts and Issues about
Mental Retardation

What is mental retardation

Many people have the false impression that mental retardation is a disease which can be spread from one person to another much like measles, mumps, or chicken pox are communicated among children. The only difference among these conditions, according to this belief, is that mental retardation consistently has more lasting, irreversible consequences than do the childhood diseases. There are other people who believe that mental retardation is the same as mental illness or insanity. Even among personnel who have had years of experience in working with the retarded, one will hear statements such as, "I feel sorry for these people who have 'gone off their rocker' and are 'nuts.'" This type of statement suggests that general confusion prevails among many people, professionals and nonprofessionals alike, about mental retardation—its nature, causes, treatment possibilities, and prognosis. Let us think about some of these areas which are so often misunderstood as a result of inaccurate information or because of the persuasive force of many old wives' tales.

First, mental retardation is not a disease. Children and adults cannot "catch it" as a result of being near someone who has been identified as being mentally retarded. This is true even with the most severely or profoundly retarded. It is not like a virus or a bacterial

condition—it is not transmitted by the wind or by touching or kissing another person.

Instead, mental retardation is a condition which results from any of a number of circumstances that have the possibility of occurring before, during, or after the birth of an infant. Mental retardation can result from a disease, infection, or virus. It is like an arm or leg that does not function properly. Either of these conditions can result from a problem with the mother or fetus during pregnancy, or they can be caused by difficulties which the infant might encounter either at birth or during any other time in his life.

Although we may not know for sure what caused the problem, we can pretty well describe a nonfunctioning arm. It has certain characteristics, some of which are identical with other disabled arms. At the same time, we could probably recognize that each injured arm differs in various subtle ways when contrasted both with normal arms and with others which are disabled. Each arm is different but yet the same in various ways. Mental retardation can be viewed similarly. Many times specialists are unable to agree on reasons for the occurrence of retardation in individual cases, although it should be recognized that more sophisticated techniques are constantly being developed so that diagnostic studies can be conducted with greater effectiveness. Indeed, there are some general characteristics of the mentally retarded; however, we should keep in mind that the condition varies in its severity, time of occurrence, and how it is manifested behaviorally among those who are retarded.

A second area of confusion for many people is in trying to relate, or separate, the concepts of mental retardation and mental illness. They are not the same. Mental retardation is a condition that is primarily characterized by subnormal functioning because an individual's basic problem is one of not being able to acquire, process, maintain, and properly use his experiences for the solution of problems. An individual may be born with disorders which restrict his ability to do these tasks efficiently and effectively, or he may have not acquired basic skills at later stages of development.

In contrast, mental illness is an emotional problem. It usually occurs after an individual has been unsuccessful in dealing with some aspect of his environment. He may not be able to work with certain other people, or he may find himself constantly in "hot water" because he cannot solve a problem of some type. Eventually he finds that he cannot deal with situations because of an inability to satisfy his own expectations or because he feels that others view him as inadequate or incompetent. This situation will often result in any of various types of unusual behavior—anger, sullenness, hostility, blaming of others, etc. It is not unusual that mental retardation and mental illness are often confused in the minds of some people, because many of the characteristics of the conditions are the same. Some retarded persons are angry, hostile, and sometimes withdrawn. Likewise, many mentally ill individuals do poorly on activities that

involve the use of intellectual skills or problem-solving techniques. Retarded persons sometimes are emotionally disturbed or mentally ill. This condition often results from the state of frustration in which they frequently find themselves; wanting to do a competent job on a certain activity in order to please themselves and others but not having all the basic skills they need in order to accomplish a task satisfactorily. This situation can be frustrating for even the most capable person; little wonder, therefore, that mentally retarded persons develop symptoms of emotional disturbance along with their intellectual subnormality. Although mental retardation and mental illness are not the same, there are numerous instances when individuals could easily be characterized as showing symptoms of either or both of these conditions.

Divergent Features   To describe in greater detail some unique characteristics of the manner in which mental retardation is expressed, direct your attention to Figure 1-1. Let us assume that we are interested in studying the characteristics of the ways mental retardation is expressed in each of these three boys. Each child has been identified as being mentally retarded and has undergone extensive testing and evaluation in many areas. Now we are ready to look at the nature of their characteristics and draw some conclusions.

First, in contrasting each boy with the other two we can see that there are certain areas in which each individual youngster is totally unlike the other two. These areas (illustrated on the diagram by letters *A, E,* and *F*) represent char-

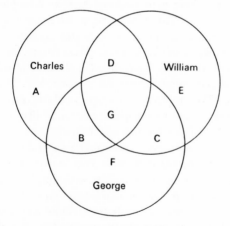

Key

A, E, and F = characteristics unique to individual children
B, C, and D = characteristics unique to two children but
              not the third
G = characteristics shared by all three children

Figure 1-1

acteristics which are peculiar to each child; William may have a significant visual problem which Charles and George do not have. Charles may have a cleft palate and a significant speech problem which are not areas of difficulty for William or George. George, on the other hand, may have no functional use of his legs. As is true with the nonretarded members of our society, the proper conclusion to be drawn from this aspect of the example is that the mentally retarded do indeed manifest any of a number of characteristics which are peculiar to individuals and which may not be shared by any other person with a similar degree of mental retardation.

A second conclusion we can reach from the diagram is that certain characteristics are shared by two of the boys and not by the third. Because we have selected three boys for study, there are only three possible ways in which individuals can be paired. George and William share certain characteristics (represented by letter C) which Charles does not seem to have. For example, they both may have great difficulty in analyzing words through a visualization or spelling approach but may have great strength in their use of a system of phonics in learning to read. This paired weakness and strength may not characterize Charles at all; in fact, we may find that he has exactly the opposite pattern of abilities and disabilities. Notice that there are two other groups of characteristics which are shared by two of the boys and not by the third. Charles and George seem to have certain similarities (represented by letter B) which are not shared by William. They may have some minimal emotional disorders which result in certain types of difficulties in getting along with authority figures or people of the opposite sex. William and Charles are also alike in ways which are foreign to George. This is represented in the diagram by letter D. In this case, as in the others, the likeness may be psychological, medical, social, physical, or educational.

Finally, there are certain characteristics which are alike for all three retarded youngsters. These areas of weakness most often represent a common denominator for many of the mentally retarded. The problems may be personal, social, intellectual, or occupational, or may pertain to other important areas of life. There are many possible reasons for this inefficiency and lack of effectiveness in dealing with problems. Some, for example, may have significant weaknesses in the whole process of taking in information from their environment. They may be unaware that a problem even exists; or they may have an eye or ear weakness, be unable to attend to aspects of their environment, or have any of several types of problems which restrict their being able to process information for future use. Others among the retarded may not be able to solve problems because of difficulties they have in storing ideas. These persons have disorders in memory functioning. Still others may have significant weaknesses in scanning their repertoire of information and selecting a response to a problem which is acceptable.

In a fundamental sense, then, the mentally retarded as a group seem to show poor general aptitude in the performance of many basic skills which most of us take for granted but which constitute vital areas for development in order that

more complex tasks can be dealt with in a satisfactory way. I am speaking of many of the skills which the nonretarded develop without intentionally offered instructional programs. Such competencies as discrimination among sounds, associating words and objects, language development, and understanding the intentions of others from their facial expressions are all illustrations of areas in which the mentally retarded often suffer from lack of skill.

Mental retardation frequently is associated with other types of problems. In fact, on an average the retarded have 2½ disabilities per individual. For example, a very large percentage of those who are intellectually retarded have significant speech and language problems which restrict them from engaging in effective communication with others. Other problems which occur with high frequency among the mentally retarded are (1) perceptual disorders, (2) motor weaknesses, (3) difficulties in attending to a task, (4) inability to transfer skills or understandings from one task to another, and (5) weaknesses in reacting to stimuli quickly.

Defining Mental Retardation From what has been said to this point, you can see how difficult it is to answer the question, "What is mental retardation?" It is not a condition that appears in the same form, to the same degree, at the same moment, because of the same circumstances, and with the same consequences for all retardates. Scientists would say that it is not a unitary entity— it varies on almost every dimension and to differing degrees. The problem of defining mental retardation is made all the more difficult because so many types of specialists are interested in medical and behavioral manifestations of mental subnormality. Obviously, each type of specialist focuses on the specific dimensions in which he is trained and interested. This has resulted in the specialists of the various disciplines defining mental retardation according to their own orientation, using language patterns and descriptions which are peculiar to their own field. For example, representatives of the medical professions focus on aspects of brain damage and malfunctions of various organic systems, psychologists emphasize maladaptive behavior in their study, sociologists talk about difficulties of the retarded within a group or in a community setting, and educators consider the manner in which the environment of a retarded individual can be modified in order to maximize possibilities for learning.

The problem of lack of agreement among the various disciplines on a general definition of mental retardation has plagued professional workers for years. The American Association on Mental Deficiency (AAMD), an interdisciplinary organization of professional workers who are concerned with the problems of mental retardation, suggested a definition which it was felt would be acceptable to the various professional groups (Heber, 1959, p. 3). This definition is as follows:

Mental retardation refers to subaverage general intellectual functioning which originates during the developmental period and is associated with impairment

in one or more of the following: (1) maturation, (2) learning, and (3) social adjustment.

To be as precise as possible, the American Association on Mental Deficiency elaborated on critical portions of the definition:

1. *Subaverage* means that a person scores in the bottom 16 percent of the population his own age on a standardized measure of general intellectual functioning.
2. *General intellectual functioning* implies that the individual has been evaluated with an instrument, or test, which is of sufficient scope to consider as many of the measurable traits of intelligence as possible or practical.
3. *Developmental period* is regarded in this definition as extending from conception to age sixteen.
4. *Maturation* refers to the rate and degree to which development of basic skills most commonly associated with infancy and early childhood occur. The focus here is on skills such as rolling over, crawling, walking, speaking, becoming toilet trained, self-feeding, and associating with peers at an acceptable level.
5. *Learning* refers to the ease with which the individual is able to gain knowledge through experience.
6. *Social adjustment* refers to how well the individual is able to exercise independence in self-maintenance within the community and in employment. During the early school years the term refers to how well the individual is able to relate to fellow students, parents, other authority figures, and younger children.

As you might expect, the definition did not gain unanimous approval by all groups in the professional community. There appeared spirited discussion in the literature both on the semantic characteristics of the definition (Kidd, 1964) and on its conceptual validity (Blatt, 1961; Garfield and Wittson, 1960; Cantor, 1960). To a significant degree, however, the AAMD definition has weathered the storm of controversy and continues to be used by most professional groups.

Recommended Readings

Blatt, B.: "Toward a More Acceptable Terminology in Mental Retardation," *Training School Bulletin,* vol. 58, 1961, pp. 47–51.

Cantor, G. M.: "A Critique of Garfield and Wittson's Reaction to the Revised Manual on Terminology and Classification," *American Journal of Mental Deficiency,* vol. 64, 1960, pp. 954–956.

Garfield, S. L., and C. Wittson: "Some Reactions to the Revised Manual on Terminology and Classification in Mental Retardation," *American Journal of Mental Deficiency,* vol. 64, 1960, pp. 951–953.

Heber, R.: "A Manual on Terminology and Classification in Mental Retardation," *Monograph Supplement to the American Journal of Mental Deficiency*, 1959, 2d ed. 1961.

Kidd, J. W.: "Toward a More Precise Definition of Mental Retardation," *Mental Retardation*, vol. 2, 1964, pp. 209–212.

Robinson, H. R., and N. M. Robinson: *The Mentally Retarded Child: A Psychological Approach*, McGraw-Hill Book Company, New York, 1964, pp. 27–40.

How frequently does mental retardation occur?

Scientists cannot give an absolute answer to this question because:

1. Groups within society do not use the same criteria for deciding who is mentally retarded.
2. Levels of social understanding and tolerance for the intellectually subnormal differ greatly among various segments of our culture. Many mentally retarded children are not viewed as handicapped by citizens in certain very rural sections of our country, but they would have great difficulty managing their affairs in a less accepting, highly urban environment.
3. The past research which has attempted to determine the prevalence of mental retardation has differed widely in the techniques that were used to identify the mentally retarded and has been restricted in scope as a result of the heavy financial necessities involved in survey research of this type.
4. It is virtually impossible to identify and evaluate groups of subjects of adequate size and at all ages in order to judge the manner in which mental retardation is distributed within various social groups.

Even with these very substantial hindrances there has been amazing consistency in the results of the most prominent studies which have sought to investigate the frequency of mental retardation (Jastak, MacPhee, Whiteman, 1963; Young, 1969; Scheerenberger, 1964). It is generally considered that roughly 2.5 to 3.5 percent of our population is mentally retarded. With a population slightly in excess of 200 million persons, we would predict that approximately 6 million individuals are intellectually retarded to some degree. A number of scientists believe that this figure is much too low (Dingman and Tarjan, 1960).

Many European scientists have systematically studied the prevalence of mental retardation in their countries. Farber (1968) reported a summary of the findings of many of the important investigations. In spite of the fact that the data collection procedures differed widely and the criteria were not identical, he reports a great deal of consistency in the results of the various studies. Moreover, findings from certain European countries are generally similar to the estimates of prevalence of intellectual subnormality in the United States.

Mental retardation is not equally distributed among all segments of our society (Lapouse and Weitzner, 1970). There are certain groups that seem to have a higher incidence of mental subnormality than other groups. Some of the reasons for this unbalanced distribution are unclear; however, a number of scientists believe the design and procedural weaknesses in various studies have contributed to this situation.

Studies on the prevalence of mental retardation are fairly consistent in their reports that fluctuations exist in the incidence of diagnosed mental retardation at different chronological ages. Relatively more children are identified as being mentally retarded during the middle elementary and junior high school years than during early childhood, late adolescence, or adulthood. Some investigators feel that these differences are the results of the relatively more comprehensive and accurate reporting procedures that usually prevail in the schools during the elementary and junior high school years. Much more testing typically goes on during this time than at any other period in a child's school career. Moreover, the trend in teacher-training institutions is to emphasize the need for procedures whereby elementary and junior high school teachers can become particularly sensitive to important diagnostic signs in children who are suspected of having school-related difficulties. This has probably resulted in more complete and systematized reporting of suspected cases of mental retardation. The same situation does not prevail during the earlier school years and at the postschool period.

As is true with most other types of handicapping conditions, the studies on the prevalence of mental retardation report that more males than females are retarded. No one seems to be certain why this occurs. It may be that our society is more aware of inadequacies among males than among females because of differences in role expectations. There is some belief that hereditary factors may be a principal influence in the differential prevalence of mental retardation between males and females.

Another characteristic of the prevalence of mental retardation is that it is not represented with uniformity throughout the various social strata. For example, there is little, if any, difference in incidence of severe retardation among the various socioeconomic levels. Nearly the same proportion of middle-socioeconomic parents as lower-socioeconomic parents have children with moderate, severe, and profound degrees of retardation. In contrast, however, we find a disproportionately higher number of mildly retarded individuals among rural families and in seriously deprived sections of the urban community. No doubt this finding is more directly related to the relative paucity of opportunities available to these families for stimulating the intellectual potential of their youngsters than it is attributable to genetic disorders.

One final point on the issue of prevalence of mental retardation: Farber (1968) suggests that we should not lose sight of the facts that the retarded tend to have a lower fertility rate and a higher death rate than nonretarded popula-

tions. He believes that these two factors may be related to the manner in which mental retardation is distributed in the society.

Recommended Readings

Dingman, H. F., and G. Tarjan: "Mental Retardation and the Normal Curve," *American Journal of Mental Deficiency,* vol. 64, 1960, pp. 991–994.

Farber, B.: *Mental Retardation: Its Social Context and Social Consequences,* Houghton Mifflin Company, Boston, 1968, pp. 43–118.

Gruenberg, E. M.: "Epidemiology," in H. A. Stevens and R. Heber (eds), *Mental Retardation,* The University of Chicago Press, Chicago, 1964, pp. 259–306.

Jastak, J. F., H. M. MacPhee, and M. Whiteman: *Mental Retardation, Its Nature and Incidence: A Population Survey of the State of Delaware,* University of Delaware Press, Newark, 1963.

Kirk, S. A., and B. B. Weiner: "The Onondaga Census—Fact or Artifact," *Exceptional Children,* vol. 25, 1959, pp. 226–228, 230–231.

Lapouse, R., and M. Weitzner: "Epidemiology," in J. Wortis (ed.), *Mental Retardation: An Annual Review,* Grune & Stratton, Inc., New York, 1970, pp. 197–223.

Masland, R. L., S. B. Sarason, and T. Gladwin: *Mental Subnormality: Biological, Psychological, and Cultural Factors,* Basic Books, Inc., Publishers, New York, 1958, pp. 145–391.

Mullen, F. A., and M. M. Nee: "Distribution of Mental Retardation in an Urban School Population," *American Journal of Mental Deficiency,* vol. 56, 1952, pp. 777–790.

Robinson, H. B., and N. M. Robinson: *The Mentally Retarded Child: A Psychological Approach,* McGraw-Hill Book Company, New York, 1964, pp. 40–48.

Scheerenberger, R. C.: "Mental Retardation: Definition, Classification, and Prevalence," *Mental Retardation Abstracts,* National Institutes of Health, Washington, vol. 1, 1964, pp. 432–440.

Wallin, J. E. W.: "Prevalence of Mental Retardates," *School and Society,* vol. 86, 1958, pp. 55–56.

Young, W. M.: "Poverty, Intelligence, and Life in the Inner City," *Mental Retardation,* vol. 7, 1969, pp. 24–29.

When does mental retardation occur in a person's development and what are some of the causes?

It has already been stated that mental retardation is expressed in numerous ways and that the frequency and conditions under which it occurs differ among vari-

ous populations within our society. We might, therefore, expect to find that the causes of mental retardation and the periods during which it occurs are equally scattered and varied in their characteristics. Stevens (1964) has stated that over 100 causes for mental retardation have been identified and that a definite diagnosis of cause, or etiology, is impossible in approximately 85 percent of the cases. Do not lose sight of the fact that one reason for this level of impreciseness in diagnosis is that many of the causal agents combine in various undefined ways to deleteriously influence the intellectual development of the growing organism. Another significant reason for difficulty in establishing a definite diagnosis is the lack of instrumentation and methodology allowing for a precise judgment about cause, even in this age of phenomenal growth in knowledge and diagnostic sophistication on the causes of complex conditions such as mental retardation.

It seems convenient to broadly classify the known causes of mental retardation according to the three major landmark time periods in a human's life. First, the period extending from conception, or perhaps even before, until the process of labor begins is called the _prenatal period._ The problems that can occur during this time and subsequently result in the birth of a retarded child are of two general varieties—genetic and/or environmental. One can be retarded as a result of unfortunate hereditary transmission of either a recessive or dominant trait. In addition, mental retardation can be caused by an intrauterine environment which is sufficiently abnormal, for any of a number of possible reasons, to damage the growth and development of the fetus. More specific information will be offered on this etiological time period in Chapter 2.

Next, conditions can prevail which will cause mental retardation during the crucial periods during labor and at birth. This period, which is called the _perinatal period,_ can be very traumatic for the infant. Not only does the fetus experience all the "tugging and pulling" associated with labor and the process of birth, but it is also important to realize that the change for the infant from a relatively warm to a cooler environment can be the source of difficulties immediately after birth. During the perinatal period various types and degrees of brain injury, which often are associated with mental retardation as well as with other conditions, can result from an overly difficult period of labor.

Finally, disorders that occur after birth and throughout an individual's life (called the _postnatal period),_ and which are often associated with intellectual subnormality, are of two major types.

1. An individual can contract any of several diseases which when associated with an unusually high "long-term" fever can cause brain damage. Trauma to the brain from lack of oxygen, a blow to the head, or a serious accident which results in neurological complications will often precipitate intellectual deterioration. Tumors, poisoning, or other atypical insults to the brain will often damage tissue and intellectual functioning. Thus there are many physical problems that an individual may experience during his lifetime which could drastically curtail

and injure intellectual development and result in a significant degree of mental retardation.

2. Mental retardation can occur during the years following birth and extending into the elementary school grades, as a result of a youngster's not having an opportunity to experience an adequate level of varied stimulation during important developmental stages. Children in this group are frequently found in poor rural areas or in pockets of serious poverty in the slums of our cities. They so often are members of large families, live in deteriorated houses, have parents who are sickly and frequently out of work, have serious nutritional problems resulting from not having enough to eat and not receiving an adequate diet, and have continual problems with diseases, infections, and other varieties of illness. These and other conditions contribute to a poor prognosis for the intellectual development of a young child who is born into this type of environment. This composite of circumstances will result in the young child's not being reared with minimal psychological requirements, i.e., not being touched enough, talked to, stimulated; not being allowed to experience colors, sounds, and other events; and being functionally isolated from those environmental components which facilitate normal intellectual development. This syndrome of conditions, which will be reviewed in greater depth in later sections of this book, is high among the principal causes of mental retardation. The children who are mentally retarded as a result of this type of postnatal deprivation constitute the largest single group among the mentally retarded. These youngsters probably represent nearly 85 percent of the mentally retarded in our society, but they do not usually have identifiable brain damage. Scientists from various disciplines are presently devoting their professional lives to a search for those aspects of a young child's environment which, when present or absent during important developmental stages, are possible contributors to the unusually high incidence of intellectual subnormality within various segments of our population.

Recommended Readings

Anderson, V. E.: "Genetics in Mental Retardation," in H. A. Stevens and R. Heber (eds.), *Mental Retardation,* The University of Chicago Press, Chicago, 1964, pp. 348–394.

Masland, R. L., S. B. Sarason and T. Gladwin: *Mental Subnormality: Biological, Psychological, and Cultural Factors,* Basic Books, Inc., Publishers, New York, 1958, pp. 34–135.

McCandless, B. R.: "Relation of Environmental Factors to Intellectual Functioning," in H. A. Stevens and R. Heber (eds.), *Mental Retardation,* The University of Chicago Press, Chicago, 1964, pp. 175–213.

Stevens, H. A.: "Overview," in H. A. Stevens and R. Heber (eds.), *Mental Retardation,* The University of Chicago Press, Chicago, 1964, p. 2.

In what ways are the mentally retarded classified?

For many years professional groups have undertaken the task of trying to meaningfully group or classify the various types of mental retardation and its associated disorders. These groups have felt that such an activity was necessary because of the wide, and often unpredictable, differences that exist among the mentally retarded in terms of (1) causes, (2) social distribution, (3) degree of intellectual severity, (4) extent of associated disorders, (5) future expectations, (6) behavioral characteristics, (7) impact on the family, and (8) appropriateness of programs for help and treatment. Because these factors fluctuate from one retarded person to another and often will change in character from one time to another for the same person, people who are concerned about the problems of mental retardation have felt the need to bring order and stability out of a confusing situation.

You probably already have some ideas on why systems of classification or categorization are felt necessary. Any list could include some of the following reasons: (1) classification of a condition such as mental retardation helps to identify common characteristics among subgroups within the larger population of retardates; (2) a system of categories helps to establish the extent to which interrelationships exist among the factors being classified and among other characteristics (for example, if a group of retarded persons were classified according to what we believed caused their condition, we might find, after testing, that more of the individuals who were retarded because of prenatal difficulties had speech and hearing disorders than those retarded persons whose problems resulted from disorders at or following birth); (3) classification offers a means for designing and studying the effects of various programs of treatment for various subgroups of retardates; (4) category systems are frequently used to help justify programs of intervention after the programs have been decided upon or are started; and (5) categories are often used to establish a range of conditions or behaviors within which laws are written to protect, treat, excuse, or exclude various segments within a much larger population. (For example, in certain states particular categories of mentally retarded children are excluded from school programs operated under the auspices of the Department of Public Instruction and are referred to educational programs within institutions.)

Problems in Classifying   Although classification systems have merit in that they help to better systematize a set of conditions and provide focus for research and treatment activities, there are several areas of potential difficulty that result from dependence on such schemes. First, one is never able to gain total agreement between people on which dimension or factors should be classified. For instance, there are some workers in the field of mental retardation who believe that the most meaningful way to classify the retarded is according to cause or etiology. Others who believe that we should group according to degree of mental

subnormality use as their primary criterion scores on intelligence tests. Still other professional workers claim that a combination of symptoms and realistic future expectations, or prognosis, leads to the design of a more meaningful program of care and treatment. Thus, there are often differences of opinion on which variables to use in a classification system.

A second problem of classification systems is that of deciding on upper and lower boundaries within subgroups. For example, people disagree on whether the lower boundary for a category called *trainable* should be at IQ point 20, 25, 30, or 35. If you use one system, the lower boundary point is at 35; if you use another classification system, the lower boundary level is at IQ 20. The implications of these differences of opinion are important to think about because they could affect the nature of incidence figures for subgroups (more would be reported if IQ 20 was used as a lower boundary than if one used IQ 35), the nature of training programs (children who score around IQ 20 may require a different program orientation than those who score at 35 or above), the character of public assistance programs (certain states or countries may provide public education programs only for children at or above IQ 35, whereas other programs may offer special education for youngsters as low as IQ 20), and the character of the training program for professional and nonprofessional workers. To be sure, boundaries are arbitrary, and there always will be imperfect agreement among people who have some concern about the development and use of systems for classifying heterogeneous conditions such as mental retardation.

A third potential difficulty with classification systems is in the assignment of individuals to a category. Since assignment must be based on information about a person, it is imperative that the information be correct and reflect a usual or typical characterization of the individual under consideration. His future destiny is so often determined by a diagnosis that if an analysis is wrong, overstated, or missed, the individual could be assigned to the wrong category. Unfortunately, such situations will result in the individual's receiving treatment in a program of management which, although it may be deemed satisfactory for the residents within the category, may be totally improper for him as a result of an inaccurate or distorted interpretation of a situation. Institutions in every state contain residents who are thought to require institutionalization because they have been misdiagnosed and erroneously classified. Many such placements are virtually irreversible and frequently result in the individual's becoming fastened to an improper program for a lifetime. Thus, the danger of misdiagnosis will seriously weaken the many advantages of using systems of classification.

Most category schemes use some measure of intelligence as the principal criterion for establishing subgroups—although the IQ range of the subgroups is often very different among systems. Figure 1-2 illustrates some differences of criteria which exist among several of the more popular classification schemes. Notice how the subgroups of the various authors use different terminology and

Proponent(s)	Intelligence quotients 95 90 85 80 75 70 65 60 55 50 45 40 35 30 25 20 15 10 5 0					
Sarason and Gladwin (1958)		Mental retardation			Mental deficiency	
Gardner and Nisonger (1962)		Border- line Retard- ed	Mildly retarded	Moderately retarded	Severely retarded	
Wechsler (1958)		Border - line retarded	Moron	Imbecile	Idiot	
American Associa- tion on Mental Deficiency (1959, 1961a, 1961b)		Borderline retarded (Level 1)	Mildly mentally retarded (Level 2)	Moderately mentally retarded (Level 3)	Severely mentally retarded (Level 4)	Profoundly mentally retarded (Level 5)
American Educators		Dull normal	Educable mentally retarded or handicapped		Trainable mentally retarded or handicapped	Custodial, dependent, or low grade

Adapted from: Gelof, M.: "Comparison of Systems of Classification Relating Degree of Retardation to Measured Intelligence," *American Journal of Mental Deficiency,* vol. 68, 1963, pp. 297-317.

Figure 1-2 *Examples of mental retardation classifications in which intelligence is the principal criterion.*

labels to describe their groups. You can sense, then, how paradoxical these systems can become—they are helpful yet confusing in many ways.

Medical Criteria   With support by the American Association on Mental Deficiency, Heber (1959, 1961a, 1961b) suggested a medical classification system for mental retardation which is based on etiological variables. Briefly this classification is as follows:

1.   Mental retardation caused by diseases and conditions due to infection, e.g., German measles
2.   Mental retardation resulting from diseases and conditions due to intoxication, e.g., carbon monoxide or lead poisoning
3.   Mental retardation caused by trauma or physical agents, e.g., birth injury due to difficult labor or brain damage resulting from postnatal accidents
4.   Mental retardation resulting from diseases or conditions due to metabolic, nutritional, or growth disorders, e.g., phenylketonuria (PKU) or malnutrition
5.   Mental retardation caused by diseases or conditions resulting from new growths

6. Mental retardation associated with diseases or conditions due to unknown prenatal disorders
7. Mental retardation associated with diseases or conditions resulting from unknown or unverifiable causes with structural reactions
8. Mental retardation due to uncertain (or presumed psychologic) cause with functional reaction alone manifest, e.g., cultural deprivation or emotional disorders, which in turn can cause mental subnormality

There are a number of ways one could regroup these eight categories. For example, (1) congenital (present at birth) or acquired (obtained after birth); (2) endogenous (genetic or subcultural without manifest brain injury) and exogenous (brain injured during either the prenatal, perinatal, or postnatal period); and (3) mental retardation (most frequently considered to be a global term to describe intellectual subnormality—others use the term to describe non-brain-injured, less severely retarded children) and mental deficiency (descriptive of persons with significant organic defects which are virtually irreversible).

Grouping According to Syndromes   Another way in which mental retardation can be classified is according to clinical symptoms, of which level of performance on an intelligence test may be only one of several related factors. Those who advocate this orientation do so on the basis of the fact that mixed, unclear patterns of cause are often related to the same clinical type. For example, it has been established that a condition known as *microcephaly,* which is characterized by a congenitally small skull and other atypical physical characteristics, has multiple causes which can occur at different time periods during the prenatal life of a child. Many people believe that because it is impossible to treat the cause after the event has occurred, a more profitable approach toward treatment or rehabilitation is to classify conditions, such as are seen among the mentally retarded, according to broad clinical symptoms.

For years it has been a common practice among medical specialists to identify certain types of mentally retarded persons according to types of signs and symptoms that characteristically occur together. The term which is used to describe this phenomenon is *syndrome.* For example, the condition known as *mongolism* or *Down's syndrome* occurs approximately once in every 600 to 700 live births. This condition prevails in nearly one-third of the cases of mental retardation in the moderately and severely retarded groups, as classified by the American Association on Mental Deficiency (refer back to Figure 1-2). Mongoloid children have a constellation of symptoms and signs which are strikingly alike, although there is some variation in type and degree of symptomatology among this group. Typical characteristics include short stature; loose, dry, and flabby skin; oriental-appearing eyes with frequent and varying ocular abnormalities; short fingers and toes with abnormal creases of the palms; large, fissured, and often protruding

tongue; small, round face; and the frequent occurrence of congenital heart problems.

In addition to these more medically oriented characteristics of the Down's syndrome retardate, certain scientists have attempted to study his psychological, social, educational, and behavioral traits. These efforts have been directed toward ascertaining if the syndrome might include unique behavioral characteristics which set the condition apart from other clinical forms of mental retardation. The research on this matter is somewhat scattered. There does seem to be an indication that compared with other types of retardates the mongoloid is significantly less aggressive and self-destructive, more moderate toward others, and less seriously mentally ill (Moore, Thuline, and Capes, 1968; Domino, 1965; Silverstein, 1964). Domino (1965) found that mongoloid children were viewed by intellectually normal young adults as being relatively happy, calm, likable, playful, affectionate, and manageable individuals. Although we would obviously expect to observe a range of behavioral characteristics among Down's syndrome children, most studies support the general belief that a recognizable pattern of behaviors does exist among the Down's syndrome population.

There are a number of other major clinical types of mental retardation, each of which can be characterized as exhibiting a unique medical, and sometimes behavioral, syndrome. The student who has an interest in pursuing this line of inquiry will find great satisfaction in reviewing the *Atlas of Mental Retardation Syndromes* (1968) as well as the writings of Carter (1965), Tredgold and Soddy (1956), Rubin (1967), and Robinson and Robinson (1964). Table 1-1 presents examples of a small selection of clinical types along with some of the usually observed signs and symptoms which characterize each. Understand, however, that the listed traits, and others, will occur in different degrees of severity, or perhaps not at all, in individuals who have been classified as representing a certain clinical type. One possible reason for this variability is that even within clinical groups, different environmental conditions can result in variable physical and/or behavioral signs.

Behavioral Classifications   Finally, another way of grouping the mentally retarded, which is still in the exploratory stage and not well developed at all, is in terms of manifested behavioral characteristics. This position differs from previous behavioral classification systems which have focused primarily, if not solely, on intelligence test performance. This new approach centers on behavioral traits and achievement in various areas including those involving perceptual-motor development (how well the person receives information from his environment and the manner in which he acts on this information), communication with others, social development, personal development and mental health, self-help skills, educational performance, and general intellectual performance. Numerous evaluative techniques are available to diagnose individual performance in these areas, and a specific profile of abilities and disabilities can be

Table 1-1 Examples and characteristics of selected clinical types of mental retardation

Clinical type	Distinctive signs
Achondroplasia	Short stature, enlarged head, prominent forehead, scooped nose, short extremities, severe defects of bones, short and broad hands
Diencephalic syndrome	Emaciation, prominent eyes, euphoric and emotionally labile behavior, inoperable tumor in region of the diencephalon, fatal usually by three years of age
Congenital hydrocephalus	Increased head size, cranial sutures fail to close, prominent scalp veins, protruding eyes with limited mobility, poor motor development, inadequately developed cortical areas
Klinefelter's syndrome	Tall stature, decreased secondary characteristics, visual defects, personality disorders, cleft palate, major skeletal deformities
Laurence-Moon-Biedl syndrome	Obesity, blindness, facial deformities, renal diseases, hypogenitalism
Microcephaly	Normal-sized face, small and sloping forehead, furrowed scalp, large and protruding ears, high-arched palate
Neurofibromatosis	Skin tumors, skeletal deformities, localized gigantism, tumors in organs, neurological complications
Phenylketonuria	Fair hair and skin, eczema, elevated blood levels of phenylalanine, obesity, musty odor, restless behavior, tremors, poor motor movement

established for each person. This profile will lead to a definite program of treatment and remediation based on results from this diagnostic effort. Obviously, other types of information, such as data from reports of physicians, physical therapists, speech pathologists, audiologists, or biochemists, can be used as part of the diagnostic profile whenever it is relevant.

A person might be classified with other retarded individuals according to primary areas of disorder and treated with an appropriate prescription of remediation. If, for example, a group of retardates have severe speech, language, and self-help weaknesses they should be treated for these problems. Classification is most meaningful, according to this position, if it leads directly to a program of intervention.

Although it is true that the type of classification approach which is advocated by the more behaviorally oriented scientists has the advantage of leading more directly to a proper program of intervention for each retarded individual, it is

likewise true that the system is relatively more difficult to implement. The reasons for this are as follows: (1) the assignment of an individual to a category within a behavioral scheme must be based on his performance on more than a single variable, (2) evaluation and subsequent classification are necessarily based on how well the diagnostician selected and administered his measuring instruments, and (3) the time, expense, and interdisciplinary cooperation that is necessary to implement this concept of classification fully are influences which hinder full acceptance of the position by most professionals.

The basic structures for a number of currently used schemes for classifying the heterogeneous condition of mental retardation have been briefly reviewed. There are numerous advantages and disadvantages of each, and differences of opinion as to which is best varies within as well as between disciplines. The list is certainly not exhaustive, and the reader might find it an interesting assignment to list various ways to classify mental retardation further so that all levels of retardation are included.

Recommended Readings

Carter, C. H.: *Medical Aspects of Mental Retardation,* Charles C Thomas, Publisher, Springfield, Ill., 1965.

Domino, G.: "Personality Traits in Institutionalized Mongoloids," *American Journal of Mental Deficiency,* vol. 69, 1965, pp. 568–570.

Gardner, W. I., and H. W. Nisonger: "A Manual on Program Development in Mental Retardation," *Monograph Supplement to the American Journal of Mental Deficiency,* vol. 66, 1962.

Gellis, S. S., and M. Feingold: *Atlas of Mental Retardation Syndromes,* U.S. Government Printing Office, 1968.

Gelof, M.: "Comparison of Systems of Classification Relating Degree of Retardation to Measured Intelligence," *American Journal of Mental Deficiency,* vol. 68, 1963, pp. 297–317.

Heber, R.: "A Manual on Terminology and Classification in Mental Retardation," *Monograph Supplement to the American Journal of Mental Deficiency,* vol. 64, 1959, pp. 55–64.

————: "Modifications in the Manual on Terminology and Classification in Mental Retardation," *American Journal of Mental Deficiency,* vol. 69, 1961a, pp. 499–500.

————: "A Manual on Terminology and Classification in Mental Retardation," 2d ed., *Monograph Supplement to the Amercian Journal of Mental Deficiency,* 1961b, pp. 55–64.

Moore, B. C., H. C. Thuline, and L. Capes: "Mongoloid and NonMongoloid Retardates: A Behavioral Comparison," *American Journal of Mental Retardation,* vol. 73, 1968, pp. 433–436.

Robinson, H. R., and H. M. Robinson: *The Mentally Retarded Child: A Psychological Approach,* McGraw-Hill Book Company, New York, 1964, pp. 207–274.

Rubin, A.: *Handbook of Congenital Malformations,* W. B. Saunders Company, Philadelphia, 1967.

Sarason, S. B., and T. Gladwin: "Psychological and Cultural Problems in Mental Subnormality," *American Journal of Mental Deficiency,* vol. 62, 1958, pp. 1113–1307.

Silverstein, A. B.: "An Empirical Test of the Mongoloid Stereotype," *American Journal of Mental Deficiency,* vol. 68, 1964, pp. 493–497.

Tredgold, R. F., and K. Soddy: *A Textbook of Mental Deficiency,* 9th ed., The Williams & Wilkins Company, Baltimore, 1956.

Wechsler, D.: *The Measurement and Appraisal of Adult Intelligence,* 4th ed., The Williams & Wilkins Company, Baltimore, 1958.

What can be done about mental retardation?

Possible answers to this question are of basic concern to parents of the mentally retarded as well as to all who have an interest in working with these individuals. The responses one might offer are of enormous significance because they reflect how pessimistic or optimistic an individual is about the whole range of possibilities for preventing mental retardation and appropriately treating the condition after it has occurred. One of the major aims of this book is to present and justify the position that a great deal can be done, within the limits of the scientific and social tools which are presently available, to deal effectively with the condition before as well as after it becomes evident in an individual. In a real sense, then, a comprehensive answer to the above question can be found in all the sections of this book. The purpose of this particular portion is to (1) help you gain an appreciation for the general picture of the field in the areas of prevention and treatment of mental retardation, and (2) aid you in developing a contemporary philosophy concerning the management and care of the retarded. The principal cornerstone of the philosophy is that the old notion that mental retardation is irreversible is no longer scientifically valid; more recent experience and study have clearly shown that a great deal can be done to change medical, intellectual, social, personal, and occupational characteristics of the mentally retarded, all which have heretofore been viewed as unresponsive to any form of intervention. This section will present some broad concepts on this issue, each of which will be dissected and studied in greater depth in subsequent sections of this book.

Preventive Measures   First, let us consider some possible ways in which individuals and society can prevent, or at least help to minimize, the occurrence of mental retardation. In 1962, the President's Panel on Mental Retardation

presented a plan for combating this condition. A major section of the report, *A Proposed Program for National Action to Combat Mental Retardation,* dealt with suggested ways in which preventive measures could be designed and immediately implemented. These suggestions, which were based on scientific evidence, included the following:

1. As a result of improved obstetric and pediatric procedures, which have a clear potential for controlling the occurrence of certain types of conditions which are related to mental retardation, the panel recommended launching nationwide programs to increase the opportunity for complete maternal care (prenatal-perinatal-postnatal) being provided all citizens, especially those who might be considered "high risk" for any of a variety of reasons.

2. Because a number of types of mental retardation result from genetic disorders, many of which can be identified before pregnancy occurs, the panel suggested that regional genetic counseling services and comprehensive diagnostic centers be established for the purpose of providing consultation to young married couples and to parents who have had a child born with a defect.

3. There is a wide range of drugs, poisons, and other teratogenic agents which are harmful to a developing fetus and to a young child during the first years of life. The panel recommended that a comprehensive program of research be undertaken to identify and develop procedures whereby these agents can be fully identified and the full impact of their influence on the growing child determined. It was further suggested that procedures be developed to inform parents and others as to the possible harmful effects of the indiscriminate or uninformed use of various chemical substances.

4. The adverse effects of too much radiation exposure on the developing fetus is of great concern to health officials. Since there is a clear relationship between radiation over-exposure and mental retardation, the panel suggested that a program be implemented to develop controls so that pregnant women will not be unnecessarily exposed to x-ray at inappropriate times. The recommendation was also made that registration and inspection of radiation devices begin as part of a comprehensive program for radiological health protection.

5. Because mental retardation is known to occur during and immediately after the birth process as a result of complications of pregnancy, difficult labor, and metabolic problems, the panel suggested that procedures be developed on a nationwide basis to provide immediate, comprehensive diagnostic services to newborns, and that proper follow-up be initiated in those instances where appropriate.

6. Childhood accidents contribute to death in more instances than any other single problem of children younger than age fourteen. After being involved in accidents in which death does not occur, youngsters frequently suffer brain dam-

age and mental retardation. The President's panel recommended that programs of prevention be developed after the causes and nature of these accidents have undergone intensive research.

7. A child's intellectual development is adversely influenced by inadequate opportunities as a result of living in a restricted or deprived environment. The panel recommended that a host of steps be taken to increase the likelihood that all citizens, and particularly those who are born into deprived circumstances, have opportunities to realize a "fair start" in physical and intellectual areas of development. The two broad recommendations made were (1) that general procedures be instituted to correct basic social, economic, and cultural conditions with which mental retardation is associated, and (2) that specific measures be developed to increase the range of experiences for those persons who reside in a "high-risk" environment. Obviously, these suggestions were long range.

Among the more short-term suggestions made by the panel were (1) the provision of preschool centers for children in rural and urban slums, (2) the greater involvement in educational programming for parents of such children, (3) the more complete coordination of public and private agencies who are concerned about mental retardation and its causes, and (4) a possible reorganization of public education in order to reflect the need to provide educational opportunities for those who will eventually become candidates for special education placement.

8. Recognizing that infants may suffer impaired intellectual development and emotional disorders while still in the hospital or in a residential facilitiy as a result of maternal deprivation or lack of stimulation, the panel recommended that hospitals and accrediting agencies give priority to making certain that problems resulting from mother-child separation be provided for in a satisfactory way. It is clear that the provision of twenty-four-hour care for infants and young children will help to alleviate emotional and intellectual disorders to a certain extent.

9. Finally, the panel felt that greater effort should be given to training greater numbers of professional and subprofessional personnel to deal with those difficulties, personal and social, which are precipitants of mental retardation. Their belief was that more personnel need to be trained at all levels and in a wide variety of disciplines. A greater utilization of available manpower, in the opinion of the panel, will go a long way toward reducing the prevalence of mental retardation in our society.

To summarize, the range of possibilities for preventing mental retardation is exceedingly wide and includes medical, psychological, family, and social programs of intervention. The problem is not only one of having adequate services available but also one of informing, educating, and dealing with negative attitudes

of those citizens who are in most desperate need of the range of services. Unfortunately, those who most urgently need the services are the most hesitant to make use of them.

Management Resources   A second aspect of any answer to the question, "What can be done about mental retardation?" involves considering the types of treatment practices that are appropriate and necessary for those persons who have been diagnosed as being mentally retarded. Again, the various approaches of care and rehabilitation will be discussed in depth in other sections of this book. As an overview, it might be helpful to briefly review a number of options which can be taken to deal with the problems encountered in an instance where mental retardation has been diagnosed and the point passed where total prevention is no longer a feasible option.

First, in instances where a child is born mentally retarded, a full range of medical attention should be made available for comprehensive diagnosis, immediate treatment, and parental consultation. Since many retarded newborns frequently have other types of disabling conditions, it is imperative that immediate plans be made and steps taken to implement an appropriate program of management. There are certain conditions which demand prompt medical intervention, or irreversible intellectual disorders will develop. For example, a metabolic disorder, phenylketonuria (PKU), if not treated immediately, will cause brain damage and mental retardation. In addition to the medical attention for the newborn or young child, definite care can and should be given to help the parents adjust to the abnormal situation, realize what reasonable options are available, and provide the baby with a program which will enhance his prognosis.

Most youngsters who suffer from mental retardation as a result of environmental deprivation can be helped, the condition being reversible to some extent for those with mild retardation and without clear-cut brain damage if proper environmental treatment is provided at as early an age as possible. The earlier the program of intervention, the more progress will be shown and the better the child's general prognosis.

Most retarded persons can be trained to take care of their own bodily needs. Obviously this is not a reasonable expectation for most of those who are profoundly retarded and nonambulatory. However, in many cases they can be trained to indicate when they are in need of help. The less retarded can develop skills which are necessary to lead reasonably normal lives in society. As the severity of retardation increases and the number of associated disabilities multiplies, the program of treatment becomes more comprehensive and lengthy, and the results of treatment are less dramatic. In every case, however, the vital factor is to begin a planned program very early and to be systematic throughout. Integration of efforts among those agencies and specialists who are concerned with the problem is essential so that a proper program of treatment can be initiated. A disjointed

and unplanned effort will be disappointing, result in parents going from one specialist to another, and cause the child not to develop skills at a level which might reasonably be predicted.

The vital components of effective management and treatment of the retarded, then, are (1) early diagnosis; (2) prompt medical, social, and environmental intervention; (3) integration of personnel and specialists who can contribute to the child's program of treatment; (4) intelligent, prompt, and properly offered counsel for the parents; and (5) continual reevaluation of the child's progress and status during treatment.

Recommended Reading

President's Panel on Mental Retardation: *A Proposed Program for National Action to Combat Mental Retardation,* 1962.

What general techniques are used to manage and control the behavior of the retarded?

There are a number of guidelines which parents, teachers, and others who deal with the mentally retarded can use to manage the behavior of these individuals. Before they are specified and discussed it might be helpful to briefly review certain general behavioral characteristics which typify many of the retarded. As you might suspect, it would be unjustifiable to claim that all retarded youngsters have these traits to the same degree and in a similar pattern. Differences exist among the retarded, and, indeed, one will frequently observe that each individual will change in character from one time to another according to the pressures and peculiarities of the moment. You can see, then, how tentative and undogmatic one must be on this issue.

Broadly speaking, the mentally retarded seem to:

1. Have difficulty focusing their attention on a task or a predominant stimulus
2. Frequently be bothered by the presence of peripheral stimuli which are either irrelevant or of secondary importance at the particular moment
3. Either overrespond or underrespond in intensity or frequency to a stimulus condition
4. Have difficulty matching a response, which would generally be considered appropriate, with a problem or situation for which some reaction is necessary
5. Have a lower tolerance for frustration and be more hesitant to participate in an unfamiliar activity because of having experienced previous failures
6. Have some difficulty in communicating their thoughts and ideas to others

As a result of the mentally retarded manifesting characteristics such as these, and of the often unpredictable and varied way in which these characteristics occur among this group, behavioral scientists have considered it particularly desirable first to have a clear picture of the strengths and weaknesses of individual youngsters before formulating a definite plan of behavioral management. This requires an opportunity to observe an individual on enough occasions and in various situations to gain an appreciation for his skill in dealing with problems and issues and to identify the areas in which his performance is especially weak. To aid in the collection of this information and to systematize the process to some extent, diagnostic specialists use various types of measuring devices, such as rating scales, check sheets, tests, questionnaires, and surveys to ascertain answers to specific questions. The procedure for collecting and recording information in an educational context is reviewed in some depth in Chapter 4.

To a very substantial degree the process of gathering information about an individual is a necessary precondition before deciding on a plan of medical as well as behavioral management. The data help one to decide the individual's needs as well as the means by which such needs can best be satisfied. When you observe and analyze the behavioral characteristics of anyone, and most certainly the mentally retarded, it is vital that you give close attention to the various components of the individual's environment. In combination with a person's unique group of weaknesses and strengths, the type of environment with which an individual is associated will influence and focus the direction of his behavior. None of us operates in an environmental vacuum; our behavior is inextricably involved with our individual surroundings.

It is reasonable, therefore, that any specific techniques one would choose in order to manage the behavior of a retarded person should be based on information that has been systematically gathered about the person and about his environment. The most efficient and effective technique is one which matches a person's characteristics with a management approach designed to help the retardate achieve a behavioral goal which you have identified. Although individualized programs of management are necessary, educational psychologists have suggested a number of procedures which seem to have general applicability when working with the retarded. It is these general techniques which we will focus on in this section.

Precursors to Behavior Management   As a preliminary to systematically dealing with the behavior of a retarded person, it is necessary for you to answer the following questions:

1. What specific behavior do I want to deal with by either increasing or decreasing its frequency? For example, you might wish to increase the frequency of hand-washing behavior, talking at proper times in the classroom, doing arithmetic work, reading aloud, or making the bed. On the other hand, you might wish to decrease the frequency of toilet accidents, throw-

ing items in the classroom or on the ward, eating too much, using the addition process when subtraction is proper, or cussing.

2. To what extent does the behavior, on which I am focusing, occur at the present time? Does it occur ten times during the day, sixteen times in an hour, three times before lunch, and so on?

3. Are there certain aspects of the retarded person's environment that seem to be related to an increase or decrease in the frequency of the behavior which I wish to change? Does it happen only at lunchtime, at home, during arithmetic periods, in the bathroom, in the presence of an authority figure, with younger children, and so on? At the same time, we would want to find out what agent, thing, or type of social contact seems to be particularly rewarding or reinforcing for the retardate. To a great extent, removal of this rewarding agent will decrease the frequency of the behavior which has preceded its removal. Likewise, administering the reinforcing agent, at an appropriate time whether it be candy, social acknowledgement, or physical contact will increase the probability of the behavior occurring with greater frequency.

A Way to Change Behavior   Suppose we consider an example of behavior which a parent of a young retarded child is interested in stimulating. Let us say that this parent wishes to teach her child to feed himself with a spoon. If he can learn how to feed himself, the parent will have more time for other activities during and after mealtimes. Also, if the child can learn to feed himself, there is a chance that the skills involved in feeding will carry over into other areas of performance. Let us make some assumptions at the beginning. First, suppose we assume that the child presently makes little or no effort to feed himself; that is, in your observation of him for a reasonable length of time, you have found that the incidence of self-feeding behavior is zero. Also, assume that the child seems to have the physical capabilities required to locate, grasp, and hold objects that are about the size of a spoon and that he has enough motion in his arms and hands to move the spoon to his mouth.

Although the parent's final goal is for the child to learn how to feed himself without taking too much time, it would be foolish to expect the youngster to suddenly discover how to do this complicated operation even if one demonstrated the process or guided his hand. The operation, while it may seem easy to most of us, is rather complicated and will take a good deal of patience on the part of a parent before the final goal is achieved. And so, the parent will have to be satisfied with small steps of progress and break down the task of feeding into very small component skills. As the child moves from one point to the next-higher-level skill, a greater degree of independence will gradually develop into self-feeding.

The parent's first goal should be to get the child to pay attention to his spoon and to become interested in it. At first the parent will have to be satisfied if the child merely looks at the spoon. As soon as this happens the parent should call

the child's attention to the fact that he likes what the child is doing by rewarding the youngster in some way. Remember, it is important to determine first what the child likes—it may be a piece of candy, a pat on the back, or a pleasant word. The first order of business is to reward the youngster for this "looking behavior" as soon as his attention has been focused on the spoon for a period of time. Very soon he will continue behaving in this way when he realizes that it will bring him something he desires. The whole process is called *reinforcement*. Next, the parent might move the spoon into different positions and reward the child immediately after he follows the object with his eyes.

Now that the parent has helped the retarded child to focus his eyes on the spoon, the next goal might be to have him touch the spoon. As the child's hands move closer and closer to the spoon, the youngster should be reinforced for this approximation of the final goal. The parent should keep up the reinforcement procedures as the child moves closer and closer to touching the spoon. It is very important for the youngster to be rewarded immediately after he does what the parent wants him to do.

When the child finally learns to grasp the spoon, the next higher goal might involve trying to get him to move the spoon toward his mouth. Just as the parent encouraged him to move his hands closer and closer to the spoon and rewarded him immediately after each successive move, it is also necessary to use the same principle to get the child to move the spoon toward his mouth. This is accomplished through the continued use of rewards each time the child comes closer and closer to his mouth with the spoon, until the final goal is achieved.

The process which has just been described is called *shaping behavior*. The parent simply cannot say, "My goal is to have the child feed himself, and so I will wait until he grabs the spoon, obtains food with it, and places the food in his mouth before I will reward him." As you probably recognize, it will result in a long wait because there is little chance that this complete behavior will occur spontaneously. The ultimate goal of self-feeding was broken down into the smaller goals of (1) looking at the spoon, (2) moving the hands toward the spoon, (3) grasping the spoon, (4) moving the spoon toward the mouth, and (5) placing the spoon in the mouth. These behaviors did not occur all at once; that is, the child did not simply move his hand to the spoon, grab it, and begin the entire process of feeding. Rather it was necessary for the parent to shape the child's behavior until the final goal was achieved. Figure 1-3 diagrams the steps which have just been described.

In a nutshell, then, the procedure of shaping behavior is simply the reinforcement or reward of closer and closer approximations toward the desired behavior. This process will be successful because the reinforcement not only strengthens the particular response that has occurred before the reward, but also increases the likelihood that the child will move closer to the desired goal the next time.

When rewarding a child for making a desired response, always remember to dispense or apply the reward *immediately after* the response has occurred; other-

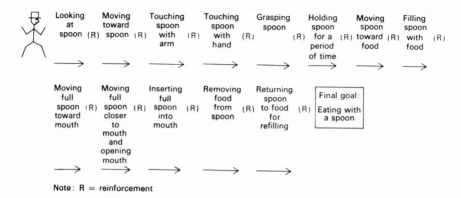

Note: R = reinforcement

Figure 1-3   *Intermediate goals associated with using a spoon.*

wise, the individual may associate the reinforcement with some other behavior or simply not associate it with anything at all. For example, if the parent had waited too long to reinforce the movement of the child's hand toward the spoon and the child looked up at the ceiling shortly after moving his hand toward the spoon, the parent would have rewarded "ceiling looking behavior" and not spoon holding. Thus, the undesired response of looking up at the ceiling would have been made and strengthened instead of the behavior the parent wished to see developed.

The procedure which has just been described is also appropriate for use with the mentally retarded in other areas of development. It can be used to manage the social behavior, emotional reactions, perceptual-motor performance, speech and language production, intellectual-skill development, and physical care of the retarded, and the nonretarded for that matter, at any level of functioning and age. It is a general strategy which seems to have applicability for the severely and profoundly retarded with the same relative effectiveness as with the mildly and moderately retarded.

There are four major components of this tactic to which specific attention must be directed if the procedure is to work. First, a clear behavioral goal must be identified. For example, you might want to identify goals such as the child's becoming toilet trained, speaking louder, doing addition problems slower, smiling at appropriate times, or dressing himself. Second, it is necessary to break the task down into its component parts and to sequence the subgoals according to when they occur in the process. In a general sense this is similar to

the same type of task analysis Henry Ford used in developing his production line for manufacturing automobiles in the early 1900s. Third, it is necessary for you to determine what is reinforcing or rewarding to the individual child. Fourth, you will need to reward the child on each occasion immediately after he has moved in the direction of achieving the subgoal which is next for him. Remember not to stop the process of moving toward the next subgoal by rewarding the child for behavior which has already been firmly established. Always require the youngster to go beyond an achievement level which he has previously reached.

Applying Appropriate Reinforcers   The use of rewards or reinforcing agents in the process of behavioral management, which has just been described, is a vital, if not central, component of the technique. Since there are often mixed feelings among groups of people on the issue of dispensing rewards to children, it might be beneficial to briefly consider some of the most predominant arguments for justifying the technique. First, since the early 1960s, psychologists have produced hundreds of reports of research studies which document the fact that the chance of a behavioral incident being repeated is increased if a person is rewarded in a way which is personally significant immediately after the specific behavior has occurred. This finding has been replicated time and time again with all types of subhuman and human subjects. A great amount of research on this subject has been conducted with mentally retarded persons in institutions as well as in public school settings. This research has been both broad or molar (such as training the retarded to become self-sufficient in an occupational setting) and molecular (such as helping the retarded to learn to discriminate between the colors green and red).

As was suggested earlier in this section, it is vital for the behavioral manager to determine what is rewarding for each child. Some children enjoy peanuts, others like candy, others Jell-O, and still others are "turned on" by a smile, a nod, or a paper clip. We all are individual in this matter; however, in a general sense the research seems to show that younger children tend to prefer some type of tangible reward, e.g., candy, toys, juice, and so on. As they grow older, their preference seems to switch to more social types of reinforcing agents and then gradually to tokens, chips, or marks on a paper which, in turn, can be traded in when enough are accumulated for an object, a privilege, or release from some usual responsibility.

There are no standardized ways for ascertaining what is rewarding to a person. Perhaps one reason for this is that we all seem to change in our preferences from time to time. The most sensible alternative seems to be one of simply observing the retarded person in various situations, and at different moments, and trying to identify what is particularly pleasing or what makes him happy on a relatively continuous basis. Directly asking the individual will probably not be particularly revealing nor accurate, certainly not more so than what you will be

able to gain through systematic observation. A colleague of the author once described an incident which dramatically validated the need for giving attention to the appropriateness of the reward one selects for the purpose of managing behavior. In connection with a college course, students were asked to select an individual, to select a specific behavioral goal, and over a period of time to try to shape the behavior of their subject towards the desired goal. Since one of the students in the class was not connected with the classroom situation, the instructor allowed her to work with someone other than a school-age child. Unfortunately, she selected her husband. When the time came to report on her project, this student expressed complete bewilderment to the other members of the class because the behavior which she was attempting to shape neither increased nor decreased in frequency from the time the project began, through the reward cycle, and until the end of the process several months later. The student had selected the behavioral goal of persuading her husband to throw his socks in the dirty clothes hamper each evening. She found at the beginning of the project that 50 percent of the time he threw his socks on the floor, and the other 50 percent of the time they landed in the hamper. At the end of the project the frequencies were exactly the same, 50 percent of the time in the hamper and 50 percent of the time on the floor. As the class analyzed the problem, they immediately raised the question of what reinforcing agent was used. The student quickly stated that she had decided to use "terms of endearment" immediately after her husband tossed his socks in the dirty clothes hamper. As soon as this fact was revealed, one of her colleagues in the back of the room promptly observed that she had apparently selected an agent which was not particularly rewarding and that if she was interested in changing her husband's sock-throwing behavior she had best consider other alternatives.

Up to this point we have discussed the value in presenting some type of positive reinforcer to the retardate following a certain behavior which we wish to see strengthened or increased in frequency. In addition to this technique of positive reinforcement other possible options for the behavioral management of the mentally retarded are conceivable. For example, whenever an aversive stimulus exists for an individual, e.g., a loud noise, too much sun, or an uncomfortable chair, there is always a potential that some action by the person will serve to reduce the discomforting situation for him. If the performance terminates or reduces the effects of the noxious stimuli, the individual will tend to perform in the same way on subsequent occasions so that the impact of the disagreeable situation is minimized. This process is called *negative reinforcment.*

To illustrate this point, suppose a retarded youngster remained quiet in a small group of his colleagues and that you desire to arrange the environment so that he is no longer hesitant to participate in vocal exchanges. After observing the child with other youngsters you may conclude that the size of the group is acting as an aversive stimulus to him and thereby causing him not to participate.

You may elect to remove some of the members of the group, particularly those who seem to be especially restricting, and to determine the impact that this has on the child's subsequent vocal behavior. In this case you have used a negative reinforcer to change his behavior. It is worth mentioning that you could have approached the problem in another way—using positive reinforcement each time the child vocalized to increasing degrees. Moreover, one could combine both procedures; i.e., remove the aversive stimuli as well as reward the desired behavior.

A third technique which most of us use to some degree with children is punishment. *Punishment* can be defined as the application of some form of aversive stimuli *after* an individual has performed or behaved in a way which we view as unacceptable. In a real sense, punishment is the presentation of an aversive stimulus after the fact. The research indicates that punishment tends to suppress rather than eliminate behavior. Further, studies have suggested that a number of possible unfortunate side effects could result from punishment. One side effect is that punishment may indirectly reinforce incompatible behaviors which are in themselves inappropriate. For example, if a child is punished for not eating his supper, he might develop maladaptive behavior patterns in other areas, such as in speech and language, relationships with members of the family, or personal or emotional development. In studies involving the use of rats and primates, animals have been known to starve to death rather than to approach food after having received an intense electric shock from the food tray. The use of punishment, then, is generally viewed as an ineffective technique for effecting satisfactory long-term change in the behavior of individuals. A much more effective technique would be the use of positive or negative reinforcement, or combinations thereof, when attempting to alter the behavior of mentally retarded persons.

Some Instructional Principles   In addition to the general techniques that have been described, a number of other principles can be distilled from the work of psychologists who specialize in this area. Although these principles of instruction and their pertinence to the retarded have been reviewed in some detail elsewhere (Smith, 1968), it might be helpful to briefly indicate some that are particularly important because of their general applicability to many behavioral situations which the retarded encounter.

First, it is inefficient to expect learning to occur in a person who is not ready to learn. Readiness involves a number of factors including (1) physical maturation, (2) the extent to which the person is able to attend to a task or stimulus, (3) how well an individual has achieved in areas which are prerequisite to those which you want him to learn, (4) the extent of a person's emotional maturity and personal adjustment, and (5) his attitude toward participating in learning types of activities.

Second, subsequent learning is more successful if a person is assured that his response is correct immediately after it has been given. This assurance is especi-

ally valuable during the first stages of learning when new ideas are first presented or new skills are in their initial stages of development. If knowledge of results is delayed, later learning will be less efficient and less effective. Of equal importance when working with the retarded is the need to emphasize success rather than failure. This means that retarded youngsters should be placed in situations in which success can be predicted. Gradually, small "doses" of failure can be introduced as soon as the retardate has fairly well grasped the nature of the activity, what is expected of him, and what a correct response is like. Finally, if failure is inordinately emphasized, the retardate will gain relatively greater skill in learning what not to do and still not have a clear grasp of what constitutes an acceptable response to a problem.

A third principle which has importance when working with the mentally retarded is the need to emphasize active instead of passive participation. Learning is very inefficient and ineffective when the learner is expected to soak up ideas and skills without having the opportunity to get actively involved. Active participation is especially desirable when working with the mentally retarded because it (1) helps to focus the child's attention on the specific activity in which you wish him to engage, (2) suggests to the child that he is an important participant in the teaching-learning process, (3) helps to provide a more emphatic means for the individual to monitor his own responses and properly correct any subsequent output, and (5) provides a means for identifying any specific weaknesses which might characterize the child's performance and which could be strengthened by applying proper remediation.

A fourth guideline to follow in the management of the behavior of mentally retarded persons is to continuously stress accuracy to the point where clear overlearning has occurred instead of speed. Unless we are told otherwise, most of us have the tendency to respond with haste in competitive situations. The retarded are not unusual in this sense. They, just as intellectually normal persons, enjoy competitive situations especially when they have not previously experienced constant failure. With respect to learning, however, it is important for the retarded to develop a repertoire of proper responses before speed or competition are ever introduced. These correct responses should be *overlearned,* i.e., practiced beyond the point of initial mastery. Do not assume that a retarded person has firmly grasped a concept on the basis of a correct response on a single occasion. Instead, you will want to present previously learned material in a variety of ways on numerous occasions and expect the retarded person to perform correctly on most of these occasions before being satisfied that the concept has been learned at a sufficient level.

Finally, learning will occur more effectively for retarded children if the subject matter to which they are being exposed is sequenced to avoid abrupt shifting between concepts and activities. Every attempt should be made to identify basic components of a task and line them up in a hierarchial or stair-step fashion so

that one skill provides all the necessities for an adequate performance to be accomplished at the next higher level. This point will be discussed in detail in Chapters 3 and 4; therefore, only brief mention of the concept is made here.

The response that has been given to the question that was posed at the beginning of this section is somewhat involved. The central features of the suggestions which have been made concerning general techniques for managing and controlling behavior of the retarded are as follows:

1. It is important to know something about the characteristics of each retarded individual with whom you will be working and the unique peculiarities of the environment which surrounds that person.
2. You must decide on a specific behavioral goal you wish the retarded individual to achieve, break this goal down into its component parts, and evaluate the extent to which the individual is presently achieving that goal.
3. A systematic program of reinforcement must be established for each child and consistently applied throughout the day whenever the child's behavior is being shaped toward a specific goal.
4. The teacher, or others who are involved in behavioral management, should consider the application of various principles of learning which educational psychologists have suggested as being desirable for purposes of facilitating behavioral change.
5. For learning to occur, and behavior to be controlled and managed at a satisfactory level, explicit attention should be given to coordination of activities in which the retarded are involved. This coordination should occur during the various units of time extending in scope from an individual moment of instruction to the retarded person's lifetime goals.

Recommended Readings

Baumeister, A. A.: "Learning Abilities of the Mentally Retarded," in A. A. Baumeister (ed.), *Mental Retardation: Appraisal, Education, and Rehabilitation,* Aldine Publishing Company, Chicago, 1967, pp. 181–211.

Ferster, C. B., and M. C. Perrott: *Behavior Principles,* Appleton-Century-Crofts, Inc., New York, 1968, pp. 101–168.

Smith, R. M.: *Clinical Teaching: Methods of Instruction for the Retarded,* McGraw-Hill Book Company, New York, 1968, pp. 54–70.

How interested has the government been in dealing with the problems of mental retardation and what types of programs does it support?

With the possible exception of the year 1958, there were relatively little federal funds prior to 1960 earmarked for the developing of new programs to train

various professional workers to deal with the mentally retarded, for enlarging the research effort in the discovery and further development of new techniques for managing this portion of our population, and for aiding states and local boards of education to upgrade their programs for those youngsters who required special services. To be sure, some relatively minimal federal monies were available from the extramural programs of the National Institutes of Health for the more medically oriented specialists who were investigating very specific, but nonetheless important, aspects of the condition. However, there was little or no emphasis given nor support available for behavioral domains involving the psychological, social, and educational aspects of mental retardation. The largest single source of federal support for behavioral research in mental retardation during the early and middle 1950s was from the Cooperative Research Bureau in the U.S. Office of Education.

The post-1958 era signaled a period of significant fiscal breakthrough for the backing of various programs dealing with education for the mentally retarded. Public Law 85-926, since amended, was enacted by Congress in 1958 and provided support for training professional personnel to work with the retarded. At that time 1 million dollars was allotted to universities, colleges, and state educational agencies to prepare leadership personnel at the graduate degree level. The law was subsequently amended to include support for training professional personnel in other areas of exceptionality, and by 1968 nearly 44,000 teachers, supervisors, specialists, and college instructors had been trained under this act. In fiscal year 1970, nearly 30 million dollars was requested from Congress to support this program.

On October 11, 1961, President John F. Kennedy expressed concern to the nation that satisfactory progress was not being made in achieving prevention, proper therapy, and appropriate educational programming for the mentally retarded. After presenting a very penetrating analysis of the problems surrounding the condition, the President appointed a panel of distinguished scientists, humanitarians, and concerned members of the laity to study the problem and to make specific recommendations with regard to (1) "the personnel needed to develop and apply the new knowledge. The present shortage of personnel is a major problem in our logistics. More physicians, nurses, social workers, educators, psychologists, and other trained workers are needed." (2) "The major areas of concern that offer the most hope; and the means, the techniques, and the private and governmental structures necessary to encourage research in these areas." (3) "The present programs of treatment, education, and rehabilitation." (4) "The relationship between the Federal Government, the States, and private resources in their common efforts to eliminate mental retardation." (A *Proposed Program for National Action to Combat Mental Retardation,* 1962, p. 201).

On October 16, 1962, the President's Panel on Mental Retardation submitted their report to President Kennedy. Under the leadership of their chairman, Dr.

Leonard W. Mayo, the panel reported on the status of mental retardation in our society from every conceivable perspective. The report was promptly received by interested citizens, concerned legislators, and various national agencies. Within a few months a ground swell of support arose from nearly all segments of the country. Significant campaigns were initiated and the Congress, under the leadership of several forward-thinking members, began to sense the public's concern over the need to provide necessary levels of competent care and treatment for the mentally retarded. It was basically because of the stimulus provided by the President's panel that the decade of the 1960s evidenced an enormous increase in federal funding for educational improvement of the handicapped including the mentally retarded. Table 1-2 summarizes most of the particularly significant public laws which Congress passed especially for the education of the handicapped.

A very important aspect of Public Law 89-10, as amended, was the creation of the Bureau of Education for the Handicapped in the U.S. Office of Education. The Bureau was charged with the responsibility for administering most of the legislation dealing with educational programs for exceptional children. Special educators view the establishment of this Bureau as one of the most important developments in the federal legislative history for this group of children. The Bureau has worked hard with professional organizations, state departments of education, and university personnel to identify priorities and establish a reasonable scope of educational programming for the handicapped. As a result of this pooling of talent, there was an increase of 114 percent in laws pertaining to the education of the handicapped between 1960 and 1969.

The federal government has moved to provide better services and facilities for the mentally retarded in areas other than education. For example, laws have been passed to:

1. Provide grants to states to determine the action needed to combat mental retardation and to coordinate state and local activities in the area of mental retardation (Public Law 88–156)
2. Provide grants to public or nonprivate institutions for construction of research facilities related to human development in the area of mental retardation (Public Law 88–164 Title 1A)
3. Provide grants for the construction of university affiliated facilities for the mentally retarded. These centers have the primary mission of training professional workers, conducting research, and providing diagnostic and remedial services to the mentally retarded (Public Law 88–164 Title 1D)
4. Provide money to support the construction of facilities for the mentally retarded and in the construction of mental health centers (Public Law 88–164 Titles 1C and 2)
5. Provide grants to state vocational rehabilitation agencies to improve services to the handicapped, including the mentally retarded (Public Law 89–333)

Table 1-2   Major federal laws supporting educational programs for the handicapped*

Programs	Authority	Purpose
Grants to states	PL 80-10 (Title VI) as amended by PL 89-750	To provide grants to states to initiate, expand, and improve programs and projects for education of the handicapped
Regional resource centers	PL 89-10 (Title VI) as amended by PL 90-247	To create regional resource centers to provide educational evaluation and assistance in developing educational strategies for handicapped children
Education of deaf-blind children	PL 89-10 (Title VI) as amended by PL 90-247	To provide for the establishment and operation of centers for children who are both deaf and blind
Recruitment and information	PL 89-10 (Title VI) as amended by PL 90-247	To provide programs to recruit personnel in special education and to disseminate information on programs in the field and to the public
Educational media for the handicapped	PL 85-905 as amended by PL 90-247	Originally to provide films and other educational media for the deaf, to act as a loan service of materials, and to research and train in the use of media. Presently expanded to all areas of the handicapped
Personnel training	PL 85-926 as amended by PL 88-164	To provide fellowships, traineeships, and institutes for the training of professional personnel for education of the handicapped
Research and demonstration	PL 88-164 (Title III)	To support research and demonstration projects on the education of the handicapped
Training and research in physical education and recreation	PL 88-164 as amended by PL 90-170 (Title V)	To provide a system of personnel training and recreation for handicapped children
Preschool education	PL 90-538	To provide grants for research and demonstration projects related to preschool and early childhood education

* As summarized by the Council for Exceptional Children.

6. Provide money to those retarded dependents of armed services personnel to contract for medical and educational services (Public Law 89–614)
7. Assist in the coverage of a program of immunization against measles and other diseases that could result in complications such as mental retardation (Public Law 89–109)
8. Establish health services for migratory workers including prenatal and post-natal clinics for the treatment of conditions which are related to mental retardation (Public Law 89–109)

As you can see, the federal government has manifested intense interest in solving problems resulting from mental retardation. Money has been appropriated to begin programs of prevention, identification, treatment, education, and re-habilitation. In addition, funds have been made available for the construction of facilities and for the administration of clinical and educational units for the mentally retarded. To a significant degree, therefore, the goals of the President's Panel on Mental Retardation have begun to be realized as a result of this inten-sive and comprehensive program of federal and state financing.

Recommended Readings

National Education Association, *Exceptional Children,* Council for Exceptional Children, vol. 32, no. 3, November, 1965.

First Annual Report, National Advisory Committee on Handicapped Children, Washington, January, 1968.

Fogarty, J. E.: "Stimulating Special Education Through Federal Legislation," *Exceptional Children,* vol. 31, no. 1, 1964, pp. 1–4.

Geer, W., L. Connor, and L. Blackman: "Recent Federal Legislation—Provisions and Implications for Special Education," *Exceptional Children,* vol. 30, no. 9, 1964, pp. 411–421.

Jordan, J.: "1966—Special Education's Greatest Legislative Year," *Exceptional Children,* vol. 33, no. 4, 1966, pp. 269–270.

Mackie, R.: "Opportunities for Education of Handicapped Under Title I, P.L. 89–10," *Exceptional Children,* vol. 32, no. 9, 1966, pp. 593–598.

————: "The Handicapped Benefit Under Compensatory Education Programs," *Exceptional Children,* vol. 34, no. 8, 1968, pp. 603–606.

Martin, E.: "Breakthrough for the Handicapped: Legislative History," *Exceptional Children,* vol. 34, no. 7, 1968, pp. 493–503.

President's Panel on Mental Retardation: *A Proposed Program for National Action to Combat Mental Retardation,* 1962, p. 201.

Scholl, G., and A. Milazzo: "The Federal Program in the Preparation of Profes-sional Personnel in the Education of Handicapped Children and Youth," *Exceptional Children,* vol. 32, no. 3, 1965, pp. 157–164.

U.S. Department of Health, Education, and Welfare: *Mental Retardation Activities of the Department of Health, Education, and Welfare,* Washington, January, 1967 and January, 1968.

―――: *Mental Retardation Grants,* parts I and II, Washington, 1967.

―――: *A Summary of Selected Legislation Relating to the Handicapped, 1963–1967,* Washington, 1968.

Which organizations are active in the field of mental retardation?

The National Association for Retarded Children (NARC) was organized by a small group of parents of retarded children who met in Minneapolis in 1950. Certainly, few of the participants at that first convention fully realized the degree to which their original efforts would multiply and expand to every section of the country in just a few years. These conferees represented parents who were concerned about their own retarded youngsters, but their concern stretched further than their individual homes. They were interested in stimulating the means by which comprehensive services of diagnosis, education, and care could be provided for the mentally retarded throughout our society. At first they called themselves the National Association of Parents and Friends of Mentally Retarded Children; later the name of the organization was shortened. The association has grown from only 42 persons in 1950, to over 100,000 in 1965, to nearly 125,000 members in 1969. There are over 1,200 local and state associations in the United States.

Because of a deluge of requests for assistance and advice by parents of retarded children, groups, and professional organizations, the NARC found it necessary by 1954 to expand their facilities and to establish a national office in New York City. Prior to that time, business of this voluntary agency had been cared for solely by its members. With the opening of the national office, NARC employed a small staff to provide for its members, answer inquiries by any citizen who needed advice on how to help himself or his retarded child, and to begin expanding their horizons to include the development of clinics, workshops, and classes. It is indeed significant that NARC members during the early development of the organization provided the stimulation, encouragement, financial resources, and political strength for the initiation of classes for trainable youngsters in many sections of the country. It is the belief of many professionals that programs for trainable children would not be as well inculcated into public education as it is if it were not for the early efforts of NARC members.

NARC is an organization which is democratically governed by delegates to the national convention and by an elected board of directors. According to the constitution and bylaws the major aims of the organization are as follows:

1. To promote the general welfare of the mentally retarded of all ages irrespective of where they might be located
2. To further the advancement of all ameliorative and preventive study, research, and therapy in the field of mental retardation
3. To develop a better understanding of the problems of mental retardation by the public and to cooperate with all public and private agencies and institutions of the federal, state, and local governments who have some interests in the problems of mental retardation
4. To further the training and education of professional and subprofessional personnel who work with the mentally retarded
5. To encourage the formation of parents' groups, to coordinate the efforts and activities of these groups, and to offer advice and assistance to parents in the solution of their problems
6. To serve as a clearinghouse for the collection and dissemination of information concerning the mentally retarded among all interested individuals.

Another organization which has had a relatively long history of active concern for various issues concerning the retarded is the American Association on Mental Deficiency. This organization was founded in 1876 by a group of six persons who were associated with institutions. The name of the organization at that time was the Association of Medical Officers of American Institutions for Idiotic and Feeble-Minded Persons. It is noteworthy that Dr. Edouard Seguin was one of its founders and an active participant in the early annual meetings of the group. The association's name was changed to the American Association for the Study of the Feeble-Minded in 1906, and in 1933 the name it presently holds was adopted.

The purposes of the association have never changed. Briefly they are (1) to promote the general welfare of the mentally retarded, (2) to stimulate research for the creation of new knowledge and to disseminate information about mental retardation, (3) to promote cooperation among persons who are interested in the mentally retarded, (4) to encourage and support the highest standards of treatment (institutional and noninstitutional) for the retarded, (5) to intensify public concern about the problems of all mentally subnormal individuals, and (6) to promote programs which develop higher level competencies among various types of professional workers.

Originally membership in the organization was restricted to medical heads of American institutions; later it was made available to other types of professionals, students, and members of the concerned laity. The association membership has increased from the original 6 in 1876, to 1,659 in 1950, and to nearly 10,000 in 1969. Nearly 50 percent of its members are classified as representing the field of education, 6.5 percent are from medicine, 9.4 percent from administrative types of positions, 14 percent represent psychology, 5 percent social work, and the remainder come from other fields including physical and occupational ther-

apy, speech and hearing, religion, physical education and therapeutic recreation, nursing, and rehabilitation.

The organization has been very active in its publication program. The *American Journal of Mental Deficiency* and *Mental Retardation* are offered to the membership bimonthly. Other publications and reports have been made available as a result of an active council and group of standing committees. Some of these efforts include:

1. *Selected Abstracts of Current Publications in the Field of Mental Retardation*
2. *Standards for State Residential Institutions for the Mentally Retarded*
3. *Manual on Terminology and Classification in Mental Deficiency*

The association has attracted a number of outside grants to conduct various special projects in several areas. Nomenclature, the system of classifying, and the development of evaluative devices have been researched by a special projects staff.

History has shown the association to be a powerful force in behalf of the mentally retarded. No doubt it will continue this legacy by actively supporting the philosophy of encouraging society to appreciate fully the needs of the mentally retarded and to make proper provisions so that they can become useful members of the open community.

A third organization which has been active in supporting the provision of adequate programs of management for the mentally retarded has been The Council for Exceptional Children (CEC). The Council, which until 1970 was a department of the National Education Association (NEA), is primarily concerned with promoting adequate education for all varieties of exceptional children. This is accomplished by (1) cooperating with various types of educational agencies and organizations, (2) facilitating articulation of programs, plans, and information among concerned persons, school systems, and organizations, (3) cooperating and participating in the establishment of proper programs of diagnosis and treatment, (4) promoting the adoption of minimum standards of professional competence by professional educational personnel, (5) stimulating, supporting, and engaging in important educationally related research, (6) disseminating information to those concerned with the problems of providing education for exceptional children, and (7) encouraging, supporting, and stimulating the passage of legislation which is favorable to exceptional children.

Membership, which in 1969 was in excess of 37,000, is open to professional personnel and others who are interested in the education of exceptional persons. Programs are planned and offered at the local, state, and national levels each year. An annual convention provides a means for sharing ideas and new knowledge in areas of common interest.

The CEC has a vigorous publication program. *Exceptional Children* is the official organ of the organization; however, numerous other publications are offered regularly and occasionally each year.

CEC headquarters houses the Educational Resources Information Center (ERIC) for exceptional children. This clearinghouse for information includes (1) a computer retrieval search service to provide information in various areas, (2) a service which prepares bibliographies on various topics, and (3) a service which prepares various publications that have pertinence to the classroom teacher.

Membership in the Division on Mental Retardation, one of several divisional units within CEC, is available to any member of the association. This division has the purpose of "advancing the education and welfare of the mentally retarded, research in the education of the mentally retarded, competency of educators in this field, public understanding of mental retardation, and legislation needed to help accomplish these goals; to encourage and promote professional growth, research, and the dissemination and utilization of research findings" (*CEC Handbook*, 1967, p. 23). As you can see, the aims of this group differ little from those of the AAMD.

This section has briefly discussed some basic facts about three of the most active organizations which have a concern for supporting the development and provision of adequate services for the retarded. They are not the only organized groups with this interest; however, within the decade of the 1960s they have probably provided the most powerful and respected voices in behalf of the mentally retarded.

Recommended Readings

CEC Handbook, National Education Association, The Council for Exceptional Children, Washington, 1967.

Voices in Chorus, The National Association for Retarded Children, New York, 1969.

History of the American Association on Mental Deficiency, American Association on Mental Deficiency, Washington, 1969.

2
The Time before and
Soon after Birth

What are some of the possible reasons for mental retardation occurring before, during, or immediately after birth?

Mention was made in Chapter 1 that mental retardation can occur for various reasons at any time from conception throughout one's lifetime. The discussion in this section will focus primarily on abnormalities that could take place before birth, during the process of birth, and soon after the neonate has been presented. You should recognize that the combined total of youngsters who are mentally retarded as a result of atypical medical conditions, arising during any of these periods, represents a relatively small percentage of all the retarded in our society. The largest group are those who have experienced serious environmental deprivation during their early formative years and have not had adequate opportunities to develop basic skills at a satisfactory level. This latter group will be considered and discussed in much greater depth in subsequent sections of this book. For now, however, let us deal briefly with the reasons for mental retardation which are more medical than environmental in a psychosocial sense.

Genetic Disorders   A certain group of the mentally retarded are irreversibly bound to be mentally subnormal at conception. This

situation stems from heredity difficulties, the consequences of which can be demonstrated at different time periods in the subsequent growth and development of the human organism. Moreover, hereditary problems can be manifested in various ways; however, the vast majority of mentally retarded individuals whose condition is caused by genetic disorders are either moderately, severely, or profoundly retarded and are most often multiply handicapped. Many handicapped youngsters who are stillborn are the product of serious genetic disorders which will not allow the organism to grow and develop in a satisfactory way during the prenatal period. Other genetically damaged children, who have been able to survive the prenatal period, present significant crisis situations at birth and are often in need of immediate medical attention.

The anomalies that are associated with mental retardation as a result of genetic disorders very frequently exhibit clusters of characteristics or syndromes. For example, the Down's syndrome child can be characterized in a relatively typical fashion not only in terms of physical characteristics but also in terms of chromosomal aberrations. In this situation various unique patterns of chromosomes are often noted. These atypical genetic characteristics lead to serious disruption of the central nervous system and combine with other systemic disorders to result in further debilitation of the organism. Other genetic disorders cause mental retardation because of the infant being unable to function without the mother. For example, a number of inborn errors of metabolism occur because the child is not able to be biochemically independent. In such instances, then, the impact of genetic disorders is not clearly manifested until the infant is required to operate independently in the environment. The classic example of phenylketonuria (PKU) illustrates this point. This defect occurs approximately once in every 10,000 live births and is a result of a rare recessive genetic problem. The consequence of this genetic disorder is that the infant's system is unable to metabolize phenylalanine. Certain injurious acids are released into the infant's body and attack the brain if the child is provided the type of diet which is normally used with infants. However, if the condition is diagnosed during the first few weeks of the infant's life, special dietary control will protect the infant from the adverse effects of the condition. Parenthetically, most states within the United States require that a test be made for PKU on each newborn prior to the child's leaving the hospital.

Many of the very rare syndromes of mental retardation happen because of certain defective dominant genes which tend to follow family lines. Examples of such situations are found in tuberous sclerosis, neurofibromatosis, congenital ectodermoses, and cerebral angiomatosis. Each of these dominantly related clinical syndromes can be expressed in varying degrees of mental retardation; however, as a rule one would expect to find relatively more individuals with any of these conditions at the severe or profound levels of retardation.

Relatively more instances of mental retardation with a genetic cause result from recessive rather than from dominant genetic disorders. We all are

carriers of varying numbers and types of recessive genes, some of which are capable of exerting serious negative influences and others of which are not of any significant import at all. For example, certain recessive genes determine certain types of inborn errors of metabolism which, as has been stated, could precipitate mental retardation in a newborn child. There are other types of recessive genes which do not exert such negative influences, such as those which produce specific eye colors. If a mother or father is a carrier of a harmful recessive gene and the other partner does not carry this same recessive gene, ordinarily the offspring will not show the characteristics associated with the deleterious recessive gene. It is possible, however, for the offspring to be a carrier of the gene without exhibiting its typical characteristics. On the other hand, if both parents are carriers of the recessive gene, by chance we can expect that one in four of their offspring will not even carry the trait, one in four will exhibit the abnormal characteristics of the trait, and two in every four of their children will just be carriers of the trait. This follows the simple Mendelian ratios. Among some of the recessive related syndromes of mental retardation are phenylketonuria, microcephaly, and hartnup disease.

Other Prenatal Complications   In addition to these genetic disturbances, there are other types of biological, chemical, and physical abnormalities which, if they occur during the prenatal period, could result in a whole range of problems for the embryo and for the fetus. Mental retardation is frequently among the consequences of such problems. In spite of the fact that science has been able to identify many of the teratogenic agents that cause mental retardation, and other handicaps as well during the prenatal period, there are still large gaps in knowledge concerning when an agent is most influential in its negative effects, how much of the agent must be present in order for the fetus to be damaged, the circumstances that allow one person to be protected from and another person vulnerable to a specific agent, and a conclusive diagnosis of the specific factor(s) which cause mental retardation in a particular situation. An enormous amount of information has been compiled on various topics concerned with prenatal disorders. Many of the studies have been done with various populations of animals and the information from this work has aided immeasurably in identifying the range and nature of prenatal problems that can result in mental retardation. With increasing frequency, however, scientists are beginning to acknowledge that animal studies have some significant limitations in applicability to man.

Most of the more severe, gross malformations result from actions of teratogenic agents which have been present prior to the eighth week of conception. It is during this time period when organ systems become differentiated and identifiable. Children with extensive multiple malformations as a result of early large doses of teratogenic agents during the first few months of fetal life will often die in utero. Beginning around the third month of pregnancy, general and gross malformations do not usually occur. By this time the major organ systems are

relatively intact. It is important to remember, because of its relevance to mental retardation, that the central nervous system, including the brain, is especially slow to mature and does not usually reach full physiologic development until well after birth. Thus, anything that is introduced into the maternal system that retards growth, development, and differentiation of systems could seriously affect brain development without significantly influencing other organs during the second and third trimester of pregnancy. Now, what are some of the agents which if present during the prenatal period could result in significant damage to an unborn child so as to cause mental retardation?

It is now well established that excessive doses of x-ray during the early stages of pregnancy will affect the central nervous system and skull development of the fetus. Animal studies have revealed that certain defects appear only at critical periods when experimental irradiation is used as a teratogenic agent. Several studies have been done on women who were pregnant at the time the atomic bombs were detonated in Japan. The data show that the incidence of mental retardation and other abnormalities increased dramatically for the offspring of those women who were closer to the center of the explosion than for those in more remote areas. Moreover, women who were 7–15 weeks pregnant bore babies with handicaps of greater severity than were observed in older fetuses. The evidence is clear that every attempt should be made to keep pregnant women from experiencing heavy doses of or continual encounters with x-ray.

The adverse effects of various chemicals and drugs on the unborn have been demonstrated on experimental animals many times. Malformations in the central nervous system can be induced in the offspring of animals through exposure of the pregnant female to agents which interfere with cell metabolism. It seems a foregone conclusion to most people that certain drugs could harm the developing embryo; this seems especially true in light of the numerous animal studies in which such relationships have been fairly self-evident. Recent evidence, however, has shown that a drug can have different results in different species of animals. For example, the use of thalidomide on certain types of experimental animals did not cause teratogenic effects as it did in humans. The same conclusion has been reached by scientists who are investigating the influence of drugs on other malformations in various species. Although the exact influence of these agents on central nervous system development in the unborn is not specifically known, large amounts of drugs, alcohol, and nicotine are known to cause changes in fetal activity, fetal heart rate, breathing, and level of activity at birth. Avoiding drugs will not assure safety; however, only under extenuating circumstances and in consultation with a physician should medication be taken by a pregnant woman.

To a great extent a healthy mother is able to protect against infection during the period of pregnancy. This type of physical robustness is an important attribute since certain chronic illnesses of the mother can be transmitted across the placenta and seriously damage the fetus. Among the infections which can alter

the intrauterine environment and cause fetal malformation, including conditions associated with mental retardation, are maternal rubella, toxoplasmosis, syphilis, Asian influenza, and infectious hepatitis. It is significant that certain viral conditions can cross the placental barrier and attack the fetus without the mother being influenced at all. In the interest of abating unnecessary fears, it should be pointed out that there are also many instances in which the pregnant woman contracts a virus of some type and the fetus is not affected. The more complete control of infectious diseases through early identification, immunization, and prompt treatment offers promise for nearly eliminating certain conditions which have serious consequences. Recent progress has been made in controlling influenza, measles, and mumps, each of which can deleteriously affect fetal development if they are contracted by a pregnant women.

Hormone imbalance of some magnitude can be teratogenic and under certain circumstances lead to disorders in the fetus or result in spontaneous abortion. Mothers who are diabetic tend to have youngsters with the higher incidence of congenital malformations. There are also increased hazards during pregnancy for mothers with thyroid disorders and pituitary problems. Although the exact cause-and-effect relationship between endocrine disorders and mental retardation is not firmly established, proper hormonal balance is helpful for a normal pregnancy and an uneventful labor and birth.

There is virtually no research evidence to provide a specific estimate of the impact that maternal trauma of a physical nature has on the incidence of mental retardation. A very few case studies appear in the literature on this particular subject, and those that discuss the relationship between the mother's receiving a heavy blow or fall and intellectual subnormality are speculative to some extent. It is difficult to document the real significance of such an event, although common sense would suggest that a pregnant woman should be particularly cautious not to engage in work which might be described as "heavy" and be cautious not to engage in any type of activity which might be a potential danger to the fetus.

Emotional stress of unusual severity for an extended period in the mother may contribute to developmental disorders in the fetus. This statement is difficult to support with reliable data on humans. The animal research, however, clearly shows that biochemical imbalances in the mother animal result from emotional stress. These imbalances seem to affect the neurological mechanisms of the unborn fetus. Experimentally produced anxiety and other stress in animals is followed with a higher incidence of fetal abnormalities than with "nonanxious" mothers. There may be, then, a physiological relationship between maternal stress and abnormalities, including mental retardation, in the offspring. Obviously, this hypothesis is difficult to prove in a methodologically satisfactory way with human subjects. Researchers who have been interested in looking at these relationships have had to interview parents after the handicapped child was born. In such a circumstance one would expect to find parents who were emotionally tense, and

they, in turn, would naturally be more inclined to report some degree of emotional stress during the pregnancy. In short, investigating a relationship between emotional stress and mental retardation after a handicapped child has been born "stacks the cards" in favor of supporting the hunch that there is a positive relationship, because the parents at that moment will not be able to report objectively on their own predelivery emotional stability.

A number of reasons have been suggested for children experiencing difficulty during the prenatal period and later manifesting mental retardation at birth. There are a multitude of other possible conditions which are related to mental retardation during the prenatal period which might have been mentioned. For example, there is evidence that loud sounds, extreme changes in maternal temperature, intrauterine complications, excessive movement, malnutrition, and blood problems in the mother may also cause mental retardation in the fetus. Those readers who are interested in becoming more familiar with the characteristics of various prenatal complications might wish to read Crome and Stern (1967), Robinson and Robinson (1964), Berg (1965), and Masland, Sarason, and Gladwin (1958).

During the process of birth there are several possible disorders that can occur and, if serious enough, conceivably result in mental retardation. The line between a normal birth and one which is inordinately difficult is a controversial issue among medical personnel. For example, some have the opinion that trauma is experienced by the newborn as a result of the difference between intrauterine temperature and the temperature in the delivery room. Others believe that the robustness of most newborns will allow them to survive most situations they encounter during delivery.

Birth Injuries   Although most pregnancies terminate in a normal way there are, at the same time, certain perinatal difficulties which can complicate labor, cause neonatal distress, and possibly result in mental retardation. Even with a relatively normal labor, a youngster can be congenitally handicapped as a result of prenatal disorders and experience real problems after delivery. It is imperative for each child to be examined immediately after birth to determine if congenital difficulties are present, if other crises are being experienced, and if immediate medical attention is needed. Apgar (1953) has developed a system for obtaining immediate data on the condition of newborns within sixty seconds after birth. Her system will allow a delivery room nurse to evaluate the degree of robustness of a neonate. She has also suggested a method whereby a delivery room physician can quickly check on whether certain critical congenital problems exist.

Brain injury is a very general term and not at all descriptive. The meaning it has for one person will inevitably differ for another; this is true even among many medical specialists. Unfortunately, the term is one which has often been adopted to explain all classes of behavior, and this has led to the misclassification of many children. Parents, for example, will often describe their handicapped

youngster as being "brain injured" instead of admitting that their child is mentally retarded. For some, the term *brain injury* seems to be a more socially accepted label. In spite of the lack of absoluteness associated with the term, it is true that a number of children are injured at birth and in certain cases the neurological structures are involved. Complicated and difficult labor, too high a level of anesthesia, internal hemorrhage, umbilical cord complications, inhalation of fluid, prematurity, use of instruments, and circumstances resulting in anoxia for the newborn can all cause central nervous system damage, mental retardation, and other abnormal conditions. It seems fair, then, to suggest that brain damage as a result of birth injury is an important cause of mental retardation; however, it is exceedingly difficult to estimate the incidence of mental retardation as a result of obstetric difficulties. Mental retardation as a result of perinatal disorders is probably decreasing because of new medical techniques.

The Time after Birth   A variety of problems can cause mental retardation after birth, i.e., during the postnatal period. The most common of the various potential hazards during the postnatal period is central nervous system infection. Meningitis and encephalitis can result in serious consequences including retarded mental development if the conditions are not diagnosed promptly and properly treated. Other infectious conditions which result in very high fever will often influence central nervous system functioning and development unless the conditions and the fever are effectively abated.

Brain problems, in addition to those involving infections, can cause mental retardation. For example, traumatic injuries to the head as a result of accidents or child abuse are often severe enough to negatively affect a child's development. Brain tumors will also result in disorders in intellectual functioning and, at times, even cause personality disorders and other complicated problems as a result of intracranial pressure. Poisons and other toxic substances will often produce serious neurological damage which can be totally irreversible. Vascular problems in the brain are often not manifested until after the child's birth; a major consequence of cerebrovascular malformations is often intellectual subnormality.

A second type of postnatal environmental disorder can result in functional mental retardation particularly among younger children. I am referring to the horribly inadequate psychological and social environment which many children who are reared in urban and rural slums experience throughout their early formative years. As a result of what many scientists have termed *sensory deprivation* these children do not develop the repertoire of experiences that most more advantaged youngsters experience. This paucity of opportunities and reduced range of stimulation, if severe enough for a substantial portion of a child's early life, apparently will result in a deterioration of cognitive functioning. Eventually the situation becomes irreversible and the child functions as if mentally retarded. This environmentally related cause is as significant in deterring intellectual development as are the more medically related causes. The manner in which a young

child's surroundings influences cognitive development is considered in greater depth in Chapter 3.

In summary of the major ideas that have been presented up to this point in this section, it has been noted that mental retardation can result from disorders during the prenatal, perinatal, and postnatal periods. Genetic problems are relatively few in contrast to environmental disorders; however, the former types of difficulties usually result in more severe and profound forms of multiple disability of which mental retardation is a part. Numerous possible prenatal problems can take place, the impact of which is dependent on when the difficulty occurs during the pregnancy and how severe an event it happens to be. During the birth process the neonate encounters numerous changes and could be damaged to varying degrees as a result of unusual circumstances. After birth, a child's intellectual development could be affected as a result of various internal disorders as well as atypical circumstances within the child's environment such as accidental poisoning, falls, etc. By far the largest portion of the mildly retarded suffer from environmental deprivation which eventually leads to intellectual retardation.

The various major categories of causes of mental retardation have been surveyed. It was not the intent here to consider comprehensively the many nuances of each type of etiology. Some of even the more common conditions were omitted. Those students with an interest in this subject are urged to consult the references which are listed at the end of this section.

Factors Contributing to a Healthy Baby   As a natural outgrowth of this discussion concerning possible reasons for mental retardation, it is only proper that some attention be given to the way in which a pregnant woman can increase the likelihood of an unborn child developing normally, both physically and intellectually. For many of you the guidelines and suggestions to be offered will seem all too self-evident after your having read the previous material. Nonetheless, focus and emphasis on protection from and prevention of mental retardation wherever and whenever possible should constantly be the aim of all who have an interest in this field.

By this time you have probably concluded that it is very difficult to attribute many instances of mental retardation to a specific factor. The physical and intellectual well-being of an unborn child results from the complex interaction of factors such as (1) the extent and type of prenatal care which the expectant mother receives, (2) the degree of nutritional inadequacies before and during the pregnancy, (3) emotional disorders, (4) the prevalence of various complications during the pregnancy, and (5) the general lack of physical robustness of the mother. For some women many of these factors are related to association with poor socioeconomic surroundings (Wortis, 1970). With this complex network of factors in operation, it is obvious why one would have difficulty in determining how much of a certain anomaly can be attributed to any one of the possible multitude of factors, such as poor nutrition, alone.

Now, how might a prospective mother improve the chances of her baby's being born in as robust a condition as possible?

1. Select a physician in the community who (1) is easily accessible to you, (2) will be able to examine you throughout your pregnancy, and (3) will be available to deliver your child. Visit this doctor no later than the third month after conception has taken place for a complete examination. Be sure to answer all his questions truthfully and thoroughly. Do not be hesitant or shy in your conversations with him. In those instances where a physician is not available or where you cannot afford to pay the doctor, you should not delay in contacting the local hospital or physician referral service for advice. Many hospitals and local agencies support prenatal clinics for citizens who are unable to pay for services. In every case, the physician should be visited on a routine basis throughout the pregnancy.

2. Do everything possible to avoid exposure to contagious diseases, particularly German measles, throughout the pregnancy but especially during the first three or four months. These conditions can seriously affect the unborn fetus. It has been estimated, for example, that nearly 50 percent of the infants born to mothers who contracted German measles during their first month of pregnancy have serious congenital malformations. The incidence of disorders caused by conditions of this sort decreases as the pregnancy moves closer to termination, but the percentage of decrease is not enough to warrant taking chances when virus or infectious diseases are involved.

3. Refrain from taking drugs and other chemical substances during the pregnancy unless your physician has given his full approval. Do not continue taking medicines that were prescribed before the pregnancy. Avoid any type of chemical substance which can be ingested or inhaled. Both tobacco and alcohol should be shunned during the pregnancy.

4. Avoid x-ray examinations and treatments especially during the first four months. Even after that period you should not be x-rayed unless your physician fully approves.

5. Get an ample amount of sleep and rest, maintain good body hygiene, avoid an association with emotionally charged situations, and exercise continually, but to a moderate degree, throughout the pregnancy.

6. Make sure that you receive an adequate diet which is especially rich in proteins, vitamins, and minerals during the period before as well as throughout your pregnancy. This guideline is a very important one for both malnutrition (inadequacy of food intake) and undernutrition (insufficient caloric intake) have the potential for affecting the unborn child. Studies dealing with caloric deficiencies consistently have found a higher incidence of fetal anomalies and complications of pregnancy in cases where the maternal diet was considered to be poor. Perhaps the most conclusive studies have been done in the area of determin-

ing the effects of protein on fetal robustness. A number of investigators have found that protein deficiencies can cause significant alterations in brain metabolism and development and eventually result in central nervous system disorders. It is important to realize that the brain functions interdependently with all organs of the body and is not an isolated entity. A condition such as serious protein deficiency and undernutrition can affect organs such as the liver and kidneys, and, in turn, negatively influence the brain as a result of an inadequate supply of oxygen reaching it via the blood stream. The impressive body of literature concerning the need for a pregnant woman's maintaining an adequate diet cannot be ignored for it clearly shows that proper nutrition provides the essential building blocks needed for the unborn child to develop all the components of a strong and healthy body.

In order to keep this proper nutritional level, a pregnant woman should maintain not less than a 2300 calorie daily diet. This should include at least three cups of milk; eight ounces of meat, fish, cheese, or eggs; one or two servings of fresh fruit; three servings of green or yellow vegetables; not less than five servings of bread and cereal; and a minimum amount of fats and sweets. Your physician will prescribe supplementary vitamins and minerals in those instances where the proper minimum diet is not being maintained.

7. Do everything possible to tolerate the usual pain associated with childbirth without requesting, on a continuing basis, heavy doses of pain-relieving medications. The evidence suggests that high levels of anesthesia before and during the process of birth will cause the newborn to be less active after birth and show a lower Apgar score. Apparently these medications do not wear off as quickly in a newborn as they do in the mother, and they cause the youngster to show a marked reduction in certain important vital signs.

Some of the major ways in which a pregnant woman can increase the likelihood of her child's being born without unusual difficulties are summarized in the latter portion of this section. Realizing all possible problems that can occur during the pregnancy is a source of real concern for many people, especially when they are listed together in a group such as presented in this section. The purpose here was not to strike fear in the hearts of those who intend to have a family but to provide some basic information concerning how they can "tip the odds" in their favor and do everything possible to prevent their child from being born with a problem such as mental retardation.

Recommended Readings

Anderson, V. E.: "Genetics in Mental Retardation," in H. A. Stevens and R. Heber (eds.), *Mental Retardation: A Review of Research,* The University of Chicago Press, Chicago, 1964, pp. 348–394.

Apgar, V.: "A Proposal for a New Method of Evaluation of the Newborn Infant," *Anesthesia and Analgesia,* vol. 32, 1953, pp. 260–267.

Berg, J. M.: "Aetiological Aspects of Mental Subnormality: Pathological Factors," in A. M. Clarke and A. D. B. Clarke (eds.), *Mental Deficiency: The Changing Outlook,* The Free Press, New York, 1965, pp. 138–165.

Crome, L., and J. Stern: *The Pathology of Mental Retardation,* J. and A. Churchill Ltd., London, 1967, pp. 1–94.

Fraser, F. C.: "Teratogenesis of the Central Nervous System," in H. A. Stevens and R. Heber (eds.), *Mental Retardation: A Review of Research,* The University of Chicago Press, Chicago, 1964, pp. 395–428.

Gottesman, I. I.: "Genetic Aspects of Intelligent Behavior," in N. R. Ellis (ed.), *Handbook of Mental Deficiency,* McGraw-Hill Book Company, New York, 1963, pp. 253–296.

Koch, R.: "The Multidisciplinary Approach to Mental Retardation," in A. A. Baumeister (ed.), *Mental Retardation: Appraisal, Education, and Rehabilitation,* Aldine Publishing Company, Chicago, 1967, pp. 20–38.

Masland, R. L., S. B. Sarason, and T. Gladwin: *Mental Subnormality: Biological, Psychological, and Cultural Factors,* Basic Books, Inc., Publishers, New York, 1958, pp. 34–135.

Robinson, H. B., and N. M. Robinson: *The Mentally Retarded Child: A Psychological Approach,* McGraw-Hill Book Company, New York, 1964, pp. 61–206.

Waisman, H. A., and T. Gerritsen: "Biochemical and Clinical Correlations," in H. A. Stevens and R. Heber (eds.), *Mental Retardation: A Review of Research,* The University of Chicago Press, Chicago, 1964, pp. 307–347.

Wortis, J.: "Poverty and Retardation: Biosocial Factors," in J. Wortis (ed.), *Mental Retardation: An Annual Review,* Grune & Stratton, Inc., New York, 1970, pp. 271–279.

What types of examinations are given before an infant is born in order to identify possible problems that might cause mental retardation?

The first visit of a pregnant woman to the obstetrician is a very important moment, not only because it is the time when the pregnancy is confirmed but also because it is the beginning of a period of extensive and intensive medical and psychological evaluation of the prospective mother. During the first visit the physician will spend a considerable amount of time taking a history of the mother and father and of their near and remote relatives. A great many questions are asked at this time so that the physician can begin to consider and predict possible complications in the pregnancy. It is also the goal of the obstetrician to collect this base-line data for purposes of comparing information and findings from subsequent examinations and to notice any gross changes in the mother's condition as the pregnancy progresses.

In addition to the historical study, the obstetrician will do a thorough internal and external examination of the mother. The aim is to ascertain if abnormalities exist which are significant enough to require attention immediately or possibly in the future. In this examination he will evaluate the mother's abdomen; pelvic area; the shape, size, and position of the uterus; the mother's breasts; blood pressure; and other visceral systems. The examination will help the obstetrician to estimate if the birth canal is of adequate size for an uneventful delivery.

The physician will also order a number of laboratory tests during the mother's first visit to his office. These tests will frequently include an examination of the mother's blood in order to determine if she is Rh negative, is anemic, or has contracted other types of significant blood disorders. The urinalysis is done in order to determine if the mother has a high level of sugar or albumin which might be indicative of conditions such as diabetes or possible kidney disorders.

The first examination is a very important one and will often extend for an hour or more. It is usually followed by monthly examinations for the first seven months of pregnancy during which time the obstetrician continues to collect data on the mother and growing fetus. Sometime after the fourth or fifth month the physician will evaluate the size of the fetus and ascertain whether the position of the unborn child in the uterus is a normal one. Continual samples of urine and blood are taken and evaluated, and an updating of the history of the pregnancy is made. The physician is able to study any dramatic changes that have occurred in the health of the mother and unborn child as a result of collecting information and data on a longitudinal basis. If potential hazards seem apparent, appropriate remedial steps can be taken immediately.

Obviously, the mother's health and that of her unborn child is enhanced according to how well the mother takes care of herself. This means that she must get plenty of sleep and rest, eat proper foods, not gain an inordinate amount of weight, stay away from children and adults with contagious diseases, not take drugs without consulting her physician, and maintain a proper level of vitamin intake. These and other commonsense practices will contribute toward a healthy intrauterine environment for the fetus.

In addition to helping to maintain an adequate physical environment for the fetus, the physician is also interested in studying the emotional characteristics of the pregnant woman. As was mentioned in the previous section, intensive and long-term psychological disorders can cause changes in the mother's biochemical makeup and, in turn, result in an atypical intrauterine environment for the fetus. The obstetrician is continually aware of possible emotional disorders and will often refer a pregnant woman and other members of her family to a counseling specialist or psychiatrist if the need is so indicated.

Finally, a number of very new procedures which are designed to evaluate the exact nature of intrauterine conditions have recently been reported in the literature. Some very successful attempts have been made at studying the amniotic fluid prior to an infant's birth in those instances where the family history or

findings from the physician's physical examination of the mother indicate that abnormalities might be present. For example, a technique has been developed to diagnose Down's syndrome in an unborn fetus. This procedure and others are very new and have not, as yet, undergone extensive laboratory testing. Nonetheless, they signal a new era in prenatal diagnosis and care for those mothers, whose yet unborn children might need some type of immediate care.

Recommended Readings

Rorvik, D. M.: "The Brave New World of the Newborn," *Look*, vol. 33, no. 22, November, 1969, pp. 74–76, 80–83.

Is it possible to detect mental retardation at birth? If so, how is this done?

Certain types of mental retardation are readily obvious at birth, especially those types which are associated with a relatively typical clinical syndrome or symptomatology. For example, Down's syndrome and microcephaly are two conditions which are present at birth, or congenital, and have a characteristic appearance. Experience has shown that children who are born with either of these conditions will be intellectually subnormal in addition to frequently having other types of disorders. The more severe conditions of mental retardation which show clear pathology as a result of prenatal difficulties are obvious at birth without a physician conducting an immediate and detailed examination. Obviously, children who are born with disorders of this magnitude should undergo comprehensive examinations by a pediatrician, or a team of specialists, in order to ascertain the extent of their anomalies and the type of immediate treatment required. There are, then, a group of congenitally affected infants in whom mental retardation can be determined immediately after birth because of the unique clinical symptoms which they manifest. These infants are characteristically multiply disabled.

There is another group of congenitally affected neonates who are especially susceptible to certain aspects of their environment which could negatively influence the effective operation of a number of their bodily systems. I am referring to those youngsters who suffer from inborn errors of metabolism which are of a genetic origin and result in the infant being particularly vulnerable to its environment. PKU has been mentioned earlier as an example of this group of conditions. Children with this disorder cannot be allowed to feed on milk and other normal forms of nourishment since their system is unable to satisfactorily process these types of food. If the condition goes undiagnosed and the proper diet is not substituted, the young child will develop progressive and irreversible brain damage. To identify if a child suffers from disorders of this type, the pedi-

atrician will usually request certain standard diagnostic laboratory tests of the infant's blood and urine. These evaluations will promptly identify whether a child suffers from an inborn error of metabolism.

During the second half of pregnancy most obstetricians will check the blood of the mother and father to see if Rh incompatibility exists. This test is necessary since the Rh factor, if undiagnosed, could cause the infant either to die before birth or to develop brain injury after birth. The problem exists when an Rh-negative mother has a baby with Rh-positive blood, like the father's. If the baby's Rh-positive blood cells mix with the mother's Rh-negative blood cells, the mother's body could produce antibodies which attack the Rh-positive blood of the infant. If this reaction is intense enough, the neonate could be born with severe leukemia, which, in turn, could damage his central nervous system. This event happens less frequently with the first pregnancy, but it usually becomes more critical in subsequent births. If the blood discrepancy is noted during pregnancy, the physician will sample the newborn's blood immediately after birth to determine its condition. In certain instances a partial or total blood transfusion is done to replace the infant's damaged blood. This treatment is typically conducted during the first few days of life, although it may have to be repeated several times.

In 1963, a pediatric researcher from New Zealand developed a new technique which allowed for a prenatal check of an infant's blood in those cases where Rh incompatibility dangers were at a potential crisis level. As a result of some very ingenious diagnostic methods, he was able to determine if an unborn was in danger of survival as a result of Rh complications. In those instances in which problems were noted, the fetus was injected with red blood cells directly through the mother's abdomen. By carefully selecting cases and as result of the utmost skill in diagnosis and treatment, a large number of babies have been saved through this procedure and now manifest no central nervous system pathology.

That part of the scientific community with an interest in problems of this sort has begun to develop some ingenious procedures for dealing with the unborn and newborn child who suffers from Rh complications. For example, one attack on this problem is presently being made by attempting to minimize the influence of the mother's antibodies prior to and during pregnancy. Through immunization, medical scientists have reported promising results from this procedure.

There is still another group of newborns which pediatricians would consider to be high-risk babies. These are youngsters who, after having received a cursory examination at birth, do not show an obvious syndrome of clinical pathology similar to those types described earlier. Experience, however, shows that this group of babies necessitates close medical observation. I am referring to infants who are born premature, i.e., those who weigh less than 5½ pounds at birth. There are several reasons for prematurity, and in every case the child will need special care to protect against various conditions which could affect his future

functioning, intellectually, emotionally, and physically. The research shows that between 60 and 70 percent of the premature who weigh less than 3½ pounds at birth subsequently suffer from various significant disorders later in life. Most hospitals, therefore, give immediate and comprehensive attention to the premature infant and intentionally guard against anything in the infant's environment that may cause conditions which could result in mental retardation later in the child's life. In fact, there is a clear trend among hospitals to establish intensive care units for children who are born premature. These units house various specialists who can give immediate attention to any crisis situation that might occur during the first few hours and days of the infant's life. Newborn special care units, such as the one at the Yale–New Haven Medical Center, are equipped to provide complete neonatal care, including pediatric surgery if necessary.

Assessing the Newborn Infant's Condition   The newborn child's condition is a matter of great concern not only to the parents but to the attending medical specialists as well. For infants who suffer from any type of crisis at birth, it is necessary that they receive immediate attention in order to prevent possible subsequent difficulties, including central nervous system involvement. It is natural, then, that attempts have been made to evaluate the child's condition immediately after birth. In the previous section mention was made of the wide use which the Newborn Scoring System has received in many delivery rooms throughout the world. Dr. Virginia Apgar, developer of the system, has attempted to objectify certain vital signs of the infant at birth and to provide a means for determining if his condition necessitates a more complete examination or, perhaps, immediate therapy. For a valid indication of the child's condition, an observer other than the delivering physician should rate the infant sixty seconds after the birth is completed.

Briefly, the dimensions of the scoring system are shown in Table 2-1.

Table 2-1   Apgar scoring chart*

	Rating		
Factor	0	1	2
Heart rate	Absent	Below 100 beats	Over 100 beats
Respiratory effort	Absent	Irregular, slow, or shallow	Good effort, cried lustily
Muscle tone	Completely flaccid	Some flexion of extremities	Active motion
Reflex irritability	No response to stimulation	Grimace	Cry
Color	Blue, pale	Body pink but extremities blue	Completely pink

* After Apgar (1953, 1968) and Apgar and James (1962).

Each infant is scored from 0 to 2 on the above dimensions according to the particular criteria. A score between 7 and 10 is considered good, from 4 to 6 is considered fair, and from 0 to 3 is viewed as poor. Studies have shown heart rate to be the most important factor and color to be least precise in the system's diagnostic predictability. The technique has been adopted by hospitals throughout the world and a great amount of research has been done to determine how predictive of future development the procedure is.

Dr. Apgar (1962) has also suggested a procedure which delivery-room physicians can use to check on hidden congenital anomalies. This five-minute screening examination helps to determine if a child has obscure birth defects such as intestinal obstructions, disorders of the esophagus, laryngeal problems, or cleft palate. While these defects may not necessarily be related to mental retardation, their occurrence signals the need for a comprehensive physical and serial examination of the newborn.

You can see, then, that the range of evaluative measures which are available to the physician at and soon after the child's birth are extensive. Those which have been mentioned in this section are but a sample of the full spectrum of diagnostic possibilities which appear in the literature. The student with an interest in this particular area will find a more comprehensive and detailed treatment of examination techniques in the following suggested readings.

Recommended Readings

Apgar, V.: "A Proposal for a New Method of Evaluation of the Newborn Infant," *Anesthesia and Analgesia,* vol. 32, 1953, pp. 260–267.

————: "Resuscitation of the Newborn," *Consultant,* January, 1962, Smith, Kline, and French Laboratories.

————: "Five-minute Diagnosis of Hidden Congenital Anomalies," *Consultant,* June, 1962, Smith, Kline, and French Laboratories.

———— and L. S. James: "Further Observations on the Newborn Scoring System," *American Journal of Diseases of Children,* vol. 104, 1962, pp. 419–428.

Downs, M. P.: "Hunt to Catch a Handicap," *Today's Health,* vol. 46, no. 1, 1968, pp. 23–27.

Drillien, C. M.: "The Incidence of Mental and Physical Handicaps in School-age Children of Very Low Birth Weights," *Pediatrics,* vol. 27, 1961, pp. 452–464.

Irwin, T.: "High Risk Care Saves Lives and Minds," *Today's Health,* vol. 46, no. 1, 1968, pp. 18–21.

Knobloch, H., and B. Pasamanick: "Neuropsychiatric Sequelae of Prematurity: A Longitudinal Study," *Journal of the American Medical Association,* vol. 161, 1956, pp. 581–585.

———— and ————: "Syndrome of Minimal Cerebral Damage in Infancy," *Journal of the American Medical Association,* vol. 170, 1959, pp. 1384–1387.

———— and ————: "The Developmental Behavioral Approach to the Neurologic Examination in Infancy," *Child Development,* vol. 33, 1962, pp. 181–198.

In cases of suspected or diagnosed mental retardation, what factors should be considered in counseling the family?

Relative to the large population of mentally retarded individuals in our society, only a very small portion is suspected of or diagnosed as being mentally retarded at birth. Even in instances of severe or profound mental retardation, a definitive diagnosis cannot always be made at or soon after the infant's delivery. Oftentimes physicians desire to systematically observe the infant's development and behavior for a relatively longer period of time before confirming that mental retardation exists. In such instances, the parents may be the first to notice that their infant is not developing or behaving as they feel he should, and they may request that their pediatrician do a comprehensive study of the child.

Factors Influencing Parents' Initial Reaction   The event of being informed that your infant is mentally retarded, or otherwise handicapped, is horribly traumatic. Unfortunately, a number of parents each day are informed of this fact in grossly primitive ways. A waiting father, for example, may become suspicious that "something has gone wrong" in the delivery as a result of subtle differences in the behavior of the attending maternity nurses. A questioning father may be told by a nurse, "The doctor will be out shortly to review the case with you." Instead of receiving warm congratulations, then, the father of a newborn retarded infant might receive a "cold-fish handshake" and be told that "your wife is fine, but we had some trouble with your child." Still other instances have been reported in which the baby has been kept from the parents for days or for weeks without explanation except that "he is too frail to leave the nursery." Whatever the technique, whether direct or unobtrusive, the initial shock is an experience which defies definition, is not necessarily the same for everyone, and is probably never completely overcome by most parents who experience the event.

The research literature is not very clear in describing the specific feelings and behavior of parents after they have been informed that their newborn infant is suspected of being mentally retarded. No doubt the initial reaction differs according to factors such as (1) whether the pregnancy was particularly difficult, (2) if suspicions were aroused before the birth, (3) whether or not the child is the parents' firstborn, (4) the extent to which earlier pregnancies have resulted in stillbirths or other handicapped children, (5) the degree of emotional and marital stability of the parents, (6) how much the parents know about mental retarda-

tion, and (7) whether they have had previous experiences with the mentally retarded. Accordingly, then, a parent's initial feelings will be highly idiosyncratic and during the first few months after having been informed of the child's condition might include all or some of the following reactions: alarm; helplessness; concern for his or her mate; anguish; disbelief; a death wish for the child; frustration as a result of not knowing what needs to be done, when, by whom, and how; and deep grief. Obviously, there are many other possible initial reactions that the mother or father might have, and if they are sufficiently severe, special medical attention might be required for relief and control.

An exceptional child has been born in my immediate family, and in my opinion the extent to which the initial family feelings are resolved, or placed within reasonable bounds, is dependent upon several very subtle but nonetheless critical factors. First, the parents, and particularly the father, in most cases will require some immediate, basic information from the physician, not a nurse or social worker, but a physician who has had experience with children with problems similar to that of his newborn infant. The exact information which the physician offers will probably differ to a great extent according to the educational level of the parent, his level of grief, the previous experiences which he has had in dealing with unusually traumatic situations, the child's prognosis, and other factors. In every case, however, it is the opinion of the author that certain very definite steps should be taken, or at least mapped out, by the physician. Even if this action is nothing more than calling in a consultant to examine the child, the father and mother can be assured that steps are being taken to properly and immediately attend to the child's problems.

Parents will be able to handle different amounts of information during the initial stages of the trauma. The anxiety and frustration of the family may be significantly increased when a physician "unloads with both barrels" and begins a recitation of the many ways in which their child is disabled and the whole range of possible problems that the parents can expect to face during the subsequent decade of the child's life. The most important aspect of the initial meeting between the father and the physician is to provide enough information to satisfy the father and to aid in alleviating some of the early concerns over management which arise, along with the expected depressing feelings which the parents experience over the event, as a result of their not knowing what to do and whether or not the advice they are receiving is dependable and valid.

A second factor which will determine the extent to which the parents' initial reactions over the event are controlled or resolved is the kind of emotional support they receive as a result of the overt initial reactions of their own parents and close friends to the report that their child is suspected of being mentally retarded. In spite of the fact that the parents may wonder about possible causes or question why it happened to them, it is not at all supportive for their friends or the child's grandparents to delineate in their presence the many ways in which viola-

tions of a physician's directions occurred during the pregnancy, to point out the manifestations of "bad blood" on one side of the family or on the other, or to offer uninformed suggestions concerning what the new parents should do or whose advice they should seek. This latter thought is important: too much input for the parents will only increase anxiety and cause them to further question whether or not the advice of their family pediatrician should be followed. In like manner, grandparents and friends of the troubled parents should never act unconcerned, nor should they ignore the degree of parental distress by not attending to their needs, acknowledging their concern, or offering support of various types. It helps the parents of the newborn defective child to know for sure that they can depend on their friends and their own parents for emotional and, perhaps, financial support in such a crisis situation.

The Range of Reactions by Parents   Numerous accounts have been presented in the professional literature regarding the nature and degree of trauma for parents arising from the birth of a child with suspected or diagnosed mental retardation (Ross, 1964; McDonald, 1962; Tisza, 1962; Olshansky, 1962; Gordon and Ullman, 1956; Goodman, 1964; Cohen, 1962). Perhaps the most thorough review on this subject and the most enlightening discussion of the implications which surround the various problems and issues of providing counsel to parents of retarded children have been offered by Wolfensberger (1967).

In looking at the continuum of possible parental reactions, Wolfensberger suggests that parents may experience one or more of three types of crisis experiences. First, and most relevant to this section, he believes that the initial reaction may precipitate a *novelty shock crisis.* This type of disorganization results from a *demolition of expectations,* i.e., the discrepancy that results between the type of expected child and the nature of the youngster that was born. In his opinion, parents who experience novelty shock crisis need basic information about the child; the nature of the condition; and emotional, physical, and financial support.

The second form of crisis primarily involves values of the parents. In this case, the youngster may either be overtly or passively rejected to some degree because of the parents' belief in what is valuable, desirable, or acceptable. The reactions of parents in this instance may be viewed as relatively extreme, ranging from total denial and immediate institutionalization of the child to oversensitization which might result in guilt due to the parents not feeling that they are providing adequate care for their youngster. Wolfensberger suggests that parents who experience this type of shock require intensive personal counseling.

Reality crisis is the third general form of difficulty which parents might experience. This type of crisis results from a realization on the part of the parents that they no longer are able to provide for, control, or effectively deal with the multitude of problems that the retarded child presents. Crises of this variety usually appear later in the retardate's life and will typically force parents into seeking realistic and practical assistance from community agencies, professional

groups, medical specialists, residential centers, and from personal friends according to the types of major difficulties which the youngster presents.

Some Thoughts on Parental Management   It is difficult to present any absolute rules or guidelines to follow when one is faced with the problem of informing parents that their child is mentally retarded. Quite naturally, you would expect the procedure to vary according to each particular circumstance. The personality and degree of emotional security of the informer as well as of the parents are indicative that differences could be expected. In dealing with novelty shock crisis, however, there are several major factors which the counselor, who is most often a physician, might wish to consider:

1.   Include both parents in the initial conference in instances which involve a confirmed diagnosis as well as in those situations in which more time is required to conduct a comprehensive medical examination of the child. In either case, the initial encounter with the parents should be handled by a physician who is well informed about the case, a gentle and warm person with whom the parents have a measure of rapport, one who is knowledgeable concerning mental retardation, and an individual who is prepared to offer the proper amount of information concerning which procedures for the immediate future are suggested by the facts.

2.   The parents should be assured that all available resources will be provided in order to properly care for their infant, and that they should not be concerned about financial affairs, contacting additional consultants, searching for alternative solutions themselves, or the future management of their child.

3.   The parents should be made aware of whom they can contact for answers to questions which will occur to them during the initial crisis period. They should be assured that no question, concern, or issue that they might have is too small or insignificant and that they will be continually informed of the child's status and included in all phases of planning which involve the welfare of themselves and their child.

4.   Under no circumstances should the parents be deceived or led to believe that the prognosis for the child is more favorable than the data indicate. It will take a very keen diagnostician to know when parents are able to satisfactorily handle information which suggests a possibility of a very dismal future for the infant. In any case, the parents should not receive anything but a true, objective, and nontechnical description of the status of their child. On this latter point, it is important for the counselor to speak in terms which are easily understood by parents and to give only that amount of technical information which the parents can satisfactorily "digest" at each particular moment of crisis.

5.   Parents will need considerable help from professional workers in the techniques that they might use to deal with potential family difficulties and other social problems arising from pressures in informing others that their newborn child may be mentally retarded. As has been suggested earlier, this is a particu-

larly difficult period for most parents since their friends, as they, were looking forward to hearing that "the mother and baby are doing well." It is therefore important that the counselor arm the parents, and particularly the father, with some suggestions for dealing with these particularly perplexing and frightfully tense situations.

6. It is especially important that the counseling physician not be mechanistic in his dealings with the parents during this initial crisis period. Instead, he must make every attempt to give the parents as much time as they need and offer the degree of warm friendship and understanding which the parents will require and subsequently seek as time progresses.

7. In spite of the fact that the physician may be aware that the research literature suggests that additional difficulties might be encountered or expected as the retarded infant grows older, this kind of information should not be presented to the parents as something they can look forward to as a future possibility. Too much information, some of which may be highly speculative, will only serve to overwhelm the parents and precipitate an inordinately high level of anxiety and frustration in spite of the fact that the child may be in highly competent medical hands.

8. Even during this initial period of crisis, certain parents may require continual information about mental retardation simply as a result of their not having had experience with or read about various aspects of the condition. It is advisable, therefore, for the parents to be given some very basic, general literature which the physician believes the parents can readily understand. Again, this suggestion is certainly not appropriate for all parents, and perhaps should not be offered to the father or mother without some clear indication that they would like to have more information later.

Discussion on the question of how to deal with the initial crisis which parents experience after the birth of a mentally retarded child indicates that procedures for counseling these parents are a highly individual matter. The degree to which it is a successful experience will be based on how effectively the counselor can diagnose the parents' needs at that particular moment and time. Diagnostic sensitivity by the counselor is not the only prerequisite for effectiveness, however; the professional worker must know a great deal about mental retardation and, specifically, be completely certain about the information on the child which is presented to the parents. It is also important that the counselor tentatively sketch out a plan of attack and gently lead the parents to consider and evaluate the alternatives which they alone must make. The initial time, however, is not the time to overwhelm the parents with technical data concerning the child and his expected prognosis. Instead, only enough information should be offered to satisfy their questions and curiosity; the counselor should be able to judge in subsequent sessions whether or not they are emotionally and intellectually prepared to

receive more detailed information on their child and alternative plans for management. As was mentioned at the beginning of this section, this period is one which is never forgotten by most parents and is so traumatic that it is difficult to describe in terms which can be understood by those who have not experienced such an event. As a result, at the beginning of comprehensive evaluation, treatment, and management of those who are mentally retarded, the problems, concerns, grief, frustrations, and anxieties which the parents will experience throughout the lifetime of their retarded child must be taken into consideration.

Recommended Readings

Bryant, K. N., and J. C. Hirschberg: "Helping the Parents of a Retarded Child," *American Journal of Diseases of Children,* vol. 102, 1961, pp. 52–66.

Cohen, P. C.: "The Impact of the Handicapped Child on the Family," *Social Caseworker,* vol. 43, 1962, pp. 137–142.

Disner, E.: "Reporting to Parents," *American Journal of Mental Deficiency,* vol. 61, 1956, pp. 362–367.

Drayer, C., and E. Schlesinger: "The Informing Interview," *American Journal of Mental Deficiency,* vol. 65, 1960, pp. 363–370.

Farber, B.: "Effects of a Severely Mentally Retarded Child on Family Integration," *Monographs of the Society for Research on Child Development,* vol. 24, no. 2, 1959.

Giannini, M. J., and L. Goodman: "Counseling Families During the Crisis Reaction to Mongolism," *American Journal of Mental Deficiency,* vol. 67, 1963, pp. 740–747.

Goodman, L.: "Continuing Treatment of Parents with Congenitally Defective Infants," *Social Worker,* vol. 9, 1964, pp. 92–97.

Gordon, E. W., and M. Ullman: "Reactions of Parents to Problems of Mental Retardation in Children," *American Journal of Mental Deficiency,* vol. 61, 1956, pp. 158–163.

Kanner, L.: "Parents' Feelings About Retarded Children," *American Journal of Mental Deficiency,* vol. 57, 1953, pp. 375–383.

Kirk, S. A., M. B. Karnes, and W. D. Kirk: *You And Your Retarded Child: A Manual for Parents of Retarded Children,* The Macmillan Company, New York, 1955.

McDonald, E. T.: *Understand Those Feelings,* Stanwix House, Pittsburgh, 1962.

Olshansky, S.: "Chronic Sorrow: A Response to Having a Mentally Defective Child," *Social Caseworker,* vol. 43, 1962, pp. 191–194.

Owens, C.: "Parents' Reactions to Defective Babies," *American Journal of Nursing,* vol. 64, 1964, pp. 83–86.

Roos, P.: "Psychological Counseling with Parents of Retarded Children," *Mental Retardation,* vol. 1, 1963, pp. 345–350.

Ross, A. V.: *The Exceptional Child in the Family,* Grune and Stratton, Inc. New York, 1964.

Tisza, V. B.: "Management of the Parents of the Chronically Ill Child," *American Journal of Orthopsychiatry,* vol. 32, 1962, pp. 53–59.

Wolfensberger, W.: "Counseling the Parents of the Retarded," in A. Baumeister (ed.), *Mental Retardation: Appraisal, Education, Rehabilitation,* Aldine Publishing Company, Chicago, 1967, pp. 329–400.

Should a child who is identified as being mentally retarded at birth be placed in an institution?

This same question will be posed in each of the next four chapters because it has pertinence to retarded children and the problems they present as preschoolers as well as during their elementary school years, as adolescents, and even into adulthood. Before the question is considered here and suggestions offered concerning the desirability of placing a retarded child in an institution at birth, suppose we review some facts and professional opinions concerning the nature of public residential facilities and services for the mentally retarded who reside in public institutions in the United States. Much of the information presented in this section will have implications for the manner in which this same question will be viewed during the other developmental periods, which are reviewed in subsequent chapters. The whole topic of residential services for the mentally retarded is a somewhat inflammatory subject, one in which there are strong emotional opinions and ties among various groups of professional workers and interested members of concerned lay organizations. The reader is urged to become familiar with the different points of view concerning suggested criteria for the placement of mentally retarded persons in institutions. Perhaps the most well-documented review of these various positions is presented by Wolfensberger (1967).

Some Demographic Characteristics of Institutions   The data which are recorded in Table 2-2 are but a few of many facts which appear in a 1969 report of the President's Committee on Mental Retardation entitled, *Changing Patterns in Residential Services for the Mentally Retarded.* Among the central themes that run throughout this status report on institutional care for the retarded are that (1) states and the federal government have been seriously negligent in allocating an adequate level of financing in order to provide a minimum level of care and comfort for most retardates who are residents of institutions; (2) this paucity of financial support has made it impossible in many regions to implement new models of residential care, significantly reduce the waiting lists, and provide minimum programs of education and training; (3) staffs have been inadequately trained and inadequately compensated for their services (this fact is

particularly true for the attendants, who most observers would consider to be the most important employees in institutions); (4) only token attempts have been presently made to train for discharge those residents who have a sufficiently high level of probability for accomplishing self-sufficiency or relative independence within a less cloistered social context than an institution; and (5) most institutions have been seriously overcrowded, devoid of an adequate level of stimulation for many residents, and have been suffering from restrictions which are imposed by buildings and facilities that are architecturally inadequate.

You can see from what has been reported so far that one cannot paint a very "rosy picture" when describing the character of many public institutions for the mentally retarded. Obviously, there are exceptions—the relatively poor and the relatively adequate residential centers exist in a number of regions in the United States. In a general sense, though, the situation is a critical one and has reached

---

Table 2-2   Some characteristics of public institutions for the mentally retarded in the United States

1. By the end of 1969, nearly 230,000 individuals resided in over 150 public institutions for the retarded.
2. Approximately 3,000 additional mental retardates are admitted to public institutions each year.
3. Most facilities for the mentally retarded are overcrowded, and many institutions contain substantially more residents than their stated capacity.
4. It is estimated that nearly 60,000 extra bed spaces are needed to reduce overcrowding and to replace inadequate facilities.
5. The average delay between application and admission is nearly three years. This figure is dependent on the types of spaces that become available more than on the types of applicants or on the nature of waiting lists.
6. The average cost of supporting institutions for the retarded in the United States is more than 500 million dollars. The average per patient per day cost is nearly $7.00, although this figure differs widely among the fifty states.
7. There are approximately 90,000 full-time employees in the public institutions for the retarded. More than 75 percent of the total supporting cost of institutions goes for their salaries.
8. Of the full-time employees, half are employed as attendants on the wards. Many attendants are paid less than $350 per month, and a good number of them earn less than they could qualify for under welfare.
9. Nearly 20 percent of the attendants in public institutions for the mentally retarded resign from their positions each year. This figure varies according to the

---

* Adapted from: E. C. Butterfield, "Basic Facts About Public Residential Facilities for the Mentally Retarded," in R. B. Kugel and W. Wolfensberger (eds.), *Changing Patterns in Residential Services for the Mentally Retarded*, President's Committee on Mental Retardation, U.S. Government Printing Office, January, 1969, pp. 15–34.

crisis proportions in many states. Realizing this degree of gravity, the National Association for Retarded Children, the American Association on Mental Deficiency, and the President's Committee on Mental Retardation have focused an enormous amount of time, energy, and financial resources in their study of the multitude of problems that surround institutions and institutional life for the retarded. In a number of ways they have not only contributed to the professional literature by describing the status of institutional life and suggesting various possible strategies for managing the most critical of the problems, but these organizations have exerted a significant degree of political pressure on various public officials and legislators in an attempt to remedy some of the most severe difficulties. Unfortunately, many institutions are faced with such an overwhelming number of problems that their cumulative influence is of such a magnitude as to make anything other than a total long-term comprehensive program with enormous financial backing relatively ineffective.

A Field Trip to an Institution   Let us assume that we decided to visit an institution for the retarded. Obviously, we could selectively choose one which has relatively ideal facilities and services. Instead of doing that, let us select a

---

policies of an institution, types of residents, salary schedule, etc. The average educational level of attendants is less than twelfth grade.

10. Approximately 11 percent of the employees in institutions for the retarded are classified as professionals, although less than 2 percent of this group are listed as physicians, psychologists, and social workers. Many of this group have not achieved the necessary credentials to be licensed to practice their profession outside of the institutions.

11. Fifty-five percent of the institutional population is male.

12. In terms of level of mental retardation represented among institutions, approximately 27 percent are profoundly retarded, 33 percent severely retarded, 22 percent moderately retarded, 13 percent mildly retarded, and 5 percent in the borderline groups. The trend is definitely toward admitting increasingly more patients at the severe and profound levels of retardation.

13. Approximately 70 percent of institutionalized retardates are above age fifteen. Less than 3 percent are below age four.

14. Variations among states in the character of their populations exist and are dependent to some degree on criteria for admission, accepted definition of mental retardation, legal requirements for admission and discharge criteria, the types of residents who die or who are discharged most frequently and thus release a bed space, the type and extent of diagnostic services as well as charges to the families, and the nature of the waiting list.

15. In excess of 50 percent of the public institutions for the mentally retarded house more than 1000 residents, although 75 percent of those institutions built since 1960 are intended for 500 or less.

---

hypothetical institution which, in a general sense, is more typical of the great majority of residential centers for the retarded across the country. What might we expect to observe?

First of all, it might take some effort to get to the institution, for many of these centers are great distances from major urban communities. Oftentimes they are converted TB sanitariums—far off into the hills or in highly rural areas. Naturally, this has certain implications for staffing of both professional and non-professional personnel. As you approach the campus you might notice great differences in the architecture among the buildings. Some of them will probably look like historical monuments, others like monasteries, and still others may look relatively new and be constructed as wards attached to a common control center. You will also notice adolescent and adult male residents who seem to be aimlessly wandering about the campus, nearly all of whom possess a transistorized radio which provides a modicum of auditory stimulation. For many it probably does not matter what kind of stimulation, so long as it is some type at an acceptable level.

If you are allowed to visit throughout the institution, you would probably quickly realize that a medical orientation prevails. Nurses would be in evidence, the superintendent would probably be a physician (most likely a psychiatrist), the total nomenclature and "in-house jargon" would ring of medical phraseology, the residents would be spoken of as patients, their dormitories would be called "wards," and even educational programs might be referred to as "treatment procedures." In addition, you probably would notice that safety was emphasized through the institution. Yards would be fenced in, light switches activated by a special key, water temperature would be centrally controlled, corners on furniture and other permanent installations would be rounded, and TV sets would be bolted to the walls just high enough from the reach of the residents to be untouchable and also nearly unseeable.

As you enter a ward your eyes might be drawn rapidly from one scene to another to a point of utter disbelief. For example, in one section of the ward you would see that the physical facilities look like an extension of a high school shower room. Tile floors and walls, windows that are too high to see out of, drains in various sections of the room, a ceiling high enough for a basketball game, and heavy benches around the large room characterize many institutional dayrooms in ward areas. Off to one side you would see bed after bed after bed lined up in close proximity to each other. And that is it; only with extreme infrequency could you expect to see individual footlockers or wall lockers for each resident.

Near the sleeping areas you would find the bathroom area. In the bathroom area you would find an array of commodes in a row hanging from the walls without floor supports and without stalls or any other attempts toward privacy. On the other side of the room you would find a number of sinks, a bathtub would

be in a prominent place and equipped with a single rubber hose, and a spraying-off area would be provided for those residents who became too soiled to use the standard facilities. Finally, off to the side, perhaps out in the hall you would find several isolation rooms. These essentially are "sensory deprivation chambers" for residents who present control difficulties. These rooms usually have no furniture, no windows, a heavily barred door, and four blank walls.

As you enter the ward area you will probably notice a unique odor which is a combination of urine, feces, and disinfectant soap. The ever present pail and mop would be obvious components of the ward scene so that the frequent accidents can be dealt with as they occur throughout the day. Usually each ward will have a ventilating fan located in one of the high windows or constructed in the ceiling. Air conditioning is not usually found in institutional ward areas in spite of the extremely oppressive heat and humidity which fill the wards during the summer months. Likewise, during the winter months many residents and workers find that the heating system for certain ward areas is ineffective, which necessitates that everyone put on extra heavy clothes during the cold season.

In those wards in which the residents are not restricted to their beds or cribs you could expect to see somewhat in excess of sixty or seventy residents milling around, lying on the floor, watching television, or generally bothering each other. Several residents may be incompletely clothed or perhaps completely nude because they have not been exposed to a systematic program which is designed to train them to dress themselves and to keep their clothes on. Some residents may be nonambulatory and be seated in wheelchairs; others may simply be seated on the floor.

The most striking observation to be made when visiting most wards in institutions for the mentally retarded is that purposeful activities of either an individual or group variety are virtually nonexistent. Organized activities on the wards are simply not a vital part of the medical model, and therefore for many residents the total future is one of sitting, rocking, and living in a truly culturally deprived environment. The more fortunate residents are allowed to participate in an institutional program such as is provided by recreational workers, occupational therapists, or speech correctionists. These organized programs, however, are often rigidly structured and so militaristic in their organization that much of the enjoyment of the activities is seriously diluted by the need for maintaining total control. As a result of this overly structured program format many residents prefer not to participate in such organized activities. One further point is worth noting with respect to the character of ward life for the resident; toys, games, and other devices of stimulation are usually not a part of a ward scene. In those instances in which activity materials are provided, the attendants are often so frightened that an incident will occur resulting in a child being hurt that they feel the safest approach is simply not to engage the youngsters in activities in which toys and equipment are used.

As you observe the general behavior of the residents on a ward, it soon becomes obvious that they are very bored people. In fact, many authorities believe that one consequence of this boredom is the frequent bizarre behavioral patterns that many institutionalized retardates exhibit, such as rocking, head banging, twirling, finger picking, and so on. This hypothesis suggests that because each human being needs a certain minimal level of stimulation to maintain psychological and physical intactness, and because the character of ward life is devoid of even the most elementary and basic levels of stimulation, the retardate is forced into a position where he must provide his own minimal level of stimulation. It is for this reason, according to the argument, that many of the institutionalized retardates exhibit such odd behavior and continue to do so to an increasing degree as length of institutionalization increases.

There are few people who would not agree with the position that the ward attendants are the most important workers in an institution for the retarded. It is they who have the responsibility for seeing that each resident is fed, clothed, kept reasonably clean, medicated properly, not hurt, toileted properly, and kept reasonably happy. In short, the attendant is often expected to act as a resident manager of the ward, parent to the residents, housekeeper, specialist on certain varieties of common medical problems, disciplinarian and fair adjudicator of conflicts, minister to those with significant emotional needs, and a therapist in the broadest sense.

These idealistic expectations are all very fine; however, it is impossible for one attendant with sixty or seventy residents for eight hours at a time to do much more than feed and keep the residents reasonably clean. On our hypothetical tour, then, you might expect to see understaffed wards with one or two attendants for sixty or more residents, half of whom cannot feed themselves and/or are not completely toilet trained. Little wonder, then, that meals are fed to those who cannot feed themselves in a very mechanical and hasty fashion. The more capable residents are often used to work with the severely retarded during these critical periods.

If you had a chance to talk with an attendant for a period of time and inquired about those things which are particularly bothersome, you might expect to hear some of the following statements:

1. "They just don't pay enough; I am one of the lowest paid people in my neighborhood and have more responsibility than anyone else. I'm really in trouble if one of those kids gets sick and I don't pick it up."
2. "I've given up; it's impossible to keep all these patients clean and dressed until they get more help in this ward."
3. "The first day I came here they stuck me in this ward without any training. They called it on-the-job training. I didn't know anything about mental

retardation and still don't. What they really need is a good training program in this institution."

4. "When a patient gets out of hand I stick him in the isolation room. I know it's not the best place for him, but what else can I do when he gets uncontrollable and I have to deal with all of the other patients' problems."

5. "We have to use straitjackets and restraints on the same patients nearly every day. Once we get the straitjackets on, things go much better that day."

6. "Institutions should have a housekeeping staff right on the ward to mop up and keep the place clean so that it doesn't smell so much. I can't keep it clean and take care of the patients—there just isn't enough time."

7. "People from the other departments in the administration building sit in their air-conditioned offices away from the smell and the problems on the ward and make decisions that affect those of us who work right on the wards. They don't really know what's going on, some of them have never visited a ward in this institution. What we need are a few legislators to come visit the wards and to shake this place up."

Most every institution has several wards for children who are bedfast. In these wards the cribs are lined in row after row with just enough room for the attendant to squeeze between two cribs. The total environment is white—the cribs, the sheets, the ceiling, and even the dress of the attendants. Many residents in these wards have seen few other colors than white; and most of them live day in and day out without toys, games, stimulating objects, or special events to which all children look forward. Many of these wards house in excess of 100 residents.

As you approach the ward you will see that certain residents are tied to or otherwise restrained in their beds. The level of noise might increase as a result of attempts by the residents to call attention to themselves. It is almost as if they sense that a visitor is in their midst. Some will begin to sing, others will cry, and still others will reach out toward you with their hands, eyes, or voices. It will become obvious to you that your attention is demanded by most of the residents. In many such wards it is clear that the young residents are actually begging for opportunities for human interaction.

As you pass through the locked doors of one ward into another you will eventually enter a wing of geriatric residents. In many instances the persons in this section will have spent their entire lifetime in the same area of the institution. These old people, many of whom are toothless and in need of bathing, sit around the dayroom staring into space, watching patterns on the television set, or attempting to intervene when two residents begin to battle. The techniques which those residents who view themselves as disciplinarians or protectors of the social order use are forceful in a physical sense and suggest that they may have learned those patterns of behavior as a result of having been handled simi-

larly by the attendants. There is very little cheer, purposeful activity, or even minimal stimulation in the wards which house the elderly retardate, many of whom could be engaged in much more productive situations on the institution grounds.

As you leave the last ward a number of questions will no doubt come to mind. You might, for example, be interested in knowing about the admission and dismissal criteria; the types of training and education programs; the extent and types of diagnostic facilities; the ancillary services such as speech, occupational therapy, physical therapy, and recreation; the extent to which the residents are required to work without pay for the institution; the degree and nature of aberrant sexual behavior among residents; how much racial difficulty exists within the institution; the character of the institutional society as it has been established by the residents themselves; the institution's policy on punishment of the residents; the relationship between the community and the institution; the attendant training program; the follow-up program for those residents who have been dismissed; and the extent to which each resident's parents are integrated into the full institutional program. Each of these areas is important and the answers that are given to the questions will in large measure help to characterize individual institutions.

As you can see from the foregoing discussion, the general picture concerning characteristics of institutions for the mentally retarded is rather bleak. One European observer who was asked to comment on what he had seen as a result of having toured a number of institutions in the United States wrote:

> Such conditions are shocking denials of human dignity. They force the retarded to function far below their levels of developmental possibilities. The large institutions where such conditions occur are no schools for proper training, nor are they hospitals for care and betterment, as they really increase mental retardation by producing further handicapping conditions for the mentally retarded. They represent a self-defeating system of shockingly dehumanizing effects. Here, hunger for experience is left unstilled; here, poverty in the life conditions is sustained; here, a cultural deprivation is created—with the taxpayer's money—with the concurrence of the medical profession, by the decisions of the responsible political bodies of society (Nirje, 1969, p. 56).

The preceding brief description of a "typical" institution was not intended to be a "muckraking exposé." Other recent accounts have been much more vivid than those described here (Blatt and Kaplan, 1967; Vail, 1967; Wolfensberger, 1969; and Dybwad, 1969). The position which is taken in this book is that a parent or physician cannot decide on whether early placement of a newborn is appropriate or not without knowing the true picture of institutional life. It is for this reason that time has been devoted to providing the brief sketch on the

"typical" institution. Hopefully it will suggest the vital need for parents and the referring physician to visit the institution into which a child at any age is being considered for admission.

Facts and Opinions about Placement   With this background, then, perhaps we can consider at a more well-informed level the desirability of institutionalizing a retarded newborn. You will recall that earlier it was mentioned that most public institutions have lengthy waiting lists and that the basis on which many new admissions are made is the type of ward in which a bed becomes available. With this in mind, then, even if it were advisable for a newborn to be committed and the parents agreed that this was best for all concerned, it may be impossible to find a public institution with a vacant bed in an appropriate ward. In fact, many candidates for emergency admission on the basis of the serious medical disorder are often kept in the hospital in which they were delivered until institutional placement is possible.

In the opinion of professionals who are informed about mental retardation, including the dimensions of family crisis resulting from the birth of a retarded child and the many nuances relative to the institutional scene, it is unwise for parents to place their newborn into an institution for the retarded. This conclusion would seem to be a logical one simply on the basis of the previous discussion regarding the character of most public facilities; however, there are other cogent reasons for adopting this general point of view. First, it is a sad commentary, but nonetheless a documented point, that physicians and social workers, whose lot it is to suggest that a child be institutionalized, themselves know relatively little about the many dimensions of mental retardation, the impact that it has on the family, and the nature of the institutions to which they refer retarded children (Saenger, 1957; 1960; Olshansky, 1962; Koch, Graliker, Sands, and Parmelee, 1959). Other references which were cited in the previous section also have pertinence to this point. It is also very true that many medical and social workers are not fully aware of the whole range of community possibilities other than institutionalization which offer assistance to the parents and to the child at birth as well as immediately thereafter. It is almost too obvious to mention that a positive and forceful recommendation from the obstetrician or pediatrician which encourages the parents to immediately institutionalize the newborn will probably be difficult for most parents not to accept. In this moment of extreme anguish they will be inclined to accept the arguments of a persuasive physician whose philosophy supports the position that early institutionalization of a retarded newborn will serve the best interests of the parents and family members.

The evidence and contemporary professional opinion among specialists who are concerned about the problems of mental retardation and who represent a variety of disciplines suggest that parents who institutionalize their mentally retarded child soon after birth tend to suffer severe emotional upheaval as a

result of immediate placement. The old adage that a child who is congenitally defective to a significant degree if taken home will result in trauma for the family members does not seem to be supported by the research (Slobody and Scanlan, 1959; Saenger, 1960). Apparently most parents would prefer to bring their defective child home before any consideration at all is given to the advantages and disadvantages of institutionalization. As soon as a proper amount of time has elapsed, which in itself is a very individual matter and will vary significantly among families, the parents may realize the inordinate difficulty in managing their retarded child and be in a better position to objectively evaluate the various alternatives which are available to them, among which may be commitment to a public institution for the mentally retarded. In a real sense, then, counselors have in the past failed to realize that placement of a newborn in an institution for the retarded does not mean that the parents will forget the event or the child and will begin life anew. In fact, the literature suggests that after having initiated immediate placement of their child, parents very often feel guilty about having given up their infant without having tried to care for the youngster themselves. Considering the various alternatives which are available will not be be as emotionally destructive for the family and will be more advantageous in the long run for their defective child.

Although the research literature in this particular subject is not well controlled and as methodologically rigorous as most scientists would wish, there is probably more to be said for keeping a retarded newborn at home than can be said for immediate placement. There is probably nothing more convincing for parents than to give them an opportunity to deal with the multitude of difficulties which the child will experience during the first few months and years of life. As they realize the range of disorders and the relatively slow rate at which development occurs in their youngster they will soon consider institutional placement or some other form of assistance. In most instances they are able to tentatively recognize the various characteristics of the child's difficulties and do not have to depend solely on the opinion of their physician or other specialists. Encouraging the parents to take the child home instead of placing the youngster in an institution could also serve the purpose of welding the family into a relatively more cohesive unit, the total energy of which is focused on a single purposeful goal, i.e., providing total care for the youngest member of the family. In contradiction to popular opinion, the birth of a defective child brings together members of a family unit more frequently than it precipitates the dissolution of an intact family. It is also quite possible that siblings of the retarded newborn will benefit greatly from having experienced with the parents the traumas that surround the event and the various means by which daily problems are met and solved. Finally, another advantage in encouraging parents to take their retarded newborn home is that it gives them more time to decide on and evaluate the full spectrum of helping services and placement possibilities which are available to them. They can conduct this evaluation, with proper guidance and counsel

from various professional workers and their close friends, in a relatively less tense environment than is characteristic of a maternity ward in a hospital. In all cases, however, the parents should be given the benefit of the various professional arguments concerning the advantages and disadvantages of placement. They should also be given an opportunity to learn about, in a very intimate way, the other community and private services which are available to them and to their child.

Table 2-3 presents a brief summary of guidelines which Wolfensberger (1969) has suggested as indicators and contraindicators for placement of a retarded child in an institution.

Table 2-3   Indications and contraindications for placement of a retarded child in an institution*

Placement is indicated if:	*Placement is inappropriate solely because of:*
1. The family is unable or unwilling to provide minimum emotional and physical care for the child	1. A child's manifesting one of the clinical syndromes such as Down's syndrome, hydrocephaly, or microcephaly
2. The family does not suffer, and the retarded youngster gains a significant physical and/or emotional advantage	2. An irrefutable diagnosis of mental retardation at birth
3. The retarded child will predictably be injured or suffer death	3. Various multiple disabilities
4. The emotional welfare of the family is threatened and all other alternatives will not result in the stabilization of the mental health of the member(s), and if there are not too severe consequences for the retardate	4. Aesthetic or cosmetic difficulties which do not have grave medical consequences or result in overwhelming, psychologically significant distress
5. The physical welfare of the family is threatened and all other alternatives are inappropriate or exhausted	5. Embarrassment to a sibling
6. The retardate has demonstrated social maladjustment to a degree that any component of society is in jeopardy.	6. Marital problems unless removal of the newborn will clearly reduce conflict and save a marriage
	7. A slight educational advantage for the retardate in contrast to the community

* From W. Wolfensberger, "Counseling Parents of the Retarded," in A. Baumeister (ed.), *Mental Retardation: Appraisal, Education, Rehabilitation*, Aldine Publishing Company, Chicago, 1967, pp. 372–374.

Recommended Readings

Blatt, B., and F. Kaplan: *Christmas in Purgatory*, Allyn and Bacon, Boston, 1967.
Butterfield, E. C.: "Basic Facts About Public Residential Facilities for the Mentally Retarded," in R. B. Kugel and W. Wolfensberger (eds.), *Changing Patterns in*

Residential Services for the Mentally Retarded, President's Committee on Mental Retardation, January, 1969, pp. 15–34.

————: "The Characteristics, Selection, and Training of Institutional Personnel," in A. Baumeister (ed.), *Mental Retardation: Appraisal, Education, Rehabilitation,* Aldine Publishing Company, Chicago, 1967, pp. 305–328.

————, C. D. Barnett, and G. J. Bensberg: "Some Objective Characteristics of Institutions for the Mentally Retarded: Implications for Attendant Turnover," *American Journal of Mental Deficiency,* vol. 70, 1966, pp. 786–794.

Dybwad, G.: "Action Implications, U. S. A. Today," in R. B. Kugel and W. Wolfensberger (eds.), *Changing Patterns in Residential Services for the Mentally Retarded,* President's Committee on Mental Retardation, January, 1969, pp. 383–428.

Koch, R., B. V. Graliker, R. Sands, and A. M. Parmelee: "Attitude Study of Parents with Mentally Retarded Children: I. Evaluation of Parental Satisfaction with Medical Care of a Retarded Child," *Pediatrics,* vol. 23, 1959, pp. 582–584.

Newman, R. W. (ed.): *Institutionalization of the Mentally Retarded,* National Association for Retarded Children, New York, 1967.

Nirje, B.: "A Scandinavian Visitor Looks at U.S. Institutions," in R. B. Kugel and W. Wolfensberger (eds.), *Changing Patterns in Residential Services for the Mentally Retarded,* President's Committee on Mental Retardation, January, 1969, pp. 51–58.

Olshansky, S.: "Chronic Sorrow: A Response to Having a Mentally Defective Child," *Social Caseworker,* vol. 43, 1963, pp. 191–194.

Saenger, G.: *The Adjustment of Severely Retarded Adults in the Community,* New York State Interdepartmental Health Resources Board, Albany, N.Y., 1957.

————: *Factors Influencing the Institutionalization of Mentally Retarded Individuals in New York City: A Study of the Effect of Services, Personal Characteristics, and Family Background on the Decision to Institutionalize,* New York State Interdepartmental Health Resources Board, Albany, N.Y., 1960.

Slobody, L., and J. Scanlan: "Consequences of Early Institutionalization," *American Journal of Mental Deficiency,* vol. 63, 1959, pp. 971–974.

Vail, D. J.: *Dehumanization and the Institutional Career,* Charles C Thomas, Springfield, Ill., 1967.

Walker, G. H.: "Some Considerations of Parental Reactions to Institutionalization of Defective Children," *American Journal of Mental Deficiency,* vol. 54, 1949, pp. 108–114.

Wolfensberger, W.: "The Origin and Nature of Our Institutional Models," in R. B. Kugel and W. Wolfensberger (eds.), *Changing Patterns in Residential Services for the Mentally Retarded,* President's Committee on Mental Retardation, January, 1969, pp. 59–172.

3
The Preschool Years

Can a child who is normal at birth later become mentally retarded? If so, how and when might this occur?

In previous sections of this book various causes for mental retardation have been specified and briefly discussed. In addition to those disorders which have a genetic relationship, there is a multitude of environmental problems that can result in mental retardation and occur prior to, during, or after birth. The most obvious types of environmental disturbances which are related to disorders of the brain and to other systems are those which have a clear medical basis. You have already been alerted to the fact that another type of atypical environment can and does greatly influence the rate and direction of intellectual growth and development in youngsters. I am referring to those physical, social, psychological, and cultural forces (or presses) which interact with the young growing organism and serve to shape and direct the specific and broad character of his intellect, achievement patterns, physical attributes, emotional temperament, attitudes, and interests. It is this person-environment interaction to which our attention will be directed in this section.

Some Behavioral Characteristics of Young Children   We can assume that the group of people to whom we are directing our attention here are born with a reasonably normal nervous system and

the other basic physiological requisites on which intellectual development is based. Obviously, we can expect that there will be substantial variability in the degree of robustness among any group of newborn infants. These differences might result from genetic idiosyncracies as well as the degree to which reasonably healthy conditions prevailed during the pregnancy. These factors help to establish the possibility of a healthy and fully developed child being presented at birth. To be sure, some children are born with greater "potential" than others because their systems are more efficient and effective interactors with their environment

Suppose that we think a bit about the behavior of infants and older preschool children. While observing a newborn children, did you ever wonder what the child was thinking, seeing, hearing, and feeling? Parents are curious about these things; siblings of an infant often wonder what the various reactions of a young child really means. It is possible to discern when the youngster is happy and satisfied and when he is uncomfortable and grumpy, but to what degree is the child able to process information from his environment soon after birth? A sizable amount of research effort has recently been devoted to studying the behavior of newborns. It has now been determined that new infants can see more than just blobs, hear, feel pain and pressure, taste, and sense temperature variations to some degree.

If you systematically observed the behavior of a relatively normal child from birth until he reached the age of approximately eighteen months, you would probably gain certain impressions about the child's behavioral development. First of all, you could expect to see that the child's very early responses were somewhat random, inefficient, and ineffective. At birth he can suck, but it takes time for him to locate the nipple and move in a parsimonious way in order to be satisfied. Gradually, however, you would see that the child interacts in a more active, definite way with aspects of his environment. It is as if he takes his "built-in characteristics" and begins to use them to influence his environment and, in turn, to have his behavior shaped and changed by environmental components. It is this reciprocal kind of relationship that develops between a child and his surroundings, each acting on and influencing the other.

The child's repertoire of experiences increases by leaps and bounds as soon as it becomes obvious to him that he can exert some control over his surroundings. Rapid development in several important areas takes place as the infant learns to master and coordinate his own body with things that are external to him. Thus, by the time the child reaches eighteen months of age he has learned to initiate activities, how to prolong an activity, how to explore his environment to some degree, how to cause something to occur, and how to proceed in a logical order to realize a goal. The accomplishment of these skills is exceedingly important, for they form the foundation on which future intellectual, social, and physical development occur.

During the first eighteen months of the child's life, sensory motor intelligence develops rapidly because at that time the child is constantly dealing with the forces, changes, and stimuli from his physical and social environment. His sense organs extract information from his surroundings which, in turn, is translated into neural impulses and quickly transmitted to the brain for processing. The brain begins the complex task of associating the incoming data with information which it has previously stored. This phenomenon results in the child developing an increasingly more complex network of information as a direct result of the affiliation which takes place with the environment. For a more detailed explanation of the theoretical issues underlying this process, the reader is referred to Smith (1968, 1969), Spitz (1963), Ellis (1963), Woodward (1963), Furth (1969), and Landreth (1967).

As the child reaches age two and advances toward the later preschool years, he moves into a period of particularly rapid growth. Bloom (1964) has studied the nature of the growth curves of certain relatively stable characteristics and has found that 50 percent of an individual's stature in physical development occurs between conception and age 2½, 50 percent of one's general intelligence develops prior to age four, and 50 percent of one's quantitative growth in general school achievement occurs before grade three. One important conclusion from the work of Bloom is that for relatively stable characteristics, such as intelligence, weight, height, school achievement, dependency, and so on, there are usually periods of relatively rapid growth and development and other periods of much slower progress. In short, he found that equal increments of advancement do not take place for each unit of time. Moreover, his findings reveal that the period of most rapid relative growth and development in many vital physical, psychological, and social areas occurs during the years from conception to age five or six.

Some Environmental Needs of Young Children   Up to this point, emphasis has been placed on two principal thoughts concerning the growth and development that takes place during the preschool years. First, the point was stressed that early learning is motoric and that the infant is an active participator with his environment. It was also emphasized that the infant requires a certain minimum level of stimuli in order to maintain his well-being in a physical, social, and psychological sense. If a young child does not have these opportunities, he could be seriously affected. Secondly, from the work of Bloom (1964) and others, it has been demonstrated that the most rapid growth and development of certain important individual characteristics occurs between conception and age five or six. During subsequent time periods relatively less development of these traits and skills can be expected to occur.

With these two thoughts in mind, then, it is not an inordinately lengthy conceptual leap to suggest that the type of stimuli to which a youngster is exposed during the first six years of his life, and the extent to which he has opportunities

to interact with his changing environment, will dictate the degree to which his brain will develop complex networks of information. Following this argument, if a young child is exposed to an environment which (1) offers a variety of stimuli, (2) encourages verbalization, (3) is generally rewarding, (4) offers chances to explore, and (5) provides opportunities to manipulate objects, we might expect him to develop a relatively extensive repertoire of information. On the other hand, if a youngster lives in an uninteresting crib, surrounded by non-complex stimuli, has few opportunities to interact with other humans, and is never talked to, held, or stimulated, we might expect him to function at a relatively low level because of these environmental restrictions.

Indeed, the research literature supports these general predictions. Kirk (1958); Spicker, Hodges, and McCandless (1966); Hebb (1949); and Skeels (1966) are a few of a lengthy list of scientists who have presented data in support of the notion that the type of early environment with which a person is associated significantly influences the extent to which characteristics such as intelligence develop. Bloom (1964) believes that the preschool years are of inestimable value because they are the period of most rapid growth and development of physical, cognitive, and emotional characteristics. He suggests that they can be more dramatically changed during the more rapid than during slower periods of growth. Bloom estimates that the difference between living in a deprived versus abundant environment between birth and age four is 10 IQ points, between four and eight years of age 6 IQ points, and between eight and seventeen years of age 4 IQ points. This amplifies the fact that as age increases an individual becomes less amenable to and affected by intervention; accordingly, Bloom believes that by age eight at least 80 percent of mature intelligence has developed.

Throughout this section the position has been taken that the type of environmental forces, conditions, and stimuli which an individual experiences, especially during periods of rapid growth, will in large measure dictate his future character intellectually, socially, emotionally, and physically. Evidence for this viewpoint has been summarized in full by Bloom (1964) and Hunt (1961). As yet the research has not specified the exact factors of an environment which makes one facilitating and another inhibiting. There are, however, certain extreme environments to which young children are exposed which are no doubt highly influential during their first six years of life and affect subsequent future performance. A powerfully stimulating environment might include factors such as the following:

1. Ample nutritional requirements, cleanliness, adequate medical care, and relatively disease-free surroundings
2. Parents who willingly interact with their children in both verbal and non-verbal areas by especially rewarding (a) spontaneity, (b) goal-directed perseverance, (c) exploration of their environment, (d) attempts toward

problem solving in areas which involve the development of new skills, and (e) by minimizing constant threats which involve externally imposed criteria of evaluation

3. A warm and accepting family environment in which the child is viewed as a real contributor and not as an alien

4. Physical surroundings which are bright, interesting, available to be handled by the child, relatively complex, and in which the child has freedom to move about and play

Some Consequences of Environmental Deprivation   Children who are born into and are reared in surroundings which are the antithesis of the characteristics of a facilitating environment can expect to suffer dramatic and serious consequences in various areas of development. The results of such a deprived, unstimulating, and disinterested environment will result in the child's being unresponsive and apthetic, late in developing skills at a level commensurate with other children of the same age, less physically robust and healthy, disinterested in participating in activities, unspontaneous, less emotionally mature and stable, and intellectually sluggish and behind. In a real sense, then, children who are victims of this overpowering physical and psychological trap of environmental deprivation can become mentally retarded in their level of functioning. If the cycle of stimulus deprivation is not broken at an early enough age, and here the position has been taken that this must occur as a result of intentionally planned intervention before age six because the child will not be able to effect a change in the environment himself, the consequences will be manifested throughout his lifetime.

The group of individuals to which attention has been directed in this section are usually called *culturally disadvantaged* or *culturally deprived*. The fact that this term is technically inappropriate to precisely describe this population is a fascinating subject but not within the domain of this particular book. Instead, one might logically view various populations of exceptional children, including those who are born mentally retarded, as being disadvantaged from the point of view of "stimulus deprivation." Allow me to elaborate on this point.

Children who are reared in seriously deprived surroundings are obviously negatively affected, in spite of the fact that they may possess excellent "raw material" at birth. Under reasonably normal circumstances these children would predictably be able to function in a moderately normal way. Because the influences of their restricted environment are so powerful, most of these young children will not realize their full potential. In a real sense, children with various types of birth defects, many of which are associated with mental retardation, are similarly deprived, that is, they are often seriously hindered in their ability to extract information from their environment, process the data which come in through their sensory mechanisms, and use the information to solve problems.

This situation prevails because their mechanisms are faulty and do not allow for a full and unencumbered interaction with their environment. Remember, one of Piaget's principal positions on the basis for cognitive development is that this reciprocity occur between an individual and his environment (Hunt, 1961; Furth, 1969).

It is of importance to consider the possible cumulative influence on growth and development which might be expected for a youngster who is born with a significantly disabling condition and who also lives in a disadvantaged environment during the preschool years. This young person is doubly affected; first, because his system is unable to effectively deal with his environment and, second, because his environment is dismal in terms of sensory stimuli which are available. From these children we might logically expect to see severe educational, psychological, emotional, and social problems which would far surpass those of retardates who are congenitally disabled, but who live in a reasonably stimulating environment, and those who are normal at birth but who live in disadvantaged surroundings.

Recommended Readings

Bloom, B. S.: *Stability and Change in Human Characteristics,* John Wiley & Sons, Inc., New York, 1964.

Casler, L.: "Maternal Deprivation: A Critical Review of the Literature," *Monographs of the Society for Research on Child Development,* vol. 26, no. 2, 1961.

Ellis, N. R.: "The Stimulus Trace and Behavioral Inadequacy," in N. R. Ellis (ed.), *Handbook of Mental Deficiency,* McGraw-Hill Book Company, New York, 1963, pp. 41–91.

Furth, H. G.: *Piaget and Knowledge: Theoretical Foundations,* Prentice-Hall, Inc., Englewood Cliffs, N.J., 1969.

Glass, D. C. (ed.): *Environmental Influences,* Rockefeller University Press and Russell Sage Foundation, New York, 1968.

Hartup, W. W., and N. L. Smothergill (eds.): *The Young Child: Reviews of Research,* National Association for the Education of Young Children, Washington, 1967.

Hebb, D. O.: *The Organization of Behavior,* John Wiley & Sons, Inc., New York, 1949.

Hess, R. D., and R. M. Bear (eds.): *Early Education: Current Theory, Research, and Action,* Aldine Publishing Company, Chicago, 1968.

Hunt, J. McV.: *Intelligence and Experience,* The Ronald Press Co., New York, 1961.

Kirk, S. A.: *Early Education of the Mentally Retarded,* The University of Illinois Press, Urbana, 1958.

Landreth, C.: *Early Childhood: Behavior and Learning,* 2d ed., Alfred A. Knopf, Inc., New York, 1967.

Scott, J. P.: *Early Experience and the Organization of Behavior,* Brooks-Cole Publishing Company, Belmont, Calif., 1968.

Skeels, H. M.: "Adult Status of Children with Contrasting Early Life Experiences," *Monographs of the Society for Research in Child Development,* no. 3, 1966.

Smith, R. M.: *Clinical Teaching: Methods of Instruction for the Retarded,* McGraw-Hill Book Company, New York, 1968, pp. 14–31.

————: *Teacher Diagnosis of Educational Difficulties,* Charles E. Merrill Books, Inc., Columbus, Ohio, 1969.

Spicker, H. H., W. L. Hodges, and B. R. McCandless: "A Diagnostically Based Curriculum For Psycho-Socially Deprived Preschool Mentally Retarded Children," *Exceptional Children,* vol. 33, 1966, pp. 215–220.

Spitz, H. H.: "Field Theory in Mental Deficiency," in N. R. Ellis (ed.), *Handbook of Mental Deficiency,* McGraw-Hill Book Company, New York, 1963, pp. 11–40.

Woodward, M.: "The Application of Piaget's Theory to Research in Mental Deficiency," in N. R. Ellis (ed.), *Handbook of Mental Deficiency,* McGraw-Hill Book Company, New York, 1963, pp. 297–324.

What are the principal differences between those children who are born mentally retarded, those who acquire mental retardation after birth, and those who are intellectually normal?

There are some important distinctions that can be detected during the preschool years between children who are born mentally retarded and those who acquire mental retardation after birth. These differences can have implications for the manner in which the retarded children are managed, medically and behaviorally. Some of the predominant characteristics of various types of retarded youngsters have been considered in previous sections of this book. The purpose of this section is to summarize some of these facts, contrast them with the usual character of intellectually normal children, and highlight their implications especially during the preschool period. Table 3-1 presents such a contrast.

Notice that several rather definite common threads run through the material which is presented in this table. First, the promise of changing the characteristics of an individual with organically based disorders even with maximum early intervention is more remote and difficult than for those youngsters who are retarded as a result of environmental deprivation (Kirk, 1958). Second, children who are congenitally retarded are usually more multiply disabled than youngsters with acquired retardation. The prognosis for the former group is less favorable than for the later.

Table 3-1 Principal differences among three groups of children

Factor	Born with mental retardation	Acquired mental retardation after birth	Normal
Etiology	Problems can be the result of infectious diseases; toxic biochemical, traumatic, nutritional, or genetic conditions; or combinations of these.	Mental retardation most frequently results from either birth injury or environmental stimulus deprivation. The later circumstance accounts for the major contribution of youngsters to this category	Children here are usually born without defects which required major decisions concerning management. This means that their hereditary characteristics and environment before and after birth were within the range of normalcy. A certain number of children in this category may be born with or acquire defects which need special attention but which do not visually impair their cognitive functioning
Physical characteristics	Youngsters here usually have more multiple handicaps, obvious clinical syndromes, brain injury; are more frequently premature; and are more vulnerable to illness and diseases	These children are typically less robust than their intellectually normal peers; have a higher incidence of prematurity at birth; may have visual, auditory, or motor problems which result from cultural deprivation and require special attention; are less multiply disordered than those with congenital problems; and most do not have the appearance of being retarded	Normal children are usually healthy at birth, without physical abnormalities; gain weight within normal limits; have few if any problems with vision, hearing, or motor development; and progress in their growth and development in a predictable fashion

Degree of intellectual impairment	Most children in this category will manifest moderate, severe, or profound degrees of mental retardation, i.e., they will typically be categorized as trainable or lower	Most youngsters with acquired mental retardation are in the mild or educable category, i.e., they usually score between 50 and 84 on most standardized intelligence tests	Children with normal intelligence, score above IQ 84 on most standardized intelligence tests and will typically have few, if any, areas of especial weakness in areas related to cognitive development
Unique behavioral characteristics	As preschoolers, children in this category will usually be either very unresponsive (hypoactive) or overly responsive (hyperactive) to their environment. As a result they often exhibit unusual behaviors such as rapid movement of their hands, whirling, thumping objects, repetitive patterns of activity, or rocking. For some of the more profoundly retarded, self-destructive behaviors are often exhibited. Their speech and language may be highly immature and, for some, nearly uncomprehensible. Many may not be able to control their bodily functions, and some will be non-ambulatory	Young children in this category will usually be unresponsive to their environment and appear to be shy, withdrawn, or lethargic. Their speech and language will usually be immature, their attention span somewhat restricted, their nonverbal performance is often relatively stronger than their verbal, and they may not spontaneously initiate activity with other children or with things	Normal preschoolers are active, energetic interactors with their environment. They are spontaneous in their activities and they seem to delight in learning how to effectively control their surroundings. They are vigorous extractors of information, they experiment with their speech and language, they enjoy manipulating objects, and they are not usually shy about interacting with other children and adults

Table 3-1 Principal differences among three groups of children (Continued)

Factor	Born with mental retardation	Acquired mental retardation after birth	Normal
Socioeconomic characteristics of the family	All social classes are represented in this group with a small, relatively higher percentage among the lower socioeconomic groups. This is probably caused by fewer opportunities for prenatal care within this group	Many more youngsters in this category come from lower socioeconomic situations than from middle or higher levels	Most socioeconomic levels are represented at this level although a relatively fewer percent are from lower than from middle and higher levels
Amenability to changes as a result of intervention	Since youngsters in this group are usually more severely disabled, they are less responsive to systematic intervention during the preschool years than either of the other two groups	If a youngster in this group is not organically impaired, i.e. brain injured, he will typically be relatively more responsive to stimulation if it is well programmed and offered prior to age five or six. Youngsters in this group who are organically involved will respond to preschool stimulation but less dramatically so than their culturally disadvantaged peers	Preschool children in this category are exceedingly amenable to change as a function of environmental intervention
Reversibility possibilities and general prognosis	The possibility of reversing the conditions of children in this group is remote. There are several types of conditions which can be controlled (PKU is an example of one) if immediate attention is given soon after birth. This will	If the children are not significantly brain injured, and if intervention occurs at a very early age, the possibilities of reversing the effects of a disadvantaged environment and the general prognosis for the child are very good. Both	The prognosis for children in this category is favorable to the degree to which the preschoolers are encouraged to interact with their environment

	of these become less favorable in those instances involving organically impaired youngsters	Preschool programs are often available for children in this group. In most instances they will later become students in a regular classroom program
Usual educational placement	not reverse the condition, only control it. The general prognosis of preschoolers in this group depends on the degree and types of defects, the immediacy of the diagnosis, the extent of needed treatment, and the availability of comprehensive services. Usually, however, these individuals will not become self-sufficient as adults	Many preschoolers in this group will have an opportunity to participate in some form of early education whether it be sponsored by the local NARC chapter, Head Start, or the public schools. Eventually they will become associated with a special class, special school, or regular classroom program
	Most frequently children with mental retardation at birth are enrolled in day-care centers as preschoolers and later transferred to classes for the trainable as they grow older. A certain number of the children will be institutionalized at or shortly after birth. These children may or may not be exposed to a systematic educational program according to the comprehensiveness of the institution's program	

Baumeister, A. A. (ed.): *Mental Retardation: Appraisal, Education, Rehabilitation,* Aldine Publishing Company, Chicago, 1967.

Jordan, T. E.: *The Mentally Retarded,* 2d ed., Charles E. Merrill Books, Inc., Columbus, Ohio, 1966.

Kirk, S. A.: *Early Education of the Mentally Retarded,* The University of Illinois Press, Urbana, 1958.

Sarason, S. B., and J. Doris: *Psychological Problems in Mental Deficiency,* 4th ed., Harper & Row, Publishers, Incorporated, New York, 1969.

What types of behavior are typical of retarded preschool children?

It is difficult to be specific and precise in describing the usual behavior of pre-school-age children who are mentally retarded. There is not a particularly unique syndrome of actions, reactions, or behavior patterns for any of the various populations of young retardates. Just as is true with most children below age six, a wide range of behaviors prevail among preschool retardates as a function of factors such as degree of intellectual subnormality, presence and extent of other disabling conditions, the degree of environmental favorableness in which the child is reared, the unique character of the child's family, the extent of central nervous system damage, and the child's chronological age. Since behavior for anyone does not occur in a vacuum, one must analyze the individual peculiarities of each person, the nature of his environment, and the manner in which the various factors involved with each of these "mix together" in order to accurately describe, study, and attempt to change the behavior of anyone, including the preschool retardate. This pinpoints one of the significant problems with that research in mental retardation which has attempted to describe "the behavior" of retardates. Much of the literature reported on very narrow and specific populations of retarded individuals to such an extent that it is impossible to generalize on other types of children who are mentally subnormal. In addition, many of the descriptive studies have failed to specify the character of the environment in which the group being researched lives (Smith and Neisworth, 1969).

Although it is impossible to describe the usual behavior of retarded preschool children in any way other than in the broadest of terms, so as not to erroneously overcharacterize them, it might be revealing to consider some of the major behavioral dimensions on which many retarded preschoolers differ from other children. To a very limited degree these characteristics are similar to the ones which were briefly discussed earlier. The reader is cautioned not to forget that behavioral stereotypes among this group are as difficult to identify and validate as they are among the intellectually normal; that manifest behavior can be viewed

as extending from horribly unacceptable to angelic and that how individuals view the behavior of others differs according to personal criteria from one moment to another; and that the behavioral character of children younger than age four is very fluid, often changing dramatically from time to time.

In a very general sense, most young retarded children fall outside of the range of normal or average behavior on many variables. They repeatedly are characterized as being "immature," insensitive to their environment and in their responses. This label is a correct descriptor in most cases; however, it is often used by parents with the implicit expectation that the "immaturity" will eventually be outgrown and that the youngster will gain the full behavioral stature of his chronological age, intellectually normal peers. In short, it is much easier for parents, and indeed for certain professionals, to explain away certain behavior by labeling it as "immature" instead of simply describing its specific manifestations; i.e., he kicks, drools, wets himself, walks only with help, or crys when he does not get his way.

There are three major ways in which preschool retarded children perform differently than other children in terms of variables related to social, cognitive, emotional, perceptual-motor, and communicative development. First, the rate at which preschool retardates develop skills is less than the speed of their non-retarded peers. Figure 3-1 describes differences in rate of skill acquisition among several groups of young children. Notice the dissimilarity in the angles of the performance curves—as the degree of retardation increases the performance curves accelerate at a less rapid rate.

The second performance characteristic of preschool retarded children can also be observed in Figure 3-1. Notice that the various groups of youngsters differ in their level of performance at every chronological age period, with the exception of during the first year. At the age of three, for example, the diagram shows that the intellectually normal subjects remember 100 percent of the words to a song, the educable youngsters remember 40 percent, the trainable 5 percent, and the severely retarded individuals are able to remember none of the words. It really does not matter which variable you select, the same general pattern of performance level will emerge for the four groups of children.

A third performance characteristic which differs among groups of individuals, such as those we have been discussing here, is the quality of their performance. There is a very subtle difference between being able to meet minimum criteria or expectations and being able to perform in an exemplary way. In contrast to the intellectually normal, the retarded consistently show poor quality performances as the level of mental retardation becomes progressively more severe. For example, at the age of five, it has been hypothesized in Figure 3-1 that the intellectually normal group will remember 100 percent of the words to a song, the educable approximately 82 percent, the trainable youngsters 50 percent, and the severely retarded individuals about 18 percent. In addition to these level differ-

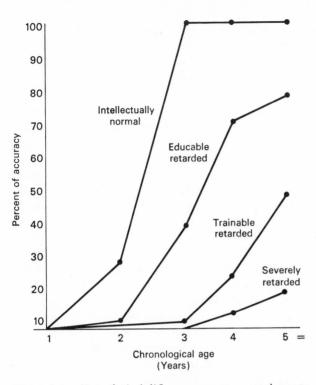

Figure 3-1 *Hypothetical differences among several groups of children in their rate of remembering words to a song.*

ences, we might expect to hear other kinds of unique patterns exhibited among the different groups as they sing a song. Variables on which these differences might occur could include clarity of singing, volume, expression or inflection, movements to the words, and others. All these factors, when combined, will effect the general quality of a child's performance.

Mention previously was made that the retarded youngsters tend to be extreme in their responses to stimuli. Reasons for some children underreacting to visual, auditory, or tactile stimuli and others overresponding are not clear. The causes for each of these conditions are no doubt different for individual children; e.g., some may overreact because of central nervous system pathology while others may respond at an identical level because their parents or siblings reward such behavior. In a similar vein, behavior of many preschool retardates tends to be repetitive or perseverative. This characteristic extends from finger-tapping, head-banging, and rocking behavior so often seen in many severely and profoundly retarded children to the single response, unvaried pattern of behavior which many higher level retarded preschoolers use in order to deal with problem situations. This latter group apparently adopts the style of responding which has worked in the

past and is accepted by parents and others. A youngster will learn to adopt this type of response pattern at a very early age during the preschool years because he finds that it works with a minimum of frustration, trauma, and anxiety for him and for others.

The social and emotional behavior of young retarded children are often relatively infantile in contrast to intellectually normal peers. A substantial number of retarded youngsters are significantly socially immature as a consequence of their not being aware of what others expect of them and because of their general social insensitivity. Among the disadvantaged this is a particularly valid conclusion, for many of these youngsters do not have adequate adult models present who are able to demonstrate to the children appropriate social and emotional behavior in various situations.

There is another possible reason for infantile emotional development and behavior among the young retardates. Parents from relatively typical surroundings and of average means often tend to treat their retarded child in a very different way than their intellectually normal siblings. For example, some parents will severely restrict the retarded preschooler's opportunity to engage in normal, usual encounters with his environment and with others. The fears that cause this "cloistering behavior" by the parents are real, often complex, and for many parents manifestations of trying their best to protect the youngsters from physical, social, and psychological harm. To be sure, for a part of the population of parents, fear for themselves being placed in an embarrassing, disagreeable, or dissonant social situation is cause enough for restricting their child's mobility. In situations where the child has been protected from encounters with others and not had a chance to develop emotionally mature responses to the environment, it is very obvious why many retarded children, when unleashed from these restrictions, either underreact, overreact, or inappropriately react to perplexing problems and situations.

As an addendum to this thought, research and clinical impressions of counselors reveal that some parents of retarded children are often more tolerant of obstreperous behaviors by their young handicapped child than they are of the same type and magnitude of misbehavior by a normal sib. Referring back to the earlier discussions concerning the development of behavioral patterns and the force which reinforcement plays in maintaining and solidifying such patterns, it is not farfetched at all to hypothesize that the unfortunate behaviors of many preschool retardates may be more a function of inept child-rearing strategies than intellectual subnormality alone. It is also not too speculative for one to suggest the crucial need for professional intervention as early as possible in this cycle in order to not cause a calcification of antisocial, emotionally inappropriate behavioral styles by the young retarded child. The evidence, as suggested earlier, points out how relatively difficult it is to alter growth and development patterns after the preschool years.

Gallagher, J. J., and L. Lucito: "Intellectual Patterns of Gifted Children Compared with Average and Retarded," *Exceptional Children,* vol. 27, 1961, pp. 479–482.

Hartup, W. W., and N. L. Smothergill (eds.): *The Young Child: Reviews of Research,* National Association for the Education of Young Children, Washington, 1967.

Hechinger, F. M. (ed.): *Preschool Education Today,* Doubleday & Company, Inc., Garden City, N.Y., 1966.

Kirk, S. A.: *Early Education of the Mentally Retarded,* The University of Illinois Press, Urbana, 1958.

Smith, R. M.: *Clinical Teaching: Methods of Instruction for the Retarded,* McGraw-Hill Book Company, New York, 1968, pp. 41–47.

————, and J. T. Neisworth: "Some Problems of and Prospects for Research in Mental Retardation," *Mental Retardation,* vol. 7, 1969, pp. 25–28.

What procedures are used to diagnose mental retardation and other possible difficulties during the preschool years?

The topics of assessment and diagnosis will be discussed both here and in a section of Chapter 4. In the latter case the focus will be on the importance of evaluative techniques for conducting diagnostic efforts which are primarily and more obviously of an educational nature. The emphasis will be on identifying the individual and environmental characteristics that hinder the retarded in their acquisition of subject matter and in use of this knowledge for the solution of problems. In this section the focus will not be on subject matter, per se; instead, the discussion first will consider some general ideas about the evaluation of the usual behavior of preschool retardates and then concentrate more specifically on some procedures by which variables at the preschool level might be observed and evaluated.

Unless the child is obviously retarded at birth or begins to show definite signs of disordered functioning during the first few years of his life, establishing a diagnosis of mental retardation may be difficult or not occur at all. In spite of the fact that the child may be slow in developing certain basic competencies, many parents and physicians are hesitant to raise the possibility than the youngster may need further more comprehensive diagnostic efforts in order to determine if developmental lags are present, and, if so, their possible cause. Parents and physicians alike often silently or aloud explain away such problems by suggesting that the child will "eventually outgrow the difficulty." It is, then, important for these two groups of individuals, i.e., parents and physicians, to report on and have follow-ups initiated when either suspects some form of mal-

functioning, inadequate development, or suspicious behavior in an infant or pre-schooler. In the final analysis parents and physicians provide the first line of diagnosis and evaluation. If they fail to correctly observe behavioral disorders or if they disregard symptoms which should be analyzed, the child may not be "picked up again" until after he has failed to perform at a reasonably satisfactory level in the elementary school. Moreover, it is always easier for parents to "wait until tomorrow" before seeking special diagnostic and remedial help if they have become accustomed to dealing with their child's disorders and weaknesses. It is almost as if they do not wish to "open an old wound" or bring to the surface the possibility that they or their child requires special help. If, however, attention is not given to many of the problems that surround mental retardation during a child's preschool years we can anticipate that serious, somewhat irreversible, repercussions will occur later in the child's development. A careful diagnosis, then, should be conducted throughout these first few years of a child's life.

A Team Effort in Gathering and Analyzing Data Medical and psychological areas hold special diagnostic interest during the retarded child's preschool years. The medical data which are collected on a youngster result from a general study of his various systems. If the pediatrician or general practitioner suspects that the child may have a congenital or acquired disorder which is evidenced by delayed developmental signs, and perhaps associated with a condition such as mental retardation, more special comprehensive evaluations may be indicated. Specialists, such as neurologists, audiologists, pediatricians, surgeons, or bio-chemists, may be asked to examine the child and study his symptoms in order to characterize the nature and extent of the disorder. As these specialists gather their data, case conferences are usually called and the entire dossier of information on the youngster is presented to representatives of the various disciplines. In addition to medical information, the reports usually include "work-ups" from profes-sionals who represent speech, social work, psychology, psychiatry, education, and other relevant disciplines. After the group has reviewed the total record on the child, a plan of remediation, recommendations for placement or further evalua-tion, and a follow-up program are developed. The responsibility for seeing that the group's recommendations are implemented usually is assigned to the social worker on the team.

As you might suspect, doing a comprehensive case study on a child who is suspected of being mentally retarded is complex because it usually involves the coordination among a number of professional specialists, expensive because it often requires the services of highly trained personnel and use of valuable equip-ment, and involved because of the need to observe and maintain records on a child for relatively long periods of time. It is worth the expenditure of time and financial resources to do an investigation of this type on a preschool child who is suspected of being mentally retarded. Without such specific information one cannot determine what, when, and how to intervene. In addition to conduct-

ing a comprehensive medical examination of the child, the diagnostic team will collect data on a number of other areas such as the child's level of intellectual performance, the achievement level of the child in various specific skill areas, his attitudes and those of others around him, the extent and quality of his socialization skills and emotional development, the character of the family milieu, and the opinions of the family members concerning their prognosis for the preschooler.

Information on these factors, and the many smaller variables that are a part of these larger dimensions, can be gathered through the use of various standard diagnostic instruments. Data from these devices can be used to construct a chronological record of the child's personal and environmental idiosyncrasies. In addition, parents and others who have an opportunity to interact with the child can be trained to provide reliable and valid observations of behavior, information from which offers valuable supplements to the results from the more formal, standardized instruments. The observations one obtains from formal and informal devices or techniques will be helpful to the degree to which they reflect the usual or typical behavior and character of the preschooler. Because this is such an important issue in the present discussion, as well as in those which appear in subsequent chapters, let us look for a moment at some of the fundament assumptions and considerations which are involved in the observation, evaluation, and diagnosis of mentally retarded individuals. Smith and Neisworth (1969) have discussed each of these points in much greater depth than is possible here.

Assumptions about Evaluation   When a person is evaluated on a test, or some other type of device, we assume that the examiner knows what he is doing. Most medical and behavioral procedures which are used in the examination require that the tester have complete knowledge of the evaluation devices, their strengths and weaknesses, and have previously demonstrated skill in using the instruments. If, for some reason, the team of specialists receives data on a child which are inaccurate, unreliable, biased, or improperly recorded, it will give a false picture of the youngster's characteristics and, perhaps, lead to remedial suggestions which are totally improper. How important it is, then, for the examiner to be one who is aware of various available instruments to measure the specific dimensions on which he desires to gather data, and that he be able to intelligently interpret the information once it is obtained.

Of importance equal to that of the examiner being skilled in administration and interpretation is that he select an appropriate instrument which is designed to measure directly what he desires to measure. Among the questions an astute diagnostician will ask of himself as he considers the various possible devices are: "Will this test get at the specific factors that I am interested in examining in a relatively more efficient and effective way than other possible devices?" "What 'trade offs' do I have to make in order to use this device?" "Does it cost more

in terms of time, money, or materials?" "Am I competent to administer and interpret the device?" "What possible biases are inherent in the instrument?" "How reliable is it?" "Are there certain errors of measurement peculiar to the device which will result in an imprecise evaluation of the youngster?" Answers to these and other such questions will aid the diagnostician to focus properly on the most appropriate assessment technique in each specific testing situation.

If we were interested in studying the behavior of a child who was suspected of being mentally retarded because he was having some difficulty dealing with his environment, most certainly we would want to accurately describe the child and the manner in which he interacts with his surroundings. Before making any statements at all about the youngster, and surely before he is classified as being mentally retarded, every caution must be exercised to assure that we have observed him on enough occasions, in various situations, and in a number of ways. We want the data to reflect his typical or usual performance, and not those behaviors which result from his having a bad day, feeling unwell, or not getting enough sleep the previous night. It does not really matter whether you talk about medical, psychological, educational, or social variables; the principle is still the same. Since it is impossible to maintain total surveillance on a child; i.e., one cannot observe the reactions of his liver on a continuous basis or how he deals with his mother and father at all meals, we need to get enough representative samples of the child's behavior to be able to characterize his total repertoire of performance. To this end, the diagnostician should (1) examine the child or observe his behavior and performance on more than a single occasion, (2) use a number of instruments and techniques to study the various dimensions, (3) evaluate the youngster at various times during the day, and (4) collect samples of performance frequently and over long periods of time.

One final point on the matter of sampling behavior that is important to ensure preciseness is that the examiner focus on a specific objective(s) throughout the process of evaluation. When a physician places the stethoscope on your chest, he has a specific objective in mind, for example, he may desire to check on the possibility that your lungs may be congested or that your heart beat is abnormal. He knows what he wants to find out, and he has devices at his disposal for obtaining the information. In a similar fashion, those professionals who specialize in behavioral problems need to formulate in clear terms what specific trait they wish to observe. After this has been decided upon, the instruments for study and the techniques for studying the specific trait can be decided upon. This procedure will reduce the possibility of a time-consuming, haphazard fishing expedition which is done under the guise of an efficient and effective diagnostic work-up.

The Use and Misuse of Intelligence Test Scores   In the section of this book which presented discussion on systems of classification, it was pointed out that for many disciplines the one most prominent criterion for determining if a

youngster is mentally retarded is how well he scores on an intelligence test. One component of the official definition of the American Association on Mental Deficiency is that an IQ score of 84 or below is indicative of mental retardation. In spite of the many who correctly argue that the IQ is an inadequate singular criterion for deciding on whether a child should be classified as mentally retarded, some of the better individual intelligence tests still offer the best predictions for determining how well a youngster will do in school. The IQ, then, continues to be used by behavioral scientists, and by others who are concerned about diagnosing mental retardation, as an important variable in deciding on degree of intellectual subnormality.

In order for the reader to fully appreciate the arguments which are used to discourage the sole use of an IQ score to diagnose mental retardation, a cursory review will be presented of some of the central concepts involved in testing intelligence, what can and cannot be determined by scores from intelligence tests, and how intelligence test data are frequently misused. Neisworth (1969) has succinctly discussed the pros and cons involved in using intelligence tests for diagnostic purposes in an interesting presentation which he labels, "The Educational Irrelevance of Intelligence."

There are many types of intelligence tests. Some are designed to be administered to groups, and others require individual administration; some evaluate verbal skills more than nonverbal (and vice versa); some are designed to evaluate infant intelligence, whereas others are designed to be used with adults; and some are appropriate for use with various groups of handicapped children while others are not. In almost all these tests one of the major problems is that the full spectrum of factors involved in the concept of intelligence is not measured. For example, infant intelligence tests are naturally more nonverbal and involve observing a child primarily in perceptual-motor types of activities. By definition, almost, they could not be expected to contain test items which involve the use of higher mental operations; the repertoire of infants does not contain such competencies. One of the problems, then, is that the results of an infant intelligence test will not accurately predict the child's performance as an adolescent or adult. In the same vein, those tests which are most frequently used on school-age children do not contain many factors which learning theorists believe to comprise one's intelligence. By using these instruments we are, at best, obtaining a general and not completely accurate portrait of an individual's promise for succeeding in school in the future.

Let us assume that a preschool retarded child is administered an intelligence test by a competent diagnostician. For the purposes of this discussion, suppose that the youngster is five years of age and scored with an IQ of 75. What does this mean? If the test was administered and scored correctly, a score of this magnitude would suggest that the child learns about three-fourths the rate of an intellectually normal youngster. We could calculate his mental age from these

data. In this case, we might reasonably expect the child to be able to function in school types of activities as a normal child of three years eight months of age. If we sampled his intelligence test performance on subsequent occasions, as we ought in order to get an adequate representation of his functioning, and found that his scores varied only slightly, we could have some confidence in these findings.

There are, however, several possible problems that could arise if you were provided with an IQ score, in this case 75. Even for people who are untrained in the nuances of diagnosis and evaluation, a score of this magnitude immediately has certain connotations. Some people would react in certain ways which implied that they did not view the child's performance as very good, that he was lacking in some way, and that one probably could not expect much from him in the future. If, on the other hand, the child had scored with an IQ of 110, a different conclusion would probably be reached. We all have rather well inculcated reference points against which we compare the performance of others. When it comes to intelligence test data, educators and others are often too prone to interpret another person's performance with flimsy and often incomplete data. The point here is that with an IQ score alone there is often a tendency among certain individuals to overinterpret or speculate about a child's background, ability, and prognosis without adequate documentation.

Moving one step further, the work of Rosenthal and Jacobson (1968) on teacher expectations is salient to this discussion. These scientists presented results from a study they conducted which strongly suggests that one's personal expectations of another person's subsequent performance are usually upheld. They divided a large group of children, all of whom were achieving at approximately the same level, into two groups. By random selection, a number of subjects from each of the groups was placed in various classrooms. The teachers were told that they could expect great things of certain youngsters who were selected from one of the groups; nothing was said to the teachers about what they could expect from the children that were selected from the other group. At the end of the school year, achievement test scores suggested that those children who had been identified as persons from whom high achievement could be expected in fact achieved significantly higher scores than the other group of subjects. Remember, at the beginning there were really no differences between these two groups in terms of school achievement. Apparently, in a very subtle way the expectations which the teachers had for the achievement of certain youngsters caused them to treat children differently. At this point, the various techniques that were used by the teachers to deal with the high expectancy children as opposed to the low expectancy children have not been identified nor measured. You might wish to speculate on what some of these possible differences might be.

There is a high likelihood that this same self-fulfilling prophecy, which

apparently was active in the experiment of Rosenthal and Jacobson, can also exert a significant force when parents, teachers, and others begin to consider appropriate management strategies for retarded preschool children. The danger in announcing that a child has an IQ of 65 and that another child has an IQ of 86 is that we begin to believe that more can be expected from the child with "a higher IQ." Unfortunately, in many cases the expectation which we have is fulfilled, not solely as a result of the difference between the level of intellectual performance between the two children but because of the indiscernibly different ways in which we treat the two children. Although the findings of this study and the implications which surround it are still tentative, those who are concerned about providing appropriate and adequate diagnostic procedures for preschool retarded children should be aware of the potential hazards involved in reporting IQ scores without supplementing this information with further, more precise documentation which offers a clearer picture of the child's behavioral characteristics.

Perhaps of equal importance to what an IQ score of 75 tells us is what it does not tell us. If one is interested in designing a program of management for the child, an IQ score alone will not tell anything about the detailed characteristics of a youngster. From this small piece of information you could not determine if he was relatively good or poor in any of the subtest areas of the intelligence test, such as auditory memory, spatial relations, arithmetic concepts, reproduction of designs, general comprehension, and so on. In order to obtain and use this valuable information one must have the child's verbatim responses or the entire test protocol. The value in having these data cannot be overstated. Extending this point a bit, we could not tell from a score of 75 if the child was organically and/or environmentally impaired, how well his communication mechanisms were intact and operating, the extent to which the youngster was social, what his family situation appeared to be like, or how eager he was to participate in the testing session. Many of these points may seem unworthy of mention and readily obvious to most of you; however, there are many concerned parents, teachers, and others who need this thought underlined because they tend to go well beyond the data into the realm of "mystic psychologizing" without any basis. An IQ score alone is not enough.

It follows logically from the position that an IQ score alone fails to truly and accurately characterize a preschool retarded child, or any other type for that matter, to the belief that the score does not lead directly to a plan of management, remediation, or control. In order to know what chemical compounds to mix in their proper proportion for a patient, a pharmacist depends on the physician to provide a very precise prescription which is based on the specific characteristic of the disorder in question. If you desire to have a prescription for the management of a retarded child's behavioral inadequacies, you would need to have a precise description of his behavioral patterns and what constitutes

reasonable management objectives. In fact, there are probably very few retarded preschoolers, who have scored on an individually administered test at around IQ 75, whose behavioral profile would suggest that each needs the same type of emphasis in a program of behavioral management or education.

Other than gaining some general indication as to a child's general rate of learning, and predicting within limits how well he should be able to do in school, what are some other advantages in administering an intelligence test to a retarded youngster? Assuming that we have the verbatim responses of the child available, and the examiners have kept rather complete notes on the testing session, we should be able to begin developing some tentative hypotheses concerning some of the important characteristics of the youngster. For example, with an entire intelligence test protocol a diagnostician should be able to gain some appreciation for areas of relative strength and weakness. At a rather general level, a child may be much higher in those areas which require verbal responses than in areas requiring nonverbal performances; or, at a more precise level, a child may have serious difficulties in remembering what he hears but not in remembering what he sees. These and other more molecular analyses can be obtained by inspecting the responses of a youngster to an intelligence test and grouping the responses according to the child's degree of success. For many youngsters, common threads will begin to emerge within those areas in which the youngster has been successful. These areas of commonality may differ significantly from the common threads that transverse through those areas in which the child has not been successful. Armed with this type of information, the examiner can begin to focus on a suggested plan for remediation and management. Again, you can see how necessary it is to dig into the child's responses for patterns which will lead logically to a suggested plan for remediation. If an intelligence test is used in this manner, as opposed to routinely reporting an IQ score alone, it can be a very valuable device for organizing and specifying the nature of an educational program for preschool children.

Intelligence tests for the most part survey a spectrum of dimensions which are related to the solution of problems, primarily those which emphasize cognitive development. There are several other major areas of performance which are important during the preschool years and which form the foundation on which subsequent development occurs. Since many retarded children tend to experience difficulty in a variety of performance areas, most plans for evaluating this group of youngsters should include measurement of the child's performance in perceptual-motor areas; communication, including speech and language; socialization; and personal-emotional factors. There are screening devices, penetrating assessment techniques, and intensive batteries of tests available to measure performance in the multitude of factors which underly each of these major areas. Smith (1968, 1969) has suggested a variety of formal and informal procedures which teachers might use to evaluate many of these dimensions. For the most

part, however, a comprehensive formal evaluation of a young retarded child requires the services of a well-trained, skilled examiner to administer, score, and interpret the data.

Suggestions for Observing Behavior   Even before a formal evaluation is made, parents will often be suspicious of their preschool child's development and behavior in instances where the youngster is mentally retarded. By systematically observing the child in an informal way, they can begin to formulate a picture of where he is predominately weak in interacting with his environment. When this information is collected, it will give some indication of appropriate sources of referral in order that more comprehensive formal evaluations can be made. The following guidelines may help to focus the observer's attention on some behavior characteristics of a preschool child that may be indicative of mental retardation, with associated disorders, and which warrant attention by a medical or behavioral specialist:

1.   Observation of a child's mannerisms should be done as much as possible in an unobtrusive way and not only by insisting that the youngster perform on a test in a somewhat contrived setting.

2.   The observer should always have a specific behavior goal in mind; just do not look for whatever happens to appear, but focus your attention on, e.g., how well the infant reaches, crawls, or hears.

3.   Look not only at a child's performance, but be aware of the environmental conditions which influence his behavior or performance. For example, does he have trouble walking up stairs but not on a level surface? Can he tolerate soft sounds but not loud noises? These kinds of questions, asked by the observer, will help specify the general influence which the surroundings have on the child.

4.   In perceptual-motor areas, look for how well the preschooler is able to maintain a certain posture (such as, for example, in sitting up); coordinate his body in motor movements; avoid obstacles; balance himself; relate what he sees to arm and leg movements; differentiate among the size, shape, color, length, and weight of objects; and move about in his environment. For a much more complete listing of perceptual-motor areas and the informal evaluative devices that might be used to measure these behaviors in preschool children, see Smith (1968, 1969), Roach and Kephart (1966); Radler and Kephart (1960), Kephart (1960), and Bayley (1969).

5.   In communication areas look for how well the child seems to hear and respond to sound, babbles, engages in other forms of vocal play, develops consonant sounds, says words in progressively more complex combinations and forms, initiates words, responds to commands, sings, expresses ideas in words or gestures, and remembers ideas in a story. These represent only a few of the

many areas which usually develop to some extent during the preschool years. A more detailed list can be found in Smith (1968), McWilliams (1969), and Van Riper (1965).

6. In emotional and social areas you might wish to be particularly sensitive to the child's disposition in relation to difficulties with his environment or with others; the degree to which he is spontaneous in initiating social interactions; his reactions to disappointment, pleasurable situations, and to strangers; the extent to which he is cooperative in play with others; his humor; and whether he is generally overly or under responsive in emotional and social areas. Again, you may wish to consult the following references for a more detailed breakdown of other social and emotional variables which are pertinent to preschool youngsters (Gordon, 1966; Baron and Bernard, 1958; and Lister, 1969).

7. There are numerous skills which do not fall specifically into any of the above three categories but which are important developmental tasks during the preschool years and warrant special attention by parents and others who may be suspicious about the extent and speed with which a child is developing. The list should include how well the child becomes toilet trained; the extent to which he engages in repetitive and nonmeaningful behavior (such as body rocking); how much he tenses his body when lifted; his visual, tactile, and auditory responsiveness; how well he learns to feed himself; his curiosity about objects and things; his anticipation of further events and rememberance of past experiences; and the extent to which he depends on others to solve his problems.

These guidelines are by no means all-inclusive nor exhaustive; they do, however, pinpoint a number of major areas on which attention should be focused during the preschool period. If a youngster is relatively weak in a group of these skills, this weakness could have some diagnostic significance and should by all means be followed up by referring the youngster to a medical or behavioral specialist.

To summarize, there is a decisive need to identify and properly diagnose mental retardation and other disorders if they are present in preschool-age children. Delay, too casual an attitude, or lack of forethought on this matter will rapidly work against optimum development for the child and be a possible cause for serious behavioral problems. Since a program of remediation and management is properly based on diagnostic findings, it is imperative that all appropriate safeguards which are involved in the observation and measurement of behavior be practiced. It is clear that referral of a youngster who exhibits uncertain behavior is dependent on how aware his parents and the family physician are to atypical traits. Parents, then, must be alerted to and taught about various techniques for informally evaluating the adequacy of their preschool child's behavior. More will be said on this matter in Chapter 4.

Baron, D., and H. W. Bernard: *Evaluation Techniques for Classroom Teachers,* McGraw-Hill Book Company, New York, 1958.

Bayley, N.: *Manual for the Bayley Scales of Infant Development,* The Psychological Corporation, New York, 1969.

Gorden, I.: *Studying the Child in School,* John Wiley & Sons, Inc., New York, 1966.

Kephart, N. C.: *The Slow Learner in the Classroom,* Charles E. Merrill Books, Inc., Columbus, Ohio, 1960.

Lister, J. J.: "Personal—Emotional—Social Skills," in R. M. Smith (ed.), *Teacher Diagnosis of Educational Difficulties,* Charles E. Merrill Books, Inc., Columbus, Ohio, 1969, pp. 171–209.

McWilliams, B. J.: "Speech and Language Disorders," in R. M. Smith (ed.), *Teacher Diagnosis of Educational Difficulties,* Charles E. Merrill Books, Inc., Columbus, Ohio, 1969, pp. 118–151.

Neisworth, J. T.: "The Educational Irrelevance of Intelligence," in R. M. Smith (ed.), *Teacher Diagnosis of Educational Difficulties,* Charles E. Merrill Books, Inc., Columbus, Ohio, 1969, pp. 30–46.

Radler, D. H., and N. C. Kephart: *Success Through Play,* Harper and Row, Publishers, Incorporated, New York, 1960.

Roach, E., and N. C. Kephart: *The Purdue Perceptual-Motor Survey,* Charles E. Merrill Books, Inc., Columbus, Ohio, 1966.

Rosenthal, R., and L. Jacobson: *Pygmalion in the Classroom,* Holt, Rinehart, and Winston, Inc., New York, 1968.

Smith, R. M.: *Clinical Teaching: Methods of Instruction for the Retarded,* McGraw-Hill Book Company, New York, 1968.

——— (ed.): *Teacher Diagnosis of Educational Difficulties,* Charles E. Merrill Books, Inc., Columbus, Ohio, 1969.

———, and J. T. Neisworth: "Some Problems of and Prospects for Research in Mental Retardation," *Mental Retardation,* vol. 7, no. 1, 1969, pp. 25–28.

Van Riper, C.: *Speech Correction: Principles and Methods,* 4th ed., Prentice-Hall, Inc., Englewood Cliffs, N.J., 1965.

What type of environment will facilitate development and what techniques are used to change the behavioral characteristics and prognosis of preschool retarded children?

It should be recognized that most mentally retarded preschoolers have the same array of physical, social, and emotional needs as the nonretarded. The obviousness of their needs may be more noticeable than with normal children because the retarded are usually less adept at dealing with their own feelings and their

surroundings. As a general rule of thumb, you can expect the retarded child's physical characteristics and needs to be closer to his chronological age than to his mental age, his intellectual needs to be nearer to his mental age, and his social and emotional requirements to lie somewhere between his chronological age and mental age. Obviously many retarded children who suffer from conditions which are multiply disabling in a physical sense often require special braces, chairs, and other apparatus for comfort or movement; greater periods for rest; increased need for or reduction in certain aspects of their diet; and adapted physical education programs.

Approaches to Understanding Needs of the Retarded   There are at least two ways to delineate the needs of mentally retarded children, particularly those who are at the preschool level of instruction. One approach is to identify what you believe to be the vast array of skills which the youngsters need to be able to perform at some minimal level in order to function in a satisfactory way as a preschool child and eventually become relatively self-sufficient in society.

If pressed, it would not be difficult for you to describe a very lengthy list of such skills, some of which follow:

1. The young mentally retarded child needs to be able to learn how to dress and undress himself.
2. The preschool mentally retarded child needs to be able to attend to his toileting needs.
3. The preschool retarded child needs to be able to feed himself in a socially acceptable way.
4. The preschool retarded child needs to be able to attend to instruction, or the pertinent stimuli, and follow directions in a reasonably satisfactory way.
5. The preschool retarded child needs to be able to play with toys in a safe way, interact with chronological-age peers appropriately, and know how to deal in socially appropriate ways with frustrating situations.
6. The preschool retarded child needs to be able to communicate his needs at a minimum level of intelligibility.
7. The preschool retarded child needs to be able to perform basic perceptual-motor skills, discrimination tasks, and association types of activities at a certain minimum level of competence.

One could go on describing the multitude of skills which most of us would agree are important for young mentally retarded children to achieve. Obviously, it is possible to fraction-down the larger skills into a myriad of subskills and, in turn, organize these into a hierarchy according to the degree of dependence which each has on the others.

The principal problem of considering the needs of exceptional children from this perspective is that the child is often blamed if he does not achieve at a

certain level in the tasks which the teacher defines. How many times have we all heard someone say about a young retarded child, "He just simply won't pay attention," "He is brain injured and is not able to perform on a certain perceptual-motor task," "There is no point in reading to him because he is mentally retarded and won't understand a word in the story," "He just can't catch on to the sequence involved in going to the bathroom himself," and "He won't listen to me when I try to help him with his speech." You see, in each of these instances the youngster has been held responsible for not achieving certain skills which the teacher might feel are vital for success at that level.

A second way of looking at the needs of young mentally retarded children is by considering the kind of environment which the individual youngster needs in order to facilitate the development of skills on his part in the most efficient and effective way possible. It is not an overstatement to suggest that the vast majority of an instructor's time should be spent in altering and manipulating the environment of a preschool retarded child in order for learning and growth to occur. If the children do not learn or are unable to achieve at a certain level which is considered desirable, the finger should be pointed to those who are responsible for managing the child's environment.

Looking at the needs of retarded children who are at the preschool level from this second point of view, suppose we list some of their principal needs:

1. Young mentally retarded children need to be exposed to "behavioral managers" who are competent and who possess a firm basis to justify structuring the environment of the youngsters in order for skills to develop on their part in a very expeditious way.

2. Young mentally retarded children need to be offered experiences which will prepare them to receive and adequately process subsequent instruction in order that the children will want to learn or will begin to see a desire to participate in activities related to school.

3. Young mentally retarded children need to be offered opportunities to participate in planned programs of intervention at the very earliest age.

4. Mentally retarded children who are of preschool age need to be exposed to a program of activities which is properly sequenced, flexible enough so that activities can be changed and modified according to each individual's diagnostic signs, continually reevaluated, and containing the proper "mix" of instructional methodology, course of study, and media.

In considering the issue of what will facilitate development of a preschool retarded child in the various areas, it is indeed appropriate to first be aware of and consider their needs. I hope that you fully realize that one of their most urgent needs is to be provided with certain environmental conditions, four broad categories of which have been mentioned above, in order that they develop basic skills which will allow them to perform in a satisfactory way later in life. The

duty is for society and its representatives, such as teachers, to provide these fundamental environmental needs through systematic intervention so that the young retardate will have opportunities to (1) see how learning can be fun and become motivated to participate in instructional activities, (2) develop a relatively efficient style for using his environment to deal with problems and situations, (3) learn how to learn, and (4) enlarge on and refine his repertoire of skills.

General Features of a Stimulating Environment   The remainder of this section will concentrate on detailing a number of the components of a generally facilitating environment for young retarded children. Toward the end of this section, special attention will be given to the more specific issue of providing some measure of formal preschool instruction for these youngsters.

Whenever scientists become interested in a new field or in a relatively unexplored subject, one can always expect a period to prevail which reflects disagreement, ambiguity, and polarization on theoretical issues and on positions resulting from empirical findings. This is a natural and expected outcome of newly emerging fields of inquiry, such as in the case of rationalizing the value of early education for the mentally retarded. The situation becomes even more complicated when various social groups exert pressure on the scientific community for immediate answers to crucial questions which suggest that certain portions of our population are not being provided for in an acceptable way.

To a large extent the literature which focuses on early childhood intervention techniques is somewhat ambiguous and certainly lacks specificity in dealing with youngsters who are diagnosed as being mentally retarded as preschoolers or who are prime candidates for acquiring characteristics of this condition. In spite of over thirty years of concentrated effort on this subject and in related areas, it is still not possible for an expert in early childhood education to particularize the absolutely essential components of an educational strategy of intervention for these subjects. There are, indeed, some relatively clear hints from the general literature concerning a number of broad conditions which facilitate or inhibit development of a young child. Likewise, various theories and curricula have been offered to the professional community for their evaluation and possible adoption. With this cautionary note in mind, then, suppose we consider some broad features of a stimulating environment with which many experts in child development and child psychology would probably have little quarrel.

1.   It is now recognized that the newborn infant is usually able to appreciate stimuli which are more complex than heretofore realized, and, in fact, prefers to deal with interesting things and people. Moreover, theory and evidence support the position that isolation of an infant from an interesting physical and social environment are associated with serious difficulties in social, cognitive, language,

and emotional areas. The environment of the newborn, then, should be visually and auditorally interesting. Bright, contrasting, and relatively complex visual figures, toys, and objects should characterize the child's crib area. Opportunities to touch and manipulate objects and toys should be provided. The child should be talked to throughout the period of infancy, and enough emphasis cannot be given to the need for increasing the amount of handling of the young child. Proper facilities and freedom should be provided to allow the infant to move his head, trunk, and limbs.

2.   As the young child gets older, the same style of behavioral management should typify his environment. This requires that the child be exposed to activities which will provide for sensory-motor stimulation which involves increasingly more complex objects and figures. Apparently, it is important for the child's surroundings to be varied in their characteristics, contain objects which can be manipulated by the youngster, and provide opportunities for reactions to occur by objects and people as a result of the child's initiating activity. Throughout the early years much attention should be given to the value in interacting with the child through verbalization. The child's speech and language development will to a large extent reflect the degree to which adult models have been provided and have related to the youngster on an individual basis. As the child's repertoire of information grows as a result of experience, the parents should intentionally verbalize what they are doing and why. This "thinking out loud" will help the youngster to develop more complex associational links between words, objects, intentions, and meaning. With intellectually normal children this type of intervention technique is not quite as important as with the mentally retarded, since the latter group typically are relatively less attentive to their environment and have greater difficulty in seeing relevant associations between abstract concepts and objects.

3.   As the child reaches the toddler stage, opportunities for learning a wide range of skills increases dramatically and should be capitalized on. He should be intentionally exposed to a wide range and variety of objects and experiences. His attention should be directed to the stimuli with which you desire him to interact. For youngsters who are "culturally deprived," a great amount of social reinforcement in the form of hugs, pats, and facial expressions indicating pleasure should be used to strengthen desired behavior. Special attention should be given to encouraging the child to complete a task before moving on to another activity. Throughout the entire process of intervention the child should not be exposed to a "pressure cooker" environment of such a magnitude that the activities and interaction with adults and others become distasteful experiences.

Your Attitude and Reactions Are Important   Whether you are a teacher or a parent, the extent to which you are effective in assisting the young retarded child to develop interests, a healthy attitude, and basic skills depends a great

deal on your own expectations for him and the style which you use in approaching the child. If you believe that "all is lost," that only very minimal change can be expected by the child, or that your time could be better spent working with someone else, you will not be very effective in your enrichment program and the child will not progress. With this attitude, although you may try to camouflage it, your influence on the youngster will diminish and deteriorate. If this defeatist attitude is severe enough, the child will begin to suspect that he is either incapable of dealing or unable to deal with aspects of his environment. This issue is important for parents whose child might be born retarded. Even in relatively affluent homes, many parents choose not to interact with their retarded infant, toddler, or preschooler, as they would with a nonretarded youngster, because they believe that the child will not gain very much. Their thought is that since the child is intellectually slow, intentional interaction of the type described in the three general statements above is a waste of time and will not make a discernible difference in his level of skill development later on. They are "dead wrong" on this issue, for the child will develop layers upon layers of disabilities. Some of these disabilities will be the result of the congenital problem; others will result because the youngster is reared in an inhibiting environment, while being surrounded by affluence. For example, if parents, realizing that their youngster is retarded at birth, fail to help him learn how to label objects because they see their time spent on the task as producing few if any results, the child will experience serious problems later on in those activities which require some minimum level of skill in this particular area. This situation will occur primarily as a result of the child not having had opportunities to engage in this type of vital activity.

Your effectiveness as a behavioral manager of a preschool-age retarded child is also dependent on the manner in which you choose to relate to the youngster. It is often difficult for the parents or a teacher to have enough patience to deal in a kindly, respectful way to their nonretarded children each day; for those who work with young retarded children, tolerance and exercising personal control is a very tough problem. It is frustrating, even for the strongest, most resistant, and flexible personality to try to communicate and direct the behavior and development of a young child who is slow, who often does not understand what is wanted, and who is frequently disinterested in participating because of his history of previous failures. Referring back to the earlier comments on needs, it is important to remember that retarded children have the same bare necessities as normal children for being shown respect for their attitudes and feelings, for being treated with patience, for not being the object of any angry outburst or a sarcastic remark, and for not being constantly "under the gun" to perform as well as another child. In fact, the statement, "We're happy when you do the very best you can," is horribly inappropriate. None of us would be able to achieve at that level even if it could be measured. This type of statement places too much pressure on the young retardate and will inevitably result in alienation

from family members and other facets of the environment from which such pressures eminate, overt dislike for engaging in activities which even hint at evaluation or competition, and a serious diminution of skill development in vital areas of functioning.

Ginott (1965) has expressed the philosophy on child rearing which seems to have applicability to the manner in which one might productively deal with young retardates. One of his main points is that you should always comment on the child's production or performance and assiduously refrain from passing judgment on the child. Suppose we look at a few examples of this point. As a teacher or parent of a preschooler, you could react to a child as follows:

1. "I enjoyed listening to you sing the song" versus "You sure are good at remembering words in songs."
2. "I think your coat looks nice hanging on your own hook" versus "What a good boy you are now; you always remember what to do with your coat."
3. "That loud noise you're making hurts my ears and makes me feel grumpy; I like quiet sounds best" versus "Why are you always so noisy; haven't you learned how to behave in school?"
4. "I like how you drew the circle today" versus "You are a good circle drawer" or "You are my best circle drawer" or "You are really good at art."
5. "I like how fast the toys were picked up today" versus "I can always depend on you as a helper."
6. "Jimmy didn't like being hit; it hurt him" versus "You are unkind" or "You are a mean child" or "Can't you keep your hands off of other people?"
7. "Blocks are for playing with and not for throwing" versus "You're much too rough."
8. "I didn't like the way you talked to me" versus "You're being nasty."

Notice that the initial reaction in each of the preceding examples reflected on how the child's behavior affected either an individual or an object's proper use. The beginning statement in each pair of reactions does not pass judgement on the child's personality, character, or ability as do the familiar sounding alternatives, some of which are listed in each of the above eight examples. Even if the child does a poor job, if you like it, he will be happy in spite of the fact that he may believe that his performance was inadequate. So, the focus should properly be on how you say you feel about his performance and not on what you think about the child. There are several pitfalls if one chooses not to follow this procedure. First, by telling a child that he is or is not capable of doing something or that he is a good boy, talented, or always dependable will cause him to lose faith in you. He knows that it is untrue. Second, it places undue pressure on the child for him to try to be like what you said he is. This is absolutely impossible for even the most talented youngster and especially difficult for the preschool retardate.

Dimensions of a Preschool Program for the Retarded   With these broad features of some of the contents of the facilitating environment in mind, suppose we turn our attention to a brief discussion of some factors one should consider in developing and providing a preschool program of instruction for young retarded children. The acquisition of skills and knowledge occurs in an accumulative fashion over time. This process begins to some extent during the prenatal period and escalates at a rapid clip during those years immediately after birth. By the time an intellectually normal child has reached the fourth, fifth, and sixth years of life, a great amount of learning has taken place in various areas of life as a result of intentional intervention by parents and others and because of incidental learning by the young child. For children with some degree of intellectual retardation this same rate and level of development does not usually occur.

The need for being concerned about providing early stimulation of youngsters who are retarded or who are candidates for future placement in special education classes has been reviewed to some degree in previous sections of this book. Scientists have known for a long time that very early stimulation of youngsters, especially those who have been associated with a deprived environment, will subsequently lead to significant advantages for the child in cognitive, affective, communicative, and motoric areas of functioning. By this time it should not be news to you that the relatively normal human organism is plastic, amenable to change as a result of intervention, and, perhaps most important of all, a vigorous extractor of stimuli from the environment. The young retarded child is similar in character although we could logically expect that he will be relatively less efficient and effective in processing information than his intellectually normal peers.

Even among normal and advanced preschoolers it is pertinent for us to consider how their time can best be spent in early instruction. Even now, after many years of research and inquiry, there exist spirited debates within the literature concerning answers to this question. I suspect, however, that most child development scientists would agree that they wish to provide a preschool environment in which the mentally retarded individual will be able to fully realize his individual aptitudes in social, cognitive, affective, personal, and communicative areas. The means by which this objective is achieved will no doubt differ according to the individual's personal philosophy concerning the proper nature of early intervention.

Irrespecitve of one's personal theoretical allegiance, in the final analysis those who are responsible for planning a preschool program for the mentally retarded must answer three questions:

1. "What to teach?" or "What competencies do I wish the youngsters to develop?"
2. "In what order should the instruction occur?"

3. "How, or in what manner, can the individual competencies best be taught so that each child's opportunity for learning skills is maximized?"

For the mentally retarded these three questions are of extreme importance because the answers one offers to each and the manner in which they are implemented will dicate how self-sufficient and independent an existence the retarded individual will be prepared for as adulthood approaches. There is no room for inefficiency or questioning whether it is necessary for the many components of the preschool educational program to be planned for maximum efficiency. We cannot waste time during this instructional period, be inefficient, or operate in a trial and error fashion. Retarded youngsters will usually begin their elementary school program later than most intellectually normal children, they will take a good deal longer to acquire foundation skills than their normal peers, many of the concepts and ideas to be learned must be intentionally presented while their normal counterparts will be able to acquire the same information and concepts at a much more rapid pace on an incidental basis, and the mentally retarded will be more susceptible to acquiring poor and cumbersome habits for developing and using skills and knowledge. At the same time, our society anticipates that those retarded individuals who are not institutionalized will be able to obey laws just like everyone else, become contributors to the community, properly rear their children, and attend to their personal business in an effective way. Do you see why the instructional program must be efficient and effective beginning even at the preschool level? The teacher is faced with the problem of providing an instructional program to a youngster who is inefficient in processing information, who takes longer to acquire basic skills, and who is delayed in his readiness to be exposed to formal components of instruction. At the same time, we anticipate that this individual as an adolescent or adult will be able to function at a satisfactory level within society. To be sure, then, systematic instruction for these youngsters must begin at the earliest possible moment and be properly programmed so that maximum learning and skill can occur.

How does one decide what to teach the young mentally retarded child in a preschool program? There are various curriculum guides available which offer advice on courses of study for preschool retardates; the major focus of some of these guides will be reviewed toward the end of this section. It should be pointed out that many people elect to use as a beginning the nursery school programs which have been designed primarily for intellectually normal children. After having had some experience with observing the intellectually retarded child, the courses of study are adapted and the procedures by which the material is presented changed in order to reflect the peculiar characteristics of the retarded children.

Another way of approaching the question of what to teach preschool retarded children is to specify in behavioral terms what you would like for them to

achieve. In the opinion of many special educators and child development authorities this approach is more pedagogically sound and prescriptive than the approach of modifying and using curriculum guides, which in many instances do not reflect the retarded child's present or future requirements. To implement the concept of using competencies as a curricular basis, identify a number of major developmental areas which are particularly appropriate for retarded children, whatever their age or level of functioning, and begin listing the basic skills that are contained within each area. You must realize, however, that the orientation and emphasis in the competencies which you list may differ among various populations of retarded children according to their different etiologies, prognoses, and placement situations.

Table 3-2 suggests some objectives for preschool retarded children in several broad areas of functioning. You will notice that it has been possible to become increasingly more specific by fractioning down some of the major areas of skill into their component parts. The list which is presented is not exhaustive, nor has it been tested out in terms of establishing validity of the order in which the skill areas progress from relatively easy to difficult. Notice that the criteria for specifying behavioral objectives, as suggested by Lindvall (1967), has been used. These criteria are:

Objectives should be worded in terms of the pupil.
Objectives should be worded in terms of the observable behavior.
Objectives should refer to the specific content to which the behavior is to apply.

The emphasis within a circumscribed group of program objectives or competencies will not be alike for the different levels of preschool retarded children, nor, for that matter, for every child within a specific class of preschoolers. You recognize, of course, that there is usually a great difference in the general levels of behavior and performance between preschool retarded children who are organically impaired and those youngsters who are medically sound but who have been reared in a deprived environment. The former group represents a population of children who are typically more substantially involved; whereas, the latter group is relatively more amenable to direct intervention in most instances. The objectives which have been described in Table 3-2 as a total group are probably more appropriate for "higher level" retarded preschoolers as opposed to those who are generally within the trainable range. On the other hand, it is true that a number of the objectives would be reasonable for most every preschooler who is mentally retarded. The basis on which one decides what should be included in the child's program is each individual youngster's profile of strengths and weaknesses. Yes, even instructors of retarded preschool children must individualize their curriculum in the same manner as teachers of retarded youngsters at other levels.

Table 3-2   Some suggested objectives for preschool retardates in six broad areas of development

---

Perceptual-motor development and physical fitness

Preschool retarded children should be able to:

1. Attend to visual stimuli and discriminate among sizes by selecting the larger(est) and smaller(est); among colors; and among shapes, triangles, squares and circles
2. Control, associate, and coordinate various body parts in visual-motor activities
   a. Maintain proper postural adjustment in general body balance and locomotion, such as actions involved in walking, jumping, hopping, skipping, and galloping
   b. Integrate various muscle systems involved in throwing, pushing, pulling, and swinging
   c. Coordinate arms and legs in movements which involve unilateral, bilateral, and crosslateral activities
   d. Locate objects in space and be able to translate from spatial to temporal dimensions, such as actions involved in batting a ball, hitting a punching clown, or catching a floating balloon
3. Respond to stimuli in a motoric way or through gesture
   a. Locomote about the environment (same as in 2a above)
   b. Express some skill in using both sides of the body in activities involving regular and irregular patterns of rhythm
   c. Express a concept or process (such as in fishing or driving a car) by using gestures
   d. Begin using small muscle groups especially in activities which involve prehension, grasping, manipulation, and other finger movements
   e. Become involved in the use of the total body in vigorous types of activities
4. Become relatively more physically fit
   a. Develop an interest in participating in activities which will help to develop speed, strength, body flexibility, and power
   b. Relax at appropriate times with less manifest tension, fatigue, and hyperactivity

---

Verbal communication

Preschool retarded children should be able to:

1. Attend to, listen for, and discriminate among various auditory stimuli
   a. Differentiate between high and low sounds, loud and soft sounds, and combinations of these
   b. Identify similarities and differences in the sounds of various parts of words
   c. Listen for familiar words and use them as clues to gain meaning from a story
   d. Listen for words that express various types of action and activities
2. Develop an increasingly more elaborate speaking vocabulary:
   a. Use different synonyms to express a concept or meaning
   b. Distinguish among the temporal meanings of certain words, e.g., as in today, tomorrow, yesterday, not yet, now, and never
   c. Connect the meaning between a concrete object and an abstract intention, e.g., as in hug and affection, hit and unkind, book and learn, or ladder and climb

3. Express ideas in an increasingly more effective way
   a. Organize their expression of an idea, story, or thought in a logical order
   b. Use proper words to express an idea
   c. Speak with increasing levels of fluency, pertinence, and elaboration of ideas
   d. Willingly engage in meaningful discussions with peers, parents, teachers, and other adults
4. Develop increasingly more precision in speaking with clarity, comprehensible enunciation, and with satisfactory voice quality

---

Cognitive skills

Preschool retarded children should be able to:
1. Develop positive attitudes toward activities which involve school work, learning new facts and information, solving problems by using new knowledge and past experiences
2. Become increasingly more sensitive toward their surroundings and initiate more complex contacts with them and with those individuals, situations, and components of their environment which foster inquiry, interest, and curiosity
3. Profit, in terms of demonstrating increasingly higher level skills for solving problems, by widened experiences, explanation, intentional instruction, suggestions, and evaluation of performances
4. Value independent thinking and the contribution of one's own ideas to group situations
5. Widen and increase their repertoire of general information, performance in associating and remembering, the comprehension and meaning of ideas, the basic components involved in quantitative thinking, and the evaluation of alternative solutions to problems.

Self-care and emotional development

Preschool retarded children should be able to:
1. Develop positive attitudes and feelings toward self-care including areas such as feeding, toileting, and grooming
2. Establish routine patterns and a satisfactory level of skill in routine health habits including such areas as brushing teeth, washing hands, toileting, blowing and wiping nose, and resting when fatigued
3. Understand why safety is essential in work and play and employ a cautious approach in activities which are potentially unsafe for himself or for others
4. Exercise some control over their emotions
   a. Tolerate and profit from constructive assistance from adults with whom they are familiar
   b. Increase in self-control and in tolerance for frustration
   c. Decrease in the incidence of the use of defense mechanisms as reactions to problems and increase in the incidence of attempting to deal with problems in a more emotionally healthy manner.

Table 3-2 Some suggested objectives for preschool retardates in six broad areas of development (*Continued*)

Social skills

Preschool retarded children should be able to:

1. Show respect for the personal and property rights of others
   a. Distinguish between one's own rights and belongings and those of others
   b. Understand that rules are helpful to everyone
   c. Defend their rights in socially appropriate ways
2. Increase the quantity and quality of interpersonal interactions with other children
   a. Engage in cooperative play, mutual activities, and participate in group projects
   b. Assume responsibilities as a leader within a group and willingly allow other children to become leaders without opposition or conflict
3. Increase spontaneous contacts with adults and exhibit interest in interacting with the teacher and other authority figures
   a. Maintain a balance between independence from and dependence on adults for solution of problems, issues, or controversies
   b. Develop a comfortable style in interacting with adults
   c. Show respect for authority figures and adults
   d. Exhibit basic social skills involving the proper use of manners in usual social situations in which preschool children might be exposed
   e. Be thoughtful and considerate of others

Aesthetic and creative development

Preschool retarded children should be able to:

1. Willingly participate in numerous and various experiences and activities in areas involving opportunities for artistic expression, e.g., as in painting, singing, clay work, acting, playing instruments, finger plays, and so on
2. Feel free from all evaluations which are externally imposed and recognize that one is free to express himself artistically in any fashion he desires, so long as it is socially acceptable
3. Develop any specific skills or competencies as fully as possible within limits of personal preference

---

There has been an increasing number of curriculum guides for preschool disadvantaged and/or retarded youngsters since the middle 1960s. Some of the programs have emphasized a language orientation (Spicker, Hodges, and McCandless, 1966; Painter, 1969; Bereiter and Engelmann, 1966), others have focused on simple concept learning (Deutsch, 1965; Gray and Klaus, 1965), a few have focused primarily on intervention with parents (Karnes, Studley, Wright, and Hodgins, 1968; Kirk, 1958), a very excellent and comprehensive program dealt with perceptual-motor skills which were developmentally ordered according to Piaget's formulations (Sprigle, Van de Riet, and Van de Riet, 1967), and a modified Montessori approach has been used successfully with

these youngsters (Kohlberg, 1968). A number of curriculum guides have been published which are aimed at these populations of children, but they do not seem to have a single characteristic orientation or emphasis; their focus seems to involve multiple techniques of intervention (Connor and Talbot, 1964; Weikart, Kamii, and Radin, 1964). Students with an interest in the various program orientations are urged to study the characteristics of each of these different programs.

Identifying Instructional Sequences   Now, what about the issue of sequencing instruction? If all the factors that are involved in the acquisition of skill and knowledge were independent of each other, i.e., if the learning of one skill in no way was related to the learning of another skill, it would be possible to present material to the learner in any random or arbitrary sequence. On the other hand, if there is a measure of dependence of one element of learning on another element of learning and still another, and so on, then it is imperative that we give attention to sequencing the elements of instruction so that the hierarchy of skills is built logically for the learner and does not force the youngster to make conceptual leaps in the absence of deliberate instruction which is needed to bridge the gap that inevitably exists between two or more concepts.

Table 3-3 describes just four of many possible sequencing patterns. These have been simplified a great deal for purposes of illustration. Each arrow represents an activity, and the placement of the arrows shows the interdependence thought to exist among each network configuration. Examples have been suggested in areas of perceptual-motor development and in communication skills. You may want to experiment with some of the other areas of development that were mentioned earlier in this section.

We can consider instructional sequencing for the retarded in terms of a vast number of units of instructional time; for example, a child's entire lifetime, one's adult life, the school years, a preschool experience, a month-long program, a weekly schedule, a daily plan, or an individual instructional encounter. From the viewpoint of the lifetime of a retarded learner, special educators are becoming increasingly more concerned about the need to provide systematically sequenced instruction and experiences from birth to death for most retarded individuals. This is particularly pertinent for those retarded persons who are moderately retarded, who often do not qualify for public instruction in their communities, whose families are unable or do not wish to care for their developmental needs, or those individuals who will spend a lifetime in a residential center or in an institution. In fact, the much closer relationship that is beginning to develop between special education and rehabilitation programs attests to the present level of interest among professionals for providing educational programs with explicit sequencing throughout the lifetime of even those individuals with mild degrees of mental retardation.

Table 3-3 Examples of selected sequencing formulations

Sequencing representations	A→B	A→{B,C}	{A,B}→C	{A,B}→{C,D}
	A B	B A C	A B C	A C B D A B
Explanation of representations	Activity B cannot begin before activity A has been achieved at some minimal level of competence	Activities B and C cannot begin before activity A has been achieved at some minimal level of competence	Activity C cannot start before activities A and B have been achieved at some minimal level of competence	Activities C and D cannot begin before activities A and B have been achieved at some minimal level of competence
Examples in perceptual-motor area	Standing (A) before walking (B)	Jumping on both feet (A) before hopping on left foot (B) and hopping on right foot (C)	Running (A) and hopping on alternate feet (B) before skipping (C)	Remembering configuration of certain shapes (A) and tracing shapes (B) before drawing a square from memory (C) and drawing a circle from memory (D)
Examples in areas of communication	Hearing sounds (A) before discriminating among words (B)	Remembering a verbal sequence (A) before carrying out a command (B) and singing a song properly (C)	Knowing the meaning of certain words (A) and understanding what is being seen (B) before associating proper labels with objects (C)	Vocally expressing meaning (A) and gesturally expressing meaning (B) before telling and showing a process like fishing (C) and role playing (D)

One could also look at sequencing learning in terms of relatively long blocks of time such as during adulthood, the high school years, the elementary grades, or throughout the preschool experiences. Conceivably it should be possible to identify units of materials or broad competencies appropriate for each of these time periods and then proceed to establish a sequence for the entire scope of training. The sequencing patterns that might be used to diagram those activities which should precede other activities would look much like the representations which appear in Table 3-3. The most obvious advantage of considering a procedure of this sort is that teachers who are responsible for each specific unit of time and instruction become informed about the scope and sequence of their responsibilities, and they can also gain some appreciation for the general criteria which teachers at lower and higher levels of instruction expect their retarded youngsters to meet before matriculating to each level. Moreover, and of immense importance, instruction becomes more efficient when one uses this approach because each teacher does not have to grope around to discover each student's level of functioning by returning to old material which the student may have had months or years before.

Moving to progressively smaller units of time, the monthly, weekly, and daily schedules of instructional activity should reflect common-sense sequencing as a very minimal expectation. It is unfortunate that the professional literature does not provide teachers with much help on this task; it will therefore be necessary for teachers of the mentally retarded at all levels to call on their practical experience, the expertise of their professional colleagues, and the very important experiences that many teachers have had as mothers and fathers to do this very important task. The first consideration should be for the teachers to specify the competencies they wish their students to be able to achieve. In the first chapter a discussion was presented on the manner in which one might identify the "behavioral bits" involved in a youngster's learning how to feed himself with a spoon. Remember, the entire complex task of using a spoon was broken down into component parts and then ordered according to their chronological sequence. This task is a relatively easier one than attempting to sequence the various complex tasks involved in verbal communication, personal and emotional development, and in socialization skills.

You can see, then, how important it is to identify a general goal or objective and begin fractioning the task down into minute component parts. In this way we can be sure that the youngster is not being forced to perform a task before he has developed skills in the predecessor activities. Especially in the preschool program we must be sure not to expect a child to use a pencil before he knows how to hold it; to speak in intelligible sentences before he has learned to discriminate among the various sounds; to go to the toilet himself before he has learned how to unzip or unbutton his pants; to attend to a task before irrelevant and obstructive peripheral stimuli have either been removed from his

surroundings or he has learned to ignore them; or to hop, jump, or skip before he has developed minimum skills in body balance, flexibility, and positioning.

Teaching Tactics   Finally, what about the issue of how to teach preschool retarded children? Possible answers to this question can only be answered after you have decided on specific goals, objectives, or competencies involved in your program. The situation is no different from the one you face when a vacation is planned. You do not plan possible routes or methods of transportation before you decide where you want to go. Only after you have decided on Seattle, Philadelphia, or Miami do you begin to think about how to get there and the advantages and disadvantages of taking various routes.

The route or method you select to use to aid a retarded youngster achieve competence in a certain skill area or master a specific goal will often differ from time to time. The same is true among different children who have been grouped together as a result of their having similar traits. To match an individual child's characteristics with an appropriate method of instruction, it would be important to consider the following:

1. The specific areas in which the child is relatively strong in performance and those in which he is relatively weak
2. The techniques or style which the child presently uses to deal with his environment and to process information
3. The types of reinforcing agents which increase or decrease the frequency and intensity of various behaviors of the child
4. Each child's pattern of multiple disabilities

Although many of the instructional needs of preschool retarded children require individual prescriptions, there are several general practices which are appropriate to enhance the learning of all young children. These are as follows:

1. Try to increase the child's attention by providing equipment and activities which are at his level of interest. See to it that the child is not constantly interrupted by other children and adults.
2. As you work with a child, frequently verbalize what you are doing and why. Think out loud.
3. Provide ample time and opportunities for the youngster to talk about what he is doing, has done, and plans to do.
4. Verbally connect activities from yesterday, today, tomorrow, and next week. Ask questions about what happened, is happening, is coming next, and characteristics of items or objects. Attempt to facilitate the development of a larger vocabulary and verbal comprehension by the children, but in the early stages of learning ignore errors of grammar and pronunciation. At first, stimulate verbal fluency.
5. Encourage listening by using games and activities that involve following

directions, identifying sounds, taking turns, and responding to a verbal stimulus.

6. Provide opportunities for the child to manipulate objects and parts of things, to place things in serial order, to compare, to measure, and to put things together.

7. Discourage constant performance comparisons among children.

Recommended Readings

Bereiter, C., and S. Englemann: *Teaching Disadvantaged Preschool Children,* Prentice-Hall, Inc., Englewood Cliffs, N.J., 1966.

Connor, F. P., and M. E. Talbot: *An Experimental Curriculum for Young Mentally Retarded Children,* Teachers College Press, Columbia University, New York, 1964.

Deutsch, M.: *Institute for Developmental Studies: Annual Report,* New York, 1965.

Ginott, H. G.: *Between Parent and Child,* The Macmillan Company, New York, 1965.

Gray, S. W., and R. A. Klaus: "An Experimental Preschool Program for Culturally Deprived Children," *Child Development,* vol. 36, 1965, pp. 887–898.

Karnes, M. B., W. M. Studley, W. R. Wright and A. S. Hodgins: "An Approach for Working with Mothers of Disadvantaged Preschool Children," *Merrill-Palmer Quarterly,* vol. 14, no. 2, 1968, pp. 174–184.

Kirk, S. A.: *Early Education of the Mentally Retarded,* The University of Illinois Press, Urbana, 1958.

Kohlberg, L.: "Montessori with the Culturally Disadvantaged: A Cognitive-Developmental Interpretation and Some Research Findings," in R. D. Hess and R. M. Bear (eds.), *Early Education,* Aldine Publishing Company, Chicago, 1968, pp. 105–118.

Lindvall, C. M.: *Measuring Pupil Achievement and Aptitude,* Harcourt, Brace & World, Inc., New York, 1967, p. 14.

Painter, G.: "The Effect of a Structured Tutorial Program on the Cognitive and Language Development of Culturally Disadvantaged Infants," *Merrill-Palmer Quarterly,* vol. 15, no. 3, 1969, pp. 279–294.

Spicker, H. H., W. L. Hodges, and B. R. McCandless: "A Diagnostically Based Curriculum for Psycho-socially Deprived Preschool Mentally Retarded Children," *Exceptional Children,* vol. 33, 1966, pp. 215–220.

Sprigle, H. A., V. Van de Riet, and H. Van de Riet: "A Sequential Learning Program for Preschool Children and an Evaluation of its Effectiveness with Culturally Disadvantaged Children," paper read at the annual meeting of the American Educational Research Association, New York, March, 1967.

Weikart, D. P., C. K. Kamii, and N. L. Radin: *Perry Preschool Project Progress Report,* Ypsilanti Public Schools, Ypsilanti, Mich., 1964.

What general considerations should be made in working with parents of preschool retarded children?

Many of the issues that were considered in preceding sections concerning parents of retarded children have a direct connection to the thoughts presented in this section. The problems which the parents may have felt to be relatively minor or inconsequential when their infant was a newborn, and in need of the normal constant attention which is directed toward most neonates, become exacerbated during the preschool period. It is at this time when the full realization of the meaning of mental retardation strikes the mother and the father of a child who is born with the condition. They begin to become aware of the extent to which their child differs from siblings and the neighborhood youngsters of the same age. The realization that younger children are becoming toilet trained, growing stronger, learning more rapidly, communicating with greater facility, and exercising an increased amount of social sophistication than their own relatively older retarded youngster is a source of anguish for the mother of a retarded preschooler.

The confusion which this situation engenders in the minds of parents will often influence their own behavior toward both the retarded child and toward the siblings with normal intelligence. The social-psychological dynamics which surround this situation have not been studied in a broad and penetrating way. The work of Farber and his associates (1960a, 1960b, 1959) is a visible exception to this statement. They have noted that the impact of having a retarded child on family relations is more substantial as the level of intellectual retardation of the child decreases. Normal family relationships and roles of the members are altered in those homes containing a severely retarded member. Likewise, other variables are affected such as marital integration, social mobility, participation in community activities, and the life goals of siblings. Among parents of mildly retarded youngsters less obvious upheaval seems evident. This, no doubt, has some relationship to the relatively higher incidence of mild degrees of retardation among the lower socioeconomic strata of society; i.e., because of instability in various areas of family life so prevalent among this group, the presence of a mildly retarded member in the family has relatively less discernible influence. Moreover, one would have difficulty separating the influence of mental retardation from other potential casual factors among this group.

Farber (1968) has revealed that the severely retarded member of a family usually becomes viewed as the youngest child irrespective of his real chronological age. Accordingly, this affects the adjustment, social and personal, of the entire family membership. Behavioral patterns which are atypical usually evolve among the various family members. You can imagine the extent of complex and dynamic pressures which parents and siblings experience at this time; the differences between normal behavior and retarded behavior become increasingly more

obvious as the preschool retardate approaches the age at which most children begin to prepare for school. This, in turn, affects the parents' behavior and clearly suggests the need for proper counseling during these crucial years.

Placement Issues   For some families, once again the problem of whether or not to seek institutionalization for their preschool-age retarded children looms as a major consideration. This issue is one to which professional workers and counselors must often direct their attention when working with many perplexed families. The indications and contraindications regarding institutional placement which were reviewed in Table 2-3 are pertinent to this discussion. Those parents who did not place their newborn in an institution at or soon after birth will usually have a firmer idea concerning how well they are able to care for the child at home, the extent to which it has disrupted family life for the rest of the family, the financial feasibility of continuing with the child at home, the prognosis for the youngster, the degree of physical and emotional strength required to maintain a routine of management, and the advantages and disadvantages of private or public placement. The first few months or years, in those instances where the child is a borderline case, are important periods for parents to experiment with home placement.

There are several additional points which should be made regarding the question of institutionalization. As the child moves toward the latter preschool years more opportunities for treatment and management exist, particularly in relatively flourishing communities. For example, as a result of federal legislation many states and local communities have established a network of day-care centers to help (1) "facilitate the adjustment of the child in his own home," and (2) "provide a developmental program for the child while he is at the center" (La-Crosse, 1964). These centers differ widely among communities; however, most seem to support the view and try to implement the concept that parents of retarded children, and especially those who are more severely handicapped, need relief from the pressures of management and the counsel of professionally trained personnel to help deal with the multitude of problems they face daily. There is also a keen interest among advocates of day-care centers to provide appropriate preschool experiences for the retarded in order to facilitate their maximum development.

The type of clients admitted to a day-care center is dependent on the community needs. In certain areas admission is reserved for handicapped youngsters who are either excused or excluded from public school. In other communities the centers are reserved for children up to a certain age whose parents must work to provide support for their families. Whatever the admission criteria, there is usually a preadmission or evaluative phase and staffing for every candidate. The fees for services usually vary according to each family's financial situation. Rarely do the day-care centers provide tuition-free programming for their clients.

Certainly an important factor for parents for preschool retardates to consider as they focus attention on the placement issue is the type and status of special education services provided by their own school system and by the various agencies within the community. This is especially applicable to those parents whose youngster is a borderline case or an obvious candidate for special class or special school placement. Parents who must eventually make a placement decision of this type should seek the advice of the family physician, membership of the local NARC chapter, special education personnel of the nearest college or university, or other parents of retarded children. If there is some possibility that the preschooler will gain admission to a public or private school program, the parents may wish to visit with the special education director and secure some information on questions which will influence the child's programming needs. Among the questions you might wish to ask the director are:

1. Does the program accept any particular philosophy of management, and to what degree is there a shared point of view among the various elements of the special education staff?

(One would hope for some commonality in thinking among the staff on the basic issues of management and intervention. Obviously, the individual implementation of the major concepts will vary among members of the staff.)

2. What criteria are used for admission, placement, promotion, and transfer?

(One should look for flexibility in the programming. Decisions in each of these areas should be based on the best interests of the youngster and not on rigid, irreversible, often unverifiable, and subjective grounds. It is important to perceive the degree to which an administration and staff are bound by tradition in spite of evidence to the contrary. Perhaps of most importance is that the youngster be given an opportunity to move from one program level to another higher or lower level according to his or her performance and not on the basis of an IQ score or some other irrelevant measure.)

3. What is the nature of the special class program?

(As you have no doubt gathered by now, an exemplary special education program should reflect a clear delineation of competencies which would have been properly ordered and lead to clear evaluative strategies. The sequencing should be obvious at all levels of instruction and be integrated wherever possible with the regular school program. Opportunity should be made available for special class students to interact with regular class children in areas where competition and various types of stigma do not exist. The program should be individualized at a realistic level to reflect the fact that each child's program of instruction is primarily based on evidence ascertained from valid and reliable sources.)

4. What kind of teachers are involved in the special education program?

(It is important that teachers of retarded children be properly trained; there-

fore, one should determine if members of a special education staff have the necessary credentials to qualify as certified instructors. If certain teachers do not hold a valid special education certificate, try to determine the extent to which they are upgrading their skills through extension programs, during summer sessions, and by inservice instruction. Examine the criteria the schools use in employing special education teachers, determine if the local NARC chapter is informally consulted on placement of personnel, and check to see how extensively the schools make the latest techniques of instruction available to their teachers. Evaluate the extent to which ancillary services, such as from speech, hearing, and psychological experts, are available to the children for purposes of diagnosis and special remediation.)

These placement issues are some of the most urgent concerns of parents whose retarded children are of preschool age. The decisions they make at this juncture of the child's life will begin a process of management which reflects a belief of the parent's concerning how they feel their child can best be cared for. There is little doubt that most parents are emotionally and experientially unable to make these grave decisions without the willing cooperation of an intelligent and informed counselor. This individual can be a member of any of many possible disciplines or a parent of a retarded child who has had experience to draw on for counsel. Throughout the child's preschool years the issue of proper placement alternatives is usually a heavy burden for most parents of the retarded.

Other Dilemmas of Parents   Factors and issues that are appropriate in viewing the counseling needs of parents of preschool retardates embrace many topics which have already been touched upon in this book, in addition to the placement question. As a result of this atypical situation many parents unknowingly or inadvertently use child rearing techniques in dealing with their retarded youngster which differ from those they use with siblings in the family. In many instances, the techniques might be characterized as overly tolerant, lenient, or indulgent. It is almost as if parents are looking at their child as a sick youngster and as a result providing special dispensation from penalty for misbehavior which in all likelihood would not escape their perception should other children in the family err in the same way.

It is precisely this issue which is so confusing to parents of young retarded children. They often ask, "Should I treat him like other children in my family?" Parents who fail to enforce the regulations regarding proper behavior in the family setting soon recognize that their young retarded child has "gotten away from them." They, like every other preschooler, will go as far as they are allowed. If they soon learn that they are going to get attention for violent, tantrum-like behavior, the frequency and intensity of this behavior will increase dramatically. If they recognize that rules are not enforced by their parents or that challenges to regulations are accepted, one can expect the young retardate to

extend his behavior to the limit. Parents of preschoolers, therefore, must be made aware of their need to (1) enforce reasonable rules just as they would with their intellectually normal children, (2) be consistent in rewarding desired behavior, (3) ignore inappropriate behavior or remove the stimuli which seems to be related to its occurrence, and (4) develop a pattern of stability in the procedures for disciplining and managing the behavior of their young child.

Parents of young retarded children often need guidance concerning how best to deal with the social consequences that surround the condition. This can be a very major problem for families whose retarded youngster misbehaves, is uncontrollable, or has a very different appearance. It takes parents with very strong personalities to go willingly with their youngster to various types of social events in public places. Perhaps the most appropriate suggestion for helping parents deal with the possibility of the youngster exhibiting obstreperous behavior is to reiterate what has been said earlier concerning providing an environment in which the child learns to understand the limits of acceptable and unacceptable behavior. One cannot expect a mentally retarded child who has been reared in a rather permissive environment in which uncontrolled behavior is accepted to suddenly know how to act in socially appropriate ways outside of the home. For this reason, then, it is important for the parents to begin an early program of social training, an important cornerstone of which should allow the child to experience opportunities for social interaction with people outside of his immediate family in an environment which is relatively new to him. During the very early preschool years, then, the young retarded child should be included in normal family social functions just as one would include an intellectually normal child of the same age.

Parents of preschool-age retarded children are often confronted with another social dilemma which could have serious implications for the degree to which they and their child are accepted by their neighbors. Many people who are unaware of their characteristics of the mentally retarded are afraid to have their intellectually normal child interact with a retarded child of the same chronological age. The parents of the retarded youngster will have to deal with this issue promptly and in a very forthright way. It is not an easy thing to do because many parents of retarded youngsters fear the reactions of their neighbors, relatives, and other members of the community. It is equally difficult to manipulate the environment in such a way as to encourage other neighborhood children to play with the preschool retarded youngster. Perhaps the most natural posture to take on this issue is to simply allow the retarded child to play in the general proximity of other youngsters of the same age. It is amazing to observe how the intellectually normal peers usually will spontaneously become involved with most neighborhood children. As a rule one could expect parents of the intellectually normal children to be more hesitant than the children themselves. If the parents are given an opportunity to see how natural the interaction between the normal and

the retarded youngsters can become, they will usually begin to see merit in allowing such an alliance to develop. As an important side benefit, many times parents of intellectually normal children become vitally interested in supporting programs for handicapped children as a result of having become friends with parents of a disabled child.

Obviously it is impossible for one to specify all of the unique problems that characterize parents of preschool-age retarded children. In this section an attempt has been made to try to consider some of the major issues which the literature reveals as being particularly perplexing for these parents. If the counselor, whether he be a member of a certain profession or a member of the laity, is a good listener to the parents, suggests reasonable alternatives as a means for solving the problems that are presented by the parents, and helps the parents to separate relevant from irrelevant information, a very important contribution will be made to the parents. In a real sense, then, a wise counselor in this instance is one who is a receptive and willing listener and who interacts with ease in a natural way by unobtrusively communicating to the parents that he is concerned for their benefit and that of their child.

Recommended Readings

Farber, B.: "Effects of a Severely Mentally Retarded Child on Family Integration," *Monographs of the Society for Research in Child Development*, no. 71, 1959.

————: *Mental Retardation: Its Social Context and Social Consequences,* Houghton-Mifflin Company, Boston, 1968, p. 174.

————: "Perceptions of Crisis and Related Variables in the Impact of a Retarded Child on the Mother," *Journal of Health and Human Behavior*, vol. 1, 1960a, pp. 108–118.

————, and S. M. Clark: "The Handicapped Child in the Family: A Literature Summary," in B. V. Sheets and B. Farber (eds.), *The Handicapped Child in the Family,* United Cerebral Palsy Research and Educational Foundation, New York, 1963, pp. 1–37.

————, W. C. Jenne, and R. Toigo: "Family Crisis and the Decision to Institutionalize the Retarded Child," *Council for Exceptional Children, NEA, Research Monograph Series*, no. A–1, 1960b.

LaCrosse, E. L.: *Day Care Centers for Mentally Retarded Children: A Guide for Development and Operation,* National Association for Retarded Children, New York, 1964, p. 6.

4
The Elementary School
Years

What unique characteristics do mentally retarded children of elementary school age tend to exhibit?

The points of view that have been expressed on the characteristics of mentally retarded persons, which have appeared elsewhere in this book, are appropriate to the children who will be discussed in this section. There are commonalities and differences in the traits, attitudes, feelings, and competencies among and within various groups of mentally retarded individuals, including those of elementary school age. Certainly the types of physical and behavioral characteristics and the extent to which they are manifested by children of this age are dependent on the interacting influences of factors such as (1) whether the child was born mentally retarded and the degree of his intellectual subnormality, (2) the extent to which the child exhibits various additional disorders, (3) how facilitating or depriving the young child's environment was during the very early years, (4) the extent to which proper medical treatment was provided the youngster during critical periods, and (5) the child's placement during the preschool years (for example, institutionalized versus foster home versus natural home placement). As was pointed out earlier, children with relatively severe problems of functioning and deprivation of experiences will typically be substantially more extreme in their

behaviors than will those individuals with less marked disorders and those who are associated with a more facilitating environment. In your thinking about characteristics you should be sure to separate these various factors; for example, you obviously would expect mild and moderately retarded children who are the same chronological age to be different in many ways. Their performance characteristics would no doubt vary not only in terms of the quantity of the performance but also in the various factors related to quality. In order to reduce inexactness as much as possible, suppose we focus on the educable-level elementary-age child at the outset and later briefly consider post-preschool youngsters who are more markedly retarded.

Some School-related Traits   In describing groups of people one must be careful not to overgeneralize on a distinctive feature or peculiarity; however, among those educable-level retarded youngsters who are candidates for special classes, we can expect to witness frequent problems in one or more of the following areas:

1. Paying attention to a stimulus
2. Using abstractions in the solution of problems
3. Seeing likenesses and differences among objects or situations
4. Discerning that one event causes a certain occurrence or a group of situations
5. Generalizing their experiences to other situations
6. Remembering what they have seen or heard
7. Learning to use and understand skills involving verbal communication
8. Being sensitive to incidental cues from their surroundings
9. Reacting to a situation with dispatch or at the most appropriate time
10. Translating the image of an object in space to its temporal counterpart (a ball thrown in the air to be batted)
11. Emotionally overreacting or underreacting to perplexing situations
12. Developing an attitude of unwillingness to participate in new activities or engagements

In these areas of performance the mildly retarded youngster will often exhibit inefficiency and ineffectiveness in dealing with situations. It is almost as if they continually operate without having gained much at all from their previous experiences with their environment. They frequently appear awake but not alert, attentive but not an active participant with their environment, willing to please but not spontaneous nor interested and curious about a phenomenon, and available but not overly enthusiastic about participating. The obvious influences of the inadequacies of the inefficient organism are often compounded by the horribly frustrating and embarrassing moments many young retardates suffer at the hands of insensitive adults, including parents and teachers alike. Little wonder,

then, that many young educable children in elementary schools begin to show signs of emotional distress in their early primary grades.

Most young elementary-age retardates will not be ready for the more formal academic aspects of instruction. In general they will manifest characteristics which suggest the negative influences derived from having lived in a substimulating environment. Their verbal skills are usually less well developed than in the nonverbal areas of performance. For the more urban disadvantaged youth, one often finds a rather well developed pattern of "street language" which attests to the impact of the child's immediate environment and frequently upsets the most stouthearted teacher.

It will take the mentally retarded longer to move from the readiness level of performance to the stage where he will be competent enough to begin initial stages of reading, writing, and arithmetic instruction. It is important that the experiences be made pleasant for the children during this lengthy period of readiness because of their tendency to reject further engagements and activities in which they have not experienced enjoyment, have not attained what they consider to be an adequate level of success in, have been required to do over and over again in order to satisfy someone else, or have been bored with beyond description. To a large extent, what happens during the lengthy readiness period will help to shape and stabilize a child's attitude toward future involvement in school-related activities. He will become eager or disinterested according to the degree to which interest has been engendered in him to participate in activities designed to develop preparatory skills.

As educable-level elementary school children move into the more formal aspects of the school program, we can expect to witness continued slowness in the acquisition and development of skills and concepts on their part. Not only will it take longer for the children to learn, but most of the youngsters will do so very inefficiently. It will probably require much more time and patience on the part of the teacher in every aspect of teaching than she has ever experienced with intellectually normal children. In addition to the retarded children being relatively lower in general achievement than their intellectually normal peers, the elementary-age retardates will frequently reveal significant learning disorders in any of various skill areas. For example, it is not atypical for these children to be lower than their general achievement level in reading. In contrast, many of them are often relatively stronger in the computational aspects of arithmetic. In short, additional weaknesses, almost superimposed on their general level of achievement, are frequent among elementary retardates and require the employment of special diagnostic procedures in the application of unique systematic remedial measures as part of the special education programming. Unless these special features are built into the regular programming, the specific learning disorders that are so common among the elementary children will become more firmly entrenched and result in even more serious disruption in learning as the youngster grows older.

Many people are curious about whether a retarded child can have special talent in, perhaps, some nonacademic area of performance. There is little evidence concerning the prevalence of such events, and perhaps this is good, for one possessing a talent of rare exception surely would not want it generally known that he or she was mentally retarded. It probably is possible for certain types of retarded children, or adults for that matter, to exhibit highly skilled performances in certain areas, such as in art, certain forms of music, dance, or athletics. This event, however, is certainly not the rule, for exceptional talent is positively related to intellectual brightness; i.e., as intellectual superiority increases, the chances of special talents being manifested also increase.

The one very rare exception to this generalization involves the phenomenon known as *idiot savant*. This term describes those retarded persons, most frequently in the moderate or below categories, who have a highly developed intellectual skill which is totally incompatible with their functioning in other areas of mental performance. Horwitz and his colleagues (1965) report on identical twins who have the unusual skills of calculating calendars. Both of these boys can identify dates and specific days of years past and future; recall if it was fair, cloudy, or rainy on a certain day; and specify other involved characteristics of calendars beyond presently existing perpetual calendars. At the same time, these boys cannot add, subtract, multiply, or divide in even the most elementary fashion. Other similar reports have been presented infrequently in the literature describing identical instances of wizardry. There have been retarded persons who are able to instantaneously multiply two eighteen-digit numbers without using pencil or paper, others who can play a musical instrument without ever having previously touched a device of this sort, and still others who can solve complex mathematical calculations and equations. There are no satisfactory explanations for the idiot savant phenomenon. The unexplainable memory which most of them seem to have in a specific area or subject apparently is not associated with their functioning in other areas. There are so few of these unique individuals and their special, but unusual and generally unproductive, talents are so obtuse that a well designed research effort on the subject is not possible nor feasible.

Environmental Vulnerability   Many young retarded children are particularly susceptible to pressures that are brought to bear by others. These types of influencing actions may be of an unobtrusive character and not directed at the retarded youngster for purposes of necessarily guiding him toward misbehavior, into committing an unethical or immoral act, or causing illegal actions on his part. Young retarded children are usually perceptive enough to gain an appreciation for what is valued by others with whom they wish to develop an association. Because they often fail in developing close comradeships, frequently suffer from failure experiences, and desire to fully participate in the affairs of their peers, the mentally retarded are a bit more easily swayed by more persuasive intellectually brighter youngsters. Moreover, as a method for gaining closer allegiance with valued peers, the mentally retarded child will often find himself unwittingly used

by others. One consequence of this situation is that many retarded youngsters seem to use more foul language than nonretarded elementary children of the same age. One of several possible reasons for this is that the retarded are less secretive about committing a social faux pas of this sort. Additionally they are often unable to separate proper from improper social behaviors.

There is no question that many mentally retarded children are influenced by their normal peers. Obviously, this influence can either be to the advantage or disadvantage of the intellectually handicapped child. The illustration of the use of foul language mentioned above, describes one way in which a retarded child can be led improperly. Too often, parents of retarded children tend to cloister their youngsters from nonretarded neighbors. They feel that the hazards are too great and that their more impressionable child will be the victim of poor influences. In like manner, parents of intellectually normal children will refuse to allow their youngsters to associate with neighborhood children who are retarded but who are of the same age. Their reasons are often identical to those held by the parents of the retarded—contamination resulting in inappropriate social and personal behaviors.

There are probably more positive, profitable, and productive reasons for retarded elementary school children becoming friends with normal children of the same age than there are negative reasons. With youngsters who are reasonably well balanced in their attitudes, desires, and needs, this type of relationship can be mutually beneficial. It can help the retarded child to develop a variety of skills at higher levels, and at the same time aid the normal child to learn how to be more accepting, willing to share, cooperative, and lenient. This type of mutual association should be encouraged in most cases. The normal child should have his questions responded to in a direct but charitable way, and the retarded child should be encouraged not to be pushy nor burdensome on the intellectually normal child's time each moment that they are together.

Some of the possible emotional consequences of being mentally retarded have been briefly alluded to previously. Whether an individual is bright or dull, if he is performing at a level which is viewed by him as being less than sufficient, and he feels it is viewed by others in the same way, possible serious mental health problems could develop. The young mentally retarded are particularly vulnerable to this situation. They soon recognize that their general performance is less substantial and sophisticated than the work of other children. This conclusion is reached through a direct comparison of their product and the way of performing with that of others. Secondly, they may also be influenced by the way in which they feel other people are viewing and evaluating their performance. If it is their opinion that others view them as satisfactory in the way they approach and perform a task, and they cherish the opinions of those other individuals, this situation will serve to foster good mental health. If the reverse is true, however, serious disorders could result. You can see how important it is for parents and

teachers to become aware of these subtle forces and to intervene at appropriate moments when the possibility of emotional upheaval is imminent. The extent to which older retarded individuals manifest good patterns of mental health is basically dependent on how much attention has been given to these matters during the time they as children were involved in the elementary school program.

The Older Retardate Those children who are of elementary school age and moderately or severely retarded may never become self-sufficient and independent. Some will benefit from special education programs within their community; others will be excluded from such programs as a result of relatively more stringent admission criteria. Discounting their prognosis for independent living and focusing mainly on the performance characteristics of these individuals, we could again expect to see grossly uneven achievement characteristics among these populations. This heterogeneity is caused by the great differences in the ways multiple disabilities are expressed among various members of these groups. Remember, as mental retardation increases in severity, multiple disabilities increase in variety and degree. Therefore, in a sense these groups of retardates may be more different on behavioral factors among themselves than the more mildly retarded children differ within their individual groups. It is true, then, that the performance profiles of moderate and severe groups of young retardates will be significantly uneven.

Just as we expect mildly retarded or educable youngsters to take longer than normal children to acquire an adequate level of competence in readiness activities, we can expect the trainable to be delayed longer than educable children in achieving a minimal level of skill on the same tasks. Some may never reach a level which will allow them to proceed to formal academic types of instruction; for most of these individuals the appropriateness of this type of orientation is even questionable. Many of the relatively more retarded children of this age will not be toilet trained, able to maintain proper dress, feed and bath themselves, and engage in more than a minimum level of social interchange. The great majority of them will spend a considerable amount of time in preschool programs or in a day-care center.

Weaknesses of the Literature Finally, a word of explanation about the enormous body of research literature which has focused on specifying characteristics of mentally retarded children and adults from every conceivable perspective and on innumerable dimensions. The behavioral literature is filled with studies of various degrees of sophistication in which attempts have been made to typify the retarded in terms of variables involving speech and language, hearing, visual performance, concept formation, reading competencies, perceptual motor development, attention, reinforcement preferences, and on an infinite array of additional factors. Attempts have been made to summarize this literature and point out the principal common threads (Stevens and Heber, 1964; Clarke and Clarke, 1965; Ellis, 1963). These efforts have been helpful to scholars and students who

have an interest in quickly becoming familiar with the status of knowledge on a particular topic.

If one digs deeply into this body of literature, however, it soon becomes apparent that mammoth discrepancies exist among the reports which have focused on similar topics. Indeed, in many instances, contradictory findings will be reported. A closer inspection of the research reports may reveal that subjects are selected from different populations of retardates, that the same instruments are not used to measure the factor on which the research focuses attention, or that the data from the various studies are analyzed using different approaches. In short, although the scientists are studying similar variables, their studies are not comparable because of internal differences which are peculiar to each investigation. The upshot of this entire matter is that the possibility of error, inadequate reporting, and bias on the status of the retarded on one or more variables is assured in those instances where an author (1) summarizes the research in a specific area but fails to obtain an adequate sample of the complete reports which represent the most current, methodologically sound studies on the subject, (2) fails to conduct an in-depth evaluation of the available studies to determine the areas in which possible sources of error and bias may be present, (3) has a point of view which he wishes to support with research and fails to consider data which support alternative positions, or (4) is unskilled in conducting an evaluative analysis of empirical research and/or is unable to identify the common threads which intermix throughout the group of studies. The purpose of this discussion is to highlight the fact that the literature on the characteristics of mentally retarded children and adults is in disagreement. This occurs to such an extent that it is virtually impossible to conclude that the mentally retarded exhibit any uniquely identifiable characteristics whether one wishes to consider a specific, rather small group of retardates or view these individuals in a much more global fashion.

Recommended Readings

Baumeister, A. A. (ed.): *Mental Retardation: Appraisal, Education, and Rehabilitation*, Aldine Publishing Company, Chicago, 1967.

Clarke, A. M., and A. D. B. Clarke (eds.): *Mental Deficiency: The Changing Outlook*, The Free Press, New York, 1965.

Ellis, N. R. (ed.): *Handbook of Mental Deficiency*, McGraw-Hill Book Company, New York, 1963.

Horwitz, W. A., C. Kestenbaum, E. Person and L. Jarvik: "Identical Twins—'Idiot Savants'—Calendar Calculators," *The American Journal of Psychiatry*, vol. 121, 1965, pp. 1075–1079.

Masland, R. L., S. B. Sarason and T. Gladwin: *Mental Subnormality: Biological,*

Psycholological, and Cultural Factors, Basic Books, Inc., Publishers, New York, 1958.

Stevens, H. A., and R. Heber (eds.): *Mental Retardation: A Review of Research,* The University of Chicago Press, Chicago, 1964.

What form does the educational testing and assessment of elementary-age retarded children take?

The major purpose of doing an educational evaluation on mentally retarded children throughout their elementary school years is to know how to manipulate their environment so that their individual behaviors can be managed effectively and with efficiency. This section will focus on the various ramifications of this process. The first segment will consider some of the management consequences of the many ways in which people vary. The later portion of the discussion will describe one plan for systematically collecting important data on elementary-age retarded youngsters and translating this information into individual programming strategies. Throughout the discussion the emphasis will be on educable or mildly retarded youngsters whose intellectual promise would lead one to expect special class or special school placement of some variety within the context of a public education program.*

Major Philosophical Tenets Suppose we begin with some assertions which seem to reflect the contemporary mood of special education for educable mentally retarded children.

1. The major responsibility of a special class teacher for the mentally retarded is to provide an environment which will allow the youngsters to develop increasingly higher levels of competence in intellectual, physical, social, personal, perceptual-motor, and communicative domains.
2. The inevitable differences that exist among mentally retarded children, who are classified on some basis into a single population or group on educationally relevant dimensions, requires that the instructional environment be designed so that each youngster's likelihood for learning is increased.
3. The nature of the instructional environment designed for each elementary-age retarded child should be based on pertinent educational information about the child being considered.
4. Special class teachers of mentally retarded children must develop sufficient diagnostic skills to allow them to systematically gather data on appropriate

---

* Much of the content in this section is a revision of the following articles and appears here with the permission of the editor of *Teaching Exceptional Children* and the Council for Exceptional Children: R. M. Smith, "The Meaning of Variability for Program Planning," *Teaching Exceptional Children,* vol. 1, 1969, pp. 83–87. *Idem.,* "Collecting Diagnostic Data in the Classroom," *Teaching Exceptional Children,* vol. 1, 1969, pp. 128–133.

educational dimensions in an informal and unencumbered way within the classroom.

5. Special education teachers who are involved in programming instruction for the mentally retarded should be sufficiently skilled to translate educational and certain psychological data into practical teaching programs for each student.

For the most part, these five assertions reflect the contemporary mood of the special education profession. Notice that they do not mention traditional disability groups, and that the concept of ability or potential is conspicuous by its absence. The principal focus is on behavior, both the teacher's and the child's, and proper remediation of educational problems has been found to follow only after germane information has been collected for each individual child.

The Characteristics of Individuality People perform or act in ways which are very similar but often for reasons which are significantly different. We cannot correctly assume that identical values, attitudes, or performances of retarded children have the same origin, cause, or characteristics. Just as it is obviously inappropriate to treat all infections with the same antibiotics or all headaches with an aspirin, it is equally naïve to consider instructing all mentally retarded children using the same curricula, identical methodology, or similar instructional media. Difficulties in learning—whether they be primarily social, cognitive, personal, communicative, or otherwise—like infections, should be treated individually, according to each child's unique diagnostic signs. This concept is the key to justifying the provision of comprehensive educational testing and assessment of every elementary-age retarded child.

To fully appreciate the reasons for special educators developing basic diagnostic skills as part of their repertoire, suppose we consider the various ways in which individuality is expressed among any group of individuals, including the retarded, and how this affects the nature and design of an instructional program. First, let us deal with the variation, on any educational dimension, that exists within a given group of children. Assume that we were interested in studying the arithmetic computational achievement of all mentally retarded children who are in their third year of public education in a large school system. For the purposes of this discussion suppose we consider this group a "population of individuals." We might administer any of several standardized arithmetic tests to each child in this population and calculate the overall arithmetic computation achievement score for each child.

On the basis of all the individual performances, it would be possible to diagram a curve of achievement for the entire group of youngsters. If we had enough subjects, we would expect to see a relatively normal distribution of scores, much like the theoretical curve of intelligence (see Figure 4-1). This curve would show that certain children do arithmetic much above the general

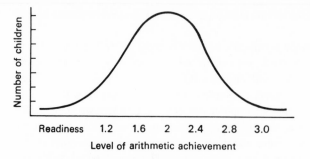

Figure 4-1 *Arithmetic achievement of a hypothetical population of mentally retarded children.*

average for the entire population of retarded children at this level; whereas, other youngsters from the same population would be performing lower than the group average. The greatest number of children might score near the second grade level, assuming that a rather large group of retarded youngsters were included in our study.

It really makes no difference what variable we elect to choose for our study. We would have seen the same type of distribution of scores if we had decided to study achievement in reading speed, perceptual-motor performance, penmanship, spelling, high jumping, digit repetition, and so on. It is a simple fact of life that we all vary in performance to different degrees when we are compared with other people who are members of a population of which we are a representative.

What might we expect to find in the arithmetic computational scores if the large population of mentally retarded children was separated into two groups on a variable which we might view as being of some particular significance? For the purposes of our illustration, let us identify one of the groups as being culturally disadvantaged and the other group as being organically impaired. Although these distinctions are not pure categories, and we might expect to find overlap between them, let us suppose that it is possible for us to make this type of differentiation. Most likely the scores of the culturally disadvantaged retarded children would again approach a normal distribution in shape, and the same type of configuration would probably prevail for the scores of those retarded youngsters who are organically defective. The most distinguishing characteristic, however, between two groups in arithmetic computation achievement might be that the relative position of the two curves would differ. Notice in Figure 4-2 that the majority of the organically impaired children scored somewhat lower than the majority of the culturally disadvantaged retarded children. At the same time, notice that both groups demonstrated a range of performance in arithmetic achievement and that both subpopulations overlap. From this illustration, then, you can see that the performance of large groups of youngsters, or populations

of subjects, not only varies within individual groups, but also the characteristics of populations differ.

To this point, then, your attention has been focused on two major types of variability. First, we notice that individuals who come from a rather broadly defined population of persons will differ in their performance on some measurable variable, in this case arithmetic computation, when contrasted with the performance of others from the same population. Second, when we divided the larger group of persons into smaller groups based on one or more variables, we found that some differences were manifested in the general performance of the subpopulations when contrasted with each other. The first type of variability might be termed *interindividual variability;* the second type of variability might be called *interpopulation variability.* Now, suppose we consider a third type of variability, one which Kirk (1962) has termed *discrepancies in growth* or *intraindividual variability.* This concept has gained increasing attention in that literature which has focused on methods for teaching the mentally retarded as well as other types of exceptional children (see, for example, Johnson and Myklebust, 1967; Smith, 1968, 1969).

As an example of the way in which intraindividual variability is exhibited, suppose we select two individuals from the population of culturally disadvantaged mentally retarded children and inspect more closely one aspect of their arithmetic computational performance. Assume for the moment that these two youngsters did relatively poorly in addition, and that the low scores on this particular dimension seemed to influence their total computational performance score. Table 4-1 summarizes, briefly, some of the characteristics of each youngster's performance in addition. This type of analysis exemplifies the form which proper educational assessment of a retarded child should take; you will notice how much valuable data the teacher will be able to gather by carefully analyzing the addition problems of each child.

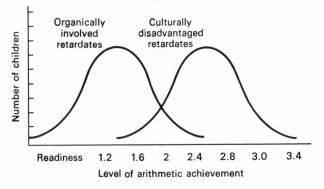

Figure 4-2   *Relative arithmetic performance of two hypothetical groups of mentally retarded children.*

Table 4-1 Profile of selected errors and habits in addition of two mentally retarded children

Types of errors and/or habits	Jack	George
1. Error in combinations	−	+
2. Used wrong process	−	+
3. Repeated work after partly done	−	+
4. Error in writing answer	−	+
5. Used scratch paper	−	+
6. Forgot to add carried number	+	0
7. Added carried number irregularly	+	0
8. Carried wrong number	+	0
9. Lost place in column	?	?
10. Disregarded column position	−	+
11. Wrote carried number in answer	+	0

KEY:

+ = Manifested the problem consistently

− = Not a consistent problem

? = Questionable weakness, worthy of follow-up

0 = Not possible to assess, either because the skill was too advanced for the child or there was not an adequate basis to sample his performance

A very quick glance at the patterns of computational strengths and weaknesses of the two boys tells us immediately that each child has a different instructional need. Jack, for example, seems to have a predominant weakness in concepts involved in understanding carrying. In contrast, George has a different constellation of problems, most of which seem to center around the lack of basic skills in understanding what addition means and the whole concept of combinations. Obviously, the proper focus for an arithmetic program which is designed to reflect Jack's problems would not necessarily deal in a forthright manner with George's problems. This is true in spite of the fact that the two youngsters may be underachieving in arithmetic, or more specifically in addition, at exactly the same level. You can see, then, why many special educators are becoming convinced that this type of variability, i.e., intra, or within, individual differences is more meaningful for instructional programs than are the more general inter-individual differences that exist among children.

Another illustration may help to amplify the importance of this concept. Suppose you have two educable mentally retarded youngsters in your class who are underachieving in reading at the same level. You cannot assume that they are both having difficulty for the same reason. One child, for example, may be having severe difficulties because of not having developed a systematic means for attacking words; whereas, the other child may have a basic visual discrimination prob-

lem which is affecting his performance. If the teacher does not become aware of the different reasons for each child's problem, there will be a tendency to provide the same instructional program for each. For example, the familiar panacea for dealing with children who are having serious achievement problems is to offer some type of individual tutorial experience or remediation. The focus, unfortunately, in these cases is not on what type of tutorial experience or how the tutor can best go about providing remedial instruction; in this instance emphasis is given to what type of tutorial experience just so long as it is "one-to-one." Remediation in itself is inadequate unless it is appropriate and considers the individual "hang-ups" of each youngster. For one child, the data might suggest that there is potential payoff in approaching the reading problem by helping the youngster develop a consistent means for attacking words through the use of a phonics approach. For another student, basic activities on visual discrimination among forms, figures, or shapes may constitute the most appropriate beginning for solving his reading problem. If the wrong approach is offered to the wrong child the entire tutorial experience will fail. It is the opinion of many thoughtful special educators that one cannot determine these facts unless an adequate program of educational testing, assessment, and interpretation takes place prior to the formulation of an instructional program.

Collecting Pertinent Diagnostic Information Teachers, then, are faced with the need to examine both the child's behavior and their own behavior in an effort to identify the possible reasons for and potential contributors to the limited performance of a youngster in some particular area of behavior. Having done this, the teacher is then confronted with the instructional problem of properly manipulating the environment of the mentally retarded youngster in order to maximize the potential for learning to occur in a proper way, in a certain period of time, and at a reasonable level. Children vary so much within themselves, not only between subject areas, but also at various times during their development, that a constant updating of diagnostic data is necessary. Prescriptive or clinical teaching depends on this type of documentation. It provides the basis for which an appropriate "mix" of subject matter, preferred instructional strategy or methodology, and appropriate instructional material or media can be offered each retarded child according to his own particular needs and in consideration of realistic educational objectives for him.

Perfunctory acknowledgement that individual differences exist within a class of mentally retarded children, whether they be located in a special education classroom or in a regular classroom, is too imprecise and in no way will lead to informed judgments concerning proper instructional programming. Moreover, the use of general achievement scores as a single criterion for deciding on the nature of an instructional program is equally vague. Most special education teachers believe to some extent that the notions which have been expressed up to this point are reasonably valid; however, many teachers are unclear as to the

form that the data collection should take and where to start in the process. Also, there is a general tendency to rely primarily on the school psychologist or some other well trained specialist for specific direction in testing, assessment, and recommending remedial steps for children who are particular problem cases. The position which will be expressed here is that the teacher can, should, and must actively participate along with others in this *diagnostic-remedial process*. A number of models have been developed to provide some structure for specifying the diagnostic-remedial process. Figure 4-3 describes a brief flow chart which delineates various stages in this process. If the information which is collected at each of the levels in this process is reliable and the observations are valid, proper educational programming for an individual mentally retarded child can be made.

Level I   The child should be screened by the teacher and others, including his parents, for relatively obvious gross disorders which could subsequently influence functioning in areas such as social, emotional, cognitive, language, or speech development. The types of problems that might be identified at this level include "the lazy-eye syndrome," serious delays in language development, unintelligible speech, constant hearing problems, developmental lags in various physical systems, constant lethargy, perpetual anger or hostility, self-destructive behavior, and nutritional disorders. It is difficult to be specific about what constitutes a "significant disorder" in any of these areas; however, if a child shows any of these types of problems for a large portion of the day, he should be referred to an appropriate specialist. The important point to consider at this first level is the necessity of doing everything possible to refer the youngster to a proper specialist as early as possible. At this level of diagnosis it is better to err on the side of overreferral than to allow a significant problem to prevail, since as the condition becomes more serious, it will begin to generate a whole galaxy of related problems which will only further complicate the child's educational future. This first stage in the diagnostic process is stressed in the previous chapter as being of inestimable importance.

Level II   Assume that all problems which were identified at level I received proper attention. At level II a determination should be made of the existence of possible problems in learning. This determination is most commonly based on each child's achievement test scores. It is not a difficult procedure at all to profile the achievement test scores of individual children in a number of educational areas. After this profiling has been completed, one can identify those areas in which an individual youngster seems to be having trouble and those in which he is particularly strong. Figure 4-4 illustrates such a profile. Notice that the youngster being described in this illustration is relatively low in reading, language, and spelling and relatively high in arithmetic and perceptual-motor development. The reader who is interested in studying the profiling procedure in greater depth will find a more thorough discussion in Kirk (1962).

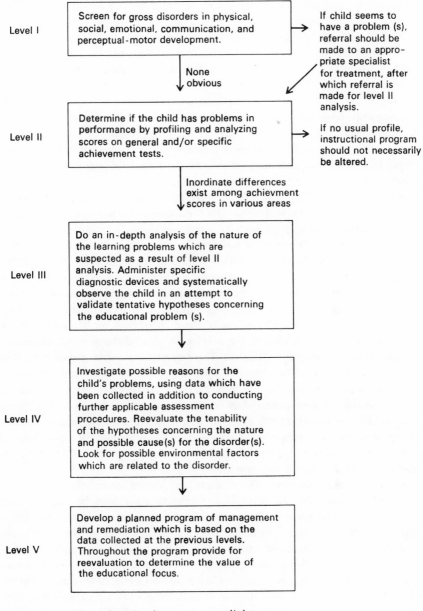

Level I	Screen for gross disorders in physical, social, emotional, communication, and perceptual-motor development.

If child seems to have a problem (s), referral should be made to an appropriate specialist for treatment, after which referral is made for level II analysis.

None obvious

Level II	Determine if the child has problems in performance by profiling and analyzing scores on general and/or specific achievement tests.

If no usual profile, instructional program should not necessarily be altered.

Inordinate differences exist among achievment scores in various areas

Level III	Do an in-depth analysis of the nature of the learning problems which are suspected as a result of level II analysis. Administer specific diagnostic devices and systematically observe the child in an attempt to validate tentative hypotheses concerning the educational problem (s).

Level IV	Investigate possible reasons for the child's problems, using data which have been collected in addition to conducting further applicable assessment procedures. Reevaluate the tenability of the hypotheses concerning the nature and possible cause(s) for the disorder(s). Look for possible environmental factors which are related to the disorder.

Level V	Develop a planned program of management and remediation which is based on the data collected at the previous levels. Throughout the program provide for reevaluation to determine the value of the educational focus.

Figure 4-3 *Flow chart for diagnostic-remedial process.*

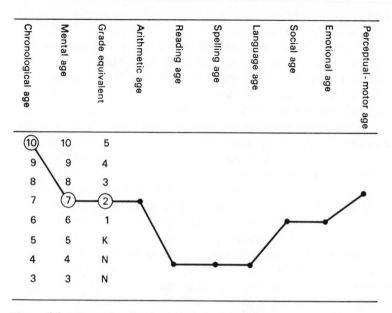

Figure 4-4 *Example of achievement scores profiled.*

Level III   The teacher will need to investigate more thoroughly the nature or particular characteristics of the learning problems in those areas in which the child shows specific weaknesses. A more penetrating analysis could involve the administration of specific formal diagnostic tests which have been designed to probe into precise skill areas, e.g., the Diagnostic Chart for Fundamental Processes in Arithmetic, Diagnostic Tests and Self-helps in Arithmetic, Spache Diagnostic Reading Scales, or Gray Oral Reading Tests.

Before proceeding into a further discussion of the other types of data that might be gathered at this and at other levels, a word or two is in order concerning the use of diagnostic tests, such as those illustrated above, by teachers. It is very true that most special education teachers have not been and are presently not being trained to administer and interpret such evaluative devices. This is unfortunate and is one real weakness of many programs that are designed to prepare teachers to work with the mentally retarded. Regretably the aura of mysteriousness and professional possessiveness has too often surrounded certain diagnostic devices to the point where many professionals have been unwilling to introduce these valuable tools into undergraduate teacher training programs. This situation has resulted in the teacher being prepared to deal with the behavior of retarded youngsters without having had exposure to and gaining skill in the use of the best diagnostic devices which are available. A careful and honest analysis of many existing assessment instruments will reveal that they are not so esoteric

and not beyond the performance levels and understanding of most students who are training to teach the mentally retarded.

As you can see, the position which is taken here is that teacher trainees should be exposed to instruments such as those mentioned above. They should feel free to use whatever portions of existing scales they feel most comfortable with and secure advice from the school psychologist concerning the interpretation of scores and possible suggestions for further evaluative steps. In addition to evaluating the responses of the youngsters on more structured evaluative devices such as have been described above, the more informal observations of the teacher and the child's parents will be of great help as data sources in analyzing the weaknesses and strengths of each youngster.

The teacher might also want to survey the child's reading performance in certain broad areas, such as silent reading, oral reading, word recognition, and comprehension. The child's production in each of these relatively broad areas can be profiled to determine if weaknesses exist in one or more of them. Closely related to the child's performance in these areas is the process which he uses in reading or in dealing with any other subject area. Two important questions to be asked are, "How does he go about attacking words?" and "What process is used to obtain a certain level of production?" At this level, then, the teacher should look at the performance or products of the child in the various areas of the subject, as well as at the process or techniques which he employs in dealing with a task.

From the diagnostic clues obtained from this type of observation, the teacher can decide in which direction to move for purposes of obtaining more information. For example, the teacher might be suspicious about a test for auditory or visual memory problems or difficulties in discrimination, visual-auditory integration, sound blending, left-to-right progression, and/or reversals. Problems in any of these specific areas could influence the child's performance in the more general aspects of the various subject areas.

Level IV An attempt should be made to identify the possible causes for the educational disorder. In the preceding three levels some attempt has been made to identify characteristics of the difficulty. Observation of a child's behavior could reveal that his educational difficulties might be caused by problems such as (1) exposure to an instructional program which is inconsistent or ambiguous, (2) association with an improperly sequenced course of study, (3) an inability to work under conditions of speed, (4) too much pressure to achieve from the child's parents, (5) difficulty in following directions, or (6) rewarding unpleasant behavior. Factors such as these might be considered as possible causes for educational difficulties. If the teacher or parent has some notion that these are possible reasons for the youngster manifesting a problem, data should be systematically collected toward that end in an attempt at trying to verify this hypothesis.

The suggestions which have just been made have been presented with some degree of trepidation. Care should be taken against forming unwarranted associations between some historical event in the child's life and his present classroom performance, as if some cause-and-effect situation is operating. Avoid engaging in mystic psychologizing with yourself or with others. Consider the conclusions you reach, as a result of the historical data you collect at each level thus far, as hypotheses. View your conclusions as educated guesses and not necessarily hard fact. The proof of the validity of these tentative conclusions will occur after you have tried and have evaluated the child's program of remediation, which is based on the hypotheses of disorder which you have formulated from the information that has been gathered from the various diagnostic devices.

Level V   From these data, then, core areas of difficulty can be delineated, and hypotheses can be generated concerning possible specific causes for a youngster doing poorly in certain subject areas. These hypotheses can be used to plan an appropriate program of placement and remediation which is based on evidence and not on impulsive or random selection of any instructional technique from those techniques which might be available to the teacher.

For example, let us assume that a teacher's observation of a child leads to the conclusion that he seems to be having problems with general use of the auditory channel but does not manifest unusual difficulty in using and processing visual stimuli. The teacher may find that the youngster is weak in one or more auditory-related skills, such as oral reading, phonic analysis, remembering what he hears, relating a sound to its appropriate visual stimuli, singing, understanding directions, or sound blending. After studying the child's record of performance, the teacher might decide that since all these areas require some degree of skill in auditory discrimination and auditory memory, a program of evaluation should be initiated to determine if either or both of these skill areas represent a common core of difficulty. Prior to that, of course, the teacher would want to have the child's hearing acuity checked by an audiologist.

If after all necessary testing has been accomplished the teacher is able to identify what might be viewed as significant weaknesses in discrimination and memory of auditory stimuli, a program of remediation in those areas should be started before the child is engaged in more complex activities, such as phonic analysis or sound blending which require a certain level of skill in more specific areas of auditory discrimination and memory. To engage a child in phonic analysis activities before he can discriminate among sounds will result only in failure and frustration. The problem that the teacher has, then, is not only to identify the core areas of difficulty but to provide remediation according to proper sequence. Again, placing a child in phonic-analysis activities before he has developed auditory-discrimination skills is definitely like putting the cart before the horse.

As has been mentioned earlier the teacher can use information from formal instruments to determine the nature of each child's educational difficulty. For

this reason, the school psychologist should report relevant information from psychological reports in language that can be easily understood by teachers. In most instances the entire protocol, including specific test scores, should be provided to the special education teacher, so that subtest performances can be analyzed and a determination made regarding the child's relative strong and weak areas. These profiles, then, will help the teacher to formulate a plan for instruction.

The teacher will find great advantage in making use of informal diagnostic strategies which might be used on a day-by-day and week-by-week basis within the classroom. There are numerous advantages in the teacher using information which has been collected in an informal way as a basis for designing an appropriate instructional environment. First of all, the teacher is in the best position to assess educational problems of the child because the rapport between herself and the student is typically stronger than between the child and other adults. Second, the teacher has more opportunity to sample characteristic behavior as opposed to extreme behaviors which are manifested by the child. Third, the classroom environment allows for observing the child's performance in a variety of situations, those which are relatively realistic and not contrived.

The kinds of activities in which a teacher engages the child in order to informally observe and diagnose behavioral disorders should be carefully considered. Smith (1969) has suggested that the following criteria be used by the teacher in selecting activities for informal diagnostic observations:

1. Every activity used for the purpose of evaluating a skill should be part of the ongoing program and should not be used in a contrived setting. Try to incorporate informal diagnostic activities into the daily classroom routine. A child may not respond with his usual behavior if he is engaged in diagnostic activities during periods which are set aside only for that type of activity.
2. Activities in which the child is engaged should be interesting so that attitudinal or motivational difficulties do not cloud his real performance. Select the content of each diagnostic activity so that it is compatible with the ongoing instructional sequences and inherently interesting to the youngster. In a real sense, then, a necessary prelude to evaluation is to determine what types of activities interest each child.
3. Activities for diagnosis should be selected to measure specific educational dimensions. For example, if you wish to evaluate the auditory memory performance of a child, he should be asked to repeat digits or remember other types of stimuli which have been presented via the auditory channel.
4. Activities should be presented so that each child's performance can be measured directly in specific skill areas. Do not select tasks which require the diagnostician to make inordinate assumptions, extrapolations, or generalizations beyond the data. For example, because the child does poorly on arith-

metic computations do not assume that he will show a faulty arithmetic reasoning performance. Determination on this specific issue can properly be ascertained only by engaging him in activities which are designed to check on arithmetic reasoning variables.

5. Every diagnostic activity should be selected for objectivity, and attempts should be made to control possible sources of bias in the collection, interpretation, and translation of the data. Report what you observe; do not succumb to the temptation of overclassifying behavior. For example, if you observe that a child plays unusually rough, throws things at other children, gets into an inordinate number of fights, and breaks many pencil points, describe those behaviors and do not engage in wild psychologizing by suggesting that the youngster is angry or anxious because his father and mother are divorced, and other equally bizarre conclusions that go too far beyond the data.

6. Activities should be varied enough so that each child does not become too familiar with the tasks. For example, if you wish to informally check on how well a child is able to borrow in subtraction, you would need to have a substantial repertoire of activities that require these skills, so that they can be used on different occasions.

7. Each child should be tested on more than one occasion in order to gain a reliable evaluation of his performance. Observations and other assessment devices are unreliable to some extent. If decisions regarding a child's future are going to be made from such data, make sure that ample opportunities have been given for sampling relevant behaviors. This implies that evaluation should be conducted frequently, unobtrusively, and at various times during the day. You would feel that it was unfair to be placed, irreversibly in many instances, into a special remedial program on the sole basis of your behavior having been observed at an inopportune moment when your performance was "off" for any of various possible reasons. This same point is pertinent when we consider the value in initiating or withholding any technique, device, or curriculum for elementary-age mentally retarded children.

To recount some of the main thoughts involved in the educational assessment of elementary-age retarded children, it should be emphasized that this form of evaluation is not the sole responsibility of the school psychologist. Indeed, it should involve everyone who has some responsibility for the youngster's management. This would include the child's teacher, speech therapist, parents, physical education teacher, physician, and others with whom the child has a significant level of contact. The important fact is that each of these individuals understand the basic requisites related to the systematic observation of behavior, many of which were reviewed in the previous chapter. Pertinent data can and should be collected both through formal and informal strategies for observation. The types of information needed and the means by which the data are collected depend on the goals which the teacher has for the youngster, the extent to which

he is disabled, and his individual profile of educationally related strengths and weaknesses. Obviously, the more severe the youngster's disorder, the more extensive the diagnostic effort will become. As these data are systematically collected, patterns begin to emerge which allow for the generation of hypotheses concerning the direction in which an educational program should proceed. As a program is implemented, it is important for continual reevaluation to take place in order to validate its appropriateness. It is only through such a marriage between diagnosis and remediation that we can expect the educational program to make an impact on individual children who require maximum effort for small increments of progress to be made.

Recommended Readings

Johnson, D. J., and H. R. Myklebust: *Learning Disabilities: Educational Principles and Practices,* Grune and Stratton, Inc., New York, 1967.

Kirk, S. A.: *Educating Exceptional Children,* Houghton Mifflin Company, Boston, 1962.

Smith, R. M.: *Clinical Teaching: Methods of Instruction for the Retarded,* McGraw-Hill Book Company, New York, 1968.

————: *Teacher Diagnosis of Educational Difficulties,* Charles E. Merrill Books, Inc., Columbus, Ohio, 1969.

————: "The Meaning of Variability for Program Planning," *Teaching Exceptional Children,* vol. 1, 1969, pp. 83–87.

————: "Collecting Diagnostic Data in the Classroom," *Teaching Exceptional Children,* vol. 1, 1969, pp. 128–133.

On what basis is placement for elementary-age retarded children decided upon and implemented?

Two issues concerning the placement of retarded children at this age will be discussed in this section. First, certain parents will be forced to make decisions about whether to apply for institutionalization for their child. Second, for most upper-level moderate retardates and those in the educable category, the problems of locating the most advantageous educational setting is of major concern for parents with a retarded child of post-preschool age.

There is a certain group of youngsters, who are severely or profoundly retarded, whose parents may have elected not to have their children institutionalized at birth or during the preschool years. These youngsters were kept at home because their parents may have felt uncomfortable about placement in a residential center, or they were found by their parents to be difficult to handle as the

age of both parties increased. Parents who are in this dilemma experience what Wolfensberger (1967) describes as a *reality crisis*. They recognize that their resources, physical, financial, and emotional, do not allow for the provision of proper management for their retarded offspring. They must again seriously consider the efficacy of institutional placement.

There is a second group of retarded children for whom institutional placement may also be a reasonable option. These are the moderately retarded youngsters who have not progressed at a satisfactory pace at home, children whose family situation may have deteriorated to such an unbearable extent that removal from the home is an absolute necessity for all concerned, or youngsters who are creating serious social problems within the community. If other options on management and control have been exhausted and found to be inappropriate or unavailable, institutionalization for this group of retardates may be necessary.

In each of these two groups the discussion on institutions and admission considerations which appeared in Chapter 2 is pertinent. By all means, before definitely deciding on institutional placement the parents should consider factors presented in Table 2-3, and in addition should:

1. Establish that no other reasonable alternative is available for maintaining a satisfactory environment for the child within the community
2. Consult with various individuals, such as physicians, psychologists, and parents of other retarded children who:
   a. are aware of the problems encountered by the child in the family
   b. are familiar with the proposed and alternative placement sites
3. Determine if institutional placement will result in disruption, disturbance, or conflict within the child's family
4. Visit the proposed placement site to determine:
   a. The philosophy of the staff on care for the retarded
   b. The extent to which medical, therapeutic, and physical care will be available
   c. How extensive the program of education and training is for residents who can reasonably profit from such experience
   d. The financial requirements necessary for maintaining an optimum level of maintenance for the child

The decision to institutionalize a post-preschool age child must be based on individual family considerations. It is impossible to delineate guidelines which will be applicable to most situations. Every family, and the individual members therein, have different tolerances, attitudes, goals, and needs. The unique personality combinations of individual family members merge into a highly idiosyncratic blend of characteristics, all of which result in the retarded youngster being located in a miniature society. For some of these groups the presence of a

severely retarded member is not out of place nor does it cause conflict or grief; for other groups, a different mix of personalities precipitates a circumstance which cannot tolerate even a mildly retarded youngster in the home. Obviously, many combinations and permutations lie between these extremes and force the need for variability in criteria and considerations concerning possible placement within an institution for mentally retarded children at this age level.

Families of retarded children are obviously concerned that their youngsters be provided with the most fully facilitating educational placement possible. To this end, it is obligatory on school systems that every option be explored to assure that their services and those of other community agencies be made available to the retarded elementary-age child and to his parents wherever most appropriate. It is vital that the concept of appropriateness be fully considered and realized with retarded children of elementary school age, for certainly one would not randomly or without reason want to refer children for placement or service without relying on supporting documentation, such as was considered in the previous section.

It is difficult to specify hard and fast rules or guidelines for the educational placement of retarded children. Among the pertinent factors involved in a placement decision are (1) the scope and extent of competently staffed and properly programmed school and agency services which are available in the community or within easy commuting distance, (2) the degree of mental subnormality exhibited in those individual children under consideration and the unique behavioral and medical traits which surround their condition, (3) the prognosis for gaining a measure of self-sufficiency of individual children, and (4) the various types of relevant resources characteristic of the child's family.

With respect to the first issue, the extent to which service alternatives are available for educational management, increasing attention is being given by many communities to the need to provide options to parents who believe their child could profit from some plan of educational and behavioral management. For example, the comprehensive mental health–mental retardation planning which has taken place in many states has resulted in the development and provision of community diagnostic centers, day-care facilities, tutorial programs for children with significant medical problems—the homebound or hospitalized—counseling services, and money for staff coordination among various groups who are concerned with problems of mutual interest relating to the mentally retarded.

Of central significance in the issue of the extent to which various educational programs are available for post-preschool retardates is the notion of the public school program. After all, most families with educable and trainable retarded children will be interested in making use of the public school programs if they are available and if they reflect contemporary thinking and planning in staffing and curricula. You will notice that many of the more important concepts related to evaluating public school special education programs have been briefly consid-

ered in the last section of Chapter 3, and so only a few of these will be highlighted at this time. One very revealing characteristic of a progressive special education program for the retarded is the extent to which a staff is available to carefully test, assess, and diagnose the educationally related traits of the retarded youngsters and how available this group of specialists is for consulting with classroom teachers who need special help in translating diagnostic data into programming plans. By this time you recognize that preciseness in educational planning cannot be accomplished without pertinent diagnostically obtained information on each retarded youngster. A second trait to look for in a school system prior to placement of the child is the degree of comprehensiveness of the program, i.e., to what extent all ages of educables and trainables are provided for within the legal limits, and how completely the ancillary services necessary for total programming of the retarded children are inculcated into the management process.

It is also important for parents to ascertain the extent to which the educational program is sequenced so that the one aspect of the curriculum flows naturally into the next segment without requiring inordinate conceptual leaps by the child nor expecting him to be exposed to the same content in one class as he was at earlier, and perhaps later, levels. Perhaps most important is the need for your assuring that any child placed in a special education program for the retarded can and will be moved to other agencies or segments of the school environment, including a regular class, if the diagnostic signs so indicate. There is nothing quite so tragic as an inflexible pattern of educational programming within which a youngster becomes "locked into a channel" on the basis of scores on a test or two and is never again evaluated or considered for alternative placement situations. Unfortunately this is a characteristic that exists in many special education programs in spite of the clear evidence documenting the changing nature of individual traits, competencies, and interests at all levels of intellectual functioning. And so, to be sure, one important indicator of an up-to-date educational program for the mentally retarded is the degree of freedom which the child has for moving vertically and horizontally from one level to the next. Finally, concerning the possible placement of a retarded child in a school program, it is important to consider the level of competency and program philosophy of the special education personnel involved in the program. Some of the tenets of the philosophy of special education and the basis on which one can determine the expertise of a teacher will be reviewed later.

Among the other factors one should consider before deciding on the type of educational placement for a retarded child is his prognosis. Obviously this is a very difficult area to focus sharply on because one must deal with possibilities and probabilities; nonetheless, it is important to gain some appreciation for factors such as an estimate of how well a youngster will be able to gain independence as adulthood approaches. The tentative answers one gives to this question

will help direct the child's early educational management. If, for example, self-sufficiency is exceedingly remote for the child, it might be important to expose him to an educational program quite different from another individual with a more favorable prognosis for independent living. During the elementary school years particularly, one can begin forcasting a child's future status by carefully observing his reactions to medical, psychological, social, and educational management procedures in addition to considering factors such as level of subnormality, extent of additional disorders, promise for living in a stimulating environment in subsequent years, and so on.

Among the practical problems surrounding the issue of preferred educational placement for a child is the character of his family. The implications of this thought should be considered in a broad perspective. It is indeed pertinent in the evaluation of placement alternatives, for children of elementary school age, to know how well the youngster is cared for at home in a physical, psychological, and social sense. Similarly, one should consider the uniqueness of the family milieu—its facilitating and/or debilitating characteristics. And, of course, it is always important to know the expectations family members have of the retarded youngster, for these will help to direct decisions concerning the format of preferred educational programs for the child and for members of his family.

To summarize, acceptable placement alternatives for retarded children at all levels can be generated only after totally comprehensive analyses have been made on the child and on his environment. Moreover, some broad judgements must be made on the child's prognosis for becoming sufficient unto himself or with minimal assistance as an adolescent and as an adult. Finally, careful analysis is required to determine the degree to which an intentional management program for the child's family is needed in conjunction with his own planned educational opportunities and experiences.

Recommended Readings

Baldwin, W. K.: "The Social Position of the Educable Mentally Retarded Child in the Regular Grades in the Public Schools," *Exceptional Children,* vol. 25, 1958, pp. 106–108, 112.

Blatt, B.: "The Physical, Personal, and Academic Status of Children Who Are Mentally Retarded Attending Special Classes as Compared With Children Who Are Mentally Retarded Attending Regular Classes," *American Journal of Mental Deficiency,* vol. 62, 1958, pp. 810–818.

Daly, W. C.: "Selection of Children for Special Class Programs," *Education,* vol. 81, 1961, pp. 489–492.

Goldstein, H., J. W. Moss, and L. J. Jordan: *The Efficacy of Special Class Training on the Development of Mentally Retarded Children,* U.S. Office of Education, Cooperative Research Project No. 619, University of Illinois, Urbana, 1965.

Holowinsky, I. Z.: "Special Child or Retarded Children? Some Problems of a Special Class Placement," *Training School Bulletin,* vol. 60, 1963, pp. 118–122.

Johnson, G. O., and S. A. Kirk: "Are Mentally Handicapped Children Segregated in the Regular Grades?" *Journal of Exceptional Children,* vol. 17, 1950, pp. 65–68, 87–88.

Kicklighter, R. H.: "Referral Needs and Assessed Intelligence of Candidates for Special Class Placement," *Journal of School Psychology,* vol. 5, 1966, pp. 39–41.

Meyerowitz, J. H.: "Self-degradation in Young Retardates and Special Class Placement," *Child Development,* vol. 33, 1962, pp. 443–451.

Meyers, E. S., and C. E. Meyers: "Problems in School Placement Arising from Divergent Conceptions of Educable Children," *Mental Retardation,* vol. 5, 1967, pp. 19–22.

Stanton, J. R., and V. N. Cassidy: "Effectiveness of Special Classes for Educable Mentally Retarded," *Mental Retardation,* vol. 2, 1964, pp. 8–13.

Wolfensberger, W.: "Counseling Parents of the Retarded," in A. Baumeister (ed.), *Mental Retardation: Appraisal, Education, and Rehabilitation,* Aldine Publishing Company, Chicago, 1967, pp. 335–337.

What practices are used by the public schools to educate retarded children at the elementary level?

Most of you recognize that it is impossible to describe with any degree of preciseness the practices that are used to educate retarded children in elementary programs. This is caused by the fact that no one really knows the types and range of teacher behaviors that occur within special education classrooms. Moreover, the educational practices that are used no doubt differ widely among school systems and individual teachers as a result of (1) differing criteria for admission to classes for the retarded resulting in the employment of various techniques and procedures for grouping, (2) exposure by teachers to dissimilar philosophies for managing the behavioral and educational problems of the mentally retarded during the time they were involved in their teacher training, (3) the extent to which administrators are knowledgeable about and committed to implementing preferred, contemporary strategies for management, and (4) the extent to which teachers within a school system are willing to be trained and retrained in the use of newer techniques of intervention. Some professionals are concerned that many existing practices which are being used in special education classes do not reflect a sound theoretical or empirical basis and may be more harmful than beneficial to certain types of retarded youngsters (Smith, 1969). For these reasons, and perhaps for others, an attempt at delineating what is being done in special classes for retarded children is not possible, nor, for that matter, might it even be desirable.

The focus of this section will be devoted to a consideration of instructional practices which seem to warrant greater application within special education

classes for the retarded, and, at the same time, are within the limits of present scientific knowledge and social consent. First, it is important to emphasize that the presentation of a "cookbook listing" of instructional procedures which if properly applied would assure success in teaching all, or even most, retarded children of this age level is highly presumptuous. There are certain broad general principles to which our attention is directed by relatively strong research efforts that are highly suggestive of the potential profit of employing certain *modus operandi* when instructing retarded children. In the discussion in Chapter 1, a number of these general techniques were reported and illustrated. The procedures involved in behavior modification and some of the principles of learning which have been distilled from the work of educational psychologists are among the most obviously germane to instructional methodology. Smith (1968) has elaborated on this matter elsewhere.

Focus of the Curriculum   By the time an educable-level retarded child is ready to move into an elementary school special class program he has become a very complex behavioral phenomenon. Individual peculiarities and the degree of variability among the retarded are more obvious and well established as they grow older. This variability and complexity of behavior result from factors such as differences in inherent strengths and weaknesses among the children, the extent and nature of systematic preschool instruction each child previously experienced, the degree to which their individual homes were facilitating or deprivating, and the proportion and types of successful and unsuccessful experiences each child encountered during the preschool years. To a large extent the type of curriculum, the manner in which instruction will proceed, and the types of materials used during the instructional encounters will be based on your observations of each child on these dimensions. Suppose we consider some of these issues in greater depth.

Attempts to isolate concepts involved in the behavioral management of retarded children, such as distinguishing between practices used to educate elementary-level children in contrast to those appropriate for preschool children, inevitably result in artificial levels and lines of demarcation. One should be careful not to establish his own conceptual clique over this matter since a great amount of overlap exists in theory and practice between various levels of instruction. It is impossible, and most certainly not desirable, to carve out a preschool or elementary course of study without considering the scope and sequence involved in other components of the total plan of education as well as each child's uniquenesses. Conclusively, then, the concepts which were expressed in the preceding section of this chapter and in other chapters are inextricably apropos to the thoughts expressed here. Perhaps the most basic tenet of the philosophy of this section and others dealing with educational management for the mentally retarded is that one cannot determine the specific nature of educational program-

ming until proper data are collected and analyzed on each child. This information, then, is used to generate reasonable alternatives concerning curriculum, methodology, and instructional materials.

There is no preferred curriculum for mentally retarded children of elementary age which is agreed upon by educators. If one inspects the various curriculum guides which have been developed by school systems throughout the country, it is difficult to find a single focus, although many common threads might be readily identifiable. In a global sense, most curricula suggest as principal goals that the retarded (1) develop a fund of general information which they can call upon quickly and at appropriate times, (2) develop those skills which are necessary to become socially, personally, and occupationally self-sufficient, and (3) develop an adequate level of performance in predicting the consequences of their behavior in all areas which require some interaction with their environment. These goals are not incongruent with the behaviors suggested as being appropriate for preschool youngsters, although the more global goals mentioned here subsume a myriad of smaller competencies which would need to be specified before instruction could proceed and evaluation of student achievement realized.

Figure 4-5 describes the general content emphasis which is characteristic of most special education curricula for the educable mentally retarded. Notice that relatively more time is usually spent on readiness activities during the early elementary years than during subsequent periods. This actually is an extension of the program which takes place in those situations in which deliberate, systematic, and intentional preschool instruction is provided for the retarded. Generally speaking, the emphasis on instruction for the development of readiness skills tapers off as the child progresses through the elementary school program. The point of emphasis here is that much more time needs to be devoted to the intentional and planned engagement of retarded youngsters in these precursive areas of performance than most special education teachers and parents of the retarded realize. It is not difficult at all to become impatient with the slow transition which many retarded youngsters make from readiness to more easily identifiable academic activities.

In order to clarify and be more specific about the types of skills involved in readiness instruction, direct your attention to the list which appears in Table 4-2. There are no precise criteria for describing what is or is not a readiness skill, per se, since in a real sense the attainment of skills at all levels is based on how well developed prerequisite competencies have become for each individual. In considering readiness skills for retarded children at the elementary level, in addition to some of those listed in Table 4-2, one might wish to consider factors such as the degree to which the child is interested in participating in an activity, how well he is able to attend to a task, the extent to which one or more of the response modalities are functioning, his emotional stability, and so on. In the

sequence of educational experiences and development, then, these specific skills must be acquired at some minimal level in order for the child to proceed to higher levels of instruction.

The transition from focus on readiness activities to those involved in the academic-tool subjects, such as reading, arithmetic, writing, and spelling, should be a smooth and gradual one. As reflected in Figure 4-5, the orientation clearly becomes more academic as the program moves closer to the junior high school years. As the child's readiness skills become better developed and more extensive he is able to deal with problems which are comparatively more complex, such as those involved in the tool-subject areas.

Perhaps no other area in the curriculum is of greater significance to the future of a retarded individual, who will eventually become self-sufficient, than reading. The impact of being unable to read is a serious one and has grave consequences for many other areas of life. It influences many of the daily living practices, to a certain extent controls the types and levels of jobs which are available to an individual, has implications for promotions at work, is used by many as a measure of intelligence, controls mobility among socioeconomic levels, regulates the political and personal influence one has over the behavior of others, and causes emotional problems in many people who have serious reading disorders. Few individuals would argue against the provision of an excellent reading program for those retarded youngsters who can gain some measure of ad-

Table 4-2   A sample of areas of readiness frequently emphasized in curricula for the mildly retarded

1. Visual and auditory discrimination (colors, shapes, sizes)
2. Visual and auditory memory
3. Separation of figure from background (auditory and visual)
4. Association among stimuli (sounds, objects, combinations)
5. Small motor movement and dexterity (cutting, sorting, copying, tracing, buttoning, block building)
6. Large motor skills (walking, balance, rhythmic motions, jumping, running, skipping)
7. Acquiring meaning from the spoken word and/or from visual stimuli
8. Expression of ideas, concepts, and processes in a meaningful and intelligible way
9. Location of an object in space
10. Labeling of common objects, letters, and numbers
11. Naming parts of the body
12. Care for toileting needs
13. Willingness to attempt a solution to problems
14. Control over emotions within reasonable limits
15. Establishment of mutually beneficial comradeships

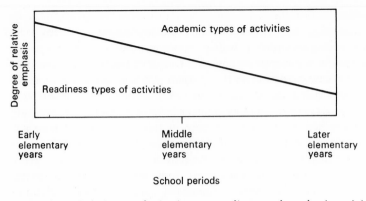

Figure 4-5 *Relative emphasis given to readiness and academic activities with mildly retarded children during the elementary years.*

vantage by virtue of acquiring reading skills. Unfortunately, there is probably no other single area of performance in which the retarded seem to have more difficulty. In spite of the fact that many retarded children, who have been exposed to adequate preschool programs, could reasonably be expected to achieve at about the fifth or sixth grade level in reading, few actually meet this expected level of performance. The reasons for this are many, complex, and no doubt individual in character. Certainly among the more predominant are (1) the inherent relative difficulty involved in learning to read as a result of the nonconcrete nature of the task, (2) the impatience of school systems to place the young retarded child into a reading program before adequate readiness skills have been developed, (3) the paucity of descriptive data about the retarded youngsters in areas which are associated with the reading process and areas in which the youngsters need intense remediation before the formal reading program begins, (4) the confusion on the part of teachers concerning the best method of teaching reading to individual retarded children, and (5) the lack of consistency in applying the most appropriate reading program to reflect each child's areas of advantage and disadvantage.

Regarding reading, then, the situation is as follows: (1) reading is a vital component for relative success for the mildly retarded individual; (2) reading at a minimum level assumes the acquisition of a whole host of complex skills most of which are very abstract; and (3) for reasons peculiar to them, their background, and the usual school instruction, retarded children usually appear to have significant problems developing an adequate level of skills in reading. The upshot of this situation is that many children who are retarded and of elementary school age are also serious remedial reading cases; i.e., they perform in reading at a level which is significantly below that which might reasonably be predicted for them.

As yet no one has identified a reading program which is best for the mentally retarded—as you might suspect—because the individual patterns of needs, competencies, and weaknesses differ so widely among members of this group. The preferred program is the one, from those that exist, that best suits a single child according to the results derived from the program of testing and assessment. For one group of children the data may show that a whole word approach will work best, for other youngsters an auditory program may be preferred, and for still other children the best approach to learning to read may involve visual and tactile components primarily. Obviously, you can imagine that the demands of the retarded elementary-age children in reading require skills of the special education teacher which transcend those usually considered adequate for instructors in regular class situations wherein almost any approach to the teaching of reading will probably be successful for the majority of the class.

Perhaps in no other area of the curriculum for the retarded has the influence of contemporary thinking and theory been so obvious as in the area of arithmetic. Prior to the early 1960s, most curriculum guides emphasized a relatively nonconceptual, mechanistic, and rote approach for arithmetic instruction. The position at that time was that rote counting, for example, was one of the most basic readiness skills involved in arithmetic processes and that educable-level retarded children should be engaged in exercises in chanting chronological sequences of numbers before proceeding to the next step of rational counting. This position was without documentation by either theory or research and was dislodged as an appropriate component of most arithmetic curricula by the well-validated positions stemming from the work of Piaget (1952) and others who have interpreted his theory (Churchill, 1961; Lovell, 1961; Woodward, 1961).

This latter, more contemporary point of view concerning arithmetic for the retarded deemphasizes those suggestions and activities which place predominance on specific computational manipulations by the children. Instead, the focus is on aiding the retarded to develop understanding in basic numerical concepts which, in turn, lead to a more solid comprehension of arithmetic reasoning skills necessary for the solution of practical problems. To this end, many of the newer curricular approaches have included intentional programs of instruction involving concepts of classification, seriation, combination, and conservation in the beginning stages of the arithmetic program.

The programs of instruction in spelling, writing, and language development require intentional and individualized attention according to the types of specific goals, skills, and competencies which the teacher believes to be reasonable for each child in the class. This suggestion is no different from that which was offered in previous sections advising how one should proceed in determining answers to the question, "What should be included in the curriculum?" Spelling, writing, and language constitute important members of the dimension of communication. If the skills that are subsumed within each broad

area are to become established and developed at increasingly higher levels, an ample array of pertinent activities will need to appear in all aspects of a child's program of study. Specific suggestions of how this might be accomplished have been delineated in other sources (Cartwright, 1969; McWilliams, 1969; Brabner, 1969; Smith, 1968).

Readiness activities and those involved in the more traditional academic areas are not the only emphases desired in a total elementary program for the mildly retarded. Certainly, deliberate attention must be given to the important areas of emotional and social development. Although these dimensions are often not willfully emphasized to any great extent in the regular class programs because intellectually normal children usually are able incidentally to acquire appropriate skills for dealing with potentially disruptive personal and social situations, the mentally retarded often lack the social sensitivity and the necessary skills required to satisfactorily grapple with various problems and issues. They must become skilled in effectively dealing with their emotions and the pressures that come from within themselves as a result of their not being able to deal with their own desires or with the expectations of those within their immediate environment. To be sure, one important aspect of every curriculum for the retarded is the provision of reasonably attainable goals and a general environment which will foster good mental health on the part of the children. Many adolescent and adult retardates suffer from significant differing degrees of emotional distress of various types as a direct result of not being able to deal with the environmental pressures and personal stresses which could have been effectively considered as part of the elementary-level instructional program. The broad area of providing means for facilitating mentally healthy responses by the retarded should be a part of their entire curriculum.

Most curriculum plans for the mentally retarded give strong emphasis to social ramifications. This segment of the instructional program is variously described as social studies, social adjustment, life adjustment skills, human living programs, and so on. Basically, the central mission of most of these programs is to engage the retarded child in progressively more complex experiences and activities involving other people and environmental situations. These involvements, which begin initially under relatively protected circumstances with a gradual broadening into a more open environment, are aimed at helping the youngster develop knowledge about himself and his surroundings and methods for effectively and properly dealing with the multitude of problems he might expect to encounter on a day-to-day basis. The extent to which a child can and should extend outward from himself into more remote and abstract components of the social order is dependent on factors such as his performance level in related areas of functioning, prognosis for eventual independence in living, past experiences, support from family members, and the availability of program supervision during important phases of the social training.

A Model of Information Processing   Because of the frequent difficulty many retarded children have in developing many skills at a satisfactory level, in spite of the effort special education teachers make to individualize the instructional program, educational psychologists and other groups of scientists have studied the means by which information is acquired and processed by the human organism. Interestingly enough, this effort has had some definite implications for the direction of curriculum planning, and the conclusions from this work have begun to be implemented in many special education programs. The global, molar curricular approach by which the teachers became "locked into" the local curriculum guide does not work with many retarded youngsters because of specific learning disorders which are superimposed on the general intellectual subnormality of these children. The realization and admission that the approach fails is one reason for the increased emphasis on studying and implementing results of the work on information processing. In a real sense these efforts by scientists and teachers have merged and resulted in a definite trend toward an analytically based molecular approach to curriculum development for the educable mentally retarded group. This means that attempts are made to identify precise weaknesses in individual children, locate the area(s) of weaknesses on a larger matrix of skill areas, evaluate the condition of each child's performance in those areas of concern, and on the basis of these data provide appropriate instructional sequences. Since a great amount of emphasis is currently being given to the components of the information processing system in curricular planning, it might be helpful to briefly describe the major segments of this instructional model (see Figure 4-6).

This book emphasizes the importance of exposing the mentally retarded to an enriched environment, i.e., one which provides a wide range of experiences and opportunities for interacting with people and other aspects of their surroundings. This position is taken in the belief that when the mentally retarded are offered increased experiences they will acquire a more extensive and complex repertoire of information, which, in turn, will aid them in the process of solving problems. One important detail which must not be overlooked, but which unfortunately is all too frequently assumed, is that the various components of the individual's system for dealing with and processing data from his environment are performing in a proper way. Since this is a dubious assumption with retarded children, as well as with other types of exceptional youngsters, it is important for curricula to reflect on these possible areas of weakness by including diagnostic and remedial activities as part of the instructional sequence. Emphasis is given particularly to these factors during the elementary school years.

Now, what about the information-processing model should be of concern to curriculum experts in mental retardation? First, it is clear that a child cannot develop an extensive repertoire of information as a result of experiences if he

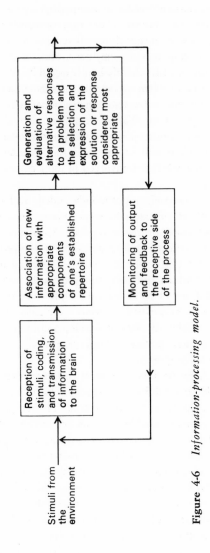

Figure 4-6 *Information-processing model.*

either lives in a nonstimulating environment or if some reason he has difficulty in extracting information from his environment. Reception of stimuli through the various sense modalities is a necessary condition and an obvious prerequisite to efficient and effective development of one's intellectual capabilities. Many retarded children have problems in adequately and accurately obtaining and using data from their surroundings. They may be unable to perceive stimuli through one or more of the sense modalities, their skill in focusing on the most relevant stimuli among many may be impaired, they may often misperceive stimulus conditions, or they will frequently be distracted by peripheral conditions. Educationally, this potential problem means that the curriculum must be designed in a way that would provide intentional instructional activities for retarded children with receptive problems. To be sure, the identification and proper remediation of a reception disorder should take priority over most every other aspect of the curriculum; it is one of the most fundamental necessities in the entire spectrum of activities which are involved in most curricula for elementary-age retarded youngsters.

After data have been received, appropriately coded, and transmitted to the brain, the complex processes of association take place. This is the least understood aspect of the information processing system. Apparently the new information that is received is evaluated and matched with components of a child's repertoire according to the pertinence and mutuality of the incoming information and the experiences which the child has previously programmed into his brain. This new material serves to enlarge the child's intellectual inventory as the various patterns of new and existing sensory experiences become firmly integrated. Understandably, as the associations develop into more complex networks as a result of the youngster having various experiences, he will have more potential for effectively solving problems.

Retarded children are often relatively weak in this integration phase. Frequently they are unable to establish associations which will be of subsequent value to them either because they have irrelevant or ambiguous stimuli introduced into their system, or are unable to relate present experiences to learning which has occurred in the past, or because their existing associational networks are not well established. It is of great significance, therefore, to include experiences which are designed to aid the retarded in the development and establishment of increasingly more involved associational patterns as part of the elementary curriculum. It is not an overstatement at all to suggest that most, if not all, disadvantaged, as well as organically impaired, retarded children will have need for intentional and systematic instruction in this important area.

In order for a person to react to a situation by expressing himself either through gesture or by voice he must have received the stimuli surrounding the situation in a reasonably accurate way, he must have related the information involved in the situation with existing associational networks, he must have

scanned his repertoire for all alternative answers which are reasonably acceptable, and he must have evaluated each alternative that he has generated to determine which one among the entire array is the most appropriate answer. The whole procedure is very complex, but it is one which must take place before a relatively meaningful response can be made. It is only after this process has occurred that the child is faced with the problem of communicating his response to those who have posed the problem. Clearly, important conditions for the utterance of an intelligible response is that the scanning, alternative generating, and evaluation components of the system be intact and be able to function well.

As you might expect, the young retardate is usually weak in those situations involving complex phenomenon such as are involved in this portion of the information processing system. Not only is it complex, but it demands spontaneity on the part of individuals. With the intellectually normal youngsters the process operates much slower than with adults, but in both instances there is an appearance that the operation of the system is relatively automatic. Not so with the retarded—they often exhibit behaviors which suggest the need for including intentional instructional sequences in their curriculum which will allow for the more complete development of the competencies required for relative mastery of the process.

Finally, you will notice in Figure 4-6 that the model suggests the need for a monitoring and feedback component. The purpose of this segment of the process is to provide a means whereby a person can match his response to the stimuli being received. If incongruence is observed between output and input, the person can promptly make adjustments to effect a more proper match. To work well, the individual must be able to perceive his own responses and modify whichever part of the process is "out of balance." Again, the mentally retarded frequently have trouble in the monitoring and feedback processes. Curricula must provide for such characteristic weaknesses on a continuous basis.

A number of direct suggestions have been made concerning other curricular needs of the mentally retarded. These suggestions are viewed as "top priority items" because of the high frequency of serious remedial cases prevalent among elementary age and older mildly retarded children. Space limitations will not permit a listing of specific competencies and their associated activities in each of the areas involved in the information processing system. The reader who is concerned about obtaining more specific information about these dimensions will find help in the work of Valett (1969), Smith (1968, 1969), Johnson and Myklebust (1967), Kephart (1960), Bush and Giles (1969), Kaluger and Kolson (1969), Early (1969), and Haring and Schiefelbusch (1967).

Suggestions on Methods   After the special education teacher has described the curricular goals appropriate for each child, the next matter for deliberation is how to structure and manipulate the youngster's environment so that the goals can most easily be attained. This issue is one concerned with instructional

methodology or the "how" of teaching. In both Chapters 1 and 3 some broad guidelines have been suggested to direct those who are involved in the behavioral management of retarded children. These suggestions are appropriate for use with elementary-level retarded youngsters. Perhaps it would be profitable to list briefly some of the more important concepts concerning management techniques or methodology:

1. Any methodology selected by a teacher for use with a retarded child as a means for helping the youngster gain a certain skill should be based on data obtained from various sources. These data should first be analyzed to determine the areas in which the child is relatively weak and strong. From this analysis instructional procedures should and can emerge.
2. Careful inspection should be made of the techniques which each child seems to use most successfully when processing information for learning. The style or process which the child uses to deal with problems, stimuli, and issues provides important bits of information and will help to specify an appropriate educational methodology for individual children.
3. The agents which increase or decrease the occurrence of a child's behavior should be identified and properly controlled so as to aid the youngster in acquiring the skills set forth.
4. The teacher must maintain constant diagnostic awareness in order to revise any instructional procedure which either is not working with the youngster or should be supplanted by a predictably better alternative method.

Instructional Materials   Another major factor involved in the provision of appropriate educational management for the mentally retarded is the use of instructional materials. There is no question about the value in and need for teachers employing various devices as a means for facilitating the rapid and stable acquisition of skills and information by the retarded child. Manufacturers and publishers have recently placed on the market an immense quantity of every conceivable variety of instructional materials, many of which are publicized as particularly appropriate for the mentally retarded. On one hand it is, indeed, a pleasant circumstance for a teacher to have many options available when it comes time to order new materials and equipment. The joy engendered from this situation is short-lived, however, when it becomes evident that documentation, theoretical and empirical, as to the efficacy of many of the instructional devices is either inconclusive, unreliable, or nonexistent. Unfortunately, the sole basis on which one can elect to choose a certain device over a second similar type of material is often hunch, intuition, and the fact that the first device looks like it might work better than the second. This situation is especially visible in the area of perceptual-motor development. Hundreds of devices have appeared on the market without proper documentation and support. In fact, one could

make a bonafide case for believing that the devices which are ostensibly designed to help a child could actually do more damage than good. Any alternative is possible; i.e., a device could enhance, reduce, or do nothing at all for a child's performance, without properly derived evidence.

This is a matter of seriousness for educators, since instructional materials constitute an important potential component of a teacher's total armament. If the proper combination of curriculum, method, and materials can be identified for each retarded child at a specific moment in time, learning will be enhanced. If one of these three major components is inadequate, improperly selected, not used at all, or inefficient, the child's performance will suffer. It is absolutely legitimate for educators to expect commercial publishers to comprehensively field test each instructional device with children in situations which simulate a market identical to the one to which they intend to direct their publicity before the device is retailed. Publishers should be able to inform teachers about the criteria they must use in selecting a certain device instead of choosing a competitor's device. Likewise, teachers should be made aware of the circumstances which suggest that materials predictably will not work. There is no reason why special educators cannot insist on the rigorous evaluation of all instructional materials in a manner similar to the expectations we have of pharmaceutical corporations and other groups who supply commodities to the public.

Other Instructional Matters   The thoughts which have been presented are obviously not all-inclusive when one considers the dimensions involved in providing optimum educational programming for the mentally retarded child of elementary school age. It is just not possible to pursue the many nuances involved in instructing these children in an introductory text of this sort. At the same time, there are a number of major issues which have not been mentioned but which are vital to the success of the total educational program. Let me elaborate a bit on this point by listing and presenting a brief point of view on several of these issues.

To what extent should an educable mentally retarded child be integrated into a regular class program in the elementary school? How you react to this question will tell a lot about the philosophical stance you choose to take. If you are unwilling to consider the possibility of regular class placement as a feasible procedure for certain retarded children, you probably do not believe that people all have different strengths and weaknesses and that these should be reflected in the management programs; you also no doubt are unconvinced that characteristics of individuals can change from time to time; and you have not realistically considered the fact that the retarded child will be seriously penalized by not having day-to-day contact with intellectually normal peers who are members of the same society in which the retarded child will eventually find himself. My bias on this point is unmistakable. If retarded children are able to perform in a reasonably satisfactory way in certain subject areas with intellectually normal peers, and if this

will not cause handicaps in other areas of performance, it seems only natural that flexible placement between special and regular classes be possible. At one extreme it might mean that a retarded child will need to spend his entire day in the special class; at the other end of the spectrum it might mean that another child will need to use the special class only as a resource room for remedial reading instruction an hour each day. The philosophy behind this type of practice will lead to retarded youngsters who are much better prepared to face the multitude of problems they can expect to encounter as adolescents and adults than if they are cloistered away for an entire school career in a special education classroom in the basement of a public school. And also, consideration for placement in a regular class program for a portion of the day is consistent with the overriding belief that individual variation must be dealt with according to the particular signs each child exhibits.

Because many retarded children have complex problems, it is often true that specially trained personnel need to become an integral part of the plan of behavioral management. The expertise of specialists such as school psychologists, speech therapists, physical therapists, hearing specialists, psychiatrists, and others will be needed not only to provide treatment to certain children but also to offer consultation to the teacher. School systems which are serious about and committed to providing total programming for special education youngsters will provide the needed resources for such services. Since these are not often high on the list of priorities for many school systems, it is usually necessary for the teacher to refer a child with a special need to a community agency, local hospital, to another school system, or to a benevolent private practitioner in order for the youngster to receive proper diagnosis and treatment for any of those conditions which exceed the training and clinical skills of the teacher.

The Preparation of Competent Teachers   In several sections of this book the position has been taken that among the most prominent needs of the mentally retarded is the need to be associated with skillful and competent teachers. It is really unfitting to discuss desirable educational practices for elementary-age retardates without spending some time on matters connected with teachers of this group of children. To a large extent the comments which follow represent a position on which professional special educators will no doubt have divided opinions.

First, suppose we look briefly at the status of special education teachers and the character of their training. Most teachers who are interested in becoming associated with special classes for the mentally retarded receive their training in colleges and universities which acknowledge that a pure mentally retarded child does not exist and that training in mental retardation, per se, is inappropriate and too restricting. The position which many institutions of higher education are currently taking is that the training program for teachers should reflect

behavioral phenomena as opposed to organizing the student's program so that they are trained to teach educable mentally retarded children or trainable mentally retarded children. It is also of some concern to many special education people that teachers are presently employed by school systems on the basis of courses which they have taken and the number of credits that they have accumulated in spite of the fact that most professionals recognize that the same course taught by the same instructor at the same institution will vary, oftentimes to a substantial degree, from one semester to the next. Using the criteria of having taken certain courses as a measure of how well one can manage the environment of a mentally retarded child in order to maximize learning requires extrapolations of the highest order. To a large extent it is equivalent to attempting to measure achievement in high jumping on the basis of whether or not a student has successfully passed a course in the principles of physics, or speculating on how well a dental student can repair a cavity on the basis of his grades in a course in which dental abnormalities and their repair were considered, or evaluating the effectiveness of the child-rearing performance of a set of parents according to how well they did on a paper-and-pencil test after having read a book on child rearing. It is clearly apparent to most professional special educators that the practices which are presently being employed in training teachers of the mentally retarded have not kept pace with current thinking on this matter.

If one were interested in identifying whether a special education teacher was ready to step into a classroom and begin managing the behavior of mentally retarded children, the first order of business would involve a delineation of the very specific competencies or skills which this teacher would need in order to deal with the youngsters effectively. The often recited goals of general education and the relatively more specific goals of special education which appear in many textbooks are fine; however, for the purposes of training teachers and evaluating their skill, these general goals are much too imprecise. The following suggestions include five or six specific competencies which some professionals might believe that teachers of mentally retarded children should demonstrate at some minimal level of skill before they are qualified to enter the special education classroom:

1. Every special education teacher of the mentally retarded should demonstrate skill in informally diagnosing educational characteristics and disorders in those processes involving basic reading and basic arithmetic. For example, the teacher of the mentally retarded should be able to identify specific problems that are related to reading such as left to right difficulties, sound blending disorders, auditory visual integration problems, and visual discrimination disorders. In arithmetic, special education teachers of the mentally retarded should be able to identify whether a child is having difficulty in adding because he does not understand the concept of zero, because he has trouble

carrying, because he subtracts instead of adds, or because he fails to place the element of algorithm in proper position on the paper.

2. Every teacher of the mentally retarded should be able to identify the technique for learning to read which seems to be most appropriate for each child and demonstrate skill in providing reading instruction using a phonics approach, a whole word approach, and a Fernald approach.

3. Every teacher of the mentally retarded should be able to properly organize, conduct, and evaluate role playing situations with mentally retarded children.

4. Every teacher of the mentally retarded should be able to maintain meaningful longitudinal records on each child and interpret the data which appear on these records into appropriate instructional strategies.

5. Every teacher of the mentally retarded should be able to demonstrate skill in changing the behavior of retarded youngsters by using procedures involving positive reinforcement, negative reinforcement, and combinations of these.

Certainly some professional special educators might disagree with one or more of the competencies which I have illustrated above. Indeed, you may feel that they are inappropriate for special education teachers. Although one could reasonably challenge their content, at the same time you must admit that they are relatively precise and when contrasted with more popular statements which are identified as special education objectives for the mentally retarded, the competencies which have been suggested above can much more readily be measured and provide a clearer behavioral statement of the goals which we might wish teachers to be able to achieve. Without such specific goals you can have the most elegant methodology and instructional materials available but be in an enormous dilemma as a result of not clearly knowing in which direction to proceed.

To be sure it is an overwhelming task to begin identifying the whole range of skills we would like special class teachers of the mentally retarded to exhibit. However, it is a task which must be done in order to have a clear and absolute picture of what we expect of teachers and whether or not they have been trained to do what we expect of them. The potential implications of assuming such an approach are unlimited. For example, retarded youngsters might be grouped on bases quite different from those which are presently used. A group of children with visual discrimination difficulties might be grouped together for a portion of the day until each child learns to discriminate among visual stimuli at a preset criterion level. Teachers could be assigned to various groups on the basis of where they, the teachers, exhibited relative strength in their teacher training program. Decisions about the relative strength of teachers in satisfying the competencies which have been described by teacher trainers could be evaluated by more systematically observing student teaching situations, requiring student teachers to respond to specific hypothetical problems which require a demonstration of how

well they are able to deal with educational disorders in the mentally retarded, through the presentation of problems using computer-assisted instruction or video taping devices or by video taping student teachers or first year teachers on the job. By identifying the specific competencies in which special education teachers for the mentally retarded should manifest skill, a teacher trainer can gain a clear picture of those areas in which the teacher has relative strength and those areas in which weaknesses are obvious. This procedure should sound very familiar to those of you who have read previous sections in this book; for the procedures that are suggested here as being applicable to the training of teachers are identical to those suggestions which were made for grouping and educating the mentally retarded children at various levels. In short, using a competencies approach for both a teacher and the mentally retarded children is more specific, easier to evaluate, and leads to more direct methodological suggestions than other approaches which are currently being used in many school systems, colleges, and universities.

For many years a number of professional educators have been dissatisfied with the criteria which have been used to certify special education teachers of the mentally retarded. It has been recognized by many that it is at best a poor second to suggest that a person is prepared or competent to teach anyone on the basis of having taken certain courses or even after having student taught. Those of you who are attracted to the suggestions that have been made concerning the need to identify and evaluate competencies for teachers of the mentally retarded will see that the certification criteria used by many states would most certainly have to change if this concept were fully implemented. If so, we might be able to do away with the familiar course names and credits as criteria for certification and require the teacher candidate to demonstrate skill in those performance areas which educators of the mentally retarded view as necessary. No longer would teachers need to worry about whether they missed a certain course or two along the way. States might be able to establish examinations or specific evaluative procedures to determine the extent to which teachers have developed the skills required for teaching the mentally retarded. The suggested procedure is much like those evaluative devices administered to our professional colleagues in the healing arts and in many of the hard sciences throughout the country. Speech pathologists, for example, require a demonstration of clinical competence by their speech correctionists before they are allowed to practice their profession.

As important as developing teacher competencies and evaluating them prior to teaching the mentally retarded is the teacher maintaining, refining, and upgrading teaching skills. This necessitates intentional, intensive, and continual reevaluation of the teacher's performance. I am not speaking of an official and infrequent visit and chat by one's supervisor or principal. Perhaps a more honest approach would be to have special education teachers demonstrate their teaching skills on a regular basis, and if the teachers are found lacking in certain specific

areas it is entirely feasible that procedures could be established on a statewide basis to help them upgrade their competence in those areas of especial weakness. One way of implementing this concept would be through the use of short courses, workshops, in-service training, and demonstrations which could be coordinated for a state or country by some central agency. With this type of central coordination a teacher might be able to predict when a special course would be offered, at what location, the specific content of the course, and other factors which might be particularly relevant, such as scholarships and college credits.

There are a number of other ways in which teachers can be aided in maintaining skill in those areas which professional educators feel are particularly important for teaching the mentally retarded. Listed are the following possibilities:

1. School systems could hire a specialist who has the principal responsibility for evaluating teacher competencies in special education and providing remediation through in-service training in those areas in which teachers are particularly weak.
2. Colleges and universities could begin to cooperate in a more intimate way with school systems and on a contractual basis offer a range of services which would help teachers, such as those involved in classes for the mentally retarded, to maintain and develop higher-level skills in behavioral management.
3. School systems might find it advantageous to hire a person with skills both in reading and understanding the research literature and in translating pertinent studies into language and procedures which are understood by teachers. A person of this sort would be able to bridge the gap that presently seems to exist between the scientific literature in special education and the practical problems that teachers face every day in the classroom.
4. Colleges and universities could provide a very significant service to the public schools by preparing and disseminating literature which summarizes in plain language those alternatives which the teacher might validly consider in order to deal with the many perplexing problems which she will inevitably face during the course of the school year.

The whole issue of preparing competent teachers is a very complex one and certainly will not change overnight. It has been stated earlier that there is substantial reason to believe that many special education teachers of the mentally retarded do not have a firm basis for making decisions about implementing certain management procedures with the mentally retarded. This is a critical problem and one which demands immediate attention. Perhaps no other issue is of greater importance in special education for the mentally retarded than that of preparing teachers who are skillful, competent, and view the mentally retarded child in a relatively optimistic fashion. A position has been taken here concerning the way in which teacher training might be reoriented. Hopefully, colleges and

universities will not feel so bound by the pressures to maintain specific course identities, to assure themselves of federal funding in specific disability areas, or to build empires that they will refuse to consider the possible advantages of an approach to the preparation of teachers of the mentally retarded such as that suggested here.

Programs for Trainable Youngsters   The discussion thus far in this section has focused on issues dealing primarily with educable-level elementary age retarded children. The intent of this book is to provide an introduction to various aspects of mental retardation. This focus and the obvious limitations of space do not allow for a more extensive and detailed account of educational practices than those which have already been described. Various texts have attempted to cover the many educational subjects from various points of view, and the curious reader may wish to explore the writings of Kirk and Johnson (1951), Smith (1968), and Baumgartner (1965).

A number of public school systems have begun providing educational opportunities for trainable mentally retarded children who are of elementary school age, i.e., somewhere between the chronological ages of eight and fourteen or fifteen. In the more progressive systems even preschool opportunities exist. When this is not the case, one will often find that the local chapter of the National Association for Retarded Children will support a preschool program. Unfortunately, programs for the trainable are very often the last to be added to a public school system and the first to go when economizing becomes necessary. As you might expect, the basic requisites for a trainable class are very expensive. The unique physical facilities which are needed, the small teacher-pupil ratio, and the extensive diagnostic-remedial ancillary services are all contributors to the expensiveness of trainable classes.

Professional educators have not been in agreement concerning the matter of who should provide programs of management for the trainable retardate. The now well-publicized debate between Goldberg and Cruickshank (1958) contains the basic rudiments of the pro and con positions. One of the most forceful arguments against the public schools providing educational programs for the trainable is that most systems are not presently "tooled up" to provide the continuum of services and training which the trainable child needs and deserves. The advocates of this position express their unwillingness to become associated with a halfhearted program which does not have the support necessary to provide total programming. In their opinion the issue is as much a moral and ethical one as it is professional and political. Those who feel in the opposite way simply rebut this argument by insisting that the educational enterprise should and must provide education and training opportunities for everyone regardless of their intellectual status and potential. It is their opinion that because services and training opportunities do not exist, this is no reason to suggest that they should not exist.

One very discouraging feature of many of the programs for trainable children that presently exists, and a factor which is subtly used as an obstructive device to the formulation of public school programs for trainable children, is the inordinately unrealistic admission criteria which many schools insist on using. For example, one school system insists on the following conditions before a young trainable child is admitted to class:

1. No lower than MA 3 and IQ 30
2. Completely toilet trained
3. Able to communicate in an intelligent and understandable way to others
4. Socially adjusted to a point where behavioral disorders are not present
5. Able to eat independently
6. Able to follow commands and function in groups
7. Not damaging to self

After considering these admission expectations, it is little wonder that school systems do not feel pressure to establish programs for the trainable. When pressed by parents, they very often "beg off" by indicating that there are too few candidates who could meet the accepted criteria for admission to classes. You can see that a "straw man" has been presented; without question, admission criteria such as these are totally inappropriate. In fact, there would no doubt be a number of regular class students who could not satisfy these criteria which many educators believe to be realistic for admission to classes for the trainable retardates.

Relatively less frequently do you find classes for the trainable housed in a regular school building than you find in a special education school. In those relatively larger school systems whose philosophy on the educational management of handicapped children supports the establishment of special schools, there is usually a full range of opportunities for trainable children extending from the preschool through sheltered workshops. A sensible program orientation for children of the age of which we have been speaking will focus on helping the youngsters to:

1. Develop self-help skills such as those involved in using the bathroom, washing, dressing, brushing teeth, and so on
2. Establish socially acceptable and mentally healthy patterns of behavior
3. Develop adequate speech and language patterns and habits
4. Achieve at progressively higher levels in specific skill areas such as are involved in perceptual-motor development, solving everyday problems, discrimination, memory, and so on
5. Gain a measure of semiindependence in those skills that are involved in nondependent behaviors, e.g., behaving in a safe way, knowing how to use the phone, knowing whom to call in an emergency, not starting fights when teased, and so on

The procedures that are commonly suggested to help the trainable children attain the goals considered to be appropriate for them are really no different from those used in managing the behavior of educable-level children. The principles are equally applicable so long as one wisely selects a reasonable behavioral objective for individual children. The crucial point, then, is to identify realistic competencies for the trainable child, such as were suggested for educable children and their teachers, and then to methodically employ the management strategies which have been sketched out in earlier sections of this book.

This section has commented on some broadly based views regarding what are considered to be realistic and appropriate educational practices for retarded children who are of elementary school age. Some of the positions which have been presented are controversial and lack firm documentation of their efficacy; others stand on solid theoretical or empirical foundations. The topic is an exhaustive one, for programs are so scattered and so frequently lack intentional focus that they defy description. Unfortunately, educational practices for the mentally retarded in many schools still operate on a trial-and-error basis. However, educational management is perhaps one of the two or three most important areas for the mentally retarded. Educational programming stands next to prevention programs in importance and, as such, demands attention from the most skilled and wise scholars, researchers, and practitioners.

Recommended Readings

Baumgartner, B. B.: *Guiding the Retarded Child,* The John Day Company, Inc., New York, 1965.

Brabner, G.: "Reading Skills," in R. M. Smith (ed.), *Teacher Diagnosis of Educational Difficulties,* Charles E. Merrill Books, Inc., Columbus, Ohio, 1969, pp. 69–94.

Bush, W. J., and M. T. Giles: *Aids To Psycholinguistic Teaching,* Charles E. Merrill Books, Inc., Columbus, Ohio, 1969.

Cartwright, G. P.: "Written Expression and Spelling," in R. M. Smith (ed.), *Teacher Diagnosis of Educational Difficulties,* Charles E. Merrill Books, Inc., Columbus, Ohio, 1969, pp. 95–117.

Churchill, E. M.: *Counting and Measurement,* University of Toronto Press, Toronto, 1961.

Early, G. H.: *Perceptual Training in the Curriculum,* Charles E. Merrill Books, Inc., Columbus, Ohio, 1969.

Goldberg, I. I., and W. M. Cruickshank: "Trainable but Noneducable," *National Education Association Journal,* vol. 47, 1958, pp. 622–623.

Haring, N. G., and R. L. Schiefelbusch: *Methods in Special Education,* McGraw-Hill Book Company, New York, 1967.

Johnson, D. J., and H. R. Myklebust: *Learning Disabilities: Educational Principles and Practices,* Grune and Stratton, New York, 1967.

Kaluger, G., and C. J. Kolson: *Reading and Learning Disabilities,* Charles E. Merrill Books, Inc., Columbus, Ohio, 1969.

Kephart, N. C.: *The Slow Learner in the Classroom,* Charles E. Merrill Books, Inc., Columbus, Ohio, 1960.

Kirk, S. A., and G. O. Johnson: *Educating the Retarded Child,* Houghton Mifflin Company, Boston, 1951.

Lovell, K.: *The Growth of Basic Mathematical and Scientific Concepts in Children,* University of London Press, Ltd., London, 1961.

McWilliams, B. J.: "Speech and Language Disorders," in R. M. Smith (ed.), *Teacher Diagnosis of Educational Difficulties,* Charles E. Merrill Books, Inc., Columbus, Ohio, 1969, pp. 118–151.

Piaget, J.: *The Child's Conception of Number,* Routledge & Kegan Paul, Ltd., London, 1952.

Smith, R. M.: *Clinical Teaching: Methods of Instruction for the Retarded,* McGraw-Hill Book Company, New York, 1968.

————: "Preparing Competent Special Education Teachers," *Education Canada,* vol. 9, 1969, pp. 31–36.

———— (ed.): *Teacher Diagnosis of Educational Difficulties,* Charles E. Merrill Books, Inc., Columbus, Ohio, 1969.

Valett, R. E.: *Programming Learning Disabilities,* Fearon Publishers, Inc., Palo Alto, Calif., 1969.

Woodward, M.: "Concepts of Number in the Mentally Subnormal Studied by Piaget's Method," *Journal of Child Psychology and Psychiatry,* vol. 2, 1961, pp. 249–259.

What are some of the needs of parents at this time in the life of their retarded child?

The parents of a retarded child have some definite counseling needs at this particular time which require precise and practical suggestions and answers by members of the professional community. They will need to have the opinions of various types of experts from several disciplines in order to have their child's condition characterized at various stages of development, his prognosis determined, and the various techniques that might be used to enhance his future considered. Perhaps as much as any other area, the difficulties that the child has in dealing with school-associated problems and in meeting the parent's expectations in educational and intellectual matters constitute areas of great concern for most parents of retarded children. It is here that many will need assistance and counsel to help chart the future for their retarded child of elementary school age. Suppose we consider some of the facets of this problem.

It is important for the schools to assume the responsibility for maintaining full and completely open channels of communication with the parents of each retarded child. More specifically, it should become the teacher's responsibility to see to it that the parents fully understand the program goals which have been delineated for their child, the general format of the school activities, the proposed manner in which the teacher intends to help the child achieve the intended goals, and how well the child has achieved and is presently achieving these aims. There are many potentially serious consequences that could ensue as a result of not maintaining close communication with parents of retarded children.

In spite of the fact that the retarded child's parents have learned to deal with many of the various crises resulting from their child's disorders by the time the youngster is in an elementary school program, they still face the daily traumas that result from their youngster's inability to deal with his environment with the same degree of skill as other children. Moreover, frustrations and anxieties occur because they see their child not performing even as well as younger normal children, they realize that the youngster is becoming bored doing the same type of school work that he was given in past years with no discernible progress, and they recognize that they are unable to control the circumstances related to his educational development and future as they would like. These are anxiety-provoking conditions, and they occur to some extent in even the most well-informed, mature parent. It is obviously important to respond to these concerns of the parents. More important, however, is that they not be recognized by the retarded child and become anxiety-provoking to him personally. Consider this problem for a moment. The basis on which we look at ourselves and consider our personal worth is in large measure according to our own personal achievement. If you think of yourself as a capable student, runner, ball player, husband, father, or hunter, it is because you can identify others around you who are worse at these professions or avocations. In terms of those individuals you know, in your opinion you consider your level of achievement to compare well with their performance. Your perception of yourself, however, is shaped by another type of dynamic interaction which has particular relevance to this discussion. In addition to the direct comparison you make with others, your view of yourself is shaped by how you think others look at you. If you believe that other people think of you as a poor basketball player, for example, and this opinion is sufficiently generalized among other people and over a period of time, in all likelihood you probably see yourself as performing at an inadequate level in that particular activity.

It is this latter type of psychosocial force that has potential for proving troublesome in parent-child interactions among the retarded populations. If the child's parents become intensely bothered about or depressed over his weak performance, and if the school fails to keep in touch with them about their child's progress and the extent to which he is reasonably satisfying well-planned

competencies, one could expect the parental anxieties to "rub off" onto the child's personality and, thereby, deleteriously influence his behavior. Every teacher of the retarded has at some time recognized either a positive self-concept or a negative self-concept in a retarded child as a direct reflection of his parent's attitude. In a large measure, then, the parents of retarded elementary-age children need to be exposed to a wide and varied spectrum of information which will help them to resolve their own personal tensions about their child and facilitate the development and maintenance of healthy attitudes which will be instrumental in enhancing their child's self-concepts.

There is one final thought on this issue that needs emphasis. If in their attitudes parents communicate to their child that education is unimportant, the youngster will quickly assume this same position. The result will be no respect at all by the child for the entire school experience or any aspect of the educational scene. On the other hand, if the child's family assumes an attitude toward education which is supportive, the child will see great value in the various aspects of the educational enterprise.

In addition to the many advantages that can ensue from an appropriate amount and type of communication among the parents, child, and school in those dimensions involving attitudes, it is important to recognize the other benefits of maintaining open channels of communication between the home and the school. The teacher and parents should both be interested in knowing about the behavioral characteristics of the youngster at home and at school. Comparing notes on these factors will enlarge the sample of representative behaviors collected on the child and (1) contribute to an evaluation of the validity of the program of management at home and at school, (2) lead to specific suggestions concerning an appropriate refocus of the home and/or school program, and (3) help the parents to more fully understand and support the school program.

Many parents of retarded children will be in a complete dilemma concerning such issues as those involving child rearing and the manner in which they can support or supplement the school program at home. They will inevitably turn to the teacher and her colleagues for help because these people are most often viewed as behavioral experts. It is very important that the parents be given advice from a proper and informed source in answer to their perplexing questions. The advice should be specific and as detailed as the parents require. It will be helpful for the teacher to demonstrate or illustrate the technique or procedures she is suggesting to the parents and, perhaps, have them redemonstrate the approach before they leave. The possibility of confusion should intentionally be minimized, and the parents should leave feeling free to consult with the teacher whenever similar issues occur.

Certain groups of parents will wish to supplement the school program by requiring their children to do homework on a scheduled basis. This is a rather obvious expectation from parents who are concerned about the progress of their

child during the school day. This inclination on their part has certain potential advantages if gingerly applied. With close cooperation and direction from the teacher, a parent can engage his child in a series of activities and experiences which will truly enhance the youngster's progress. It must be emphasized, however, that extreme care should be taken not to place the child in a pressured situation. If the child does not achieve, he soon begins to realize that his parents are disappointed with his performance, and this could inflame a variety of areas, including interfamily relationships, interest on the part of the child in attending school, eagerness to work on individual projects, self-care, and personal behavior. As simple guidelines concerning the engagement of a retarded youngster in school-like experiences at home, consider the following:

1. Check with the child's teacher concerning the advisability of working with the youngster at home. Get specific directions concerning what to do, when, how, and the amount of time to spend on each activity. It is essential that the school and home not work at cross-purposes.
2. Make every experience in which the child is engaged a gamelike situation, or at least make certain that the encounters are pleasant for him.
3. If the child acts negatively toward homework experiences, do not force the issue. This will serve only to exacerbate the problem. Under no circumstances should the youngster feel pressured to perform with the subtle hint, implied or assumed, that if he does not participate, his parent's love or support will be lost, or some other equally horrible type of reprisal will occur.
4. Be sure to look for loss of interest on the child's part and, forthwith, stop the activity or switch immediately to another. Do not make the sessions inordinately long; usually anything extending beyond twenty to thirty minutes will result in diminished payoff for both the child and for his parental tutor.
5. Place the youngster in situations in which success is guaranteed at first and then only subtly introduce progressively more difficult situations in which failure might occur to a small degree. Reinforce proper performances and ignore, or give minimal attention to, incorrectness. It is important that the child not learn how not to respond to situations, but instead that he learn and practice proper responses.
6. Never compare the retarded child with his peers in terms of achievement, level of attention, interest in participating in activities, or future status.
7. If questions occur concerning how a situation should be handled, stop the activity and seek the opinion of the child's teacher at the earliest moment.

Naturally, guidance concerning the educational aspect of a retarded child's life is not the only dimension on which parents are in need of assistance. Periodically review with parents is necessary on the total general plan for therapy, remediation, and education as further data become available. This procedure will allow the parent to gain some reasonable perspective on immediate and long-

range goals for their child as seen by their profesisonal counselors. It will also help them to gain a clearer appreciation of how their present and future situation and that of other members of the family can fit into various aspects of the planned educational and occupational programs for their retarded child. Finally, keeping the parents informed will help them to establish or reestablish more realistic goals for their retarded youngster. So frequently parents of the retarded elementary school-age child have totally unrealistic expectations for their youngster in spite of the direct attention given by many professional workers toward helping them fully appreciate the real status of their child's development. These unrealistic hopes must be promptly dealt with as soon as they are discovered. Feeding information to the parents about their child's progress, the school's program of instruction for him, and future plans will help the parents to gain a realistic appreciation of their offspring's level of performance. It will also help to "set the stage" for clearer thinking on their part concerning the child's future situation as he moves toward adolescence and young adulthood.

Recommended Readings

Begab, M. J.: "The Mentally Retarded and the Family," in I. Philips (ed.), *Prevention and Treatment of Mental Retardation,* Basic Books, Inc., Publishers, New York, 1966, pp. 71–84.

Kirk, S. A., M. B. Karnes, and W. D. Kirk: *You and Your Retarded Child: A Manual for Parents of Retarded Children,* The Macmillan Company, New York, 1955.

McDonald, E. T.: *Understand Those Feelings,* Stanwix House, Pittsburgh, 1962.

Wolfensberger, W.: "Counseling the Parents of the Retarded," in A. Baumeister (ed.), *Mental Retardation: Appraisal, Education, and Rehabilitation,* Aldine Publishing Company, Chicago, 1967, pp. 329–400.

———, and R. A. Kurtz: *Management of The Family of the Mentally Retarded,* Follett Publishing Company, Chicago, 1969.

5
The Mentally Retarded Adolescent

What are some characteristics of mentally retarded junior and senior high school youngsters?

Adolescence is a particularly perplexing period for most young people. It is a time when an individual is trapped in a horribly complex overlapping situation. On one hand the individual's physical systems are racing ahead into adulthood and his psychosocial desires and interests are more akin to those of adults; on the other hand the experiential immaturity and naïvity of childhood is obviously present and is often totally incongruent with the individual's adult-like characteristics. This highly polarized, ambivalent situation that depicts most adolescents is a source of great personal strife and often results in patterns of significant social, emotional, and family disorders among intellectually normal teenagers.

Consequences of Unsatisfied Needs   The intensity and types of problems peculiar to adolescents are magnified many times for those youngsters with mild degrees of mental retardation. They face the usual issues and difficulties experienced by their intellectually normal peers; in addition, the mentally retarded often find themselves in a more complicated situation. To be more specific, the retarded teenager has the same feelings, attitudes, and desires as other children his chronological age. His social desires to interact with peers, to

actively engage in usual teenager activities, and to be considered a valued member of a group are usually more closely affiliated with "life age" than mental age, especially for those with mild degrees of mental retardation.

Holding this thought for a moment, next consider the potential serious consequences of failing to be able to solve various types of practical, day-to-day problems in a satisfactory way; of not doing well enough in school to be included in the mainstream of the educational program; being of generally smaller stature, less physically appealing to the opposite sex, and relatively weaker; of not being looked up to by others as a leader or as leadership material; and of never being sought after or intentionally selected by those other persons whose opinions and attention are generally valued. And so, the dimensions of this powerful discordancy unfold with definiteness. On the one hand there are the strong social needs, which in some retarded children may be more pronounced than in their normal peers who have tasted the sweet fruits of social success. At odds with this natural need are those cognitive inadequacies which restrict the retarded adolescent in satisfactorily responding to problems and issues. Whether the inappropriate or inadequate solutions are of a social nature or not, the consequences are identical, viz., loss of prestige, support, and value in the opinions of the youngster's nonretarded peers. Perhaps Figure 5-1 will help to clarify some of the dimensions of this issue.

If a retarded adolescent is unable to satisfy the normal needs and desires that are associated with this age of development because the physical, social, and/or personal barriers that are constructed by himself or by others are too imposing,

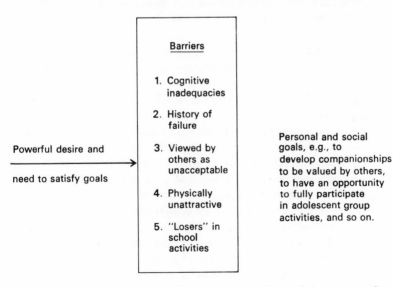

Figure 5-1   *A way to view problems characteristic of adolescent retardates.*

if his needs are of sufficient strength to result in continual attempts on his part to try to satisfy them, and if he is constantly frustrated in his struggle to achieve, an enormous amount of psychological tension can be expected to follow. The result of this type of situation is that maladaptive behavior becomes noticeable with increasing frequency and magnitude as the frustration levels rise. When normal social needs are blocked for some reason, retarded adolescents will then develop unacceptable patterns of social behavior as a definite style and/or manifest significant emotional disorders. For example, behavior such as the following could be expected according to one's level of frustration and degree of intellectual retardation:

1. Overt expressions of aggression directed toward those individuals who play a major role in causing the retarded teenager not to achieve social desires.
2. Overt and/or passive aggressive acts toward things or institutions within his environment which he feels are contributing to his frustration, e.g., the school, the bus, or the lunch program.
3. Aggressive behavior directed toward himself because he blames himself for not being able to achieve a need or desire and feels that self-punishment is a proper or at least a satisfactory reaction to the frustration. These acts could include physically hurting himself, self-derogatory remarks, self-pity, placing himself in jeopardous positions where injury can occur, and so on, thus calling attention to himself.
4. Sullenness, withdrawn, and/or isolationistic behaviors resulting from not being able to accomplish a satisfying level of social interaction and status.
5. Substitution of a desired goal or approach to satisfying a goal in place of usual social desires and practices.

There are then opposing forces at work in the life of most adolescent retardates. On the one hand there are the intellectual inadequacies; on the other hand there are the expectations which the child has for himself and those which others have for him. The sum of the forces in this dissonant situation is the emergence of involved and damaging secondary traits which impede the effective processing of information on the part of the teenager and hamper the development and maintenance of all aspects of the processes involved in problem solving. Secondary characteristics which are frequent among teenage retardates include a low tolerance for frustration; unwillingness to consider new ideas, approaches to a problem, or engagement in new activities; regression to earlier more satisfying and successful styles of behavior; a relatively more keen awareness of how not to deal with problems as opposed to proper and successful solutions to situations; low concepts of self-worth, ability, and chance for success; and a general lack of spontaneity.

As the retarded individual approaches and proceeds through adolescence, these secondary characteristics become more obvious, complicated, and difficult to

deal with in direct proportions to the extent to which the two forces, mentioned in the preceding paragraph, have operated throughout the child's earlier years. If, for example, the child's parents have continuously expected higher levels of achievement from the youngster than he was able to deliver, one could reasonably expect to observe serious and extensive side effects in the form of secondary characteristics. In contrast, if the child's parents and/or teachers describe reasonable expectations for the youngster according to his intellectual resources and other personal characteristics, it would be more common to see a child of this sort with less obvious and relatively more simple secondary disorders. Explicitly, attention then should be given early in the management process to the precipitants of and procedures by which secondary characteristics might be controlled and eliminated, if at all possible.

Self-concept   Throughout this book mention has been made about the need for parents and others to be attentive to the self-concept problem so prevalent among the retarded. In the last chapter it was pointed out that one's concept of self develops, to a large extent, on the basis of direct comparisons the retarded child makes of his performance with the performance of others. Secondly, self-concept is formed according to how the retardate believes others view him. If he thinks other people look at him as inadequate or incompetent, and he values their judgements, he will begin to view himself as an inadequate or incompetent person. These psychological-social dynamics are particularly powerful and influential in those situations and areas in which the youngster believes a satisfactory performance is irrefutably necessary. So, if he has been led to believe that a certain level of reading achievement is vitally important, and he is unable to perform at this level, he will become a candidate for self-concept problems.

To a large extent, self-concept is related to the degree to which the retarded teenager has experienced success and to how many continual encounters with failure have been a part of his earlier development. This implies that the types of goals which the individual has imposed on himself, or accepts for himself, will tend to enhance or detract from the establishment of a healthy view of self. If the goals are too long-range, too difficult to realize, or improper, and modifications in them do not occur, the child will perpetually fail and lose faith in himself and in his ability to subsequently perform in a reasonably satisfactory way.

Social Difficulties   Mentally retarded adolescents often have social problems ranging from the normal difficulties almost everyone has in getting along with others to serious misdemeanors. The range of social disorders is the same as those for the average population; however, the mildly retarded population tends to be slightly diverted in the direction of a relatively higher incidence of social disorders. This, of course, is not unexpected, for such increases in social misconduct can be explained by the retarded:

1. Frequently not realizing or understanding the difference between right and wrong behavior
2. Being relatively more prone toward misunderstanding or forgetting
3. Not having experienced a wide range of social situations which offer opportunities to practice appropriate responses
4. Being told how not to behave with greater frequency and intensity than what constitutes a proper manner of behavior
5. Being more apt to be "taken in" or "used" by unscrupulous individuals, who want to find someone to do their "dirty work" and take risks
6. Seeming to be more susceptible to the belief that the easiest way to get something is the best, most appropriate practice to follow

The fact that retarded teenagers tend to be more responsive to affiliating with others who are troublemakers, ruffians, or agitators can be accounted for using the behavior modification model which was discussed in a general way in the first chapter. The chain of reasoning on this issue is as follows. Assume that behavior will increase in frequency and intensity following a reward which is personally satisfying and decrease in frequency and intensity when no reinforcement is offered or a type of punishment occurs after the behavioral incident. For many retarded teenagers, attempting to behave in socially proper ways has not been a rewarding experience at all. Indeed, for many, the whole situation surrounding attempts at manifesting proper behavior is usually followed by statements by others suggesting personal disappointment at the retardate's exhibiting such a low-level attempt at proper behavior, offering no feedback or ignoring the child following a response, or directly punishing the child for not operating at what they consider to be "his real ability level." The result of this type of management practice is that the child is literally "turned off" from subsequently attempting to approximate the final goal which others have set for him in areas of social development. A principal error parents and teachers make is that of not reinforcing successive approximations as the child approaches the goal.

This same situation often prevails for the retarded in social interaction with intellectually normal peers. To the normal child, the retarded youngster is usually not particularly deserving of reward. The normal child ignores, or at least refrains from rewarding, proper behavior exhibited by the retardates. This occurs for at least two possible reasons. First, the normal child will usually have higher criteria for acceptable social behavior than can reasonably be expected of the retardate and, thus, will be intolerant of clumsy, imperfect performances. Second, many normal children consider it to be of low potential in terms of social prestige with "those who count" to affiliate with someone, like a retarded teenager, who is "different" and not a readily accepted member of a desired social clique. In fact, for some teenagers who are especially conscious about their social

status, alliance with a retarded colleague will result in their being banished from a valued social group.

To satisfy their normal adolescent needs for social attachments many retardates will actively, and quite naturally, seek out persons who either overlook or are not critical of their social faux pas. This results in many retardates becoming members of antisocial groups who are without scruples and good intentions. The retarded youngster is used to carry out "missions" and, if successful, is rewarded by being given attention, tangible reinforcers like money, and promises for the future. For once in the lives of many teenage retardates they are stars and valued. They have been successful, and this is rewarding in itself. The whole pattern, then, emerges into more frequent and larger varieties of delinquent acts by the relatively naïve retarded teenager. You can see how contrasting the two social situations are when one views them from a reward-punishment–behavior-modification perspective.

There is relatively no solid evidence to suggest that mentally retarded adolescents have a higher incidence of sexual perversion than one could expect to find among other populations within our society. Obviously, the degree of mental retardation is related to the incidence of self-play, masturbation, and other similar varieties of behavior. Within most institutions instances of open self-play occur with great frequency without the residents sensing any social ramifications of these acts. In order to protect themselves from self-destructive types of behavior, many severely and profoundly retarded residents must be placed in restrictive devices.

School Learning Problems   To a very broad degree the learning characteristics of mildly retarded teenagers are similar in pattern to those youngsters who have been discussed in previous sections. As a group they seem (1) to have difficulty using abstractions in solving problems and tend to resort to concrete reference points, (2) to be relatively poor in use of verbal symbolizations as opposed to their usual level of functioning in the manipulation of nonverbal stimuli, (3) to lack powers of generalization and transfer, (4) to have a weak repertoire of general information which they can call upon to deal with problems of living, (5) to be unskillful in generating possible alternative solutions to problems and evaluating the worth of each, and (6) not particularly eager to engage in school-related activities.

Many mildly retarded adolescents are in need of special remedial programs that are designed to alleviate the frequently expressed learning disorders which seriously hinder these youngsters in moving ahead in their school program. In spite of the fact that most educable retarded children can be expected eventually to read at around the fifth-grade level, perform the basic reading process in a satisfactory way, demonstrate a minimal level of competence in language and be able to deal with personal and social problems in a reasonably mature way, it is still clear that most school-age retarded teenagers suffer from specific learning and

behavioral problems that exceed those which directly result from mental retardation, per se. These two specific problems may be caused by poor teaching, inadequate diagnosis, exposure to a school program which is without sequence, emotional problems caused by undue pressure, and so on. Whatever the cause, these learning disorders are important enough to warrant intentional planning for their diagnosis, characterization, and remediation. When discovered and after being analyzed, proper instructional modifications must be made in order to minimize their impact and control their future development.

This section has briefly reviewed some of the more global characteristics of retarded adolescents. Emphasis was given to those youngsters who are usually located in educational programs. It should be realized that the retarded populations tend to become relatively more heterogeneous in their characteristics as the youngsters reach higher chronological ages. Thus, it is much more difficult to specify a unique trait as being peculiar to the mentally retarded teenager because of the relatively larger number of populations of which they are representatives.

Recommended Readings

Beier, D. C.: "Behavioral Disturbances in the Mentally Retarded," in H. A. Stevens and R. Heber (eds), *Mental Retardation: A Review of Research,* The University of Chicago Press, Chicago, 1964, pp. 453–487.

Blackhurst, A. E.: "Mental Retardation and Delinquency," *The Journal of Special Education,* vol. 2, 1968, pp. 379–391.

Goldstein, H.: "Social and Occupational Adjustment," in H. A. Stevens and R. Heber (eds.), *Mental Retardation: A Review of Research,* The University of Chicago Press, Chicago, 1964, pp. 214–258.

Quay, H. C., and D. R. Peterson: "Personality Factors in the Study of Juvenile Delinquency," *Exceptional Children,* vol. 26, 1960, pp. 472–476.

Sternlight, M.: "Fantasy Aggression in Delinquent and Nondelinquent Retardates," *American Journal of Mental Deficiency,* vol. 70, 1966, pp. 819–821.

What particular problems do parents face with a retarded adolescent?

The types and the degree of seriousness of problems faced by mentally retarded adolescents and by their parents depend on several factors. First, there are those obvious problems and issues that surface during the adolescent period which are largely related to this particular developmental time. Although physical growth and development are influential in giving adolescent problems visibility, the types, causes, and means by which the child deals with them are basically de-

pendent on factors such as the individual child's degree of retardation, family situations, previous experiences, concept of self, emotional adjustment, history of success and failure, and other variables, many of which have been touched upon in earlier sections of this book. It is this uniquely complex interaction that occurs among these and other dimensions which results in the problems of adolescents such as those involving sexual matters, physical unattractiveness, social acceptance, and a desire to become more independent and to have better control over their environments. To a great extent, then, the behavioral problems of a retarded adolescent cannot be entirely attributed to the child or to his condition, but they are as much a function of the family milieu which the parents have provided and the types of educational experiences which are offered by the school. As you might expect, as age increases the problems of the retarded adolescent become increasingly more complex.

The point was emphasized earlier that many retarded teenagers have significant social problems. For some, this comes as a result of their having too few chances at home to engage in social interaction with all members of their family. In some homes the retarded adolescent may be treated as a nonmember either by literally being required to remain in his or her room during periods when the family entertains; by being required to eat his or her meals at a separate table, at a different time than other members of the family eat, or with much younger siblings; or by not being allowed opportunities to learn the basic social amenities in a pragmatic way. Reasons for such treatment of the retarded adolescent by his parents may be that (1) they do not wish to present a situation in which they or their guests will be embarrassed, (2) they want to insulate their other children against possible social consequences occasioned by a social "goof" by the retarded sibling, or (3) they wish to protect the retarded child from being placed in a possibly uncomfortable social situation by potentially imperceptive persons. Whatever the motive of the parents, it should be obvious to you that their method for dealing with the situation is unfortunate and will probably do more harm than good for them and for their children.

Concerns of and for Normal Siblings   There are other potential family difficulties caused by a retarded teenager's presence with which parents must deal. I am referring to the possibility of certain members of the family becoming antagonistic or embittered over what they view as inequitable treatment and attention being given to the retarded child and not to them. It is difficult, indeed, for parents to be totally evenhanded in distributing themselves in what each person in the family would consider to be a fair way. The retarded adolescent in most cases will require relatively more attention than the nonretarded siblings. This fact will cause frequent disruptions in the balance of the family milieu and possibly result in misunderstandings and hard feelings. It is important, then, that parents direct their attention to this potential problem by intentionally including all family members in various activities; behaving in ways which communicate

to their children that their opinions, attention, and contributions to the family welfare are valued and needed; judiciously avoiding open conflicts between husband and wife over issues on which they disagree, such as what each parent believes to be appropriate procedures for managing the retarded member of the family; intentionally including the retarded child in all aspects of the family activities; and minimizing the importance of differences which characterize the retarded person in the family, focusing on what he or she can do in a reasonable way. Parents should recognize that the time may come when the family situation becomes so inflamed that professional advice is needed. These occasions should be predicted and proper counsel obtained by members of the family.

Of especial critical concern to parents of a retarded adolescent are those problems with which the intellectually normal adolescent siblings have to cope. These youngsters represent a particular population with very unique problems. Many of the normal siblings will not have worked through the psychological and social strains which prevail as a result of their family situation. These anxieties may be caused by jealousy; by resentment; by guilt feelings; and by lack of knowledge and understanding on the siblings' parts concerning what happens to their retarded brother or sister, when the situation occurs, how to deal with it, and the general prognosis.

Not only is the normal sibling faced with the fact that he has to learn to deal with his personal feelings about the condition and establish a reasonably acceptable style for interacting with the retarded sib, but he is burdened with the many social concerns which emerge more forcefully as adolescence approaches for him. For example, issues such as the following are common among intellectually normal adolescents whose brother or sister is mentally retarded:

1. In what way can I best tell my boy and girl friends about my brother or sister?

2. What information about my retarded sibling and our family problems and concerns can I discuss with my friends in an open way, and which of these problems and issues should I consider to be confidential and remain within the family circle?

3. How can I introduce my retarded brother or sister to some of my teenage friends so that he or she can enjoy fun and companionships without fear of being teased, taunted, or ridiculed, and without my having to fear becoming ostracized by my own friends?

Many times normal adolescents are able to consider and deal with problems with a clearer eye and in a relatively more forthright way than their parents. It is not atypical for certain types of teenagers to be more blunt in their consideration of issues and expression of concern on issues such as those caused by having a retarded brother or sister in the family. The following problems are illustra-

tions of the depth of individual concern which many young people have for their retarded brother or sister. Notice that these statements are focused on family variables which, if given proper attention by their parents, could be discussed, considered, and perhaps resolved.

1. What can I do to help my parents openly admit that my brother or sister is retarded and is in need of special help? How can I help them to candidly discuss their own feelings, concerns, and desires over this problem?
2. How can I help my parents realize that they are expecting too much (or too little) from my retarded brother or sister?
3. What is a reasonable way to make my parents realize that they are being too possessive of my retarded brother or sister and that this is causing him or her to become a more dependent person and alienating other members of the family? (This same type of problem occurs in those situations in which the retarded child is ignored by his parents.)
4. To what degree should my parents expect me to care for my retarded sibling, and what is a reasonable role for me to assume in this respect?
5. How far into the future am I going to have to be responsible for my brother or sister?

There are other concerns which intellectually normal teenagers have that suggest their need for certain basic information about mental retardation. In their opinion the direction of the answers to these issues have implications for choices that are available to them in their own personal and professional lives. For example, normal adolescents might be concerned about:

1. Should I marry and have children? Does the fact that a member of my immediate family is retarded increase the likelihood of any of my future children becoming mentally retarded? What are the chances of this occurring?
2. What will eventually happen to my retarded brother or sister? Should I consider my retarded sibling in any of my own future plans?
3. Can I depend on my parents to provide for me during my college years?
4. How do I tell when to seek professional counseling for myself, to recommend it for members of my family, and for my retarded brother or sister?

Notice that many of the questions which have been raised as illustrative of the types of concerns held by the normal adolescent siblings of a retarded child could be answered and resolved through an open, informed, and honest series of discussions among members of the family. In most of these cases the normal teenager requires some fundamental information, which if he does not receive will only result in him becoming confused; being especially susceptible to misnomers, inaccuracies, and suspicions; and developing an abundance of frustra-

tions and anxieties which could seriously damage his own mental health, social interaction effectiveness, and general performance in school. It is important for parents of retarded children to realize their obligation to aid their normal teenage siblings in dealing with these difficult and inevitable problems. They must provide ample opportunities for a dialogue to occur between all members of the family on any issue that bothers any individual. It is only in this way that problems can be resolved and potentially tense situations dealt with before they become so severe as to psychologically cripple any member of the family.

Lastly on this topic, there are parents who are concerned about the possibility of the retarded child adversely affecting the normal siblings, teenagers or otherwise. This is a concern in some homes for the following reasons:

1. There are certain impressionable intellectually normal adolescents who have specific needs which are not completely fulfilled. They may observe that their retarded sibling is getting a disproportionate amount of attention from other members of the family. This could result in the manifestation of abnormal behavioral patterns being developed by the normal sib as a way of attracting attention to himself and away from the retarded brother or sister.

2. There are those very concerned normal adolescent siblings who, for any of a variety of possible reasons, are so interested in the situation and future of their retarded brother or sister that they devote an inordinate amount of time and effort in behalf of their handicapped sib. This they may do with the total disregard for their own personal benefit, future, and pleasure. This type of behavior may not be a healthful reaction on their part, and the child's parents should be alert to the possible need for this normal sibling to receive professional attention.

School-related Responsibilities of the Parents   Ideally, parents of a mentally retarded adolescent should be actively involved in the whole process of preparing their child for the problems of adulthood. The attainment of the instructional goals which the school believes to be appropriate for each retarded teenager will be achieved with greater facility and less trauma, discouragement, and difficulty if the parents are able to support and supplement the school's program objectives and methods within the home. In fact, there are certain problems involving training and instruction which possibly can best be accomplished at home, but at the very least the child's family can reinforce the school's program objectives without too much burden. One of the important areas of concern in this regard is the need for the retarded adolescent to experience opportunities for independently making decisions. As adults, most mildly retarded individuals can be expected to perform independently in various social and vocational areas; it is therefore essential that they be given the necessary instruction and experiences to aid in the development of a style for solving problems

which will serve them well throughout adulthood, irrespective of the nature of the problem demanding their attention.

The adolescent period for a retarded child is as important to vocational as it is to social and emotional development. During this time period the youngster begins to practice using the tools with which he has developed some measure of competence and understanding during his earlier school years. The means by which this evolution from emphasis on tool subjects to occupational practice within the school program takes place will be considered later on. This whole area is introduced here simply to point out the ways in which the teenager's parents can help to support the smooth transition of the youngster into the beginning stages of occupational training and the later phases of relatively more pure vocational education. So often parents are confused about their proper role throughout this process.

At the outset, we may as well admit that few if any standards have been adopted on this issue. Some schools and teachers would be especially grateful to receive the moral and tangible support of parents in this regard; at the same time other school systems and teachers would prefer that the parents remain relatively free from obvious involvement. A commonsense approach on the part of both parties seems to be most reasonable; i.e., close consultation should occur between the home and the school concerning the child's status on occupationally related matters, the tentative indicators and contraindicators concerning specific occupational training, the short and long term goals which are reasonable for the child, the predicted sequence of events in an occupational sense, and the specific ways in which the home and school programs can work together to train the child toward similar goals using methods which are proper, compatible, and most parsimonious. As a concluding thought it is important for the parents to closely monitor how well the child is developing the social and vocational skills that are within the scope of the school program and appropriate for his particular age. I am not suggesting an "undercover operation" in which constant surveillance on the part of the parents takes place. It is reasonable, however, to take the position that the parents have a duty to see that their child receives a reasonable school program—one which provides the teenager with proper experiences leading to the development of those competencies necessary for becoming as self-sufficient a person as is humanly possible.

The parents' responsibilities go beyond the simple monitoring of the child's program at school. The home program should foster in the adolescent the establishment of proper work habits, assuming responsibilities for completing a job, taking the initiative and working alone, getting along with other people while at work, and demonstrating willingness to participate in distasteful but necessary tasks. This means that opportunities need to be provided at home for the child to work under a somewhat controlled setting on jobs that will gradually allow for the building of confidence on his part and progressively more complex skills.

An important factor for the parents to realize is that they should not impose too much pressure to achieve a certain level of excellence. A fine line exists between a proper level of encouragement and a totally volunteer environment in which the child elects whether or not he wishes to participate. It is impossible to delineate where this line exists for retarded teenagers, because of their individual differences and the changing character of their dispositions, skills, successes, failures, and the previous ways in which the parents have elected to manage their child's behavior.

In many communities, local, state, federal, and private agencies of various types are available to provide services, resources, and support to retarded teenagers and to their parents whenever necessary. Unfortunately, many people who can qualify for such services are either unaware that they exist or hesitant for some reason to make use of them. This is very unfortunate since their principal mission is to do whatever is necessary to assist the retardate and his family during periods of particular crisis. The retarded child's parents should not be shy about taking the initiative to seek out these agencies, initiate the necessary contacts, and determine what assistance they can have made available to them. It is wrong to assume that someone else will make the contact with the agency for them, that it will happen automatically, that they will not qualify because the father of the family makes too high a salary, or that a physician has not referred them for services and therefore they do not qualify. Indeed, it may be the case that a parent, family, or teenager will not meet the minimum criteria for having the benefit of the services of an agency; however, parents should explore every possible avenue to make sure that their child has the best planned and implemented program available. Among the types of agency services which are often found in a community and available to the retarded and to their family are those which offer (1) family counseling services, (2) medical diagnosis and therapy, (3) work-study programs, (4) family nursing services, (5) day-care facilities, (6) services of a housekeeper for families in temporary crisis situations, (7) psychological and psychiatric services of various types, (8) financial and tax advice, and (9) religious counseling.

Sex Education   Few other issues are more frightening to parents and approached with greater trepidation than those dealing with sex education. This is a subject on which you can be sure to get strong opinions expressed by almost anyone. Members of school boards, teachers within the same schools, PTA members, junior and senior high school students, politicians, and even husbands and wives are often found to be in conflict, at loggerheads, and at opposite ends of the spectrum of opinion concerning the matter of who should offer sex education to school children, when should it occur, and what nature should the content take. The relationship between home instruction and school instruction, and the particular responsibilities of each, is at the heart of this controversy. In the discussion here, these issues will not be considered. Not that they are not im-

portant; however, the intent of this section is to focus on certain other "knotty problems" concerning sexual matters which are unique to parents with retarded adolescents and, then, to suggest possible ways in which they might react to and deal with these matters in a reasonably healthful way. Those of you who might be interested in reading about the wide issues involved in providing sex education in the public schools may wish to refer to Collier (1968), Ginott (1969), Arnstein (1967), Lorand (1965), Pike (1965), and Gendel (1968a, 1968b).

Sex education for the mentally retarded, and for any other child for that matter, begins much earlier than during the teenage period. It starts with the kinds of attitudes which the parents bring to their marriage and the nature of their own behaviors and those which they accept by their children in the home. If the parents consider matters having to do with the physical body and the normal functions in a light which suggests shame, unestheticness, total secretiveness, embarrassment, "not to be enjoyed," "not to be touched," "sin," "dirty," "smelly," "disgusting," and so on, then it is very likely that their offspring will adopt a similar attitude toward his own body and its normal processes. In contrast, if parents are open, responsive to the questions of their child about his body and its functions, considerate of their child's interest in exploring his body, not impatient or disgusted over issues dealing with elimination, frank in establishing rules for privacy, and not overprotective of the child, then one might reasonably expect the child to feel free to frankly discuss with his parents his own concerns, feelings, misunderstandings, and needs regarding sexual matters.

There is no question that the problems surrounding sex education are complicated. There is also no doubt that parental attitudes have an important influence on the direction of a child's motivation for knowledge about, attitudes concerning, and control over his sexuality. These parental influences are inextricably bound to the family styles and habits regarding activities around the home and the manner in which parents deal with and react to matters dealing with the body, elimination, nudity, privacy, peeping, questions about sexual matters, and so on.

Sex education for the retarded should go well beyond considerations of matters such as the sex act, conception, reproduction, birth, menstruation, and nocturnal emission. Nor are the proper motives for providing sex education for retarded adolescents those aimed singularly at controlling sexual behaviors which are considered socially improper and minimizing the possibility that pregnancy will occur or that diseases will be caught. The more rational reason for providing sex education for retardates is to help them learn more about themselves and the expected role and associated behaviors of males and females in our society. Naturally, this broad objective should involve somewhat more detailed and pointed instructional sequences dealing with bodily functions related to sexual matters at the proper time. The point of particular importance to be stressed is that an error is often made in viewing sex education programs as constituting only emphasis on sexual intercourse, reproduction, and other related topics.

It is not possible to provide a single procedure for parents of retarded teenagers to use in dealing with issues concerning sex education. As with other areas of instruction, the child's level of retardation, interest in the subject, background of experiences, and family situation suggest that the focus and scope of every sex education program at home or at school will vary accordingly. Perhaps one of the most helpful sets of general guidelines for parents of retarded children who are interested in providing an effective environment for the development of a basic understanding and healthy attitude toward sexuality has been offered by Gendel (1968b). In reflecting on some of the essential components of a home and school program on sex, she feels that the following should be included:*

1. The idea that love and affection nurture a sense of self-worth for the child and enhance his life experience at whatever level it occurs.

2. The concept of responding to a child's curiosity and questions about sex to be answered at any age. Parents should not evade or dismiss them but should answer directly and honestly. When the parent truly does not know the answer he should let the child know it and proceed to find the information he needs and share it (Gendel, 1968a). Concise, brief answers are the most meaningful, and will have to be repeated many, many times. The main point to stress is that learning about sexuality is a part of the general learning process, no matter how slowly it may progress or how poorly it seems to be comprehended. Granting the child the dignity of receiving an answer to his query helps to create a healthy attitude—whereas discomfort and evasion by the parents is interpreted by the child as rejection of himself as a person. It also places a special connotation on sexuality associated with the rejection.

3. Parents must also feel free to initiate discussion on sexuality whether or not questions are ever asked. Having acquainted themselves with expected developmental tasks they can make use of discussion of neighborhood and family pregnancies or other events as they occur, to bring about the dialogue they wish to elicit. Animal families are not as good for discussion as the retarded child has limited capacities in relating one subject to another—or in interpreting concepts from one area to another.

4. A knowledge of sex-related behaviors such as masturbation, which may begin for the younger 4–6 year old as a pleasurable exploration of the genitals along with other body areas represents one example of the confrontation parents must experience.

    They need to know that this activity is normal and not limited to mentally retarded children. That it cannot harm the child physically or mentally. When practiced to an excess of total preoccupation for most waking

*The suggestions, numbered 1 through 11, which appear on the following pages have been quoted directly from the following source and are presented here with kind permission of Dr. Gendel and the National Association for Retarded Children: E. S. Gendel, *Sex Education of the Mentally Retarded Child in the Home,* National Association for Retarded Children, New York, 1969, pp. 5–9.

hours, it is a symptom of anxiety and other problems—it is not a problem per se. Ordinarily as children grow, their interests broaden, and they may not experience this intense urge to self-manipulation for release and pleasure until puberty and thereafter. As their socialization with peers and with adults outside of the family expands, they can be taught that masturbation, like toilet needs, must be taken care of in private. Most retarded children who are adapting to the culture recognize, for instance, that it is not acceptable for them to urinate in public. The same kind of learning or training can be acquired concerning masturbation. Parents of both normal and retarded children are asked to follow the most difficult advice which can be given—to ignore the masturbatory activity to overcome their own reactions of fear, or shame, and to resist punishing or threatening their children or "falling apart" themselves.

5. Earlier reference was made to keeping the family patterns of modesty, privacy and/or openness about sex, or about states of dress, or bathroom habits unaltered in any radical way. Only where excessive overstimulation or frightening restriction are the family styles should parents be counselled toward changes.

6. Creating a feeling of trust of the child's abilities as they manifest themselves is critical to his concept of being male or female.

7. Listening to his concerns about family roles, to the impressions he has received about sex from other children is an important part of the parent's support. Much of the peer-group gossip will have little meaning for the mentally retarded child but the manner in which the other children relate it, the vulgarized responses often displayed by them, will influence his impressions of sexuality. He cannot be shielded from these contacts as they are the experience of living—but parent's sensitivity and anticipatory explanations are helpful in maintaining respect for the human body and its functions, and for people as individuals.

8. Parents also cannot isolate the child from the mass media sex messages of our time. Rather than bemoan their influences—especially since we do not know their effect, we must accept them as the "real world" and assist the child in strengthening his positive responses to the sexual scene (Gendel, 1968b).

9. At puberty the tasks which are universal to all children must also be met by the retarded adolescent—assuming independence, identifying self, choosing a vocation and maturing sexually. Parents of normal and retarded children are equally concerned about this period. The mentally retarded child must have information and understanding of these changes to whatever degree he can absorb them. This is why simple information on body characteristics in a context of appreciation of self must be given as early as four or five years of age chronologically, to strengthen the child's self-concept.

Material presented objectively and in the early years of healthy curiosity can help to stabilize the social and emotional factors later. The adolescent boy hears about sexual intercourse, and experiences his own nocturnal emis-

sions and penile erections. The more prepared he is for the impact of these happenings the better he will cope with his own feelings. For girls, the circumstance of menstruation is so concrete that there is no hesitation in informing and training them for this event—but even here we often wait too long, and we narrow the idea to the mechanics of menstrual cycle. A sequential pattern of repetition and reinforcement is needed which will provide a foundation for both boys and girls upon which future discussions of social behavior, dating, marriage, and family planning can take place.

10. We are all familiar with the case of a child who has been living at home and has become accepted in the neighborhood and by friends for a number of years. At sexual maturity and the teen years he is suddenly looked upon by a previously accepting group as a less desirable associate because they suddenly recognize that the slow, pleasant child is now a sexual person whose judgment and impulses are limited. Their fears may not be justified but the child should be helped to understand the possibility of community reaction. He should learn that his sexual feelings are part of his makeup as an individual, and that everyone has them—they are not to be feared or characterized by shame or guilt, but to be understood to the degree possible.

11. In the post-adolescent years, parents who have tried to expand the knowledge of sexuality for themselves and their child are in a position to help them make the life decisions which lie in the future. Depending on the condition of retardation—but certainly in the mild cases—many retarded wish to consider marriage (Bass, 1963). They need all of the background and experience which they can handle to reach the most realistic and happy conclusions. The comfort and communication of marriage enhance the lives of many couples. Even the most successful adjustments, however, cannot tolerate the extra burden of children to care for. They need opportunities to be advised on contraception and sterilization. These decisions affect job aspirations, possibilities for independence from the family and for the further growth of potential as an individual.

For the subnormal adult, in the few studies which are available, marriage is common.

Planning for the Child's Future   For many parents of retarded children one of the concerns holding especial prominence as their child approaches the adolescent years is how best to provide for his future when they are gone. There are several facets of this whole issue to which parents must give consideration. First, it is necessary to provide for the child's financial support and the proper protection of the estate from which he may benefit as a result of the death of one or both of his parents. Second, the parents of certain teenage retarded children should begin planning to assure that the youngster will receive personal protection, comfort, love, guidance, and have his other basic needs supplied throughout his adult life. These two "wings" of a protection assurance program

require careful and detailed planning in order to mitigate the possibility of financial waste, grief and hardship, and emotional disorders occurring for the child as he approaches adulthood.

Many mildly retarded children will predictably be able to care for themselves and for their families as adults. For this group, a complex protection plan may not be necessary unless a large enough estate is left and there is some fear that the retardate may spend money unwisely or become prey to designing persons. In such instances, the child's parents may wish to establish a partial trust arrangement in order to assure that the rights, liberties, and resources of the retardate are protected as fully as necessary. For other relatively more retarded individuals, there is need for intentional planning for lifetime care.

A first step in executing a plan for the future care of the retardate is to seek the advice of an attorney in order to determine the type of options available to you, as parents, in the state in which you are a resident and to ascertain the procedures which are required to implement the option you select as being most appropriate for your situation and child. Usually it will be necessary to establish that the retarded child is mentally incompetent and does not have the capacity to handle his own affairs. The statutory definitions of mental incompetence, the provisions among various states, the means by which incompetency proceedings are initiated and conducted, and the definition of the term "incompetent" differ greatly among states and among jurisdictions. The purposes of the incompetency determination are similar, however, and are established (1) to safeguard the assets of the retarded individual who cannot manage his own affairs, and (2) to protect him by methods which are short of hospitalization or institutionalization.

Naturally, the process of going through an incompetency hearing is not a pleasant experience for most parents. It is an event on which one can procrastinate, but sooner or later parents face the fact that future planning must take place. There are wide differences in the nature of incompetency hearings and in the types of data required. Usually the evidence to support incompetency comes from medical, psychological, and social information which has been gathered on the basis of longitudinal evaluations of the child. The parent's attorney may request additional supporting data from other professional specialists by whom the child has previously been examined. Parents of retarded children usually elect to initiate this formal proceeding at some time during the late adolescent years of the child. This is particularly advisable in those instances where some questions may exist concerning the child's promise for self-sufficiency as an adult. There are always those "fine line cases" which suggest the advisability of waiting until the data are more obvious. In any case, however, it is desirable to obtain a judicial determination of mental incompetence prior to the child reaching age eighteen, if at all possible.

The second step in providing for the retardate who is incompetent to manage

his own affairs is for the parents to declare that a legal guardian be appointed. By doing so, the child's parents request that the court designate an individual, usually the parents' choice but not necessarily so in certain cases where the parents have died without a will or having established a guardianship, who is willing and able to protect the rights of the retarded and/or provide for the child's other needs. The legal guardian, then, assumes a responsibility which the child's parents have held during their lifetime. It is important to realize that various types of guardianship arrangements are possible, from those in which complete control over and responsibility for the management of the retardate is desired to those which involve a much smaller scope of responsibility, for example, in certain restricted financial matters dealing with investments or other business interests. It is also not required that the guardian be a single person; many parents choose to use a board of trustees, business partners, or members of an association in whom they have confidence as guardians.

It is important for parents of a retarded child to leave a will at death. This allows for the disposition of the parents' estate according to their personal wishes and provides the guardian with specific indicators concerning the plan that the parents prefer to be implemented for their retarded child. It is vital that the parents maintain an up-to-date version of their will at all times, and they should periodically consult with their attorney concerning the most advantageous methods available for dealing with the estate, the means by which their wishes for the retarded individual can be assured, and other important matters.

The other factors which parents of a retarded adolescent, adjudged to be mentally incompetent, must consider in arranging for his future are (1) how much life insurance they and their child should carry, (2) the advantages and disadvantages of the various savings plans available to them, (3) the advisability of establishing trust funds, (4) the extent to which government benefits are applicable in the case of their own retarded child, and (5) the degree of hospital insurance necessary for proper coverage.

In this whole matter of providing for the child's future, the parents should take every step and precaution to assure that no legal confusion exists between their desires and the determinations which have been made by the courts during the process of establishing mental incompetence and in assigning a guardian for their child. It is also wise for the parents to assure themselves that every possible legal safeguard has been considered for their youngster, and that he will be represented by a capable counsel should possible trouble or confusion occur later on. In cases of vagueness in the child's legal status, steps should be taken by the parents to promptly clarify any possible areas of legal concern.

In this section some of the major problems faced by parents of retarded teenagers have been reviewed and discussed. It should be realized by the reader that the genesis of many of these problems that were considered here occurs much earlier than suddenly during the teenage years. In many cases they are the con-

sequence of the parents not dealing with subtle hints of problems during the youngster's preschool and elementary school years. Certainly one vivid illustration of this point is the whole range of potential sexual problems which parents of retarded teenagers often encounter during this particular time period. As was pointed out, many of these troublesome issues which blossom during the teenage years could have been greatly controlled by the parents had they acknowledged them and begun dealing with them during those periods in which maximum growth and development occurred for the child.

Recommended Readings

Arnstein, H. S.: *Your Growing Child and Sex,* The Bobbs–Merrill Company, Inc., Indianapolis, 1967.

Bass, M. S.: "Marriage, Parenthood, and Prevention of Pregnancy," *American Journal of Mental Deficiency,* vol. 68, 1963, pp. 318–331.

Boggs, E. M.: "Legal Aspects of Mental Retardation," in I. Phillips (ed.), *Prevention and Treatment of Mental Retardation,* Basic Books, Inc., Publishers, New York, 1966, pp. 407–428.

Collier, J. L.: *Sex Education U.S.A.—A Community Approach,* Harcourt, Brace and World, Inc., New York, 1968.

Gendel, E. S.: *Sex Education of the Mentally Retarded Child in the Home,* National Association for Retarded Children, New York, 1969.

————: "Parents Are Human Beings," *Journal of the American Medical Women's Association,* February, 1968a.

————: "Sex Education Is Character Education," *Kansas Teacher,* March 1968b, pp. 23–28.

Ginott, H.: *Between Parent and Teenager,* The Macmillan Company, New York, 1969.

————: *Between Parent and Child,* The Macmillan Company, New York, 1965.

Jacobs, A. M.: "Legal Aspects," in J. Wortis (ed.), *Mental Retardation: An Annual Review,* Grune & Stratton, Inc., New York, 1970, pp. 250–261.

Lindman, F. T., and D. M. McIntyre: *The Mentally Disabled and the Law,* The University of Chicago Press, Chicago, 1961.

Lorand, R. L.: *Love, Sex, and the Teenager,* The Macmillan Company, New York, 1965.

Marino, L., and B. Green: *How to Provide for Their Future,* National Association for Retarded Children, New York, 1964.

Pike, J. A.: *Teenagers and Sex,* Prentice-Hall, Inc., Englewood Cliffs, N.J., 1965.

President's Panel on Mental Retardation, *Report on the Task Force on the Law,* U.S. Department of Health, Education, and Welfare, Washington, 1963.

How are mentally retarded adolescents placed?

By the time a mentally retarded person has reached the adolescent stage of life, ideally he should have been exposed to numerous diagnostic checks within the educational program. Unfortunately this desire is often not fulfilled, for many retardates are placed in different situations on the basis of scores from intelligence tests which were administered on only a few occasions. Obviously, this approach does not adequately respond to the issue of proper placement of a retarded person. Again, then, we must face the fact that a discrepancy often exists between the current, predominantly used method for deciding on placement and those which the literature suggests as being relatively more suitable and certainly within the limits of social and scientific acceptance. Consider some of the dimensions of this discrepancy.

First, it is a fact that many retarded youngsters are placed in special education programs, institutions, day-care centers, or even excluded from any of these, as a direct result of their having scored poorly on an intelligence test. It is equally true that many of the assumptions of intelligence tests and their administration are violated during the course of such evaluations (Neisworth and Smith, 1969). The upshot of this situation is that many young children are misclassified; most of the errors in classification probably result because scores have been reported too low rather than too high. Furthermore, in many school systems the continual reevaluation of the initial placement of a child is not a systematically executed component of the school program. Thus, many adolescents find themselves in a certain type of program as a result of (1) a placement decision made years earlier on the basis of scores on an intelligence test (which may not be accurate because it may have been misadministered, misscored, and/or misinterpreted), (2) not being consistently reevaluated at subsequent time periods with instruments which provide pertinent information about present and predicted achievement levels, and (3) being placed in a relatively irreversible "program channel" which does not allow for other placement alternatives.

This procedure for placement is in disagreement with present knowledge concerning the fallibility of using intelligence test scores as the sole determinant of one's potential or even his academic, social, and vocational needs. Of equal significance in the support of positions which question the advisability of using these methods for placement are the data which describe the great potential for change that can and does take place as an individual grows older and becomes exposed to environmental changes throughout his lifetime. The substantial alterations that can be expected to occur in physical, intellectual, social, and emotional areas are enough to warrant many individuals being reclassified, exposed to revised educational programs, and becoming candidates for a much different future than previously had been predicted. The rationale and evidence supporting

the arguments concerning individual change as a result of environmental intervention have been represented in an earlier chapter.

To summarize the problem, on one hand there is the unfortunate situation which prevails in many settings of a mentally retarded adolescent being irreversibly placed, or not being placed into a program of study at all, on the basis of data which may be suspicious, invalid, or unreliable. This method for placement and the consequences that emerge from it "fly in the face" of facts which authenticate the position that change in the characteristics, needs, attitudes, and future status of mentally retarded persons can be effected and that placement decisions which are too premature, which use inappropriate criteria, or which are beyond recall in the future should be artfully guarded against.

The placement problem is one facet of the whole issue of providing the most appropriate program of management for the mentally retarded. A position that has been emphasized throughout this book is that a specific plan of management must be decided upon for individual retardates and not for groups of persons, that any plan decided upon must undergo continual and systematic reevaluation, and that the only basis for deciding on a specific plan of management is the nature of the data which are obtained on individual retardates. We certainly should be satisfied with nothing less than those determinants in the formulation of curriculum and methods. In like manner, since the issue of proper placement of a retarded person is an instance of the general issue of management, we can only decide where and when certain placement decisions should be implemented after having first collected and analyzed information or data which are pertinent to these problems. "What kind of curriculum does he need?" "How should I teach him?" "Where should he be placed and when?" These important questions can be answered only after the psychologist or educator has arrived at suitable responses to the following questions: "What are his important and unique characteristics?" "What goals do I want him to be able to achieve and when?" "At what level is he presently achieving in those areas in which I want him to perform at increasingly higher degrees of competence?"

The placement problems are much more complex for the adolescent than they are for younger retardates. The effects of inept prior management on the part of teachers and others surface during this period and must be dealt with in an effective and expeditious way. For example, a certain number of junior and senior high school level retardates will inevitably have severe learning disorders or have remedial problems, which if properly attended to could be reduced in their seriousness. Not only does this pose a definite instructional problem in terms of the type of curriculum and methodology that is most appropriate for them, but this type of difficulty will be sufficiently widespread among most secondary-age retardates to affect the placement options available to the educator. Still other retarded adolescents may have problems which stem from previous management strategies as a result of their having been located in primary and intermediate

classrooms within which curricula were not clearly enough delineated in terms of sequence and scope to allow for full integration among various classes and levels; they may have been exposed to poor teaching because their teacher had not been trained to deal with the specific learning problems of the retardate or to apply an instructional methodology consistently; they may have been improperly placed as a result of an inadequate evaluative system used by the school system; or the youngsters may not have been exposed to a continual reevaluation of their performance which provides the logical documentation for effecting necessary program adjustments.

Since there is such great similarity between the factors used in deciding on an appropriate instructional program and those used to determine where a child might best be placed within the spectrum of available situations, and inasmuch as each of the factors have been discussed in some depth in previous sections, only a brief recapitulation of the most salient parts will be made here. What, then, is of especial concern in deciding on the type of placement for an adolescent retarded person?

1. The individual's characteristics including personal factors, socialization skills, emotional traits, levels of achievement in school-related subjects, competence in communication, and history of gaining from exposure to a systematic instructional program, are all important indicators of present and past levels of performance.

2. It is uniquely important during the adolescent years to try to predict the kind of future situation (occupational, personal-familial, social, and so on) in which the teenager will fit most comfortably upon reaching adulthood. This will have direct bearing on what constitutes the most appropriate placement circumstances for him.

3. Mentioned earlier, but certainly worthy of reemphasis, is the need to ascertain those areas in which the teenager is performing so low that special remedial programs will have to be designed and provided on a systematic and intentional basis.

4. The types of interest, needs, current pressures, and future desires of the youngster should be surveyed and seriously considered before a definite placement decision is formulated.

5. It is especially important to consider the specific goals or skills which are reasonable for the younger to achieve during the course of secondary school instruction as well as when he reaches adulthood.

6. Of no less importance than all the above factors is the need to survey what placement alternatives are available, the strengths and weaknesses of each situation, the degree to which the placement position will facilitate the accomplishments of the stated goals in terms of desired student behaviors, and the degree of congruence between the characteristics of each adolescent and those of the different placement situations.

The precise emphasis and possibilities for program breadth within the junior and senior high schools differ so widely among communities that it would not be meaningful to specify firm regulations or criteria for admission to and dismissal from the program. The broad guidelines outlined above should help to focus attention on the components of importance. The responsibility for gathering data germane to each of the areas belongs to everyone who has concern for a particular retarded adolescent. It should fall to the school psychologist or special education teacher to see to it that data from the parents, teachers, guidance counselors, employers, physicians, speech therapists, and others are collated, brought to the attention of those individuals for whom the data have especial meaning, correctly interpreted, and rigorously acted upon for the adolescent's advantage.

The discussion to this point has centered on the issues involved in placing the more mildly retarded adolescents who are usually more compliant with the program goals and existing instructional requirements of a special class situation. There are, however, several different types of retarded adolescents who are unable to profit from or gain admission to these educational programs. I am speaking of those youngsters whose parents believe that they should be placed in an institution for the retarded or mentally ill, those teenagers whose social behavior is so out of control that they or others are in jeopardy, and those trainable adolescents whose local community has not seen fit to provide the necessary programming to meet their needs. The placement problems for these groups of youngsters are as serious as are those for the less retarded group about whom we have previously spoken.

As in every other instance mentioned in this and in other chapters, one cannot intelligently make decisions about placement and decide on alternatives until information about the child, his situation, and promise for the future has been collected and deliberated upon. Then, one would want to survey the community and state to determine the range of services available for children who fall into these difficult placement groups. In each instance mentioned above, the indicators and contraindicators concerning institutionalization which were listed in Table 2-3 are appropriate for adolescents. Many parents with older, stronger, trainable children, or lower-level educable teenagers who constantly violate the law, find it impossible to deal with their offspring in the home and must face the inevitable fact of commitment to an institution. In certain instances this is not an unfortunate option, for certain institutions are able to provide a respectable social and occupational program. As was emphasized earlier, however, many of the programs are far from exemplary in the attention they give to the basic needs of the adolescent children for whom they have responsibility.

Finally, in those instances where institutionalization is not a viable alternative, it is very often possible for the adolescent to be placed in some form of a day-care center. Usually, however, states will admit only those adolescents who do not qualify for public school programs. If a child can gain admission to a day-care

center, it is very often possible for him to receive specific occupational training as well as instruction in other important tangential areas. If satisfactory progress is made by the teenage retarded person, it may be possible for him to eventually become employed in a sheltered workshop or in some other type of semiindependent occupational setting. In those situations in which parents face a "brick wall" concerning the evaluation of their teenager and the identification of possible placement sites, they can usually find help from such groups as community mental health agencies, the local chapter of the National Association for Retarded Children, or the Department of Maternal and Child Care in their state.

Recommended Readings

Goldstein, H.: "Issues in the Education of the Educable Mentally Retarded," *Mental Retardation,* vol. 1, 1963, pp. 10–12, 52–53.

Mayer, C. L.: "The Relationship of Early Special Class Placement and the Self Concepts of Mentally Handicapped Children," *Exceptional Children,* vol. 33, 1966, pp. 77–81.

Meyerowitz, J. H.: "Peer Groups and Special Classes," *Mental Retardation,* vol. 5, 1967, pp. 23–26.

Meyers, E. S., and C. E. Meyers: "Problems in School Placement Arising From Divergent Conceptions of Educable Children," *Mental Retardation,* vol. 5, 1967, pp. 19–22.

Neisworth, J. T., and R. M. Smith: "Fundamentals of Informal Educational Assessment," in R. M. Smith (ed.), *Teacher Diagnosis of Educational Difficulties,* Charles E. Merrill Books, Inc., Columbus, Ohio, 1969, pp. 1–29.

What issues are salient in the special education and rehabilitation of retarded adolescents?

In order for the continuum of special education and rehabilitation, from the preschool years into adulthood, to be maximally effective, a great amount of intentional planning and coordination must occur among many individuals and agencies. The philosophy underlying such a lengthy plan of management is most ideal and in reality is extremely difficult to fully implement. Aside from the practical problems involved in identifying the scope, sequence, and specific responsibilities of all who are involved in the total program, this type of comprehensive program is difficult to develop and carry out for another important reason. Unfortunately, most retarded individuals are identified for special education programming consideration sometime after their preschool years, and, moreover, they often become dropouts or are dismissed from the special education–

rehabilitation programs prior to adulthood. This situation places great strain on the total plan of management, for it requires that the system make available proper diagnosis and management at all program levels and on a continuous basis so that each retardate's needs are properly responded to and his future opportunities maximized for gaining self-sufficiency as an adult.

Focus of the Secondary School Program   As is true at each previous level of the education program, the junior and senior high school habilitation sequence has assumed antecedents. Adolescents who are matriculated into these secondary programs should have been exposed to earlier programs which helped them to develop a sufficient level of skill in prerequisite areas. The secondary instructors should not be confronted with retarded adolescents who need training in the various basic skills which have been reviewed earlier as being within the domain of the preschool or elementary programs. For example, no adolescent who has been involved in earlier phases of the management continuum should have undiagnosed visual or hearing problems, have inordinate or unattended to discrimination or memory problems, be unable to do simple addition and sub-traction, or be inordinately weak in interacting with his peers at an acceptable level. These and other foundation areas should be dealt with in a large measure during earlier program periods. It is, however, a fact of life that a substantial number of adolescent retardates reach the junior and senior high school levels without having achieved a minimum level of competence in various of these basic-skill areas. The schools must provide instructional sequences to handle these programs, although it is blatantly obvious that the time spent on this aspect of student needs subtracts from that available for other vocationally oriented com-ponents of the program. It is equally true that relatively less progress can be expected from this type of student in areas of particular deficiency because of the lateness with which the difficult-to-remediate weaknesses were identified and pedagogically attacked.

In order to grasp the general relationship that usually exists among the differ-ent special education-rehabilitation components of the secondary program and its evolution from the elementary sequence, direct your attention to Figure 5-2. This general time-line sequence shows that great emphasis is given during the late elementary school years and during most of the junior high school program in helping the mildly retarded children acquire skills and understandings related to certain important tool-subject areas. These areas were briefly considered in the previous chapter and include such familiar subjects as reading, writing, arith-metic, language and speech, social studies, spelling, and so on. Emphasis on the acquisition of specific skills in tool subjects diminishes relatively as the youngster progresses through the program into the senior high school years.

The second major focus during the secondary school years is on the area of occupational training, or vocational preparation, and on the broad area of sociali-zation. For most educable retardates general concepts and skills pertaining to the

world of work are intentionally introduced near the beginning of the junior high school years; for certain youngsters this may occur a bit earlier. At this time primary emphasis is given to how one can use the tool-subject skills in dealing with practical, personal, vocational, social, and family issues and problems. Parenthetically it must be understood that sharp lines of demarcation should not exist between the instruction dealing with tool subjects and that which emphasizes occupational and social training, as may be implied by the lines in Figure 5-2. Instructional activities and sequences should be planned to intentionally show students the various practical relationships that exist among concepts, skills, issues, and solutions characteristic of both major curricular thrusts within the secondary program. As the student proceeds through the senior high school years, notice that a relatively greater portion of his time is spent on vocational preparation and less on learning new academic skills, per se. A certain portion of the final years in the senior high school, however, should be devoted to remediating any particular tool-subject areas with which the retarded adolescent still has difficulty or may have acquired bad habits of execution.

To add relatively more specificity to the time line of curricular focus during the secondary school program for mildly retarded adolescents, the instructional areas of a number of respected programs in the United States have been listed in Table 5-1. There are other similar types of secondary program plans which are equally well considered and which should definitely be studied by those readers with a keen interest in this area (Harvey, 1964; Heber, 1963; Peck, 1966; Clark, 1967; Deno et al, 1965; and Neuhaus, 1965, 1967).

You have probably noticed that a great amount of stress is placed on occupational preparation during the secondary school program. This intentional emphasis is justified by the belief that the retarded person will view himself and will be viewed by others in a more positive way if he is gainfully employed. If unable

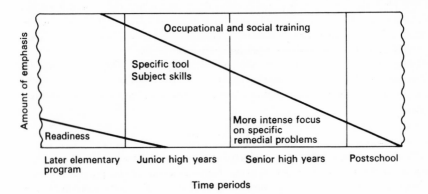

Figure 5-2 *Relative emphasis and relationship among components of the secondary school program.*

Table 5-1 General focus of selected secondary school programs for the mildly retarded

---

*The Texas Plan**

---

1. Levels 1, 2, and 3 are located in the elementary schools and are concerned with readiness as well as basic tool-subject instruction.
2. Level 4 occurs in the junior high school, and the students are engaged in activities which emphasize the following: (a) introduction to vocations including basic occupational information, social relationships, and the relationship of vocational proficiency to life situations, (b) certain manipulative types of activities, via art, industrial education, and home economics, which are incorporated into the program, (c) a functional rather than academic focus on the tool-subject skills, and (d) participation of the retarded adolescent with regular class peers in at least one comparatively noncompetitive class.
3. Level 5 also takes place in the junior high school and is an extension, with broader scope, of the types of activities focused upon in level 4. At level 5 emphasis is given to (a) the placement of a retarded adolescent on "work stations" within the school environment from which he will be able to gain experience in various social-vocational areas and be evaluated in terms of his dependability, tolerance for work, attitude, occupationally related weaknesses, relationships with others, and in his ability to accept and follow directions, (b) integrating various subject areas into a more occupational orientation and format, and (c) providing continual and more extensive associations with regular class students.
4. Level 6 occurs on the high school campus and is usually reserved for adolescents beyond age sixteen. It is characterized by (a) on the job training for part-day or full-day sessions in training stations on the campus and in the community, (b) particular emphasis is given to vocational evaluation, occupational planning, adjustment to the world of work, and the development of the full spectrum of skills required to effectively deal with the requirements of work, and (c) introduction to the vocational rehabilitation services available to the retarded adolescent.
5. Level 7 is the employment phase during which time is focused on securing a job, competing in the labor marketplace, behaving in a socially and personally acceptable fashion, dealing with specific job-related problems, using leisure time wisely, and becoming an increasingly more productive employee.
6. Level 8 is the postschool evaluation and follow-up period. During this time the vocational rehabilitation counselor keeps tabs on the retardate until he is satisfied that the client is functioning in an independent way and has a satisfactory prognosis.

The Fairfax Plan†

---

1. This program was designed exclusively for the senior high school level and, thus, is at three grade levels. When reported, it was an experimental program aimed at helping older adolescent educable-level retardates (a) to become more productive citizens, (b) to become more flexible and sophisticated in occupational areas, and (c) to view work, employment, and themselves in a more positive way.

Table 5-1   General focus of selected secondary school programs for the mildly retarded (*Continued*)

The Fairfax Plan (Continued)

---

2. In the first year the program focused on the following areas: (a) enhancement of oral and written communication skills with especial emphasis on their vocational applicability, (b) further development and applicability of arithmetic concepts associated with various jobs, (c) the primary functions of contributing citizenship, (d) remedial and/or developmental reading according to individual student needs, (e) introduction to hand and power tools, simple repairs, and individual industrial art projects (for the boys) and introduction to homemaking requirements and competencies, such as those in cooking, sewing, cleaning, and grooming (for the girls), and (f) regular physical education and recreation.

3. The second year of the Fairfax Plan emphasized the following: (a) continuation of communication with focus on letter writing, using the telephone, and interviewing for a job, (b) extension of earlier arithmetic programs to include budgeting, banking, insurance, taxes, and payment plans, (c) the required role and involvement of a contributing citizen within one's community, (d) factors related to seeking and gaining a job, (e) continuation of vocational training for boys and girls with involvement in more difficult types of activities including engine repair, welding, maintaining tools and equipment, auto body repair, appliance repair (for the boys) and machine sewing, nurse's-aides work, child care, nutrition, preparation of meals, and grooming (for the girls), and (f) regular physical education.

4. During the third year the tasks became more complete and the student expectations were higher. At this time the program was as follows: (a) emphasis was again given to the development of higher and more extensive skills of communication and reading, (b) a specific period was set aside for dealing with problems and issues which students need to resolve in order to become successful employees, (c) each student was encouraged to select an elective course (in consultation with an advisor) in which he was especially interested, and (d) every student was required to have four job experiences which were chosen by the student and his counselor and supervised carefully by special education and vocational rehabilitation personnel.

Southern Illinois Plan‡

---

1. The program suggested here is a four-year high school sequence. During the first year the retarded adolescent spends one period a day in each of three relatively academic areas—reading, arithmetic, and social studies. The content offered in these subject areas is integrated into the occupational focus of the remaining program during this period. Two periods a day during the freshman year are given to vocational information, and the same amount of time is devoted to the important area of prevocational evaluation.

2. In both the sophomore and junior years the students average half-time on a job and half-time in classroom activities. The classroom program is tailored to each student's particular needs, but it most usually involves the youngster carrying subjects such as language arts, reading, arithmetic, and social studies. The focus of the content in the classes is on the various requirements for securing and holding a job.

Table 5-1   General focus of selected secondary school programs for the mildly retarded (*Continued*)

Southern Illinois Plan (Continued)

Vocational information, vocational-adjustment training, or job tryout constitute the remainder of the program during these two years. It is not uncommon for students to experience six to eight different job situations during these two years.

3. During the senior year the student is placed in a vocational situation for four to eight hours a day. His performance is closely supervised by the schools, by his vocational rehabilitation program, and by his employer. Remedial courses in the tool subjects are provided by the special education program and are available to each student according to his individual needs. Any additional vocational training required is also available at the school, should the employer be unable to provide such instruction.

* Eskridge and Partridge, 1963.
† Capobianco and Jacoby, 1966.
‡ Kolstoe and Frey, 1965.

to secure a job the retardate will probably be a relatively less happy and well adjusted individual, have little or no social status within his family or community, be an economic burden to others, and be susceptible to patterns of social and personal misbehavior. Moreover, the economic consequences of an individual being unable to work and requiring care by agencies within the society are substantial (Wolfensberger, 1967). The position has been taken by most professional authorities that every attempt should be made to train and provide meaningful work opportunities for the mentally retarded at all levels of competence. It is the belief of Wolfensberger (1967) that any retardate who is capable of basic self-care can also be trained to work, albeit it may be in a somewhat sheltered environment; that adolescents who can perform arts and crafts activities should also be candidates for work training and experience; and that walking, speech and language, and incontinence problems are not satisfactory indicators of one's vocational aptitudes and promise.

If one adopts the position that every possible attempt should be made to prepare the retarded, and especially those with mild degrees of subnormality, to become gainfully employed, you can imagine the enormous array of problems that must be considered and resolved. For example:

1. In order to provide a full and proper program of training, the schools must provide appropriate prevocational evaluations of the adolescents who will be and are involved in the occupational training program. Further, continual reappraisals must be made of the youngster's performance and the degree to which the program is congruent with the individual's needs.

2. As alluded to earlier, there is no specific training program which is considered to be most appropriate for different levels of retardates. Not only is there spirited debate among work-study experts on the proper entrance and exit criteria to an occupational program and the sequence of experiences deemed advisable throughout the training, but the content of the occupational curriculum varies widely among individuals and school systems. For example, there exists professional disagreement on issues such as (a) should trainees be provided with work experiences which are relatively wide range or should they focus on a specific professional; (b) is it best to introduce the trainee to out-of-school work before the senior year or should that activity wait; (c) to what degree should the curriculum contain intentionally planned courses for the remediation of learning disorders, at what level of performance should the instructors be satisfied that further effort is unwise, and whose responsibility is it to see that appropriate remediation takes place; (d) to what degree, when, and how should actual work situations be simulated within the school before the trainee is placed on a job; and (e) should sex education be part of the secondary work-study curriculum?

3. To a great extent, the success of the secondary work-study program depends on how effectively the coordinators have been able to identify and establish relationships among employers. The recruitment of employers and developing and maintaining their interest and support are vital components of the work-study program. Payne and Chaffin (1968) have presented an approach which they use to establish good employer-school relations.

4. Introducing a trainee to his first job and providing the necessary follow-up are areas which require meticulous attention. There are many factors involved in judging when and where students would best be placed. The situation requires not only careful preparation of the employee but also of the employer and supervisor. Among the various specific problems to be considered are (a) the type of work expected of the employee, (b) the basis for pay, (c) the legal complications (such as those possibly related to minimum wage laws), (d) union demands and/or restrictions, (e) the possible need for an employee to interact with other employees or the public, (f) the accessibility of the employment site to the employees home, (g) the previous history of success with the employer, and (h) whether or not the work is of a seasonal nature.

Occupational Problems of the Retarded   If satisfactory placement cannot be found for the retardate, and if the worker is unhappy with the job or unstable in his employment, the training sequence and all effort behind it will have failed. At all levels of the secondary program, constant analysis and reanalysis of the employment scene in the environment surrounding the work-study program, as well as the general employment trend on a state and national basis, must take place. It is vital to the relevance and stability of the secondary program that the

influence of automation, employee competition, unemployment levels, types of jobs available or closed, long-range employment prospects, legislative conditions, government subsidy programs, and the possibility for and types of new industry be estimated and appropriate changes made in the program components to enhance the retardate's employment possibilities. A number of follow-up studies have reported on the occupational status of retardates who were formerly associated with a work-study program (Strickland and Arrell, 1967; Peck, 1966; and Gruenberg, 1964). Briefly, the major results of these studies are as follows:

1. The retarded are found most frequently in unskilled and semiskilled occupations, with the greatest proportion being associated with service occupations and factory employment. The prospects for successfully placing retarded trainees and employees in agricultural occupations is presently very dismal.

2. Automation has reduced the possibility of retardates being employed in certain jobs which heretofore have been available to this group; at the same time this event has created a certain number of semiskilled jobs which previously were not possible for the retarded to handle. It is difficult to estimate the proportion of gain or loss as a result of this development in various industries.

3. Longitudinal data reported on trainees from the Texas Plan (Strickland and Arrell, 1967) suggest the following:

   a. Within certain limits it is possible to identify which jobs mentally retarded adolescents can perform prior to their being placed on a full-time job.

   b. Following the Texas Plan, it is possible to place approximately 80 percent of the students in jobs for which they have been trained.

   c. Some trainees were placed in jobs for which they were not trained. They were unable to relate learnings from jobs for which they were trained to the jobs in which they were placed.

   d. Ten percent of the trainees required only counseling, guidance, and direct job placement in order to maintain employment productivity.

   e. Training and employment were equally successful for both sexes.

4. There is a higher probability of subsequent success with employers if the initial placement has been judged by the employer to be a positive experience for all parties involved. There is a clear need for coordinators of work-study programs to "lead" with their strongest candidates into new placement situations.

*The Role of Vocational Rehabilitation**   The fulfillment of a comprehensive secondary program which is designed to deal with the vocational and social needs of retarded youth necessarily involves the commitment of many

* Appreciation is expressed to Professor Gerald Robine for his counsel on matters related to vocational rehabilitation.

types of specialists. In addition to the various members of the school staff, every state in the Union offers counseling, testing, training, placement, and follow-up assistance to certain groups of disabled adolescents and adults, including the retarded, under the auspices of the Bureau of Vocational Rehabilitation. The intent of this program is to foster a situation and provide the basic necessities which will allow the retarded to become economically and socially integrated into their community.

The vocational rehabilitation services which are offered to the mentally retarded are supported cooperatively by state and federal agencies. Most state Bureaus of Rehabilitation are divided into districts, each of which has an administrator and several counselors. The counselors within districts usually specialize in terms of the types of clients each deals with. For example, a relatively large district may have a counselor for cardiac clients, one for the physically disabled, and another for mentally retarded youth and adults. In many districts a rehabilitation counselor may have responsibility for coordinating the services offered by the Bureau of Vocational Rehabilitation with those available from the schools. As you might suspect, this type of close coordination is desired and should be encouraged so that full continuity can take place between the various levels of services.

Certainly for the senior high school adolescent, as well as for the special education teacher, the rehabilitation counselor is a key person. It is he who will be able to help in the identification of training sites in the community; it is he who will be able to implement necessary vocational, psychological, and social evaluations which each child might require; and it is he who can provide the means for gaining any special training or management services which the schools cannot offer but which are needed by the youth for maximum integration to occur in the community. Most contemporary rehabilitation plans have positions for this type of coordinator who can bridge the gap between the schools and full-time work. This rehabilitation specialist has the responsibility for effecting an easy transition from special class placement to full affiliation with the Bureau of Vocational Rehabilitation. He also serves as an important agent for follow-up in order to assure that the retardate maintains his position and skills in the community and to check on the efficacy of the training sequence to which he has been exposed.

You remember that it has previously been mentioned that the development of prevocational skills is to be emphasized, along with certain academic competencies, during the junior high school special education program. At this time children are usually given some measure of responsibility for vocational duties within the school. They are encouraged to develop skills in following directions, arriving on time, accepting responsibility, getting along with others, and so on. It is at this time that the vocational rehabilitation counselors should begin to learn about their future clients. The special class teacher should contact the district office and begin a process of close collaboration with the agency. Data which the school has

should be shared and tentative plans made for future evaluative steps and possible management procedures.

By the time the retardate has reached the senior high school work-study program, the rehabilitation counselor should become a more active participant in the process. It is at this time that a full vocational evaluation should take place and all services offered by the various community and state agencies brought to bear on the problems of individual students. Through counseling, testing, and coordinating, the rehabilitation specialist and the special class teacher can establish training experiences and priorities which will be most appropriate for each youth. It should be clearly understood that the school has the principal duty to begin the process by introducing the prospective rehabilitation client to the Bureau of Vocational Rehabilitation.

There are basically eight phases involved in the plan of the Bureau of Vocational Rehabilitation. They all may not be required for certain disabled or retarded individuals who qualify for eligibility. Various combinations of these stages are indicated according to each individual's characteristics and employment requirements. Briefly, these stages are as follows:

1. The first stage in the process is locating the potential client and making proper referral. This should take place as early as possible but certainly before the individual becomes unduly exposed to an environment which fosters laziness, disinterest, hopelessness, or distrust of others. As mentioned earlier, it is possible for referral to be made to the Bureau of Vocational Rehabilitation by anyone, including the client himself.

2. The next phase involves determining the extent to which the client is disabled; it, in effect, involves establishing a characterization of the individual by means of physical, vocational, and psychological diagnostic procedures. The procedures usually involve interviews and examinations. A principal goal at this point is for the rehabilitation to draw some tentative conclusions as to possible successful jobs which might suit the client and match his interests, disabilities, strengths, and aptitudes.

3. The counseling and guidance phase is a continuation of the preceding stage. It dovetails into other components of the process as well, ending only after a thoroughly successful job placement has occurred for the client. The rehabilitation counselor will employ various strategies at different times in working with the client. These could include conducting intensive interviews, doing comprehensive case studies, formulating intensive vocational plans, making use of community resources for further evaluation of the client, and using occupational data from the community in directing the individual to consider reasonable vocational options.

4. This stage of the rehabilitation plan involves the provision of restoration and treatment wherever an obvious employment handicap exists. This treatment could include medical, psychiatric, and surgical services. Other care might involve

the provision of physical, occupational, speech, and hearing therapy; care in nursing or convalescent homes; and braces, artificial limbs, glasses, and hearing aids.

5. The possibilities for the training phase of vocational rehabilitation are unlimited. It could include almost any type of situation ranging from tutorial sessions in remedial reading to college-level instruction. The rehabilitation counselor makes every effort to identify and provide the most suitable occupational training for the individual client.

6. At this level money is often provided for tuition, books, material, transportation, adjustment training, workshops, licenses, tools, equipment, and even maintenance while in training and on the job. The degree to which these auxiliary provisions are made is a totally individual matter and dependent on the client's resources, needs and prognosis.

7. Selective job placement is the next step in the process. It could be effected in various ways, two of which are by the individual rehabilitation counselor or through some cooperative agency other than the Bureau of Vocational Rehabilitation. In certain instances the bureau will pay for tools, equipment, and supplies or stocks needed to initially support the functioning of the client.

8. The final step in the rehabilitation process involves follow-up of the individual for a reasonable length of time. If necessary, the bureau will provide additional medical attention or training opportunities to supplement the employment situation. Other types of adjustments, such as replacement of a client, will often be made during this follow-up period.

You can see that the Bureau of Vocational Rehabilitation provides a very valuable service to the community. It has the potential for offering comprehensive, individual, and selective services to many groups of mentally retarded persons. Unfortunately, the cases seen by most bureaus of vocational rehabilitation do not reflect that as much relative use is being made of the services it can offer for the retarded as for other groups of disabled adolescents and adults. It appears as if the major problem in this regard is at the referral stage of the process, which, evidently, is not the responsibility of the bureau but of other agencies and groups within the community who have closer contact with the retarded during the earlier years.

Recommended Readings

Capobianco, R. J., and H. B. Jacoby: "The Fairfax Plan: A High School Program for Mildly Retarded Youth," *Mental Retardation*, vol. 4, 1966, pp. 15–20.

Clark, G. M.: "A State-wide School-Work Program for the Mentally Retarded," *Mental Retardation*, vol. 5, 1967, pp. 7–10.

Deno, E., R. Henze, G. Krantz, K. Barklind: *Retarded Youth: Their School-rehabilitation Needs,* Minneapolis Public Schools, Minneapolis, 1965.

Eskridge, C. S., and D. L. Partridge: "Vocational Rehabilitation for Exceptional Children through Special Education," *Exceptional Children,* vol. 29, 1963, pp. 452–458.

Gill, R. C.: "Individualizing the Curriculum for Educable Mentally Retarded High School Students through Prevocational Evaluation," *Education and Training of the Mentally Retarded,* vol. 3, 1968, pp. 169–179.

Gruenberg, E. M.: "Epidemiology," in H. A. Stevens and R. Heber (eds.), *Mental Retardation: A Review of Research,* The University of Chicago Press, Chicago, 1964, pp. 259–306.

Harvey, J.: *Special Class Curriculum and Environment and Vocational Rehabilitation of Mentally Retarded Young Adults,* University of Alabama, University, 1964.

Heber, R. F.: *Proceedings of a Conference on Special Problems in Vocational Rehabilitation of the Mentally Retarded,* Rehabilitation Service Series Number 63–62, Vocational Rehabilitation Administration, Washington, 1963.

Kokaska, C.: "In-school Work Experience: A Tool for Community Adjustment," *Mental Retardation,* vol. 2, 1964, pp. 365–369.

Kolstoe, O. P., and R. M. Frey: *A High School Work-Study Program for Mentally Subnormal Students,* Southern Illinois University Press, Carbondale, 1965.

Neuhaus, E. C.: "A Unique Pre-vocational Program for Educable Retardates," *Mental Retardation,* vol. 3, 1965, pp. 19–21.

———: "Training the Mentally Retarded for Competitive Employment," *Exceptional Children,* vol. 33, 1967, pp. 625–628.

Payne, J. S., and J. D. Chaffin: "Developing Employer Relations in a Work-Study Program for the Educable Mentally Retarded," *Education and Training of the Mentally Retarded,* vol. 3, 1968, pp. 127–133.

Peck, J. R.: "The Work-Study Program—A Critical Phase of Preparation," *Education and Training of the Mentally Retarded,* vol. 1, 1966, pp. 68–74.

Peterson, R. O., and E. M. Jones: *Guide to Jobs for the Mentally Retarded,* American Institute for Research, Pittsburgh, 1964.

Shawn, B.: "Review of a Work-Experience Program," *Mental Retardation,* vol. 2, 1964, pp. 360–364.

Strickland, C. G.: "Job Training Placement for Retarded Youth," *Exceptional Children,* vol. 31, 1964, pp. 83–86.

——— and V. M. Arrell: "Employment of the Mentally Retarded," *Exceptional Children,* vol. 34, 1967, pp. 21–24.

Switzer, M. E.: "The Coordination of Vocational Rehabilitation and Special Education Services for the Mentally Retarded," *Education and Training of the Mentally Retarded,* vol. 1, 1966, pp. 155–160.

Wolfensberger, W.: "Vocational Preparation and Occupation," in A. Baumeister (ed.), *Mental Retardation: Appraisal, Education and Rehabilitation,* Aldine Publishing Company, Chicago, 1967, pp. 232–273.

What is the character of institutionalized adolescents?

The many problems that were cited in attempting to characterize the institution-alized mentally retarded during the preschool and elementary years are salient to this discussion. Even if it were possible to collect descriptive data on these individuals, it would be hazardous to interpret it in a way that would suggest institutionalized retarded adolescents as constituting a homogeneous population. They obviously are not alike in physical, psychological, and social factors because of the enormous disparity among these adolescents in individual constitutional dimensions and in the extent to which their early environment has been a facilitating one. The interaction of these two major forces, their impact on growth and development, and the implication each of these forces has on deciding the best way to deal with the mentally retarded have all been thoroughly discussed in previous sections.

The weight of the environmental forces in shaping and directing behavior among the adolescent retardates within an institution should not be underestimated. The age at which a youngster is placed in an institution and the kind of environment which the child encounters during his early years will direct his behavioral patterns and to a large extent dictate the favorableness of his prognosis. There are, no doubt, a significant number of adolescent retardates who have been placed in institutions that are lacking so many of the basic necessities, which most people assume are available to all individuals in our society, that the youngsters live in an environment which is seriously deprived. In fact, clinical observation of certain teenage retardates who are members of this type of institutional community suggests to many specialists that their intellectual performance actually deteriorates as they grow older. As a result, then, one might reasonably anticipate significant differences between those retarded adolescents who are placed at an early age into an institutional environment which has poor facilities, services, and programming in contrast to those retarded teenagers who, at the same age, became members of a much more progressive residential center for the mentally retarded.

Tenets of a Progressive Philosophy on Institutional Management Since the middle 1960s, there has been increasing public pressure exerted by individuals, agencies, commissions, and professional organizations for state and federal governments to begin providing optimum programs within institutions for the mentally retarded. There is a continuing suggestion in the professional literature that behavioral scientists have been able to describe the character of a facilitating institutional environment with respectable validity and reliability, but that the implementation of these concepts has not been realized because the whole issue is not a priority item for the governing bodies in most states and in pertinent federal agencies. Some of the topics relevant to this issue have already been dwelt on; however, since the consequences of living in a horribly lacking institutional environment are so severe and obviously manifested during the teenage years of

many retardates, allow me to briefly recapitulate some of the major objectives of particularly progressive institutions for the retarded, placing a special focus on those youngsters of adolescent years. The broad goals of these types of programs are:

1. To aid adolescent residents in developing increasingly higher levels of skill in solving practical problems with as much independence as possible and by using the competencies which they have gained as a result of exposure to a systematic formal and informal instructional program during their early years.
2. To aid retarded adolescents in developing those skills required to become involved in some form of occupational usefulness to the degree of self-sufficiency appropriate for each individual.
3. To aid the retarded teenagers in effectively dealing with personal, emotional, and social problems and issues with the degree of independence which is consistent with the character, needs, situation, and prognosis of each person.
4. To help the retarded adolescents gain a reasonable prospective on the proper use of leisure time.

Some of the means by which progressive institutions attempt to provide for attainment of these broad goals to some extent with each retardate are:

1. Making their institutional environment as natural and homelike as possible by placing residents in smaller, more homogeneous groups with house parents who live with the residents in individual cottages.
2. Increasing the contact which residents have with individuals in the community on all fronts—socially, in terms of services provided by and for the residents, shopping, school placement, religious training, and so on.
3. Introducing a full range of instructional experiences which are provided to youngsters at appropriate times and in appropriate ways according to the diagnostically observed characteristics of each resident.
4. Increasing the opportunity for teenagers, as well as younger children, to have wider natural experiences with members of the opposite sex in social, educational, and occupational contexts.
5. More actively encouraging and supporting the development and maintenance of those competencies which are appropriate for various types of institutional employees.
6. Encouraging realization on the part of the institutional staff that intelligence is a trait which can be developed to an extent which was not believed a decade or so ago.

The kinds of characteristics exhibited by institutionalized retarded adolescents, then, to a large extent will reflect the degree to which institutional personnel

have adopted and implemented a progressive philosophy of management. If this point of view is accepted and translated into practical programming throughout the institutional environment, by simply observing and talking with a number of adolescent residents almost any outside observer will be able to detect whether the institution has accepted a more progressive model or held to the traditional modes of treatment. Just recently, the author had an opportunity to observe similar behavioral incidents in two institutions, one of which might be viewed as relatively more progressive than the other. Both situations involved the need for a retarded adolescent to use the telephone for purposes of ordering a supply of food for six girls who were involved in a work-study type of program on the institution grounds. The young lady from the progressive institution was confident in what she had to do, had no trouble in executing the necessary steps involved in calling another party on the telephone, communicated her needs to the storekeeper in a proper way, and looked upon the event as not out of the ordinary or anything to be afraid of. The other young ladies involved in the program went about their business while Sandra placed her order; they had obviously experienced a full range of previous activities that led logically to the point where one might describe their behavior as being like that of any other adolescent with a similar type of responsibility. Ruth, the young lady with an identical duty to that of Sandra, manifested very different behavior under the same circumstances. Apparently, as a result of not having experienced a sequence of activities which was designed to prepare her for adultlike responsibilities, Ruth literally panicked over the thought of using the telephone. In spite of the beautiful lecture which was rendered by her teacher and fellow work-study students, Ruth could not bring herself to use the telephone, and, when asked, neither could her colleagues. You see, the differences in the behaviors between these two adolescents reflect the unique relationships each has had with an environment that is based on a philosophy of management that varies in significant ways from the other situation.

Institutional Sociology   You must recognize that the behavioral incident that has just been reported represents a whole syndrome of behaviors in which adolescents involved in the two types of institutions will differ. Those who are associated with a more restricting institutional environment will grow up to become adolescents who are institutionally bound—who are neither self-confident nor self-sufficient, who are unable to bring themselves to a point where they can carry on a conversation with adults or opposite sex peers, who do not have a minimum knowledge of or skills required for becoming self-sufficient, and who become totally dependent on others for almost every aspect of life. In a real sense, youngsters who are reared in such an environment are more dependent as adolescents and adults than one could reasonably expect had they been exposed to a more progressive program of management. In direct contrast, those institutionalized adolescents who are mildly or moderately retarded and who have

profited from a program which is more optimistic and progressively based will manifest characteristics in a general style of behavior which exudes confidence, self-esteem, and reflects the acquisition of many of the basic skills required for occupational and social self-sufficiency to a degree heretofore considered by many to be impossible. By the adolescent period the differences in the ways institutionalized retardates have been treated and managed during their most formative years are very obvious from their manifested behaviors. Whereas intellectually normal adolescents often build up a facade to cover up for weaknesses, the institutionalized adolescents are typically more obvious in demonstrating areas of weakness and less adept at using the normal adjustive mechanisms which all of us employ to hide our problem areas and psychologically protect ourselves.

A rather interesting sociological phenomenon apparently occurs in many institutions and particularly among higher-level adolescent populations. Marden and Farber (1961); Edgerton (1963); and Edgerton, Dingman, and Tarjan (1961) have discussed the various ramifications of the type of social system which develops and is maintained within an institution under the sponsorship of certain groups of residents and usually without any formal authorization or support from the institutional staff. Not much empirical and systematic research has been done on this aspect of an institution's character, but apparently the phenomenon is a larger and more complicated version of the one which many special education teachers have observed in classes of adolescent retardates. I am referring to the way in which members of the school class tend to label and classify each other according to their individual levels of intelligence, areas in which each can be depended on to be strong or weak, their social sophistication, and so on. Since the work of Edgerton (1963) is relatively comprehensive in its description of a social system which is active in one institution, most of the discussion on this point will come from his interesting article on the subject. Be sure that you recognize, however, that other institutions may not have the same type of social subsystem, may have a social system which is based on a different set of variables (e.g., homosexual-heterosexual dimensions), or may have no discernible social structure which has been established and maintained by the residents (Shelton, Schoenherr, and North, 1965).

Using a variety of behavioral science observational and evaluative techniques, Edgerton was able to identify a group of residents at a large hospital for the mentally retarded who had established themselves at the top of the residential hierarchy and were looked upon by the staff, other residents, and themselves as "the elite." Careful investigation of this group in contrast with nonmembers of the group revealed the following:

1. Members of the group associated almost completely with other members and rarely, if ever, with nonmembers.
2. Members shared patterns of dress, behaviors, attitudes toward nonmembers, habits, and values.

6

The Retarded Adult

What are retarded adults like, and can they lead a full and productive life?

In many respects it is difficult to comment on issues related to retarded adults. First, different people consider adulthood in different ways. The legal profession considers an adult as one who has passed his twenty-first birthday (eighteenth in some states), educators usually view adults as individuals who have completed their years of mandated schooling, physicians use anatomic and physiologic criteria, and psychologists typically consider emotional stability and maturity of some magnitude to be fair indicators of adulthood. There is, then, lack of agreement on what criteria should be used to describe adults. For certain, whatever criteria are adopted, chronological age alone is probably not an adequate basis on which to make a decision regarding whether or not one is an adult. A second very important problem that makes comment on the retarded adult an especially formidable task is the lack of research and study that has been reported on these individuals. This is in stark contrast to the relatively higher quantity and quality of the professional literature on the mentally retarded at other age levels. The possible reasons for this discrepancy include (1) the enormous relative difficulties scientists have in locating retarded adults after they have been discharged

adulthood. The degree to which this occurs will obviously depend on the types of educational provisions that are made during preceding years.)

These are a few of the most important factors and conditions on which the degree of favorableness of the retarded adult's characteristics are contingent. Harkening back to a point made earlier, after considering the many conditions which are influential in directing the character and destiny of retarded adults, you can readily see why these adults, especially adults with mild and moderate degrees of retardation, are so heterogeneous a group.

Some Broadly Based Needs   Retarded adults have the same type of needs, wishes, desires, and attitudes as most other adult populations. In terms of needs, they have identical requirements as other humans for water, sleep, food, protection, and warmth. In most situations these are usually provided to a minimal extent. Other vital needs of the retarded adult, however, are often overlooked; the fact that many of these are not provided at an adequate level has serious potential consequences. Those of particular potential concern are such essentials for life as love, belongingness, recognition by others, usefulness, praise, and opportunities to be actively and meaningfully involved in a task. These needs must not be frustrated; they must be satisfied through intentional programming in order for the adult to have contact with an environment which is full of meaning for him and which will always allow him to grow toward a greater measure of independence. There are other needs of the adult retardate, most of which are taken for granted by the intellectually normal, that should be recognized and provided for in all instances. Such needs as freedom to explore, to satisfy one's curiosity, to learn about new and interesting things, to find satisfaction through religious experiences, and to create something are all important and of no less significance to the retarded than they are to the normal adult. Inability to perform or produce in an obvious and tangible way, as is frequently the case with many retarded adults, should not be construed to mean that their basic needs, such as those just cited, do not exist or should not be satisfied on a regular and intentional basis.

In addition to these basic needs, mentally retarded adults who are members of the open community require security in a financial sense, need appropriate advice and counsel during certain critical periods, often find additional training and retraining necessary, require opportunities for leisure-time activities which are appropriate and need exposure to an accepting family milieu. In a real sense, then, these needs and characteristics of the retarded adult translate clearly into program goals for both special education and vocational rehabilitation throughout the lifetime of the retarded individual.

Social and Occupational Characteristics   In the previous chapter many of the primary issues concerning the employment of the mildly retarded were discussed. The thoughts expressed for the retarded adolescent have pertinence for

the adult retardate. Many of the higher-level retarded adults are capable of acquiring and being maintained on a job which can provide an adequate level of economic self-sufficiency so long as they act wisely in their use of money. Certainly those adults who have received assistance from special education programs and vocational rehabilitation will be better potential candidates for successful work placement. There is often movement from job to job immediately after the initial job placement; however, the adult retardate tends to soon find satisfaction in a job setting, especially in those circumstances in which the employer is sympathetic, understanding, and supportive. Obviously, the condition of the labor market, the increasing trend towards specialization, and the wider use of automatic machines have forced many retarded adults into different types of occupations, many of which require skills which heretofore have not been included in the work-study sequence in junior and senior high schools.

There is a distinct tendency especially among poorly trained retarded adults to have difficulty in satisfying the usual social requirements expected of adults who live in an open community. They tend to commit more minor crimes and have more problems with others at work. It is almost as if certain types of adult retardates either overreact or underreact and as a consequence become set apart in the eyes of their fellow workers. As you can imagine, this often penalizes them in future encounters with others, and they become the most likely candidates for teasing, taunting, practical jokes, and fights. These difficulties often end with the retarded adult being chastised by the employer or foreman while the perpetrators dissolve from the scene of the encounters. Little wonder that certain retarded adults have "short fuses," social problems because they cannot get along with others, mental health difficulties, trouble taking orders, and frequent instances of becoming perplexed more quickly than intellectually normal peers who are of the same age.

Although the retarded adult is often in a difficult position in many ways, it is still reasonable to expect that most of the mildly retarded could lead a full and productive life. The extent to which this goal can be fully realized is dependent on how properly shaped each individual's education and training program has been during previous crucial phases. Unfortunately many adults were not provided with an ideal program of total intervention during their early and adolescent years because (1) their individual problems were not properly identified, (2) school programs based on individual diagnostic signs were not widely available, (3) programs of intervention lacked proper sequencing and continuity among the various segments, and (4) state financing for total special education programming was inadequate, seriously jeopardizing the range of available opportunities.

Marriage and Matters Related to Parenthood   The issues surrounding marriage, controlling pregnancy, and being responsible parents have great significance in our considerations concerning the degree to which mildly retarded adults

can be helped to lead full and productive lives. There is no question that many higher-level retarded adults, particularly those from lower socioeconomic areas, whose etiology is more environmental than constitutional, will marry and have family responsibilities. Many of these adults will marry relatively early, certain persons in this group will acquire partners who are relatively higher intellectually, and a significant number will have large families for which their support will be required. Since marriage for the severely and profoundly retarded is highly unlikely, and for the trainable retarded is nearly as remote, the focus of this discussion will be on concerns related to the educable or mildly retarded population. In addition, you probably recognize that the ramifications of the topics of marriage, pregnancy control, and child rearing involve complex, interrelated personal and social phenomena; therefore, only a superficial consideration of these subjects is possible in this book.

There are a few studies which have been reported in the professional literature concerning the capabilities of the retarded for developing and sustaining a satisfactory marital relationship (Shaw and Wright, 1960; Charles, 1957; Dinger, 1961; Mickelson, 1947, 1949). As you can see, many of these studies were done some time ago and, thus, do not necessarily reflect the current status on this subject with regard to mentally retarded adults. There is a definite need for more systematic and contemporary research on the multitude of issues involved in the marital status of retarded adults.

In a scholarly and understandable way, Bass (1963, 1964) has reviewed and summarized most of the definitive literature dealing with marriage and parenthood for the mentally retarded. She points out that evidence is accumulating to suggest that a large percentage of the mildly retarded can be successful in marriage. This is especially true for those retardates who are reasonably mature and stable and for individuals who are not completely inundated by problems arising from the need to care for a large number of children. In the opinion of several authorities, the stresses engendered by dealing with problems of providing for the health and welfare of a group of children is probably beyond the capacity of many retarded adults and is a prime precipitant for marital discordance. Obviously, the degree to which marital integration and harmony take place within a family in which mental retardation is present on the part of one or both parents is dependent on factors in addition to intelligence alone. Chronological age, tolerance for frustration, willingness to compromise, emotional sensitivity and robustness, and other traits are important determinants of the degree to which material stability is developed and maintained within a home. All these factors are characteristic of individuals who are mentally retarded in different degrees and because of different conditions; therefore, one should recommend or not recommend marriage for the retarded adolescent and adult only after careful study has been given to each individual situation. It is worth recognizing, however, that in spite of the accumulating evidence which predicts a more opti-

mistic future of material stability among many retarded adults, three states still have legal statutes which prohibit marriage for the "weakminded" and the laws in fifteen other states can be interpreted to imply that it is probably illegal for marriage to take place between those persons with such characteristics (Strubing and Scully, 1960).

The adequacy of the child-rearing techniques used by parents is not solely determined by their level of intelligence. At the same time, although in the absence of adequate longitudinal data, the clinical impression of many behavioral scientists is that one could expect relatively more parent-child problems of a significant magnitude among married retarded adults than among other populations. The research that is available on this issue lacks clear definition as to the magnitude of this problem (Harper, 1959; Hathaway, 1947; Dinger, 1961; Mickelson, 1947). In a more contemporary study, Peck and Stephens (1965) found that retarded adults, from a population whose IQ scores range from 50 to 75, showed basic inabilities to deal with the requirements of parenthood in spite of what otherwise appeared to be a reasonably satisfactory marriage on their part. In the opinion of Peck and Stephens (1965), the position taken by Hill (1950, p. 403) is particularly appropriate, "A mentally deficient person is not a suitable parent for either a normal or a subnormal child, and children would be an added burden to an already handicapped individual who does well to support himself."

The evidence that is available on this subject seems to point to a real need to implement a program of intentional contraceptive measures with certain married retarded adults in order to reduce the possibility of their becoming overburdened with children. In the opinion of Bass (1963), it is too great an expectation of the retarded that they be expected to consistently and properly use oral or mechanical contraceptive devices. Their temperament, character, and frequent lack of foresight mitigate the probable adequacy of temporary, artificial methods for controlling pregnancy. The position of the Catholic Church notwithstanding, there are significant and persuasive arguments to justify the provision of a voluntary plan for birth control through the use of sterilization procedures to be made available to retarded adults. Among the arguments used to rationalize this position are the following:

1. The retarded adult is preoccupied with making an adequate social and vocational adjustment and maintaining reasonable stability between himself and his wife. The introduction of children into the family will produce a new set of responsibilities with which, in most instances, the mentally retarded father and/or mother will have had little or no experience. The tensions and anxieties engendered by various situations arising as a result of having a family will tend to overwhelm the retardate's available resources. The consequences of such frustrations which come from the responsibilities of parenthood may disrupt the

delicate adjustment balance between the retarded husband and/or wife and cause any of a whole host of individual and family disorders.

2. As a result of their frequent lack of experience and competence in dealing with young children, mentally retarded husbands and wives are poor risks to become responsible parents who are sensitive to the physical, mental, and social needs of young children. Their limited experience and intellectual prowess do not lend themselves to the kind of awareness and sensitivity demanded of parents with young children.

3. Among retarded adults whose etiology is more environmental than constitutional, the possibility of the offspring eventually acquiring some degree of mental retardation is high. This is a consequence of the parents not understanding the full ramifications involved in providing minimal stimulation to the infants from birth through ages six or seven. This lack of early stimulation, as has been noted in previous sections, will result in definite manifestation of retarded behavior later on in the child's development.

Notice that reasons for suggesting voluntary sterilization for married retarded adults were based on the future health and welfare of the individuals and their marriage. Additionally, this position was taken in order to control the inevitable consequences of their offspring suffering from serious inadequacies which could result in developmental lags, physical and mental disorders, accidents, and intellectual retardation during the formative years. For many infants who are born to retarded parents, a destiny of this type, or some variation thereof, is reasonably predictable. It is worth emphasizing that no claim is made here that sterilization is appropriate primarily to significantly reduce the prevalence of mental retardation in our society. To make such a claim involves tenuous assumptions, although it should be realized that in certain instances indictations for sterilization are quite valid when obvious genetic complications on the part of certain parents will result in handicapping conditions in subsequent offspring.

The topics of marriage, contraception, and parenthood for the retarded adult involve complex issues and personal attitudes which are polemic among the best of friends. One of the obvious reasons for differences of opinion on these topics is that the scientific community has not contributed basic knowledge on such subjects through more contemporary research efforts. There are still many questions in these issues that have not been answered. Among the more important are: What antecedents to marriage on the part of the retarded are related to successful or unsuccessful family experiences? To what extent are the mentally retarded able to deal with family problems in our contemporary society? What specific child-rearing difficulties do retarded parents experience, and to what extent do these factors influence the development of their children? What attitudes do retarded parents have toward assuming responsibilities of parenthood,

and how can the community agencies provide the means for maximizing success in this regard? What is the attitude of retarded adults concerning voluntary sterilization, and what factors are indicative or contraindicative for recommending such a procedure to a retarded husband and wife? What are the possible consequences of married retarded adults living in a community in which their friends and neighbors are more intellectually sophisticated than they?

In this section attention has been focused on certain of the more predominant needs of mild and moderately retarded adults. A number of difficult problems and issues have been pointed out and some general recommendations and positions have been taken for dealing with these problems. Since other authors have taken rather definite positions with respect to various characteristics of retarded adults, the reader is encouraged to consult the following list of readings for further discussions on these topics.

Recommended Readings

Bass, M. S.: "Marriage, Parenthood, and Prevention of Pregnancy," *American Journal of Mental Deficiency,* vol. 68, 1963, pp. 318–333.

———: "Marriage for the Mentally Deficient," *Mental Retardation,* vol. 2, 1964, pp. 198–202.

Charles, D. C.: "Adult Adjustment of Some Deficient American Children," *American Journal of Mental Deficiency,* vol. 62, 1957, pp. 300–304.

Dinger, J. D.: "Post-school Adjustment of Former Educable Retarded," *Exceptional Children,* vol. 27, 1961, pp. 353–360.

Harper, R. D.: "The Responsibilities of Parenthood: A Marriage Counselor's View," *Eugenics Quarterly,* vol. 6, 1959, pp. 8–13.

Hathaway, S. B.: "Planned Parenthood and Mental Deficiency," *American Journal of Mental Deficiency,* vol. 52, 1947, pp. 182–186.

Hill, I. B.: "Sterilization in Oregon," *American Journal of Mental Deficiency,* vol. 54, 1950, pp. 399–403.

Katz, E.: *The Retarded Adult in the Community,* Charles C Thomas, Publisher, Springfield, Ill., 1968.

Mickelson, P.: "The Feeble-minded Parent, A Study of 90 Family Cases: An Attempt to Isolate Those Factors Associated with Their Successful and Unsuccessful Parenthood," *American Journal of Mental Deficiency,* vol. 51, 1947, pp. 644–653.

———: "Can Mentally Deficient Parents Be Helped to Give Their Children Better Care?," *American Journal of Mental Deficiency,* vol. 53, 1949, pp. 516–534.

Peck, J. R., and W. B. Stephens: "Marriage of Young Adult Male Retardates," *American Journal of Mental Deficiency,* vol. 69, 1965, pp. 818–827.

Shaw, C. H., and C. H. Wright: "The Married Mental Defective: A Follow-up Study," *Lancet,* vol. 1, 1960, pp. 273–274.

Strubing, P. H., and D. W. Scully: *Marriage of Morons,* Human Betterment Association for Voluntary Sterilization, New York, 1960.

How might the community provide for retarded adults?

Upon reaching adulthood most people are expected to have developed a whole host of competencies which can be used, with a minimal degree of effectiveness, in dealing with personal, social, and occupational issues. The acquisition of such skills occurs as a result of an individual undergoing a wide range of experiences and activities most of which are made possible through systematic as well as informal intervention by one's family, peers, schools, and community agencies. To a great extent, the degree to which an individual eventually develops into a competent performer is dictated by the quantity and quality of these interactions throughout his lifetime.

The point has been made in various sections of this book that our society has a clear responsibility to the mentally retarded to maximize their opportunities for interacting with those components of the environment which will facilitate the attainment of such problem-solving skills. These learning experiences must be provided on an intentional basis, and they must begin during the first few years of life to be really effective. To optimize conditions for learning by the retarded, or those youngsters who are potential candidates for special education classes, it will be necessary for many families to look to various agencies within the community for direction and various types of support. Some of the ways in which assistance is provided to parents by community groups have been mentioned in other sections and include (1) comprehensive medical and behavioral diagnostic services, (2) training opportunities for children who are excluded from the public schools, (3) day-care centers, (4) counseling opportunities for parents of retarded children, (5) free medical consultation and treatment for those families who are unable to pay for such services, and (6) vocational training.

Although many of the mildly retarded adults in our society will be able to function with total independence, there still exists a significant number of adults with varying degrees of retardation who will require attention and services by the community beyond their adolescent years. Among this group are those retarded males and females who are able to work but who are unemployed because of lack of previous training, serious adjustment difficulties, or inability to find a satisfactory position. Other types of retarded adults for whom the community may need to provide programming are those who have been released from an institution to their homes, those who are moderately or severely retarded and

who do not qualify for sheltered workshop placement, those whose parents or guardians need any of a number of forms of relief, those who are driven to antisocial behavior because of family or social frustrations, and those who are suffering from the many burdens and problems occasioned by having too large a family. With these broad needs in mind, then, community programming for retarded adults might include vocational guidance services, training and retraining for employment in addition to that offered by the schools or vocational rehabilitation agencies, placement in a sheltered workshop, social adjustment programs and mental health counsel, various types of community activity programs, and adult education for parents and their retarded offspring (Gardner and Nisonger, 1962).

Earlier it was mentioned that the schools usually assume the principal responsibilities for preparing mildly retarded adolescents for the world of work. In combination with the resources from the Bureau of Vocational Rehabilitation, it is usually possible for most young adults to be placed on a job after having finished their formal schooling. For some, more intensive specific job training is necessary and may be available from an employer with previous experience in providing on-the-job training for retardates. Usually a rehabilitation counselor will individually, or in concert with the school work-study coordinator, provide supervision, support, and counsel to the employee and employer. For still other young retardates, much more comprehensive services may be required before job placement. Usually the Bureau of Vocational Rehabilitation is able to provide such assistance either in the community or at one of their regional centers. It should be recognized, however, that the Bureau of Vocational Rehabilitation will not accept a client merely because he is disabled. It is necessary to document that a clear vocational handicap exists, and that the services which the bureau can provide will significantly increase the individual's employment possibilities.

There is another employable group of retarded adults which we have not mentioned thus far, but toward whom the discussion in the next section will be directed. I am referring to those retarded adults who are unable to maintain themselves in a totally independent way, but who are able to become partially self-supporting in a relatively more restricted environment. These adults may be moderately or severely retarded and reside either in an institution or in the community. They may also be a group of mildly retarded and emotionally or socially disturbed adults who require a similar type of vocational atmosphere. In terms of employment, these adults are most frequently candidates for a sheltered workshop. More will be said later about this facet of a community plan for retarded adults.

Activity Centers   In many respects most of these adults would legally qualify for placement in an institution as a result of their having serious handicapping conditions or requiring continuous care and treatment. In fact, some will eventually be placed in residential centers or institutions as their require-

ments become too great a burden for those members of the family who must provide care. Any comprehensive philosophy of management would certainly dictate that provisions be made for increasing the level of skill development and enhancing the social contacts of these homebound seriously handicapped adults. As a result, many communities have established activity programs which have objectives such as:

1. Helping the retarded develop socially acceptable patterns for daily living
2. Aiding the retarded and their parents in developing good patterns of mental health
3. Helping the parents to better understand and accept the idiosyncrasies of their retarded offspring
4. Providing the parents who have elected not to place their child in an institution with some periods of relief from the rigors of constant care
5. Providing the retarded adult with opportunities to participate in simple group activities outside of the home
6. Preparing certain of the retardates with specific skill training which, for some, could lead to eventual placement in a sheltered workshop

Cortazzo (1963, 1968) has suggested some guidelines for developing an activity program and has analyzed the characteristics of those activity programs which are presently operating. The first step involved in establishing an activity center is to survey the community to determine (1) the number of retarded adolescents and adults who can benefit from the services provided by the program, and (2) the status of existing services and facilities available to retarded adults through private and public agencies. After these data are collected and analyzed, and a decision made concerning the feasibility of establishing some form of activity program, an interdisciplinary planning committee should begin to consider issues such as:

1. Who will sponsor, finance, and be responsible for the activity center program?
2. What will be the specific focus and purposes of the center's program?
3. To what extent and for whom should tuition be charged?
4. What organizational pattern is most feasible and to whom will the center relate for services either formally or informally?
5. What criteria should be used in the employment of the center staff?
6. Where should the center be located and how will this be financed?
7. What criteria will be used for the admission of clients?
8. What legal provisions are required in areas relating to accidents, contracting for services, insurance, transportation, and health of clients?
9. What priority should be established in terms of program commitment?
10. How can community support and participation be maximized?

11. To what extent and in what manner can the activity center relate to other community programs who serve similar groups of adults?

As you might expect with any relatively new program, the analysis which Cortazzo (1968) made of activity programs revealed a number of significant problems. Among these were problems involving transportation, inability to finance the centers at a level which would allow for the full realization of the individual program objectives, lack of intergration with other community agencies, problems in employing adequately trained staff, and difficulties in implementing the necessary steps to allow for full evaluation of the potential of trainees. There is no question that these problems are not insurmountable, and that most communities fully support an activity center which is designed to provide programs for the social, personal, self-care, and vocational skill development of retarded adults who would otherwise spend their entire lifetime within a house or as a resident of an institution.

Adult Education   The mildly retarded, especially, can profit from adult education in specific areas. Many larger communities have the resources and inclination to provide evening instruction for adults in subjects that range from those which are very job specific and difficult to others which are broader in scope and offer general information and counsel on subjects involving daily living practices. These courses are very often offered by the public schools, libraries, Young Men's Christian Association (YMCA), Young Women's Christian Association (YWCA), certain employers, community groups, and church organizations.

No single person or organization should be given the responsibility for assuring that retarded adults enroll in adult education courses when there is a need or a belief that an individual could profit from such experiences. Instead, it is the proper role of everyone with whom the adult comes into contact to show the kind of initiative required to see to it that the retarded adult is aware of and provided with the means which will allow for enrollment in appropriate adult education courses. The community leaders have a responsibility to alert parents, clergy, teachers, counselors, employers, and others who come into contact with the retarded adult about some of the frequent postschool educational needs of this segment of the community's population and the nature of the opporunities that presently exist.

Social and Recreational Programs   There is often a tendency on the part of the retarded adults who are relatively self-sufficient to either withdraw from social and recreational experiences in their leisure hours or to become associated with questionable and potentially damaging persons, situations, and activities. Obviously, either of these circumstances could cause difficulties or result in serious problems which might deleteriously influence the adult's level of functioning at work and with others. In spite of the school's programs which are

designed to militate against such eventualities, retarded adults are not unlike others in this regard; i.e., they will succumb to pressures which are subtly applied by the attraction of questionable social practices or remain totally apart from any interpersonal activity because of their own unsurenesses.

The need for opportunities to engage in satisfying social contacts and recreational opportunities by the retarded adult is definite and of significant magnitude for many who live alone. There is no rational reason why most of the mildly retarded cannot participate—they may be unaware that these opportunities exist and that they are welcome to partake in various social events, or they may be unsure about imitating the process of becoming involved in an activity or event in which they will be expected to participate with other people. Again, the initiative for including the retarded adult in recreational and social activities and programs should come from members of the community. A person-to-person interest in the welfare of others in the long run will be much more effective than attempts at trying to dictate or administratively organize social interaction for them. Among the agencies with exising programs and resources which could be made available to many mildly retarded adults are the YMCA, YWCA, church groups, community recreation and park agencies, social clubs, and volunteer groups.

Recommended Readings

Cortazzo, A. D.: *A Guide to Establishing an Activity Program for the Mentally Retarded Adults,* National Association for Retarded Children, Inc., New York, 1963.

————: "An Analysis of Activity Programs for Mentally Retarded Adults," *Mental Retardation,* vol. 6, 1968, pp. 31–34.

DiMichael, S. G.: *Preparation of Mentally Retarded Youth for Gainful Employment,* U.S. Department of Health, Education, and Welfare, 1959

Dybwad, G.: "Rehabilitation for the Adult Retardate," *American Journal of Public Health,* vol. 51, 1961, pp. 998–1004.

————: "Administrative and Legislative Problems in the Case of Adult and Aged Mental Retardates," *American Journal of Mental Deficiency,* vol. 66, 1962, pp. 716–721.

Gardner, W. I., and H. W. Nisonger: *A Manual on Program Development in Mental Retardation, Monograph Supplement to the American Journal of Mental Deficiency,* January, 1962.

Smith, R. M.: *Clinical Teaching: Methods of Instruction for the Retarded,* McGraw-Hill Book Company, 1968, chaps. 10 and 11.

Tobias, J., and A. D. Cortazzo: "Training Severely Retarded Adults for Greater Independence in Community Living," *The Training School Bulletin,* vol. 60, pp. 23–37.

In what ways can a sheltered workshop be responsive to the needs of retarded adults?

Throughout this book mention has been made of various plans, techniques, and resources available to the different specialists and parents who are concerned about providing proper management strategies for the mentally retarded at all age levels. There is a large degree of singularity in purpose among such groups as are represented in special education programs within public schools, community mental health–mental retardation groups, medical and psychological diagnostic clinics, professional organizations which are concerned about the mentally retarded, and the National Association for Retarded Children. All these groups are interested in seeing that complete services are available to the retarded and to their families so that a firm diagnosis of individual characteristics can be made and procedures of management established. This section will focus on another of the many ways in which the rehabilitation professions have sought to provide for certain retarded adolescents and adults. Our discussion here of sheltered workshop programs could legitimately have appeared in the previous chapter inasmuch as many of the workshop clients are of adolescent age, but it was placed in this chapter in order to emphasize the manner in which the community can exercise leadership in providing retarded adults with needed services beyond the mandated public school age. A conceptual companion to the sheltered workshop program in this respect is the activity center which was discussed earlier.

In their most comprehensive and informative handbook, the National Association of Sheltered Workshops and Homebound Programs defines a sheltered workshop thusly:

> A sheltered workshop is a work-oriented rehabilitation facility with a controlled working environment and individual goals which utilizes work experience and related services for assisting the handicapped person to progress toward normal living and productive vocational status (*Sheltered Workshops—A Handbook*, 1966, p. 1).

Gellman (1965a, 1965b, 1967) has noted the manner in which the philosophy and future of sheltered workshops has recently changed after having had rather static objectives for a century and a half. Prior to the late 1950s, sheltered workshops were considered solely as situations in which severely handicapped (mentally and/or physically) adolescents and adults could be employed without having to be exposed to the multitude of difficulties related to the competitive employment scene. This extended or terminal employment situation was viewed as an end unto itself, and graduation or movement of the workshop clients into the competitive marketplace was not considered part of the workshop's mission.

In the middle 1950s, there was a rather marked departure from this prevailing philosophy; provision was made for clients who could benefit from having more training in an occupational setting before placement in the open labor market was effected. This transformation and emphasis reflected a definite realization on the part of rehabilitation specialists that the sheltered workshop has a real potential for contributing to the future employability of its clients than heretofore recognized.

Some specialists have gone a step further in this emerging philosophy by conceptualizing the sheltered workshop from a more clinical perspective. With this model, focus is placed on analyzing and evaluating the kinds of environments required by each client in order to fulfill their individual psychological, social, and vocational needs. This involves the manipulation of the type of work, nature of the supervision, extent and variety of social and vocational pressures, character of colleagues, degree of success required by each individual, and tolerance for frustration. It requires careful articulation of information and services among the various types of social, emotional, and vocational counselors. The individualized plan is regularly evaluated and changes are made according to the type of therapeutic milieu which each adult requires.

These various philosophical tenets are totally compatible with the broad community needs of various groups of retarded adults. Some will be totally unable to progress into a competitive vocational setting, but they may find great congruence with and benefit from the extended component of a workshop program. Other retarded adults may be excellent candidates for the transitional sequence of activities within the workshop as a result of their having demonstrated a minimum level skill development in certain crucial areas. A third group may require a program of assistance which is highly specific, i.e., one which needs to be tailor-made to respond to a definite area(s) of weakness. There is no reason why a sheltered workshop needs to adhere only to one of these directional thrusts. A shrewd community group and the workshop's staff will mold their program so that all components are represented in order to more clearly reflect the needs of disabled clients within the community and to provide optimum opportunities for their individual development.

Although there are a few, sheltered workshops are usually not operated to serve a single disability group such as the blind, retarded, or deaf. Workshops which admit groups of clients with varying disabilities will usually find that they are serving the community in a relatively more comprehensive way, that opportunities exist for a wider range and assortment of work, that costs will be more evenly shared among interested agencies, and that more competent staff can be attracted when broader challenges are available.

To a large extent, the establishment of a sheltered workshop will follow the same type of steps which are suggested as being appropriate for community activity centers. After someone or some organization in the community feels that

a need exists in this direction, some form of a planning committee will usually emerge. In the beginning phases of the project, it will be necessary to have wide community representation and to initiate a survey in order to determine the need and extent to which supportive services and possible personnel are available. A careful investigation must be made concerning other issues such as (1) What community resources are available which might obviate the need for a sheltered workshop being established? (2) Is work available in the community and surrounding areas which might suit the needs of the workshop and serve to enhance the skills of the clients? (3) What type of workshop should be developed to respond best to the predicted needs of the clients? (4) What types of supportive services will be required on the workshop grounds, what kind will need to be purchased from other agencies, and to what extent will they be needed? (5) What type of staff will be required to operate the workshop, what are appropriate job specifications for each, and where can the best available candidates be recruited? (6) What financial arrangements can be made between various governmental agencies and groups within the community to provide an adequate level of support for the program? (7) How much and what type of physical space is needed, should it be rented or constructed, and how can it best serve the objectives of the workshop and at the same time reflect the needs and problems of the clients?

As part of their suggested working plan for sheltered workshops, The National Association for Retarded Children recommends that programming for retarded adults include the following phases:

1. Screening for admission to a sheltered workshop should include a comprehensive analysis of data obtained from medical, psychological, social, educational, and vocational sources. A team of professional consultants who represent pertinent rehabilitation specialities should participate in this total evaluation of potential workshop candidates.

2. After the workshop trainee has gained admission, a great amount of time and effort should be devoted to analyzing the type of training he will need in order to become as self-sufficient as possible. This phase of the program involves the intentional observation of the trainee by the workshop staff as the individual participates in various types of social and occupational activities. This pragmatic approach lends itself to the definition of a relatively accurate picture of the future training requirements and placement possibilities for individual trainees.

3. One of the two training phases which focuses on the personal adjustment of retarded adults includes instruction which is directed to helping these individuals gain wider social experiences within which they are expected to demonstrate satisfactory patterns of behavior. Because of the high relationship between normal work demands and atypical patterns of reactions which basically are the result of an inability on the part of the retarded to deal with various frustrations,

those trainees who are involved in sheltered workshop programs usually receive a heavy dose of personal-adjustment training.

4. The second phase in the training sequence typical of most sheltered workshop programs focuses on vocational or job training. By conducting a comprehensive job analysis, the workshop staff can determine, within reasonable limits, the trainees' specific and general competencies, job interests, and training needs. With this information, then, they attempt to match each trainee's needs with an appropriate job. Obviously, the congruence of this match will depend on the types of work in which the workshop is participating at a certain time. This crucial need has clear implications for the varieties of work situations which the workshop's staff agrees to perform.

5. Emerging from the various evaluations and training phases is the placement aspect of the sheltered workshop program. A number of options for placement are possible in most comprehensive workshop settings. The trainee could be placed within the open labor market. It is also possible in many communities for the trainee to be placed on a job in the workshop. Whatever the placement situation, the trainee's highest level of skills should always be utilized.

6. The workshop staff has a responsibility to see that each trainee receives proper follow-up care. Both the employee and the employer should be satisfied, and steps should be taken by the professional personnel to see that any problems with either party are dealt with before they become inflamed or uncontrolled.

A successful sheltered workshop requires that the staff and board of directors adhere to sound business principles in all aspects of management. The central focus of providing services to those in the community with disabilities must be maintained and should not be sacrificed because of fiscal problems. Workshop-planning groups may need to seek various sources for support to adequately subsidize the level of programming needed. The Federal Vocational Rehabilitation Act contains provisions for funding. This act will partially support the establishment of, improvement of, and assistance to various types of sheltered workshops.

The type of work conducted in the workshop depends to a great extent on the character of the community. In heavily populated metropolitan areas, industrial subcontracting often serves as the principal work focus. In other centers, the work will involve the manufacture of new goods, such as Christmas decorations, aprons, wooden chairs, containers, or birdhouses. Still other workshop staffs prefer to focus attention on the renovation of used materials for resale. Aside from the degree to which these patterns of work are relatively lucrative for a workshop, the staff must gauge their work activities according to the nature of the objectives considered appropriate for the trainees involved in the program.

As you can see, the establishment and operation of a sheltered workshop is exceedingly complex. It requires the services of a director and staff with skills in education, business management, trade and industrial procedures, evaluation

of client functioning, and public relations. The training and commitment of the staff is of unmeasured value of the success of the workshop operation, perhaps more so than the character of the physical plant. If the community is prepared to support the aims of the workshop program in spirit and in tangible ways, there is no reason why it cannot provide valuable services to many retarded adults who would otherwise spend their mature years in unproductive and unfulfilling activities.

Recommended Readings

Gellman, W.: "New Directions for Workshops Meeting the Rehabilitation Challenge of the Future," *Rehabilitation Literature,* vol. 28, 1967, pp. 283–287.

————: "Rehabilitation Services in a Workshop Setting," *Journal of Rehabilitation,* vol. 31, 1965a, pp. 34–37.

————: "The Workshop As a Clinical Rehabilitation Tool," *Rehabilitation Literature,* vol. 26, 1965b, pp. 34–38.

Organizing a Sheltered Workshop, National Association for Retarded Children, New York, 1968.

Sheltered Workshops—A Handbook, revised ed., National Association of Sheltered Workshops and Homebound Programs, Inc., Washington, 1966.

Appendixes

Appendix A

Some Issues Pertaining to Research in Mental Retardation*

Many disciplines have a concern for contributing to a growing understanding of mental retardation from various perspectives. An increasing amount of cooperative research and interdisciplinary sharing has
begun to yield more rapid solutions to the vast array of problems
related to the condition. Unfortunately the convergence of disciplines toward cooperatively solving problems too frequently awaits
crises such as impending periods of war, economic collapse, epi-
demics, urban disasters, and similar types of emergencies. It would
seem that we could preempt crises; that cross-disciplinary research,
even with moderate or limited funding, would be capable of asking
and answering the relevant problems before they escalate to the crisis
stage. Where early and continual cooperative research has existed,
the strategy has been to bring together related specialists to work on
common problems. Too often these specialists have been working *in
vacuo* for so long that they have difficulty in seeing and appreciating
the relevance of one discipline to another.

* The material presented in this section is a revision of the following article
and appears here with the permission of the American Association on Mental
Deficiency: R. M. Smith and J. T. Neisworth, "Some Problems of and Prospects for Research in Mental Retardation," *Mental Retardation,* vol. 7, 1969,
pp. 25–28.

It is probably wise for scientists who represent fields of great research activity and expenditure to periodically step away from their current specific interests and involvement to consider the total matrix of activity and need in their field. There is a great deal to be gained by the researcher periodically "taking stock" of the direction in which his field is moving or could move and reconsidering his own specific interests and activities accordingly.

The potential hazard of being functionally "out of touch" with the important issues in the field is particularly relevant to those areas of inquiry in which several disciplines have research interests. This is true in the field of mental retardation; representatives from a variety of disciplines are heavily committed to the study of the phenomena from their own professional perspectives.

This situation results in a certain unevenness in the research; i.e., individual disciplines tend to focus their research attention on a single entity within a broader area, the results of which at times exceed the relative contribution of other disciplines who may less aggressively be investigating the same entity from their own perspective. Medical research, for example, may have reached a relatively higher conceptual level in medical knowledge about Down's syndrome than have the fields of education, psychology, or sociology in their consideration of the behavioral aspects of the condition. This disproportionality in research, along with the lack of communication among disciplines, has resulted in scientists not sharing their research findings even though they may be of great significance to someone else in another field. At the same time, this lack of intradiscipline and interdiscipline communication can result in experimenters becoming functionally locked in on a specific problem which may be of low-order priority.

There is, then, an urgent need for scientists who are interested in the study of mental retardation to share continually the results of their research efforts and to chart mutually the preferred direction for future investigations. By studying the same entity from a variety of perspectives, a researcher in one field can contribute to knowledge in other fields of inquiry in a way that could significantly alter the direction and emphasis of research in each discipline.

This section will focus on two issues which are of concern to researchers in the field of mental retardation. First, the discussion will present a number of design and methodological problems which are frequently of central concern to scientists in various disciplines. Second, attention is directed to several topics which represent crucial ongoing and imminent research areas in which more intentional investigation is needed.

Complications in the conduct of mental retardation studies

Selection of Research Populations   An enormous amount of research has been conducted by psychologists, sociologists, and educators on the behavior of the mentally retarded. Most of the investigations have sampled from very specific

populations of the retarded because of their desire to control for possible contaminating variables or because certain groups of subjects are more readily accessible. In many instances, scientists have chosen to use institutionalized retardates as subjects in their investigations. This is a frequent pattern in the psychological research literature, which has a history of being more basic than applied, whereby studies tend to focus on a single variable or a restricted constellation of factors in a more molecular area of inquiry.

The number of investigations that have used the mentally retarded who are located in the community as subjects of study are relatively fewer. Among the possible reasons for investigators tending to shy away from using subjects of this type for study are the following:

1. The difficulty inherent in conducting intervention-type research which requires the random assignment of subjects to either an experimental or control group when it is administratively impossible to separate intact public school classes
2. The problems scientists have in generalizing their findings to larger populations of subjects because of experimenter bias or because of other influential variables
3. The greater heterogeneity expressed among the mentally retarded located in the community as contrasted with those in institutions (this is a result of etiological differences as well as environmental variation)
4. The difficult logistics problem researchers face in attempting to conduct research when the validity of the results are so closely tied to the degree to which cooperation is given by administrators and teachers, who may or may not be overly sympathetic to this type of endeavor

Because of this situation, a great deal of the research in mental retardation lacks obvious practical application because of the hazards faced in extrapolating findings to populations other than those on whom the research was originally conducted. For example, one must be very cautious in taking results from research conducted on institutionalized subjects and concluding that the findings are equally relevant to those retardates who are located in an open community. Moreover, by controlling many of the active variables that might have been influential in the performance of children on the dependent variables, experimenters restrict the generalizability of their findings because of the contrived nature of many experiments. Many research findings, then, are not of obvious and immediate practical benefit because the studies have been designed in such a way as to control many of the variables that are usually present and which perhaps influence the retarded individual's behavior as a result of this complicated interaction that occurs with the environment.

There is, then, a need for future research in mental retardation to consider using designs that reflect more realistic environmental settings. Moreover, the

problems in using results of studies conducted on very specific populations of the mentally retarded in formulating programs for other groups of retarded, who may be quite different in certain significant characteristics, suggests that samples should be chosen with more thought given to the types of individuals about whom the scientist wishes to generalize his findings. Experimental samples must be randomly drawn from the populations about which the investigator wishes to generalize. This will provide consumers of research with some assurance that suggestions emerging from research may have applicability.

Heterogeneity of Experimental Subjects   Evidence is accumulating from almost every discipline which is concerned with the study of mental retardation that hazards exist in trying to characterize the condition as a single entity. Even within specific categories extreme variation is often expressed in terms of etiology, characteristics, and appropriate treatment procedures. The educable mentally retarded child, for example, could be subnormal for reasons that might include trauma, infection, biochemical abnormalities, or sensory deprivation. Similarly, children classified as being educable mentally retarded can, and often do, manifest characteristics of behavior at either extreme of whatever dimension one might wish to choose. Certain of these youngsters may be hypoactive, whereas others may be hyperactive. Certain may have specific learning disabilities which overlay their general intellectual subnormality, whereas other educable retarded youngsters may learn at a rate which is consistent with or beyond that which is predicted.

The design of experiments which use the mentally retarded as subjects is further complicated by variation in the types and degree of multiple disability that is expressed among the subjects. There is no unique syndrome of disabilities that will adequately describe the retarded irrespective of their degree of intellectual subnormality. Even within the category of the mildly retarded a variety of disabilities are detectable. A great amount of the past research has tended to disregard these associated disabilities, which implicitly leaves one with the belief that the subjects in the study were only intellectually subnormal and that the presence of any other possible disabilities in individual subjects in no way contributed to their performance on the dependent variables.

In order for subsequent research to be definitive and suggest specific procedures for treatment and care of those children who are regarded as retarded, scientists must carefully consider the manner in which this heterogeneity influences the generalizability of their findings. If crucial experiments are to be replicated, the influential variables which actively contribute to this within and between various populations of the retarded should be more clearly identified. This means that experimenters must more precisely define the characteristics of each population from which their samples were selected, assuming such samples are randomly drawn. If experimental samples are not randomly selected, the scientist is obliged to describe the research samples in sufficient detail to permit, perhaps, some possible generalization on the basis of logic.

Interaction Effects   Heterogeneity of experimental groups and failure to identify possible relevant status variables suggest still another topic, interaction effects, which has pertinence to problems of generalization and to the analysis of the experimental data.

Behavioral research in mental retardation has traditionally tested the influence of special programs by comparing the pretest and posttest performance of a group of experimental subjects against scores of a control group who had not received the special treatment. The usual method has been to measure differences between the means of the two groups and to subject these data to some type of statistical procedure to determine if the differences are significant. Certain programs of treatment or intervention which are theoretically promising have not shown significant advantages for experimental subjects when the data are analyzed in this fashion. The possibility exists that the treatment program may have been highly influential but that differences between the groups were not apparent because the investigators failed to consider the possible interaction of the treatment with other variables, all of which influenced the subjects' scores on the dependent variable(s).

To illustrate this point, an investigator might wish to initiate a program which is designed to stimulate productive thinking in young mentally retarded youngsters. The performance of the subjects might be evaluated at the termination of the program and their scores compared with a group of youngsters who had not received this unique program. Assume that a comparison of the mean scores of two groups reveals that no differences exist. The investigator, then, might logically conclude that the special program did not stimulate productive thinking in the retarded youngsters. His report to this effect in the literature would probably have the influence of dampening further research on the influence of this special program on productive thinking among the retarded. It is possible, however, that in this investigation the male subjects may have been highly stimulated by the program; however, the females might have reacted to the special treatment in an entirely opposite manner. Collapsing the data for both sexes (rather than leveling on sex) would yield no main (treatment) effect and might obscure a significant interaction of sex with treatment. In fact, the special program might have been highly influential for a defined subgroup of the sample.

This example serves to illustrate the need that more systematic attention should be given to the possible interaction that can occur between a treatment procedure and other potentially important variables. No longer can investigators be satisfied with testing for differences between means alone and basing their conclusions on the efficacy of a certain program without routinely analyzing possible interactions. This type of analysis will allow more precise statements to be made about the influence of specific intervention procedures in terms of those segments of the population which were most or least influenced by the treatment program.

Cross-sectional Research   Psychological and educational research has clearly described the magnitude of the learning problems of most populations of mentally retarded individuals. The findings of this research leads to the clear implication that the effects of any type of environmental intervention will remain stable only under the circumstances of longitudinal treatment. This is most obviously true for low-grade retarded subjects. The stability of differences between experimental and control groups over time has been exceedingly disappointing, even with the mildly retarded, when the treatment has been of short-term duration. The findings of such *in situ* research are consistent with the results of that basic research which has considered the various learning problems of the retarded.

In order for education and treatment of the mentally retarded to be definitive, future research of an intervention type will need to be more longitudinal than cross-sectional. This is true for the retarded at all levels of severity. One should be cautious in basing management programs on the results of research which has been for short-term duration and in those cases where stability scores on the results of intervention have not been reported. In many instances which involve this type of research effort, the subsequent evaluation of the retarded subjects has shown that the control and experimental groups return to an equal performance level even though significant differences may have been observed after the immediate termination of the treatment program. Research that employs any type of intervention, then, should be designed for longitudinal study so that an accurate determination can be made of the influence of the treatment procedures.

Critical behavioral research needs in mental retardation

Early Intervention   The advantages which accrue from the manipulation of a young child's environment in such a fashion as to provide increased stimulation are no longer in dispute. Numerous studies have supported the efficacy of intervention of some type at a very early age. In fact, the suggestion has often been made that the preschool education of deprived and potentially retarded children might be started soon after birth.

It is somewhat ironic, however, that research has not systematically considered the nature of the stimulation or environmental intervention that is most necessary for optimum cognitive development. This, in spite of the repeated assumption that early stimulation is the basis on which subsequent intellectual development occurs.

There is, then, an urgent need for more research effort to be devoted to a determination of the specific types of programs most desirable for young children who are reared in nonstimulating circumstances. Empirically and theoretically based courses of study need to be designed for deprived preschool youngsters.

With such materials, the researcher could then systematically evaluate the impact of various specific curricula on the development of children from a disadvantaged environment whose diagnosis or prognosis is mental retardation. A research effort of this sort would require both cross-sectional and longitudinal programs in order to thoroughly evaluate the value of early stimulus-intervention programs.

Sequentially Based Curricula   Courses of study which have been developed for educable and trainable youngsters are somewhat speculative and usually are not based on empirical documentation or on some systematic theory. Curricula for the retarded rarely have been subjected to experimental evaluation, are often biased in terms that are peculiar to individual teachers, are sensitive to pressures that are brought to bear by groups outside of the schools, and lack systematic sequencing within classrooms and between levels of instruction.

Primary research emphasis should not be devoted to the construction of more courses of study; instead, the major research thrust should focus on the development of a theoretical rationale for curriculum. The most urgent task for behavioral scientists in this area is to identify and test instructional sequences suggested by theories of cognitive development, concept attainment, verbal learning, and behavioral acquisition.

Programs in the Home   Even with the most propitious type of school setting, the mentally retarded will be significantly influenced by other components of the environment. The nature of the child's family situation is an important part of his life, whether he comes from an advantaged or disadvantaged home. Programs to alter behavior, or to prevent the acquisition of retarded behavior, must necessarily include the home and begin at the earliest possible moment.

Programs of early stimulation that might appropriately be offered in the child's home constitute legitimate and necessary areas for research activity. The role of the parents in providing stimulation to neonates, who show early indications of intellectual disability, needs to be studied. These issues demand a programmatic effort on the part of special educators in university and public school programs alike.

Clinical Teaching   With an increased sophistication in their understanding of the significance of diagnostic data, teachers are becoming more aware that retarded children no longer can be satisfactorily grouped or taught according to traditional classification systems. Not only do the youngsters vary on most educationally important variables when compared with their peers, but the retarded are often discrepant within themselves. No single teaching procedure will work for all retardates even though children may be similarly categorized. These youngsters, then, have learning difficulties which clearly warrant clinical educational diagnosis and individualized prescriptive teaching. Teachers need to be taught to recognize which educational variables are especially important, the manner in which educational weaknesses of various types can be remediated most effectively, and the range of appropriate evaluative techniques available to

measure the stability of changes resulting from various intervention practices.

Research in teaching methodology, then, must give more attention to the educational implications of heterogeneous ability and disability profiles among the mentally retarded. Accordingly, educators must begin to develop and evaluate specific educational strategies that are suitable for children with various diagnostic profiles.

New Instructional Technology   Rapid advances recently have taken place in the development of instructional concepts and devices, such as are illustrated by teaching machines and computer-assisted instruction. These techniques suggest potentially fruitful areas for educating and training the retarded at various levels in different subject areas. Once programmed, the devices show great promise for accommodating the wide individual differences observed among the mentally retarded in a way heretofore not thought possible. Research by special educators must be directed toward answering questions such as:

1. What criteria should be used in developing instructional sequences?
2. Which types of children will profit most from programmed instruction?
3. Are there certain subject areas which can more effectively or efficiently be taught through computer-assisted instruction than through traditional methods?
4. What is the longitudinal impact of using programmed instruction with mentally retarded youngsters?

A forecast of research focus in mental retardation

In prescribing the direction of future research in mental retardation, clear attention should be given toward effecting closer collaboration among disciplines. The different specialists will want to know about and make use of data and theories from other fields. This type of integration of efforts will aid in the development of potentially effective programs. To this end, there is a clear need to begin preparing specialists who are responsible for translating and synthesizing the literature from the various fields into programs and practices with a common focus.

Three somewhat divergent but potentially fruitful suggestions are given here for the direction future research in mental retardation might take. The first two suggestions could be implemented immediately; the third suggestion will require the continuation of certain basic research activities in the biological sciences.

Computer-based Programs   Even now a number of programmed instructional devices are being used in various ways with the mentally retarded. The procedures range from employing a scrambled textbook to help the retarded develop a number of basic skills to the use of a talking typewriter which pro-

vides the subject with both auditory and visual input and output. The value in using these techniques with the mentally retarded has not been clearly documented.

There is another way in which this new educational technology might be used with the mentally retarded on a broader basis. The storage, analysis, and quick retrieval characteristics of the computer suggest the great potential this device offers for individualizing instruction. More specifically, appropriate data on any number of children could be stored and analyzed according to the strengths and weaknesses of individual students or a group of youngsters. Based on an a priori analysis of various possible profiles, the computer could be programmed to relate specific remedial procedures to individual profiles. This type of analysis would provide teachers with a print-out of specific, sequentially presented remedial procedures which each child's pattern of strengths and weaknesses suggests as being most desirable.

After the suggested program had been tried for a specified time period, the teacher might evaluate each child's progress using techniques which the computer has suggested. These data could be entered into the computer, related to each child's earlier profile and remedial program, and analyzed to provide the teacher with suggestions for each student's subsequent program in terms that are specific to instructional methodology, courses of study, and recommended instructional media.

Technology has reached a level of sophistication where a system of this type could be made available to every teacher in the country. By locating computers in various regions, teachers could have accessibility to facilities for data storage, analysis, and retrieval by using a telephone or teletype system. Normative data could be systematically and continually gathered and the efficacy of each remedial suggestion evaluated in terms of various psychological and educational profiles.

A system of this sort would allow small schools, as well as overcrowded urban school systems, to provide prescriptive teaching for children with various types and degrees of learning difficulties. Every child within a school system would be reevaluated when a need exists; moreover, the teacher or psychologist would be provided with suggested evaluative procedures to use in each circumstance.

The development and implementation of this system obviously presents numerous complex problems. The best professional minds would need to be used to suggest remedial steps appropriate for the various profiles. Expertise in psychological and educational evaluation would be required to identify appropriate instrumentation. Pilot work in the development of systematic evaluations would be needed. All these and other considerations would precede the effective operation of such a diagnostic and remedial service. This type of system, however, is presently needed; the technology is now available and the advantages are unlimited.

Behavioral Engineering   Since about 1940, there has been a rapid expansion of research in behavior modification. Out of such research have come a number of principles that may be used to explain, predict, and control behavior. The more important principles concern the nature and effect of primary and token reinforcers, various reinforcement schedules, the delay of reinforcement, and the role of stimuli as cues for the onset of behavior. The acquisition, maintenance, and extinction of even some complex human behavior is now possible through the use of strategies based on these behavioral principles. Compared with older and other current explanations of behavior that usually invoke hypothetical mechanisms and forces, the behavioristic approach is far more simple, objective, and verifiable. In other words, a true empirically based science of behavior is emerging.

Recently, this new approach has been focused on the problems of the moderately retarded and emotionally disturbed with dramatic success. Although research and demonstration of this type in special education have been thus far only token (no pun intended), they could be the vanguard of a vast and potent array of techniques for the prevention and remediation of problems exhibited by exceptional children.

It is clear that special education is an intensely fertile area for the study and use of behavioral techniques. A concentrated research effort of this type could result in a new breed of special educators: "behavioral engineers" capable of making great strides toward the normalization of deviant behavior.

Biological Bases for Altering Behavior   All sciences are evidencing increased sophistication in the description, prediction, and control of phenomena. The biological sciences have shown particular growth in this regard, especially in their analysis of the relationship between environmental and physiological variables. Even at this initial stage of inquiry, there is some reason to believe that future educators will look more and more to biological scientists for answers concerning how cognitive development takes place, aspects of the environment that facilitate or inhibit intellectual development, and the most opportune period in the life of an organism to promote the development of various capabilities.

Recent studies with animals have suggested that marked alterations can be made in the learning rate of an organism as a result of being reared in different types of environments. Not only have dramatic changes been made in their rate of learning, but it is particularly interesting that definite modifications occurred in the brain biochemistry of the animals as a function of association with an enriched environment. Experiments are presently being conducted to identify the exact nature of the influence various environmental settings have on the neural-chemical systems of animals.

There will probably come a time when it will be possible to predict with assurance the type of environments necessary for optimum neural transmission at specific periods in the life of an organism. When this stage of sophistication

is reached, biochemists may be able to provide educators with specific guidelines concerning the nature of environmental variables which will effect optimum neural-chemical balances and, thus, establish an advantageous physiological basis for learning. With these types of data, specific curricular and methodological procedures can be designed for individuals who exhibit various patterns of characteristics. This possibility has special importance for education of the mentally retarded since the literature is replete with documentation concerning the efficacy of placing young retarded children in an enriched environment.

Although this latter speculation on the possible direction of future research in mental retardation may seem ludicrous to some, if one will allow himself a peek a generation or more beyond the existing data, it is not farfetched at all. A decade ago many would have scoffed at the suggestion that man would eventually reach the point of being able to control genetic transmission. Scientists presently have developed techniques whereby certain genetic traits can be controlled; it is not at all hazardous to speculate that the biochemist will eventually be a member of a diagnostic and remedial team of the future. Indeed, his contributions may be most significant, especially if the biochemist is able to describe the type of environment that will optimize neurological transmission. The possible influence of this scientific breakthrough will far exceed the potential advantages of being able to control genetic transmission. To be sure, this dream already has an empirically based superstructure.

Appendix B

Summary of Recommendations for Planning, Developing, and Coordinating Programs for the Mentally Retarded

In 1962, the American Association on Mental Deficiency developed a manual on program development in mental retardation. The principal purpose of this document was to explore some of the central problems involved in programming for the mentally retarded at all levels. The discussion throughout the manual is comprehensive and penetrating, and the recommendations which are offered are as applicable for the decade of the 1970s as they were in 1962. It was felt, therefore, that the final summary and recommendations which appeared in this manual would offer an appropriate conclusion to this book since there is great similarity between these two documents in philosophy.*

1. *Prevention*

Substantial progress has been made in the discovery of specific determinants of mental defect and retardation and in the development

---

* The material appearing in this section is reproduced from the following source and permission to use the material has been granted by the authors and by the American Association on Mental Deficiency: W. I. Gardner and H. W. Nisonger, *A Manual on Program Development in Mental Retardation, Monograph Supplement to the American Journal of Mental Deficiency,* January, 1962, pp. 3–8.

of methods for their prevention and/or treatment. However, mental defect and retardation are associated with a multiplicity of causal factors, some of which are still unknown. Consequently, for these, no preventive measures are available. Prevention must be approached on a broad front. *Maximum efforts of state and community officials, professional workers in mental retardation and the general public should be focused in the following directions:*

a. *In supporting expanded programs of research in areas where the etiologies or causal factors and the methods of prevention and/or treatment are unknown.*

b. *In strengthening those general community services—medical, health, education, and welfare—which have potentials for prevention.*

c. *In providing adequate programs for early identification, diagnosis and treatment, education and training, rehabilitation and care, which serve to mitigate the damaging effects of the disability.*

2. Statewide Approach to Program Development

States provide services to the retarded and their parents either directly or through financial assistance to communities for the development of local services. Local governmental agencies provide services to the retarded either from local taxes alone or with financial assistance from the state and federal governments. Some services are also provided by private agencies. Collectively these represent the total resources for the retarded within a state. *Responsible state officials are urged to provide the necessary leadership in making a statewide approach (state, regional, local) in the assessment of total needs of the retarded and in future program planning for all mentally retarded within the state.*

3. Delineation of State and Local Governmental Responsibility

Some state services for the retarded are being administered by state departments of government which have no counterparts in local government and no established working channels with local governmental units. Many new local services are being established without local governmental responsibility being clearly defined or fixed by law which often leads to confusion. *State legislatures and state officials are urged to delineate more clearly the responsibilities of state and local governmental units for specific services to the retarded and their parents and for working relations of local government agencies with their counterparts in state government.*

4. Utilization of Existing Agencies

Many of the medical, health, education, and social service needs of the mentally retarded are similar to those of the general population, and maximum

use should be made of the existing and long-established general services. Also many specialized services are required to meet the specific needs of the retarded. *Those responsible for program planning are urged to provide for the maximum utilization of existing services and in the establishment of specialized services, incorporating them whenever feasible within the administrative framework of existing and generally accepted agencies.*

5. Early Identification

The significance of early identification of the mentally retarded has increased with expanding knowledge about the etiology, methods of treatment, education and care. Few communities have any systematic method of identifying the retarded unless the disabilities are highly visible. *Community leaders are urged to develop systematic methods of early identification through existing medical, health, education and welfare services and through the development of special services where necessary.*

6. Diagnostic Services

Sound prognosis, treatment, and planning for mentally retarded individuals must be based upon adequate diagnostic data. Diagnostic or clinical services have been greatly expanded in recent years, but in terms of total needs they seriously lack completeness, coordination, continuity, and coverage. *State officials in cooperation with community leaders are urged to assume leadership in the development of a statewide plan for adequate clinical services (state, regional, local) which can be made available to the retarded and their parents wherever they may live.*

7. Parent Counseling

The counseling needs of parents are manifold. Some of these may involve counseling with respect to specific problems such as interpreting the nature of mental retardation, diagnostic evaluation, medical treatment, provision for schooling, family adjustments, and institutionalization. Others may involve continuous long-term planning for the needs of the child. Counseling services are being provided with varying degrees of adequacy by the family physician, specialized and general mental health clinics, special education teacher, home visitor, nurse and social worker. *Responsible community leaders should take necessary steps to insure adequate counseling services, both short-term and long-term, for parents either through the existing community services and/or through specialized services where necessary.*

8. Home Training

Whether mental retardation results from a damaged nervous system or from cultural deficiencies, parents frequently are unable to stimulate adequate development of whatever potential the child has available. This not only adds to the child's gross inadequacy but also places a terrific strain upon the mental health of the entire family. Assistance with home-training problems, especially during the preschool period, becomes highly significant to both the child and the parents. *Responsible community leaders should provide for home-training services to parents of preschool-age retarded children through existing community agencies and/or through a specialized agency.*

9. Education and Training

School programs for mildly retarded or educable children have made phenomenal growth in the last decade. However, national statistics indicate that only about one-third of those eligible are enrolled in special classes. Similarly, school programs for moderately retarded or trainable children have expanded rapidly in recent years. *Responsible state officials and local boards of education are urged to continue the improvement and expansion of these programs.*

10. Preparation for Employment

The early development of public school programs for the educable mentally retarded largely benefited children of the elementary-age levels. The expansion of special programs to include the older groups in the secondary schools has taken place more recently. At present a number of secondary schools have provision for part-time school and part-time supervised work experiences during the last year in school in order to better prepare mentally retarded individuals for full-time employment. In this task many schools are ably assisted by the vocational rehabilitation agency and other community agencies. *School officials and other community leaders are urged to provide similar part-time school and part-time supervised work programs designed to better prepare mentally retarded individuals for full-time employment.*

11. Sheltered Workshops

There are two groups of mentally retarded individuals who need sheltered workshop programs. DiMichael refers to them as (a) the deferred placeable group (educable) who will need further training beyond what the school can provide, and (b) the sheltered employable group (trainable) who will need

continuing employment in a carefully supervised environment of a sheltered workshop. During the last decade many communities throughout the country have established sheltered workshops to meet this urgent need. Most of them have been developed under private auspices. Public support is needed and is likely to come in the near future. *Responsible community leaders including officials of government should make provisions in their program plans for adequate sheltered workshop facilities for these two groups of retarded individuals.*

12. Selective Placement

Because of the inadequacy of home conditions it sometimes becomes necessary to place retarded individuals outside their natural homes. The traditional reaction is to have them committed to a state residential institution for care. However, here are other possible resources which should be explored such as foster homes, boarding homes, and private residential institutions. *State officials and community leaders should set up a selective placement system based upon the specific developmental needs of the retarded individuals to be placed and the potential resources available.*

13. Role of State Residential Institutions

Residential institutions have performed a very significant role in the care of the mentally retarded and will continue to do so in the future. However, their specific role may be changing due to advanced knowledge concerning the developmental needs of the retarded, the rapid expansion of community facilities and changes in the composition of new admissions. *In planning future institutional facilities and programs, state officials should consider the modern role of residential institutions in the light of current knowledge, changing conditions and general trends.*

14. Need for Community Residential Facilities at Community Level

Communities, especially the larger ones, have many uses for small residential units. Examples are (a) for temporary care of retarded individuals awaiting admission to state institutions, (b) for temporary care in periods of crises in families, (c) for temporary care while individuals are under intensive study and evaluation, and (d) for temporary care and orientation to the community after release from state institutions. *Responsible state and local officials should consider seriously in their program planning provisions for local residential facilities, preferably in a community center associated with other services for the retarded.*

15. State Administration

Many of the state services for the mentally retarded are administered as part of the state's mental health program. Within such a mental health program the position of chief administrator for services to the retarded should be on a relatively high echelon in the departmental table of organization. *State legislatures and responsible state officials are urged to place this position on an administrative level of authority and responsibility which is consistent with its needs for effective program planning, decision making, and administrative action.*

16. Coordination of State Services

For historical reasons state services to the retarded are administered by several different departments of government usually with little provision for joint planning and coordination. *State officials are urged to establish some kind of official interdepartmental committee, council, or board to facilitate joint planning and coordination of these services.*

17. Planning and Coordination at Community Level

At the community level, especially in the larger communities, there are many public and private institutions, agencies, and organizations involved in services to the retarded and their parents. New services often are established independently with little regard for how they fit into a plan for meeting the total community needs of the mentally retarded. This may lead to duplication of effort and even conflict. *Community officials and other responsible leaders are urged to provide for a sound and orderly development of programs for the retarded through community-wide planning either by utilizing existing community planning councils or by establishing planning agencies for this purpose.*

18. Research in Mental Retardation

Research is a major key to progress in prevention, diagnosis, treatment, education and care in the field of mental retardation. The resources for research in this field, especially the medical aspects, have expanded greatly in recent years. Much more emphasis should be given to research in the behavioral area. This calls for state-level initiative and responsibility. *Responsible state officials in cooperation with research institutions are urged to assume leadership in planning essential research programs and in securing appropriations for their implementation.*

19. *Professional Training*

Progress in mental retardation, including research, is largely dependent upon an adequate supply of trained personnel. Because of the multidiscipline character of mental retardation, training programs in many disciplines are involved. Recent expansions and improvements in professional training programs have greatly increased the numbers of available qualified personnel in all disciplines, yet the current demand far exceeds the supply. This calls for state-level initiative and responsibility. *Responsible state officials in cooperation with professional training institutions are urged to assume leadership in the development of expanded professional training facilities and in securing the necessary appropriations for their implementation.*

20. *Facilities for Research and Professional Training*

Research and training of professional personnel in mental retardation require access to human subjects. Such access may be secured in institutions and agencies serving the mentally retarded such as residential institutions for the retarded, various types of clinics, and special education classes in the public schools. Colleges and universities are the focus for professional training and for much of the research in mental retardation. Universities must have access to institutions and agencies serving the retarded in order to do effective professional training and research. It is, therefore, of paramount importance that universities, institutions, and agencies serving the retarded establish close working relations. *Responsible state and university officials are urged to cooperate in planning adequate laboratory facilities for research and professional training programs, especially when new facilities are contemplated.*

21. *In-service Training*

In a complex and rapidly growing field such as mental retardation, it is impossible for university graduates to remain up-to-date for very long periods of time without further systematic study. Recognizing this need, many universities and professional organizations provide opportunities for in-service education through the publication of professional journals and through periodic seminars, workshops, and conferences. Most states have organized programs of in-service training for their institutional and clinic personnel. *Responsible state officials and community leaders are urged to work cooperatively with their universities in the development of more adequate in-service training programs for professional and voluntary personnel in both state and local services.*

22. *Nomenclature and Classification*

Every branch of knowledge has its own vocabulary of technical terms, usually referred to as its terminology or nomenclature. Nomenclature is the basis for the classification of knowledge and for communication among members of the profession in a given field. At present there is great disparity in the definition and use of terms in mental retardation. *Institutions and agencies and professional personnel serving the retarded are urged to cooperate with efforts now underway by AAMD toward the establishment of a more uniform system of nomenclature and classification and in its continuous development and refinement.*

23. *Statistical Reporting*

More adequate statistical data on the mentally retarded population are needed for research, for program planning and for administrative purposes. The Biometrics Branch, National Institute of Mental Health, United States Public Health Service, which is responsible for assembling national statistics on the mentally retarded, revised its report forms in 1960 to provide for more adequate data. *Institutions and agencies are urged to cooperate with the Biometrics Branch in supplying the data requested.*

24. *Legal Reform*

Since public services for the retarded are expanding rapidly and since public programs in research, professional training, and state and/or local programs of prevention, diagnosis, treatment, education, rehabilitation and care must be established within the framework of law, the adequacy of state legal codes is of great importance. The laws must be based upon modern concepts of mental retardation and permit the modernization of practices as new knowledge becomes available. Legislative provisions for the retarded have existed in most states for over a century. Most of the early laws were oriented toward institutional care. As new scientific facts became available and the demands for new services developed, existing laws were amended or new ones added to meet the changing situation. This piecemeal procedure has often resulted in gross inadequacies and even inconsistencies. *State legislatures and state officials are urged to assume leadership in the periodic review of state legislative provisions for the mentally retarded in order to keep them abreast of modern concepts, scientific knowledge, and up-to-date practices in this field.*

INDEX

INDEX

Apgar, Virginia, 46, 55–56
Apgar scoring chart, 55–56
Arithmetic, 139, 152, 154
Arnstein, H. S., 188
Arrell, V. M., 206
Asian influenza, 45
Association of Medical Officers of
    American Institutions for Idiotic
    and Feeble-Minded Persons, 38
*Atlas of Mental Retardation
    Syndromes,* 16
Atomic bombs, 44

Baron, D., 99
"Basic Facts about Public Residential
    Facilities for the Mentally
    Retarded" (Butterfield), 64–65
Bass, M. S., 191, 222, 223
Baumgartner, B. B., 167
Bayley, N., 98
Behavior:
    of adolescents, 175–181
    consequences of unsatisfied needs,
        175–178
    in institutions, 211–216
    school learning problems,
        180–181
    self-concept, 178
    social difficulties, 178–180
    of adults, 218–220
    changing, 25–28, 100–117
    biological bases for, 248–249
    classifications of, 16–18
    cloistering, 89
    control, 23–32
    during elementary school years,
        124–130
    individuality, 132–136
    management, 23–32
    appropriate reinforcers, 28–30

Behavior:
    management: instructional principles,
        30–32
    precursors to, 24–25
    observing, 98–99
    obstreperous, 89
    during preschool years, 75–77
    changing, 100–117
    typical, 86–90
    sampling, 93
    shaping, 26
Behavioral engineering, 248
Behavioral goals, 25–27
Behavioral research, 244–246
    clinical teaching, 245–246
    early intervention, 244–245
    home programs, 245
    new instructional technology, 246
Bereiter, C., 112
Berg, J. M., 46
Bernard, H. W., 99
Birth control, 223–225
Birth injuries, 46–47
Birth process, 36–37, 46–48
Blatt, B., 6, 70
Blood, 46
    Rh factor, 52, 54
    tests of, 52, 54
Bloom, B. S., 77, 78
Brabner, G., 155
Brain:
    damage, 46–47
    accidents, 20–21
    phenylketonuria (PKU), 17, 22,
        42, 43, 53–54
    interdependent functioning of, 50
    slow maturity of, 44
    tumors, 47
    vascular problems in, 47
Bureau of Education for the Handi-
    capped, 34

Neisworth, J. T., 86, 92, 94, 195, 239n.
Neuhaus, E. C., 201
Neurofibromatosis, 17, 42
Newborn Scoring System, 55–56
Nicotine, 44, 49
Nirje, B., 70
Nisonger, H. W., 227, 250n.
North, G. E., 214
Nutrition, 48–50, 52

Obstreperous behavior, 89
Occupational characteristics, 220–221
Occupational problems, 205–209
  preparation for, 253
Olshansky, 59, 71
Overlearning, 31

Painter, G., 112
Parents:
  and the adolescent period, 181–194
    concern for normal siblings, 182–185
    planning for the future, 191–194
    school-related responsibilities, 185–187
    sex education, 187–191
  counseling of, 252
  educational programs for, 21
  and the elementary school years, 170–174
  family counseling, 57–62
  importance of attitudes of, 104–106
  initial reaction of, to a retarded baby, 57–59, 61–62
  management, 60–61
  the mentally retarded as, 221–225
  placement issues, 119–121
    during elementary school years, 144–148
  program for the retarded, 107–113

Parents:
  range of reactions of, 59
  reality crisis, 59–60, 145
  working with, 118–123
Parmelee, A. M., 71
Partridge, D. L., 204
Payne, J. S., 205
Peck, J. R., 201, 206, 223
Perceptual disorders, 5
Perceptual-motor development, 110
Performance:
  level of, 87–88
  quality of, 87–88
Perinatal period, 10, 46–47
  detecting mental retardation during, 53–56
  prematurity and, 54–55
Phenylalanine, 42
Phenylketonuria (PKU), 17, 22, 42, 43, 53–54
Physicians, selecting, 49
Piaget, J., 80, 112, 154
Pike, J. A., 188
Pituitary problems, 45
Placement, 63–73, 119–121
  of adolescents, 195–199
  demographic characteristics of institutions, 63–65
  elementary school years, 144–148
  facts about, 71–73
  field trip to an institution, 65–71
  opinions about, 71–73
  selective, 254
Planning:
  community, 255
  for the future, 191–194
Poisons, 20, 47
Positive reinforcement, 26–29
Postnatal period, 10–11, 47–48
  assessing the newborn infant's condition, 55–56

Prematurity, 54–55
Prenatal period, 10, 41–46, 48
 data gathering, 51–53
 examinations during, 51–53
 factors contributing to a healthy
  baby, 48–50
Preschool centers, 21
Preschool years, 75–123
 and aesthetic development, 112
 behavioral characteristics during,
  75–77
  changing, 100–117
  typical, 86–90
 cognitive skills, 111
 creative development, 112
 diagnostic procedures, 90–99
  analyzing data, 91–92
  assumptions about evaluation,
   92–93
  gathering data, 91–92
  intelligence test scores, 93–98
  observing behavior, 98–99
 dimensions of a program for,
  107–113
 distinctions during, 81–86
 emotional development during, 111
 environmental needs, 77–79, 102
  deprivation consequences, 79–80
  to facilitate development, 100–117
 perceptual-motor development, 110
 physical fitness, 110
 self-care, 111
 skills, 87–88
  needs for, 101
  social, 112
 understanding needs, 101–103
 verbal communication, 110–111
 working with parents, 118–123
President's Panel on Mental Retardation, 19–21, 33–34, 36, 63–65
Preventive measures, 19–22, 250–251

*Proposed Program for National Action
 to Combat Mental Retardation, A,*
 20–21, 33
Protein, 50
Public Law 80–10, Title VI, 35
Public Law 85–905, 35
Public Law 85–926, 35
Public Law 88–156, 34
Public Law 88–164:
 Title 1A, 34
 Titles 1C and 2, 34
 Title 1D, 34
 Title III, 35
Public Law 89–10, 34
 Title VI, 35
Public Law 89–109, 35
Public Law 89–333, 34
Public Law 89–614, 36
Public Law 89–750, 35
Public Law 90–170, Title V, 35
Public Law 90–247, 35
Public Law 90–538, 35
Public school practices, 149–169
 focus of the curriculum, 150–155
 information processing, 156–159
 instructional materials, 160–161
 integration problems, 161–162
 method suggestions, 159–160
 programs for trainable youngsters,
  167–169
 responsibilities of parents, 185–187
 teacher preparation, 162–167
Punishment, 30
 defined, 30

Radiation, 20
Radin, N. L., 113
Radler, D. H., 98
Readiness learning, 30, 152–155

Trauma:
   initial reaction to a retarded baby,
      57–59, 61–62
   maternal, 45
Tredgold, R. F., 16
Tuberous sclerosis, 42
Tumors, brain, 47

Ullman, M., 59
Umbilical cord complications, 47
Undernutrition, 49, 50
U.S. Office of Education, 33, 34
Urinalysis, prenatal period, 52

Vail, D. J., 70
Valett, R. E., 159
Van de Riet, H., 112
Van de Riet, V., 112
Van Riper, C., 99
Variability:
   interindividual, 134
   interpopulation, 134
   intraindividual, 134

Verbal skills, 110–111, 126
Viruses, 45
Vitamins, 50, 52
Vocational rehabilitation, 206–209

Weikart, D. P., 113
Weitzner, M., 8
Whiteman, M., 7
Wittson, C., 6
Wolfensberger, W., 59, 63–65, 70,
   73, 145, 204
Woodward, M., 77, 154
Workshops, sheltered, 231–235,
   253–254
Wortis, J., 48
Wright, C. H., 222
Wright, W. R., 112
Writing, 152, 154–155

X-rays, 44, 49

Yale–New Haven Medical Center, 55
Young, W. M., 7

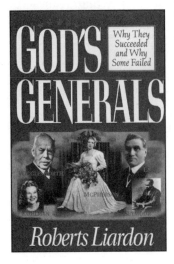

God's Generals:
Why They Succeeded and Why Some Failed
Roberts Liardon

Some of the most powerful ministers ever to ignite the fires of revival did so by dynamically demonstrating the Holy Spirit's power. Roberts Liardon faithfully chronicles the lives and spiritual journeys of twelve of *God's Generals,* including William J. Seymour, the son of ex-slaves, who turned a tiny horse stable on Azusa Street, Los Angeles, into an internationally famous center of revival; Aimee Semple McPherson, the glamorous, flamboyant founder of the Foursquare Church and the nation's first Christian radio station; and Smith Wigglesworth, the plumber who read no book but the Bible—and raised the dead!

ISBN: 0-88368-944-8 • Hardcover • 416 pages

God's Generals II:
The Roaring Reformers
Roberts Liardon

The basic truths of the Protestant faith—the things you believe and base your life on—were not always accepted and readily taught. Here are six of *God's Generals* who fought to reestablish the core beliefs and principles of the early church in an atmosphere of oppression, ignorance, and corruption that pervaded the medieval church. As you read about these *Roaring Reformers,* men who sacrificed everything in their fight for God, you will appreciate the freedom you have to worship, find encouragement for your spiritual battles, and be motivated to find biblical truth in your own life.

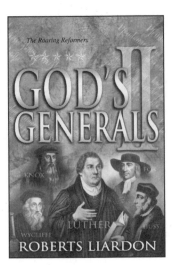

ISBN: 0-88368-945-6 • Hardcover • 416 pages

"To do so would": *George Mueller: Man of Faith,* edited by A. Sims (Chicago: Moody Press, n.d.), 7–9.

"Hours every day": Ibid., 11–13.

"When I first": Ibid., 27–29.

"Faith is the assurance": "Real Faith" <http://theoldtimegospel.org/studies/serm6.html> (24 May 2005)

Arthur T. Pierson, *George Muller of Bristol* (Old Tappan, N. J.: Fleming H. Revell Company), 18–39, 44–372.

Roger Steer, *George Muller: Delighted in God!* (Wheaton, Ill.: Harold Shaw Publishers, 1975), 11–307.

George Mueller: Man of Faith, edited by A. Sims (Chicago: Moody Press, n.d.).

CHAPTER 80

Lois Hoadley Dick, "Live," *Radiant Life* 65, no. 4.

Fred Ward, "In Long-Forbidden Tibet," *National Geographic* 157, no. 2.

The New Encyclopaedia Britannica, 15th ed., s. v. "Tibet."

CHAPTER 83

Bruce Olson, *Bruchko* (Lake Mary, Fla.: Charisma House, 1973), 22–28, 31–148.

CHAPTER 84

Paul Lee Tan, *Encyclopedia of 7700 Illustrations: Signs of the Times* (Rockville, Md.: Assurance Publishers, 1988), 887.

CHAPTER 86

James Alexander Stewart, D.D., *I Must Tell* (Asheville, N. C.: Gospel Projects, n.d.), 3–46.

Edith Deen, *Great Women of the Christian Faith* (Uhrichsville, Ohio: Barbour and Company, Inc., 1959), 164–71.

CHAPTER 72

Edith Deen, *Great Women of the Christian Faith* (Uhrichsville, Ohio: Barbour and Company, Inc., 1959), 285.

Ernest K. Emurian, *Hymn Festivals* (Natick, Mass.: W. A. Wilde Company, 1961), 40–41.

Kenneth W. Osbeck, *101 Hymn Stories* (Grand Rapids, Mich.: Kregel Publications, 1982), 146–147.

CHAPTER 74

John S. Tompkins, "Our Kindest City," *Reader's Digest*, July 1994.

CHAPTER 75

"A revival is not": Allen C. Guelzo, "The Making of a Revivalist," *Christian History* 7, no. 20 (1988): 30.

"You tell me": Charles Finney, "Lectures on Revivals of Religion," *Christian History* 7, no. 20 (1988): 31.

"Ingratitude" through *"Hindering Others"*: *Sound of the Trumpet* 4, no. 4 (1975): 3.

Charles G. Finney, *Charles G. Finney: An Autobiography* (Old Tappan, N. J.: Fleming H. Revell Company, 1876).

"Charles Grandison Finney: 19th Century Giant of American Revivalism," *Christian History* 7, no. 20 (1988): 6–12, 22–23, 31–32, 37.

The New Encyclopaedia Britannica, 15th ed., s. v. "Charles Grandison Finney."

Paul Lee Tan, *Encyclopedia of 7700 Illustrations: Signs of the Times* (Rockville, Md.: Assurance Publishers, 1988), 687–688.

Charles Finney, "Lectures on Revivals of Religion," *Christian History* 7, no. 20 (1988): 31–32.

CHAPTER 77

"This shall be my argument": Roger Steer, *George Muller: Delighted in God!* (Wheaton, Ill.: Harold Shaw Publishers, 1975), 85–86.

"Such a thing is": Ibid., 102–103.

"It is worth": Ibid., 117.

"For nearly seventy years": *George Mueller: Man of Faith*, edited by A. Sims (Chicago: Moody Press, n.d.), 7–9.

"Why, madam": *Today in the Word* <http://www.sermonillustrations.com/a-z/w/will_of_God.htm> (24 May 2005)

"Shall I, for fear": <http://www.bibleword.com/maxims2.htm (24 May 2005)>

Issue Devoted to John Wesley, *Christian History* 2, no. 1 (1983): 4, 6.

"The Holy Club," *Christian History* 2, no. 1 (1983): 16.

"John Wesley and Women," *Christian History* 2, no. 1 (1983): 25–27.

Wesley L. Duewel, *Ablaze for God* (Grand Rapids, Mich.: Zondervan, 1989).

"John & Charles Wesley," *Christian History* 9, no. 28 (1990): 44.

Roger J. Green, "Experience Conversions," *Christian History* 9, no. 28 (1990): 45.

The New Encyclopaedia Britannica, 15th ed., s. v. "Charles Wesley."

The New Encyclopaedia Britannica, 15th ed., s. v. "John Wesley."

Howard A. Snyder, *The Radical Wesley and Patterns for Church Renewal* (Downers Grove, Ill.: Intervarsity Press, 1980), 1–4, 13–52.

Edith Deen, *Great Women of the Christian Faith* (Uhrichsville, Ohio: Barbour and Company, Inc., 1959), 141–148.

CHAPTER 64

"Whoever intends to enter": Martin Luther <http://www.wwnet.net/~kipf/luther.htm> (18 May 2005)

CHAPTER 66

John Newton, paraphrased by Dick Bohrer, *John Newton: Letters of a Slave Trader Freed by God's Grace* (Chicago: The Moody Bible Institute, 1983), vii–viii, 7–76.

John Newton, *Out of the Depths* (New Canaan, Conn.: Keats Publishing, Inc., 1981), 3, 11–14, 128.

Ernest K. Emurian, *Hymn Festivals* (Natick, Mass.: W. A. Wilde Company, 1961), 65–73.

Kenneth W. Osbeck, *101 Hymn Stories* (Grand Rapids, Mich.: Kregel Publications, 1982), 28–29.

CHAPTER 69

"I saw the greatest": Edith Deen, *Great Women of the Christian Faith* (Uhrichsville, Ohio: Barbour and Company, Inc., 1959), 166.

Ruth A. Tucker, *From Jerusalem to Irian Jaya* (Grand Rapids, Mich.: Zondervan, 1983), 68, 70.

Auguste Hermann Francke, "Overwhelmed as with a Stream of Joy, An Autobiography," *Christian History* 59, no. 2 (1986): 7–8, 33–34.

CHAPTER 56

"I would gladly": "The Moravians and John Wesley," *Christian History* 1, no. 1 (1982): 30.

The New Encyclopaedia Britannica, 15th ed., s. v. "Zinzendorf, Nikolaus Ludwig Graf von."

"The Rich Young Ruler Who Said Yes," *Christian History* 1, no. 1 (1986): 7–9.

"The Moravians and John Wesley," *Christian History* 1, no. 1 (1982): 30–32.

Leslie K. Tarr, "A Prayer Meeting That Lasted 100 Years," *Christian History* 1, no. 1 (1986): 18.

"A Day in the Life of Early Herrnhut," *Christian History* 1, no. 1 (1986): 19.

"Gallery of Leading Figures," *Christian History* 1, no. 1 (1986): 20.

"My Zeal Has Not Cooled," *Christian History* 1, no. 1 (1986): 35.

Ruth A. Tucker, *From Jerusalem to Irian Jaya* (Grand Rapids, Mich.: Zondervan, 1983), 69–74.

Kenneth W. Osbeck, *101 Hymn Stories* (Grand Rapids, Mich.: Kregel Publications, 1982), 141.

CHAPTER 58

"The thirteenth chapter": *John G. Lake: The Complete Collection of His Life Teachings*, compiled by Roberts Liardon (New Kensington, Pa.: Whitaker House, forthcoming), 36–41.

CHAPTER 59

Winifred M. Pearce, *David Brainerd* (Grand Rapids, Mich.: Zondervan, 1953), 10–96.

Jonathan Edwards, *The Life and Diary of David Brainerd* (Chicago: Moody Press, 1949), 43–54.

The New Encyclopaedia Britannica, 15th ed., s. v. "David Brainerd."

CHAPTER 62

"Monday, January 1, 1739": Howard A. Snyder, *The Radical Wesley and Patterns for Church Renewal* (Downers Grove, Ill.: Intervarsity Press, 1980), 30.

"A Letter from Prison in Tyndale's Own Hand," *Christian History* 6, no. 16 (1987): 32.

"From the Obedience of a Christian Man," *Christian History* 6, no. 16 (1987): 35.

The New Encyclopaedia Britannica, 15th ed., s. v. "William Tyndale."

John Fox, *Fox's Book of Martyrs* (Philadelphia, PA: Universal Book and Bible House, 1926), 176–184.

Bruce L. Shelley, *Church History in Plain Language* (Dallas, Tex.: Word, Inc., 1982), 286–287.

Henry C. Sheldon, *History of the Christian Church*, vol. 2, *The Mediaeval Church* (Peabody, Mass.: Hendrickson Publishers, 1988), 421–422.

CHAPTER 50

"Massachusetts School Law," *Annals of America 1493–1754* (Chicago: Encyclopaedia Britannica, Inc., 1976), 184.

CHAPTER 51

"When our Lord": Dr. Martin Luther, *Disputation of Doctor Martin Luther on the Power and Efficacy of Indulgences,* as published in *Works of Martin Luther*, vol. 1, edited and translated by Adolph Spaeth, L. D. Reed, Henry Eyster Jacobs, et al. (Philadelphia: A. J. Holman Company, 1915), 29–38.

"It is a good thing": Martin Luther "How I Pray: Counsel on Approaching the Almighty," *Christian History* 12, no. 39 (1993): 45–47.

"Martin Luther: The Later Years and Legacy," *Christian History* 12, no. 39 (1993): 6, 8, 10–37, 45.

Eric W. Gritsch, "Luther Posts the 95 Theses," *Christian History* 9, no. 28 (1990): 35–37.

Henry C. Sheldon, *History of the Christian Church*, Volume 2, *The Modern Church Part One* (Peabody, Mass.: Hendrickson Publishers, 1988), 45–107.

The New Encyclopaedia Britannica, 15th ed., s. v. "Martin Luther."

Merle Severy, "The World of Luther," *National Geographic* 104, no. 4.

C. Douglas Weaver, *A Cloud of Witnesses: Sermon Illustrations and Devotionals from the Christian Heritage* (Macon, Ga.: Abingdon Press, 1993), 71–73.

CHAPTER 53

"Faith is a living": Auguste Hermann Francke, "Overwhelmed as with a Stream of Joy, An Autobiography," *Christian History* 59, no. 2 (1986): 33.

"My Lord Jesus Christ": *Foxe's Book of Martyrs* <http://www.churchofgodpro-claimed.org/miscwriters/foxes_book_martrs/chap8.html> (May 24 2005)

"But I do commend": http://www.myfortress.org/JohnHuss.html (May 24 2005)

The New Encyclopaedia Britannica, 15th ed., s.v. "Jan Hus."

Bruce L. Shelley, *Church History in Plain Language* (Dallas, Tex.: Word, Inc., 1982), 249–251.

Henry C. Sheldon, *History of the Christian Church*, vol. 2, *The Mediaeval Church* (Peabody, Mass.: Hendrickson Publishers, 1988), 427–429, 433–451.

John Fox, *Fox's Book of Martyrs* (Philadelphia, Pa.: Universal Book and Bible House, 1926), 140–144.

CHAPTER 47

"The church will be scourged": *The New Encyclopaedia Britannica*, 15th ed., s. v. "Girolamo Savonarola."

Justo L. Gonzalez, *The Story of Christianity*, vol. 1, *The Early Church to the Dawn of the Reformation* (New York, N.Y.: HarperCollins Publishers, 1984), 353–356.

The New Encyclopaedia Britannica, 15th ed., s. v. "Girolamo Savonarola."

Henry C. Sheldon, *History of the Christian Church*, vol. 2, *The Mediaeval Church* (Peabody, Mass.: Hendrickson Publishers, 1988), 473–478.

CHAPTER 48

"Whereas we all came": "The New England Confederation Articles of Confederation," *Annals of America 1493–1754* (Chicago: Encyclopaedia Britannica, Inc., 1976), 172.

"If we will not": William J. Federer, *America's God and Country Encyclopedia of Quotations* (Coppell, Tex.: FAME Publishing, Inc.), 500.

"I am much afraid": Ibid., 404.

CHAPTER 49

Issue devoted to William Tyndale, *Christian History* 6, no. 16 (1987): 2–4.

Tony Lane, "A Man for All People: Introducing William Tyndale," *Christian History* 6, no. 16 (1987): 6–9.

Brian Edwards, "Tyndale's Betrayal and Death," *Christian History* 6, no. 16 (1987): 12–15.

Donald Smeeton, "The Bible Translatory Who Shook Henry VIII," *Christian History* 6, no. 16 (1987): 16–23.

Regulations at Yale College, from "Of A Religious and Virtuous Life," *Annals of America 1493–1754* (Chicago: Encyclopaedia Britannica, Inc., 1976), 464–65.

"Every one shall": Paul Lee Tan, *Encyclopedia of 7700 Illustrations: Signs of the Times* (Rockville, Md.: Assurance Publishers, 1988), 158.

CHAPTER 43

"The Bible is necessary": <http://logosresourcepages.org/IronPen/ironpen56.htm> (18 May 2005)

"Christ gave His gospel": "Why Wycliffe Translated the Bible into English," *Christian History* 2, no. 3 (1983): 26.

"Who must be plucked": John Foxe, *The Acts and Monuments of John Foxe*, vol. 3 (New York: AMS Press, 1965), 5.

"First, when you are": "A Short Rule of Life for Priests, Lords, and Laborers," *Christian History* 2, no. 3 (1983): 23.

"It is not confession": "On Confesssionals," *Christian History* 2, no. 3 (1983): 25.

"That pestilent and most wretched": "What Medieval Critics Said of Wycliffe's Bible," *Christian History* 2, no. 3 (1983): 26.

"We decree and ordain": Ibid.

"They burnt his bones": Fuller, as quoted by Dr. Donald L. Roberts, "Wycliff and the Reformation" *Christian History* 2, no. 3 (1983): 30.

"About John Wycliffe: Did You Know?" *Christian History* 2, no. 3 (1983): 4.

John Fox, *Fox's Book of Martyrs* (Philadelphia, Pa.: Universal Book and Bible House, 1926), 135–139.

Dr. Donald L. Roberts, "Wycliff and the Reformation," *Christian History* 2, no. 3 (1983): 10–13.

The New Encyclopaedia Britannica, 15th ed., s. v. "John Wycliffe."

Henry C. Sheldon, *History of the Christian Church*, vol. 2, *The Mediaeval Church* (Peabody, Mass.: Hendrickson Publishers, 1988), 400–426.

Bruce L. Shelley, *Church History in Plain Language* (Dallas, Tex.: Word, Inc. 1982), 243, 248.

CHAPTER 45

"I am attracted": Henry C. Sheldon, *History of the Christian Church*, vol. 2, *The Mediaeval Church* (Peabody, Mass.: Hendrickson Publishers, 1988), 433–434.

"Receive the honorable man": Ibid., 444–445.

CHAPTER 37

John Fox, *Fox's Book of Martyrs* (Philadelphia, Pa.: Universal Book and Bible House, 1926), 42.

CHAPTER 38

"The oftener we are mown": "Tertullian: Colorful, Controversial, Early African Christian," *Christian History* <http://chi.gospelcom.net/GLIMPSEF/Glimpses/glmps053.shtml> (18 May 2005)

John Fox, *Fox's Book of Martyrs* (Philadelphia, Pa.: Universal Book and Bible House, 1926), 42–43.

CHAPTER 41

"Waldo was a rich man": "Remembered by Their Enemies," Christian History 8, no. 22 (1989): 4.

"Remembered by Their Enemies," *Christian History* 8, no. 22 (1989): 4.

"A Prophet without Honor: Waldo of Lyons," *Christian History* 8, no. 22 (1989): 6–7.

Bruce L. Shelley, *Church History in Plain Language* (Dallas, Tex., Word, Inc., 1982), 226–227.

CHAPTER 42

"It is impossible to rightly govern the world": William J. Federer, *America's God and Country Encyclopedia of Quotations* (Coppell, Tex.: FAME Publishing, Inc.), 660.

"So great is my veneration": Ibid., 16.

"That book, sir, is the rock": Ibid., 311.

"I believe the Bible is the best gift": Ibid., 388.

"It is impossible to mentally": Ibid., 266.

"I ask every man and woman": Paul Lee Tan, *Encyclopedia of 7700 Illustrations: Signs of the Times* (Rockville, Md.: Assurance Publishers, 1988), 192.

"Believe me, sir, never a night": Ibid.

"The whole of the inspiration": Ibid.

"Young man, my advice": "Benjamin Franklin" <http://www.geocities.com/Athens/Parthenon/6528/fund63.htm> (18 May 2005)

"Cursed be all": "Presbyterian" <http://www.otweb.com/bible/atpcem/Church4.html> (18 May 2005)

CHAPTER 28

"Everywhere we see tribulation": Bruce L. Shelley, *Church History in Plain Language* (Dallas, Tex.: Word, Inc., 1982), 184.

"I have been unable": Ibid., 185.

"Universal pope": Ibid., 185–86.

"Pride, which we have": Ibid., 186.

"A spiritual leader": Ibid., 182.

The New Encyclopaedia Britannica, 15th ed., s. v. "Gregory I."

Bruce L. Shelley, *Church History in Plain Language* (Dallas, Tex., Word, Inc., 1982), 181–86.

CHAPTER 30

The New Encyclopaedia Britannica, 15th ed., s. v. "Saint Boniface."

John Fox, *Fox's Book of Martyrs* (Philadelphia, Pa.: Universal Book and Bible House, 1926), 39–40.

CHAPTER 32

The New Encyclopaedia Britannica, 15th ed., s. v. "Saint Ansgar."

Ruth A. Tucker, *From Jerusalem to Irian Jaya* (Grand Rapids, Mich.: Zondervan, 1983), 49, 52.

CHAPTER 33

Paul Lee Tan, *Encyclopedia of 7700 Illustrations: Signs of the Times* (Rockville, Md.: Assurance Publishers, 1988), 1,307.

CHAPTER 34

The New Encyclopaedia Britannica, 15th ed., s. v. "Saint Adalbert."

John Fox, *Fox's Book of Martyrs* (Philadelphia, Pa.: Universal Book and Bible House, 1926), 40–41.

CHAPTER 35

James Reapsome, "Persecuted Christians Today," *Christian History* 9, no. 27 (1990): 37.

CHAPTER 36

John Fox, *Fox's Book of Martyrs* (Philadelphia, Pa.: Universal Book and Bible House, 1926), 41–42.

The New Encyclopaedia Britannica, 15th ed., s. v. "Saint Aelfheah."